THE TROJAN PEACE:

HALF-LIGHT

JILL BARTELT

CALYMENE PRESS

Kewanee, Illinois

Publisher's Cataloging-in-Publication data

Names: Bartelt, Jill, author.
Title: The Trojan peace : half light / Jill Bartelt.
Description: Kewanee, IL: Calymene Press, 2016.
Identifiers: ISBN 978-0-9982932-1-9 | LCCN 2016920186
Subjects: LCSH Troy (Extinct city)--Fiction. | Greece--History--To 146 B.C.--Fiction. | Mythology (Greek)--Fiction. | Andromache (Legendary character)--Fiction. | Hector (Legendary character)--Fiction. | Penthesilea, Queen of the Amazons--Fiction. | Cassandra (Legendary character)--Fiction. | BISAC FICTION / Historical.
Classification: LCC PS3602.A83858 T76 2016 | DDC 813.6--dc23

For Marc and Luke

Contents

PART ONE:

The Tamer
of Horses

Winter

Chapter 1

The sky was a pale grey color, the air brisk. Wind was gusting down from the north, pulling Andromache's long hair loose and swirling it around her shoulders.

What now? she thought, looking around. The place was hardly familiar to her — she'd been there only once. The high plateau where she was standing fell away on two sides toward the sea. Before her, though, the land stretched out broad and flat. Some sections of it had been smoothed by the work of farmers, while others had a wild and tousled look. In spring, she could tell, the latter would be thick with herbs and flowers and alive with a host of animals.

As for what lay behind her —

"Troy," she murmured aloud. For well over a year, now, she'd lived inside the city's towering grey walls. They'd signified safety — protection — shelter from the dangers of the world.

Had she been wrong to leave all that behind?

No! she told herself. *Don't say that — not after everything you went through to get here.*

Andromache turned around, eyeing the little cottage behind her. It looked so ordinary, so innocent. No one ever would have guessed the secret it concealed...

She was walking down a dark passageway, lit only by the small, flickering lamp in her hand. It seemed so fragile. One breath would be enough to extinguish it. One breath, and she would be alone in the dark...

Hurriedly, she turned her face to the side, breathing as shallowly as possible. If she lost the light, she would be trapped down there, and no one would ever find her — or at least, not for a long, long time.

How often was the tunnel used? She didn't know. He hadn't said.

She pulled her cloak tighter, glad for its warmth in the chilly subterranean air. I must be coming to the end, *she thought, hoping she was right.* It can't be too much farther.

Up ahead, though, she saw only deeper blackness. The passageway didn't continue — it ended in a wall! What had she done wrong? Had she missed a turn? As she spun around, searching for the way out, the patch of deeper blackness caught her eye again. The passage did end, she realized — but only on her level. A set of stairs led up to the world above.

At the top, there was a panel blocking the way. She had to stop for a moment to remember the knock he'd shown her, a series of long and short raps: craaaaack, crick crick, craaaaack, crick, craaaaack!

The panel was lifted away, and a hand plunged down into the darkness of the stairway.

Gasping, she drew back.

A face appeared in the hole. 'Need help?' the man asked kindly.

'N-no thanks,' she stammered.

The man moved back, allowing her to clamber through the hole. She stepped out into a dim, quiet room, where the man had been sitting with his companion. Neither of the guards questioned why she was there. She'd known the right knock, which told them all they needed to know: she was there with their commander's blessing. Wordlessly, the first man replaced the floorboard and took her lamp from her, leaving her to walk out the door and onto the windswept Trojan plateau…

Andromache shivered slightly at the memory of her recent trip through the tunnel. The day before, it hadn't seemed so long, or so dark. Perhaps she'd made a mistake in coming here…

No! she told herself. *This is what you wanted, isn't it?*

The freedom to run around out in the countryside — yes, Andromache had wanted that, badly enough to start a fight with Hector over it. *This is where it all began,* she thought to herself. *All the yelling, all the crying. We weren't too far from the gateway cottage.*

She turned to gaze at the steep, grassy northern hillside. From where she was, she couldn't quite see the rock — her special rock. It was there she'd sat with Hector, after their fight. It was there she'd first learned that he was her friend.

Her friend! It was a startling thought. Hector was her friend. _Always, always_...

Since the moment Hector had come into her life, a year and a half earlier, he'd been many things to her — a gore-spattered monster, a noble commander, a hardworking student of her native language, Lukkan. The role he played was always changing, but never, ever, had he been her friend.

Or so she'd thought.

Andromache had often reflected that she and Hector _should_ have been friends. He was funny and kind; he seemed to understand her. Their relationship, though, had been burdened by layers of guilt, pain, and fear. _If only we hadn't met the way we did_, she'd often lamented. If only she hadn't seen him for the first time during a raid. If only Hector hadn't blamed himself for the destruction of her village, Lyrnassa. If only he hadn't learned Lukkan from her as a way of atoning for his failures...

Now, she knew that these '_if onlys_' had sprung from a misunderstanding. But how could she have guessed that? Hector had never explained himself — at least, not until after their fight.

Andromache smiled softly as she looked once more in the direction of the rock.

Painful though that fight had been, it had allowed many truths to pour out. Hector had told her that he wasn't studying Lukkan in order to assuage his guilt or to punish himself — no, he liked speaking it and always had! Best of all, though, was how he truly felt about _her_...

'Hector?' _she asked him._ 'Do you like me? Are we friends?'
'_Always_, always _we abre friends!' was his reply._

To Hector, who seldom bothered to differentiate past, present, and future when he spoke Lukkan, '_always we abre friends_' meant not only that they were friends in that moment, but that they always had been and always would be. In his mind, the way they'd met had never mattered. _Always, always we abre friends_...

Andromache smiled again. It was strange, the effect a few simple words could have. Because of what Hector had said, she no longer _needed_ access to the countryside. She no longer _needed_ to run. For much of her life, running had been her only means of solace when she felt worried, anxious, or depressed; this time, the right words had made those feelings melt away.

No, Andromache didn't *need* to be here, now — yet she'd come back. She'd braved the tunnel, she'd fumbled through the dark, she'd stifled her fears, and again, it was because of her talk with Hector. Somehow, sitting on the rock with him had revived an old, lost part of her. She'd caught glimpses of a little girl, down in the Lukka lands — a girl who had run around all day for the sheer joy of it. A girl who had seen life in a honey-gold light.

A girl who had disappeared, the day her parents died. Who had slipped further into the past with each successive tragedy…

For years, Andromache had been a very different person — fearful, untrusting, and suspicious. She had her reasons. Now, though, she could feel her world shifting once more. She might never again be that laughing little girl, but at least — at very least — she'd *found* her. "Today is the start of a whole new era," she said aloud.

And with that, she knew just what to do. She knew how to spend her first morning alone on the Trojan plateau. *I'll find that rock*, she thought. Her rock — hers, and Hector's.

Andromache took a deep breath and gathered her hem in her hand, preparing to run. She was ready — she was set — she was —

"Kreeeeeeeeeeh!"

Andromache let her breath out in a strangled scream. *What was that?* she wondered. The sound had come from behind her. Deep in her belly, she felt the old boiling of fear. A voice in her mind cried out, '*Run, Ahndromahk! Run!*'

"Kreeeeeeeh!" the sound persisted, loud and shrill. "Kreeeh! Kreeeeeeeeeeeeh!"

Something was after her! Something was *chasing* her! In horror, Andromache whipped around, and —

All she saw was a hawk, wheeling in the grey sky.

"Fool!" she rebuked herself. "Panicking over a bird!" A bird — it was ridiculous! Panicking *at all* was ridiculous! There was nothing out here to be scared of. Hector wouldn't have shown her the tunnel if he thought the countryside was dangerous. He cared about her — he was her *friend.*

But that time, the word had no effect on her. Andromache's heart was racing, and her legs had turned to wood. She couldn't move. Not a step. In her mind, she saw what might happen if she did…

She was running across the plateau. The earth spread wide and flat on either side of her. Trees were sparse, but there were many clumps of old, dead grass. As she passed by one of them, a hand reached out to seize her. She was dragged into the tall grass by a hideous, brutish man — a raider, an enemy of Troy. He gagged her and bound her hands behind her back. He then loomed over her, trying to decide what to do — whether to drag her off, far from home, or simply kill her there. He had a knife in his hand. She pictured it slicing across her throat. Days from now, a Trojan patrol might find her corpse, drained of blood, lying facedown in the grass. But how often did they come this way? Perhaps no one would ever find her…

Andromache choked back another scream. She *had* been stupid to leave Troy's walls! What was the tunnel, compared to the horrors of the open countryside? In the tunnel, darkness had been the only enemy. Out here, foes were limitless. Anyone or anything might be lurking in that broad expanse of grass, and threats could appear from any direction. Why, oh why, had she come out here?

Andromache looked around, searching for the beauty she'd seen the day before, with Hector. It was gone. All she saw now was malevolence.

In that moment, she knew — her life hadn't changed. She hadn't entered a new era. At heart, she was still the same timid creature she'd been when she first came to Troy. She was still the cringing, battered refugee who hadn't dared set foot outside the house — who'd sensed danger around every corner — who'd been so reclusive, she'd earned the nickname Hermie, '*as in hermit.*' She was damaged beyond repair.

It's not fair, she thought, tears of frustration rolling down her cheeks. *It's not fair!* Her old instinct to flee was overwhelming. It didn't matter what her dreams were, who her friends were, or what she had to pass through on the way — all that mattered now was getting back to Troy.

"It's not fair!" she cried, kicking at a long patch of grass. As if in response, the hawk gave another loud, "Kreeeeeeeeeh!" and flew away.

℧

LESS THAN HALF an hour later, Andromache once again found herself knocking on the underside of a board. This time, though, the trapdoor opened up into a small outpost stable within the walls of Troy. She was back home. She was safe — and defeated. She was a failure.

As she left the outpost stable, she was attacked by a flock of swallows that nested near the doorway. She shrieked, covered her face, and sprinted away. Even once she'd moved beyond the birds, though, she kept the hood of her cloak low over her face. What if she passed Hector's father, Priam, on his way to the temple? Or his mother, Hecuba, out checking on one of her patients? What would they think of her cowardice? What if she ran into Hector's sister, Cassandra, or their brother, Paris? Andromache knew just the sort of thing *he* would say: '*Hey, Hermie — where are you slinking off to?*'

What if she saw Hector himself?

Andromache sped up. Not *him* — especially not *him*! She couldn't bear to think about what *he* would say! Not after she'd wheedled, cajoled, and finally fought him for the right to leave the city! Not after all the assurances she'd made that she would be fine, outside the city walls! Not after all the trouble he'd gone to, to see that she had a way out!

Early as it was, the streets were almost empty, and Andromache — to her great relief — didn't pass anyone she knew. No one noticed her until she arrived home, where her dog, Cutie, gave her a boisterous greeting. The little creature yipped in disapproval of Andromache's outing. '*Where have you been?*' she seemed to be saying. '*How dare you leave me?*'

"Sssssssssh!" hissed Andromache. "Calm down! I'm back now. Sssssssssssh! All right, all right, I get it — you need to run around. Let's go out to the courtyard."

Compared to the wild countryside beyond the city walls, the courtyard was miniscule. Dead calm. So thoroughly enclosed that Andromache could barely see the pale winter sun above her…

(*At least no mean, nasty hawks can get you, here,*) said the snide little Voice that sometimes invaded her thoughts.

Oh, go away! she snapped. Mentally turning her back to the Voice, she knelt down beside the myrtle shrub and pulled off a few dead leaves.

Long ago, when Andromache was barely a teenager, she'd lost her parents. She and her Auntie had left their Lukkan village, Hurapi, to visit the market in a nearby town. While they were gone, a rockslide from the mountain behind her house had buried her parents in a storm of rocks, debris, and rubble. Auntie had taken Andromache far away from the Lukka lands, far away from the heartache. Her plan had been to settle in Troy, the city where Andromache's father was born, but they hadn't quite made it. Instead, they'd stopped in the quiet northern village of Lyrnassa. There, years later, Auntie herself had died.

Andromache missed her family every day, but there were times when she especially ached for them. With her family, she'd always felt warm and safe. How many thousands of times had she gone out walking with her mom — in a land often troubled by raiders — and yet she'd never felt afraid. Danger had never crossed her mind! In retrospect, Andromache was certain that her mom had kept a constant vigil, and, to be sure, no voice had goaded her more fiercely if raiders were actually spotted: *'Run, Ahndromahk, run! If they catch you, they'll tear your throat out and drink your blood!'* her mom had cried to her. Still, in normal times, she'd never mentioned keeping watch. Instead, she'd pointed out different types of rock. She'd shown Andromache which berries were safe to eat and which plants gave good dyes. Always, she'd looked upon the world with a keen, admiring eye…

'Look, Ahndromahk,' she said softly, gesturing to a dew-covered shrub.
'Look at what, Mom? The branches?'
'No, between the branches. There's a perfect spider web.'

With her mom, Andromache had never seen anything but beauty around her. *If only mom had been with me today!* she thought. Instead of squandering the morning in fear, Andromache would have seen rocks — plants — creatures — other beings who called the Trojan countryside home. As it was, all those things were still alien to her. She'd wasted time. She'd missed out. She'd failed, and not just herself, but her mom, too.

(*And you failed* him, *too*,) the Voice reminded her. (*After all the trouble he went to*.)

Him. Andromache knew who it meant. *Him*…In a few short hours, she would have to see *him* for his Lukkan lesson. What would he think of her? What would he say to her?

You'll find out soon enough, Andromache sighed to herself. Listlessly, she went back to trimming dead leaves.

ℰℴ

LATE IN THE AFTERNOON, Andromache trudged up to the library. The door was slightly ajar, and when she pushed it open, she saw that Hector was already sitting at the table. His head was bent over a text, and a lock of hair was flopping into his eyes.

The boy with hair in his face, Andromache remembered, smiling. That was what her Auntie had called him, years before Lyrnassa was invaded, when Hector had visited the village with his patrol. While there, he'd carried water for an old woman, who'd been charmed by him and had never forgotten him: *'The sweet boy with hair in his face.'*

And Auntie had been right about him — Hector *was* sweet! He'd seen Andromache at her worst — angry, feeble, injured, sick, despondent — and yet none of it had fazed him. He liked her anyway. He knew what made her cry; he could always make her laugh. He was her confidant and the best friend she'd ever had.

"Hay-lo, Ahndromahk," he said.

He'd heard her come in — had caught her smiling — was smiling back at her. And oh, it was the most wonderful smile! A sweet smile — a warm, sunny smile. A friend's smile!

In her mind, Andromache could hear his voice: *'Always, always, we ahre friends.'* Joy flooded through her, such joy that she felt dizzy. Had she really spent the whole morning scolding herself? What a ridiculous creature she was! There was nothing to cry about! The world was full of beauty — swathed in beauty! Sooner or later, she would learn to be comfortable out in the countryside. It might just take a little time. After all, the streets of

Troy had once terrified her, yet now she didn't think twice about walking around the city. So she'd failed on her first trip out to the countryside! Had she *really* been worried that Hector would fault her for that? Hector, with his boundless patience? Hector, who was her *friend?*

"Hay-lo, Ahndromahk?" he said again, a hint of laughter in his voice.

"Hello," she murmured.

"You ahre walking in sleep?"

"Sleepwalking? No, just daydreaming…"

"Dreaming? On what?"

About my friend, she thought but was too embarrassed to say.

Hector saved her by asking her another question: "Cutie is where?"

"She's out on the courtyard, chasing birds."

"Oh." Hector looked disappointed.

Andromache felt another strong flooding of warmth toward him. He'd always loved Cutie, from the moment Andromache had brought her home. He'd even been the one to give the little dog her name. "I'll make sure she comes tomorrow."

"Good," said Hector.

Andromache sat down across the table from him. "What are you reading?" she asked.

He held his text out to her. "The stohry ohff a hohrse wiff wings."

She smiled at his accent, still thick after more than a year of lessons. "Is it a good story?"

"I haff not reaaded mahch, yet. It is new. You want to read it fohr lessons?"

"Sure," said Andromache. "Why not?" Their lessons had always been free-form. When Priam and Hecuba had taken her in, after the raid on Lyrnassa, the only thing they'd asked of her was that she teach Lukkan to their eldest son. Hector, like all Trojans, had grown up speaking Truvan, but unlike most of his compatriots, he'd never gained fluency in a foreign language. His parents had wanted to fill that gap in his education. Other than requesting that Hector be taught '*phrases of politeness and refinement,*' though, they hadn't laid down any guidelines about how lessons should be structured. Everything was left to Andromache's judgment. Her favorite thing to do was to read and discuss texts with Hector. The readings were in Truvan, since Lukkan had no written form, but their discussions were in Lukkan — and they were always fascinating, no matter what the subject matter. The story of a winged horse sounded like as good a choice as any. "Unless —" Andromache hesitated. "Weren't we already reading something?"

"I know not," said Hector, a rueful smile on his face.

Andromache blushed. The past few Lukkan lessons were a blur to her, as well. All throughout their week-long fight, she'd devoted most of her time to making Hector miserable. "Let's just start fresh, then," she murmured. A fresh start with Hector, in lessons as well as in life.

Hector nodded. "All rahght."

"The flying horse text sounds interesting. I like horses."

Hector smiled. "Then some time, you mahst come again to the hohrse house. Buzzy and Thisbe, they want to see you."

Buzzy and Thisbe — Hector's horse and pony. Andromache hadn't seen the two of them in over a week, now. "I'll come soon," she promised. "And I'll bring apples for them, if you have any left in storage."

"Bring one also for Xanthus," Hector advised her. "In winter, he can be sahch a lobster…"

"Lobster?" Andromache raised her eyebrows. Xanthus, the old stable master, had always reminded her of a lobster, but she was surprised to hear Hector make the same comparison.

"He's cranky," said Hector. "Grouchy."

"Oh!" Andromache giggled. "Then you mean '*crabby*.' He's a crab."

Hector nodded. "Yes, a crab! So, you can bring fohr him apples? Breads wiff honey? Somefing to make him sweet?"

"Wine?" Andromache suggested.

Laughing, Hector shook his head. "No — that is fohr the hohrses."

Andromache *tsk*-ed in disbelief. "Taruisha —" she used the Lukkan word "— is the only place I've *ever* heard of where people mix wine into the horse feed!"

"And Taruisha has the hohrses the best in all the world!" Hector said smugly. "A hohrse is proud to be from Taruisha. He can hold his head so high!"

"That's just because he's light-headed from all the wine," Andromache retorted.

Hector groaned, then laughed. "You win," he said.

She shot him a triumphant look.

"All right, all right!" He raised an eyebrow. "Just don't go and get *drunk* on your victory."

It was Andromache's turn to groan. Had they always teased each other this way? She couldn't remember. Even if they had, everything felt different to her now that she knew where she stood with him. She could enjoy their jokes without fearing any hidden motives.

(*Your lessons could* always *have been like this, if you hadn't waited so long to talk to him*,) taunted the snide little Voice. (*You wasted a lot of time*.)

Better late than never! Andromache thought at the Voice, although she knew that it was right. She *had* wasted a lot of time...

"What?" Hector asked her.

Andromache blinked. "What, what?"

"You say somefing I cannot hear."

Blushing, Andromache realized that she must have muttered aloud to the Voice. "Nothing much," she said to Hector. "I was just reminding myself of what to bring Xanthus if I go down to the stables, later."

"Oh."

"How crabby is he, today?"

Hector shrugged. "I know not. Today, I do not see him — I sleep all day. Yesterday, I haff training in the afternoon, then petrolling, late, in the hills."

"That's right," said Andromache, remembering. "I can see why you needed to catch up on sleep."

"And you?" asked Hector. "You go out there, today? To the hills?" His eyes were expectant. Eager. He was hoping to see her happy, hoping that she'd gone running out in the countryside she claimed to love so much.

"Not very far," Andromache said softly.

Hector frowned. "Somefing is wrong?"

"Just my dress," Andromache explained — lied. "My long dress..." She let her words trail off, hoping he would remember the way she'd tripped over her hem and skinned her knee the day before. When he nodded gravely, she gave a soft sigh. Lying to him made her feel rotten. *I'll just have to learn to love it out there*, she told herself. *Then I won't have to lie, anymore*. But even if she failed, and Hector found out — even if he was annoyed with her for not going out to the hills, after all the effort he'd made to give her access — the world wouldn't end. He wouldn't stop liking her. They'd entered a whole new era.

Andromache smiled. "Back to the text," she said. "Does it mention what the winged horses eat?"

"Why?"

"I was wondering if they ever have wine with their grain."

"Ohff couhrse!" said Hector. "How else can they feel lahght enough to fly?"

Chapter 2

The next morning, as Andromache was braiding her hair to go to market, she was interrupted by a sudden racket at her door.

Crack, crack, crack.

"Just a moment, all right?" she hollered, assuming that the visitor was Paris. He'd never come up to her room to rouse her for marketing, before — ordinarily, she was the one trying to get *him* out the door at a decent hour. *There must be a sexy new honey cake vendor,* she thought sourly. *Nothing else could get him this excited.* He was certainly never as focused on shopping as on flirting...

Crack, crack, crack.

"I said, one moment!" cried Andromache. "Your little girlfriend will just have to wait!"

"Andromache? Can I come in?"

Andromache frowned. The person at her door wasn't Paris — wasn't a man at all. She knew the voice from somewhere. It was familiar, but she couldn't place it. Was it one of Cassandra's friends? Or maybe one of Hecuba's? Curious, she dropped her half-braided hair and said, "Come in."

The door swung open to reveal a very tall, stunning woman dressed in riding clothes.

"P-Penthesilea!" gasped Andromache. Penthesilea, Hector's fiancée and comrade-in-arms; he usually called her *Lee*. Penthesilea, the woman who had brought Andromache to Troy in the first place. Penthesilea — there was no mistaking her.

Penthesilea nodded a greeting.

"Do — are — is there —" Unsure what to say, Andromache closed her mouth. What was Penthesilea doing at her door?

They hadn't spoken in well over a year. *The last time*, thought Andromache, *she offered me a place to stay if I wasn't happy in the citadel. Is she here to check on me? Or does she have some other business in mind?* One thing was certain: Penthesilea must have a mission. She wasn't the type to stop by for an idle chat. "Do — do —" Andromache gulped. "Do you — need something?"

Penthesilea frowned. "Didn't Hector tell you I'd be coming? To bring you running clothes?"

Andromache shook her head.

"Oh," said Penthesilea. "Well — he asked me to bring you this." She gestured to a bundle that was tucked under her arm. "He said all your dresses are too long, and it's dangerous for you to go running."

Cringing, Andromache imagined Hector and Penthesilea — *Lee* — discussing the spill she'd taken, two days earlier. What an oaf she was! Someone like *Lee* would never trip on her own hemline! "Thanks," she mumbled, embarrassed. "So — what did you bring?"

Penthesilea held out several knee-length dresses and a pair of thick-soled sandals, but Andromache didn't take them. Borrowing clothes from Cassandra was one thing, but she hardly knew Penthesilea. Did the woman even *want* to lend her anything, or had Hector coerced her? Or perhaps she just felt sorry for poor, gawky Andromache...

"They're all right?" asked Penthesilea, looking concerned.

"Oh — oh, yes, they're good," said Andromache. "But — but — I mean, are you sure *you* don't need them?"

Penthesilea shook her head. "They're army issue, not mine."

"Oh — thank you," said Andromache finally accepting the bundle.

Nodding, Penthesilea said, "Let me know if you need anything else."

How about your height? Andromache thought bitterly. If she were as tall and strong as Penthesilea, the countryside wouldn't terrify her! She could run blithely through the wilds, never worrying about raiders or brigands. She would have nothing to fear. If only —

Andromache paused mid-thought. An idea had come to her, the solution to all her problems: *she* could never be as strong and fearless as Penthesilea, but what if the woman came with her?

Penthesilea was a warrior, one of Hector's comrades. Andromache wouldn't have to worry about thugs or raiders as long as Penthesilea was beside her! She would be as safe as she'd been with Hector himself. Meanwhile, she could get to know the countryside.

Even better, she could get to know Penthesilea. The two of them had a lot in common. They were both transplants to the city of Troy, both outsiders to the citadel. Who knew? — they might even become friends, and Andromache found herself suddenly greedy for friends.

"Actually," said Andromache. "Maybe there is something."

Penthesilea cocked her head. "What's that?"

"Do *you* ever run there, out in the countryside?" asked Andromache. "To train, or for fun, or —"

The woman was nodding. "Sometimes."

"The next time you do, could I go with you?"

"All right," said Penthesilea. "I'm busy this morning, but this afternoon —"

"I have Lukkan lessons."

"Oh." Penthesilea's face took on a catlike look. "Then how about tomorrow morning?"

"At dawn? At the outpost stable?"

"Sounds good," said Penthesilea. "See you there."

∽

ANDROMACHE'S HOPES for friendship were somewhat dampened by Penthesilea, who ran with steadfast focus and had no spare energy for chitchat. As they wound through fields and down into ravines — and, Andromache noticed, past the rock where she'd sat with Hector — Penthesilea said nothing more than the occasional, "Watch out! Stump!"

Still, Andromache refused to let herself feel disappointed. Having company, even quiet company, made a pleasant change from running alone. She also liked the challenge of running with a partner. On the flat stretches, she lagged behind. There was no help for it; Penthesilea's legs were much longer than hers. On the steeper sections, though, Andromache was pleased to find herself in the lead. All of those stairs she'd run during her first months in Troy were paying off.

She felt good. She felt confident. She felt almost brave.

Before passing back into the city, she and Penthesilea decided to meet at the same time the next day.

Andromache was there early, and she brought Cutie with her. During the run, she pushed herself harder than ever. She knew the terrain, now, and she was growing reaccustomed to the feel of running on grass. What was more, she was full of energy — good energy, for once. She was happy with her life, with her home, with her dog — with her *friends* — and now she had the freedom of the countryside, too.

"Good run," Penthesilea said afterward.

Andromache nodded.

"Want to come back tomorrow?"

"Tomorrow," Andromache agreed.

The two women crossed back under the walls and went their separate ways.

Chapter 3

L ife was smiling on Andromache as she moved further into her new era. In the first part of the rainy season, she'd begun a weaving project, a cloth with stripes of green and white. She wasn't yet sure what she was going to make it into — perhaps a blanket — but so far she was happy with the result of her weaving. Smooth, even, and soft, the cloth would have made her mother proud. What would her mom have said?

'This is lovely, Ahndromahk. I always knew you'd do good work, once you had a little more patience.'

Her Auntie, too, would have given a nod of approval, if a slightly grudging one:

'You've done a good job, girl, but it's too bad you made stripes. If you'd stuck to one color, you'd be twice as far along by now. I suppose it was your mom who taught you about stripes — her with her fancy ways!'

Even her dad would have chimed in:

'Don't listen to your Auntie, Little Cricket! Stripes might not make your blanket any warmer, but they make it more beautiful. You should never feel bad about making the world more beautiful.'

The imagined compliments and teasing meant even more to Andromache than the blanket itself. If she closed her eyes, she could see her Auntie's wrinkled face. She could see her mom's smile, weary but warm. She could see her parents' shoulders pressed together. They were all so close to her, closer than they'd been in months.

She suspected that clearing the air with Hector had drawn them near. Lukkan was a joy, again. Lessons were a joy. Andromache only wished that her family could have listened in on one. They would have been intrigued by the text she and Hector were reading, the one about winged horses. Although only her dad could have read it — her mom and Auntie had never learned to read — they would have loved hearing about the strange homeland of the horses:

> *These exceptional creatures live on the flank of a mountain no less wondrous than they. Upon this mountain lie pockets of unquenchable flame that can be extinguished neither by wind nor by smothering earth. Sailors on the sea at night believe these flames to be the flares of fire nymphs, warning ships of their approach to land…*

What would her family have thought about that passage? Andromache had been fascinated. Hector, meanwhile, had laughed himself sick over '*fire nymphs*':

> *'Fahre girls? Fahre girls! That is crazy,' said Hector, once he'd calmed down enough to speak. 'Baht not so crazy as a fahre who cannot go out.'*
>
> *'What's so crazy about that?' asked Andromache.*
>
> *'You can fink ohff a reason fohr this fahre?' he challenged. 'Fohr why it cannot go out?'*
>
> *'No,' she admitted. 'Unless — '*
>
> *'Ahnless?'*
>
> *'Unless the mountain sits above a bottomless spring of wine.'*
>
> *He laughed harder than ever. 'Oh, Ahndromahk! I say this mountain is a dream some guy has after he drinks a bottomless spring ohff wine!'*
>
> *'Why couldn't there be a mountain of unquenchable fire? Just inland from it, there's a whole palace made of ice, remember?'*
>
> *'No, I do not. You read fahrther than me.'*
>
> *'Oh. Travelers who went inland from the fire mountain saw a palace made of ice. It's as tall as a cliff and has lots of terraces. Behind the palace, there are hot springs, and their water dribbles down to fill the terraces.'*

'Hot water dribbling down ices?' Hector snorted. *'Oh, this is fahnny! Lahke the sahmmer is attacking the winter!'*

'Maybe you're right,' Andromache mused. *'Maybe the ice palace is a symbol for the change of seasons.'*

Hector made a face. *'Ohr maybe the guy who writes this text is jahst crazy,'* he said.

'Or maybe the so-called ice palace is really made of salt. Salt wouldn't wash away as fast as ice,' she retorted.

'Maybe,' he agreed cautiously. *'Maybe there is sahch a palace.'*

Before Andromache could revel in her victory, though, Hector added, *'Baht there can be no fahre mountain, no home fohr flying hohrses. Why? Becahse there can be no flying hohrses.'*

'Why not?'

'Troy has good hohrses. Many, many good hohrses. Herds ohff good hohrses.'

'So?'

'So, they ahre here. On the earff. Fink about dahcks.'

'Ducks?' Andromache frowned. *'Why should I think about ducks?'*

'Becahse,' Hector said triumphantly. *'When dahcks ahre in the sky, and they see dahcks on the earff — maybe on a lake — they fly down. They want to see the dahcks on the earff.'*

'So?' Andromache said again.

'So, no flying hohrses come to see the hohrses ohff Troy. Neffer, neffer do they come. Why not? Becahse there ahre *no flying hohrses!'*

Andromache bit her lip. She wasn't convinced that flying horses — assuming there was such a thing — would be attracted to land-bound horses the same way ducks in flight were drawn to ducks swimming on a lake. Then again, she had no way of proving Hector wrong, and he knew a lot more than she did about horses. Rather than tackling an argument she had little chance of winning, she asked a question:

'If there *were flying horses, and you could ride one, where would you want it to take you?'*

Hector's answer was both prompt and flattering: *'To the lands ohff Lukká.'*

Andromache, too, wished he could fly there — and not only in space, but also back in time. She wished they could fly there together, just for a day, to a little cottage up on a rocky hillside.

ℰℭ

ANDROMACHE WAS NO STRANGER to the main stables of Troy. For months, she'd been making occasional trips there to play roodles with the old stable master, Xanthus. He'd invited her — requested her — stored up complaints and grumblings to regale her with. Still, she hadn't felt truly at home there. The stables were Hector's domain, after all, and she hadn't wanted to overstay her welcome.

Now that she knew that Hector liked her, she felt at ease in the stables. She went there whenever she pleased and spent lots of time with the horses — except for Penthesilea's horse, Battleblaze. Battleblaze was terrified of her; she bucked and whinnied whenever Andromache came near. *'She remembers you,'* Hector had explained. Battleblaze remembered being ridden from Lyrnassa to Troy, remembered the way Andromache had fought to stay astride, remembered her pulling out handfuls of hair in the process. Not wanting to upset the poor creature any further, Andromache stayed away from her. She avoided the whole middle aisle, where Battleblaze had a stall.

It's all right, she murmured to the horse from afar. *We all have our secret fears*. She could certainly sympathize with feelings of fear and anxiety. Even now, one thing about the stables still made her nervous: combat practice. Soldiers gathered on a field behind the stables to train with spears, swords, clubs, and an array of other gruesome instruments. Under Hector's command, they learned the best ways to kill or disarm an enemy — and then they practiced the moves on each other.

Andromache hated the very thought of it. She didn't want to be reminded of the Hector she'd met near Lyrnassa…

He was hulking, a giant, with two black hollows for eyes. His bronze armor was smoke-streaked and covered with blood. He reeked of sweat, of gore. He was a monster…

The Raider, as she'd called him back then, had haunted her nightmares for months. Even now that she knew Troy's army was used to defend, never to attack or invade — and even now that she knew how sweet Hector really was — she didn't like to think about the vision she'd seen.

Still worse than Hector's frightful appearance, though, were all the ghastly things that might happen *to* him on the battlefield. Andromache thought of the long, worm-pink scar on his arm, and how much more hideous the wound might have been. She thought of his skin slashed open — his bones crushed — his blood spilling out onto the ground.

Hector was commander of half the city's forces, and war was a part of his life, but Andromache hated to think about it — and she most assuredly did *not* want to see him dressed for combat practice. Once, she almost had. He'd come back inside when she was by Buzzy's stall, and she'd fled only just in the nick of time. As long as she was mindful of his schedule, though, and alert to what was going on in the stables, she didn't think she would be caught like that again. She was free to visit Buzzy and Thisbe and to play countless matches of roodles with Xanthus.

The grumpy old stable master couldn't make up his mind whether to scowl at or praise her ever-increasing skill. He hated to lose, but, on the other hand, he liked to see a young person whose head wasn't full of fluff.

If he was ambivalent about Andromache, though, Cassandra completely bewildered him. He met the girl one rainy evening when Andromache coaxed her down to the stables. Cassandra giggled through the old man's rantings, and she played well each time she was at the board, but whenever a boy walked by, she made eyes at him. She hadn't spent much time in the stables until Andromache brought her down there, and the constant flow of young men was a revelation to her.

"I've never seen such a flirt," Xanthus complained to Andromache, the next day. "If she'd watched the board the way she was watching those soldiers —"

"She would've creamed you," Andromache said impishly.

Xanthus glowered at her. "That is *not* what I was going to say, Missy. In any case, it's just as well that that little hotsy-totsy doesn't come down here as much as *you* do, or the whole place would go to hell, what with her goggling at the soldiers and them goggling right back — and no work getting done. Hmmmph!"

"I roodle you," murmured Andromache.

Huffily, the stable master reset the board.

"Anyway," said Andromache, "I wouldn't worry. None of the guys goggled back at her."

Xanthus froze mid-play. "Eh? Is that a fact? Then they're even dimmer than I thought." He shook his head in disgust. "There's no hope for the city. None at all."

Andromache smiled. She suspected that the young men had *wanted* to flirt back with the beautiful Cassandra, but, knowing whose sister she was, they hadn't dared.

Cassandra, too, had mixed feelings about her trip to the stables. "I love that stable master!" she cooed to Andromache, afterward. "He's a funny old dear, isn't he? Really, honey — the things he said! And there are *so many* cute boys down there!" The girl sighed. "I just wish they'd been friendlier. It wouldn't have hurt them to *smile* once or twice! I mean, *he* wasn't even there!"

Cassandra loved her brothers dearly, but she saw Hector as a damper to her love life. Intentionally or not, he terrified the boys who might otherwise have flirted with her — in particular the boys who were his subordinates.

"They just wanted to be careful," Andromache chided. "He could've come in at any time."

"It's so unfair!" moaned Cassandra.

"If you don't want to go back there, that's fine," said Andromache. "You don't have to."

"I never said I don't want to go back!"

"But —"

"Listen, honey — you know the sculpture garden?"

Andromache thought of the park where there were dozens of carved stone blocks, sculptures of famous Trojans past and present. "What about it?" she asked.

"You don't go there expecting the sculptures to smile at you, let alone to kiss with you," Cassandra said gravely. "You go there to *appreciate*. I'll just have to adjust my expectations for the stables."

Andromache hid a smile. "Xanthus will be delighted!"

ANDROMACHE'S NEW ERA was also turning out to be the age of Penthesilea.

Before, the other woman had been just a shadowy presence in her life — usually unseen, seldom mentioned. Now, Andromache had frequent encounters with her. On fair days, they went running together out in the countryside; while on rainy days, they sometimes crossed paths in the stables. Penthesilea wasn't there as often as Hector or Xanthus, but she made her rounds.

Even when Andromache didn't actually see the woman, she was popping up in conversations with Hector.

"I wish the rain would take a break," Andromache lamented to him one afternoon. "Honestly, six days in a row! The hills will be nothing but mud by the time I get back out there."

"So, you go there sometimes?" Hector asked casually.

Andromache stifled a cough. Assuming that the outpost stable guards made reports to their commander, Hector was already well aware of her trips to the countryside. She supposed, however, that he didn't want to seem like he was spying on her.

"Yes, I've been running with —" For no good reason, she choked on the name. But why would Hector care who her running partner was? Besides, he probably already knew. "I've been running with Penthesilea."

Hector merely nodded. He didn't seem to find the pairing strange at all. "Good. That is fahn?" he asked.

More confidently, Andromache went on. "Yes, it's nice. I like her." And she did. Talking to Penthesilea didn't come easily, but the woman was calm and steady, and Andromache liked being around her.

"Mm-hmm," Hector agreed. "She is so great."

"She *is* great. A really good runner, too."

"She can keep ahp wiff you?"

"She tries," said Andromache, smiling.

Hector smiled back. "You talk wiff her, in your rahnnings?" he asked.

Andromache shook her head. "Not much."

Hector nodded. His face was inscrutable, but somehow Andromache got the impression that he was relieved.

Later, as Andromache was reflecting on that conversation, the strangeness of it hit her. Why was Hector glad that the two women weren't talking? Why would he care? And what did he mean by *'She is so great?'*

'She is so great.' The words themselves didn't surprise Andromache. Hector often cloaked high praise in simple language. The other day, she'd been fussing over Buzzy: *'He's just beautiful! I love the way his mane curls over his shoulder. And what a sweetheart, too!'* Hector had agreed, saying, *'Buzzy is a nice hohrse.'* That was it. But oh, how his eyes had softened, and how tenderly he'd said the words!

'She is so great' hadn't sounded tender at all. Then again, Hector never showed much affection for his fiancée, other than by calling her the pet name, *'Lee.'* When Andromache saw the two of them in the stables, she could tell that they had a perfect understanding of each other. With a few simple nods and a half-finished sentence, they could communicate a whole day's worth of activities. The nods, however, never progressed to sweet looks or caresses. Neither Penthesilea nor Hector brushed slyly against the other's shoulder.

Maybe they don't know how to be affectionate, mused Andromache, thinking of the stiff pat and stiffer waves Hector had occasionally given her. *Maybe they're not affectionate people.*

The snide little Voice in her mind gave a knowing snort. As it did, Andromache thought back to a moment when she'd been out in the countryside, with Hector...

His hand was on her back. It was warm, so warm that she could feel it through two layers of cloth...

That — that wasn't affection, Andromache protested. *That was fear. He was worried about me when I fell, and —*

(*Of course,*) the Voice said smugly. (*But I think you see my point. He knows how to be —* ahem *— affectionate. He and Penthesilea just doesn't do it in front of other people — especially not in the stables. That wouldn't be very professional, would it? No — they wait until nighttime and meet in dark places, where they can be alone.*)

The Voice was right, as Andromache well knew. The whole *city* knew! A pair of nosy Trojan matrons had once complained to Hecuba that Hector was *'living in disorder,'* meeting his woman in secret rather than marrying her properly. Paris, too, had made sly remarks about his brother running off to an evening rendez-vous with Penthesilea — and Hector hadn't denied it.

Andromache felt strangely bothered by the whole idea. *Well, if that's what they're up to at night, you'd think they'd at least give each other a sweet look or two during the day,* she snapped.

(*That's not how it works here, remember?*) said the Voice. (*Serious couples show restraint — at least in public.*)

Again, the Voice had a point. Young Trojans were known for sneaking out of parties to kiss in the stairwell, just for fun — Cassandra unabashedly kissed as many young men as she could. Once a couple was serious about each other, however, the stairway kissing stopped. Demuchus, Andromache's one-time companion, had long put off kissing her because he'd wanted to marry her. The less overt kissing a relationship involved, the more serious it was. According to Cassandra, Hector and Penthesilea had been engaged for almost three years, now —

(*And, by the look of it, their relationship is about as serious as they come,*) the Voice opined.

Andromache felt another wave of irritation. *Then why don't they just get married, and done with it?* she said crossly.

(*You know why...*)

And of course, she did. She knew that Hector wanted to get married — she'd known ever since the day he explained Trojan wedding symbolism to her. '*Blue is fohr the happy,*' he'd said wistfully, as though despairing ever to have such happiness for himself. *Because Penthesilea doesn't want to move to the citadel,* thought Andromache. *She doesn't like Hector's neighbors. She thinks they're hard on outsiders.* Which was true. Andromache and even Hecuba had suffered at the hands of the Trojan elite. But while the two of them had learned to cope with all the snobbery, Penthesilea apparently hadn't. *It's strange that Hector doesn't just move down to live with her, then.*

(*Maybe he doesn't like her neighbors,*) sneered the Voice. (*Maybe they're hard on the Taruishan elite.*)

Oh, shut up, said Andromache. More likely, as a commander of Troy's army, Hector was required to live up on the citadel. Yes, that was it! He might not have the freedom to leave, even if he wanted to. If so, the choice was Penthesilea's to make, and the woman seemed unwilling even to try. It was almost as though she didn't *want* to live with Hector —

Andromache's eyes widened. Was that it? Penthesilea didn't feel the same way Hector did — didn't yearn for marriage — perhaps didn't even love him? It was possible. People got married for all kinds of different reasons. Andromache's own parents had fallen instantly and passionately in love, and had then run off together, but other people got married for convenience, or for political gain, or —

(*Or to be rescued,*) the Voice reminded her.

Rescued. The word conjured up a host of frightful images: a prodding tongue — a wagon — her dress, covered in blood, as she shambled down the path to Lyrnassa —

Shut up! she huffed at the Voice. *That's not what I was going to say. I'm sure that* Penthesilea *doesn't need to be rescued!*

The Voice seemed to grin at her dismay. (*Then what's her reason for getting engaged?*)

Because, said Andromache, pausing for effect. Her off-the-cuff conclusion made a lot of sense. *It gives her an edge in the army.* Surely Hector's fiancée would be better positioned than most warriors to rise through the ranks. And if Penthesilea wanted to keep her status without having to live in the citadel, her best option was to stay engaged forever.

Andromache could sympathize with Penthesilea's situation. Her own father had been born in Troy, the bastard son of a master luthier. The luthier — her grandfather — was dead, but Andromache knew roughly where his shop had been. She'd gone down many times to search for it, yet she'd never truly wanted to find it. What if it was decrepit and dirty? What if the neighbors were nasty people who hadn't liked her dad? What if no one remembered him? Andromache had spun various fantasies about her dad's childhood in Troy, some so vivid that she'd actually *seen* him as a little boy. The visions made her feel close to him, and she didn't want a harsh reality to destroy them.

Oh, yes, she could sympathize with the desire to live in a half-world — to seek something without really wanting to find it. The difference was that her fantasies didn't hurt anyone, while Penthesilea's *did.* If Penthesilea — *Lee* — felt nothing for Hector and didn't really want to marry him, the decent thing would be to cut him loose. He didn't deserve to be strung along, to be met only in dark places, at night, as though his fiancée were ashamed of him.

(*Why do you care?*) demanded the Voice.

Because he's my friend, Andromache replied tartly. Aside from that, he was a good person. He was warm, and funny, and bright, and he deserved better.

(*Maybe you're wrong about how he feels,*) the Voice argued. (*Maybe he's happy with how things are, secret meetings and all. Maybe he's getting more than you think out of the arrangement...*)

Andromache blushed. *If that's it, fine!* she thought. *I don't care what they do, if they're both happy!* They could stay engaged forever or get married tomorrow, for all she cared. Now that she knew Hector liked speaking Lukkan, she was no longer worried that his marriage would bring an end to their Lukkan lessons. She wouldn't be affected, no matter what they did. Her only concern was for Hector's well-being.

Andromache knew that voices couldn't smirk, but the one in her head seemed to be doing just that.

Chapter 4

On the first clear day after a week of rain, Andromache took Cutie and headed to the outpost stable, hoping Penthesilea would be there. She was.

"Morning," said Andromache.

"You're here to go running?" asked Penthesilea.

Andromache nodded.

"Let's go, then."

They passed through the tunnel and out into the open countryside. While the two women ran, Cutie sniffed around, joyous at her first taste of freedom after days spent moldering in the house. Andromache, too, was so pleased to be out in the fresh air that she paid little heed to where she was stepping — and promptly ran right through a nest of thorns. "Eeeek!" she cried.

"Rock?" asked Penthesilea.

"No," said Andromache. "Butcher's thorn!" She stopped to inspect the scrapes on her legs, muttering, "I didn't know *that* grew up here!"

Penthesilea, too, stopped. "And I've never heard of butcher's thorn."

"You wouldn't want to! It's the worst kind of prickle plant. I used to gather butcher's thorn for my aunt so she could make it into a tea. She said it helped her fall asleep." Reluctantly, Andromache added, "Maybe I should bring some back for Hecuba." Hecuba used many different plants in her healing salves, poultices, and tonics, and she would undoubtedly be glad for a new type of sleeping aid. The danger was that she would then want butcher's thorn cultivated in her garden…

"You sure know a lot about plants," said Penthesilea with respect.

Humbly, Andromache shook her head. "I have so much to learn. I've never even heard of half the stuff they sell down in the herb market."

"Oh, is *that* why you come down to my neighborhood?" asked Penthesilea. "To visit the herb market?"

Andromache blushed furiously. She'd been seen! She'd been seen conducting her secret, private mission. She'd been seen wandering through the neighborhood where her grandfather's lute shop had once been. Penthesilea, who lived down there, had seen her!

"I was wondering why you kept showing up down there," said Penthesilea.

Kept showing up? The woman knew it was a habit! And she could no doubt sense that Andromache was up to something strange. How many other people in the neighborhood had noticed her? No one else there knew her, but they might have begun to recognize her. By now, she might have a reputation as the crazy woman who muttered to herself. Oh, it was so unfair! Andromache hadn't even been down there in weeks — not since her reconciliation with Hector!

"I figured it must be for something important," said Penthesilea. "It's not the kind of neighborhood people stroll through for fun."

Andromache hesitated. Penthesilea, if anyone, would understand her true errand down in that quarter: to look for but not find the luthier's shop. The woman had a similarly strange goal, to be engaged but not married to Hector. If Andromache told her about the shop, though, she would inevitably have to explain her family's whole twisted history. She would have to tell Penthesilea about the master luthier who had taken advantage of his servant girl — about the child who had been trained for years in the luthier's craft but had ultimately been disowned — about the bitter young man who had stolen his father's tools and secrets and fled to the Lukka lands. She hardly knew Penthesilea and didn't want to expose this sordid past to her.

"I thought maybe you'd changed your mind about living in the citadel," Penthesilea suggested. "If you have, I can help —"

"No—I haven't changed my mind!" Andromache interrupted. Just because Penthesilea couldn't reconcile herself to living there didn't mean Andromache couldn't! She didn't fit in with the Trojan elite, but neither were they hostile to her. She was happy living just where she was. She loved her house and her host family, and she *never* wanted to leave!

Hoping to close the matter once and for all, she stood and started running again. Penthesilea soon caught up, and the two women ran side by side, not speaking, just looking straight ahead into the distance. Neither broke the silence, not even to warn the other about a stump or a rock. Andromache finally began to scold herself:

Penthesilea was trying to talk to you! She was asking you about your life. She was trying to be friends *with you! Isn't that what you wanted?* Penthesilea hadn't been making idle conversation; the woman didn't do *anything* idly. She'd been trying to make a connection. After all those days of running in silence, there had finally been a breakthrough, and Andromache had ruined it. *So, fix it!* she told herself. *Ask* her *something!*

Andromache cleared her throat. "So," she began, trying to think of what to say. "You — I mean — How was —" Useless! Nothing was coming to her! Nothing, except a very bland question, one unlikely to spur on further conversation. At best, it would earn Andromache a nod. Since she had nothing better, though, she turned to Penthesilea and asked, "You're from Santiya, right?" Santiya was Hecuba's home country, a land to the east where her brother still ruled as king. According to Cassandra, it was there that Hector had first met Penthesilea.

But Penthesilea didn't nod. She looked startled by the question, even dismayed.

"I'm sorry," whispered Andromache. Why, oh why, had she chosen *that* question? She knew better than most people how sensitive a matter origins could be! She wanted to speed up, to outrun Penthesilea and not have to look at her, but they were on the flat and she didn't stand a chance. She kept her eyes locked on the dead, fallen leaves littering the ground. They were halfway back to the gateway cottage, now. If she could just hang in a little longer, the run would end, and she could escape the embarrassment she'd caused them both.

A few moments later, though, Penthesilea surprised her by saying, "I'm from all over."

"Oh," murmured Andromache, nodding. She could sympathize with *that*, as well as with not wanting to talk about it.

But Penthesilea went on: "Have you heard of the Munnanda Sea? Through the straits, to the northeast?"

"I've read about it," said Andromache.

"I lived there for a while, before I went to Santiya."

"Oh." Andromache paused. She didn't know how best to respond, but Penthesilea was making an effort, so she would do the same. "Is the Munnanda Sea pretty?" she asked cautiously.

Penthesilea shrugged. "It's big."

"Oh," said Andromache, feeling encouraged. At very least, the conversation hadn't ground to a halt. "So, is that where you were born?"

The other woman shook her head. "I was born near Percote, down the straits from Troy."

"Then Truvan is your native language!" Andromache exclaimed. The news came as a surprise. She'd always assumed that Penthesilea had learned Truvan later in life, perhaps at the Santiyan court.

"Yes," said Penthesilea. "It's my native language."

"I've never been to Percote," said Andromache. "What's it like?"

"I don't remember," Penthesilea said softly. "Raiders took my mother and me when I was little, and I haven't been back since."

No mention of her father — and Andromache knew what that meant. Raiders who took women and children usually killed the men. "Oh," she whispered. "I'm so — sorry." She didn't know what else to say. She'd been on the receiving end of many similar awkward sentiments; now she knew that giving them was just as awkward.

Penthesilea faced forward, her eyes expressionless. For the next half-hour, she said nothing, and Andromache didn't dare pose any more questions. At the door to the gateway cottage, however, Penthesilea asked, just like always, "Tomorrow?"

Andromache nodded. "Tomorrow." Perhaps by then, she would have thought of a topic that didn't make either of them uncomfortable.

AS THE DAY drew to a close, though, Andromache lay down and sighed. She still had no idea of what to say to Penthesilea during their next run. The problem wasn't that they had too little in common. Far from it, Penthesilea was an alternate version of her, the person Andromache might have become if her father had been killed by raiders, if she and her mother had been captured and held as slaves. Even with that difference, her life was hauntingly similar to Penthesilea's. They'd both been orphaned. They'd both survived raids. They'd both moved around from place to place to place. They shared a wealth of grim, traumatic experiences.

Perhaps that was itself the problem. Neither of them wanted to relive the things they had in common.

Knowing both of them as well as he did, Hector might have been able to suggest a suitable conversation topic, but Andromache hadn't wanted to ask him. Earlier that day, she'd gone to the stables to visit Xanthus and had instead seen Hector and Penthesilea in the midst of a fight — at least, it looked like a fight. They weren't yelling, but they were stalking around, haughty and unnaturally stiff with each other. On the spot, she'd decided not to mention Penthesilea during lessons. What if Hector got mad at *her*, Andromache, because she brought up a sore subject?

Andromache shook her head. That afternoon, she'd spent several perfect hours discussing winged horses and fire-breathing goats with Hector. She was glad she hadn't spoiled their time together by mentioning Penthesilea. That matter would just have to sort itself out on its own.

Chapter 5

Andromache felt queasy as she walked down to the outpost stable the next morning. She half expected Penthesilea not to meet her, but the woman was there, looking as calm and steady as ever. Her face showed no lingering discomfort from their failed conversation the day before.

Well, good, thought Andromache. *Maybe we can try again*. As they ran, she watched the landscape for something to discuss with Penthesilea — the scrub oaks, perhaps, with their prickly leaves. Or maybe not the oaks themselves, but the squirrels running up and down them. That might —

"Have you ever thought about joining the army?" Penthesilea asked suddenly, interrupting Andromache's thoughts.

The what? Andromache stopped running to turn and stare at her companion.

"Well, have you?" prodded Penthesilea.

"No!" Andromache shook her head vehemently.

"Never?"

"No, never!"

"Maybe you should," said Penthesilea. "The way you run, you'd make a fine courier."

Andromache shook her head again, less to say '*no*' than in sheer disbelief of what she was hearing. Penthesilea knew her best as a weak, cringing little creature, a terrified mess. Yet now, out of the blue, here was Penthesilea, inviting her to join the army! The *army*! Had the woman lost her mind?

"You'd make a fine courier," Penthesilea repeated. "More, if you wanted, if you had the right training."

More, if she wanted? Andromache *didn't* want — not more, not anything! She didn't even like to *think* about armies! If an enemy were ever to appear before her, she would trip over herself trying to flee. She didn't want to be in the army, and the army wouldn't want her! She shook her head until her ears started ringing.

"It's true," said Penthesilea. She had a look of ineffable patience, as though she'd waited years for this moment.

"No!" Andromache insisted. "I mean, thank you, but — but — I wouldn't be any use."

"I think you would," Penthesilea said earnestly.

"You can't be serious!"

"Why not?"

Andromache stared openmouthed. "I'm a *wimp*!" she cried.

Penthesilea shook her head. "You punched Hector, the day we found you near Lyrnassa."

"That was a reflex," muttered Andromache, blushing.

"Most people would've fainted, or screamed." Penthesilea gave her a long, hard look. "I've always known you were tougher than that. You know how Hector told me to take you to Thebe, that day?"

Andromache nodded. She remembered, although faintly.

"He wanted *me* to take you because after the way you reacted to *him*, he thought you'd pass out if he came near you."

Andromache blushed again. Hector had undoubtedly been right.

"And he wanted you taken to Thebe," Penthesilea went on, "because he thought you'd never make it all the way to Troy from Lyrnassa. He thought you were too sick."

"But then you brought me here anyway," said Andromache. "You brought me to Hecuba, so she could heal me."

Penthesilea nodded. "Even then, Hector said you were still in danger of dying — and that if you did, it would be *my* fault, for not taking you to Thebe in the first place. I was never worried, though. I knew you'd be fine. You're tougher than people think. Maybe not in the obvious way, but tough all the same."

Penthesilea obviously *had* gone mad — either that, or she'd gone out drinking before the run. Andromache, tough? She was the very *opposite* of tough, a trembling little ball of fear who fled at the first sign of a hawk! "No!" she argued. "I'm not tough in *any* way!"

"You lost your family. Your village. You were badly hurt." Penthesilea paused. "You've been hurt by men, too — haven't you?"

Andromache nearly fainted. "That's *my* business!" she cried.

Penthesilea held her hands up. "You're right. The point is, you're still here, after everything you've been through. You could have shriveled up and died, but you didn't."

Andromache's cheeks flushed with shame. How could Penthesilea call her tough, when her greatest accomplishment was simply that she hadn't shriveled up and died? And she couldn't even claim that small victory as her own! "I have Hecuba and Priam to thank for that," she mumbled.

Penthesilea shook her head. "They gave you a place to live, but *you* made a life out of it. You look different than you used to — you look happy. It takes toughness to be happy after living through a raid, after losing your family. You have to work at it. It's much easier to be angry."

Andromache shook her head, stubbornly refusing the word '*tough*.' Without Hector's family, she wouldn't be where she was now. They'd encouraged her. They'd given her safety and the feeling of home. And even if even if she alone were responsible for creating her new life, how did that qualify her for the *army*? Her pastimes consisted of gardening, weaving, reading, playing with Cutie, marketing, and teaching Lukkan — none of which had anything to do with the *army*! Gardening had given her calluses, not the ability to wield a spear!

But Penthesilea was equally stubborn. "You have natural resilience. In the army, you could build it up further. You wouldn't have to be a courier. Maybe you'd want to be a healer, since you know so much about plants."

"I know how to *grow* plants, not how to heal!" Andromache cried in exasperation. "All I do is grow whatever Hecuba tells me. And I'm a *wimp*! I asked to go running with you because I was too scared to come out here by myself!"

Penthesilea's eyes took on their catlike look. "Are you still scared, out here?" she asked.

Andromache thought about it and decided that she wasn't. Not at the moment. But what did that prove, when she had a rugged warrior woman beside her? She hadn't been scared with Hector there, either. "I guess not," she said reluctantly.

Penthesilea's eyes flashed in triumph. "Aha! — that's what I thought!" she said. "There's no reason you *should* feel afraid. All you need to do is build a little on the toughness you already have."

Andromache bristled. Whether or not she had toughness — which was debatable — she didn't want to be told what to do with it. She liked her life just the way it was. "Listen!" she protested. "I'm really not —"

Penthesilea cut her off. "I've already talked to Hector about it."

"About *what?*" gasped Andromache.

"About you — joining the army."

Talked to Hector? About her, joining the army? What was Penthesilea *thinking?* In horror, Andromache spluttered, "Wh-what did he say?"

Penthesilea hesitated. "He said, '*No effing way.*'"

'*No effing way…*' Andromache wasn't sure what '*effing*' meant — it was probably Truvan slang — but she could tell by the tone that it was *not* a word to say in front of Hecuba. It was probably even worse than '*sucks*,' that other word of slang that had once gotten her into trouble. On some level, she felt insulted. She wouldn't have expected Hector to want her in the army, but the vehemence of his refusal still stung. "Well," she said. "There you go."

"That doesn't have to be the last word." Penthesilea's face was lit by a strange intensity. "If the two of us teamed up, he couldn't oppose us for long."

Team up? Wasn't Penthesilea supposed to be teaming up with Hector — her colleague and fiancé? The way she was talking, she sounded like she wanted to overthrow him, instead. Why on earth would she jeopardize their relationship by insisting that Andromache join the army? She couldn't seriously think that Andromache's skills were worth it!

"Troy's army has a few women already," said Penthesilea. "But so many others would benefit from joining. If they saw you in the ranks…"

So, that was it! Take the least likely person — take timid little Hermie — and fit her out with army gear. If she could make it, anyone could! "Listen," said Andromache, shaking her head. "I don't —"

"Think about it," Penthesilea said firmly. "This could be a whole new era for you. It was for me. It changed my life. Think about it, and we'll talk tomorrow."

℘

THIS COULD BE a whole new era for you,' Penthesilea had said. A whole new era...

Andromache shook her head in disbelief. For years, back in Lyrnassa, and then for months and months in Troy, her life had moved along slowly without changing much. But now, new eras were coming one after the next! She'd never had so many opportunities to make big changes in her life.

But I don't want big changes! she thought. *Not now — not anymore.* She finally had just the life she wanted, and she was *not* about to spoil it by joining the army! She couldn't deny that it felt good to imagine herself brash and unafraid, running wild across the countryside, but the rest of it made her sick. Riding out to battle — poking spears into people — watching their blood drain onto the sand...

Andromache shuddered. Joining the army would be one new era too many!

Not that she really had a choice. Hector had said *'no effing way,'* and whatever his reasons for making that decision, he was in charge. She would have challenged him — would have risked a fight — for something she wanted, but not for this. She wondered again why Penthesilea *was* willing to take that risk. Was she really just acting out of kindness, trying to help a timid person find courage, trying to inspire more women to join the army? Or was there a darker truth? Was her real motive to cause a rift between Andromache and —

Don't be silly! snapped Andromache. She looked out her window. The courtyard trees were casting long shadows in the rays of the setting sun. The fig seemed to stretch past the spring, the apples clear to the other side of the garden. *Shadow bridges,* she thought. They were beautiful. The courtyard was beautiful. Her world was beautiful. She had everything she could ever want, and there was no more room in her life for new eras.

℘

THE NEXT MORNING, as Andromache walked toward the outpost stable, she thought of all that Penthesilea had done for her. The woman had brought her running clothes — had loaned her shoes and a cloak. Several times, she'd offered to find Andromache new housing. Before all the other favors, though, she'd endured the long, bumpy ride from Lyrnassa to Troy just to bring Andromache to a healer.

Andromache had made her decision. As she thought back through her history with Penthesilea, though, she almost regretted not being able to give a different answer. She didn't want the woman to hate her, now.

"I — I can't join the army," she said softly, when Penthesilea gave her an expectant look. "But I wanted to say thank you, for — for asking me — and for everything you've done for me."

More catlike than ever, Penthesilea responded: "I've done what I can."

The two women didn't stop running together, after that, but they went less often. Neither mentioned the army or Hector ever again, and Andromache didn't tell Hector about the strange episode. Since she would never, *ever* try to join the army, there was no need to stir up tension between him and Penthesilea. There was no need for him to be upset. There was no need to disrupt Lukkan lessons with anything unpleasant.

As time passed, the incident with Penthesilea slipped farther and farther to the back of Andromache's mind. She had other things to focus on. Spring was coming! Soon, all of Troy would be flooded with colors. She and Cutie would be able to spend the whole day tending her gardens, out in the light, warm breezes. Even better, for the first time, she would get to run through fields of flowers on the Trojan plateau. Then, after a long day outside, she would go to the library. The cool, shady library, where she would while away the late afternoon speaking Lukkan — with her *friend*.

No, she had no time for worrying about Penthesilea. As suddenly as the woman had become a real presence in her life, she was once again relegated to the fringes. She was a faint presence, a shadow moving through the dim light of the stables.

Early spring

Chapter 6

There came an evening that, during the height of summer, might have felt cool, but that seemed warm after the eternal mists and rains of winter. Night had almost fallen. The sky was still blue, but such a dark, rich blue that it looked almost black. Andromache was sneaking out onto the courtyard. She had to find a hiding place before Cassandra found *her*...

'Please come,' begged Cassandra. 'Tonight will be the first soiree we've had in such a long time! It's finally nice outside.'

'Oh, Cassandra — you know I can't.' Andromache wouldn't have minded going to a soiree, as the Trojan youth called their evening discussion groups. Cassandra's friends intimidated her, it was true — they'd been tutored in every conceivable subject and all hoped one day to join the Trojan city council. She was horribly outclassed by them. Still, the discussions were interesting enough, and she would gladly have accompanied Cassandra if not for Demuchus.

Demuchus was the leader of the soirees and Andromache's former suitor. The autumn before, she'd refused his proposal of marriage. Worse, when he'd offered, she'd laughed hysterically in his face. In retaliation, he'd spread a false rumor that she was a die-hard monarchist. Most of the young would-be council members loathed kings and queens above all else. They believed that a council such as Troy's was the only proper form of government. Once Demuchus's rumor had made its rounds, then, Andromache was no longer welcome at soirees.

But even if Demuchus himself had invited her back, she would have balked — she had no desire to see him! *In proposing to her, he'd given her a truly abominable kiss; she still shuddered at the thought of his tongue slinking around in her mouth. And then there was everything he'd done to Hector when they were boys, like throwing him into manure, and mocking him for how he smelled, and —*

'Of course you can come with me tonight, honey!' Cassandra was saying. 'The ban against you has been lifted!'

'The ban?' asked Andromache. 'There was actually a ban?'

'Oh, no, not really! I'm just teasing. Everyone's forgotten about the incident, that's all I meant. You never really seemed like a monarchist. Oh, you have *to come!'*

And risk running into Demuchus? No way! *thought Andromache. But Cassandra might not understand her reluctance; the girl seemed to think the whole affair had blown over. 'I — I can't,' she stammered. 'I need to take a nap. Lessons took a lot out of me, today.' It was a lie. Talking with Hector had never been so easy.*

'Then go lie down for a while, and I'll knock on your door when it's time to leave,' said Cassandra.

Andromache nodded, relieved. All she would have to do was not *answer her door, and Cassandra would go on alone to her soiree. She wouldn't want to show up late...*

By evening, though, the weather was so beautiful that Andromache couldn't stand to stay indoors. Who knew if the next day would bring back the chilly winds and rain?

Furtively, with Cutie in her arms so that the clicking of dog toenails wouldn't betray her, Andromache crept downstairs and out onto the courtyard. Once there, she traversed the labyrinth of shrubs and vegetable boxes in search of a place to hide.

Here? No, too close to the house. Not enough cover, there. Now, that's all right — wait! Ew! Never mind! Maybe a little farther —

Suddenly, Cutie wriggled out of her grasp and bolted.

"Cutie? Where are you going, stupid dog?" hissed Andromache. "I swear to you, if I get stuck going out with Cassandra because of you...then you'd better *stay* lost!"

But the dog had disappeared behind a row of myrtle shrubs.

Andromache paused thoughtfully. Disappeared? That was what *she* wanted to do! Rather than cursing Cutie, she decided to follow her.

"Cutie?" she whispered, dodging past the shrubs and winding around boxes, benches, and trees. She couldn't see the dog anywhere, but she could hear her — high-pitched yips and moans. She'd found something. A bird, perhaps?

"Cutie! Hey!" Andromache ran on. She was getting closer. Between the yips, she could now hear muffled, piglike noises. She kept going and at last found the dog, who was furiously licking the ground. No, not the ground —

"Hector?" asked Andromache, in shock. "Are you sick?" He was lying down, flat on his back. Andromache had rarely even seen him *sitting* down, outside of lessons or meals.

"No," said Hector. "I was looking for hazy sky jellies — at least, till your dog blocked my view." He ruffled Cutie's ears while she licked his chin.

Hazy jellies — did he mean the Lorani? The most exciting text Andromache had ever read was a treatise called *On Lorani*, which described certain creatures living out in the celestial ocean. The Lorani, which looked like small, hazy blotches of light, were actually gigantic, luminous beings, rather like jellyfish. They lived far from the earth and could be difficult to find in the night sky. So difficult, in fact, that Hector had never seen one. He claimed not to believe in them, despite the fact that Andromache had seen them many times — despite the fact that even the Mudders had a word for them. Mudders! Those horrible, brutish raiders from across the Western Sea! Granted, their word was silly — '*galaxias*' — but one couldn't expect much from a people whose only talents were raiding and making clay pots.

As for Hector, his interest in the Lorani that evening perplexed her. He'd always denied their existence. What could possibly have possessed him to search for them? "Cutie's not the reason you can't see them," Andromache said cautiously. "It's not quite dark enough, and even once it is, the trees and walls here block a lot of the sky. You'd have better luck if you went out to the countryside."

Hector shook his head. "Not tonight," he said, gesturing to a jar on the ground beside him.

"Ah!" said Andromache. "Wine." She was relieved. It was perfectly reasonable for a drunken man, even Hector, to lie on his back, searching the sky above for something he didn't think was there.

With a nod, Hector said, "Yes — I thought it might help me find them."

So, his Lorani hunt idea had come *before* the wine? Andromache frowned. The situation had lost any sense it was beginning to make. "How would *wine* help you?" she asked.

"Because," he explained. "It makes everything look hazy."

Andromache rolled her eyes. He was joking! The wine itself had been his reason for coming out — a sip of cool wine on a warm spring evening. He'd brought up the Lorani only to tease her. "Well, is it working?" she asked sarcastically. "Does the sky look hazy enough?"

"I can't tell," said Hector, with a winning smile. "Now *you're* blocking my view."

"Sorry." Andromache sat down on the other side of Cutie. "Is that better?"

Hector squinted. "Not really," he said, sighing. "So there's no chance of seeing them from here?"

"I don't know," said Andromache. "It's worth a try, anyway." She lay down. Delighted, Cutie licked her forehead — her chin — her lips. "Ick!" cried Andromache. "Dog breath!"

Hector snorted, and Cutie slunk to Andromache's feet in shame.

"So dramatic!" said Andromache. "Here. Come here, girl — I'm sorry. Please, come over here." She patted the ground beside her.

Cutie looked away.

"She is mean at you, my baby?" simpered Hector. "Oh, poor Cutie!"

A sick look on her face, Cutie crawled forward until she was once again between them but closer to Hector. Her ears were slicked to her head, and her eyes were mournful.

"Oh, for pity's sake!" Andromache scoffed. "To hear her tell it, I'm the meanest person in the city."

"No," said Hector. "The meanest in all ohff the earff."

"No, wait — the meanest in the whole celestial ocean!"

Laughing, Hector turned his face skyward once more. Andromache did the same, and for a long time they lay there, silently watching the stars appear. It was a rare treat to be spending time with Hector this way. Even now, she seldom saw him outside of lessons. She felt like a young girl again, stretched out in a clearing beside her childhood friend, Haliosh.

"I still don't see any Lorani," she said after a while.

Hector offered her the wine. "You can use this."

"Thanks," she said, accepting the jar. To her surprise, it was nearly untouched.

"I haff no, er, drinkers," Hector apologized. "That is to say, no *cahps*."

"That's all right. Who needs cups?" Andromache sat up and took a drink, setting the jar beside Hector when she was done.

"Ahndromahk?"

"Hmm?"

"*You* ahre out here, why?"

"I'm hiding from Cassandra."

"Why?"

"She wants me to go out with her."

Hector laughed. "And you do not want to go, why? Too mahch talk on the taxing ohff pahppies?"

"'*Pahppies*?'" Andromache giggled. "Do you mean '*puppies*' or '*poppies*?'"

Shrugging, Hector answered: "Either. Boff."

The wine had begun to take effect, filling Andromache with a sense of giddiness. "They aren't discussing puppies *or* poppies," she said, giggling once more. "I just didn't want to risk seeing my would-be husband, Demuchus."

Abruptly, Hector stopped laughing. "Oh," he said. "I see." His pause at the end of the sentence was explosive: plainly he hadn't said all he wanted to say.

"What is it?" asked Andromache. Why was Hector refusing to share in her joke? He knew how she felt about Demuchus. They'd laughed about him together other times.

"It is that you ahre making me to fink on Lyrnash," Hector said slowly.

"Oh," murmured Andromache, guarded now, despite the wine. Lyrnash…Lyrnassa…the village where she'd lived before coming to Troy. The village that had been destroyed by raiders. "What about it?"

Hector took a deep breath. "There, you lose — a man — that is to say, a — a husband…"

The words were so hesitant that Andromache wasn't sure whether they formed a question or a statement, not that it mattered. For months, she'd been dreading this conversation, yet hoping Hector had forgotten the comment she'd let slip during one of their fights…

'Cassandra told Demuchus I wanted to marry him,' Andromache sighed.
'Do you?' asked Hector.
'No.'
'You're sure?'
'Yes.'
'Really sure?'
'Yes, dammit! I don't need another husband saving me from my life!'

Evidently, Hector hadn't forgotten — and now she would have to explain. "No…I didn't lose a husband in Lyrnash."

"Baht —" Hector shook his head and switched to Truvan: "But that day, you said you didn't want '*another husband.*' Which means you'd already *had* one."

"I guess," sighed Andromache, reaching for the wine. She took a drink, then told Hector about the dark days following her parents' death. She told him about the wagoner who had driven her and her Auntie to Lyrnassa — who had given them food in exchange for their help loading and unloading his wagon — and who had been, she guessed, her husband.

It was a story she'd tried very hard not to think about, although certain details had never fully faded. Her dress, covered in blood — her stumbling walk down to Lyrnassa — the wagon, that hateful wagon. Even in her happiest moments, she couldn't quite keep those memories at bay.

Now, she gave in to all the hurt and shame. She let it engulf her. She let it spill out toward Hector.

She left out a lot of details. She didn't tell Hector just how lonely and heartbroken the loss of her parents had left her, or how she hadn't wanted to cry in front of her equally heartbroken aunt, or how the wagoner had held and comforted her when he'd found her crying late one night.

It hadn't seemed strange that he should put his arm around her. She'd been the neighbors' pet, back home — everyone had hugged her, held her, danced with her. She'd once been like Cassandra, surrounded by innocent affection, loved and adored by all. It hadn't seemed strange for the wagoner to hold her.

Nothing more had happened until Auntie fell ill. Then, certain that Auntie, too, would die and leave her to fend for herself, Andromache had cried and cried. The wagoner had asked her what was wrong — had offered to marry her, to take care of her and Auntie. Defenseless, Andromache had agreed. Better to have a husband than to be left all alone! Where she was from, a lot of people married young. And so what if the wagoner was old enough to be her grandfather? That just made him all the more able to care for her. Andromache was pragmatic, and the wagoner had offered her a solution to her problem.

Or so she'd thought. In fact, he'd only made her troubles worse. She'd soon realized that he wasn't much interested in taking care of her — what he'd wanted was to be her *husband*. Andromache hadn't really thought about what it would mean to be his wife. She hadn't known. The education she'd received from watching farm animals hadn't taught her much at all…

Andromache told Hector the essentials — whom she'd married, and when, and why — but she left out the grittiest details. She told him the end of the story, how the wagoner had left her and Auntie on the cliffs above Lyrnassa, but she didn't tell him why. She didn't tell him that once Auntie had finally recovered, the wagoner had stopped touching her — but it was too late. *The thing* was already inside her, growing.

She didn't tell Hector about *the thing*, nor about wishing it away, nor about waking one morning in a pool of blood and crying with relief.

She didn't tell Hector that the wagoner had yelled at her, cursed her, wept, and finally prodded her and Auntie out of the wagon — or that her relief had then turned to despair. She'd fallen, sobbing, to her knees, begging the wagoner not to leave them there, but he'd refused: *'All I wanted was a son, useless girl! I'll take you no further with me. Go see if one of the villages down by the shore will have you!'* He'd turned his wagon northward and jolted off, away from the coast.

Andromache left out many details of the story.

She didn't tell Hector that Auntie had been livid when she found out everything the wagoner had done — that she'd yelled at Andromache, cried, and held her, moaning all the while about the defilement of her poor dead sister's little girl. She'd then hurled stones in the wagoner's direction until she slumped to the ground in exhaustion.

It was in this condition — weak, with Andromache covered in blood — that they'd somehow stumbled down to Lyrnassa. Practical people on the whole, the villagers had recognized the worth of Auntie's weaving and had allowed the two women to stay. Andromache, however, was believed to be cursed. Lyrnassans feared blood, especially strangers' blood; they saw it as the sign of an angry god. In all the time Andromache had lived there, the villagers had neither forgotten her shocking entrance nor made her feel welcome.

The blood had stained Andromache in her own mind, too. No memory filled her with more shame. It wasn't just the horror and filth of the act itself, or even the humiliation of begging her tormentor not to leave. The episode shamed her most because it hadn't just happened to her — she'd brought it upon herself. She'd agreed to be the wagoner's wife. As for *the thing*, not for a moment did she regret losing it. She'd been so weak and grief-stricken that having it probably would have killed her, and surviving would have been no better. A lifetime with the wagoner. More *things* with the wagoner. Dozens more until he finally grew too old and died. No, far better to have lost the first *thing* early! Even so, she still felt guilty for having wished it away...

Andromache sighed and closed her eyes. The pain of those memories had dimmed but never truly vanished.

Hector stayed silent throughout her story and for a long time even after it had ended. When he did finally speak, his words held immeasurable disgust: "When you were a *little girl?*"

From the direction of Hector's voice, Andromache could tell that he was looking at her. She kept her own eyes tightly shut. She couldn't stand to meet his accusatory gaze — to see him condemning her as sick, as a freak. She cursed Cutie for running over to Hector in the first place. She cursed the Lorani — and the fall of night — and Cassandra — and Demuchus — and everything else that had brought about this hellish moment.

"Ahndromahk?" persisted Hector, his voice terrible.

"Thirteen," she murmured. "Maybe fourteen."

Silent revulsion from Hector's corner.

"People get married young, in the Lukka lands," she argued, trying to defend herself.

"I'm sure you looked every bit of six," came the mordant reply.

Tears welled up. Hector was mad at her, and it wasn't fair.

"And how old was *he*? Forty?"

Andromache didn't answer.

"Fifty?" Hector's voice hardened further. "I'll bet he was at least fifty. He sounds like the type."

Andromache swallowed. "Your dad's a lot older than your mom," she whispered.

"My mom wasn't a baby in diapers when they got married," Hector retorted.

Andromache finally looked at him and saw that his torso was raised up, now, and his face had drained to a gruesome grayish-white. He was plainly sickened by her.

In anguish, she clutched Cutie so tightly that the dog made a grunt of protest and struggled away, pressing herself to Hector's leg. *So, you're against me, too!* thought Andromache. Before the tears could flood out, she turned to her other side, so that she wouldn't have to face either one of her accusers.

"Who was this asshole?" asked Hector, his voice thick with loathing. "Did he give you a name?"

Andromache screwed her eyes shut and clamped her lips together, refusing to cry.

Still, Hector kept at her: "Do you know where he went?"

She curled into a ball. Several moments passed, then something moved lightly in the ends of her hair; Cutie's foot, she thought, stirring as the dog resettled herself.

Hector spoke again: "Ahndromahk…"

"Go back to your Lorani hunt!" she snapped. "I'm done talking about my former husband."

"Don't call *him* your *husband*!" Hector snapped back.

"Why, because we didn't have all your fancy Trojan rituals?" cried Andromache, rising to face him. She was fed up with Trojans and their stupid wedding snobbery! Her dad's life had been ruined — he'd been disinherited — and for what? Because his mother hadn't been the master luthier's lawful wife. She'd never worn a blue dress or a crown of leaves or performed any of the other wedding rituals. That was the only reason! Well, Andromache couldn't take it anymore! "So that marriage doesn't count?"

she snarled at Hector. "Just go ahead and say it, if you think I'm a whore!"

"Ahndromahk!" he said sharply.

She ignored him. "Call me a bastard, too, because my parents had the same kind of marriage. Oh, and while you're at it, call my mom a slut! Call my dad a —"

"Ahndromahk, stop!" cried Hector. "Please! I don't give a shit about rituals, and I don't call people names like that! That's not what I meant *at all!*"

"But you said —"

"What I meant is that you shouldn't call him your husband because he doesn't *deserve* to be called that. He never acted like a husband!"

Andromache shriveled inside. What did *Hector* know about it? *He* was living in disorder! He had no right to criticize anyone else's arrangements!

Hector went on: "Husbands talk to their wives, and listen to them, and laugh with them, and love them, and protect them. Husbands don't desert their wives on the side of a cliff. They don't force themselves on lonely little girls!"

Once more, Andromache turned away. Hector's pity was worse than his revulsion. "No one forced me," she hissed. "It was my decision." She took a drink, and wine dribbled down her chin. Numbly, she wiped it away.

"Ahndromahk..." whispered Hector.

She turned toward him. For several long breaths, he neither spoke nor broke eye contact with her. She began to feel a hint of nervousness. He seemed to be on the brink of saying something important —

"Demuchus wouldn't do that," he finally said, lowering his eyes. "Desert you, I mean. If that's what you were worried about — if that's why you didn't marry him." Tentatively, he added, "And I'm sure that — if you told him you'd lost a —" *cough* "— husband — before coming here, and were a little —" *cough, cough* "— sensitive — about the subject, he'd forget about the whole —" *cough* "— laughing thing."

Whatever Andromache had been expecting Hector to say, *this wasn't it!* Her eyes blazed. She was disappointed. Furious! She pictured a little boy, floundering in a pile of manure while Demuchus sneered and snickered at him. "I don't *want* him to forget that I laughed at him!" she cried. "He deserved it, after the way he —" She stopped short. Despite everything that Hector had just put her through, between his disgust and his pity, she didn't want to force him to relive the manure incident.

Hector tilted his head, waiting for her to finish.

"After the lousy kiss he gave me," she said crossly. "Don't you remember?"

Hector laughed. It was a golden laugh that flooded through Andromache, warming her just as the wine had. "Oh, yes, <u>Ahndromahk</u>," he said. "I remember. You told me he smelled like sweat and lamb."

"Sweat and lamb," she agreed, adding, "You'd think with all the kissing that goes on in Troy, the people here would know how to do it right!"

Pause. "Some do," said Hector.

Andromache felt another, stronger, flutter of unease. "<u>Do you see any</u> Lorani <u>yet</u>?" she asked.

"<u>Not yet</u>."

"<u>More wine — is there</u>?"

"<u>Here</u>."

To Andromache's relief, talk turned away from sensitive subjects like her past. Like *kissing*. Instead, as the level of wine in the jar receded, Hector told her all about what life was like in his uncle's country of Santiya. He named the animals he'd seen while out riding through the wild lands near Troy and described the many pranks Paris had pulled during his adolescence.

The breeze was light, bringing now the scent of loamy earth, now a hint of salt from the sea, now the scent of cedar trees, now mint from the stash Hector was perpetually chewing. Andromache lay flat against the ground, listening to Hector's voice until he, too, lapsed into silence. The stars were at their height, a river of silver running across the sky. Now was the time, if any, to hunt for the Lorani…

But just then, Hector took the last glug of wine. "<u>I cannot be in lessons fohr a while</u>," he said softly.

Andromache shivered, noticing for the first time a chill to the night air. "<u>Patrol inspection</u>?" she whispered. Sometimes Hector had to leave for a few days, to check up on the soldiers who were guarding Trojan lands. But if *that* wasn't why —

"<u>No</u>," he said.

With that one word, Andromache knew: a Trojan ally had called for help, and Hector was answering with his army. He was leaving! Instead of sitting under the stars, talking with her, he would be out on a battlefield, surrounded by a host of spear-wielding murderers.

(_He'll be one of them,_) said the hateful little Voice. (_Don't you remember the Raider?_)

The Raider! That monster who had found her on the cliffs above Lyrnassa — the armor-covered giant, smoke-streaked and slick with blood—that face with two black hollows where there should have been eyes —

Shut up! thought Andromache. _He's not a monster — he fights the monsters! He defends people who are being attacked! And he has to wear that armor to protect himself!_ She thought of Hector's scar, the long, worm-pink scar on his arm. He'd come home with it the last time he'd left on a military campaign. She imagined his arm laid open, his blood leaking out. She imagined him screaming in pain.

Andromache blinked back tears. She felt dazed and nauseous from the wine she'd drunk, and, reasonably or not, she felt angry. Why had Hector told her _now_? Why had he ruined the beautiful evening they'd just spent together? Why couldn't he have waited till morning, at least, to say that he was leaving?

"Where are you going?" she asked.

"Souff," said Hector.

"South." Andromache closed her eyes so as not to risk seeing his scar. "How long will you be gone?"

He shook his head. "I know not."

"Oh…"

"Please, you can do somefing fohr me?"

"What?"

"You can see Grandma Thisbe sometimes? She is so lonely, wiffout Buzzy."

Her stomach roiling at the thought of the forsaken pony, Andromache murmured, "Of course."

"You can giff to her the wine ohff Buzzy," Hector teased. "The wine fohr his grains."

Andromache didn't laugh with him. She didn't even look at him. All she could do was stare up at the sky. The entire celestial ocean seemed to be pouring into her lungs, suffocating her…

Suddenly, she couldn't stand to be anywhere near Hector. "'M t'red," she mumbled, wobbling to her feet and wishing only for the mercy of being alone when all the wine she'd drunk that evening came back up.

$$\wp$$

LATE THE NEXT morning, Andromache awoke, groggy from a nightmare she'd been having, where Hector was grabbing her arm, helping her to stand...

> '*Stay in my room,' he was saying. 'It's closer. I'll go to a spare room.'*
> *She shook her head wildly. 'I want Stripey!' she wailed, stamping her* foot.
> '*What's a stripey?'*
> '*My blanket! My favorite blanket, the one with shtripes!' She was starting to slur, now. 'I want Shtripey! Go ahead — laugh!'*
> *Hector didn't laugh, but he smiled — smiled! — and backed away...*

Andromache's head was pounding. Her mouth and eyes were painfully dry. Ugh! What a terrible dream! At least, she hoped it was a dream...

Stripey! <u>*Honestly, Ahndromahk! If that wasn't a dream — oh, gods!*</u> *— <u>what would</u> Hector <u>think, if —</u>*

Hector. Hector wouldn't think anything at all about it. Hector was leaving again.

No longer too dry, her eyes filled with tears. She wrapped Stripey around herself, but the blanket's comfort wasn't enough. "<u>Cutie</u>?" she called.

The dog wasn't there.

Unbothered by how disheveled she must look, Andromache leapt out of bed and ran down the stairs. "<u>Cutie</u>?"

Cutie wasn't in the stairwell, the banquet hall, or the kitchen. Andromache finally found her curled up beside the main door, her snout tucked under her tail.

"He's gone — isn't he," said Andromache, sinking down to the floor, beside Cutie. Eyes closed, she stroked the dog's soft, white fur.

Chapter 7

Only two years earlier, the Trojan army had been a different institution. A man named Laoganus had been supreme commander, in charge of defending Troy as well as the city's allies and its protectorate. Hector had been one of many patrol captains out riding Trojan lands. When Lyrnassa was attacked, he'd taken his patrol down to defend it. They'd been too late to save the village from burning but had managed to defeat the invaders. Impressed with Hector, the city council had promoted him to commander. Laoganus remained in charge of defending Troy, but Hector was made responsible for any campaigns outside the city. The current mission was his second as commander.

During Hector's absence the previous spring, life on the home front had been strained. This time was no different. Cassandra turned into a quiet, brooding creature who made dreary predictions about what the future would be like if her brother never returned. Priam and Hecuba, while less dramatic than Cassandra, were also tense. Neither spent much time at home. Hecuba marched from house to house, taking healing salves and ointments to those in need, while Priam — who was Troy's high priest — more or less moved into the temple. Andromache supposed that they were taking on extra work to avoid having free time to worry about their son.

She could sympathize. Lately, whenever she was idle, her thoughts turned to Hector and the brutal raiders that he was facing. The first time he was away, she hadn't worried about him at all. She'd thought he was invincible, so skilled at battle that no one could hurt him. When he'd come home with his arm torn from elbow to shoulder, though, she'd realized that he was as vulnerable as anyone else. She couldn't bear to think about what might be happening to him, now, and constantly sought ways to occupy herself.

Paris offered one such opportunity. Without Hector there to goad him out of bed for archery practice, Paris was sleeping late and shirking his household chores. The vendors were sold out by the time he stumbled down to the market, each day. Stale bread, limp salad greens — those were all he ever managed to bring home.

He'd pulled the same tricks the year before, and Andromache had done her best to fill the gaps in the family's diet. She'd worked extra hours in her garden, weeding, transplanting, trimming, and thinning in order to supply everyone with spring vegetables. She'd slipped fresh herbs into Paris's watery stews. Back then, however, she'd still been afraid to leave the house, and her ways of helping out had been limited.

They're not limited anymore, she thought one morning, as she climbed the stairs to Paris's room to rouse him for marketing.

"Wake up! Get up! It's time!" she hollered, ruthlessly banging on the door. When that racket failed to elicit a response, she opened his door a crack and let Cutie in. "Lick him, girl! Lick that sleeping slug awake!"

Cutie joyfully obeyed.

At last, Paris shuffled to the door, one eye squinting and the other bulging. When he grumbled, "This had better be good, Taskmistress," Andromache felt a twinge of pride. '*Taskmaster*' was Paris's favorite nickname for Hector.

For the next few mornings, Paris tried to sleep in, but Andromache gave him the same wake-up call each time. Eventually, she came downstairs at sunrise to find him waiting for her in the kitchen, wearing a sour expression and his marketing clothes.

Paris never slept late, after that, but he also didn't let Andromache savor her victory. Indeed, he found a particularly nasty way of getting back at her: by refusing to play his lute for her. Paris didn't know that his lute had been made by Andromache's grandfather, or that the instrument sounded uncannily like the ones her own father had made. Paris had no idea that his music sent her spinning through time and space, to the pine-covered mountains of the Lukka lands, where she'd once lived. He didn't realize that he had the power to reunite her — however briefly — with her long-lost family. All he knew was that Andromache loved his music, and that he could hurt her by withholding it.

Damn that Paris! she thought each time she saw his scowling face, but she didn't stop waking him to go marketing. It was the best way she had of helping Hecuba, Priam, and Cassandra.

Besides, while Paris could deprive Andromache of her family's music, he couldn't wholly separate her from them — at least not from her dad. Every day, she walked down toward Penthesilea's house — no one was there to spy on her, now that Penthesilea was away with the army! — where she wandered through the neighborhood that had once housed the luthier's shop. She had many more visions of her dad...

He was a teenager, coming out of his gawky phase — he was strutting through the streets, flirting with neighborhood girls while the women his mother's age laughed softly at him. He was a serious student, mastering the art of lute-making — he was frowning as he shaped the instrument's neck and scoured its bowl...

When Andromache wasn't busy wrangling Paris or daydreaming about her dad, she spent time with Thisbe, just as she'd promised to do. She fed and petted the little pony and even took her on short walks around the pasture. The excursions were Xanthus's idea; Andromache still remembered the terror of her long ride to Troy and so was nervous around unstalled horses. Thisbe, however, was as gentle and quiet as could be. She walked along docilely beside Andromache and never bucked or pulled.

If Cassandra was around, Andromache brought her along to the stables to play roodles against Xanthus. Andromache won most of the matches, as neither opponent gave her much of a challenge. The stable master was even grumpier than usual, and more distracted. On normal days, the stables buzzed with the sounds of clattering hooves, bantering soldiers, and equipment being shelved or taken down. Now, few people came to the stables, and few horses remained there to be tended. The place was quiet — too quiet for Xanthus, who startled at every tiny noise emerging from the stillness. He took such sounds as both an ill portent and a personal insult and complained bitterly about all of them.

Cassandra — when she agreed to play roodles in the first place — put up even less resistance in their matches. While moving her game piece, she would mutter gloomily about all the ways she'd failed Hector: *I never thanked him for helping me with that poetry text. He was so good at explaining it! I never would've understood it without him, and now* — 'By the time she remembered that she was in the middle of a game, she would often lose interest and forfeit.

Andromache tried to shut her ears against such comments. They made her think hideous thoughts...

Spears thrusting — swords hacking — slashed skin — torn flesh — blood, everywhere blood, a body drained of blood —

Yes, Andromache could sympathize with the need to keep busy, to avoid having too much time to think.

Even so, worry occasionally overwhelmed her, and in those moments, she found herself drifting up to the library; it was there that she'd spent the most time with Hector. She would sit at the table, trying to summon his face — to see it, across from her, where it so often had been. No matter how hard she concentrated, though, his whole face never appeared to her. She could see his nose and ears, but never his eyes. She couldn't even remember their exact color. Every time she tried to picture them, she saw the Raider's two dark hollows, surrounded by streaks of blood and smoke...

How she hated the Voice for reminding her of that image!

Once Andromache gave up trying to see Hector, she would imagine telling him things. The conversations weren't about anything serious, just funny or strange little details from her day.

You'll never guess what Cutie did, she told him, one afternoon, after he'd been away for several weeks. *She kept me awake all night, barking at a beetle. Yes, that's right, there was a beetle that got stuck in my room and fluttered around all night, trying to find a way out. Can you imagine? And every time I tried to catch the thing, so I could let it out the window, it would fly off to another corner of my room, where I couldn't see it. Anyway, the stupid dog would just get settled down when the stupid beetle would start rustling around again, and then Cutie would wail her head off. It was awful! I'm sure you could've heard her from your side of the courtyard, if you'd been here. Your parents heard her. They weren't mean about it, or anything, but they definitely noticed. Your dad joked about how stressful it must be to be so small, so threatened by every little thing in the world. Your mom didn't say anything, but she looked terrible. She hasn't been getting a lot of sleep as it is, so it didn't help —*

No, *that* wasn't a good thing to tell Hector! If he knew his mom wasn't sleeping, he might worry. He might get distracted.

Andromache changed topics.

I've been reading a lot, and I have some ideas for what we can read together when you get back. There's one text that won't be on the list, though! It's the history of a village just east of where I used to live in Lukká. Anyway, the text said that that whole village was full of cannibals! I went and showed it to your dad because I thought he ought to know that one of his texts was wrong. I used to go there with my mom or Auntie to the market, and it was a normal place. No one there was a cannibal. My mom never would've taken me to a cannibal village! Anyway, your dad was surprised, but he thanked me and asked me all about what those people were really like, so he could write a correction to the text. He said that that's one of the problems with reading histories — you don't always know how accurate they are. He said it can be a really hard problem to fix, too. That village was illiterate. How would they know to correct a text they couldn't even read? If I hadn't happened to read it, Trojans for all time would've had the wrong idea about that place. Your dad says he's suspicious of every history text. The writer might report facts without really understanding the meaning behind them and end up giving the wrong impression. Or, the writer might misrepresent things on purpose. Your dad gave a silly example — the history of a roodles match — and said the winner might represent the loser as nobler, more treacherous, cleverer, or stupider than he or she really was, all to make the winner look better. If the loser doesn't hear about the account or isn't around to —

Again, Andromache broke off her thoughts. '*Winning*' and '*losing*' and the loser '*not being around*' weren't comforting ideas when Hector was away with the army.

Paris is up to his usual tricks, she said instead. *You know, trying to sleep late, doing more carousing than shopping at the market. Yesterday, he snuck a hunk of lamb into my basket. He thought it was so funny! When I opened it, he —*

But this new line of thought was as bad as the others. Hector had shown only compassion when she'd told him the story of the goat she'd had to kill, and he'd never mocked her for refusing to eat meat, afterward. He'd understood...

Andromache sighed — she was tired of talking to empty space! There was only one thing left to say. *I miss you. Hurry back.*

Glancing outside, she saw the faded orange of an evening sky. *Dinner time*, she thought. She went downstairs to the kitchen, where she found Cassandra and Hecuba. Each woman gave her a clipped greeting:

"Hi."

"Evening, dear."

"Hello," answered Andromache. Cassandra and her mother were clearly in the midst of an argument. Andromache wanted to leave but didn't think she could without making the situation even more awkward.

For a few moments, all three women picked at the food on their plates. It was Cassandra who broke the silence.

"I'm not going," she said to her mother.

"Yes, you are," Hecuba insisted. "You mustn't fall behind."

"I won't."

"Well, stewing around the house isn't doing you any good — and it's not doing any of *us* any good to watch you."

"I'm not stewing!" Cassandra protested. "I just don't feel like going out, tonight."

"Oh, you'll go, if I have to shove you out the door myself!" Hecuba was gritting her teeth. She meant what she said.

Knowing she'd lost, Cassandra slumped against the table. "Honey?" she whispered.

Andromache froze. She didn't want to be involved in this. "Wh-what?"

"You'll come with me?" Cassandra's eyes were pleading.

"Where?"

"To a soiree…"

Andromache shook her head. She would just tell Cassandra the truth, this time, and hope she understood. "Demuchus —"

"Doesn't host soirees anymore," said Cassandra. "He hasn't for a while, now. They're held at Phegeus's place."

Who Phegeus was didn't matter. So long as Andromache was in no danger of seeing Demuchus, she had no good reason not to go. "All right," she sighed, with a strange feeling that she would live to regret those words.

"What a fine idea!" approved Hecuba. "You girls had better hurry."

Chapter 8

When they arrived at Phegeus's house, Andromache recognized their host: he was Demuchus's acolyte, a man who'd come to every previous soiree wearing robes of a toxic green hue. As a mark of his new status — or so Andromache presumed — his robes were now raucous yellow in color.

Inside, Andromache suffered through the greetings and the insincerely bright choruses of *'How we've missed you!'* She was sure the group hadn't really missed her, as she'd never contributed much to their discussions. Once everyone had arrived, Phegeus led the group out onto his courtyard. His parents, unlike Demuchus's uncle, didn't seem to mind noise; they'd provided the young people with several jars of wine.

Knowing what might happen if she drank too much, Andromache took only a tiny cup. It was one thing to mention Stripey in front of Hector, if indeed she'd done so. Cassandra's friends would be much less understanding.

Once everyone had found a seat, the conversation began. Andromache hadn't read the text the others were discussing, so rather than listening, she peered into the nearby banquet hall. Demuchus's house, she remembered, was full of Mudder pottery — beautiful vases and urns, true masterpieces. Phegeus's family also had vases, but they were of lower quality. The designs on their sides had a cheap look. Imitations of Demuchus's treasures, they'd been painted by an unskilled hand.

Andromache sighed and shifted on her bench. It was even worse than the ones on Demuchus's courtyard! Not only was it hard, it was also covered by a thin, twiny wool pad whose crisscross lines dug deep into the backs of her thighs. She looked around, but none of the others were fidgeting. How could they stand it?

'*They haff asses ohff stone,*' answered Hector's voice, from deep within her memory.

"…a threat of immense proportions," one of the guests was saying aloud.

Andromache frowned. Threat? What threat? Was it in the text, or had they moved on to something else?

"Come now," someone else scoffed. "They're no threat to us. All the Mudders really know how to do is throw pots!"

Phegeus cleared his throat. "I must insist that we call them by their proper name, Achaeans."

"Whatever you call them, they know how to raid a village," the first voice argued.

Andromache shut her eyes. She wanted to shut her ears, her memory. *Don't talk about that day,* she thought at the others. She didn't want to see the ship full of Mudders, bristling with spears, bearing down on Lyrnassa. Or bearing down, now, on Hector —

"They've even attacked our protectorate," said someone else.

Lyrnassa — Lyrnassa was within the Trojan protectorate —

"And look what happened when they *did!*" yet another voice retorted.

Everyone nodded solemnly. They all knew the story of the Achaean raiders, defeated at Lyrnassa.

"Our city has the finest walls that have ever been built," declared Phegeus. "But even if we didn't, the Achaeans wouldn't *dare* attack us. They know they wouldn't get far, with your brother —" He nodded to Cassandra. "— protecting us."

"Paris *is* a good shot," Cassandra joked nervously, and they all laughed.

"I've heard that," Phegeus responded. "But you know who I mean. Hector, the warrior! Hector, the man who is *defined* by his heroism!"

Andromache stiffened. Defined by? Hector had a heroic side, there was no doubt about it. He'd rushed down to Lyrnassa to save the villagers from Mudder invaders, and even now, he was off defending yet another village somewhere. Andromache couldn't deny his heroism, but she never would have said that it *defined* him.

He was much, much more than just a warrior or a hero! He was a man who read texts; who drank wine; who looked at the stars; who loved horses, and teasing, and laughing. He was a sweet boy who helped little old ladies carry water — a *'sweet boy with hair in his face.'* He was Andromache's confidant, the only one who knew all the miseries she'd endured: her parents' death, the wounded goat, and even the wagoner. Hector was the best friend she'd ever had. Didn't Phegeus care about such things? Or was he too busy showing off his learnedness to notice? Yes, that was it! His mouth was just as loud as his raucous yellow clothing!

"He's the greatest warrior — and the greatest commander — Troy has ever seen," Phegeus declared to a chorus of nods.

And you have the biggest mouth Troy has ever seen, you Raucous Yellow Man! Andromache thought scathingly. When even that name sounded too dignified, she mentally shortened it to 'RYM.'

"But isn't Laoganus in charge of defending Troy?" someone objected.

"Everyone knows who Troy's true protector is," the RYM pontificated. "Laoganus is merely a figurehead."

Another attendee sighed, "What an honor for your family, Cassandra!"

Honor? More like horror, *you idiot!* Andromache shook her head, thinking of the two Trojan ladies who had visited Hecuba during Hector's previous campaign: *'He'll come back covered in glory!'* the old biddies had squealed in delight, even as Hecuba grimaced. Now, the latest saying was *'What an honor!'* Xanthus had been right all along: the young people of Troy were even stupider than their elders. Their heads were full of fluff, and everything was going to hell!

Cassandra gave a wan smile.

"Of course it's an honor!" crowed the RYM. "But nothing compared to the honor they'll know when he brings back another stunning victory."

Brings back? Andromache scoffed. *How? In a basket? Maybe they can decorate it with string and dried berries — or maybe garland, so it's covered in glory!*

"Is he handsome?" a breathy voice chimed in.

Andromache turned toward the sound and saw someone she'd never met before, a young woman who must have joined the group during Andromache's period of banishment. The girl's dewy little face raised her hackles. *If that's the kind of thing you're worried about, little Newbie*, Andromache thought sourly, *then I'll be leaving Troy the day you join the council!*

"Well, I don't know if you'd say *handsome*…"

"Pretty ordinary, really."

Ordinary! Andromache's eyes lit with scorn.

"Paris is much handsomer."

Slicker, Andromache corrected. *Puffier.*

"But I don't know what Paris looks like, either," the Newbie admitted with appealing frankness.

Oooooh, I don't know what Paris looks like, either! Andromache mimicked silently.

"Wait a moment! You've seen him."

"Who, Paris?"

"No! Hector."

"I have?"

"On the practice field. He's the one running it."

"Oh — *him*."

That *him*, laced with delectation — Andromache didn't like it, not one bit! What business did the Newbie have down at the practice field, ogling people she didn't even know? Watching them flail about, half-dressed? But outrage was quickly followed by shame and jealousy: the Newbie, for all her silliness, *did* know Hector in a way that she, Andromache, did not.

"But I still don't know if he's handsome," giggled the Newbie. "I never thought to look at his *face*."

And while Andromache had seen Hector's face a thousand times, she hadn't been able to picture it, lately. She didn't even have *that* to hold over the Newbie!

"Oh! — you'll know it soon enough," proclaimed the RYM. "When it finds its place in the sculpture garden."

The sculpture garden? Andromache knew the carvings of the sculpture garden. They formed a simpering marble horde of Trojan councilmen and generals, all of whom looked identical — freakishly proportioned and uncannily smooth. Hector didn't belong there! *What a joke!*

When the group members turned toward her, surprised, Andromache realized in horror that she must have spoken aloud.

"What did you say?" the RYM asked politely.

"I — I said, are you serious? About the sculpture? Of —"

"Of course! What kind of city would we be if we didn't all know our protector?"

Know him? Andromache laughed to herself. How did they expect to know him from a sculpture like the ones in the garden, the ones that were all the same? Once the artist had erased Hector's ugly — or was it shameful? — scars, what would he edit next? Would he pare away a bit of nose? Tack back the ears a little? The legs were doomed, of course. The sculptor would carve a pair of trunk-like limbs to match those of the garden's graceless demigods — ugly, heavy legs that could never sprint up a hill. Finished, the false Hector would lurk there in the garden, silent, bloated, blank-eyed, and smelling of stone.

"How would he be posed?" someone asked.

"That's hard to say," mused Phegeus. "Possibly on horseback—"

That wouldn't be the worst, thought Andromache. That way, less attention would be drawn to the sculpture's insipid face.

"— or with a sword, or a spear. To honor our greatest citizens, the options are many."

And each one stupider than the last, Andromache added sneeringly to herself.

"And yet, some countries still surpass us in the art of sculpting," the RYM opined. "In my travels far across the sea —" He paused modestly while some, including the Newbie, murmured over the scope of his travels — "I saw the most moving tribute, a sculpture depicting a young hero who had died in battle, and who was being carried back on —"

"What?" cried Andromache. "Where were you traveling, the land of ghouls?"

"Ghouls?" asked the RYM. "What do you mean?"

"Who else would want to look at *that*? At a dead man? It's terrible! It's sick!"

"It was beautiful," the RYM corrected, nevertheless looking at Andromache with new respect. Rarely had she spoken up at soirees, much less to challenge the leader.

"Then you're a ghoul, too," she accused him. Pink was rising in her cheeks. "Corpses *aren't* beautiful!" In her mind, she saw a waxy-white body, drained of blood, facedown upon the earth.

"You simply do not understand the aesthetics of the sculpture," the RYM explained patiently. "Allow me to describe it in more detail. There he was, frozen in youthful perfection, his father and brother carrying him in on a bier, his mother weeping on the ground beside him —"

"I've heard enough!" Andromache interrupted. "Any normal person who saw that would get sick!"

"Exactly!" exclaimed the RYM. "The sculpture elicits sorrow — tears — anguish. Centuries from now, people will still know how deeply the young hero was loved and honored."

"What difference does that make to *him*?" Andromache's voice was trembling.

"What difference?" the RYM asked pedantically. "But who *doesn't* dream of eternal glory?"

Andromache was running low on retorts. She didn't have the type of argument that would silence this fool and wanted — no, expected — Cassandra to burst in and help her. *Say something!* raged Andromache, but Cassandra just sat there.

"To cheat death even in embracing it," the RYM rhapsodized. "To live forever in —"

"Shut up!" shrieked Andromache, her fury unmistakable, though no one there could understand her words of Lukkan. She was now on her feet, her hands clenched into fists, ready to take a swing.

Everyone stared. "What's wrong?" the RYM asked mildly, trying to calm her. He seemed to think they'd been having an ordinary, cordial debate.

"What's *wrong*?" Andromache fumed at him. "What do you mean, '*what's wrong*,' you effing —"

"Let's not overreact," the RYM chided. "Let's be civilized."

Andromache stared open-mouthed for a moment before erupting into brittle laughter. *Civilized?* She was laughing so hard that she barely felt Cassandra's hand tearing her away from the others and hustling her out the door.

"Let's go, honey," the girl whispered. "You need to calm down."

But Andromache wasn't ready to calm down. "Why did you let him say all that?" she demanded, as they hurried home.

"All what?"

"All that stuff about dead heroes!"

"Oh, that," said Cassandra.

"Yes, *that*. Didn't it bother you?"

"Not really…"

"They were talking about your *brother!*"

"No, they weren't! They were talking about a guy from —"

"Oh, stuff it, Cassandra! On some level, they were talking about *him*, and you know it!"

Cassandra sighed. "Even if you're right, it's easiest just to let it go. Phegeus thinks he's paying people — like my brother — a compliment."

"What a wonderful way to honor people, wishing they were dead!" snapped Andromache. "Gods, Cassandra, that friend of yours is *almost* as human as the sculptures he loves so much!"

"He doesn't wish that my — he doesn't wish *anyone* — was dead!" Cassandra said hotly. "All he meant was that he found that particular work moving. If anything ever happened to — *anyone* — they'd all be devastated."

"I bet! Devastated that Hector doesn't have a *wife* to add her tears to the mix while his mangled corpse is being hauled around on a bier." Andromache threw the words out like a jab. "A wife weeping over his broken body would really complete the work!"

"Stop it!" Cassandra's voice rose.

"Why?" cried Andromache. "Those people don't care about Hector, as long as they can have a sculpture of him! Some hideous hunk of stone that doesn't even have the right *legs!*"

Trying to return the conversation to reason, Cassandra took a deep breath and said, "Look, all I'm saying is that if I were to make a scene like that every time —"

"There wouldn't *be* other times if you stamped out the first one!" Andromache retorted. "Admit it — you're *glad* I yelled at them!"

"I have my own way of dealing with things."

"Or of *not* dealing with them!"

"What's it to *you?*" Cassandra whirled on her, breaking the contact of their hands. "He's *my* brother, not yours." She glared at Andromache, waiting for a response.

Andromache stood there, trembling. What was it to *her?* The RYM's comments had been a violation — a greasy handprint left on a clean, white wall — that's what it was to *her!* Matching the fury of Cassandra's glare, she spat, "If you like listening to that kind of thing, then go back and tell everyone you're sorry. Tell them you've given that horrible foreign girl the slip. Tell them she won't be interrupting any more *civilized* gatherings. I'm going home!"

Although not yet ready to make amends with Andromache, Cassandra seemed equally reluctant to return to her friends. "I'm tired," she said haughtily, finding a third option. "I didn't really want to go out in the first place."

"Fine," Andromache hissed.

Neither spoke a word the rest of the way home. The instant they stepped through the door, Andromache split off from Cassandra and fled to her room. Once there, she burst into tears. All she could think of was the poor, mangled corpse, lugged around on a bier, seeping blood from a thousand ragged cuts.

Lashing out at Cassandra — attacking her with that hideous image — had only made Andromache's own pain worse, and now, on top of that, she hated herself. She'd hurt a friend for no reason at all! As soon as she was calm — as soon as she could pull herself together — she would go down to Cassandra's room and apologize. As soon as she was calm. As soon as she was *calm*! As soon as she could stop thinking about the corpse —

The tears kept pouring out and wouldn't stop.

Cutie licked them away. Ever faithful, she'd leapt onto the bed and glued herself to Andromache's side. Even Cutie's comfort wasn't enough, though. Andromache needed a tonic, one of Hecuba's sleeping potions. She needed something stronger than butcher's thorn — something that would erase all the pictures in her mind.

Cutie gave a small yip and turned her ears toward the door. She'd heard something.

Hecuba? wondered Andromache. She hoped so.

Scritch, scritch, scratch.

"Andromache?" It was Cassandra.

Andromache wasn't ready. She hadn't calmed down. Her apology was going to come out in a torrent of weeping, but there was no help for it. She couldn't send Cassandra away. "C-c-come — in," she stammered, wiping her nose.

Cassandra flung the door open and ran in. "I'm so sorry!" she cried, throwing her arms around Andromache.

Dizzy with relief, Andromache hugged the girl back. "No," she wailed. "No, Cassandra, no, it's *me* who's sorry!"

"No, honey — it's my fault. I'm *so* sorry! No wonder you were upset. Oh, honey! I didn't *know*."

Cassandra put a troubling emphasis on the last word. *Know?* "Know *what?*" Andromache asked warily.

"Know how you feel about my brother."

Andromache stopped cold. "Paris?" she whispered, mimicking Cassandra's own feigned confusion from earlier.

Cassandra snorted. "Don't be silly."

The room began to waver.

"I knew you were good friends with him," the girl went on, "but I didn't realize —"

"What, you — oh, no, you think —" Andromache gave a reedy laugh. "Oh, no — no!"

"No? Even with his — as you said — '*sexy legs?*'" teased Cassandra.

"I never said *that!*" cried Andromache.

"Oh, but honey, you *meant* it!"

Andromache's face was lost in a rush of crimson.

"It's so obvious to me, now, why you didn't want to marry Demuchus!"

"Cassandra! Please!" Andromache implored. "Go away!"

"Oh, all right! All right," said Cassandra, in the bland, comforting tone one uses on the insane. "But honey? Do you forgive me, about — about *earlier?*"

"Mm-hmm," mumbled Andromache.

With another hug, Cassandra left. "Sleep well," she whispered from the doorway.

Sleep? *Sleep?* Hah! That would have been nice! What was wrong with Cassandra? '*I didn't know how you feel about my brother'.*'

What a stupid thing to say, Andromache thought shakily, trying to reassure herself. *She knows full well how I feel about* Hector. *He's my friend.*

(*Ahem,*) came a sly little cough.

Andromache frowned. She hated to acknowledge the protest, but it was warranted. *All right — my good friend.*

This time, the Voice didn't cough. It snorted.

My best friend, thought Andromache, biting her bottom lip.

(*If you say so,*) was the snarky reply.

Well, what's wrong with that? He's a nice person.

(*There are lots of nice people in Troy. There's Xanthus, Cassandra, her parents…*)

Maybe, admitted Andromache. *But Hector is the one I can talk to best.*

(*Ah. Talk.*)

That's what I said, yes! Talk. It means 'open your mouth and make words come out.'

(*Hmmm…*)

What?

(*So it's only the talking that you like…*)

Andromache thought about the day she'd gone to the countryside with Hector, and the night of the Lorani hunt, and how some of their best moments together had been silent. *With your close friends*, she thought slowly, *you don't always have to talk because you understand each other. Silence is comfortable, too.*

(*Is Cassandra a close friend?*)

Of course.

(*How much time have you spent silently reveling in her company?*)

The impertinent question made Andromache flush. *I don't revel, with him!*

(*Snort!*)

I don't!

(*You don't take lingering breaths whenever he's around?*)

Andromache thought of the green smell that meant Hector to her, a mingling of cedar trees and mint. The red in her cheeks deepened to purple. *So he smells nice! It's hard not to notice that. It's not my fault, and it doesn't mean anything.*

(*Oh, no?*) taunted the Voice.

Andromache had never appreciated, till then, just how much the Voice sounded like Paris. *So what?* she snapped. *So what if he smells nice, and so what if I like being with him? Why wouldn't I? We laugh a lot together. Besides, he's special. He met my Auntie, and she liked him.*

(*And you love him!*)

Of course I love him —

(*A-hah!*)

He's my friend, stupid Voice! You'd love your friends, too, if you had any! Andromache loved her *friend* — that was all! Romantic love, the kind her parents had known, was something that happened instantaneously. You fell into a delirium and ran away to a foreign city with your lover, and that was how it worked — end of story. Running away with Hector had never crossed her mind!

(Why did your parents run away together, exactly?)

Because, Andromache thought peevishly, *the next day, my mom was going back to her village. My dad never would've seen her again, if he hadn't left with her.*

(Hmm,) said the Voice, as though it now understood all the secrets of the universe.

What, hmm?

(And if those were your choices — to run away with Hector, *or never see him again?)*

Shut up! Andromache had already answered that question, hadn't she, back when Demuchus proposed marriage? When she hadn't been able to resign herself to a Hector-less life? But still, she couldn't let the Voice think it had won. *That's a stupid question. Anyone would run away with her friends, rather than never seeing them again.*

(Oh, I see. So you would run away with Cassandra? *Or with* Paris? *They're your friends too, aren't they?)*

Not my best *friends.*

For one blessed moment, there was silence in her head. The Voice seemed to have no retort for her, and she thought she'd finally squelched it. Until —

(So…) The thing spoke up again, more impudently than ever. *(What happens if your* — ahem! — *best friend doesn't make it back here?)*

He will!

(Maybe. Maybe not,) sneered the Voice.

Yes, he will!

(And if not?)

Once more, Andromache saw the mangled corpse —

No, there just *had* to be something else to think about! She turned violently onto her side and stared out the window, at the tree tips poking up into the sky, at their leaves waving lightly in the breeze. *Ah — trees. Trees are good. Trees are calm.* She imagined herself floating out the window, away from the badgering Voice, to lie peacefully under the trees. She thought back to the platana grove in Lyrnassa — to the mountain pines of the Lukka lands. Her nerves had just begun to calm when she remembered that many of those trees were gone now, burned or buried by a rock-slide.

If this place, the house of Hecuba and Priam, ever lost its trees, then everything that made it beautiful would be gone. The courtyard would be drab and lifeless. If these trees were ever chopped down — or buried — or burned, leaving only a ribbon of smoke in the sky — then the whole house might as well go with them — all of Troy might as well go with them, because without them, it would be ugly!

Andromache began to cry.

(*You see?*) crowed the Voice. This was its hour of triumph.

Yes — you win. She saw. She knew. She *knew*! Hector meant the world to her. He understood her and made her feel good about herself. Fighting with him was miserable; his anger tore her insides to a raw and bloody pulp. But a smile from him — a laugh! — sent her floating past the stars.

She understood, now. Everything made sense. All her bitterness and hurt, back when she'd thought he was using her — learning Lukkan to punish himself — those feelings had come from thwarted love. And then, when he'd told her that he *did* like her, and she'd been lit from within by that dazzling, light-footed happiness…

I thought it was because we were finally friends, she moaned to herself. *Real friends.* Friendship was something worth glowing about, wasn't it? Of course it was!

Andromache chewed her bottom lip. Of course friendship was worth glowing about, but being friends with Hector didn't mean he wasn't her love. She saw now that love didn't have to happen fast, like it had for her parents. It could creep up little by little. It could catch you from behind —

(*You turned your back,*) taunted the Voice. (*You didn't want to see it. I tried to tell you.*)

Of course I turned my back! snapped Andromache. For so long, she hadn't even thought he *liked* her! She hadn't dared take too much pleasure in being with him, let alone question what her feelings for him meant! She'd never thought of him that way before — him or any other man. *What else was I supposed to do? And what am I supposed to do* now?

(*What do you want to do?*)

I don't know.

(*Come on.*)
I don't know!
(*Really? You don't want to hug him? Hold him? Kiss him?*)

Andromache thought of the warmth of Hector's hand on her back, out in the countryside — that brief touch that had burned down to her skin. She thought of the unease she felt around him, whenever kissing came up. She thought of what kissing with him would be like — how joyous and alive he was, how tightly he would hold her. She imagined a kiss like the one she'd once witnessed in the stairwell, when Paris and his little girlfriend had been slithering against each other — except now it was her, kissing Hector. Her hands on Hector's back, in his hair...

The picture wasn't all that different from what she'd seen.

Andromache clapped her hand to her mouth. Oh, gods, no wonder she'd been jealous, that night! No wonder she'd thrown her shoe at the lovers! The dim light — the dark-haired boy — the girl wound all around him...

(*From behind, Paris and Hector look a lot alike,*) the Voice helpfully reminded her.

Shut up! thought Andromache, but the Voice was right. She felt stupid for not having seen the connection sooner. Everything about Hector had unsettled her that night, from his smile at the doorway, to his cedar tree smell, to his whispered words as they sat together on the stairs. The whole time, she'd been lusting after *him* — and *this* was no mediocre lust that could be solved with time or laughter.

(*So, I see you know what you want after all,*) taunted the Voice.

Andromache's cheeks flushed an almost painful shade of red. She knew, all right. She wanted *him*. She wanted everything about him.

(*I wonder what Penthesilea would think about that.*)

Andromache turned pale. Penthesilea. Hector's fiancée.

(*His beautiful fiancée,*) corrected the Voice.

Yes. Beautiful.

(*And talented.*)

Very talented,

(*Not to mention nice. She gave you clothes, didn't she?*)

Yes, murmured Andromache.

(*And offered you shelter?*)

Yes.

(*And saved your life?*)

Yes, yes, yes! snapped Andromache.

(*She brought you here when* he *didn't want you.*)

He likes me now, Andromache retorted. *He said so.*

(*That's true. He's your* friend,) the Voice said with a sneer.

'*Always, always we ahre friends,*' Hector had said. Before, his remark had enchanted her; now, it left her feeling dull and luster-less. Always, always, she and Hector would be friends. *Friends!* Nothing more.

(*More? Who are you kidding? Just be glad he even wants to be friends with you, after everything he's seen and heard!*)

The Voice was right again! Hector had been there for her first night in Troy, when she was bloodied, sunburned, and faint-ing. He'd watched her languishing for all those months when she was too scared to leave the house. He knew about her family — about the wagoner. The last image he had of her was a drunk girl weeping for her blanket: '*I want Shtripey!*' She was certain, now, that the incident was real. She couldn't merely have dreamed it. She wasn't that lucky.

(*He belongs with* Penthesilea. *She's strong. She can handle things without falling apart.*)

Their relationship is stupid! snarled Andromache. *They're still not married, after all this time.*

(*You don't know the whole story.*)

I know they have as much spark together as two dead and bloated fish!

The Voice began to cackle. It was obviously enjoying itself. (*They must have their reasons for staying together.*)

Andromache had no retort to make. The Voice was surely right. "Just go away!" she cried, immediately embarrassed at her outburst. *Leave me alone.*

Andromache waited a moment — then another — and then one more. The Voice didn't return. Finally, it seemed to be gone. *Hah!* She thought. It was a victory, but a small one. In truth, she knew, her torment had only just begun. What good could possi-bly come of these feelings for Hector? What could they possibly bring her but humiliation? No wonder she'd been slow to pick up on the signs! Hector would never love her back. Denial had been her shield, her lone protection against heartbreak.

An hour or so after the fatal phrase — *'I didn't know how you feel about my brother'* — had been uttered, Andromache emerged tearily from her room and tiptoed to Cassandra's. Since *she* had been the one to cause all this, the least she could do was offer comfort. Andromache knocked on the door. When no one answered, she knocked again. Still no answer. Slowly, Andromache opened the door. When she could just squeeze past it, she entered Cassandra's room and sat on her bed. "Cassandra," she whispered to the sleeping girl.

"Aaaaaah!" cried Cassandra. "Oh — it's you, honey." She rubbed her eyes groggily. "What are you doing here? Is something wrong?"

Andromache started to cry again.

"Oh, honey," murmured Cassandra, hugging her. "Oh, honey! I'll talk to him, when he gets back, and —"

"No!" shrieked Andromache. When Cassandra had tried to fix her up with Demuchus, the results had been disastrous. The last thing she wanted was another, worse catastrophe. Above all, Andromache could *not* let Hector find out how she felt! Being around her would make him uncomfortable. He would stop taking Lukkan lessons, and she would lose his friendship.

"Why not?"

"Because!"

"Honey…"

"I mean it, Cassandra!"

"All right. I won't say anything."

"Promise?"

"I promise."

But even if Cassandra said nothing, she couldn't guarantee the same for her friends. "We need a cover story," whispered Andromache.

"What do you mean?"

"A cover story! You know, to explain why I said whatever I said at the soiree tonight. We need a story in case any of your stupid friends blab everything to *him*, when he gets back. Something that will make them — and *him* — think the opposite of what *you* think."

"Andromache…"

"Just help me, please!"

"All right," said Cassandra, sitting upright. "Let's see…I can tell them you were coming down with a fever," she offered.

Andromache nodded. "That's good," she said. "Simple. Do you think they'll buy it?"

Cassandra furrowed her brow. "You should probably stay in bed for a couple days, to be on the safe side," she finally said. "Then, I don't see why they wouldn't. You were acting pretty crazy, tonight."

There was too much truth in Cassandra's words for Andromache to be offended by them. Besides, a few days in bed, away from everyone else, suited her perfectly. "Will they gossip about it?"

"Oh, probably not much. Fevers are too common to be exciting," Cassandra assured her.

"Do you think that's enough? The fever, I mean?"

"I'll think of something, if it seems like the story needs embellishment. Don't worry."

Andromache nodded gratefully.

"Honey?"

"Hmm?"

"It's going to be all right."

Chapter 9

When Andromache awoke, her mouth felt as dry as sun-shriveled seaweed. Her hands, in contrast, were slick. Dog saliva. "Cutie," she groaned, without much force.

The dog's ears stood up straight. Forsaking Andromache's hands, she went instead for the nose.

"Cutie! Cut it out!"

The red-brown ears went back.

"Oh, don't look like that," sighed Andromache. "Here — come here."

Cutie, forgiven, nuzzled Andromache's chin and lay down to groom herself.

The whole scene was so ordinary that Andromache concluded she *must* have gotten drunk the night before and hallucinated everything. Surely, she hadn't menaced the RYM! Or heard voices! Or run weeping to Cassandra's room in the middle of the night! Or hatched a plan to be feverish for a week!

Ridiculous, she thought. Lie around, pretending to be feverish, indeed! What she needed to do was open the curtains and —

Pain exploded in her head. *Ouch! Headache. Drunk, all right.* Hastily, she snapped the curtains shut. The pain lessened, but doubt began to gnaw at her. Other than the headache, she didn't really feel hung over.

Maybe she *hadn't* been hallucinating! She didn't remember having drunk much wine the night before, and weeping, at any rate, sounded like something she would do. The Voice? She'd heard it many times before, so that, too, was plausible. As for threatening the RYM, she couldn't blame herself if she had. He was insufferable! Especially after the way he'd talked about —

Andromache swallowed hard on her leathery tongue. Hector! *That* flood of feeling had been no hallucination, and neither were the sudden warmth and dizziness that overcame her as, finally, she was able to picture his whole face, even his eyes.

She *loved* Hector! She loved him so madly that, if he asked, she would run away with him to any foreign city of his choosing. It was the same feeling that must have taken hold of her parents, the day they eloped: an all-consuming need to be with the other person. To spend each day together, talking, and laughing, and loving…

Andromache let out a long, slow breath. In spite of herself, she'd entered yet another new era: the era of loving Hector. Overnight, her life had been transformed. Cassandra had assured her that everything would be all right, but she didn't see how. The best she could hope for now was for her love to stay hidden, as though it were shameful and indecent. What a dismal hope to cling to!

She was suddenly glad to be spending the next week alone in her room. There, she could think about Hector without having to face all the reasons that it was stupid to think about him. She could enjoy a short while with him, undisturbed.

Cutie curled into a ball at Andromache's side.

"Good idea," said Andromache. "I'm supposed to be sick, you know. Practice looking sorry for me, will you?"

The little dog sighed and closed her eyes.

"Not bad," said Andromache. "Not bad at all."

CUTIE EVENTUALLY WANDERED downstairs, but Andromache stayed in bed all day. While she was lying there, Cassandra, true to her word, set about sowing the seeds of their cover story. That afternoon, she stopped by Andromache's room to tell her about it. She looked rosy and cheerful, quite like her old self, not gloomy as she'd been for the past several weeks. Having a project had restored her.

"I told everyone — well, not everyone, but the *right people*, you know — anyway, I got to them early this morning and told them about the fever. But just in case that wasn't enough, I added a few touches."

"Like what?"

"For one, that when you lost your baby brother —"

"Cassandra!" interrupted Andromache. "I *never* had a brother, baby or otherwise!" Her mom had in fact lost a baby once, but she'd never told Cassandra about that — and in any case, Cassandra didn't seem to have been talking about a miscarriage.

"Oh, well!" said the girl. "It doesn't matter — no one here knows that, do they? Anyway, when you lost him, the people in your village all raved about how beautiful he was, lying in his little shroud, and so when Phegeus said that that sculpture of the dead man was beautiful, it touched a nerve with you."

The story was both nutty and brilliant, and, unbeknownst to Cassandra, it even had a whisper of truth. Back in the Lukka lands, when Andromache was a little girl, she had indeed been scarred by the sight of a corpse. That waxy-pale corpse, its blood drained by raiders…

In a hushed voice, Andromache asked, "Did anyone believe you?"

Cassandra giggled. "This afternoon, when I went down to the dressmaker for a fitting — and oh, honey, aren't you glad it's time for summer clothes, again? — but anyway, this woman I hardly know stopped me on the street and asked me to give you her sympathy on the loss of your five brothers."

Andromache didn't know whether to laugh or groan. The cover story seemed to be working, but she worried that Cassandra's '*embellishments*' would somehow come back to bite her.

"But it's time for me to run, honey," sang the girl. "I have to get ready for tonight's soiree. I can't wait to hear what everyone is saying!"

As Cassandra danced off, Andromache sighed. *I'm glad someone's getting pleasure out of this mess!*

HECUBA CAME to the room an hour later. "My daughter says you have a fever," she said, touching Andromache's forehead, then frowning. "It doesn't feel like it to me."

"I'm sick," Andromache insisted.

Hecuba narrowed her eyes. "Whatever's the matter, you aren't ill. Did one of her friends say something to upset you?"

Andromache shook her head.

"Dear," said Hecuba, more gently this time. "You can tell me. I know what it's like to be a foreigner, here in the citadel."

"I'm *sick*," Andromache insisted, moaning slightly for emphasis. "I *am*."

Hecuba threw her hands up in disgust. "Very well! Never mind all the Trojans who are suffering real ailments while you're up here, neglecting your herb garden!"

Andromache felt a pang of guilt, but it was shaded with relief. Hecuba hadn't guessed! Oh, she knew the fever was a hoax, but she hadn't connected it in any way to Hector. Andromache's world might have been turned on its head, but she would at least be spared the humiliation of a public, unrequited love. "I'll be better soon," she promised Hecuba.

The woman sniffed. "See that you are."

$$\wp\mathbb{O}$$

DURING ANDROMACHE'S phony convalescence, Cassandra made many trips up to her room. She brought meals, extra blankets, and jars of Hecuba's healing tonic, as well as news of how their cover story was spreading.

"The whole city knows that you're feverish!" she cried in delight. "No one would believe a word you said, right now. And you're up to seven brothers!"

Andromache groaned. "Oh, Cassandra!"

"What? It's what you wanted, right?"

"I guess so," said Andromache, although the story had gotten a little out of hand.

Still, she preferred news of her false illness to the other stories Cassandra had begun to share.

"You know Echepolus?" she whispered one night. "He's really smart, isn't he? And so sexy! I kissed with him, once. Mom would pop a vein, if she knew — I was only thirteen!"

The next evening, it was a sighed, "I don't know what to do! Echepolus is sexy, but not half as cute as Periphas, and Periphas won't even *look* at me! I think I might *die* if he doesn't. What do you think I should *do*, honey?"

Andromache could only shrug. Cassandra's so-called secrets, she knew, had one purpose — to tempt Andromache into spilling her guts about Hector. They were a trade in the gossip market: *I'll tell you about my crush, then you tell me about yours.*

Andromache didn't dare make such a bargain. It wasn't that she didn't want to talk to Cassandra. She would have liked to have a confidant for her feelings about Hector — someone on her side — someone who wasn't the Voice.

Cassandra, however, was far too great a risk. She might let something slip to her friends — to her *brothers*. In spite of her promise, she might even try to meddle, once Hector came home. No, the less she knew, the better. Let her think that Andromache had developed a silly little crush, one that would fizzle out in due course.

When Andromache gave nothing in return, Cassandra tried enticing her with ever-juicier morsels.

"I heard Lycon is getting married, and the horror of it is, I never had a chance to kiss with him! Oh, honey! And to think, he might have been my *one true love*. I've always wondered what it's like to have one of those! The library has *thousands* of beautiful love poems, of course, but I don't feel like I'd really *know* what it's like to have a *one true love* just by reading them. On the other hand, if I could talk to someone who *did*…"

On it went for days, until Andromache had no choice but to declare herself well.

Life more or less went back to normal once Andromache returned to the lower levels of the house. She had to endure Paris's dramatic refusal to kiss her cheek —

Don't come near me, Hermie. I don't want to catch your fever!

— and his jibes —

'You're not the prettiest girl around, anymore, Hermie. I heard there's a corpse down the road who's absolutely gorgeous!"

— but at least she could scurry the other way when she saw Cassandra coming.

Chapter 10

She clambered from one stair to the next, trying not to fall through the gap between them, a gap as large as her lower leg was long. And another one — even larger, it seemed — between the next two stairs.

What was beneath her? She looked down, gasping in horror when she saw only sky. Oh, gods, the whole stairway was suspended in air! She knew what was going to happen before it did: with her next step, she would fall through the gap into nothingness. Sure enough, her foot slipped in its sandal, dragging her downward...

Andromache awoke in a sweat. Her heart was thudding and beside her, Cutie was whimpering. Andromache bowed her head in shame. She'd scared the dog! It was a new low. And because of what, a nightmare about stairs? Stairs! Hadn't Hector once teased her for a similar dream? If only he were there, right now, to remind her how silly it was!

Andromache gulped. No, even if he talked to her, it might not be enough, this time — but maybe if he *held* her, instead of just talking to her...

She imagined Hector there, his arms around her, her face pressed so tightly to his neck that she almost couldn't breathe. In no time, she was fast asleep.

FROM THEN on, whenever Andromache was scared or lonely, she pictured herself in Hector's arms and soon felt happy again. Glowingly happy. Even, as it turned out, dangerously happy.

"What's up with you, Hermie?" asked Paris one afternoon, when he surprised her with a look of particular contentment on her face. As her expression turned to guilt, he became fascinated. All day long he pestered her, trying to discover what she'd been thinking about.

(*This is nothing!*) laughed the Voice, once Paris had finally grown tired of bothering her. (*Just you wait.*)

Wait for what? asked Andromache.

(*Wait for how awkward it'll be once* he gets back.)

As always, the Voice was right. If the mere thought of Hector could put a guilty look on her face, what would the sight of him do? Paris was no fool, and he loved to gossip. He was more than capable of ferreting out her secret and blabbing it to Hector — in which case, Andromache would die of mortification.

(*Penthesilea wasn't here, either,*) the Voice observed.

Penthesilea. Andromache's insides quivered at the thought of the warrior woman — so beautiful, so lethal. How would *she* react, if she intercepted a too-sweet look? Andromache probably wouldn't survive that, either.

Nothing could bring her more happiness than Hector's return to Troy. At the same time, nothing could bring her more danger.

Mid-spring

Chapter 11

When word of the army's homecoming spread through Troy, Andromache was out by herself, in the herb market. It was a stroke of luck. If she'd been at home, Cassandra would have pounced on her. There would have been endless chirpings and squealings of '*Oh, honey!*' Now, she would be alone when she spotted Hector's orange commander's cloak — or, if not alone, she would at least be with people who didn't know her secret.

As Andromache climbed to the top of the grey city walls, she found herself pressed on all sides by Trojans. For a moment, her old fear of crowds — of being trampled — overcame her, but then the feeling waned. The crowd was thick but calm. No one kicked or elbowed her as they stood watching, waiting for the army to arrive.

Soon, it happened. A wave of people, horses, chariots, and gear poured through the gate. Andromache looked and looked, scanning the chaotic scene for a bright swath of orange, but she didn't see it.

It's all right, she told herself. *I'm sure he's just letting everyone else in first.* That seemed like something Hector would do.

When a quarter-hour had passed, then a half-hour, and still no sign of Hector, Andromache's insides bunched into a solid knot of fear. How stupid she'd been, to see his homecoming as dangerous! So what if he found out about her feelings? So what if Paris found out? So what if she got embarrassed? None of that mattered! But if she didn't spot his orange cloak soon! — if he hadn't made it home with the others —

At three quarters of an hour, Andromache began to panic. Where *was* he? Had it taken so long the first time? If only she'd gone with Cassandra, back then, she would know if such a long wait was normal.

An hour — surely, this was too long! Andromache couldn't breathe. The air had turned to syrup. Beside her, a man started dancing wildly and jabbed her twice in the shoulder, but she didn't care. She would gladly have suffered jabs — let her feet be stomped, her shins bruised — if it somehow meant that Hector would come home. She would have given anything — *anything* —

Andromache's thoughts broke off abruptly. There he was! She saw him! At last, she saw him, on horseback, far to the back of the crowd, pinioned against the walls. He was safe — he was *there*! She watched as the mob swelled around him, lapped at his ankles, and then finally began to ripple away. She stared at him for as long as she could, knowing it might be her very last chance to do so.

℘

"WHERE ON EARTH HAVE YOU BEEN?" Hecuba clucked when Andromache finally returned home. "My goodness!"

"Stuck in the crowds," muttered Andromache, avoiding the woman's eye.

"Yes, well! The streets aren't empty today, it's true." Hecuba nodded, smiling. "You're in time to help, anyway. Would you mind seeing to the garden boxes? Cutie is already out there."

Andromache eagerly agreed. Now that Hector was safely back in Troy, she was scared once more of seeing him face-to-face. She couldn't imagine meeting him in the entry hall, as she had after his last campaign. The tiny, bare entry hall...no, anywhere but there! True, the courtyard had its own risks — Hector's bedroom was out in a little building on the far side. He might well head over there after greeting his family. Still, the courtyard would at least provide weeds to pluck, stones to scrub, the dog to pet, and a thousand other reasons not to look Hector in the eye.

While the others set out food and lamps in the banquet hall, Andromache tackled the gardens. She pulled weeds, vegetables, and herbs indiscriminately. There was no question of focusing. Every sound distracted her from her task; any of them might have been *him*. She startled when a noisy bird launched itself from a bush. She shrieked when one of last year's wizened apricots plopped to the ground beside her. Gasping, she saw that the fruit's mealy flesh had split open.

She shuddered.

Leaving the apricot where it lay, she called for Cutie and fled upstairs to her room. Once the door was slammed shut, she fell against it, trembling. She was never going to be able to make it through the night.

ℂℂ

"HONEY? ARE YOU THERE?"

Cassandra had noticed her disappearance. Wild-eyed, Andromache opened the door for her.

"What are you doing up here? Hector will be home soon!"

At the sound of his name, Andromache flushed.

"Oh, honey…"

"I-I can't — I can't —" Andromache stammered. Already the evening was a disaster, and she hadn't even left her room, yet!

"You should at least take a bath," said Cassandra. "It might help you calm down."

Andromache shook her head vehemently. "I can't go down there."

"Oh, honey!"

"Could — could you bring me some water for a sponge bath?" Andromache beseeched. "I'll do anything you want! I'll do all your dishes — make you breakfast in bed. Anything!"

"Don't be silly! Of course I can do that," said Cassandra, running back down the stairs. Cutie followed her.

Just moments later, Andromache heard a commotion down on the first floor. Cutie had begun to yip. Even muffled by distance, her odd mix of welcome and anger was unmistakable.

He's home, Andromache thought to herself. She could hear Cutie yelling at Hector for having left her and imagined the dog bouncing off his calves and slathering him with kisses. With a touch of envy, she remarked how easy it was for dogs to greet the ones they loved. Dogs didn't have to hide their feelings.

It's better that I'm up here, thought Andromache. *That way, I don't have to try to hide anything.* At the same time, she felt sorry that she wasn't downstairs. The last time Hector had come home, he'd given her such a sweet smile! Who was he smiling at, now? Who was he hugging? Was he wondering about her, why she wasn't at the door with her broom?

Andromache sighed and waited.

"Sorry I'm late!" sang Cassandra, when she finally got back to the room. She was carrying a basin of water, a sponge, and an assortment of oils. "He's here!" As she plunked down the basin, half its contents sloshed onto the floor. "Oops! Oh, honey, I'm sorry!" She laughed and tried to mop up the water with her skirt. "Do you need anything? I could brush your hair, if you want."

"No, no — that's all right," said Andromache. Her nerves would unravel if Cassandra were there much longer, dancing in circles. "Go ahead downstairs. Go talk to —"

"All right!" Cassandra agreed. "I'll see you in a little bit."

Andromache swallowed hard. Alone again, she began her toilette in earnest. Her hair took the longest. It was a mess of tangles and required all of her patience to brush and braid. The sponge bath, on the other hand, relaxed her, and as she rubbed a little of her favorite oil into her skin, the thought of facing Hector seemed less daunting.

Muted cries and laughter drifted up from the courtyard. The first guests had arrived.

Andromache pawed through her clothing chest. *Nothing*, she thought miserably, when she saw the dull heap of dresses inside it. *Nothing at all!* — she was going to be a grey rock in the flower garden of Trojan girls. After searching for another moment or two, hoping something prettier might appear, she gave up.

The sounds grew louder. It was time for her to go downstairs.

୫ଠ

ANDROMACHE SLIPPED OUT to the courtyard. If this party was anything like the last one, Hector would be stuck in the banquet hall for another few hours, surrounded by friends and well-wishers. It was a scene that Andromache wanted to avoid. She was still too nervous to talk to Hector, and she certainly didn't care to watch Priam's oration. Hector and Penthesilea — Lee — would be standing beside each other while Priam honored the army's leaders, and Lee would be so stunning and graceful that it would make Andromache retch.

I'll find Hector later, she told herself. It would be easier to face him once she'd had a little wine. In the meantime, she would stay out on the courtyard, where it was quiet.

Not many people were outside in the brisk spring air. Andromache was able to linger there, unnoticed, as the evening sky turned from gold to deep blue. While meandering around, she came upon the broken apricot. No one had picked it up. Gently, she nudged it under one of the benches, where it wouldn't get stepped on.

Then, a sweet, familiar scent filled her nostrils. *Hector!* she thought, turning around so hurriedly that she backed into the bench and sat down on it, hard. *Great, Ahndromahk,* she rebuked herself, but her stumble didn't matter. No one was there to see it.

Confused, she looked around. *But — I'm sure I smelled — oh.* The garden box behind her was full of mint. No wonder she'd thought of Hector! Andromache took a sprig and put it between her teeth, then took it out again. She pulled off one of the leaves, nibbled it furtively, and balled up the rest of the stem in her fist.

By the time the music had struck up in earnest, Andromache still hadn't laid eyes on Hector. She was beginning to feel thwarted by her success at avoiding him. *I have to see him,* she thought, suddenly heedless of the risks. *If I don't see him now, I'll explode.*

She passed from the courtyard to the banquet hall. Inside, it was loud, hot, and crowded. She skulked at the edges of the room, circling it several times in the hope of finding Hector. There was no sign of him, though, not even among the throng of Cassandra's beautiful young friends.

He must be out there somewhere, Andromache sighed to herself. *If only I were a little taller —*

(*Like* Lee?) taunted the Voice.

Shut up! thought Andromache, making her way to the staircase. *Lee* wasn't the only one who could be tall! From the third stair, Andromache could see out into the crowd.

(*They're looking at you, too,*) said the Voice. (*They're wondering what you're doing up there, and why you're staring at them. Maybe* he *can see you staring.*)

Andromache fell to the ground so quickly that she bumped her tailbone again. A tear leaked out and she buried her face in her hands. While she was sitting there, pair after pair of sandaled feet passed by her, some shuffling ponderously and others dancing. She imagined a room full of disembodied feet, blown about by the wind.

I must be going crazy, she told herself. *That's a crazy thing to think.*

Yet another pair of sandals scuffed by. Unlike the others, though, it slowed its course and backed up. Someone had noticed her! The owner of the feet then sat down beside her and laughed. "The life of the party!" said a man's voice.

The comment might easily have come from Paris, but Andromache knew that it hadn't. Paris didn't smell like cedar trees.

"You lahke this stairs a lot." Another laugh.

If only the damn stairs would engulf her, fool that she was! This was *exactly* where she'd been sitting at the last party, when Hector had come over to talk to her! It probably looked like she'd been *waiting* for him! She opened her eyes and noticed the broken mint sprig, which had fallen from her hand. She moved her foot to conceal it, but was she too late? Had he seen it?

"Always ready fohr escape," said Hector, trying again.

He's waiting for me to say something. Andromache sucked in her breath. She couldn't think of anything to say but managed to look up at him and offer a feeble smile. Her smile deepened when she got a good look at him. His beard had grown in, and his head was shaven, but he wasn't wearing a cloak, the way he had when his arm was wounded. His only cover was the shoulder wrap Trojans wore on cool evenings. *He must be all right!* she thought with relief. *He's not hiding any wounds, this time*. His knees were scabbed over, but otherwise the legs looked fine. Actually, more than fine — they looked — they looked — *sexy*. She bit her lip. *Damn* that Cassandra! Why had she joked about that?

"Ahndromahk?" said Hector.

"Hi," Andromache said back. Her greeting had come far too late to pass for normal, but her voice sounded all right — at least for someone whose insides had melted together. Now that Hector was there, beside her, with his warmth seeping into the air between them and the sweetness of mint leaves teasing her every time he spoke, Andromache knew that she'd been right about feeling no mediocre lust for him. What she felt was a raging, burning, drastic, dizzying lust. She ached to take his hand and pull him up the stairs. *The Make-Out stairs,* she thought, remembering the kiss she'd once witnessed there. What she wouldn't give for a few moments, writhing against Hector's body in the darkened alcove. A few moments? An hour! The whole ni —

"Hi," the oblivious Hector said back.

Andromache knew she'd been staring again when he ran a hand over the stubble on his head and explained, a little sheepishly, "Befohre, I haff hair bahgs. To caht the hair off is mohre easy than to —" He pantomimed combing.

"Hair bugs?" she repeated. "You mean lice?"

Hector nodded.

"Oh, no!" Andromache exclaimed. "Lice *suck*." The instant the words left her mouth, she wished them back in. Lice suck? Of *course* they sucked! Had she actually *said* that? Hector was going to think she was dimwitted instead of taking her comment the way she'd meant it, as Truvan slang for, '*Lice are awful.*'

But Hector only shrugged in resignation. "The worst is, I'm stuck with a beard again until the hair grows back — unless I want a naked head, that is."

At the word '*naked,*' Andromache flushed.

"You ahre not there today," said Hector after another moment of silence. "In the hall ohff entry."

"I know." Andromache gulped. So, he *had* been thinking about her, wondering why she wasn't sweeping out the entry hall. "I was — I was taking a nap. I felt a little weird this afternoon." That, at least, was no lie!

"You ahre still sleepy?" he asked. "You can go to your betroom." He nodded toward the stairway behind them.

The Make-Out stairs, Andromache thought once again. Forget sleep! Forget her bedroom! She wondered if anyone was in the dark alcove right now, or if she could take Hector's hand and —

Stop it, Ahndromahk! she warned herself, shaking her head firmly.

"You ahre not sleepy?" asked Hector, in response to her gesture.

"Not really," she murmured. What else could she say, at that point? "Are you?"

"Yes, ohff couhrse." He coughed. "Baht these people, they leaff *neffer*. All night, they sit in front ohff my betroom door, and I cannot go in."

Ah! The guests — that was a safer topic. "They always do that, don't they," Andromache said sympathetically. At the last such party, Hector had complained about guests blocking the way to his bedroom. If he tried to get through, he'd said, they would catch him and gabble his ear off. No matter how tired he was, he had little choice but to stay at the party.

"Always," he said ruefully.

"Maybe you should drug the wine," Andromache suggested. Hector laughed until he coughed again. "A good idea…"

When his voice trailed off, Andromache thought desperately of something else to ask — *anything*. Now that he was there, she didn't want him to leave. "How's Buzzy?"

"Good, so good. He is happy now, in the hohrse house. He is wiff Thisbe."

"Oh, that's good! She missed him."

"You see her, when I am gone?"

"Yes. A lot."

"Good."

Andromache nodded. After a pause, she asked, "How are you?" Again, the question had come too late in the conversation to sound normal, but at least things were getting back on track.

"This time, I am *entahre*," joked Hector, holding up his arms for inspection. Except for a few shield chafe-marks, nothing was marring the healthy brown glow of his skin.

Automatically, as though she'd done so a thousand times before, Andromache ran her hand down the length of his forearm.

He flinched away.

Oh shit! Andromache cried to herself. *Oh* shit! Her mind was thrashing about for an excuse — any excuse! — for having stroked his arm when she noticed something else. The collar of Hector's wrap had shifted as he recoiled, exposing a large, blackish bruise. "Hector!" Her voice came out high and sharp.

"What?" he asked, nudging his collar back into place and coughing again.

She hesitated. Should she ask him ask him what had happened? Probably not, unless she wanted to alienate him further. He knew she'd seen the bruise and would have explained if he'd wanted to. It wasn't as though she could help him, anyway —she wasn't a healer. "Nothing," she finally mumbled. "Welcome back." She hoped that the phrase was bland enough to hide the tremor in her voice and make him forget that she'd touched him.

"Oh. Yes. Back."

Why wasn't he leaving? In his place, she would have left by now. It was plain from the uncomfortable way he was shifting that he wanted to. He was just too kind to hurt her feelings by making a hasty exit. *I'll make it easy, then,* thought Andromache. *I'll give him an out.* "See you tomorrow," she whispered, unable to keep herself from peering at his neck again.

He pretended not to notice. "Ah-ee prahctice — a — a leetle," he said.

She stared uncomprehendingly. Why had his accent suddenly gone thick?

"Lukkan," he said. "I practiced Lukkan."

"Oh…"

"Eensahde the head. Eensahde *mah-ee* head."

"Oh. Inside your head. Good. I'm sure you'll be fine." Why wasn't he leaving, after the opening she'd given him? Gods, why wasn't he leaving?

Nodding, he repeated, "Fine."

Andromache looked at the floor.

"Yeuh trah the — oh, what's that word?" Hector sighed. "Bread wiff plahnts?"

He got another blank look from her.

"Herb bread," he said softly, squirming again.

"Uh — uh — no," said Andromache. "No, I didn't try it. Is it good?"

"Eet ees all rahght." But he looked so miserable that she couldn't take the recommendation seriously.

"Oh." *It's afternoon,* Andromache told herself, to keep from crying. *It's afternoon and you haven't left your room yet. You fell asleep on your bed, and you're having a nightmare.* She closed her eyes for a moment to collect herself. When she opened them again, several distinguished, older men were huddled together, eyeing Hector. "I think they want to talk to you," she said.

"Great," he muttered, adding, "I wish someone had drugged *their* wine."

Andromache smiled feebly. "See you later, then, I guess," she murmured.

Hector nodded. "See you." With a sigh, he stood to leave.

As Andromache watched him walk away, she noticed once more just how sexy his legs were...not to mention the rest of him. His clothes were as shabby as ever, but she saw for the first time how well-cut the tunic was, how it hugged his narrow hips. The sight made her want to —

Stop it! she snapped at herself. *Look where that kind of thing already got you! Now's not the time!* Not that there *was* a good time to think such thoughts, but *that* moment was particularly bad. What she had to do was focus on damage control: she had to make sure that no one, including Hector, would think twice about the fact that she'd stroked his arm.

Andromache groaned. Only one solution came to her, and she didn't like it at all.

ℂ

"WOW, HERMIE. THIS is quite the night for you," hooted Paris, hours later.

Immediately, Andromache's hackles rose.

"Still up at this hour!" he went on. "And you look almost social."

"Thanks," she muttered.

"I'm not the only one who thinks so."

Her breathing stopped. "What do you mean?"

"I'm actually here on a mission."

"A mission?" she croaked.

"I'm an emissary — for someone too spineless to tell you he wants to make out with you."

Blood pounded in Andromache's ears. She leaned over to avoid passing out. Emissary! This wasn't the first time Paris had been an emissary! *Oh, gods — what do I — what do I —*

"I have to say, Hermie — I'm impressed with you. I never thought you'd have the guts to just feel him up like that."

Guts? Had he liked it?

"Go on over to him!" Paris gestured toward a gangly man with bright red hair. Andromache didn't remember having talked to him, let alone having touched him. In all fairness, though, she'd touched a lot of people by then — on their shoulders, their hands, and most of all their arms. She'd been trying desperately to hide the caress she'd given Hector among a thousand similar caresses.

Andromache turned away from the red-haired man. "No thanks," she said to Paris.

"Well, well! Aren't *we* a little tease!"

"Shut up, Paris," she snapped. "Whatever he told you, I never felt him up."

"You still could. He's quite a catch."

"Forget it, I said!"

"Relax, Hermie. This one doesn't want to marry you. He just wants to go up the stairs and suck muzzles for a while."

What irony! Here was her chance for a fabled Trojan stairway kiss, and she wanted nothing to do with it! "I don't want to kiss *him*," muttered Andromache, unintentionally stressing the last word.

Paris raised an eyebrow.

"I don't want to *kiss*!" she amended.

"You're putting me in a bad position. I already agreed on your behalf."

Andromache glared at him. "That's not my fault! *You* go suck muzzles with him if you're so worried about what he'll think."

Paris sighed. "There's only one way I can get you out of this."

Andromache was wary of his help, but he'd left her little choice. She was literally backed into a corner, with the red-haired man sizing her up.

"It'll involve dancing," said Paris.

"No way! I'm *not* dancing!"

"Then I'll leave you to Firelocks."

Andromache cringed. "All right! Just not on the tables."

"Who told you I dance on the tables?"

Blushing, Andromache remembered how Hector had once warned her about Paris's table-dancing. How he'd whispered conspiratorially to her. How she'd felt his breath on her cheek —

"Ouch, Hermie! I need that foot! Watch what you're doing, or the deal's off."

"Sorry," murmured Andromache.

The room blurred as Paris spun her through the crowd. If the night hadn't been so tense, Andromache would have enjoyed herself. She used to dance all the time and missed the thrill of twirling and leaping. With everything that had happened, though, she was relieved when Paris left her by the back staircase. She was far too dazed to thank him, or even to look back. When her foot touched the stair where she'd sat earlier with Hector, she stopped breathing.

She didn't take another breath until the door to her room was shut behind her.

Chapter 12

E arly in the morning of his first full day back, Hector sent word via his mother that he wouldn't have time to meet for tutoring that day but would see Andromache the next.

"It's just as well," sighed Hecuba. "This morning he was in one of those foul moods, again." Her son's humor seemed to strike her as regrettable but unsurprising.

Andromache, on the other hand, felt like throwing up. Her plan had failed, and now, in the wake of the arm-touching incident, Hector was avoiding her.

"But then, he'll actually see you before tomorrow," Hecuba went on.

In a rush of panic, Andromache asked, "What? Why?"

"At the family dinner tonight, dear," said Hecuba, wrinkling her brow. "You'll be there, of course." It wasn't a question but a statement.

"O-of course," murmured Andromache. She was doomed. Hector would now have to face her in front of his whole family! The awkwardness between them would be on display. Cassandra would take note, and probably Paris, too — Andromache's odd behavior at the party had already aroused his suspicions…

Andromache spent the day dreading and planning for the family dinner. Above all, she couldn't let herself be placed next to Hector. Sitting across from him was risky, because then she would have to see him, but at least there would be no danger of touching him again. If their elbows were to bump during dinner, after what had happened at the party…Andromache didn't even want to think about that!

As evening approached, the family members brought platters, cups, and jars to the table and took their seats. Andromache claimed a spot between Cassandra and Priam. The priest gave one of his usual lovely orations, but Andromache didn't listen to a word of it. Instead, she counted the olives sitting in the bowl before her.

Forty-six...forty-seven...forty-eight... She was still counting even once the prayer had ended, even when the platters of food began to circulate.

"Andromache." Priam gently tapped her arm.

Her head jerked upward and she gave a startled, "Oh!"

"Are you feeling all right, little one?"

All eyes fixed on her, including Hector's. *So dark*, thought Andromache. *So warm...*

"Andromache, dear?" asked Hecuba. "What's wrong? Paris, did you slip lamb onto her plate again? What did I tell you about teasing her?"

"I didn't! I didn't do *anything* to Catatonia over there! Why do I get blamed for everything? There are other people around who might be responsible for her stupor!"

"I'm not in a stupor!" cried Andromache, wishing she could die.

"There, there," said Priam. "You were lost in thought, that's all. Here, will you pass this to my daughter?"

Andromache passed the platter without taking anything from it. Nor from the next one, nor from the one after that. She tuned out the family's chatter and went upstairs to bed as early as she graciously could.

Her last thought, before falling asleep, was to wonder if the next day would be easier, and to comfort herself that it probably couldn't get any worse.

Chapter 13

*A*ndromache *wandered down the stairs, into the kitchen. She sat there with Cassandra, waiting to go to a soiree.*

'We all read the treatise,' Cassandra bragged. 'Didn't you?'

Andromache shook her head in shame.

'You should've had almonds for dinner,' Cassandra reproached her.

Andromache knew that, but there was no way to change what she'd eaten. And she just couldn't *go to the soiree, where everyone would know her disgrace!*

'You have to come!' Cassandra pleaded.

Andromache shook her head.

'You have to!'

'Here is your drinker,' murmured Hector, who was suddenly there, holding out a cup, while Cassandra just as suddenly was gone. The next thing Andromache knew, she was lying on the ground with Hector, and his face was blocking out the light...

Andromache awoke out of breath, her heart pounding as it had countless other times. A nightmare about Hector! What was wrong with her, to start having nightmares about him again? Except — she paused doubtfully — *had* it been a nightmare?

Of course it was! she rebuked herself. *How could* that *not be a nightmare? It's the very definition of a nightmare!*

But it hadn't *felt* like a nightmare...

It was a nightmare! she insisted. It would have been one thing, to dream about kissing Hector — touching him — slithering against him in the stairwell, even. But *that?* Not *that!* She'd had her fill of *that*, years ago, in the back of the wagon. The thought of *that* brought forth a stream of ugly memories. Embarrassing, painful memories.

But —

But there were other memories, too, dim ones suddenly surging from a hidden part of her mind. *The man in the tent*...

When Andromache was ten or so, her mom had taken her to a nearby town to sell lutes and woolens at the market. She'd been wandering around during a lull, looking at the other booths' wares, when she noticed a tent set up behind one of them. A woman was standing in it, looking downward. A hand reached up and pulled her to the ground. The woman giggled. More giggles came up from the floor of the tent — the woman's, and a man's. Curious about what was making them laugh — was it a game? — Andromache had been trying to peer inside the tent when her mom had found her and hustled her away...

'Mind your own onions, Ahndromahk!' she scolded. 'Leave those poor people alone.'

'What are they doing?'

Her mom looked tired but answered frankly: 'They're making love.'

'Is that a game?'

Laughing, her mom said, 'Not exactly.'

'But I heard them giggling!'

'That's a good sign.'

'What? Why?'

'You'll understand when you're married,' her mom assured her with a kiss on the forehead.

'But, Mom —'

'I need you back at the stall, Little Cricket. Come on — I'll get you a jelly tart on the way!'

'All right.'

The jelly tart had distracted Andromache only so long before she again began to wonder what '*making love*' meant. She'd asked and asked until her exasperated mother had told her to go to the goat pasture...

'Why, Mom?'

'Watch the billies with the nannies...you'll see what I mean.'

Andromache did as she was told, but her afternoon at the goat pasture left her sorely disappointed. She'd seen the same thing a thousand times before. Billies — fast and rough. Nannies — pained and absent.

'I saw what you meant,' she informed her mom later.

'Good. So you understand?'

'I guess, but — '

'But what?'

'The goats weren't laughing, Mom!'

Andromache's mother had stared at her for a moment before letting out the loudest shriek of laughter Andromache had ever heard. Embarrassed, she'd never again broached the subject, but privately she'd kept wishing to get married — and soon — so she could find out what 'making love' really was.

Andromache let out a bitter sigh. She'd gotten her wish, or half of it, anyway. Marriage hadn't enlightened her at all about the goings-on in that tent. The wagoner had been no different than a billy goat. When he'd abandoned her on the cliffs above Lyrnassa, her only comfort had been that she would never again have to do *that*. All she had to do was avoid men, avoid marriage, and she would be free from *that*.

However much she'd been thinking about Hector, lately, she hadn't thought once about *that*. And however delightful his version of marriage sounded — with all the talking, laughing, and loving — she hadn't imagined being his wife in that way. Why spoil her pleasant daydreams with *that*?

Andromache caught her breath. She was not at all sure that her sleep that night had been spoiled.

(*It was a* dream,) sneered the Voice. (*It wasn't real. You know what the reality is like.*)

Not all men are like the wagoner, Andromache retorted. *The man in the tent wasn't like that.* She could imagine Hector laughing from the floor of a tent. He loved laughing! He had a sweet temper, too, and gentle ways. His touch was slow and soothing when he groomed Buzzy. And oh, how warm his hand had been on her back, that day out in the countryside…

(*Dream whatever you want,*) said the Voice. (*It's not like you're ever going to find out for sure.*)

Andromache's cheeks flamed.

After a final, knowing cough, the Voice fell silent again. Andromache resolved not to dwell any more on the nightmare — or dream — or whatever it had been — and was so unsuccessful that she never fell back to sleep.

Chapter 14

"H ay-lo? Ahndromahk?" whispered Hector. "Hay-lo? You ahre there?"
Andromache awoke with a small cry, blushing hotly when she realized where she was, and with whom. "Yes, I'm here," she said, immediately cursing herself. *Fool! What a stupid thing to say! Obviously you're here! He really meant, what's wrong with you? Why are you sleeping in the library?*

She'd come to the library a little early for Lukkan lessons, and, after her fitful sleep the night before, she'd decided to lay her head on the table. Just for a moment or two...

"How ahre you?" asked Hector.

"Fine." Andromache tried not to look at him, so he couldn't tell that she was lying. Far from fine, she felt completely disconcerted. Her insides were too large in a most pleasant way. She was relieved that Hector had come, after missing the day before — he must have moved past the whole arm-touching incident! Still, she didn't know what to say to him. "So when — that is, what — er —" What she needed was a nice, casual question; what she produced was a bizarre non sequitur: "What did you have for breakfast?"

After blinking in surprise, Hector said, "Fruits and cheeses."

Unfortunately for Andromache, she was so nervous that she repeated the question several more times.

"Breads," answered Hector, and then, "Wine," and then, "Hay." He seemed intrigued by her behavior and amused by her funny little quiz.

Andromache was far too flustered to joke with him, though, and with horrible inevitability, she asked the question again.

"Almonds," said Hector, obviously pleased with himself for having remembered the word.

Almonds! Andromache nearly fainted. *'You should have had almonds for dinner!'* Cassandra had chided in her dream — and once Andromache remembered *that*, all the other lurid details came flooding back.

With a gasp she looked down, away from Hector's face, but that was no better. His hands were there on the tabletop, busily fiddling with the dust — and she couldn't help imagining them on *her*. Her heart began to pound, and her cheeks turned red. Mortified, she looked out the window.

"It was a rock," said Hector, finally exasperated by her fluttering little glances.

The comment cut through Andromache's daze. In horror, she looked at his neck. She'd forgotten all about the bruise!

"It's no big deal," he said in response to her agonized look, but a coughing fit belied his words. His eyes still looked pinched, too. Tired.

Andromache said nothing — she'd never felt so small. *He's hurt. He thinks I'm worried. He thinks I'm a concerned friend, when all I'm doing is sitting here in this stupid erotic fog. This is exactly why I don't deserve a lover. No!* she snapped at herself. *You don't get to cry. You don't get to make him feel sorry for you!*

"You're sure?" she finally whispered. "You're *sure* it's no big deal?"

"Yeah."

Andromache wove her fingers together and looked once more at the bruise. She pictured Hector alone on the field, falling to his knees, vomiting blood onto the ground. She had to bite her lip to keep a sob from escaping.

After an awkward silence, Hector spoke up. "Cassandra say you go out wiff her again?"

Andromache's cheeks burned. Cassandra had told him *what?* What was *wrong* with her? They'd agreed to tell him about Andromache's last soiree *only* if he caught wind of it elsewhere, first!

"I say somefing bad?" asked Hector, noticing her agitation.

"No, not you!" cried Andromache. She couldn't let Hector think he'd done something *bad!* "It's just — with her friends —"

"Someone is mean at you?" Hector's tone was ominous.

"No!" Andromache said hastily, even as she cursed herself. She'd overreacted. She'd been wrong about Cassandra and how much the girl had blabbed. Hector didn't seem to know *what* had happened at the soiree — and now he looked ready to menace whoever had supposedly been mean to her! She had to fix things, and fast. "No one was mean. I just — I disgraced myself." With any luck, Hector would accept that answer and move on.

"Deesgrice?"

"Humiliate, shame," she explained. "I looked"— there was really no other word for it — "foalish." '*Foalish*'... the word Hector had once mistaken for '*foolish*.' '*Foalish?*' he'd asked her. *Lah-ke a baby hohrse?*'

Hector's eyes lit up at the word, and Andromache felt better, despite the mess she was in.

"You look foalish why?" he asked.

Andromache cringed. The cover story she and Cassandra had concocted now seemed flimsy protection. "I was yelling at someone," she mumbled.

Hector squinted. Coughed. "Yelling? *You?*"

"He called a corpse '*beautiful!*'"

"Oh," said Hector, bewildered. He coughed again.

"It reminded me of what happened years ago, when my little brother died and all the villagers in Hurapi said his body was '*just beautiful*,'" Andromache injected a tremor into her voice. "I got really upset."

"Wait, wait — slow down. Did you said '*brahther?*'" Hector frowned. "But I thought you were an only child."

"*Cousin*," howled Andromache, bemoaning his fine memory. "You heard me wrong. I said *cousin*!"

"Oh," said Hector, still baffled. "I'm sorry, Ahndromahk." He coughed. "Don't get mad. I'm out of practice with Lukkan, that's all."

She swallowed hard on her guilt. "Th-that's all right," she stammered. "It'll come back."

Hector nodded and graciously changed the subject again. "Paris fink you ahre crazy."

"What?" shrieked Andromache, in fresh alarm. What good could possibly come of *that* statement?

"He say, '*Hermie's been possessed.*'"

"Why! Why would he say that?"

"Becahse." Hector's eyes sparkled. "You ahre dancing, at the pahrty."

Andromache sighed in relief — Paris might have said something much, much worse. "Maybe...but it'll *never* happen again."

For the first time that afternoon, Hector laughed. "Neffer you can say '*neffer*,'" he admonished.

Never say never. The words sent Andromache straight back into a daze. She wondered if he was right.

℘

IMMEDIATELY AFTER THE LESSON, Andromache walked down the hall to Cassandra's room, where she had a less dreamy matter to attend to. "Cassandra!" she hollered, pounding on the door. "Open up!"

"Oh, honey — what's wrong?" Cassandra flew out to her. "Did something happen to Cutie?"

"Cutie's fine. She went down to the kitchen with —" Andromache gulped. She couldn't say his name. "What were you *thinking?*"

"About what?" Cassandra's eyes widened. "What did I do?"

"You weren't supposed to mention that soiree to him!"

"Who?"

"Who do you *think?*"

"Oh — him."

"Yes, *him!*"

"All I said about *you* was that you'd gone with me."

Andromache knew that that was true — *she'd* been the one to blow her own cover! "But — but you weren't supposed to say *anything!*" she stammered. "He started asking me all these questions — and it sounded so stupid — and — and —"

"Breathe! That's it, honey — breathe."

Andromache made a choking sound.

"It's going to be all right," said Cassandra, slipping an arm around Andromache's shoulders. "Why don't you lie down for a while?"

"But —"

"It's just what you need."

"All right," mumbled Andromache. The air was exploding around her. Everything was too bright. Cassandra was right. She needed to lie down. She needed to close her eyes.

ℰℴ

AFTER A NAP, Andromache felt better. It was late evening. The first floor would be empty, now. Cassandra would have gone to a soiree, and Paris would be out carousing. Their parents would be off studying the sky and taking healing draughts to sick neighbors. As for Hector —

Andromache closed her eyes. She didn't want to think about where *he* would be, at this hour, or with whom. She didn't want to think of Penthesilea — *Lee* — with her arms around him…

Andromache walked downstairs. "Hey, little girl!" she cried to Cutie, when the dog greeted her at the entrance to the courtyard. "How are you?"

Cutie gave a dog smile and nibbled playfully at Andromache's fingers.

"What's going on, out here?"

Cutie bounded over to a shrub and spooked a moth, which she then chased. Meanwhile, Andromache sat on the edge of a box of lettuces and began weeding. She hadn't properly tended the garden for almost a week, now. Her thrashing efforts the day of Hector's return did *not* count.

Once finished with the lettuces, she sailed on to the daisies, the celery, and the rosebush, plucking with an energy she hadn't had for weeks.

Only when she arrived at the mint did she pause. The mint — now, what was she supposed to do with *that*? She didn't want to neglect it — oh, no! She wanted to water it, inspect each leaf tenderly, and trim those that were wilted so the healthy ones could get more sun. But then again, she couldn't appear too eager to cultivate that particular plant.

At an impasse, Andromache sat down beside the mint. She glanced toward Hector's room and saw that the window was dark. Where on earth *was* he? Someone with an injury like *his* really shouldn't be out late — he should come home! Andromache nodded to herself. *Yes, home!* And if he *did* come home while she was still out there, maybe he would sit and talk to her. Or not talk. Maybe he would —

Abruptly, she rose to her feet and hurried back upstairs.

℘

THE NEXT afternoon, however, Andromache returned to the mint bed out on the courtyard. She crushed one of the plant's leaves, inhaled, and, just that quickly, Hector was beside her...

His arms were around her, and he was kissing her — and kissing her — and kissing her. He knew how to do it right, too — his tongue didn't slime her, as Demuchus's had. It stayed respectably within its own mouth, leaving her free to focus on how his lips felt, and how nice he smelled, and —

"Honey?"

Andromache flinched, fanning the heat from her face.

"It's warm, today," observed Cassandra. She sat next to Andromache, on the opposite side from where her brother — in Andromache's mind, anyway — had been. "I came out here to get some fresh air," the girl went on. "A breeze, you know? But I don't think there is one."

Andromache shook her head.

"The library's an oven."

"Oh," Andromache said softly. "The library..."

Cassandra clapped a hand to her cheek. "Oh, that's right! You'll be up there, later today!" she remarked as if in surprise.

Sensing now that the conversation had always been headed there, Andromache warily agreed. "Mm-hmm."

"Are you glad to be tutoring again?"

Not trusting herself to make a casual remark — look what had happened the day before! — Andromache nodded.

"I'll bet! It's so good to have Hector back, isn't it?" trilled Cassandra. "The house just seems empty when he's gone, don't you think?"

So, the girl had *not* abandoned her quest to learn Andromache's deepest secrets — she'd merely deferred it. Until she was satisfied, she would dog Andromache's footsteps, waiting for a moment of weakness.

"Don't you *think*?" prompted Cassandra.

"You know what? I forgot — I have to read something before he — before your brother comes to — Hector, I mean — I have to read something." With that exceptionally feeble excuse, Andromache ducked away from Cassandra and went to the library to wait for Hector.

The lesson that afternoon went better than the one the day before. Despite the heat, Hector was wearing the wrap around his neck and shoulders. It bothered Andromache that she'd become someone he had to cloak his wounds around; she didn't want him to think she found him ugly! At the same time, it was easier to hold a conversation without the bruise right there in front of her.

As the afternoon wore on, though, the heat of the library affected her. She found herself focusing less on Hector's words than on his lips. They looked soft, except at the corners, where they were cracked — the kind of crack that took an eternity to heal, because it reopened every time one spoke or ate. Andromache felt sorry for him that his lips were sore, and that made her think of how she'd split his lip once, long ago, and she felt sorry for that, too. She wished she could —

"Ahndromahk?"

"Huh?"

Cough. "You fink what?"

"About what?"

"This," he said patiently, indicating the text they were supposed to be discussing.

"Oh." Although Andromache had read it, she couldn't remember a single word. "I don't know."

"You ahre not wiff me today," teased Hector. His eyes lost their pinched look for a moment and sparkled. With his shaven head, they looked more remarkable than ever.

Andromache turned away to hide her flaming cheeks. Not with him? Oh, if only he knew just how with him she was! She was stroking his hair — rubbing his shoulders — leaning against him to read their text — lying beside him on the courtyard — pressing her lips to his —

"So maybe we ahre done wiff this text," Hector suggested, coughing.

"It's too hot to concentrate on it," Andromache was quick to agree.

He gave her a thoughtful look. "What on the mohrning?" he asked. "It is too hot then to rahn?"

"Why?" Did he want to go running with her? If so, she didn't care how hot it was, or when!

"Lee say, '*Ask Ahndromahk to rahn tomorrow wiff me.* "

Lee. Penthesilea. Hector's fiancée was invading their lessons! Why wasn't she content with what she already had? Why did she have to break her way in here, as well? Go running with *Lee*? Be forced to admire her beauty, her athleticism, even while hating her? "I can't," said Andromache.

"All rahght," said Hector, shrugging.

Venomously, Andromache added. "I don't want to go out to the countryside, anymore."

At that, Hector's expression turned sad. "You do not lahke it?"

Dammit! Andromache cursed herself. Once again, she'd said too much, and he was now insulted! *He* was the one who'd originally taken her there, after all. "Not right now — too many bees are out," she explained hastily.

Hector's frown softened. "You do not want the stings," he said.

"No," agreed Andromache, shaking her head. That said, if *he'd* wanted to go running with her, a thousand swarms of bees wouldn't have stopped her.

Late spring

Chapter 15

Andromache laid her text down on the table and rubbed her feet against Cutie. The little dog rolled over onto her back, groaning as she did.

Andromache, too, felt like groaning. "<u>I don't know why he wanted to read *this*</u>," she sighed.

Hector had chosen the text. He'd described it as a series of adventures, the collected tales of an eastern wanderer. He'd told her to expect strange lands, weird creatures, and even weirder people. At first, she'd been excited, thinking that a fantastical setting would be just the place for an imaginary rendezvous with Hector, but her hopes had soon been dashed. The text was dull — mind-numbing — and no hint of weirdness within had been enough to save it.

As much as Andromache disliked the text, though, she read it because Hector had chosen it. She wanted to do something nice for him, and reading *Tales of an Eastern Wanderer* seemed to make him happy. His eyes were losing their tight look. He wasn't coughing anymore, either, and he'd stopped wearing his wrap. The bruise on his neck had faded to yellow, barely visible except to those who made a habit of studying his skin.

His hair had grown out to the soft stage that looked so velvety to the touch…

Andromache smiled to herself. Just weeks ago, the thought of stroking Hector's hair would have made her quiver and blush; by now, though, she was able to take such things in stride, even if she was talking to Hector at the time.

Being around him felt normal, again. It had surprised her a little to discover that he was still the same person she'd always talked to and laughed with. A new dimension had been added to the way she saw him, but nothing underneath had changed.

Still, there were threats to her renewed ease with Hector, many of which came from Cassandra. The girl was even nosier now than she'd been during Andromache's fake fever…

'I'm so sorry I disturbed you and my brother this afternoon, getting that stupid history text!' said Cassandra, as she and Andromache were cleaning up after dinner. 'I had no choice, though. We're set to talk about it at the soiree, and I'd forgotten to read it. Ooooops!'

'Ooooooops,' Andromache repeated, giving the girl a spiky glare. She hadn't been at all pleased by Cassandra's sudden appearance in the library.

'I couldn't help hearing him speak, though, and my! It really seems like he's getting good! Not that I know Lukkan, of course, but I know other languages, and how they work, and he just seems — comfortable.*'*

Andromache ignored the emphasis that Cassandra had placed on 'comfortable.' *Objecting to the word would only allow the girl to defend it. 'You're right,' she said. 'He's getting good.'*

'You see?' sang Cassandra. 'Remember when you first started teaching him, and everyone told you he wouldn't last? They were so mean to you! Now, the joke's on them. It just goes to show you that it pays to hope for the best — don't you think?' Cassandra winked; Andromache scowled back at her.

Andromache returned to the present, to the library, where Cutie was licking her feet. "<u>Stop that</u>," she protested.

The little dog grunted but didn't stop.

Andromache sighed. At least it wasn't hot. There had been a heat wave, an early taste of summer, the previous week. Hector had moved combat practice to the evening hours, when breezes were cool — and Cassandra had tried to turn *that*, too, to her prying, snooping advantage…

'Honey?' asked the girl. 'Did my brother tell you that he's got training tonight?'

'Yes. He did.'

'It's just that sometimes he forgets things like that.'

'He told me.'

'Oh…'

'What is it?' Andromache asked warily: Cassandra's "oh" had a sly undertone.

'It's just — oh, this is so embarrassing! Mom won't let me go to the training field by myself, remember? She thinks it distracts me from my studies — as if watching a couple cute boys is enough to make me forget the tin trade — honestly!' Cassandra rolled her eyes. 'But she won't budge, and Dad's with her, and Hector might tell on me if he sees me there by myself. Or worse, he'd send me home. Can you imagine the humiliation, to be singled out in front of all those people and sent home, like a naughty cow, getting chased out of a barley field? Oh, honey! I couldn't stand it!'

'Isn't Paris going with you?'

'Not tonight.' Cassandra sighed tragically. 'He's refusing to go.'

Now certain of where the conversation was headed, Andromache cut it off. 'Well, I can't go either.'

'Why not? Are you sick?'

'I don't like fighting,' Andromache said bluntly. Fighting terrified her and brought back gruesome memories: brutish raiders in the mountains of the Lukka lands — burned huts — a waxy-pale corpse — blood and soot and cavernous eyes —

Even fake fighting was a part of that world. It was too close to the real thing, and Andromache didn't want to watch it — especially not with Hector there. Her new feelings for him were strange and sometimes embarrassing, but pleasant, too. She didn't want to ruin them by watching him spar with his comrades — even if there was a chance of seeing him half-dressed.

'Oh, heavens! They don't hurt each other, honey! They just try to outmaneuver each other.'

Feeling as though Cassandra was about to outmaneuver her, Andromache nevertheless stayed firm. 'I can't.'

'You're sure?' the girl whined. 'I could watch the boys, and you could cheer for — '

'Good night, Cassandra,' Andromache interrupted.

Cutie began to make strange popping noises; her lips curled and uncurled, and her eyelids flickered. She was having a dream.

"It's all right, baby girl," soothed Andromache.

The little dog stirred and let out a long sigh.

Andromache sighed with her. Although she hadn't said so to Cassandra, another reason she couldn't bear going to the training field was her dread of seeing Hector and Penthesilea —

Lee — together. For the same reason, she'd been avoiding the stables, except when she knew for certain that neither of them would be there. Those occasions were so rare — a few scattered patrol trainings — that she hadn't seen much of Xanthus, lately, either. At their last meeting, he'd griped at her: *'You're as flighty as all the other young sprogs in Troy, these days!'* Andromache had had no choice but to apologize. She certainly couldn't tell Xanthus the truth, that she was trying to avoid seeing Hector with his beloved *Lee.*

No, that didn't go far enough — she didn't want to see *Lee* at all! Hector had passed along several more requests for her to go running, all of which she'd refused. He didn't press the issue, but he did mention casually that he hadn't seen many '*sting flies*' the last time he was out.

Andromache looked back at *Tales of an Eastern Wanderer.* In one section, the traveler had had to climb over a mountain so tall that on the other side of it, he'd found yesterday. Andromache scoffed. Compared to a nosy sister and a beautiful fiancée, such a mountain seemed a puny obstacle indeed.

Chapter 16

For days, whenever Andromache had free time, she slogged on in *Tales of an Eastern Wanderer*. It was a very long text, bone dry throughout. Many times, she found her head nodding and her eyes blinking too rapidly, especially when she took the text up to her bedroom to read. She didn't try to fight her weariness. She told herself that a short nap might help her concentrate better, but the truth was that with sleep came the possibility of another dream about Hector.

Weeks had passed since her first such dream, and the feeling it had given her was fading. She wanted to refresh it. But while she still went out to the mint bed to imagine kissing with Hector, she was too timid — too guilty — to picture more than that. Dreams were different — excusable. She couldn't help what she saw in them, and neither could she be blamed. Lately, though, all her dreams had been inane — marketing with Paris or dusting breakfast plates.

One night, when she'd gone to bed with especially high hopes, she had the most insipid dream of all…

She was digging holes in the courtyard. She dug a hundred or so, then filled them in again, then dug them once more. The ground was spotted with holes. She'd just begun filling them again when —

Scritch, scritch.

Andromache shook herself awake and looked toward her bedroom door.

Scritch, scritch.

"Cassandra?" she asked.

"Yes! Can I come in?"

"Sure."

The door squeaked open, and Cassandra slipped in. "I just wanted to ask you about something. I have to read this text on healing herbs, and there are a few I can't keep straight. I was going to ask Mom, but she was on her way out. There's another baby to deliver! It's the mother's fourth, so Mom doesn't expect any problems, but you never know."

"I can try to help you," said Andromache. "What were the names of the herbs?"

But Cassandra's attention had seized on something else. "What's that?" she asked, pointing at the text by Andromache's bedside.

"Oh," Andromache said lightly. "It's called *Tales of an Eastern Wanderer.*"

"Oh my, I've never read that!" said Cassandra. "Are you reading it for fun, or —"

"With Hector," Andromache admitted in a low voice.

Cassandra pursed her lips. Lately, she'd been giving Andromache a devious smile whenever Hector's name came up, but just then, her face was pensive. "I wish you could've seen the way he looked at you," she sighed. "In the kitchen, after your lesson, when he thought no one was watching."

"Cassandra!" Andromache hissed in protest.

"What? I thought you should know. I mean, boys don't just look like *that* for nothing."

"Like what, exactly?"

"Like he was covered in fire ants, and you were a soothing pool of mud."

In spite of her embarrassment, Andromache had to laugh. "Maybe Paris put too many hot peppers in the stew."

"Honey, I'm serious!"

"Oh, Cassandra…"

The girl took a deep breath. "I think you should tell him," she said solemnly. Her face was as earnest as only it could be. "He might not know how you feel. Boys can be dumb about that sort of thing."

"*Tell* him?" cried Andromache, forgetting her resolution not to talk about Hector with Cassandra. "But he's got a fiancée!"

"Oh, *her*," Cassandra pooh-poohed. "He's never looked at *her* like that."

"How would you know?" Andromache said sourly. "It's not like you've seen every look he's ever given her."

"I've seen enough."

"Oh, who *cares* what you think you saw! They're engaged, right? That's what *you* told me."

Cassandra batted away the objection with a wave of her hand. "Don't you think if they were *really* going to get married, they'd have done it by now?"

"How should I know?" snapped Andromache.

"Well, I know what I *saw*."

"You'd see a five-headed flying tortoise if that's what you wanted to see!"

Cassandra smiled serenely, unbothered by the insult. "Just promise me one thing."

Andromache sighed. "What?"

"Find a way to peek at him — on the sly, of course — and then you'll see what I mean, about the way he's looking at you."

"Oh, Cassandra — I —"

"Promise — please?"

"Fine, I promise," said Andromache, although she had no intention of keeping the promise. She was too afraid of what she would or wouldn't see on Hector's face.

Chapter 17

*There were two hundred foot soldiers, each clad in a
wool tunic that hung to the knees. On his feet, each
soldier wore sandals of tanned leather. The number of
straps on the sandals varied from three to ten. This
number indicated not the rank of the soldier, but his
personal wealth. The sandals varied in thickness from
one half finger to two fingers. The thickness was another indication of the soldier's personal wealth...*

Andromache set *Tales of an Eastern Wanderer* down on the
library table. She needed a break. In the passage she'd
just read, the wanderer had climbed up to a mountain
stronghold and joined the local king's army. The author hadn't
bothered to describe the local scenery, the king's palace, or the
personalities of the soldiers — although he'd rendered a stitch-
by-stitch image of their uniforms...

I don't know how much more of this I can take, thought Andromache. *Even for Hector's sake.* But the thought of Hector so galva-
nized her that she picked up the text and started reading again.
As she was skimming through a painfully detailed description of
the soldiers' shields, a line farther down leapt out at her:

> *And so Gemasila disguised herself as a soldier so that
> she might go with her lover, the wanderer.*

What? thought Andromache. *Who's that? What did I miss?*
Frantically, she scanned the nearby lines, searching for any other
mention of Gemasila, but she found none. After devoting fifty-

odd lines to the soldiers' uniforms, the author had allotted only one to the wanderer's lover! Andromache sighed in frustration.

"What is abohff?"

She let out a startled cry.

"I scare you? Sohrry," said Hector.

"You always come in so quietly," she complained.

"You always fink so deep," he countered.

He was right — she *had* been deep in thought. "The text finally got good."

"Finally?" Hector's eyes twinkled at the word. "You lahke what?"

"Well, I'd just read through a *very* long section on what these soldiers were wearing, and it was all so dull — no offense."

He laughed. "I take no offense."

"But then there was a line about Gemasila — whoever that is, the wanderer's lover, I guess — dressing up like a soldier to go with him."

"Oh, yes," said Hector, remembering the passage.

"Does the text say anything else about her?" asked Andromache. "I couldn't find a word."

"No," said Hector. "Noffing else."

"That's weird."

Hector furrowed his brow. "Maybe long ago there is mohre on Gemasila. Baht then somehow that pahrt is lost. Maybe it is on a scroll that burns. Then some person makes a copy ohff *Tales of an Eastern Wanderer*. Baht the pahrt on Gemasila is gone, so he cannot copy it. He does not know it. And Dad buys the new stohry." Hector held up the text Andromache had been studying.

Andromache nodded. Hector's explanation made a lot of sense. Somewhere along the line, the Gemasila passage had been lost, so later copies of *Tales of an Eastern Wanderer* couldn't include it. The only way to ever learn more about the mysterious woman would be to find a copy made very early on, before the passage with her story had disappeared.

"We'll probably never know much about her," Andromache said with regret.

Hector shook his head. "Probably not."

"Just that she '*disguised herself as a soldier*' to go with him." Andromache frowned. "'*Disguised*' — does that mean she dressed up as a man? That soldiers had to be men?"

"Yes, I fink so."

"Hmm. That's interesting," said Andromache. "In Taruisha, she wouldn't have to do that. She could just join the army."

Hector snorted.

"What's wrong? You don't think women should be in the army?" That was news to her — and interesting, considering his fiancée!

"No, not that — it is —" Hector took a deep breath and, as he sometimes did when his feelings on a topic were especially strong, he broke into Truvan: "I'd kick both their asses out, if anyone tried that in *my* army."

Andromache stared at him. "Tried *what?*"

"To be *lahffers,*" he said scornfully. "I do not permit this."

He didn't permit lovers to be together in his army? Wondering if she'd misunderstood, Andromache said, "Don't you think that's hypocritical?"

"It is what?"

"Hypocritical. When one person condemns — sorry, um, rebukes — criticizes — denounces — oh, fine, condemns — condemns — when one person *condemns* another person for what the first person is also doing." When Hector turned a blank look on her, Andromache gave up. "Hypocritical."

"Oh." He cleared his throat. "All rahght, my rule is — ahm — hippo-*risical,* why?"

Andromache narrowed her eyes. "Are you joking?"

"No."

"Penthesilea."

"What on her?"

"Oh, come on, now!" snapped Andromache, furious at being driven to say the words: "If you two can — can be *lovers,* why can't the rest of the poor bastards in your army?"

Hector eyed her curiously. "Who say that we ahre lahffers?"

"Your sister," said Andromache.

He snorted.

"*And* your mom!"

He began to laugh.

"Why is that so funny?" Andromache exploded. "Your uncle sent her here to be your fiancée. Everyone knows that!"

Hector shook his head. "Uncle sent her here to be my *combat partner* — and my lieutenant, if I were ever in a position to need one. Anyone who thinks otherwise has made a stupid assumption along the way." Pausing to look at Andromache, he added, "Except you. You were just given false information *based on a stupid assumption.*"

Flabbergasted, Andromache kept opening her mouth, only to close it again when she couldn't think of what to say. *Now's not the time to look like a fish, Ahndromahk!* she warned herself, but it was hard not to gape. His combat partner? His sister-in-arms? His lieutenant? It explained their lack of heat...

But then, Hector *wanted* to get married, didn't he? Why else would he have looked wistful when explaining Trojan weddings to her? Andromache sucked in her breath and forced her mouth shut.

"Ahndromahk?" said Hector, with a hint of concern.

"You're *not* engaged to Penthesilea?" she managed to croak.

"No."

"And you never have been — never plan to be?"

"No."

"Did you — did you know — people —"

"Did I know what people were saying?"

Andromache nodded.

"I guess."

"Then why — why — why didn't you — I don't know — *correct* — the assumptions, then?"

"Oh, Ahndromahk...you've lived in Troy long enough to know how much people gossip, here. I can't waste my time correcting everything anyone says about me. I have too much to do. Besides, with rumors, the more you fight them, the stronger they get. It's better to ignore them and get on with your work. They die down eventually."

Andromache shook her head. "They haven't died down! Some of your mom's friends were up here, last year, asking when you and Penthesilea were going to get married."

Hector shrugged. "If *that's* all they have to worry about in life, then they're lucky."

"But your *mom!*" Andromache protested. "You couldn't at least tell *her?*"

"Of *course* I would've told her, if she'd ever asked." Hector now looked and sounded annoyed. "But she never did — whenever she brought up Lee, it was generic little questions like,

'How's Penthesilea doing?' Am I supposed to leap from that to *'By the way, Mom, we're not engaged?'*"

Knowing her voice would sound thick, Andromache tried to disguise it by switching back to Lukkan. "It's only *natural* for her to think Penthesilea is your lover. She's beautiful, and you're —" She broke off abruptly, afraid of what might slip out.

Hector raised an eyebrow.

"A man," she finished lamely.

He laughed. "So…you noticed!"

Andromache had never felt so self-conscious. "She's *beautiful!*" she insisted, switching languages yet again.

Hector shrugged. "Lee looks how she looks. That doesn't mean I lust after her."

Oh, the easy way he said '*lust!*'

"I've put my life in her hands," he went on. "But nothing else."

Andromache squirmed and turned toward the window, as much to avoid looking at Hector's hands as to hide her flaming cheeks. If this went any further, she would die! Summoning all the dignity she could muster, she argued, "Well, you *seem* very close to her."

"I *am*," said Hector. "We've been through things together. We care about each other — the same way we both care about Medon, and Dolops, and Palmys, and Thaeus."

"I don't hear you giving *them* pet names, like you do for *Lee*," Andromache muttered darkly, poking at the dust-covered table.

Hector laughed again. "Thaeus's full name is *Orthaeus*."

Andromache blinked. "Oh," she said.

"Soldiers *need* short names," Hector explained. "Just imagine if I had to say, *'To my left, Penthesilea!'* By the time I got the whole thing out, the battle would be over. A short name isn't *always* a pet name — *Ahndromahk*."

Andromache looked up in shock. She'd long since grown used to hearing Hector say her Lukkan name. This time, though, he'd put a heavy and deliberate stress on it. *He was flirting with her!*

She'd seen Paris flirt in the market a thousand times, and the signs were unmistakable. It wasn't just the way Hector had said '*Ahndromahk*.' There were also the dancing eyes that never left hers, no matter how hard she tried to look away. There was the supple insouciance of his bearing. He was flirting with *her*, and he didn't love Penthesilea — Cassandra was right, after all!

No — you can't trust Cassandra, Andromache warned herself. *And you shouldn't read into all the flirting. Maybe he's just in that kind of mood, today…*

She cleared her throat and said primly, "Well, there's still no reason to laugh at your mom, for thinking what she thought."

"Mom!" Hector shook his head. "She is so — so — hippo-*fetical*."

"Hypocritical? Why?"

He gave a superior smile. "She say always, *'Women can be anyfing. Women can do anyfing. Cassandra, you can do anyfing. You can stahdy. You can learn. You can join the council. You can marry later if you want to, baht you need no man.'* Then, Lee comes here — and she can fight, she can rahn. She is the soldier the best ohff the world, better than men. Baht what does Mom fink on her? Mom fink Lee comes fohr to be a — a — a woman married —" He looked to Andromache for help.

"A wife," she supplied, unable to keep the color from her cheeks.

Hector nodded. "Mom's first assumption was that Lee came here to get married. If Uncle sent her here, it *must* be to marry his nephew. It *couldn't* be to work with him — to *fight* with him!"

"All the more reason to set your mom straight, if you were *that* annoyed with her!" Andromache argued.

Hector looked sheepish.

"Well?"

"It's been nice, these past three years," he said. "You don't know what it was like, before! For some reason, Mom got it in her head that marriage would be good for me. She was relentless, harassing me about all the neighborhood girls, and Cassandra's friends, and every she-creature on two legs from here to the end of the world. Then, suddenly —" Mid-narration, he clapped his hands. "Lee came, and it all stopped. I could breathe again."

"You let your mom believe in a fake relationship so she wouldn't keep pushing real ones?" cried Andromache in disbelief. "You're terrible!"

"Yes," said Hector with a winning smile. "Baht I am not hippo-*fekital*."

They were back to where they'd started — Gemasila and the wanderer. Andromache leapt to their defense. "I still don't see a problem with lovers being in the army together," she said.

Hector looked at her as though she were stupid. "They'd endanger everyone around them, Ahndromahk. All they'd be thinking about is each other. They'd get so worried about whether their love cabbage was all right, they wouldn't be able to do their job."

For the thousandth time that afternoon, Andromache found herself gaping. *Wouldn't be able to do their job.'* The phrase took her back to the fight she'd had with Hector when she was asking him to help her go outside the city walls. *There've been murders down there,'* he'd said about the outer market. *'How can I do my job if I know you're down there?'* Back then, the phrase had rankled. She'd thought his concern boiled down to nothing more than guilt or responsibility. Now, though, after the revelation about Penthesilea — not to mention the flirting! — his words had a different ring.

Other memories were coming to her, too, like how Hector had said *'No effing way'* to the thought of Andromache joining the army. Why didn't he want her, there? Was it merely because she would be useless, or was he afraid of being distracted by her?

And then there was his remark about *some* Trojans being able to kiss — his supposed fire-ant look — his hatred of Demuchus — his near-limitless patience with her — his fury at the nitwit twins who had attacked her and Cutie —

No! Andromache told herself. *Don't get all excited. It's a coincidence, the 'Wouldn't be able to do their job' thing. It's just a phrase he likes. You know how he gets stuck on things! And of course he'd worry about you, if he thought you might be in danger! You're his friend. You always were, even when you had that fight. He said so. None of this makes you his — what was the word? Love cabbage…*

Andromache chewed her lip. *Or does it?*

"Ahndromahk?" said Hector, when she'd been silent for too long. "You ahre all rahght?"

She looked up at him. "If you're *not* hypocritical — *Ector,*" she murmured, pronouncing his name the Lukkan way for the first time. "Then how do you know what those lovers would be thinking?"

Hector gave her a slow, sweet smile. All the joking about pet names and body parts and irritation toward his mother was gone. "I *know*," he said simply.

Andromache stopped breathing. There were so many questions that she wanted to ask him — so much that she longed to tell him — so much that she didn't know where to start. It all flailed around in her mind like a pot full of earthworms, with no ends or beginnings for her to seize on. *Something!* she hissed to herself. *Say something, before the moment ends! Anything! Anything!*

"Where do you go at night?" she finally whispered. "I always thought you went somewhere with *her*."

"To a tavern, with Xanthus or Paris," said Hector. "Or to the river, with Buzzy." Pause. "I didn't know you thought about it." His eyes, always dark, were black, and when he looked at her, she felt naked — and liked it. With no more words to say, and none needed, Andromache just gazed back at him. What now? Would he touch her hand? Kiss her? Take her in his arms and —

"Cutie!" hollered Hecuba, from down on the courtyard. "What's gotten into you, digging up Priam's prize poppies! How *dare* you! What's your mama going to say about that, you naughty little creature?"

"I should go," sighed Andromache. *Damned dog!* she thought viciously. *Damned, damned dog!*

Hector nodded. His eyes had gone back to normal.

Chapter 18

In fact, everything returned to normal.

Every day, Andromache gardened, walked Cutie, went marketing with Paris, played roodles with Xanthus or Cassandra, ate dinner with whichever family members were around, and read for a while before going to sleep. In the middle of it all, she had lessons with Hector, and while he continued to progress in Lukkan — making greater leaps than ever, she thought — he didn't try to kiss her or make hinting eyes toward alcoves. Life went on as before.

At the same time, everything had changed. Hector was now walking with just the hint of a swagger, enough to betray his excitement without quite making him look ridiculous. He came to dinner almost every night, saying casually that he'd finally, after almost two years, gotten a handle on his duties as commander. If he was sitting across from Andromache, and she caught him looking at her, he didn't turn away. If he was sitting beside her, he ate with whichever hand would cause their elbows to bump. Each time, Andromache silently gave thanks that Hector was ambidextrous.

The contact was fleeting, a brief touch of skin to skin. Yet as stiff as he'd always been with her before, Andromache saw the change as portentous. Indeed, more light caresses followed the first. She noticed their shoulders grazing while they were looking at a text together, and sometimes Hector's foot rested against hers under the table.

She never would have thought that such subtle, almost incidental, touches could be so erotic, yet any desire she'd felt before paled in comparison to the lust now tearing through her. Each day left her more impatient to kiss with him.

Still, she knew that for Trojans, not kissing was *more* serious rather than less. If Hector had just wanted a stairway fling, he would have kissed her by now. She realized, too, that their situation was complicated by the fact that she was living in his family's home. He would know when the time was right, and until then, she would just have to wait.

After a week of sweet looks and elbow bumps, though, Andromache was at her limit with waiting. She tried running out her lust down at the exercise arena, but that didn't work. The circuit was too dull. There were no holes to avoid, no thorn bushes to skirt, no snakes, and few rocks. No matter how hard she ran, she couldn't keep her mind from wandering toward Hector.

She needed a more challenging place to exercise. Even better, she needed a partner to push her to her limits…

"Can I ask a favor?" she said to Hector at their next lesson.

He raised his eyebrow with interest.

She blushed, mumbling, "Can you ask Penthesilea to meet me at the outpost stable, tomorrow morning?"

"You want to go rahn?" Hector looked amused. "Again, you lahke the cahntryside?"

"I never *didn't* like it," said Andromache. "It was just —"

"The sting flies."

"Bees," she agreed. "So — you'll —"

"I can ask. Yes."

"Good. Thank you."

⁌

ANDROMACHE ARRIVED EARLY at the outpost stable. She was worried that Penthesilea wouldn't come, or that she would be angry after all the times Andromache had snubbed her, recently. However, the woman came right on time, showing no obvious signs of resentment. Once out in the countryside, they ran their standard route across the fields of the Trojan plateau.

Dodging obstacles didn't distract Andromache as much as she'd hoped. She found herself thinking as much as ever about Hector while stumbling over rocks in the bargain. She didn't mind the bumps and scrapes, though. Running felt good, and running outside in the sun and wind felt especially good.

"You've been training," puffed Penthesilea, as they were finishing up. "Have you given any more thought to —"

No effing way! thought Andromache. Aloud, though, she only giggled.

Penthesilea looked at her like she was insane. With a slight hesitation, she asked, "Same time tomorrow?"

Andromache beamed. "All right!"

℥℥

"ISN'T IT PRETTY UP HERE?" said Andromache, the next day. Penthesilea was looking as remote and taciturn as ever, but Andromache didn't care. She had to talk, had to chatter. She was too giddy not to.

Overnight, it seemed, the hillsides had turned purple. A few flowers must have been open the day before, but she hadn't noticed them. Today, they were everywhere — sprays of purple, bobbing in the wind. She'd seen the first clump while running past the rock where she'd once sat with Hector. Growing at its base were several of the plants he'd held between his toes, the plants he'd told her bloomed with purple flowers. The sight of them made Andromache feel as dizzy as she had that day.

"Pretty?" said Penthesilea, in response to her question. "I guess."

"There are a lot of nice places, though. The Lukka lands are so beautiful. Have you ever been down there?"

"No."

"Oh," said Andromache. "Well, I've never been to Santiya. Did you like it there?"

"Yes."

"Because it's pretty?"

Penthesilea slowed. "Because the people there value women. They don't expect women to be helpless, like in some places. Santiyan women can do anything the men do — rule the country, fight in the army. *Command* the army."

"Oh," said Andromache, suddenly cautious. She didn't want to encourage too much talk of women in the army, for fear that Penthesilea might once again ask her to join. She turned her attention back to the sprays of purple flowers. *I wonder what they smell like. When we stop, I'll have to pick a few — they'd look pretty in my room. Or maybe I could even transplant some into the garden. What would Hector — Ector — say if he saw them outside his door?* The thought of him so electrified her that she had to start talking again. "Why did you come to Troy, then?" she asked Penthesilea.

"They respect women here, too. Not as many women fight in the army as in Santiya, but they're allowed to."

The army, again! Andromache gave a wary nod.

"Besides," Penthesilea went on, "it's not in every city that women can be on the council."

To that, Andromache gave a wholehearted nod. Her first spring in Troy, she'd begun to realize how special her adoptive city was. Herself, she never would have wanted to join the council. She was a quiet person who hated to be the center of attention; if she'd been born a man, she would have felt the same way. However, she liked living somewhere that those women who *did* crave power and notoriety could attain them. Penthesilea could be a captain in the army — Hecuba could be a healer and an ambassador — Cassandra and the Newbie could join the city council — and Andromache could teach and grow things in her garden. There was a place for everyone.

"There's still a long way to go for women in Troy," Penthesilea admitted. "You probably noticed on your first night here that the council is mostly men."

Andromache hadn't noticed. She remembered only a few men from that night — Hector, Laoganus, Priam, and a council member with a sharp, white voice. As for women, the only one she could recall was Hecuba. Everyone else had just sounded angry. She hadn't thought to distinguish men from women.

"But that's changing," said Penthesilea. "In twenty years, the mix will be different."

Andromache nodded. There were just as many girls as boys at the soiree discussion groups.

"Women and girls have a chance in Troy," said Penthesilea. "That's why I came. There's also more for me to do here than in Santiya. More room to move up. There, the Santiyan royal family takes priority — and it's a big family, with lots of children."

It took Andromache a moment to realize that Penthesilea was talking about Hector's family, about the hordes of humorless princess cousins he'd claimed to have. "That's right," she said. "That's what Hector told me."

Penthesilea seemed to bristle. "He'd know." She then sped up again, explaining, "I need to get back."

The pace made talking difficult, so Andromache was left to her thoughts. She reflected on what might have upset Penthesilea: *It was when I mentioned Ector...maybe she's still mad that he refused to let me join the army. Yes, that must be it. She must be lonely, here. It sounds like there were a lot more women in the* Santiyan *army, even if most of them were princesses. Princesses! Ector's cousins! I wonder what they're like — if they're as boring as he said. And I wonder what they could tell me about* him! *They probably knew him as a teenager, or even a little boy...*

In short, Andromache's mind turned in the direction it was always turning, of late. She forgot everything that Penthesilea had been talking about, as well as the woman's abrupt change in humor.

When they arrived back at the gateway cottage, Penthesilea made a move to go inside, but Andromache lingered away from the door.

"Aren't you coming?" Penthesilea asked.

Andromache shook her head. "I think I'll stay awhile."

"Oh. Tomorrow, then?"

"All right."

Penthesilea disappeared into the cottage, and Andromache walked back to her rock. She knelt by the flowers at its base, held a spray of them to her nose, and inhaled. The scent startled her.

My bath oil! she realized. *But I always thought that was made from yellow flowers!* Again, she breathed in, but there was no mistaking it: the flowers smelled just like her bath oil. Had Hector noticed, the way she'd noticed his cedar trees?

Andromache looked up at the rock. He'd been sitting right there. He'd touched his hand to her back. What would have happened if she'd turned toward him, then, instead of wrenching away? She sighed but comforted herself with the thought that he liked her. He'd given her a pet name. He wanted to kiss with her. There would be other chances.

Still kneeling, she gathered a bouquet of the flowers.

℁

AS ANDROMACHE CLIMBED up into the outpost stable and handed her lamp to the guards, she realized how late it was — far too late to go marketing with Paris.

I'll be hearing about that *later,* she thought, but there was no help for it now. The best she could do was avoid him for a while. She could wander down to the herb market — or, no — better yet, the main stables. Thisbe would be glad to see her, and so would Xanthus. The old stable master had been clamoring for a roodles rematch; she'd won their last three games.

Best of all, at the stables, she stood a chance of seeing *him.*

℁

"DIDN'T THINK YOU'D BE SHOWING your face around here, Missy — not after last time!" taunted Xanthus, as though he were the reigning roodles champion.

"It's good to see you, too," Andromache replied.

"Hmph," he said, setting up the game board.

His first move was bold, but she was able to counter. He went again, then she did, in a rhythm as regular as rowing. The game had grown easy. Andromache could have played it in her sleep.

She found herself focusing less on her next move than on the sounds around her: munching, crunching, whinnying, chattering, griping. Above all, griping. Xanthus's favorite tavern had closed, and he was livid. With every breath, he proclaimed that the world was going to hell.

"…and it's just unacceptable, Missy! I suppose a man *has* to hand over his business to the younger generation eventually," he said with a grudging air. "But for that young lout to close a perfectly good tavern so he can move out to the countryside? Milk robins, or whatever he thinks he's going to do? I give him one rainy season, Missy — you mark my words, one rainy season! — before he slinks back here, begging for his old life. But *I* won't be giving it to him, no thank you, not after he closed the only decent tavern left in this sorry place." Xanthus thumped a game piece down onto the board.

Andromache countered. "I roodle you," she said softly.

"Eh? Now look here, Missy —"

"She's clobbering you!" exclaimed a different voice. Deep. Husky.

Andromache caught her breath.

"You think she's a patsy, do you?" Xanthus shook a lobstery old fist at Hector. "*You* sit down and play her! See for yourself what a ruthless little schemer she is."

Blushing, Andromache protested, "Oh, no! I'm sure you're busy —"

"He'll tell you that, Missy, but don't believe it — he's just afraid to show you that his game's gone to hell."

"I have a little time," said Hector. He and Xanthus switched places.

Andromache's hands were trembling as she reset the board. What now? Would it be better to win, or to lose? She didn't want Hector to think she was a *'patsy,'* but *'ruthless little schemer'* wasn't flattering, either.

Since she'd won the last match, the first play was Hector's. He moved, then she did, and again Andromache found herself slipping into the familiar pattern of gaming. She hardly had to think, which was fortunate, since she couldn't — at least not about anything besides Hector.

He was sitting so close! If she shifted slightly, their knees would be touching. His face was turned three-quarters toward her, eyes lowered to the board in contemplation. Before each turn, he brushed a hand over his face, as though forgetting that the stray lock of hair hadn't grown back yet. The game pieces looked small in his hands, but he moved them gently. He never slammed them against the board the way Xanthus did.

Back and forth, his turn, her turn, until finally —

"I roodle you," she murmured. And suddenly, she wished that they were alone, so she could say another word besides 'roodle.' The waiting and the tension had gone on long enough. It was time they told each other the truth.

Hector nodded once to acknowledge her victory. His eyes were still downcast, hidden from her.

"See?" cackled Xanthus. "I told you!"

"You were right," said Hector, smiling.

"Don't beat yourself up about it, though. It's not our fault. She brought a good luck charm with her. No use fighting someone with tricks like that, eh?"

"Good luck charm?" asked Hector, looking from Andromache to Xanthus and back again.

Xanthus pointed triumphantly to the floor beside Andromache's feet. As one, she and Hector craned their necks downward and saw the forgotten bouquet of flowers.

The air in the stable grew thick. Andromache knew that she was blushing, but she looked over at Hector anyway. His dark cheeks, too, were flushed. "They're pretty," he murmured.

"Pretty?" Xanthus scoffed. "I suppose it doesn't bother either of you that they're giving me the sneezes!"

Hector's laugh had a strange, hollow sound to it.

"Weeds in the stable and a barkeep out to pasture," muttered Xanthus. "I never thought I'd live to see such dark days!"

Hector laughed again, more normally this time. "It's a wonder you can keep your cheery nature," he teased.

"It's a wonder I don't box your ears."

"Go ahead and try it!"

"Eh? Wait till later and see if I don't!"

Hector cocked his head. He looked genuinely confused. "Later?"

"At training," Xanthus reminded him.

Hector sighed and rubbed the back of his neck. To Andromache, he said, "I forgot. There's evening training."

"Oh," she murmured.

Frowning pensively, he went on. "I don't want to squeeze in a lesson this afternoon —"

"We can reschedule."

"I was thinking tonight, after training, if you're free…" His voice was heavy — suggestive.

Tonight, thought Andromache. Tonight, when it would be dark, and quiet, and they would be alone…

"That is all rahght?" he asked.

Andromache nodded. Her throat was far too tight for her to speak.

"Good," snapped Xanthus. "Now that *that's* settled, I want a rematch, Missy. And the weeds have got to go."

Chapter 19

While waiting for Hector, that night, Andromache went out to the courtyard to look up at the sky. She saw no Lorani, but there was a fair smattering of stars — tiny, glowing specks in the celestial sea.

Then, as she lay there, another strange orb caught her eye. It was hazy and luminous, like the Lorani, but it had a tail. How could she have missed it, before? And what *was* it? She would have to make a stop at the library the next day to see if *On Lorani* mentioned any such creatures.

"Ahndromahk?"

She screeched. Once again, Hector had caught her by surprise! She hoped her dress was straight but didn't want to draw attention to it now by fixing it.

"You ahre doing what?" he asked.

"Looking at that thing." She indicated the hazy orb. "What is it?"

Hector sat on the ground, beside the bench where she was lying. Their heads were close together, and suddenly Andromache didn't care about the sky.

"I know not," he said. "Baht it is — how does one say? — evil."

"What?" Evil? It wasn't a word Hector had ever used, in any language. The gravity of it jarred Andromache from her thoughts about kissing. When she looked over at him, though, she saw that his eyes were dancing.

"This is as Dad says," he added.

Andromache frowned. "Priam thinks it's evil?"

"Yes, *eefil.*"

"But it's so pretty!"

Hector shrugged.

"How can he think it's evil?"

"Maybe not eefil — maybe a *sign* ohff eefil to come."

"That's ridiculous," said Andromache. "Whatever it is, it's *interesting.* I was thinking it might be a cousin to the Lorani."

"Oh, Ahndromahk," teased Hector. "Still you say there is Lorani? Neffer do *I* see one."

"Well, *I* have."

Hector shook his head. "You joke so mahch. You fink, '*Silly boy, he belieff anyfing I tell to him.*'"

Andromache swatted playfully at his head; he laughed and ducked. Straightening again, he glanced at the single purple flower woven into her braid, then caught her eyes. She held his gaze as long as she could — several breaths — before her eyes began to drift toward his lips.

"Hector!" boomed a voice, as sonorous and severe as Andromache had heard it only one other time.

Hector sighed. "Dad sent me out to find you," he said to Andromache. "Everyone's in the kitchen. We're not allowed to be out, tonight."

"You're serious?"

"Yes, I'm serious! He's scared of that fuzzy thing up there, and he wants us all in the kitchen."

Andromache, too, sighed. "I was comfortable, out here."

"I don't even get to sleep in my own bed," Hector complained. "He's making me use one of the spare rooms."

Don't say it, Andromache warned herself. *Don't make a fool of yourself by offering to share yours!*

"Hector! Where are you, son? Haven't you found her?"

"Yes!" Hector bellowed back to his father. "Finally. We'll be right in." In a murmur, he added, "I know, this is all insane. But it's better just to humor him when he gets like this. Do you mind going in?"

"No." Andromache shook her head. "Why did they send *you* to find me?" she whispered.

"Because they were worried that Paris might anger the fuzzy thing," Hector whispered back.

They walked into the kitchen, where the whole family had gathered. Even Cutie was there. When the little dog saw Andromache, she ran over and danced around her legs. Andromache reached down to pet her and was rewarded with a fervent *schlurp*!

"Thank the stars you're back," said Priam, looking so genuinely worried that Andromache regretted having mocked him. "What took you so long?"

"I couldn't find her," said Hector. "She was off in a corner, looking up at the — the — *thing*."

Paris snorted, but Priam looked at Andromache with concern. "Do you know the danger it represents, little one?"

She shook her head. As far as she was concerned, the fuzzy thing was a *good* omen. It had brought Hector wonderfully close to kissing her.

"Well, in any case, all is well," said Hecuba. "They're here, now. Let's have something to eat, and then we can get out the roodles board." She closed the curtains.

"Mom! Are you kidding?" Paris protested.

"About roodles? Why on earth would I joke about that?"

"Not roodles! I meant the curtains! It's way too hot in here. You're going to melt the Songbird."

Cassandra did indeed have beads of sweat on her upper lip.

"We can't be too careful, son," said Priam.

"Who cares if the fuzzy thing gets us, if we suffocate first?" griped Paris. "This is the craziest thing anyone in our crazy family has ever done!"

"No," Cassandra contradicted. "*That* was back when Hector opened the wasp nest."

Andromache gave Hector a questioning look.

"I wanted to see what it was like inside," he said with a shrug.

"You've always had such curiosity about the world." Priam smiled. He was tranquil again, now that the whole family was safely indoors.

Hecuba grimaced.

"Did they sting you?" Andromache asked Hector.

"His face looked like the harvest moon," sighed Hecuba. "He was in poultices for a week."

"And scarred for life," added Paris. "You'd probably never believe it, Hermie, but my poor brother used to be a living god of beauty, before the wasps got him."

"It's true," said Hector, ruefully shaking his head. "And *my* poor brother used to be a regular god of wisdom before that one wasp crawled into his ear and punched holes in his brain."

"Boys — enough!"

"Sorry, Mom."

"Sorry."

Andromache smiled softly as she took in the faces around her. She felt warm inside and didn't mind that Priam's shouting had thwarted her kiss. This was something more. At the same time, being with Hector's family made her all the more anxious to tell him that she loved him. She decided to do so the next time they were alone.

The story of the wasp nest led into one about a very young Cassandra getting lost in the library, and the roodles board was forgotten. An hour later, Hecuba and Priam went to bed, after making another admonition against anyone leaving the house.

Cassandra ran upstairs to fetch the roodles board. "Let's play!" she cried, as soon as she was back in the kitchen. "We can do teams!"

"I get Hermie," said Paris.

"Oh." Cassandra pursed her lips, looking stymied. "I was going to say Hector —"

"Forget it, Songbird. I don't want him. I heard about what happened in the stables, this morning, and I don't want to *lose*."

Hector fixed his brother with a stony look. "<u>You go to in the hell</u>," he muttered.

Andromache giggled. So did Cassandra. Although the girl didn't know quite what her eldest brother had said, she could tell that he'd successfully mocked the middle one.

"Your move," said Hector. "And Paris, don't cheat. The fuzzy thing in the sky is watching you."

Chapter 20

ell him! thought Andromache, during Lukkan lessons the next day. Hector was sitting right across from her. They were alone — it would be so easy — *Tell him!*

But without the thrilling danger of the fuzzy thing and the warmth of family all around, she found her courage flagging. The words made their way to her lips at least seven times, only to be swallowed when something prevented her from saying them. Hector had to adjust his sandal, which was cutting into his foot — Cutie knocked a scroll to the floor while chasing a bug — Andromache sneezed. And so on, and so on.

Afterward, Hector walked down to the kitchen with her. They were early. No one else was there, yet, but other family members were sure to stop in soon, for dinner. *This is my last chance*, thought Andromache, panicking. *I have to tell him!*

"Ector?" she said. Her voice sounded thin and webby.

"Hmm?"

Tell him. Do it! "I — I —" She swallowed. "What are you doing tonight?" *You coward!* she admonished herself.

But Hector had sensed a hidden meaning to her words, perhaps because she'd used his Lukkan name. He paused with a piece of bread midway to his mouth and stared at her. Still, his tone was casual as he answered: "I was thinking of taking Buzzy to the river."

"Oh. That sounds fun."

"You can come, if you want," he said off-handedly.

Never mind, never mind! You did fine, Ahndromahk! The river, far away from everyone else! Where they could talk privately, and maybe even —

"All right," she said. "I'll go."

"Go where?" asked Cassandra, who had just walked in.

"To the river," blurted Hector. "After dinner." A little too quickly, he added, "Uh — you — you want to come?"

It was an awkward moment all around. Ordinarily, as Andromache knew, Cassandra prized few things more than spending time with her brothers. The girl didn't like going outside the city walls, though, and as much as she might enjoy the occasional spying mission, she didn't seem to want to play chaperone. "Uh — I —" she stammered, looking at her feet.

But if Cassandra was uncomfortable, Andromache was in anguish. All along, Hector had been mocking her! Playing with her! He so hated the thought of spending time alone with her that he'd asked his *sister* to join them! Gods, how stupid she'd been, and how glad she was that she hadn't managed to spit out the dreaded words!

"You know what? You two go," Andromache heard herself saying as she stood and backed out of the room. "I'm not feeling well. I must've eaten something bad for lunch."

Once she felt the open space of the banquet hall around her, she turned and fled to her room. There, she stared out the window, toward the flat plain and Scamander, the river where she *wouldn't* be walking. Where she *wouldn't* be kissing Hector, where she *wouldn't* be telling him that she loved him, because he didn't want to go there with her.

She'd been so sure! What had she done wrong?

Fiercely, she snapped the curtains shut. Everything out there was grey, and she didn't want to look at it. She wasn't going to cry! She *wasn't* going to —

For the next hour, she lay curled in a ball, weeping. She was stupid, a fool, an idiotic wretch. Who was she, to think Hector would love *her*?

Cutie, who had followed her upstairs, tried repeatedly to lick her face, but Andromache kept pushing her away. "Even *you* don't really love me," she finally whimpered. "You're just here for the salt. I know how dogs are."

Cutie wagged her tail and gave Andromache's cheek another *schluuurp*!

Just then, Andromache heard a soft *tap, tappa, tap* coming from the doorway. She sat up sharply, then sagged. It couldn't be *him*, of course. Not after the way he'd treated her!

Tap, tap.

Still, it wouldn't hurt to run her fingers through her hair, a little...just in case.

Tap, tappa, tap. "Honey?"

Sighing, Andromache let her arms fall slack. "Come in."

Cassandra opened the door a crack and slipped inside. "I just wanted to check on you."

"What for?" asked Andromache, trying to sound breezy.

"To see if you were feeling better." Cassandra coughed. "You know, from your *lunch*."

"Oh." Andromache shrugged. "I guess. And how was *your* evening?"

Cassandra smiled. "Uneventful. I read up a little on comets — that's what the '*fuzzy thing*' is really called, you know. I'd never seen one before, but apparently they're quite common. I have so many questions to ask my astronomy tutor, tomorrow! It's spooky, all the things that have happened when comets came around. We'll be busy." Cassandra nodded with grim satisfaction. "Anyway, all that reading got me so stir-crazy, I just *had* to move around a little. So here I am!"

"The walk to the river didn't stretch your legs enough?" Andromache asked sourly.

"Oh, I didn't go. My brother had to back out. Some work thing came up, as usual. He was all, '*Maybe some other time.*'" Cassandra tried to look disappointed, as she always was when Hector uttered that phrase, but she wound up beaming instead.

"Oh," said Andromache, feeling her hope revive. "That's too bad."

"Oh, yes! It's just *dreadful*." Cassandra sighed theatrically. "Anyway, I have to get back to my reading." With a giggle, she skipped out of the room.

Andromache re-opened the curtains and breathed deeply, smelling the lush scent of growing plants. She felt green inside, too. Things were stirring back to life.

Chapter 21

At the first hint of pale morning light, Andromache crept downstairs. She was eager to give Hector another chance — to give *herself* another chance — to try again.

Please be there, she begged him silently. *And please be alone*...

Luck was with her, that time: as she stepped into the kitchen, she saw Hector sitting at the table. By himself. "<u>Ector</u>," she said softly.

He turned toward her. "<u>Ahndromahk</u>..."

She nodded, unable to say more.

"<u>You were sick</u>," he murmured.

Nodding again, she went over to him.

"<u>You feel better</u>?" he asked, his voice strangely thick.

"<u>Yes</u>," she said. Her tone was forgiving — inviting.

He smiled. "<u>It is going to be a nice efening</u>."

"<u>Yes</u>."

"Buzzy <u>cannot go in the riffer, last night</u>." Pause. "<u>Maybe he want to go this night</u>." Pause. "<u>You feel better</u>." Pause. "<u>So, you want to come, too</u>?" The tone was casual; the pauses were not, and so Andromache blushed. "<u>You want to say yes? Ohr no</u>?" teased Hector. His eyes were dancing.

"<u>What's</u> Cassandra <u>up to, today</u>?" asked Andromache, just to be sure.

Hector gave a disdainful shrug. "<u>I know not</u>."

"<u>Then yes</u>," she whispered.

"<u>We can go in place ohff our lesson</u>," he decided. His voice was strange again, and he didn't look at her. "<u>Jahst befohre the sahn is to fall</u>..."

$$\wp$$

JUST BEFORE THE SUN IS TO FALL…

"Hermie?"

"Oh! Sorry! What did you say?"

"Are you coming to the market with me, or what?"

"Oh…I don't think I have time today."

"Mom has you grooming the herbs again?"

"No, I just — I need a bath."

Paris squinted at her. "Unless you're a lot dirtier than you look, there'll be plenty of time for that after we go marketing."

"I'm not dirty!" Andromache howled. "I just want — I just want —"

"What?"

"I don't know. Forget it. Let's go."

"If you say so, Hermie."

At the market, rather than marching Paris straight to the food stalls, keeping him on task as was her habit, Andromache found herself drifting among the booths that sold baubles — shining necklaces and silken sashes, rings of every size and color.

"Hermie?" called Paris, who had lost her in the crowd and was coming back to collect her. "What's with you, today?"

"Nothing," she said, her cheeks coloring. "Sorry, I just got — distracted." Her eyes swept over a display of beads.

Paris stood still, assessing her. "Are you trying to look pretty, Hermie?" he asked. His tone held disbelief but, for once, no mockery. He actually sounded sympathetic.

Andromache nodded. There was no use trying to hide such truths from Paris.

"All right, then. Hmmm." He scrutinized the tables. "None of this. No, let's head over there. Something subtle, I think, for you. Sorry, Hermie. You just aren't the flashy type."

Far from offended, she was relieved to have his help. She wanted to look pretty, not cheap.

Giving nothing but a sneer to the first dozen stalls, Paris finally stopped before a table of cloth goods. He chose and then pretended to spurn a wine-colored sash, impossibly fine and soft.

"No — never mind," he said to Andromache, curling his lip. "This thing smells like goat's breath."

The vendor's eyes bulged; Paris seemed to grin. After much intense haggling, the sash was his, and he turned it over to Andromache. She caressed its fabric the whole way home, imagining how it would look against her dress in the evening light, waving in the breezes near the river.

"After your bath, wash your hair, and brush it — a *lot* — and then leave it down. You'll be glad you did. Trust me," counseled Paris, once they were back inside the house. "Oh, and Hermie? Be a sport. Don't tie the knots too tight…"

He gave her new sash a blushworthy wink and disappeared up the stairs, leaving Andromache to picture Hector, fumbling with her sash as he'd once done with a box of tangled ropes, down at the stables.

℘

ANDROMACHE WAS READY. She'd bathed, brushed her hair to a high sheen, scrubbed her nails, and wound and rewound the sash around her waist. With the longed-for, magical hour approaching, she decided to wait for Hector in the entry hall. He would be back at any moment, and she wanted to see him as soon as he came through the door.

Andromache sat. She sat, and sat, and sat on the bench until her bottom ached and her feet began to fall asleep. Evening fell; the sky darkened. *He's late,* she thought.

(*He changed his mind,*) the Voice inside her head corrected snidely.

He's just late!

(*Hours late. He's not coming.*)

Yes, he is! I know *it!*

In all the racket of her argument with the Voice, Andromache almost failed to hear the door open. She gasped — straightened her shoulders — hastily smoothed her hair — and sank back into a slouch as Hector walked in on the heels of his parents. Always! There was always a family member around to —

151

"Come, little one," murmured Priam, in passing. His wife hustled ahead without a word. Neither seemed to have noticed her change in appearance. Hector, on the other hand, acknowledged her hair and sash with a single, impenetrable look before following his parents.

Andromache hurried to catch up. "What's going on?" she whispered frantically to Hector.

"Cassandra!" Hecuba was hollering. "Paris! Get down here immediately! Now, I say!"

"Emergency council meeting," was all Hector whispered back. He was no longer the sweet, playful boy of that morning, but a stranger with hooded eyes who hardly seemed to notice her.

"Oh," said Andromache. She understood. Hector was leaving. It wasn't the family who had intervened, this time, but Mudders — brutal Mudders, invading one of Troy's allies. Mudders, or perhaps some other raiders. What difference did it make, who they were? All that mattered was that Hector wouldn't be kissing her, tonight — not for weeks — might *never* kiss her, now. Might never —

Don't! she warned herself. *Hold it together, for his sake. Don't make this any harder on him. Try to look calm. Happy, even. That's how you want him to think of you*…

In entering the banquet hall, Andromache affixed a smile so broad that the muscles of her face began trembling from the strain. She knew it looked appalling, but it was the best she could do. Hector's other family members had had more practice. Their smiles were fake, but not as frightful as hers.

"Do you need help getting ready, son?" asked Priam.

Hector shook his head. "No thanks, Dad. I can get it."

"So you're leaving tonight?" whispered Cassandra.

Hector nodded. "As soon as we can."

"That's sudden."

He nodded again. Neither he nor his parents volunteered any details. "I just have to get a few things from the shed."

"I suppose the rest of us ought to let you, then," said Hecuba. It was the cue for everyone to wish Hector farewell.

While the others moved to surround him, Andromache slipped off toward the back staircase. She had to rip off that stupid sash — had to stuff it under the bed, out of sight — had to tie her hair back before she tore it out in disgust — had to get upstairs before her face went into spasms!

But her room brought her no peace, just thoughts of Hector's neck, bruised — his arm, laid open — his blood, pouring out —

_No!_

Tears poured down her cheeks. How could it be true? How could this be happening? That morning, her world had been so bright, so alive with possibilities; now, all was ominous and bleak. Hector was leaving. Leaving! And she hadn't even —

From her window, she looked down onto the courtyard and saw light shining through the doorway to Hector's shed.

There's still time, she thought.

(_Time for what?_) sneered the Voice.

To tell him.

(_Tell him what?_)

That I love him, stupid Voice! What else would I be telling him?

(_Great idea! Dump that on him right before he leaves! Just face the facts — it's too late, now._)

Shut up! snapped Andromache. She _had_ to go down there! She at least had to _see_ him!

She crept down the stairs and out to the shed where Hector was making a few last preparations. Timidly, she stepped inside and whispered, "Ector."

Hector looked over in surprise. "Ahndromahk! What are you doing out here?"

"I don't know. I saw a light, and — and —" She gulped. "I thought I'd see if you needed any help."

"Thanks," he said, smiling.

She wanted desperately to smile back, but the sight of him, stooped beneath the shed's beetle-eaten rafters, brought on another surge of tears. With great effort, she held them back. "S-so, what can I do?" she asked softly.

"Uh —" Hector looked around, but there was little left to pack. Even his armor had already been stowed. "Uh — you could hand me that blanket," he finally said, gesturing to a heap of grey fabric at Andromache's feet.

She passed him the blanket, and he turned around to stow it with his other things. While he was facing away from her, she watched him, feverishly taking in the sight of him — the movement of his arms, the gleam of scars as they tensed and flexed in the lamp light. This time, she would remember everything about him! This time —

He turned back toward her, so abruptly that he had to have caught her staring. "Ahndromahk…" he said.

"Hmm?"

"Promise me you won't go out into the countryside while I'm gone. Promise me." His face was grave. "I don't want to think about you alone out there."

Andromache looked down. "I promise, Ector," she murmured. She knew then that she'd come too late. The Voice was right. Hector couldn't afford to think about her, just then. He needed a clear mind; his life depended on it. The worst thing she could do was to distract him from his mission. But to let him leave without giving him a sign of what he meant to her — no, she couldn't do that, either!

Impulsively, she touched her hand to his cheek. He turned slightly, so that she could just feel the curve of his lips against her palm. "Be well and come back quickly, Ector," she said, trying to fill the traditional Lukkan farewell with everything she'd waited too long to say.

Hector nodded once, and without another word, Andromache hurried back to the house. As she fled, she kept seeing the image of him, framed by the rafters of the storage shed. *I hate that place!* she sobbed to herself. *I hate it! It's the last place I'll ever see him. He's not coming back, this time — I just know it!*

She tripped several times running up the stairs, which grew blurrier and blurrier as she climbed. When she reached her door, she opened it with her left hand rather than the right, so as not to rub off the warm, rough feeling of Hector's cheek.

He's not coming back, she thought again. She pictured the scene in the shed over and over until she sobbed herself sick. Grabbing for a basin, she knelt in front of it and retched until her stomach was empty. Even then, she continued to heave.

The night was a torment. Whenever she told herself, *I have to stop thinking about the shed!* she thought about it all the more. She also thought about the date she and Hector hadn't had, the secrets she hadn't told him — like that he'd once met her Auntie! She thought about all the times she'd been mean to him and all the horrible things she'd said to him during their fights. Each thought pushed her into another round of violent, stomach-wrenching sobs.

I have to think about something else, she told herself. *Something happy.* But everything that made her happiest — Cutie, Troy's countryside, the library, the stables, the courtyard — held too much of Hector to be comforting. Reaching back before she'd known him, she thought of the platana grove beside the river in Lyrnassa and the pine trees of her childhood home in the Lukka lands, but those thoughts just reminded her of everything she'd already lost.

Eventually, she wore herself out and fell asleep on the floor, her cheek resting on her open left hand.

ℰᴐ

WHEN ANDROMACHE AWOKE the next morning, her head ached, and her back was stiff from sleeping on the floor. She wanted just to lie there in misery but was afraid Hecuba would come to check on her. She would ask pointed questions about why Andromache had been so sick...

Slowly, Andromache stood and trudged downstairs to the kitchen. The family was already gathered there, Paris included. Andromache was grateful to see him. Somehow, he'd figured out her secret, yet he'd been nice to her about it — Paris, nice! He'd helped her look pretty for her date with Hector, and because of that, now, he was an unexpected source of comfort.

"Good morning, dear," said Hecuba. "Are you hungry? What would you like?"

"Not the cherries," said Paris. "I called dibs. Pass them over!"

"But surely you don't need *all* of them," Hecuba chided. "I've never seen such gluttony!"

"That's all right," murmured Andromache. Paris could have the cherries; he deserved them. Still refusing to touch anything with her right hand, she took the bowl in her left, which was weaker. Her grip faltered, and the fruit spilled all over Paris.

"Whoa!" he protested.

"Sorry."

"What's wrong with your right hand, Gimpy?"

"Nothing!" cried Andromache, feeling as stupid as only Paris could make her feel. Hot tears threatened to spill down her cheeks. Paris? A *comfort*? How could she have been so deluded?

"Are you all right, dear?" asked Hecuba, concerned.

"I'm fine. I just slept on my arm." Andromache shot Paris an acid look. "It's stiff, that's all."

He shrugged.

"Paris, leave her alone," Hecuba scolded.

Paris obediently turned to Cassandra, who had been sipping fruit juice and nibbling a piece of cheese. "How's it going, Songbird?" he asked.

"Oh, fine. I was just thinking of everything I have to do today." Her smile was peculiarly bright: she was engaging Paris, to take his attention away from Andromache. Andromache would have been grateful, too, if Cassandra hadn't added, "I should really go upstairs to prepare for lessons."

Lessons. Andromache choked down a sob, thinking of the long, dismal afternoon ahead of her. Of the weeks of dismal afternoons. Perhaps months.

(*Perhaps forever…*)

Chapter 22

As Andromache had known it would, the one empty afternoon stretched into several, then many. Every day, she gardened before going down to visit the stables, but she neither read much nor roused Paris early for marketing. She didn't care when he went to the market, as she had no intention of joining him. Her garden had served the family well enough the first time Hector went away; they would have to make do with it once more. In all likelihood, they wouldn't even notice.

Other than the stables, the only place she ever went was the luthier's quarter. While she wandered around down there, she saw visions of her dad. He was a young man, now, walking arm in arm with a woman, small and bright-eyed. _Mom!_ thought Andromache, but she'd never seen her mom looking so young, so carefree. _Mom, you're here!_

In truth, of course, her mom had never been to Troy — had never left the Lukka lands. That glimpse of her was nothing but a dream. A might-have-been...

ℰℴ

ANDROMACHE WAS HAUNTED by might-have-beens. So much in her life could have — should have — gone differently! If only she hadn't listened to the Voice...

She was in the shed, with Hector. He was packing to leave. Knowing he might not be back for weeks, or months, or more, she threw her arms around him.

'I love you,' she said. 'I love you, Ector!'

'I lahff you, too,' he murmured. Then, he kissed her, and when he had to leave, a few moments later, they at least had the feel of that kiss to hold onto.

Andromache kicked a loose rock. How stupid she'd been! How could she ever have thought it would burden him, knowing she loved him? It might even have strengthened him. Who wouldn't want to be loved?

I should have told him, she thought. *If only I could go back!*

She replayed the scene in her mind with dozens of variations — different words, more or fewer of them, and different lengths of kisses. Sometimes, Hector didn't leave at all. Enchanted by her kisses, he held her all through the night and long into the next day, not letting go until a message came that the danger had passed, and he no longer had to leave.

Rewriting the past made Andromache feel better, at least for a while. She began to look back on other moments she and Hector had shared...

He was in the library, standing beside the window, waiting for her. She came into the room, but instead of sitting down at the table, she walked over to him and slipped her arms around his waist, letting her head rest on his shoulder...

She was out on the courtyard, hunting for Lorani with Hector. 'You'd think Trojans would know how to kiss right,' she said. 'Some do,' he murmured. His tone was suggestive and made her nervous, but she didn't turn away. Instead, she leaned toward him, and he leaned toward her, until their lips were touching...

She was out in the countryside with Hector. His hand was on her back. She turned over so that it was on her stomach, instead. 'Ahndromahk...' He bent down, and then they were kissing — and kissing — and kissing. They kissed for hours until finally Andromache fell asleep, wrapped in the sun-warm skin of Hector's arms...

(*It was cold that day*,) the Voice reminded her.

Shut up!

158

(*And you're really on the courtyard. Alone.*)

Andromache sighed. She had no energy for quarreling with the Voice; she was worn out from the nightmares she'd been having, lately. In the worst one, Hector had lost a leg and had come home unable to walk. Then, he'd thrown the leg into the sea, to bury it, and it had kicked back up to the surface. She'd awoken screaming, with Cutie licking her face. *It's just a dream, Ahndromahk*, she'd told herself, but the thought of it still made her sick.

(*You're crazy, too,*) prodded the Voice. (*Crazy and alone…*)

Shut up, Andromache said tiredly. *I won't be alone forever. You'll see. Everything will change once I tell him I love him.*

The Voice's answer was simple but effective: (*When?*)

℥

AS TIME WORE ON, Andromache's nightmares worsened while her fantasies sobered. She thought less about kissing Hector than about eating breakfast with him, or visiting him in the stables, or laughing together over silly texts. But even those thoughts never soothed her, because with them came the Voice:

(*When?*) it echoed snidely. (*When?*)

Although she didn't mean to, Cassandra sometimes added to Andromache's fears. "How are you doing, honey?" the girl asked one night.

"Fine," said Andromache, although she wasn't.

"I know these past few weeks have been hard on you…"

Andromache sighed.

"Why wouldn't they be? Even without —" In horror, Cassandra clapped a hand over her mouth. As she often did, she'd clearly said too much.

"Without what?" asked Andromache.

Cassandra shook her head.

"Tell me!" Andromache insisted. She was beginning to feel truly frightened.

"Without the comet," Cassandra mumbled.

"Oh — that." Andromache almost laughed. "You don't still think it's an evil omen, do you?"

Cassandra frowned. "I have to admit, I was a little skeptical at first, despite other cases having been thoroughly documented, but facts are facts. The comet came, then Hector left, and —"

"Was there a comet in the sky, the last time he went away?" Andromache interrupted.

Cassandra thought back. "No," she said.

"Well, there you go. The comet had nothing to do with his leaving."

"There must have been another sign, that time."

"There were other signs this time."

"What?" gasped Cassandra.

"Your dad is on the council. And your mom goes to the meetings, too, sometimes, doesn't she?"

"Yes — she's an ambassador. So?"

"So, they probably heard reports of trouble brewing, and then when your dad saw the comet, he called it a sign of what he knew would happen anyway." The solution had come to Andromache on the fly, and she was proud of it. She thought Hector, too, would approve.

Cassandra eyed her suspiciously. "How do you know?"

"Because comets are just creatures, Cassandra. Big creatures that live in the celestial ocean."

The girl looked thoughtful. "Maybe. But —"

"But what?"

"But why was it swimming so close to us, just as the — *trouble* — started brewing?"

"Chance," said Andromache.

Cassandra nodded slowly. "Yes," she said. "That must be it."

Andromache could tell by her tone that she wasn't convinced — that she'd only agreed with Andromache because she didn't want to worry her — which of course made Andromache worry all the more. The appearance of the comet, which hadn't bothered her before, began to weigh on her. She wondered what it might mean for her — for Hector.

There aren't bad omens, she told herself fiercely. *Just bad times. And the good times will come back.* Hector would come back. Andromache would be with him once more. She would sit with him again, speaking Lukkan in the library. She would smile and laugh with him.

(*When?*) sneered the Voice.

ઈ)

IN THE END, Andromache's hopes and daydreams gave way wholly to nightmares. She was plagued by many strange, unsettling things. Five tornadoes twisted around each other in the air as she stood, rooted, unable to run for cover. Water crashed up over the walls of Troy. Cutie's tail broke off in her hand. Paris served her a plate of goat's heads, their blank eyes staring at her.

The worst dreams, though, were about Hector. In one, the earth moved, the courtyard spring stopped flowing, and Hector was buried in a rockslide. Andromache awoke from that dream so terrified that she ran outside to check the spring. It was flowing as usual, but she could still see Hector, crushed and struggling for breath...

She had only one way to combat such nightmares: running. Exhausting herself to the point where she could no longer think. It was her old way of handling trauma. She'd promised Hector not to leave the city walls, so she went instead to the exercise arena, where she ran for hours at a time, trying to deaden her horror of what the future might bring.

High summer

Chapter 23

As Andromache finished her last lap, she sank beneath a tree. She was exhausted. She'd spent the night thrashing in a shallow, troubled sleep...

Hector was back. He'd been carried into Troy on a blanket. He wasn't dead, but his mind was gone and he lay unresponsive on a narrow bed, his body growing soft, unable to live or die. His mother told them, with false hopefulness, that he'd gained a little weight, as though this were a sign that he might grow strong again. But Andromache knew that he would never really return. He would never talk to them again, or laugh. He would only lie there, growing softer, and softer, and softer...

Andromache repressed a wave of nausea. The nightmare still made her sick, no matter how many times she told herself that it wasn't real.

No mind — lying on a narrow bed.

Even after a whole morning's run, the dream remained sickeningly fresh.

Soft — unresponsive.

Abruptly, she rose and took off once more around the arena. *Faster, dammit, faster!* she told herself.

Unable to talk or laugh.

She didn't care if she fainted — if she collapsed and hit her head — so long as she didn't have to see the dream anymore.

Drooling — thick and flabby.

She went faster — faster — faster!

162

His parents still loved him. His mother was stroking his hair, which had begun to fall out.

Finally, Andromache had to stop again to catch her breath. While she sat there on the ground, her pulse made a terrible racket, pounding in her ears like drumbeats — or hooves. She closed her eyes and lay back. At last, her heartbeat slowed, but the clamor continued.

She sat up. Was it coming from her — or from outside the arena?

Other people had begun to notice, too. From the scraps of their conversation, she heard one often-repeated word: *gates*.

The gates? The gates! Could it be —

"They're back!" someone cried, running out of the arena.

Andromache followed. In her haste to reach the streets — then the *gates!* — she fell, tearing skin from her knees and hands. Without pausing to look at the wounds, she leapt up and kept running. She no longer felt winded.

"They're back — they're back!" she shrieked to the city at large, even as blood soaked through her dress. Those who saw her glanced hurriedly away. She looked like a madwoman.

She ran on, always downhill. She wasn't going to watch for Hector from above, on the wall. Oh, no! She was going to run straight to him. She would be jostled, and jabbed, and pushed around by the mob at the gates, but she didn't care. She wasn't going to waste any more time.

(*You're assuming he'll be there*,) taunted the snide Voice. (*But maybe —*)

Shut up! she snapped. *He'll be there.*

(*Just like in your dream — carried in on a blanket —*)

Lying on a narrow bed. Slack.

No! she thought to herself. *Forget about the dream!*

Ahead, Andromache saw a welcome sight: soldiers. Some had already made it up there from the gates. She ran on, dodging reunited families along the way. A grey-haired man was hugging a boy in his late teens; it was probably his first time out with the army. Several steps further, a young woman was both laughing and crying in the arms of her husband. Andromache wondered vaguely which of them had been away and which had stayed — the woman looked just as rugged as Penthesilea. Perhaps sensing

Andromache's gaze, the woman glanced up. She gave Andromache a look of pity before burying her face in the man's neck.

What does she know? Why did she look at me that way?

A hornet buzzed around inside Andromache's stomach, and she quickened her pace. The closer she got to the gates, the more Trojans she saw. A few, she noticed, were stumbling alone and confused, ghostlike. They'd already been down to the gates, only to find that they no longer had anyone to welcome. None of those people paid any attention to her. They shuffled along, their hollow eyes fixed downward, or else they sat in doorways, crying.

Demighosts. Andromache tried not to look at them. She ran on until she arrived at the edge of the crowd near the main gate.

No orange.

On her tiptoes, she looked in every direction, bobbing and leaping to see past the swarm of people.

Still nothing.

She couldn't breathe. Another hornet circled around the first — and then a whole swarm of them began to roil when Andromache saw that the gates were closed. The entire army had come in, but no orange.

A useless body, slack — carried in on a blanket.

Overwhelmed by a surge of nausea, Andromache stepped backward and ran into a woman who was jubilantly embracing her son. He was intact, if a little dirty, and never had Andromache hated anyone so bitterly as she hated his mother.

Ector's got to be here, she told herself desperately, looking around again. She still saw no orange, but this time she did see Penthesilea, deep in the middle of the milling throng.

Penthesilea! she thought, ruthlessly kicking and elbowing to get to the woman's side. If anyone would know where Hector was, Penthesilea would. The woman was holding the reins of a large, stomping horse, though, and Andromache was afraid to go too close. "Lee! Lee!" she screamed. "Lee!" Finally, Penthesilea heard her voice over the hubbub and turned toward her. It was then that Andromache recognized the horse — Buzzy.

Hector's horse was riderless.

Andromache looked into Penthesilea's eyes and saw utter desolation. In that instant, she realized two things: Hector really *was* dead, and Penthesilea had loved him all along.

Andromache's stomach turned to stone. Her lungs froze. She backed up, colliding with a donkey and crashing to her still-bloody knees. Dimly, she heard Penthesilea calling out to her, but she got up and kept running. She fought through the crowd, retracing her steps.

She had to get away! Not just away from this horde — no! She had to get away from Troy — away from the house where there might already be strings of mourners, where Hector's family would be walking around like ghosts, where she might have to see his broken body.

She passed by more reunited families, hardly noticing them. They weren't really there. No one was there. The city was empty, now that Hector was dead.

His body laid out. His clothes arranged to hide the many wounds — or perhaps just one mortal one. Neighbors weeping, Cassandra's face streaked with tears, Priam tearing out the garden plants and stomping them under his feet.

Andromache gasped. Her field of vision went red, and she nearly fell once more. She teetered — swayed — then, somehow, her head cleared and she was able to stand.

Don't think about it, she told herself. *Just go.* There was only one place she knew of to go, where she would be able to escape.

Ⅎ⁎

SWALLOWS DARTED through the door of the outpost stable, swooping down at Andromache when she passed by them. She hoped that the guards wouldn't ask why she was leaving, why she wasn't back at the house with the others, mourning Hector. She hoped that they would just let her go.

Inside, the place felt wrong. *It's too quiet*, she thought. Had the guards deserted the stable to watch at the main gate? Or had they already heard the news — *Hector, stiff and still, red blood dried to black in the gash on his throat* — *the whole city draped in black* — *Hecuba, smashing plates against the wall and falling down amongst the shards* — and left to grieve for him?

Andromache crumpled. Before her, the air was once again a shimmering red. *Just go. Get away. Take a lamp and go.* With sudden dread, she worried that the guards hadn't left a lamp. She wouldn't be able to pass through the tunnel without one! She would be stuck in Troy…

Slowly, she picked her way to the back of the stable. As she neared the tunnel's trapdoor entrance, she saw that the guards had indeed left a lamp — a dim one, burning low, but it would be enough to get her through the underground passage.

Seeing something else, she stopped short. One of the guards had stayed behind, after all! He was huddled on the floor, forehead pressed to his knees, arms wrapped around his bent legs. Plainly, he was grieving for his commander. Andromache felt no pity for him, though, only irritation — he was sitting almost on top of the trapdoor. *Move!* she thought, wishing him away. What was his sorrow, compared to hers? He didn't love Hector the way she did! He had no right to block her in! *Move, damn you!*

The guard shifted slightly, revealing a puddle of vomit on the floor in front of him.

Please, move! begged Andromache. *Please, just go!*

The guard began massaging his temple. As he did, a line of worm pink tissue gleamed on his upper arm.

Andromache gasped. *She knew that scar! But it can't be!* she told herself. *I must be dreaming — it can't be him!* Buzzy *was — and* Penthesilea —

In disbelief, Andromache blinked several times, expecting the scar to disappear. It didn't. "Hector?" she croaked.

The man turned toward her, and Andromache gaped. Even with the strange new line of stitches on his forehead, his face was unmistakable. Hector was there, before her — grimy, sweat-stained, blood-caked, but alive. She didn't know what he was doing there and didn't care.

"Ector!" In her frenzy to reach him, Andromache tripped, landing squarely on her injured knees. "Ector!" she yelped, half in pain, half in joy. She threw her arms around him and kissed his shoulder, heedless of the filth. "Ector…Ector…Ector…" she babbled, unable to say anything more.

"Go away," he growled, breaking contact with her.

Her stomach churned. Why was he saying that? Didn't he recognize her? Maybe he'd lost his memory when he hurt his head! Or maybe he was in too much pain — that would explain the vomit and the hollow look in his eyes. Whatever the problem was, he obviously needed help. She had to get him home, to his mother. Hecuba would know what to do. "Ector, it's me — Ahndromahk," she murmured, stroking his arm.

"Go away."

"No." Once more, she pressed her cheek to his shoulder. "I'm not leaving you here. I love you — I *love* you."

He pulled roughly away.

"Ector —"

"Go!"

Andromache drew back. After an excruciating silence, she whispered, "All right. I understand." She struggled to her feet and backed away from him, hoping he would stop her.

He didn't.

When she reached the door to the stable, she exited numbly, not bothering to duck the swallows diving for her head.

Her head...her head! It had *all* been in her head — the flirtation, the heavy pauses, the simmering looks. The heat in his hand. He didn't love her or want her.

(*Of course not, you fool!*) sneered the Voice. (*He never said he did! He never touched you on purpose, except once, to make sure you were all right. He never tried to kiss you. It was all in your head.*)

Her head. Her poor, stupid, lovesick head...

(*So, what's your plan now?*) taunted the Voice, relishing her misery.

I'll go home, she thought dully. *I'll pack, get a little sleep, and then come back here tonight. He'll be gone, by then. He can't stay here forever...*

If she could just keep going a few more hours — and endure the hornets in her belly — she could escape the living Hector the same way she'd planned to flee the dead one.

ഇ

"HONEY, YOU'RE HERE!" trilled Cassandra, when Andromache arrived home. "We've been looking all over for you!

There's so much to do for the party! Honey?" The girl stopped abruptly. "What on earth happened to you?"

Andromache shook her head, imagining what she must look like, from the cuts on her hands and the blood-soaked knee of her dress, to her face — tearstained, flushed, and sweaty from all her running.

"Here, come with me." Without questioning Andromache further, Cassandra led her through the banquet hall and across the courtyard, to the bath chamber. "I just got a bath ready for you, anyway. Hop in the tub and relax, honey — I'll bring you some food."

As soon as Cassandra was gone, Andromache shrugged her soiled dress off her wooden limbs and sank into the water. She closed her eyes and let herself slip deeper...deeper...deeper...

"Honey?" said Cassandra.

Andromache's eyelids fluttered open.

Cassandra was walking over to the tub. She'd brought not only food but also fresh clothes and ointment for Andromache's wounds. "There, is that enough of a soak?" she asked.

Andromache didn't answer.

"Well, come on out and put this dress on. I brought you the nicest one I could find."

Andromache did as she was told, even though she knew the dress wouldn't fit her. It was nicer than her other clothes because she'd never worn it — it had been made too large, and she'd never gotten around to having it altered.

"Oh, no!" cried Cassandra, when she saw the dress sagging on Andromache's shoulders.

"It doesn't matter," mumbled Andromache.

"You're right," said Cassandra. "It doesn't — not just for going upstairs." The girl then took out the ointment and began rubbing it into Andromache's cuts and scrapes. "What happened, honey?" she asked softly.

"I — I fell," said Andromache.

Cassandra nodded. "And you've probably been out in the sun all day, watching the soldiers come home." She spoke with great compassion. "So, now you're heat-sick."

It was a plausible story. Andromache found herself nodding.

"You should sleep for a little while," Cassandra suggested. "That way, you'll be rested for the party tonight." She brushed

Andromache's hair off her face, adding, "I'll come up, if you want, and help you get ready."

Listlessly, Andromache said, "I can't go to the party. I don't feel well."

"Oh." Cassandra swallowed hard. She picked up the tray of food. "I can take this back to the kitchen, if you want."

Knowing that she wouldn't eat a bite, anyway, Andromache nodded. "Thank you, Cassandra," she said, her eyes lingering for a moment on the girl she loved like a sister — and would never see again.

Cassandra kissed her cheek. "Get some rest."

Andromache passed back through the courtyard and up the stairs to her bedroom, mercifully running into none of the other family members. Once in the safety of her room, she collapsed onto the bed.

Cutie, who had been taking a nap there, nuzzled her happily.

"Go back to sleep," Andromache told her. "In a few hours, we'll be taking a very long walk."

Chapter 24

Andromache awoke to a dark room, lit only by a streak of moonlight. *That's pretty,* she thought, looking out at the sky.

A familiar mix of party sounds drifted up from the court-yard below. This would be the last time she ever heard them, she realized with a pang. Still, the decision to leave couldn't be un-made. She couldn't keep living under the same roof as Hector, not after what had happened in the outpost stable.

Sighing, she tore her eyes away from the moon. She trudged over to the clothing chest, opened it, and pulled out a few dress-es, along with her warm grey cloak. Everything else would have to stay behind. Demuchus's poems belonged to another era, and as for the drawings she and Hector had made during his earliest Lukkan lessons…well, even if the potsherds weren't too heavy to carry, the memories they evoked were now too painful to bear.

As Andromache folded her dresses, she thought she heard a soft tapping at the door, but she ignored it. Either she'd imag-ined the sound, or it was Cassandra, coming up to check on her again. *'Honey?'* the girl had whispered through the door, earlier. *'Are you sure you don't want to come down?'* Andromache hadn't an-swered, and Cassandra had left. Hopefully, she would do the same this time. Andromache didn't want to have to explain why she was packing her clothes…

Creak.

Andromache gasped. The door was opening!

Creak, creeeeak!

Torn between irritation and dismay, Andromache turned around, and —

"Oh, gods!" she whispered, dropping her clothes.

The visitor wasn't Cassandra, after all, but Hector. His face looked solemn in the light of the lamp he was holding. From the bed, Cutie barked a joyous greeting, but Hector ignored her. His eyes were fixed on Andromache. "Ahndromahk," he whispered, entering the room. "You're awake."

Ahndromahk...Her insides leapt at the sound of his voice, at the clean scent drifting in with him. She looked away. "Don't worry," she said in a low voice. "I'm not coming to the party — I'm leaving."

"Ahndromahk —"

She turned back to her dresses, frenziedly clutching them as she stammered, "I-I can't stay here — I won't. It would be stupid — I'm Demuchus to your me. I understand — I do, I —"

"No, you don't," said Hector, moving to block the doorway. The message was clear. Andromache could gather all the clothing she wanted, but she wouldn't be allowed to leave.

Defeated, she let the chest lid fall shut, sank down onto it, and dropped her dresses in a heap. "Yes, I *do*! I'm Demuchus to your Ahndromahk." Her head was bowed low, and her lips were trembling. She gripped the chest until her knuckles went white.

"Why do you keep saying that?" asked Hector.

He had set the lamp down but was still standing in front of the door. If Andromache didn't answer him, he might stay there all night, just to torment her. "You remember Demuchus?" she asked. Her words were muffled by the curtain of hair over her face.

Hector grunted.

"Then I shouldn't have to explain it!" Andromache's voice rose in frustration. It must give him pleasure, to watch her demean herself this way! "He wanted me, but I was disgusted by him. Now *I'm* like Demuchus, and you're like —"

"You're *nothing* like Demuchus," said Hector.

"Oh, *thanks*!" hissed Andromache. Her wound was far too deep to be soothed by such paltry consolation. "What are you doing here?"

"Making sure you're all right. You had me so worried." Hector had the audacity to sound reproachful. "I looked all over the city for you. I had them shut the gates. I never thought you'd be here."

Oh, I'll bet he was worried! thought Andromache. *Worried about explaining to his parents why I'd gone missing!* "Well, I'm fine!" she snapped. "So you can go."

Hector paused. "I saw Lee, today, after — after you left."

Lee, who had loved Hector all along! Andromache's cheeks flamed, and she kicked at the ground. "Oh, good!" she said. "I hope things went better for *her!*"

Ignoring both comment and kick, Hector continued. "She said she'd seen you — and that you looked terrible —"

"How *nice* of her!" Andromache flared.

"Hurt," Hector clarified hastily. "Bleeding. Crying. And — and something about a donkey."

Certain that she would die of ridicule, Andromache shrank downward, toward the chest.

Hector went on. "She said you ran away from her —"

"Obviously not fast enough!"

"— and that you seemed really upset."

"Upset?" shrieked Andromache. "Of course I was upset! I thought you were *dead!*"

Hector blanched. "That's what she was afraid of — that you hadn't heard her. She was trying to tell you that I was coming back another way."

Blood rushed to Andromache's ears. She buried her face in her hands. *That* was what Penthesilea had been trying to say? If only Andromache had heard her — if only she'd listened! — she never would have gone to the outpost stable, and the whole abominable scene there would have been avoided! If only she'd listened to Penthesilea, she wouldn't have disgraced herself! She wouldn't now be forced to leave Troy!

(*It wasn't just* Penthesilea *you ignored,*) sneered the Voice. (*Everyone at the gate would have been screaming if* Hector *had actually died.*)

The Voice was right. Of course it was! If only she'd stopped to *think!* "No," murmured Andromache. "I didn't hear her." She sniffled several times. "I'm so stupid…"

"No — <u>Ahndromahk</u>, no, it's *me* who's stupid," Hector said softly. "It's all my fault! I told her I was going back through the tunnel to talk to the guards and make sure there hadn't been any problems."

Andromache stared up at him in horror. "*Have* there been?"

"No," he assured her. "No. The city is safe."

"The guards never saw any —"

"I never expected them to." Hector sighed. "I lied to Lee about why I was going there."

"What *were* you doing, then?" Andromache didn't bother to mask the combative note in her voice. What did she have to lose, at this point, when she'd already lost her self-respect, her home, and Hector?

"I needed to be alone," he said.

Something in his tone stilled Andromache's anger. "Because of your head?" she asked, more gently. She could now see just how hideous his wound was, with the crooked, sewn-up gash, the bruises, and the scrapes. No wonder he'd hidden in the outpost stable! The din at the city gates would have been agonizing for him.

Hector looked away. "Yes, my head. I wasn't myself."

"I'm sorry," whispered Andromache. "I-I didn't mean to bother you."

"You could never bother me," said Hector, turning back toward her. He fixed her with his somber eyes and asked, "Why were you bleeding?"

"What?"

"Lee said your hands and knees were bleeding. Was it because of the donkey?"

Incensed once more, Andromache didn't answer.

Hector persisted. "Did it kick you?"

"No!"

"Bite you?"

"No — no — *no!*" She flushed a furious shade of red. "I ran into the damn donkey and fell down. That's it!"

"And that's why you were bleeding?"

Andromache sighed. What did it matter, after the way she'd thrown herself at him, earlier? Maybe once he heard the whole story, he would finally have his fill of her misery and leave. "I was in the exercise arena, and I heard some people say that the army was back. I fell down when I was running out to find you."

Hector looked stricken. "Let me see," he murmured.

"It's just a few scrapes."

"Let me see." He knelt down beside her and gently took her hands.

As he examined them, she could feel his breath — and then his fingers — grazing the hurt places. Her mutinous skin tingled where he was touching her. "Don't," she whispered, pulling back from him. "I'm fine."

Hector shook his head. "You're *hurt*," he said. "And heat-sick, too. Cassandra told me. You were out there in the sun, running around, and —"

"It's my own fault," Andromache interrupted. She wasn't going to let him have an excuse to feel guilty! "Everything's my own fault! I have no one to blame but myself. I ran too fast. I stayed out in the sun too long. I bumped into a donkey because I wasn't watching where I was going." She fought back tears. "And I read too much into our friendship. I got carried away, seeing things that weren't there. It's —"

"Ahndromahk, no!" cried Hector. "They're there — they've *always* been there!"

Her tears began to fall. She covered her face to hide them and whispered once more, "Don't!"

"Ahndromahk…"

She let out a sob.

"Ahndromahk, look at me." He pulled her hands away from her face. "I love you."

Andromache blinked. Through her veil of tears, she saw the blurred lines of a face that had never looked more serious. More truthful. More sincere. But —

"I've *always* loved you, ever since you came to Troy."

Always? She stared at him. *Always?*

"Always!" he said again. "I just couldn't tell you. Not right away. You would've thought I was crazy! We hardly knew each other. Besides, after everything that had happened to you, I thought you'd want space. Time to think things through. Time to be mad. It took you months to smile, Ahndromahk, let alone to laugh. I didn't see how it would help you to have some man chasing after you."

Hector was right. She'd been a wreck! Always crying, always cringing — and, worst of all, terrified of *him*. If he'd told her that he loved her, back then, she probably would have shattered to bits.

"But there'd be these moments, these looks," he said, his voice lowering. "It all made me think, *Just be patient — wait for the right time.'* So I waited. But then, whenever I thought the time had come, something would happen. You'd get a boyfriend, or we'd have a fight, or I'd have to leave."

Andromache thought back to their encounter in Hector's storage shed. *Not now,* she'd warned herself. *Don't tell him you love him right before he leaves. Now's not a good time...*

"I shouldn't have worried about timing," Hector said bleakly. "It all came out in the worst way, anyway. I was filthy. I was a mess. I wasn't myself."

You were alive, thought Andromache. In her mind, she still saw the nightmare images of Hector. *His body slack and soft, carried back into Troy on a blanket — his hair falling out — his voice gone — his laughter gone —*

"I was humiliated," he said. "To have you find me like that — you, of all people!"

Drooling — flabby — his mind gone —

"Then you said the most beautiful things — things I wanted more than anything to hear! And I —" He winced. "I yelled at you. I ruined everything. I don't blame you for hating me."

Did she hate him?

"But I just — I— you deserved to know the truth. That's why I came here tonight..."

How could she hate him? He was there, before her, safe and alive. He was there, with his dark, familiar hair — his warm, familiar voice — his green, familiar smell. He was there, and he loved her, and he always had. Andromache started to cry. Without another thought, she leaned into him, her lips just touching his. There was a flare of heat. She drew back and looked into his eyes.

Chapter 25

Andromache snuggled deeper into the dark warmth of her bed. She couldn't go downstairs, yet — the family might question why she was up so early, sick as she'd been the day before.

I could get dressed, though, she thought. *That way, I'll be ready to go when it's time*.

Peeking out from under the covers, she saw three or four dresses still lying on the floor. They were the dresses she'd been packing for her journey. She'd never gotten around to refolding them, let alone to leaving Troy…

Hector's eyes were wild. Her own were wild, too. For a long moment they looked at each other, their breath coming faster and faster — and then, he was kissing her.

At once, it became clear how trivial most other kisses were — even the one she'd seen Paris giving his girlfriend, long ago, in the stairway. For all its outward passion, that kiss had been empty of meaning. Paris, like some overstuffed rat, had abandoned his tidbit at the first sign of trouble: the clattering to earth of a poorly aimed shoe.

But with Hector, no mere shoe — not even all the shoes in Troy, falling in thunderous unison — could have made him scuttle from Andromache's side. He kissed her mouth, her neck, her shoulders, her arms, losing himself utterly to the caresses he'd been waiting two years to give her.

Two years! Why had they waited two years? How had they waited two years? Now that he was finally kissing her, Andromache never wanted him to stop. She wanted the kissing to go on forever, with Hector's arms tight around her, his lips and tongue teasing her skin. His tongue! His tongue…

After the slimy, repellent kiss Demuchus had once given her, Andromache had sworn off tongues. Nothing, she'd thought, could ever make her reconsider! But Hector knew how to kiss — and kiss — and kiss. She found herself melting, little by little, until at last, she slid partway off the clothing chest.

Hector steadied her. The shoulder of her dress slipped down.

'Oops,' he murmured, straightening the dress.

As he did, his fingers skimmed across her bare arm, and she nearly collapsed again. Oh gods! Her skin was burning. Her heart was racing, and she couldn't breathe. She couldn't *just keep kissing him —*

'Ector...' She leaned slightly away from him. Looking up into his eyes, she pulled the dress back down — farther, and on both sides, this time — and watched his expression change from bewilderment, to shock, to joy...

Andromache shrieked. Her daydream evaporated as cold rain blew through the window onto her face. Cold rain, in summer! She snapped the curtain shut and hurried into one of the dresses littering her floor. Still not warm enough, she threw on her grey woolen cloak as well and dove back under her blanket. When even this combination failed to stop her shivering, she tried to coax Cutie onto the bed with her. The dog turned her back on Andromache as if on a traitor.

Andromache smiled, unbothered by Cutie's ill will. It was late enough, now, wasn't it? She could go down to the kitchen, where it was warm — where there was a fire — where Hector might now be eating breakfast.

I could have breakfast with Ector...

That did it! Andromache was out of bed at once, unable to wait any longer to see him. With each stair step came a thought of him...

Their stumbling embrace toward the bed — Hector, heaving Cutie unceremoniously off of it — his clothes torn off — hers removed tenderly, little by little — his hands and lips all over her — different kissing — harder, faster kissing — a feeling, impossibly good; so good she dug her fingers into his shoulder and bruised it — and only then the whole lengths of their bodies touching — her arms around his back — her legs around his legs — his hips on her hips — his body moving inside her body — the whispered love word, 'Ahndromahk...'

There was a kettle bubbling over a fire in the kitchen hearth, although Andromache saw no one tending it. *He's been here*, she thought. *And I bet he'll be right back. I'll wait for him.* As she stood beside the shelf, tracing a cup with her fingertips, she imagined sitting in the warm kitchen with Hector — pouring a hot drink for Hector...

Lying in bed with Hector on top of her, his arms strewn about her shoulders. He seemed to be sleeping. He was heavy, but she didn't want him to move. Not ever.

She ran her fingers through his hair and listened to the music drifting up from the courtyard. It was — well, 'pretty' wasn't quite the right word. 'Fun,' maybe, and definitely 'familiar.' If the singer would just sing a little louder, so she could hear the —

A giggle caught in the back of her throat as she recognized the tune. A drinking song! A filthy, lecherous, and undeniably catchy drinking song. She giggled again and began drumming her fingers against Hector's scalp, keeping time to the music.

The next thing she knew, the lyrics were resonating against her shoulder as well as coming in through the window. Hector was awake. Andromache marched her fingers up and down his spine, hopping from vertebra to vertebra.

He writhed — or rather, wrenched — away from her touch.

He's ticklish! Andromache realized. Her legs were still wrapped around his. He couldn't get away! Giggling, she tickled him again, until he finally ended the torment by pinning her wrists to the bed. She closed her eyes, bracing for payback.

Nothing.

When at last she opened one cautious eye, she saw that he was staring down at her — bending toward her — kissing her —

Andromache gasped at the sudden sound of footsteps. A tall, dark-haired man came into her peripheral vision, and she turned, dewy-eyed, to face him.

"We-ell!" crowed Paris. "Hello to you, too! Is there a kiss with that?" He offered her a set of noxiously pursed lips.

Andromache blocked them with her hand. "Go cook yourself an egg!"

"What's with the look, then, Hermie?"

"I'm just in a good mood," she said, her expression turning guilty.

"I'll say," Paris said slyly. "The night has done wonders for you."

Had Paris seen something? Someone leaving her room, for instance? Anxiously, she cried, "What's *that* supposed to mean?"

"Sleep, Hermie," Paris explained. "You obviously needed some, after getting sick yesterday."

"Oh, *that!*" Andromache sighed in relief. "Yes. I feel much better now."

Paris raised an eyebrow but said nothing further. He took the cup she'd been caressing and filled it with liquid from the kettle.

"What is it, wine?" Andromache wrinkled her nose.

Paris laughed. "Just hot water, mint leaves, and a few other herbs. A new concoction. I think you'll like it, partial as you are to the taste of *mint.*"

A singular shade of crimson stained Andromache's cheeks. She moved closer to the fire's heat, hoping to camouflage her blush.

Paris went on as though he hadn't noticed anything: "And, of course, it settles the stomach."

First blowing over the cup to cool its contents, Andromache took a small sip. "That's good!" she said.

"You don't have to sound surprised, Hermie."

"Sorry." She was far too happy to quarrel. Dishes heaped with food sat before her. The beverage was warming her insides while the fire blazed at her back. Best of all, Hector would soon be there with her…

Hector was lying beside her, facing her, gently stroking her hair. She was in bliss.

'You ahre smiling,' he whispered.

'This is perfect,' she whispered back.

'Perfect…'

'Except — '

'Yes?'

'Except I could really go for a jelly tart.' Andromache smiled again, thinking back to when she was ten, walking through the market, peppering her mom with questions she now knew the answers to.

'I can get this fohr you,' offered Hector.

'No, don't,' said Andromache, laughing softly. *'It was just a joke. I don't want you to leave.'* Not for any reason! If he went downstairs, one of the guests would almost certainly trap him, and she wouldn't see him again till morning. The thought of the partygoers then gave her a twinge of guilt. *'Do you think they're missing you?'* she asked. *'Downstairs, I mean.'*

In response, Hector ran his fingers from her shoulder to her hip, whispering, *'You haff the skin the softest ohff the world.'*

She blushed — and forgot all about the party, as Hector had no doubt meant her to do. The wind outside grew cooler. She shivered, and he pulled a blanket over them.

'Stripey?' he asked.

Her cheeks burned. *'Stripey,'* she admitted.

'I lahff this Stripey,' he said, with such tenderness that she asked drily: *'Do you want me to leave you alone with it?'*

He laughed. *'I am serious.'*

'I love it, too. Cassandra gave it to me, the day Muka died.'

'No.'

'Yes. I was sleeping, and when I woke up, Stripey was there.'

'Me, I did this,' said Hector.

'You?'

He nodded. *'I bring it, then leaff quick.'*

'But why?'

'Becahse I am not supposed to be in your room,' he said demurely.

Andromache shook her head. *'Not "why did you leave quickly." I meant, "why did you bring it to me?"'*

'Becahse I take — took — yours.' Hector had, in effect, taken her blanket to use as a shroud for her first dog, Muka. He went on: *'So, I giff to you mine.'*

'Your old one?' she teased, stroking the worn fabric.

'My best one,' he corrected. He pressed the blanket to her skin with his hand. *'The softest one.'*

With those words, Andromache finally understood why Hector always wore threadbare clothes, despite his family's wealth. It wasn't out of laziness or rebellion, but because he liked the texture. Only the softest cloth would do, and nothing — neither his mom's complaints, nor Demuchus's jeering — could dissuade him. She realized, too, what a sacrifice it must have been, to give up a blanket that he'd spent years breaking in...to have to start over with a new, scratchy one. If that wasn't love, she didn't know what was. *'I can't believe you did that,'* she murmured, kissing him.

'I — oh — well — ' he spluttered, surprised at the warmth of her response. 'It's nothing. You needed a blanket, and I didn't know how else to help you.'

'You helped me bury Muka.' He'd carried the large dog all the way down to the sea...

'I mean after, back at the house. You were crying so hard.'

Andromache vividly remembered coming inside, slumping against the front door, and sobbing for what felt like hours. At the time, she'd thought Muka was the last being on earth who loved her. 'You heard me crying?' she asked.

Hector nodded.

'But I thought you left after you dropped me off there.'

'I didn't leave,' he said. 'I stayed outside the front door.'

'For how long?'

'Pretty much the whole day, except when my sister was taking you upstairs. That's when I got — um, Stripey — from my room.'

Andromache gaped at him. 'You sat there in the cold, all day? But why?'

'Because.' He hugged her fiercely. 'I was worried about you. When we were down by the sea, you looked at it like you wanted to jump in. I had to make sure you didn't leave the house again, just in case.'

Andromache lowered her eyes in shame. He was right about how she'd been feeling, that day — and he'd sat outside for hours in the cold spring air to protect her from herself. 'You froze for me,' she said solemnly.

'It wasn't that bad.'

'That's why your face was raw, that night,' she whispered, looking at him once more. 'I-I thought it was because you'd gone out riding, but you didn't. You froze for me!'

Hector's eyes darkened. 'It was worth it. That was the night you told me you liked me.'

'I did?'

'You don't remember? At the dinner table? You mouthed it.'

And then, Andromache remembered — she remembered mouthing "Thank you," and Hector mouthing it back — except that he'd apparently seen "Like you," and mouthed that back. She remembered the bright smile he'd given her...

'You remember,' he declared, stroking her hair.

She nodded. Why take away something that made him happy, when the truth was she had liked him, then, anyway?

'I was relieved when you said that,' he murmured. 'You seemed mad at me when you first came to dinner.'

'I was,' she admitted. 'I was mad that you left me by the door, after we buried Muka. I know — I shouldn't have been mad. I had no right to be. You'd done so much for me already, that day, but — '

'But what?'

'But I really wanted you to come in and sit with me. Why didn't you? It would have been a lot easier than freezing to death on the doorstep.'

Hector gave a strange laugh. 'I was afraid you'd want me to put my arm around you, like Paris did that morning.'

Andromache remembered the comforting hug Paris had given her; Hector, meanwhile, had barely patted her hand.

'I remembered what it was like to hold you,' he went on, 'and I was afraid — '

"Remembered?"' Andromache interrupted. 'What do you mean, "remembered?" You never held me before tonight.'

Hector shook his head. 'There was one other time.'

'When?'

'The night you came to Troy.'

Andromache blinked. On her first night in Troy, she'd been sick and traumatized. Her village had just been burned by raiders, and she'd been terrified of anyone in armor — particularly Hector. Surely she would have remembered being held by him, that night!

'Lee brought you to the house,' said Hector, seeing Andromache's confusion. 'There was a council meeting going on, down in the banquet hall.'

'I remember that.'

'They asked you some questions.'

Andromache nodded.

'But you were too sick and hurt to make it through the meeting.'

'I passed out.'

'Yes,' said Hector. 'And then I carried you upstairs, so Mom could take care of you.'

Andromache felt stupid. Sometime after collapsing in the banquet hall, she'd awoken in a bed on the second floor. It had never occurred to her to ask how she'd gotten there. 'You carried me,' she whispered.

He nodded. 'I carried you. I held you. Your cheek was on my shoulder, and my cheek was touching your hair. You were hanging onto my neck with your poor bruised, burned arms. When I laid you on the bed, you didn't want to let go. I had to tear away.' Pause. 'I didn't want to, Ahndromahk. I wanted to stay there and hold you while you slept...'

'But you left?'

'Of course I left! Mom came in and yelled at me. "Hector, thank you. You've done your part — now, get out, so I can bathe the poor girl!" *'*

'I don't remember any of this.' Andromache chewed her lip.

'I know,' said Hector. 'You were pretty out of it. And I know the only reason you held on like that was because you didn't want to be alone. You were scared. But me — ' He took a deep breath. 'Oh, <u>Ahndromahk</u>! That council meeting was so loud! Everyone was yelling, everyone was screaming, everyone was shouting. Then I held you, and the world went quiet. I wanted to be yours.'

Andromache didn't know what to say. She was startled — humbled.

'So that's why I didn't come in to sit with you, the day Muka died,' said Hector. 'I was afraid you'd want me to put my arm around you, and I'd feel like I did the first time I held you. I was afraid you'd know — and it would freak you out. I was afraid of doing even stupider things, too, like kissing you. I could only imagine what would have happened if you were sitting there crying, and clinging to me, and your face was so close to mine...'

'Maybe I wouldn't have minded,' murmured Andromache. 'I felt so sad and lonely, that day. A kiss would've been nice.'

'You mean a comfort kiss,' Hector said scornfully. 'I wanted to give you a love kiss, <u>Ahndromahk</u>, not a comfort kiss.'

'What's the difference?'

Rather than explaining, Hector gave her two kisses. The first was pleasant; the second, volcanic.

'<u>I see what you mean</u>,' she sighed.

Hector smiled, showing a dimple Andromache had never seen before.

She burrowed closer to him and said, '<u>You should give me lots of kisses now, to make up for the ones you couldn't give that day</u>.'

'<u>How many do you want</u>?' he asked.

'<u>A thousand.</u>'

He kissed her.

'<u>Two thousand</u> — '

"Ahem!" Paris coughed. "I said, what do you think?"

"A-about what?" asked Andromache. *About comfort kisses?* she mused. *Love kisses?*

Paris raised an eyebrow at her. "Well, you're certainly on the moon, today! I asked you what you thought about the parties —

whether they're better when everyone's jammed together in the banquet hall, or when some people go out onto the courtyard."

"Oh. I don't know," she said. "They're both fine."

"That's what I love most about you, Hermie — your strong opinions."

Andromache shrugged. "Was it nice?" she asked innocently. "The party, I mean?"

"So-so. My parents set out plenty of wine, so no problem there. The music wasn't bad, at least once *I* joined in — and some of my sister's friends looked pretty sexy." Paris paused to let Andromache scold him. She gave a token roll of the eyes, and he went on with his story: "The guest of honor was definitely at his most charming after he left. Early on, he planted himself by the door to the entry hall. He just sat there, ready to bolt, and hardly said a word to anyone. At some point he disappeared, but like I said, that was no great loss to the party. At least we didn't have to listen to his grunting." With that, Paris tossed a dried fig up into the air and caught it in his mouth.

"How many hours did you waste perfecting *that* little trick?" Andromache asked venomously. She suspected the truth of what Hector had been up to, guarding the only exit so she couldn't slip out, just as he'd done the day of Muka's burial. He deserved better than mockery for it.

Paris's retort was slowed by the half-chewed fig. Before he could answer, his mother and sister had swept into the kitchen.

"Oh, who knows!" Hecuba was saying. "Who *ever* knows! Don't waste your time speculating, Cassandra. And, while we're at it, don't say '*girlfriend.*' It sounds crass. People quarrel, after all, if indeed that's what happened. I'm sure it — oh, good morning, you two." Hecuba interrupted herself to give a pleasant smile to Andromache. "How are you feeling, dear? We were so worried about you."

Andromache felt a stab of guilt. She was saved having to answer, though, when Hecuba fixed a stern eye on Paris. He smiled back in his most disarming way.

"Tisane, Mom?" he asked.

Caught off guard, Hecuba stammered, "Oh — oh, well, yes. Thank you, dear. Can you *believe* the weather we're having?" She sniffed, frowning out the window as if personally insulted by the rain.

While Paris poured his mother a drink, Cassandra skipped over and hugged Andromache. "You look so much better than yesterday!" she sang. "You just needed some sleep."

"Mm-hmm," said Andromache, avoiding Cassandra's gaze. The family members were multiplying around her, but still no Hector. Where was he? He should be there, by now. She loved these people — all of them, even Paris — but they had become *her lover's family!* She didn't know how to relate to them, now! None of the love poems she'd read in the library could help her. They had scads of useless information about perfumeries of the evening wind and honey in the glint of a lover's eye, and even warnings for those who would fall in love with their family's bitter enemy. Not a single text, however, gave advice on what to do if the lover's family was kind but nosy — and one *lived* with them.

"Here, Songbird." Paris gave his sister a hug and her own cup of tisane. "Where's Dad?"

"Down at the temple," said Hecuba.

"Is he putting in an order for new weather, I hope?"

Hecuba cast her son a glare that matched the rain chill for chill. "Just see that there's enough tisane for when he comes back! He'll be frigorified." Muttering, she added, "The way the men in this family disappear!"

Another wave of guilt shot through Andromache's stomach.

Paris rose obediently from his seat and began fussing with the pot of hot water, while Cassandra interrogated her mother about the agenda for that evening's council meeting. For the next half-hour or so, Hecuba chatted with her two children while Andromache shoveled food into her mouth and daydreamed contentedly…

Hector was curled around her back, holding her tightly with one arm. Against her neck, she could feel the ridgeline of his nose. She was warm even though Stripey had been kicked to the foot of the bed. Stripey…

'Ector?' she asked, skimming her fingers over his arm.

'Hmm?'

'Are there any other things like the blanket?'

'You mean what? Warm fings?'

She smiled. 'Other love secrets, like the way you came to bring me the blanket.'

Hector brushed his lips against the nape of her neck and breathed deeply. 'Purple flowers,' he murmured. 'On your hair. On your skin. Always around you. So beautiful.'

She flushed with pleasure at the fact that he'd noticed — and liked — her perfume. This time, though, she didn't let herself be diverted by his compliment. 'Tell me another love secret.'

He cleared his throat. 'You know that day when I come home, after I am away — wiff the ahrmy?'

'Which time?'

'The first time. When I see you near to the door.'

'I remember,' she said softly. 'You came in when I was sweeping the entry hall, before your party.'

'Yes. And you ahre so pretty, and I miss you so mahch, that almost, I kiss you.'

She turned over to face him. 'Which kind of kiss? Comfort or love?'

He laughed. 'Lahff, ohff couhrse!'

'But you didn't do it.'

'No. Too soon, Dad is there. But if only he is not there, no pahrty fohr you and me...'

Hector was joking about that last part, but Andromache wondered what would have happened if he'd kissed her back then. She hadn't been nearly as close to him; officially, they weren't even friends yet. Would she have slapped him? Or just stood there, looking foolish? That seemed a likely option! But then she thought back to that night, and how strange Hector had made her feel. Maybe he was right about skipping the party...

'What if we'd gone to the river?' she asked abruptly. 'If we'd gone down there alone together, would you have kissed me?'

'Ohff couhrse!' he said, as though she should have known better than to ask.

'I wasn't sure you wanted to,' she teased. 'The night before, you invited your sister along, to chaperone!'

'An accident!' Hector groaned. 'I am so nerffous, that night, I do not know what I am saying!'

'I got nervous, too, sometimes,' said Andromache.

'When, fohr example?'

'For example, when we were sitting on the staircase.'

'You mean when you touch me on my ahrm?'

She nodded. 'I was a wreck, that night. I could barely talk to you! Don't you remember that awful conversation we had? I thought you were crazy for not leaving sooner.'

Hector laughed.

'What's so funny?'

'Oh, <u>Ahndromahk</u>! It really was an awful conversation.'

'I know!'

He laughed again, then said, 'The reason I stayed was so I wouldn't embarrass myself by standing up.'

Andromache's cheeks flushed crimson as she realized what he meant. 'Because I touched your arm?' she whispered. 'That's all it took?'

Hector caught her arm and returned the caress she'd given him months earlier.

'Oh,' she murmured in surprise. <u>'That's…nice.'</u>

<u>'You see?'</u> he asked, adding his lips and tongue.

<u>'I see,'</u> she sighed. <u>'I see…'</u>

Hector kissed upward from her elbow to her shoulder. When his lips reached her neck, she gave a soft sigh. She wanted him to keep kissing her, but she was also curious about something. <u>'Ector?'</u> she asked.

'Hmm?'

<u>'Were there any other times you were</u> — embarrassed — <u>by me?'</u>

He smiled a contented smile and lay back against the pillows. 'Oh, <u>Ahndromahk</u>! Constantly. Like a fifteen-year-old boy.'

With that, he fell silent, leaving Andromache to assume that fifteen was the pinnacle of embarrassment for boys. She smiled to herself and gently began running her fingers over his forearm. <u>'Ector?'</u> she whispered.

'Hmm?'

<u>'Are you getting</u> — embarrassed — <u>now?'</u>

He laughed and hugged her with the arm she'd been caressing. 'Oh, my sweetheart! I'm exhausted.'

'Oh.'

'Aren't you?'

She nodded. In fact, she wasn't tired, but she loved the thought of lying in Hector's arms. <u>'I'll get the blanket,'</u> she whispered, sitting up to retrieve it.

She meant to cover Hector and let him sleep. She did! But just as she was about to draw the blanket over his body, she stopped. Until now, she hadn't really had a chance to look at him. She'd seen him many hundreds of times, of course, but never like this, bare in the flickering lamp light. There was the darkness of his hair against her pillow — the lighter brown of his arms and shoulders — the rise and fall of his chest — the valley between his ribs — his hard stomach — the divot of his belly button —

He coughed.

Startled, Andromache turned her face back up to his. His eyes were open. Perhaps he'd begun to feel chilly, blanketless as he was, or perhaps he'd felt her staring. Either way, he was now fixing her with his own curious gaze.

'I like how you look,' she blurted.

His dimple appeared. 'I lahke how you look, too.'

Andromache felt herself blushing. 'Ector?' she murmured.

'Hmm?'

'You're embarrassing me…'

Andromache's pulse raced. She imagined pressing her hands to Hector's chest — feeling the heat of his hands, covering hers — stretching out on top of him — kissing him — making him forget his exhaustion —

Meanwhile, the voices of his family droned on around her.

"…council…what…need to read?"

"No, no…rest. Whereas you, Paris, must…"

"…market? …kidding me? …rain!"

"Well, who else…"

"…not crazy!"

A hush fell over the voices.

"Did you hear that?" asked Hecuba. "Someone just came in the front door. It must be your father. Priam?" she called out.

"No, Mom," came the reply. "It's me."

Andromache, who had just seized an apricot, now dropped it. *Ector!* He was there, at last! She sat on her hands, hoping to hide their trembling from Paris's eagle eye. *Stay calm! They aren't supposed to know, yet,* she reminded herself. *He made that clear when he left your room this morning. He said that no one would know he'd been there.*

"Hector!" cried Hecuba, sounding delighted. "Come in here, dear, sit by the fire! Have something hot to drink. Paris!" she barked. "Get your brother a cup of tisane."

Paris sighed but shuffled over to the fire.

As Hector's footsteps came closer, Andromache dove suddenly for the fallen apricot. *I'm not ready for this! I'm not ready for this! They'll know as soon as he's in here, and then what will they say? Will they hate me? Will they kick me out, even in the rain?* She peeked out from behind the table to watch Hector enter the room.

"Hi, Mom," he said, walking over to Hecuba and bending to kiss her cheek. With a cluck of mild reproof, she smoothed his rain-dark hair. Cassandra threw her arms around him, heedless of his soggy clothes. Even Paris looked welcoming as he passed Hector the tisane.

In all of the hubbub, Hector hadn't yet seen Andromache, crouched behind the table, clutching the now-bruised apricot to her chest. What would happen once he spied her there? What would happen to him — to his family — to *her*?

"It's nice to see you for breakfast, like this," said Hecuba. "Sit, sit. Have something to eat."

"Mom, I just came home to change clothes. The rain —"

"Hector, sit *down*, since you had to leave the party so early last night." Hecuba took an imperious tone. "Sit with your family. We're all here except your father, and he'll be back soon. For goodness' sake, even Andromache is feeling well enough to join us, although — now, where did she go? Oh, there you are. What on earth are you doing, hunched behind the table like that? You aren't vomiting, are you, dear?"

"No!" cried Andromache, aggrieved. *Vomiting!*

Hector was now facing her. His cheeks looked hollow, and the grey circles beneath his eyes had darkened. The eyes themselves were blank, and they refused to make contact with hers.

Andromache felt a hornet stirring inside her belly. *He won't look at me because then everyone would know, and we're not ready for that yet,* she told herself. It was for that same reason that Hector had left her room so early. And yet — how her stomach churned at the thought! — wasn't he taking things a step too far? He looked almost as miserable as he had the day before, when she'd found him in the outpost stable. *He's just acting,* she told herself. *Acting!*

As he so often did, Paris made a bad situation worse for her. "Hurry," he said to Hector. "You'd better sit down, if you want something to eat. Hermie's been gobbling everything in sight!"

"That's not true!" Andromache bristled. *Vomiting* and *gobbling,* just when she most wanted to feel delicate — graceful — attractive! Thrusting the apricot behind her, she returned to her seat.

"How many plates have you had?" Paris demanded.

"I — who cares?"

"It's a lot, anyway."

"I didn't eat much, yesterday," she snapped, hoping her answer would satisfy Paris and shut him up.

"Of course she didn't!" Cassandra declared. "She was heat-sick. People don't eat when they're heat-sick."

"Heat-sick," Hector muttered. He didn't look at Andromache's face, although his eyes flicked briefly to her hands. He sat down at last, on the far side of the table.

He's acting, she repeated silently, to quell the hornets buzzing around in her stomach. *One look would give us away!*

"Honestly, you three, she's looking peaked again! Give the poor girl a moment's peace. In any case, none of us will be suffering from heat-sickness today." Hecuba made the pronouncement with a grim sort of satisfaction. She then turned back to her eldest son. "How's your head?" she asked, frowning at the crooked gash on his temple.

"Fine," he said dully.

Andromache's heart stirred with compassion and relief. *Ah!* she thought. The wound was clean and stitched but still fresh. Still sore. And Hector had spent a whole night without soothing salve or poultices! Of *course* his head was hurting him! No wonder he looked so grey!

Hecuba tried again to engage him in conversation. "What have you been up to this morning?"

"Not much."

Hecuba sighed. "Hector," she began tentatively, "I've been thinking maybe it would be nice for you if you stayed with your uncle for a while. I know he'd love to see you, and — and —"

Hector said nothing, allowing his mother to stammer on.

"It would be good for you," she finished, showing a rare amount of strain. "I'm — well, I'm concerned about you, about your health. I know you have your duties here, but surely someone can take care of them. The opportunity to relax a little —"

"Fine, Mom," said Hector, more listlessly than before.

"Oh. Well, then," spluttered Hecuba, blinking in surprise. She seemed to have been expecting a fight.

Andromache sucked in her breath. Hornets were bombarding her insides. Hector's head wasn't the problem, no! He just didn't love her, after all! He couldn't possibly love her, if he was willing to travel to Santiya to visit his uncle! *No! It's part of the act!* she told herself. *He's not really going!* Desperately, she sought his eyes, hoping he might wink at her — *something!* — but his gaze remained fixed on the table.

It was then that a terrifying new thought struck Andromache: had she dreamed it all? Had the night before been nothing but the delusion of a heat-sick mind? Had none of it — the secrets, the jokes, let alone the kissing, the loving — been real?

It was real! she told herself frantically. *It had to be! I could never have thought up everything he told me, or everything that happened!*

"I should get going," muttered Hector.

(*It doesn't matter whether it was real or not,*) the snide Voice inside Andromache's head piped up. (*Either way, he obviously hates you now.*)

Shut up! thought Andromache, but without much force.

"Well, it was nice to see you, dear," Hecuba said gently. "We didn't expect you till later this evening, for the meeting. I assumed you'd be off with —" She cleared her throat. "With your comrades."

"Oh. I'm working alone today," said Hector.

"Ah!" said Paris.

"Ah, what?" snapped Hector.

"Cassandra thinks you had a spat with a certain — *comrade,*" Paris explained. "And now I'm thinking she must be right."

"Paris!" Cassandra gasped in outrage. "I never said —"

"Hush, both of you!" barked Hecuba.

Hector had gone back to staring at the table. Meanwhile, the hornets were roiling inside Andromache. Who else could Paris have meant but Penthesilea? He'd said that just to torment her, yet Hector wasn't protesting — wasn't telling Paris to shut up — wasn't reassuring her — wasn't saying anything at all!

Hecuba drew a deep breath. "Hector, dear," she said, her voice low and soothing, "If you *have* had a quarrel, all the more reason to see your uncle — he might be able to help you with that."

Wordlessly, Hector closed his eyes; Andromache blinked hard to keep from crying.

Sighing, Hecuba added, "He must know her as well as anyone. He's the one who introduced you to her, and he'd probably have the best advice regarding your — *fiancée.*"

"Enough!" bawled Hector.

Andromache blinked again, this time in relief. Oh, this was progress! He *had* to tell them, now. *You've got it wrong, Mom. Andromache is the one. We love each other. I slept in her room last night, and I'm going to again tonight. Every night.* His family could make all the impertinent remarks they wanted! Andromache didn't care what they said, if it meant that Hector would be hers again!

"Hector, dear, what's the matter?"

"Dammit, Mom!"

"Watch your language!"

"Fine. Dammit, *Mother*! I don't want to hear another word about my so-called fiancée!"

"So you *have* had a quarrel!"

"No — no — *no*! There was no quarrel, and no fiancée! On the heads of a thousand courtyard chickens, Lee — Penthesilea — is just my *colleague*!"

Hecuba frowned. "But my brother sent her here —"

"To *fight* with me!" Hector interrupted. "In the army! To be my combat partner, my left hand on the battlefield! And that's all she's ever been!"

Andromache choked down a sob. Even though Hector had denied loving Penthesilea, he hadn't admitted to loving *her*. The Voice must be right after all.

"Oh," said Hecuba, nonplussed but not displeased. "Your colleague. I see."

"I knew it!" crowed Paris. "That woman's a *goddess*! I always thought you were aiming too high!"

"Yes," Hector said scathingly. "Oh, yes — why don't *you* enlighten us on the subject of *aiming*."

"Oh, *both* of you, for the sake of all that spins!" their mother exclaimed in disgust.

"Sorry, Mom." Paris pretended to be chastened.

Hector looked as though he'd just swallowed a prickle plant. "I have to get to the stables," he grunted. Without another word, he walked out the door to the banquet hall.

Helplessly, Andromache watched him leave. He was gone — not just from the room, but from *her*. Angry hornets swept through her insides, stinging her mercilessly. Hector was gone.

Unable to vent her irritation directly on Hector, Hecuba griped, "And after all that, he didn't even remember to change his clothes! I suppose he'll come back an icicle and blame me for that, as well!"

"I could heat more water, Mom," offered Paris.

"That would be a start." Hecuba sniffed.

"You know, at first I thought I was really going to like this tisane. But now that I've *had* it —" Paris looked squarely at Andromache. "I guess I don't."

Andromache's face turned bright red. She shot up from the table.

"Andromache?" asked Hecuba. "What's wrong?"

"Still sick," she mumbled. "Need rest."

"Of course, dear. Go. Get some sleep."

Once in the banquet hall, though, Andromache didn't head for the stairway. Instead, she turned to leave the house. *Liar!* she thought at Paris as she made her way through the streets. *Ignoramus! You don't know anything about* anything! Whatever Paris had seen or guessed, he had no idea how things really were between her and Hector. He had *no idea!*

'I thought I was really going to like this tisane. But now that I've had *it —* '

Oh, she was furious! If Paris thought he'd crushed her, he was wrong — his nasty remark had only opened her eyes. If Hector had wanted to toss her aside, he could have left her room after the first time — or the second — or the third — let alone the fourth! — rather than staying to hold her, and kiss her, and talk to her, and fall asleep beside her.

(Then why is he so miserable?) asked the snide Voice.

Andromache gritted her teeth. *That* was all she needed, a lecture from the Voice! She couldn't just tune it out, though. It was right. Hector was definitely miserable. The gloom had been no act.

Still that doesn't mean he's miserable about me! she retorted. Something else must have happened to Hector, and now she had to find him! She hoped he was still in the stables. If only the rain would let up, so she could get there faster — she'd never seen such a downpour! Water was streaming over the tops of her feet and up her calves. With every step, the hem of her sodden cloak thwacked against her shins, half tripping her. She was thoroughly soaked by the time she reached the stables.

Several horses whinnied when she entered, but no guard came to greet her. In fact, the place looked deserted. Andromache frowned. Surely Hector wouldn't have left the stables unattended! That wasn't like him — not that she could be certain of what was like him, anymore! But no, if the guards weren't there, then he *must* be. Unless — oh gods! What if he was sick again? He might be crouched on the floor — vomiting — in pain! He might have fainted!

"<u>Ector</u>?" she called out.

Nothing.

<u>Where</u> is <u>he</u>? she thought frantically. The obvious place to start looking was Buzzy's stall. As she ran back toward it, she noticed several horses with fresh dabs of healing salve, a sign that Hector had recently passed by. Her panic eased a little. Rounding the corner of the leftmost aisle, she at last caught sight of Buzzy's stall, and her knees went weak with relief. Hector! He was there, engrossed in spreading salve on Buzzy's hide. He must not have heard her come in. "<u>Ector</u>?" she murmured.

Both Hector and Buzzy turned toward her. "I'm sorry," Hector said tonelessly, before Andromache could say another word. "It never should've happened."

Andromache reeled as though he'd slapped her. *Sorry?* she thought, in anguish. *Sorry?* So, Paris had been right after all!

(*<u>Of course he was</u>!*) sneered the Voice. (*Hector <u>doesn't want you</u>! He never wanted you, except maybe for a little fun. Paris <u>was right</u>. He knows men better than you. He knows Hector <u>better than you</u>. You don't know anything! You're just a —*)

<u>No</u>! Andromache shrieked at the Voice. Tears were welling in her eyes, and if Hector didn't want her anymore, then she was *not* going to let him see her cry! "Oh," she said aloud, and then, again, "Oh." What a fool she'd been, not to realize that this, too, would be taken from her, along with everything else good in her life! "You're sorry." *Sniff, sniff.* "Well — I'm sorry I wasn't up to your standards!"

Hector's eyes gave a momentary flare and then went flat. "Don't do this," he said hollowly, rubbing his forehead. "Don't say things you know I don't mean, just to be cruel."

Now, not only hurt but also confused, Andromache stammered, "I — I wasn't —"

"We both know why you're here," Hector broke in. "You spared me in front of my family, but now there's no one around. So get it over with."

Andromache was too appalled to speak.

"Then I'll say it for you." Hector's eyes glassed over, but beneath the dull surface, they were burning. "You do not want a screamy man."

Screamy man? Screamy man? What does that *mean?* "I don't understand!" cried Andromache. "What do you mean? I don't —"

Then, all at once, she did…

Just before sunrise, Hector gave a yell and shot bolt upright. He raised one hand to his temple while thrusting the other behind him, to steady himself. The second hand dug into Andromache's stomach.

Oh, gods! she thought, grimacing and curling into a ball. Never in her life had she felt such an urgent need to pee! What am I going to do? What am I going to do?!

Perhaps if she and Hector had been lovers for weeks instead of hours, she could simply have told him to excuse her for a moment. Even last night, in the midst of all the euphoria, it might have been possible. Now, though, the sun was coming up. Reality was setting in, and Andromache was too ashamed to tell him. He might be disgusted; he might never want to touch her or kiss her, ever again.

Miserably, she sat up and clamped her knees to her chest. While she was huddled there on the bed, she heard a rustling sound, followed by the squeak of her door. She looked up. Hector was halfway out into the hall. 'Don't worry,' he whispered. 'No one will know I was here.'

He was gone before she could reply, but that didn't matter — she understood. Morning had come. The family would soon be awake, and Hector didn't want to be seen leaving her room. He didn't want everyone to start gossiping.

Thank goodness, she sighed to herself. She wasn't ready to be talked about, yet. She wanted time to savor everything that had just happened.

More importantly, she was now alone. Hector had spared her the humiliation of having to tell him about her problem…

"Oh, gods," whispered Andromache. If she'd known what Hector was really thinking, she would have peed right there in front of him — she would have peed in front of the whole city, rather than letting him leave! "Oh, Ector — so you had a nightmare! That doesn't change how I feel about you." The words were bitter to say. How often had she dreamed of the comfort Hector could give *her* if she woke up screaming, without once thinking about how to comfort *him*?

"The look you gave me said it all," he croaked. "You were disgusted by me."

Andromache moaned. Oh, those moments the night before! The way Hector had looked at her, as though she were the love-liest, most exquisite being on earth! It hurt to throw that onto the fire, but she couldn't just stand there, watching him disinte-grate. "You don't understand," she murmured.

"Understand *what*?"

With dread, she said the fatal words: "I had to pee."

Hector blinked. "Pee?"

She nodded. "When you — your hand landed on my stom-ach, and — but I just *couldn't* tell you! I thought you'd never want to — to — kiss me ever again if you knew, and so I —"

Hector stared at her. His eyes had an odd look, as though he was about to cry. "Pee," he said. "You had to pee!"

She nodded again.

"You crazy woman!" His voice shook, then broke. "You crazy woman!"

Before she could respond, he was kissing her, hard — much harder than he had the night before. She kissed him back, seizing him with both hands to pull him in as close as she could.

The horses whickered in surprise when Andromache's sod-den cloak hit the floor, but neither she nor Hector turned to comfort them. By then, her dress was up around her hips and her legs were around his waist. She wasn't sure exactly how it all had happened, but she'd never felt so much like she was flying.

Chapter 26

Andromache slid her hand up Hector's arm, to his shoulder, and grazed the bruise there with her fingertips. "Still purple," he murmured.

She glanced up to see if she was hurting him. Far from it, he looked delighted. "Do you *like* being purple?" she asked, curling deeper into his lap and resting her head on his other shoulder.

He tightened his arms around her. "I lahke when *you* lahke," he said.

Her cheeks reddened. "I liked just now," she whispered shyly, in case he hadn't been able to tell.

His dimple popped out. "And I lahke your chest."

She blushed harder. "I've noticed."

"You can bring it. Downstairs."

"Of course," she said, furrowing her eyebrows. "It goes where I go."

Hector didn't notice her confusion; his dreamy expression never changed. "It is the first place that I kiss you."

Andromache shook her head and smiled obliquely. Favorite? Maybe, but not the first. "No, that was my lips. After that, you kissed me here." She pointed to her neck. "And here. And here." Her shoulders. Her arms. "Before you ever kissed my — uh — *chest*."

Hector's eyes opened wide. "What?"

"Breasts," she hissed. "You used the wrong word."

"I was talking about your furniture," he said, laughing. "The clothing chest in your room, where we sat...and kissed."

"Oh," Andromache said awkwardly. "Well, yes, in that case, you used the right word."

Hector's serene smile returned. "I thought so. If I'd meant '*breasts*,' I would've said <u>tatas</u>, like you taught me."

"What!" cried Andromache. "I never taught you *that*!"

"Then where did I learn it?"

"Maybe you just guessed and got lucky," said Andromache. "I shouldn't be surprised. You've always learned the bad words, first. Remember? '*Life is a bag of goat shit…* '"

"That's true," said Hector. "But there's *nothing* bad about <u>ta-tas</u> — especially yours." He eyed her as though she had no dress on.

Andromache blushed again. "Back to the clothing chest," she said. That subject, so risqué moments earlier, now seemed safe by comparison. "Why should I bring it downstairs?"

Hector stroked her hair, playing with the strands that had come loose from her braid. "Because, your room is nice and all, but I could never stay there. Your bed is horrible."

"No, it's not! I love my bed."

"It's like sleeping on a tree trunk — hard and thin."

"You didn't give it a fair chance," argued Andromache. "It's not like we slept much."

Hector kissed her ear. "True. But, in any case, you know I was banished from the house years ago."

"Oh," said Andromache. "Right — because of all the noise you made with your army gear."

He nodded. " '*Move out to the courtyard so we can sleep, for the sake of the dimmest stars!* '" His voice came out as a hybrid of his mother's and his father's.

Andromache giggled.

"So, you'll have to move downstairs," said Hector. "Outside. With me. And I thought you'd like to bring your chest."

"Move downstairs…"

Hector's face turned serious. "<u>Fohr to be — fohr to be my</u> — oh, *dammit*!" he swore in disgust. "I forget the word for '*wife*.'"

Andromache laughed. "That's fine. I'll be your '*oh dammit*.'"

He was beaming. "Then you are," he said. "Right? That's how it works, in the Lukka lands?"

She nodded. "That's how it works. Once people decide to be married, they are."

"Then tonight, after the meeting, I'll tell my whole family," he murmured in her ear. "I'll tell them that my wife and her chest are moving downstairs."

His family! Suddenly, Andromache felt a twinge of misgiving. Kind as his family had always been to her, there was no telling how they would receive *this* news. A tutor was one thing; a wife, another. "Will they be upset?" she asked faintly.

Hector laughed. "Upset? No. They gave the chest to you. You should get to keep it."

"I'm serious! Enough with the chest, already!"

"Well, if you don't want me to say <u>tatas</u> —"

"<u>Ector</u>!" she pleaded.

He relented. "They love you…and you heard my mom this morning."

"I heard her tell you to go to your uncle's," said Andromache. In a small voice, she added, "And I heard you agree."

"I'm not going to Uncle's," said Hector. "This morning, I didn't care where I was — but everything's different, now." He hugged her tightly.

She hugged him back. "Then what did you mean about your mom?"

"You heard all her talk about fiancées. She wants me to be married."

Andromache sighed. "Maybe — but she thought you'd be marrying *Penthesilea*, not me."

"I know," said Hector. "But I'm sure she'd rather have *you* for a daughter-in-law. She loves you, <u>Ahndromahk</u> — my whole family loves you!"

"Paris doesn't," muttered Andromache. "He said I was your one-time tisane."

"My *what?*"

Briefly, she explained the jibe.

"He'll pay for *that!*" Hector said ominously. "I don't know what little game he's trying to play! He knows better."

"What do you mean?"

Hector laughed. "My brother caught me staring at you during a family dinner, a month or so after you came to Troy. Ever since, he's been hassling me about you, usually when we're down on the archery range."

"You talked to him about me?" Andromache wasn't sure whether to be alarmed or flattered.

"No, not exactly. He talked — mostly to call me stupid for not making a move — and I told him to shut up, and go to hell, and watch where he was aiming." Hector, who had been smiling, frowned. "Anyway, I don't know why he said that to you this morning, but he'll be sorry."

"Oh, let it go," murmured Andromache. She was feeling magnanimous.

Hector kissed her. "So…can you meet me in the kitchen, tonight?"

She nodded.

"Oh, <u>Ahndromahk</u>! I'm so happy!"

"Me, too."

Buzzy whickered.

"And Buzzy's the happiest of all," said Hector. "Or else he's telling me that I should get back to work. He's probably right."

"What do you have left to do?"

"Well, I already gave the horses their salve," he said. "But some need burrs picked out of their tails, or knots combed out of their manes. That kind of thing. I like to give them extra attention, after we get back." His expression turned grave. "They don't ask to go with us."

Andromache felt a shiver run through her.

"We only use them to move us from place to place," Hector went on. "We do everything we can to keep them safe, but as you can see…"

Andromache followed his gaze to a spot of salve on Buzzy's hide.

Hector coughed. "They don't ask to go with us. Combing out a few knots is the least I can do for them."

Andromache squeezed his hand. He squeezed back.

"This seemed like a good day to do it, when I was alone, down here," said Hector. "I hate to ask Thoas to help me. He's a good guy, but so nervous. He makes the horses jumpy — and the last thing you want when you're picking out burrs is a horse that feels like dancing."

"Why *are* you here alone?" asked Andromache.

Hector's face turned sheepish. "I couldn't stand to look at anyone, after making an ass of myself in front of you. I told everyone to get lost for a couple hours."

"You sent them away?"

"Mm-hmm."

"You really *are* in charge, here!"

"Sometimes Xanthus lets me think so."

Andromache smiled at him, and he kissed her.

"Ector?" she asked, a breath or two later.

"Hmm?"

"Can I stay? To help with the horses?"

He gave her a long, tender look. "Of course," he said. "Of course you can stay."

℘

"CUTIE!" SQUAWKED ANDROMACHE.

The dog flattened her ears and raised her muzzle skyward. "Bad dog!"

Cutie tucked one front leg up to her chest. Before her lay the remains of Andromache's wine-colored sash — the same one Paris had bought for her to wear on her date with Hector. Andromache hadn't seen it since that night, when she'd thrown it under the bed in despair.

"How could you?" she asked Cutie.

The dog's head pivoted so that it still pointed upward, but toward the other corner of the room.

Andromache sighed. "It's all right. It's not your fault. Come here." She sat on the ground.

Joyous that she'd been pardoned, Cutie flopped onto Andromache's lap and licked her chin.

"Hi, to you too, sweetie." Andromache giggled. "I'm sorry I was gone all day. I know, I know — I missed you, too."

Cutie lowered her head to the ground and began to burrow, writhing until she was lying fully on the floor. As Andromache reached out to pet the dog's belly, Cutie snuffled happily at her hands, savoring the scents of the stable.

"I know, I know. I need a bath." Andromache sighed. "And a change of clothes." Oh, did she ever! Soon, she was going to have to meet with Hector — and his parents. His parents. His parents! She'd hardly had time to enjoy being Hector's wife before becoming *their* daughter-in-law.

Back in the stables, she'd spent a few blissful hours caring for the horses with Hector — her *husband!* All too soon, though, the guards had shown up, reminding Hector of the council meeting he had to attend — and reminding Andromache of her own meeting later that night...

"A change of clothes," she repeated. Her dress was soaked from the rain, and it smelled of horses. She didn't want to wear it in front of her new in-laws. But what *was* she supposed to wear? The sash would have been nice, now that the sight of it no longer made her cry, but Cutie had utterly shredded it. Well, regardless, she needed to find a dress! Several still lay sprawled across the floor, where she'd dropped them the night before. She scooped them up, realizing as she did that every last one of them was covered in dog hair.

Andromache sighed. "You could've had the whole bed to yourself — and instead, you take a nap on my clothes!" she said to Cutie.

The little dog wagged her tail.

Andromache appraised the dresses, choosing the one with the least amount of white hair and picking off as much as she could. It was a fruitless task. "How do you have any fur left?" she demanded crossly, thrusting the dress out at Cutie. "You left it all on *here!*"

Delighted, Cutie lunged for the dress.

Andromache snatched it away just in time. "I don't think so. You already got the sash."

A gust of wind blew in through the curtains. It had finally stopped raining, but the air was still cold. Shivering, Andromache eyed her cloak, now a sad, sodden heap of grey wool. To wear it would be unthinkable.

She groaned. There was only one other option — Cassandra's old magenta cloak, the one she'd worn during her first few months in Troy. It looked hideous on her. *But not as awful as shivering would look,* she told herself. *Just imagine what Hecuba would say if she caught you freezing to death in her kitchen!*

Andromache knelt beside her clothing chest — ran a hand tenderly over the top of it — and rummaged around inside. At the bottom, she felt the scratch of wool and tugged. Her face fell when she saw the cloak. Its color was blinding, much worse than she'd remembered.

Anxiously, she scanned her room for something — *anything!* — that might salvage her outfit. Her eyes lit on a pair of sandals tucked under the bed. They were thick-soled and new, a recent gift from Hecuba. Andromache hadn't even tried them on yet, preferring to wait until her old ones were in tatters, but tonight was undoubtedly the right time to start wearing them.

Cutie licked her hand.

"Thank you," said Andromache. "You knew I needed a little comfort, didn't you? Or are you still just licking off the horse smell?"

The intensity of Cutie's next *schluuuurp!* was her answer.

"All right, then!" Andromache laughed. "Time for a bath." She gathered up her clothing and headed downstairs.

℘

AFTER HER BATH, Andromache went straight to the kitchen. She wasn't sure when Hector and his parents would be home and didn't want to keep them waiting. Besides, even her horrid pink cloak wasn't warm enough, on such a chilly evening. She needed to sit by the fire.

"Hi, Hermie. Nice threads," called a voice from the table.

Paris, thought Andromache, with a dark sense of déjà-vu. *Just who I need to help me relax!*

"I see you're going with the understated look," he jeered.

"And *you're* going with the understated snack," snapped Andromache, glaring at the mound of food before him.

Paris nodded. "I need my energy."

"Oh, I'll bet!"

His eyes began to gleam in a wicked way. "Much like *you* needed it, at breakfast —"

The color on Andromache's face approached the vivid hue of her cloak.

"— so you could go horse around in the stables, afterward."

Even as her blush deepened to crimson, Andromache felt a sudden flood of warmth for Paris. It was *his* jibe, after all, that had stung her into following Hector to the stables. The fact that Hector was now her husband was linked, however indirectly, to Paris.

Or, she wondered with a start, *was it more than that?*

She took a sidelong look at Paris. On several other occasions, his rotten behavior had pushed her closer to Hector. He'd played tricks on her; he'd given her false messages. At the time, she'd thought he was just trying to make her look silly, but now she wasn't sure. She thought about what Hector had told her: *'Ever since you came here, Paris has been hassling me about you....He called me stupid for not making a move.'*

Again, Andromache took stock of Paris. What was he, really? Some warped little god of love, or just an ordinary jerk?

"See something you like, Hermie?" he taunted, as he caught her staring.

Andromache rolled her eyes. Whatever the truth, Paris was unlikely to reveal it — and either way, he was still Paris. *Paris*, she thought, now smiling. Her brother-in-law. The pesky little brother she'd never had. Strangely moved, she walked over to kiss him on the cheek.

"What's *that* for?" he asked.

Andromache smiled. "I'm not sure."

"Oh. That sounds normal, for you." Paris kissed her cheek in turn and then, without another word, he left.

CREEEAK! THE FRONT DOOR SHUT. Andromache huddled closer to the table, her whole body humming with tension. *Will bread and fruit and chickpea stew be enough?* she fretted, scrutinizing the snack she'd laid out for Hector's parents — for her in-laws — in case they were hungry after the meeting. In case they wanted to celebrate her marriage to Hector with a meal, in the Lukkan way. *I should've put out cakes. Why didn't Paris get any cakes at the market, today?*

Voices were coming near. Had Hector already told his parents about the marriage, or was he going to include her in the big moment? She hoped he *had* already told them. That way, they would have time to mask their disappointment before seeing her. They were certain to be disappointed — anyone in their position would be! Their son had chosen to marry a woman of origins so humble, she hadn't even been wearing shoes the day they met.

At least I'm wearing them now, sighed Andromache. She hoped the family would notice.

The voices arrived at the kitchen door. Andromache shot to her feet.

"Hello, little one," said Priam, the first one in. "I'm glad to see you aren't frozen solid."

"Indeed," said Hecuba, glaring at the darkened window. "But never mind this frightful weather! It looks like that nap earlier was just what you needed — the roses are back in your cheeks."

Great! Andromache groaned to herself. *Blushing already.* As if the pink of her cloak wasn't hideous enough!

Cassandra, who had evidently run into her parents after the meeting and walked home with them, gave Andromache a mysterious little smile.

What's that about? wondered Andromache. *Did he tell them already? And where is he?*

"Yes, you look much better," Hecuba declared. "At least we can cross *you* off our list of people to worry about!"

Priam nodded gravely. "Andromache?"

"Y-yes?" she stammered. Was this it?

"Have you noticed anything — well, *different* — about our son?"

Andromache's mouth went dry. "Which one?" she asked weakly, to stall for time.

"Touché!" Priam laughed. "I meant Hector."

Andromache shook her head. Over the past two days, she had indeed noticed many new things about Hector, but she was pretty sure his parents wouldn't want to hear about them. In any case, they didn't seem to know about *her* yet — and Hector still hadn't arrived to tell them. Too anxious to face them alone any longer, she busied herself retrieving a jar of wine from the shelf.

"Well, *I* have!" said Hecuba. "I mean, the moping is one thing — goodness knows he's done *that* before! — but the gibbering and the chattering? Our son does *not* chatter, Priam," she said stoutly.

Priam nodded. "He tends not to."

"Tends? *Tends?* He *never* chatters."

"It *is* a little strange."

"That's putting it mildly! This morning, he was as sour as a bowl of green apples, wasn't he, girls?"

"Pretty sour," Cassandra agreed.

Andromache reshelved the jar she'd chosen and took another.

"And yet, tonight, he was all aflutter. He looked downright odd, and did you *hear* him, Priam?"

Great! thought Andromache. Marrying her had made Hector *odd!*

"What exactly did he say, Mom?" asked Cassandra, with a smile half-innocent, half-sly.

Well she *obviously knows something — or has guessed.*

"What did he say? He said it's time to talk seriously about marriage, and we should do so right after the meeting, if you can believe that! Oh — wine — good idea, dear," said Hecuba, taking the jar from Andromache. "We'll be needing some of that, once *he* arrives! Although, that could be awhile — Thymoetes caught him at the door, and the way that man blathers on —" Hecuba sniffed in frustration. "Andromache, dear, would you mind bringing over some cups, while you're up?"

Andromache was only too happy to linger away from the table.

"He's mocking me," said Hecuba, narrowing her eyes. "I know it! You should've seen his face this morning when I mentioned the word '*fiancée.*' He looked like I'd suggested he choose a foot to sever from his body. And now he wants to talk about *marriage?* These theatrics are all just to spite me!"

Andromache pretended to have trouble finding the necessary number of cups.

"Oh, my dear," said Priam. "I know he likes to tease, but surely you don't think —"

Hecuba cut him off. "Andromache," she said, with sudden vigor.

Andromache let out a gasp. The cups rattled in her hands, and she had to set them down.

"Andromache," Hecuba repeated. "I believe you've been here all night. Has that Penthesilea come by, or has anyone said she'd be coming?"

"Mom, it's not *her*," Cassandra protested. "You heard what he said about her — they're just colleagues."

"Yes, and yet a lot of his tunes have changed since this morning," insisted Hecuba. "Well, dear? Have you heard anything from or about that woman?"

Andromache shook her head miserably.

"I think I hear *him*, now," Priam interjected.

Sure enough, Andromache heard a set of footsteps coming from the main door. Good! Let *him* deal with this! Feeling better, she scooped up the cups.

"So, the mystery will soon be solved." Priam was smiling.

"Maybe he's brought her with," Hecuba said wryly. "Unless he's tricked some poor market vendoress into playing the part of his fiancée…"

When Hector entered the kitchen — alone, of course — Andromache couldn't help but stare. He didn't look odd at all. From his light, quick step to his radiant face, Hector was dazzling. Her arms went weak; the cups slid dangerously.

"*There* you are!" said Hecuba, at the same time as Priam said, "Hello, son."

But Hector, who had eyes only for Andromache, ran over to rescue her. After setting her cups on the table, he wrapped his arms around her and kissed her tenderly, as though that were the first thing he always did upon returning home.

Hecuba made a sound of disgust. "Oh, enough already," she snapped. "Leave Andromache out of your comedy routines."

"What comedy routines?" asked Hector. "I told you — I want to talk about marriage."

The family fell silent. *They hate it*, thought Andromache. *They hate* me. She buried her face in Hector's chest and didn't move until she heard a soft laugh from Priam.

"Andromache?" he said, sounding awestruck.

She turned her face to see Hector's father beaming at her. At his side, Cassandra was speechless with her own form of joy, shining and tear-streaked.

"Is it true, little one?" asked Priam. Eyes twinkling, he added, "Are you the one my son's been gibbering about?"

Blushing, Andromache nodded. The word '*gibbering*' was horrendous, but at least Priam looked happy about it.

"I must say, I often thought —" The priest shook his head. "But no, things must happen in their own time. Come, sit down, both of you, so we can toast your happy news! Sit, little one. Your cups are safe!" He laughed and motioned to the seat across from him.

Awkwardly, Andromache sat. Hector slid in beside her.

"I *knew* the stars foretold happiness in your coming here," said Priam in a reverent voice.

"*Great* happiness," Cassandra added impishly.

Hector grimaced at his sister, and Andromache fiddled with her cloak, which seemed more garish with each passing moment.

"Great happiness," Priam agreed.

"So," said Hecuba. "Why didn't you tell us sooner about this — *happiness*?" She made the last word sound like a disease.

Andromache shrank, and even Hector stiffened. "There was nothing to tell, sooner," he said.

Hecuba snorted.

"Mom?" asked Hector, now on guard. "What is it?"

"You're telling *me*," she began, her voice acrid, "that all of a sudden, after two years of '*nothing*,' you develop such passion for this woman that you leap straight to gibbering about marriage and canoodling with her in our kitchen?"

This woman. Andromache shuddered — she'd become a *this woman*. And as for *canoodling*…

"No," said Hector. "That's *not* how it was."

"I see! You have the audacity to admit it! And I suppose all of Troy is laughing at your father's and my credulity for condoning the charade of your lessons! Behind our very backs, Priam! Trysting in the *library*!" Her tone made it clear that the location worsened the crime.

Andromache's lungs deflated. Her tongue went thick. The evening was turning into a nightmare!

"Oh, come on, Mom — '*charade*?'" Hector scoffed. "Bring in any Lukkan person you want and watch me talk to him!"

"Son," Priam said soothingly. "I'm sure your mother knows that you've learned a great deal of Lukkan."

"Well, how does she think I learned it, then — by swallowing a magic herb?"

Hecuba glared at her son. "Perhaps it was a magic herb that inspired this sudden ardor."

This isn't happening. Andromache closed her eyes. *This isn't happening.*

"What I meant before," snapped Hector, "is that the feeling *isn't* sudden. I've been in love with Andromache since her first night here —"

His mother's face passed from purple to grey.

"— I just didn't tell her."

"Well, of course!" Hecuba snarled. "*That's* the sensible thing to do!"

"There was never the right moment," said Hector. "For a lot of reasons. But I finally told her, and now I'm telling *you*."

Priam turned to his wife. Soothingly, he explained, "Coming home from war can make a man realize certain things —"

"Don't — *don't!* — don't you *dare* speak to me as if I know nothing of war!" shrieked Hecuba, fixing her husband with an erosive glare. "Or as if men are the only ones that do! — as if *you* do for that matter, sitting there in your priestly robes!" Tears poured down her cheeks, and she buried her face in her hands. Her whole body was shaking with fury or agony.

"Mom!" Cassandra cried in horror.

Andromache clamped her lips together, sure that she was going to be sick. She thought back to how gently Hecuba had tended her wounds when she first came to Troy — how the woman had encouraged Andromache to read — how she'd often visited her room, just to chat. Now, Hecuba hated her. It was as though the skin was being ripped from her feet all over again.

"It is all rahght," Hector murmured in Andromache's ear. He wrapped his arms around her. "Sssh…it is all rahght."

"Hecuba," said Priam. "Let's go upstairs."

Wordlessly, Hecuba swept out of the room.

"It is all rahght…"

"Son?"

"Hmm?" said Hector, barely looking up.

"I need to talk with your mother, now."

Hector gave a curt nod.

"I think she's just a little surprised." Priam sighed. "You know how she can be with surprises. But she'll come around."

"Unless the stars don't will it. Right, Dad?"

"Hector, please — she just needs some time." Priam bent down to kiss first Andromache, then Hector, on the cheek. "A thousand blessings to you both," he said, before following his wife upstairs.

Bitterly, Andromache wondered if that would be enough.

"It is all rahght," Hector said again, when he heard or felt her sigh. "I lahff you."

"I love you, too." Andromache's voice cracked a little. He still loved her, after *that*! She hadn't doubted that he would, not really, but it was nice to know for sure.

"Hector?" someone murmured from across the table.

They looked up to see Cassandra, whose presence they'd both forgotten.

The girl was pouring three cups of wine. She had a mournful expression on her face.

"What is it?" asked Hector.

"You know how high-strung Mom can be, but I'm sure Dad will talk sense into her. *I'll* talk to her too, if you want. Every day, seven times a day at *least*, until she gets over this — this stupid snit."

Hector tried to smile at his sister. "Thanks," he said, downing his wine.

Andromache did the same.

"It'll blow over!" Cassandra insisted. "It always does. Think of all the times Paris has done something stupid." Realizing what her words implied, she hastened to add, "Not that I think what *you've* done — that *that's* stupid — I mean, *that* is wonderful! It's how things should have been all along! Oh honey, *you* know I think that you — you —"

"I know," Andromache reassured her.

"Then tell my brother I didn't mean —"

"I know that, silly," Hector said affectionately.

Cassandra gave a faint smile.

"But what *do* you think is going on?" he asked. "You're the best at deciphering Mom."

"Mom?" Cassandra gulped. "Well, you know she hates to be sur —"

"Surprised," he interrupted. "Yes, I know. Is that all it is?"

"Probably," said Cassandra. "She was *really* surprised! Maybe the problem was how you —" *Cough!* "— *introduced* the subject."

"I didn't plan to kiss Andromache like that," said Hector, a haze of red spreading on his cheeks. "It just happened! Those stupid cups!"

Cassandra giggled. "It was so cute!"

"Anyway, what difference does it make?" argued Hector, redder than ever. "I thought Mom *liked* Andromache."

Andromache had thought so, too.

"Of course she likes her!" said Cassandra.

"Just not as much as she likes making people miserable."

"Hector, stop," Andromache implored. She didn't want him to rile himself up again.

"Hermie?" asked Paris, from the kitchen doorway. "Is my brother bothering you? Do you need me to protect you from him?"

Oh, gods, thought Andromache. *Paris! That's all we need!*

"Enough with the 'Hermie' crap, Paris!" snapped Hector. "She's got a real name."

"No, It's all right. I don't mind '*Hermie*,'" said Andromache, afraid of what dreadful nickname Paris might come up with to take its place. Especially *now*!

"And neither does my brother," said Paris, eyeing them slyly. "He doesn't seem to mind Hermie at all. In fact, he looks pretty pleased with himself to be sitting by her."

Hector gave in and laughed. "Fair enough," he said, kissing the top of Andromache's head. "So what were *you* up to tonight, little brother?"

"Proving myself right."

"That's going to take a lot longer than one night."

"Ha, ha."

"Proving yourself right about what?" asked Cassandra.

"About the only thing that counts, Songbird — music. Last night, that worthless old Selagus came to *our* house and absolutely *butchered* the words to my favorite song — except he kept insisting that he had them right."

"Oh. What song was it?"

As soon as Paris hummed the first few notes, Andromache recognized the tune. Coyly, so that the others wouldn't see, she marched her fingers up Hector's spine. He didn't wriggle away.

"I'm not always ticklish," he whispered, switching to Lukkan to add: "Only when —"

"Ahem! I was going to finish my story, if you two don't mind!" Paris interrupted. "Anyway, I made a survey of the city's taverns, and in every locale, people were singing that song the way *I* know it." He poured himself a splash of wine and sang the first two verses.

"Stop it, Paris!" Cassandra protested. "That's terrible!"

Paris laughed. "All right, Songbird — you show us how it's done!"

"*I'm* not singing *that*," she said primly.

"Don't like all the nasty, nasty words?" teased Paris. "Maybe Hermie can sing it, then. That kind of thing doesn't bother *her*."

Andromache glared at him.

"Watch it, little brother," said Hector.

"That's cute, defending your girlfriend. Oh, sorry. I didn't mean to be crass — your consort."

Hector corrected him: "My *wife*."

Giggling, Andromache whispered, "Your '*oh dammit.*'"

Hector gave her a squeeze.

"Your *wife*? What did you have to bribe her to get her to agree to *that*?"

Cassandra rolled her eyes. "Can't you quit making your stupid jokes, just this once?"

"No, Cassandra, he can't help himself," said Hector. "It's his natural state." Muttering, he added, "Better this than what Mom said."

"Mom?" asked Paris.

"She didn't — take the news — as well as one might have expected," Cassandra said delicately.

"She ran out, frothing like a she-dragon," Hector amended.

"You'd think she'd be ecstatic!" Paris frowned. "To get you married off before your back hunches over."

"You'd *think*," Hector agreed.

"Well, if it makes you feel any better, *I'm* happy."

"Oh, yes, that *is* a comfort."

"It's true." Paris's grey eyes twinkled. "Of all the women you might have wound up with, I like Hermie the most."

Andromache almost let herself be touched by Paris's words, but then she remembered to wait for the sting.

"I mean, your colleague probably would've hurt me if I teased her. And even if she didn't, she wouldn't have blushed. You, on the other hand, Hermie —" Paris gave her a wicked grin. "You have a soft spot for me. And you can *certainly* blush — unless it's just that my brother gave up shaving again."

"*You* have a soft spot in your head if you think you get to tease her!" Hector menaced his brother with an apricot; he was the first person all night to touch Andromache's wedding snack.

Paris laughed. "It's not teasing, if it's true."

"It's *not* true!" Andromache retorted, even as her cheeks went red.

"*Isn't* it, brother? I bet she blushes beet red when —" Paris's impudent leer vanished as the apricot struck his head. "Gods!" he protested, rubbing his temple. Then, after a moment, he added grudgingly, "You've got a good arm, I'll say that for you. A bit lower and we'd be twins."

"You wish."

"Oh, now *that's* funny!"

"What's funny is how flabby your arms have gotten." Hector scrutinized his brother from across the table. "Have you been practicing every day, like you were supposed to?"

"Well, of course," said Paris, in his usual lazy drawl.

"All you ever practiced was *napping!*" hissed Andromache, still irked by the '*blushing*' comment and furious with Paris for mocking Hector's wound — even though Hector himself hadn't seemed to mind the teasing.

Hector snorted. "Tomorrow, little brother. You and me."

Paris glared at Andromache. "Conspiracies," he muttered. "Perhaps I *don't* like this new alliance."

"Get some sleep," Hector advised.

Rising from his seat, Paris flashed a sour look, huffed a curt '*Congratulations*' and stalked out of the room.

Cassandra yawned. "I'm sleepy, too," she said. "It's been quite a night!" She gave her brother and Andromache each a kiss on the cheek, saying, "Things will sort themselves out, you'll see."

Hector nodded for Cassandra's benefit, but as soon as she was gone, he sighed. "I'm so sorry — about my mom, I mean."

Andromache shook her head, refusing the apology.

"You should never have had to go through all that. I really thought she'd be happy." Hector's face clouded over. "But Cassandra's right. I should've known not to surprise her. Tomorrow, I'll talk to her. I'll apologize, and things will work out."

Andromache moved over onto his lap. "This kind of thing runs in my family," she said. "My dad didn't get a good reception either."

"Your dad? Why?"

"Well, when he met my mom, he was poor and disheveled. He'd run away from his father in Taruisha."

"I remember," said Hector.

"The guys who helped my dad run away were from Lukká. They lived in his neighborhood in Taruisha, and he was friends with them — that's how he learned Lukkana. Then, when they decided to go back to Lukká, he went with them." Andromache paused. "He met Mom in Lukká. She was working at a market, and he went over to talk to her. In Lukkana, of course." Laughing, Andromache added, "And Dad could *talk*! He was there all day, scaring off the other customers. Her sister — my Auntie — finally guilted him into buying something. Like I said, he was poor, so he picked out the littlest thing they had and left. But the next day, he was back, and the next, and the next, until they were so wild about each other that he ended up leaving with her when she went back to her home village. That's why Mom never let me go alone to sell their things at the market — *'You never know what you'll come back with,'* she always said." Andromache imitated the look of tender suspicion her mom had flashed at her dad in saying those words.

Hector laughed. "She is fahnny. Lahke you."

The phrase gave Andromache a jolt. *Lahke you.* Was it true? Was she at all like her mom, or her dad? Her memories were those of a child. She wondered if she would even recognize her parents, now that she was an adult, or if they would recognize *her*. How much remained of that girl she'd been down in the Lukka lands?

"You ahre all rahght?" Hector asked gently.

Andromache nodded. "Mom *was* funny," she said. "But her parents weren't laughing when she showed up with a bum from who-knows-where, who they'd never met before, and insisted that he was her husband."

"They were mad, her parents?"

"They let Auntie have it. She told me the whole story. *What were you thinking, letting her bring that tramp home? He looks completely useless! And what's he carrying in that horrible leather bag?'* When they asked about the bag, he interrupted — he opened it up to show them. It had all of his lute-making tools inside."

"The parents say what?" asked Hector.

"Well, as soon as he started explaining what the tools were for, they heard his accent. They were even less excited to have their daughter marry a foreign bum than a local bum, so they thought up a trick to make him look silly in front of my mom. It would be best, they thought, if *she* made the decision to boot him out. Anyway, they asked him if he was any good at lute-making, and he said yes. My grandpa ran to the neighbors, borrowed a lute, took off all the strings, and brought the whole mess back to my dad to see if he could put it back together. He could, of course, and he even made a few little adjustments. In the end, it sounded better than before."

"Then what?" asked Hector.

"My grandparents gave in to the inevitable. My dad was very charming. They were starting to like him, whether they wanted to or not. Besides, they were afraid of driving Mom away. So instead of kicking my dad out, they fetched some wine, called over the neighbors, and everyone drank, sang, and danced all night. Dad provided most of the music, of course."

"So, in the end, they lahke him," said Hector, hinting that their own story might turn out just as well.

Andromache nodded. "They liked him. At least, that's what Auntie told me. I never talked to my grandparents about it. They died before I was old enough to know them very well. I don't have much luck with family members," Andromache said ruefully. "Maybe that's why your mom doesn't like me. She's worried. Maybe she should be."

"Ssh…" Hector kissed her softly on the lips. What began as a simple comfort kiss, however, quickly morphed into something else. Andromache forgot all about fights and angry parents. She forgot about everything except Hector's lips and tongue — his green scent — the heat of his hands through her dress —

Too soon, he backed away from her. Andromache kept her eyes closed for a moment; when she opened them, Hector was smiling.

She blinked a little bashfully and asked, "Where was I?"

His dimple appeared. "Your grandparents."

"Oh." Andromache had no idea what she'd been saying about them.

"You did not know them…"

"Oh. Yes. They died of old age. Mom was their youngest."

Hector nodded. "Ahndromahk," he asked tentatively. "Your family will — would, I mean —"

"Would?"

"Thanks. Your family *would* fink what on me? Fohr your hahsband?" He cleared his throat. "They *would* lahke me?"

Andromache took a deep breath. It was high time he knew: "Auntie liked you," she murmured.

"What?"

"The woman you fetched water for, in Lyrnash. You know, the tiny old woman who bandaged your leg after you fell. The one who took you to a shack with no windows, and bunches and bunches of wool, and a little tan rug in the corner."

Hector's eyes widened. He'd never described the inside of the woman's house to her.

Andromache went on. "That woman was my Auntie — and she really liked you." Auntie had never forgotten the kindness of the Trojan boy. She'd often spoken of him…

'It's a shame we didn't make it to Taruisha,' sighed Auntie.

'Why?'

'City people have better manners than the ones here.'

'Oh, Auntie! Not the hairy boy again!'

'The boy with hair in his face,' Auntie corrected. *'The* sweet *boy with hair in his face.'*

'All right. Sorry.'

Auntie fixed her eyes on Andromache. *'We could still go there,'* she said.

'Go where?'

'To Taruisha. You could be with a larger group of people — a better *group of people.'*

'I'm fine here, Auntie. I have you. I don't need anyone else.'

'What would my poor sister think of me? What would your dad say about how I've cared for you?' moaned Auntie. *'Still a young woman, and you've turned into a lonely old owl, like me.'*

'I like owls,' said Andromache. *"And I like you…'*

Andromache looked up at Hector. He was speechless, staring at her. "Auntie never spoke a word of Táruvan, even though she understood it all right," she said. "That's why she didn't say anything to you."

Hector nodded mutely.

"And you remember the cloth she wore wound around her head?"

He nodded again.

"She had a fever, back when we were traveling with the — you know when. I chopped off her hair, and she never let it grow back, afterward. That's why she kept her head covered."

"The lady with the scarf was your *aunt*," Hector finally managed to say.

Andromache nodded.

He let out a long breath. "I always wondered," he said. "The way you ran out of the courtyard, the day I told you about her, I thought she must have been special to you. I thought she was your friend, or maybe —" He fell silent once more.

Andromache looked up at him. "Are you mad I didn't tell you sooner?"

"No, no, no." He kissed her forehead. "I know why you did not. It is weird. It is hahrd."

"She really liked you," whispered Andromache. "She told me how sweet you'd been to her, and she said you had nice manners. She wanted to move to Taruisha so I could be around people like you. If she knew we were married, she would be so happy."

This time, Hector kissed Andromache's lips. "So, she lahkes me."

"A lot," said Andromache. "I think she might even have had a little crush on you."

He laughed.

Andromache took his hand. "My parents would've liked you, too," she said softly. "They really would've liked you." Hector would have fit so easily into their life: the days of hard work, the nights of music, dancing, and wine. Lying in the grass, looking up at the sky. Walking in the hills. Reading. Laughing. How much laughter there had been, in their tiny mountain cottage! She could almost hear Hector's laughter blending with her family's! She wished more than anything that she could have introduced him to them — had a meal with them to celebrate her marriage — danced around with their neighbors while her dad played jaunty music on his lute...

As her tears threatened to spill over, Andromache nodded again. "They would've liked you a lot, but — Dad — would —"

Hector stroked her hair. "Would what, pretty wife?" he asked softly.

"Um, he w-would've been jealous of your horse, and your library."

"Oh, yes," said Hector. "I remember. It is him who teaches you to read."

Andromache nodded.

"And he lahkes — lahked — hohrses?"

"He liked all animals, but especially horses," said Andromache. "He always wished we could have one, but it never really made sense." She sniffled once or twice and cleared her throat. "Because he was — hurt."

"In the legs, rahght?"

Andromache nodded. "He would've liked to feed Buzzy an apple, though."

"Greedy yellow hohrse," muttered Hector.

Andromache laughed as a few last tears rolled down her cheeks.

Hector held her close. "And your mom?" he murmured in her ear. "She would fink what?"

"My mom," replied Andromache, "would've said your Lukkana accent was cute, but —"

"Wait, wait," said Hector, drawing back from her.

"What?"

"What on you?" he asked, with a playful look. "Do you fink my accent is cute?"

Andromache blushed. "Adorable," she murmured.

"The first time you heard it, you burst into tears," he said, laughing.

"That wasn't about *you!*" she cried. "You know I was a mess back then!"

"I know," he said soothingly. "I was only teasing, my sweetheart."

"Well, fine! I wasn't. I *love* your accent."

He flashed a flirtatious look. "*Yours* is cute, too."

"I don't have an accent!" she protested.

"Oh no? *'ello, 'ectorrrr. Want to 'old 'ands?*" mimicked Hector, reaching for Andromache's hands.

"Stop that!" she giggled. "I don't sound like that!" She tried — although not very hard — to keep her hands away from him.

He grabbed them and pulled her in close. "*Orrrr should we kish?*" he asked, planting a playful kiss on her nose.

"At leasht give me a real kish," Andromache teased back.

Hector obliged. "I'm glad you think my accent's cute," he whispered, after a while.

"It is," she whispered back. "But what I was going to say before is that my mom was a weaver, and no matter what she thought of your accent, she would've warned me against marrying someone who can't unknot thread."

"What? Thread?"

"Don't you remember? The first time I ever went down to the stables? You couldn't get the knots out of those ropes, even after I showed you the right way to do it. I'm sure you'd be just as bad with thread."

"Oh, *that.*" Hector smiled. "What makes you think I was really trying, after you showed me the right way?"

"What do you mean?"

"Maybe I did the ropes wrong to get your attention."

"To get my attention?"

"Mm-hmm."

Andromache could tell by his smug look that he knew how successful he'd been. "In that case," she said, poking him in the chest, "maybe Mom would've warned me against marrying a flirt."

"A what?"

"A flirt," she repeated in Truvan.

"Oh," said Hector. "I suppose you're right." With a laugh, he added, "<u>A jaylous fleert</u>."

"<u>Jealous? Of who</u>, Demuchus?" As she recalled, Hector had brought the box of tangled ropes home, that evening. He'd been working on them in the kitchen when Demuchus had arrived to escort her to a soiree. "<u>You had nothing to be jealous of</u>," she said. "<u>I hardly even knew</u> Demuchus <u>was there</u>."

"Paris <u>says that</u>," Hector agreed.

Paris again! What else had he blabbed to his brother over the years? "<u>Then why *were* you jealous</u>?" she asked.

"The wormy way Demuchus grabbed your arm!" Hector said with disgust. "I don't know what I would've done if Cassandra hadn't been going along with you guys. She's so nosy, she made the perfect chaperone."

"Maybe *you* should've grabbed my arm!" said Andromache.

"Maybe I will now." Instead of grabbing her arm, though, he kissed her neck.

"Ector?" she murmured.

"Hmm?"

"*You're* the reason I laughed at Demuchus, out on the courtyard."

Hector stopped kissing her. "What do you mean?"

"You know, the night he asked me to marry him?"

"Yes…"

"Well, earlier that evening, you made a comment — something about his face, and wax — and it popped into my head right then, when he was —" Andromache gulped to avoid saying what Demuchus had been up to when she laughed at him. "Anyway, it was just so —"

"Fitting," Hector suggested.

"Yes."

"Well," he said soberly. "I didn't mean to make you laugh at him like that, but —"

"But you're not sorry."

"To say the least."

Andromache smiled, but as she thought back to other moments of her past with Hector and Demuchus, her smile faded.

"What's wrong?" asked Hector.

"It's just —" She cleared her throat. "Well, there were times you kind of pushed me to be with him…"

Hector said nothing.

"At least, that's how it felt to me…"

Still, he said nothing.

"Why did you do that?" she prodded.

"Oh, <u>Ahndromahk</u>!" he finally sighed. "I never *assumed* anything would happen with you and me, but in case it ever did, I wanted you to be sure you were through with Demuchus, first."

"Oh, for goodness' sake!" she exclaimed. "You honestly thought I wasn't through with him?"

He shrugged.

"Well, what would you have done if I *had* taken your advice and married him?" she asked tartly.

He kissed her. "<u>Cutie</u> never would have allowed it."

The dog, who had just sauntered in from the banquet hall, wagged her tail at the sound of her name.

"It's true, she doesn't like Demuchus," Andromache agreed. "But she's not so fond of you either, right now, after the way you chucked her off the bed."

"She'll get over it," said Hector, smiling.

Andromache smiled back and said, "I'll cuddle her a little extra tonight, to make up for it." Shivering, she added, "I'll need to anyway, for my own sake. It's freezing up in my room."

Hector gave her an odd look.

"What?" she asked.

"I thought you were coming with me."

Blushing, Andromache stammered, "I just thought, I — I mean, after what your mom said —" She was too embarrassed to repeat the phrase, *'Trysting in the library'* — let alone *'living in disorder'* — but Hector seemed to understand.

"You'd rather wait to move out there," he said.

"I don't *want* to, I just —" Tears welled up again. Andromache swiped at them in annoyance. She wasn't even sure why she was crying. Fear of disappointing Hector? Fear of scandalizing his family?

"Sssh…" Hector kissed her forehead. "I understand."

The tears began streaming down Andromache's face.

"Oh, my sweetheart," murmured Hector. "Ssh, it's all right. Here." He moved her gently out of his lap. "<u>You can sleep, now. And I can sleep.</u>" He stood beside her, giving her a warm — but not fiery — embrace. "<u>And tomorrow, I can fix Mom.</u>"

Andromache wiped her eyes on his shoulder. "<u>All right</u>," she whispered.

He kissed the top of her head. "<u>Good night</u>," he said. "<u>I lahff you</u>."

"<u>I love you, too</u>."

As Hector walked out onto the courtyard, toward his bed chamber, Andromache found herself doing the same thing she'd done that morning: sitting there dumbly, watching him leave.

(*This morning, you didn't just watch,*) the snide little Voice reminded her.

I can't go after him, this time, she said.

(*Why not?*) jeered the Voice. (*What's so hard about it? All you have to do is move your feet a little. Unless…*)

Unless what?

(*Unless you don't* want *to be with him.*)

Of course I do! she snapped. She thought about the night before, with all the kissing — the whispering — the feel of Hector's skin against hers. *I want it more than anything! I'm just —*

(*Just scared of being called a few nasty names,*) sneered the Voice. (*You care more about that* than *you do about* him.)

No, I don't!

(*Then why are you sitting here in the kitchen on your wedding night?*)

Andromache bit her lip. She hadn't thought about it quite that way, but the Voice was right. She was spurning Hector on the very night he'd asked to be her husband!

(*And now he's off in his room, wishing he hadn't bothered!*)

That did it. Without another word, Andromache ran out onto the courtyard. Cutie chased after her. Their feet pounded past the garden's herbs, fruit trees, and shrubberies.

"<u>Come on, girl — let's go!</u>" cried Andromache when Cutie stopped to sniff at the roses, but she didn't look back to make sure the dog was following her. Her new sandals flopped and slapped against the paving stones, making a terrible commotion. She raced on in spite of them, and in spite of the water that splashed up her legs each time she landed in a puddle. She didn't stop running until she'd reached the door on the far side of the courtyard. Hector's door.

There, she had a moment of trepidation. His was one of the few doors in the house she'd never opened; in fact, she'd rarely even approached it. To do so now felt like trespassing.

He might not even want me here, right now, she thought.

(*Why* would *he?*)

Shut up! she snapped at the Voice, before hastily opening the door. It squeaked. Andromache gasped. Cutie ran into the dim room just as a blanketed form flew up from the bed, demanding:

"Who's there?"

"Me," said Andromache.

"Oh — hay-lo, Me," said Hector, his voice softening.

Andromache shut the door but continued to hover near it. Her teeth chattered in the chilly air.

"You ahre cold?" asked Hector, lifting one side of the blanket as an invitation.

Andromache dove under the covers, as much from relief as from cold. Hector didn't seem to be upset with her. Once again, she'd panicked over nothing. Hector's arm slid around her, and she kissed him on the shoulder.

It was bare.

She snuggled closer to his chest.

Also bare.

Lightly, she touched her fingers to his hip bone.

Bare.

"Ector?"

"Hmm?"

"You're *naked!*" she whispered.

"I know," he whispered back. "That's how I sleep."

Andromache couldn't help giggling. "You sleep *naked?*"

"Mm-hmm."

"Every night?"

"Mm-hmm. Whenever I used to sleep with clothes on, the stupid fabric would bunch up under me. I'd spend half the night awake, trying to fix it."

Andromache giggled again.

"Besides," Hector added. "The linens feel nice."

"Especially the oldest ones, right?" she asked, thinking of Stripey.

"Exactly." He fell silent for a few moments before asking, "You're warm, now?"

"Mm-hmm."

"Good." Pause. "Ahndromahk?"

"Hmm?"

"What are you doing out here? When we were in the kitchen just now, you said —"

"You're my husband," she interrupted.

Hector propped himself up on an elbow and looked down at her. "I know," he said, sounding awed.

"It's our wedding night," she added, her voice dropping.

"Oh, <u>Ahndromahk</u>, I know that, too, but that can wait. Like you said, things are weird right now."

"I was wrong to say that. I don't care how weird things are."

"Well, *I* do. This is your house. I want you to feel comfortable in it — and with the other people that live here."

"I *am* comfortable," insisted Andromache. In a softer voice, she added, "<u>Very comfortable — except this stupid cloak is bunching up</u> —"

"I'm serious," said Hector, refusing to flirt. "That can wait until you don't feel like you have to sneak out here, like we're two teenagers, up to no good."

Andromache sobered. Hector had his pride. He wanted her there, but not if it meant reducing their love to some sleazy, secret affair. That morning, after his nightmare, he'd thought she was ashamed of him; she didn't want there to be any question of that, now. "I didn't sneak," she said quietly.

Pause. "You didn't?"

"No," she said. "I ran. I yelled at Cutie. Didn't you hear all the racket?"

Hector shook his head. "Honestly, I fell asleep just as soon as I was in bed."

"Well, I splashed through at least two dozen puddles, and the way my sandals were smacking against the ground, I must have sounded like a herd of giants."

"What? Giants?" asked Hector. By now, a hint of flirtation had crept into his voice.

"Giants," Andromache confirmed.

"I told you long ago —" He kissed her lightly on the lips. "There's no such thing as giants." *Kiss.* Pause. "And no sandals allowed in this bed." *Kiss, kiss.* "So, if you're going to stay —"

"All right." Andromache sat up to kick off her shoes. For good measure, she shinnied out of her clothing and threw it, too, onto the floor. Hector's arm slid around her as soon as she was back under the covers.

"Gentle giants!" he said hoarsely. "Now — *you're* —"

"Naked. I know," she whispered back. "I want to feel your linens."

"'*Feel* — *my* — *linens?*'" Hector repeated slowly, with feigned indignation. "Oh, <u>Ahndromahk</u> — that's obscene!"

She giggled. "<u>So? It's our wedding night</u>..."

"<u>I know</u>." He laughed, holding her close. Kissing her. "<u>I know. I lahff you, pretty wife</u>."

Chapter 27

himper. Whimper.

It was dark. Groggily, Andromache poked her toes around, searching for Cutie, hoping to comfort the dog quickly so she could go back to sleep. But instead of dog fur, Andromache felt feet — a *man's* feet. And the whimpers weren't coming from Cutie, but instead from the owner of the feet.

Hector was in the grips of another nightmare.

Andromache leaned over him. While she never, ever would have wished this on him, she wasn't going to pass up the opportunity to redeem herself. "Ector," she murmured, gently shaking his shoulder. "Wake up."

"Shit! Shit!" he cried, panting, still mostly asleep. Then, a moment later, "Shit."

She stroked his arm. "Ector…"

He gasped. "Ahndromahk?"

"Are you all right?"

Palpating his wounded temple, Hector croaked, "Fine. Just — just dreaming about Mom." He forced a laugh. It was nothing like the strong black laugh that had first intrigued Andromache, or the golden one that had often warmed her. This one was feeble and a pasty yellowish-grey. It sounded diseased.

Andromache wrapped her arm around him and pressed her cheek to his chest; she was too afraid of making things worse to ask what he'd really seen in his nightmare. She didn't want to upset him by forcing him to think about it. She didn't want him to push her away again, either, as he had at the outpost stable. "I had nightmares when you were gone," she whispered.

Hector's arms closed around her. "Bad?"

She nodded.

"On what — the goat?"

Andromache furrowed her brow. She hadn't told Hector about Paris and the plate of goat's heads, had she? "What goat?"

"The baby. When you ahre a little girl."

"Oh. That goat." The one that had been screaming in pain — the one she'd killed to end his suffering. "I used to have a lot of nightmares about him, but not as much lately." Andromache lowered her voice. "Lately, they've been about clusters of tornadoes — never just one, but five or six, swirling around each other. About falling through rotten wood. About Cutie's body parts breaking off." *About you,* she added to herself.

Hector stroked her hair as though she were the one who had just woken up in a sweat. They lay like that, not sleeping, for the rest of the night.

℘

"I MAHST GO," whispered Hector, as soon as the first bird chirped.

"Go where?" asked Andromache.

"Work stahff." He sighed.

"It's not even light yet."

"I know. Baht there is so mahch. I haff been away."

Andromache could tell by the yellowish-grey sound of his voice that he was still thinking about the nightmare. It must have been a bad one, the kind that would stay with him awhile. She understood all too well. Even days later, with a live Hector beside her, the dream where he'd come back to Troy on a blanket still made her sick. She hugged him. "I'll miss you," she said.

"My Ahndromahk," he said, gently stroking her hair. "I am going to come back in a few years."

"What!" she cried in anguish. "Years?"

"Hours!" he corrected hastily.

"Oh," she sighed. "Can I walk you to the door?"

"Ohff couhrse."

Andromache reached for her cloak and rumpled dress, still in a heap at the side of the bed, and hurriedly threw them on. Meanwhile, Hector was in a struggle for his own clothing: Cutie, having evidently forgiven him for chucking her to the floor two nights earlier, was lying in a nest she'd made from his tunic. Oh, the reproachful look when he once again evicted her from her bed! If the mood hadn't been so gloomy, Andromache would have laughed.

Not wanting to wake anyone, they crossed the dark courtyard in silence. Hector took nothing from the kitchen as they passed through it. He didn't even glance at the table, still covered with fruit and bread.

"All right," said Andromache, when they'd reached the main door. "I'll see you later."

Hector was rubbing his temple.

"Oh, no," she murmured. "Your head — is it hurting?"

"No, no," said Hector, brushing off her concern. A moment later, he offered, "Maybe noon…"

Andromache frowned. "What? Noon? Does your head hurt more in the afternoon?"

Hector shook his head. "No — '*noon*' is fohr you. You can come to the hohrse house then?"

"O-o-o-oh! Noon," she agreed.

"If it is hot today, you can come a little befohre and wait fohr me. We can stay in the hohrse house until efening, when it is cool. I haff some work to do, baht —"

"We can be there together," Andromache finished. "I'd love to. Maybe I can help. Maybe there are some ropes that you need me to untangle."

Hector gave her a faint smile. He then embraced her with sudden fervor, as though he hadn't misspoken earlier and actually *would* be gone for years. He kissed her and touched her face, giving her a look so long and tender that she almost had to turn away. Just as she was about to, Cutie threw her front feet up on Hector's legs. *Notice me! Me, me, me!* the little creature seemed to be pleading, as her ears flattened back against her head.

Andromache laughed around the lump in her throat, and even Hector seemed to brighten a shade or two.

"And later," he said. "I can fix the stahff wiff Mom."

Andromache nodded. "I'll see you at noon."

Once Hector had left, Andromache went back to the kitchen for a lamp and a snack and then coaxed Cutie up to the library. At that hour, there was little risk of running into the other family members. She could read there in peace and try to distract herself.

She chose a text, sat down at the table — *The table. We spent so much time together, here* — and started reading:

Swashmuckers yabulli skaggentor thod —

So much time. He loved me the whole time — wanted me the whole time! Now he has me, but what good is it doing him? He's almost as miserable today as he was yesterday, when he thought I'd broken up with him.

Whiskor slertum tooit grakellont —

Where did he go?

Grommitt slockle whiskator —

It's not time for him to meet with Paris, yet. Maybe he went down to the training field early, to blow off some steam and try to get that nightmare out of his head. Or maybe he went running — that's what I'd do. Then again, maybe he's just checking on the horses. No, wait — he said to come to the stable at noon, so he probably isn't there yet.

Grenettit fomni ovnior shambit —

He could've at least told me where he was going! It wouldn't have been that hard. Don't husbands tell their wives what they're up to? Maybe not, in Taruisha. I hope he's all right! I hope he wasn't lying about his head, when he said it didn't hurt.

Illit radyad phronic —

Maybe that's it — he's somewhere getting treatments for his head. No, that's silly! If it was bothering him, he'd just have his mom look at it.

Yaka yaka simly sod —

Oh, gods, his mom! That'll be fun, later, when he talks to her! She'll have had a whole night to cook up new insults.

> *Grattit, ohheh graattit, hiskin rattletat granianet sook oatta.*

Enough! thought Andromache, dropping the text in disgust. The first sentence had taken her forever to read, and she hadn't understood a word of it. *It's no use,* she decided. *I'll just straighten up a little.*

The table was once again piled high with texts. Andromache left the ones that were obviously for Cassandra's lessons but set about reshelving the others. To her surprise, at the bottom of a stack on Hector's side of the table, she found an old favorite of hers: *On Lorani.* Hector had always hated the text as much as she loved it. Had he hidden it there, before his last trip out with the army? Had he been giving it another try, as a way of feeling close to her? Andromache smiled at the happy thought. Instead of reshelving the rest of the texts, she sat down at the table and began to read:

> *Many people have stood on our earthly seashore at night, in awe of the luminous creatures drifting on or beneath the waves. In like manner, an observer on the shore of the celestial ocean might watch the great Lorani drift serenely past each other, luminous like certain creatures in our terrestrial seas. Our world would be invisible, being comparable, as mentioned before, to a tiny mote within a bubble of air...*

AFTER AN HOUR or so, Cutie stirred and ran to the library door, which was ajar. She barked once and pushed her way out into the hall.

"What are *you* doing here?" hissed a male voice. "Not allowed in the new digs?"

Andromache hurried over to the door and opened it a little wider. "Hey, Paris," she said.

He raised an eyebrow. "Hermie? You aren't allowed there, either? I've always known my brother is peculiar, but *that* —"

"He left already."

"Oh."

"I'm just up here reading."

"I see."

"Are you going down to meet with him, now?" asked Andromache.

Paris glowered. "Yes, thanks to you."

"Be nice to him, today. He's — I don't know, upset."

"Now, Hermie! Don't get all wrinkled up. He's upset? Mom can have that effect on people. Just give it a few days and the whole thing will blow over."

"Just promise that you'll be *nice*."

"What makes you think I wouldn't be?"

Andromache gave him a stern look. He held up his hands in surrender and left.

I should get going too, thought Andromache. She couldn't stay much longer in the library because soon, Cassandra and her tutors would need to use it. But where else could she go? Not to the kitchen, where she might encounter Hecuba. Not to Hector's room, where she didn't quite belong, yet. Not to her old room, which now seemed too lonely.

The courtyard, she decided. *It's not raining, today*. Even if someone was in the kitchen, she could slip out through the banquet hall and hide in a quiet corner of the courtyard until it was time to meet Hector. *I'll take Cutie with me*. When she looked around, though, the dog was nowhere to be seen.

I'll bet she's in my old bedroom, poor confused little thing, thought Andromache. *She probably went up there after she saw Paris. Well, I'll just leave her there. Hiding will be easier without her, anyway.*

ANDROMACHE GROANED herself awake. Her head was bent at an awkward angle, and drool was pooling on the paving stones. Her bottom half ranged from numb to sore from the way she'd been lying on the hard ground. She shook her head and frowned. What time was it, anyway? Late morning? Her stomach growled. *Time to eat.* She stood, letting the blood trickle painfully back into her legs, and was about to plod over to the kitchen when she heard two voices coming from inside it.

Hector was in there, talking to his mother.

Andromache didn't dare barge in on them. At the same time, she didn't want to miss what they were saying. *I'll just hide behind a shrub,* she decided.

"What have you been up to today, dear?" Hecuba asked pleasantly.

"Not much," said Hector. "Just a few work things." His tone was guarded — wary.

Hecuba sighed and changed the subject. "Well, thank you for coming back."

"Paris said you needed me."

Ah! So Hecuba had intercepted Paris on the way to archery lessons — just as well Andromache hadn't gone to the kitchen after the library! She would have run into both of them at once.

"Is Andromache here?" asked Hector.

"I haven't seen her, dear."

"I can only talk a little while, then. If she's not here, it's because she's trying to meet me down at the stables."

"That's a shame. It would've been nice to have her with us, considering all that we have to talk about." Hecuba sighed again. "Well — *you're* here, and you can discuss these things with her when you see her. First and foremost, we need to plan a date for the wedding ceremony. You'll want it to be soon, I'm sure."

She actually sounded apologetic. Maybe she *had* just been taken by surprise, the night before!

"Yes," said Hector, softening. "I'll help Andromache move her things downstairs tonight."

His mother paused. "That wasn't quite what I meant. Moving is hardly a ceremony."

"Oh. Well, we could have a family dinner to celebrate, too," offered Hector.

"Yes, of course, dear," said Hecuba. "But I didn't mean that, either. I meant a proper wedding ceremony, complete with all the rituals."

"Oh, Mom! Can't we just skip all the pageantry?"

"Pageantry!" huffed Hecuba, clearly piqued but making an effort to keep calm. "Hector, dear —"

"It isn't pageantry to show honor to the gods, son," Priam intervened.

Both parents? Andromache frowned. Was Priam just there as a buffer, or was something larger afoot?

"Or to hold a lawful ceremony," his wife added.

Hector sighed.

"What are you sighing about?" asked Hecuba. "I don't see the problem, and I don't see why you wouldn't want to invite your friends and relatives to share in this momentous occasion."

A Taruishan wedding ceremony... thought Andromache. Well, why not, even if she was already Hector's wife? True, some of the rituals were silly, but she and Hector could laugh about them, afterward. It might be fun. Plus, a second wedding meant a second wedding night. Andromache smiled to herself, and her cheeks went pink. She definitely wouldn't mind having another one of those...

Hector, however, was unconvinced. "*Your* friends, you mean," he muttered.

"Pardon?" said Hecuba. "I don't think I heard you."

"I said, *your* friends. Not mine."

"Hector," his father said sternly, but Hecuba cut him off. "It's all right, Priam," she said. "Let him make his point."

"My point," said Hector, "is that *my* friends don't need to see Andromache and me prancing around with weeds on our heads. Only *your* friends care about that kind of thing."

"Prancing around? Weeds? Honestly, Hector!" His mother sniffed twice but bit back a sharper retort.

"What are you so upset about, son?" asked Priam.

Andromache had been wondering the same thing.

"Look," said Hector. "Where she comes from, there aren't ceremonies. You tell your families you want to be married, and then you are. Just like that. We're already married, Mom and Dad — she's already my wife. What's the point of a ceremony?"

"We understand your desire to respect her traditions," Priam said gently, "but it's important to honor yours as well. What harm does it do to have a Trojan ceremony, so that you're married in both cultures?"

"Did *you* have two ceremonies? One for Mom's culture, one for yours?"

Priam hedged. "We brought in elements from your mother's culture — which we'd certainly want to do for Andromache — but we just had one ceremony. The traditions were more similar, between your mother's land and mine, than between yours and Andromache's."

"You mean that Mom's traditions were *better* than Andromache's," Hector said cuttingly.

During the moment of silence that followed, Andromache cursed herself. She finally understood why he was so opposed to a Trojan ceremony — and it was all *her* doing. She'd sown the seeds of this conflict months earlier, when she and Hector had been lying out on the courtyard, drinking too much wine, and she'd told him about the wagoner…

'*Don't call* him *your* husband!' *Hector shouted.*

'*Oh, so that marriage doesn't count?' she shouted back. 'Well, go ahead and say it, if you think I'm a whore!*'

'*That's not what I meant!' Hector cried in horror. 'I meant he didn't treat you like husbands should treat their wives. He doesn't deserve to be called your husband…*'

But even though they'd cleared things up, he apparently still felt the need to prove himself. Andromache wished that she could take back her words. *You don't have to do this*, she thought at Hector, silently pleading with him to calm down. *I was drunk. I didn't understand why you were so mad about the wagoner, or why you didn't want me to call him my husband. I didn't know you wanted to be my husband! It all makes sense, now. You don't have to do this, Ector!*

"Son," Priam said softly, "consider that Andromache might *want* to participate in Trojan traditions —"

"*Trojan* traditions, my ass!"

"Hector," warned Hecuba.

"Sorry — my *ankle*. Is that all right, to say *ankle*?"

"Make your point, Hector," said his father, less gently than before.

Andromache cringed. Priam sounded dangerously close to yelling — Priam, who *never* yelled! What was going on with Hector? Even if he disagreed with his parents — even if he wanted to prove something — it wasn't like him to be nasty to them.

"Fine, Dad, here it is. Most so-called Trojans have the same traditions *my wife* does. Most of my soldiers, for instance, can't afford carnivals like the ones *your* friends put on. Am I supposed to run around, letting my wife and soldiers think I despise them? That I'm better than they are?"

Hecuba inhaled. "Hector, dear," she said, miraculously calm. "It costs very little to have your union blessed at the city temple. I imagine that your soldiers do this, whether you know it or not. But even if what you say is true, I doubt they would fault you for doing things differently. Expectations aren't the same for someone in a position such as yours."

"You *don't* say," said Hector, so scathingly that his parents fell silent.

"What about Andromache?" Priam risked saying, after a moment.

"What about her?" Hector growled.

"Don't you want her, as much as possible, to feel a part of things?"

"A part of things?"

"She might feel more comfortable among our friends and neighbors if she's gone through the same rituals as they have."

"What you mean is that *you* would feel more comfortable." Hector's voice was soft, now — dangerous. "What you've *really* been saying all along is that if we drown her in enough ritual bullshit —"

"Hector, honestly!"

"— your *friends* might forget that she's an orphan from nowhere instead of the daughter of some rich Trojan. You can pretend she's whoever you *really* wanted for a daughter-in-law."

"You don't know us at all," whispered Hecuba. "You think we're monsters."

"We always told you we would welcome whomever you chose to be your wife," Priam reminded his son. "And we meant it."

"Hold your noses and welcome her!"

"Hector!" cried his father, in disbelief. "You know how we feel about Andromache. She was sent here by the stars."

"There you go again, rewriting her history to make it more palatable to you! The truth is, she was hauled here on Lee's horse from a tiny little dead-end village. And I love her." Hector's voice broke.

"We love her, too," said Priam.

Hector didn't respond.

"And if *you* are serious about loving her, think about her well-being."

"What do you think I'm doing, Dad? I'm the only one here who's showing any respect for her customs — her traditions — her family."

"By respecting them to this degree, you're going to end up hurting her."

"*Me*, hurt her?" Hector gave a horrible, sharp laugh. "What a load of —"

"Oh, enough!" snapped Hecuba. "Delicacy is lost on him, Priam. Very well, Hector, we cede. Let the entire city think that you're embarrassed by Andromache, if that's what you want. Let them think that you don't really want her but feel obligated to keep her around because you've put her in a *predicament*."

"Mom!"

Andromache winced.

"So, you don't like that word?" taunted Hecuba. "That's the very *least* of what people will say about her if you don't have a public Trojan ceremony, my boy! And there's nothing you, or I, or your father, can do about it."

There was a sudden, loud *thwack*, presumably of Hector's elbows hitting the table.

"Dammit!" he cried. "Dammit, dammit, *dammit*! Damn them *all*!"

The pain in his voice brought Andromache to her feet. Just as she was about to launch herself toward the kitchen, though, Hecuba spoke.

"Ssssh, I know," she soothed, overlooking Hector's profanity. "I know. I've never seen such an infestation of gossips as there are in this city. But there's nothing you can do about them, Hector, dear, except try to prevent them from hurting Andromache." Hecuba sighed. "I honestly thought you'd grasp that without our having to scream at each other."

"Well, I didn't," muttered Hector, sounding weary and defeated. "You should've just said what you meant right away."

Andromache sat down. Hector was unhappy but calm. If she ran in now, with his parents there, he would probably work himself up again. *Just wait till noon,* she told herself. *You can hug and kiss him then, after everything's settled with his parents. Don't run in and stir things up.*

"You're right," Hecuba said graciously. "I should have just said what I meant. Let's start over, dear — we've come full circle, anyway. Let's decide when the ceremony will be."

"My wife and I are free tonight," said Hector.

"Son…" Priam demurred.

"You've thrown together parties with a lot less notice than that," countered Hector, with new signs of agitation in his voice. "Every time I come home from a campaign, the house is clogged with people, food, and wine — even if you only had a few hours' notice — even if I'd rather just sleep."

Wounded though she must have been by his jabs, Hecuba kept her cool, saying only, "Very well — we won't bother, next time. But *this* isn't just another party! *This* isn't something one simply throws together!"

"Tomorrow, then," said Hector. "This is only a formality, anyway. I'm sure all the ritual bu —" He stopped himself. "*Business* — can be arranged by tomorrow."

"I doubt it very much," his mother said primly.

"For one thing, I don't know offhand if the date is auspicious," Priam added.

"Oh, I don't give a flying —"

"In any case, that isn't the only issue," Hecuba interrupted. "Neither you nor I have seen my brother, your uncle Asius, for some time —"

"I'll stop you right there, because I'm *not* going to visit him. I only said I would before because of a misunderstanding with Andromache. But now that's cleared up, and I'm staying here. With *her.*"

"Under the circumstances, I can see why you wouldn't want to go to Santiya for a long visit —"

"Damn right, I wouldn't!"

"Son, hush!" Priam broke in. "Your uncle needs to come *here*. For the wedding."

"Oh," said Hector. "Well, of course. Of course. As long as he gets here *soon*."

"You may go whenever you like to fetch him and bring him back," said Hecuba.

Andromache was dumbfounded. Up until that moment, Hector's parents had sounded reasonable — far more reasonable than Hector — but Hecuba's comment changed everything.

Equally stunned, Hector said nothing at first. "*Me*? Fetch him? From Santiya?" he finally spluttered.

"Yes."

"You're joking. You *must* be joking."

"No, my dear, I am *not*."

"Tell me she's joking, Dad."

"Son —"

"Then at least tell me *you're* not in on this!"

"Your mother and I are in agreement."

"Well, I'm not going," Hector snarled. "I *just* got back here, and you're nuts if you think I'm leaving again. Send someone else — anyone! Send the baker. Send Paris."

"Asius won't believe *them* if they tell him you're getting married," argued Hecuba. "For the past three years, now you've given every appearance of courting Penthesilea. Yes, yes — I know, she's your colleague, no more! But I for one believe that Asius had other motives in sending her here. Last time I saw him, years ago, we both agreed that marriage would be good for you."

"Oh, thank you for deciding that," Hector said sarcastically.

"You're welcome," said Hecuba, matching his tone. "In any case, Asius has no reason to believe Paris, or the baker, or anyone else but *you* that you're suddenly in a rush to marry some girl he's never even heard of."

Hector scoffed. "That's *his* problem."

"He deserves far more respect from you than *that*," huffed Hecuba. "He's been like a second father to you."

"I'm not going!" cried Hector, his voice rising on the last word.

Behind her shrub, Andromache was reeling, both with fury and with love. Now she knew what his parents had been up to all along! Their kindness had just been a ruse. A trap. The whole time, they'd been maneuvering Hector into leaving *her* behind. They'd wheedled, schemed, and steered until they thought they had him in a position where he couldn't refuse. It hurt. It hurt that they were so opposed to the marriage — especially Priam, who'd seemed happy about it the night before and had plainly been corrupted by his wife. It hurt, but not unbearably, because Hector wasn't falling for it. He was choosing *her*.

Hecuba, meanwhile, tried a different tack: "Besides all that, Hector, since it's *your* wedding, it's also your duty to see that your uncle arrives here safely."

"Screw my duty! And screw my uncle!"

"Hector!" boomed Priam, finally goaded into yelling. It was a terrible sound. "That's enough!"

"It's all right, Priam." Hecuba said quietly. "His filthy mouth won't hurt anyone but himself. Please, Hector, be reasonable —"

"I *am*!" Hector shot back. "I *am* being reasonable! Just when I thought I'd finally had it, something good happened. And now, all I want is to stay here — with *my wife*. What's so fucking unreasonable about that?"

'Had it?' Just what does that mean? wondered Andromache, feeling sick.

"Oh, Hector...your poor head," murmured Hecuba.

Was that what he'd meant by '*had it*' — that the wound was even worse than it looked? That he'd barely made it back? Was that why he'd wanted to be alone, in the outpost stable? Was that what all his nightmares were about? Was that why he'd been so quick to think that Andromache was dumping him, after the first nightmare? Because his nerves were frayed from reliving his own near-death?

Andromache's eyelids fluttered as she fought back tears. She wanted more than ever to run to Hector, but she was still scared of making things harder for him. *Wait. Just wait. See him later. Comfort him later. Talk to him later...*

"Your poor head," Hecuba repeated.

"Stop talking about my head!" Hector roared.

Silence in the kitchen.

Andromache began to shake. *Leave him alone!* she wanted to scream at his parents. *Just leave him alone!*

Strangely, it was Hector who tried to make peace. "Look," he said. "I'm sorry for yelling. I'm sorry for swearing. We can have a ceremony whenever you want — just drop the Uncle idea. Please."

Do it, Andromache thought to his parents. *He loves me. If you try to make him leave me, you'll hurt him.*

"If Cassandra's child were getting married, she would stop at nothing to have *you* there," Hecuba reasoned.

Hector sighed. "Fine — but I wouldn't care if it was my nephew who came for me or a wide green sea monster. Send someone else."

Do it! thought Andromache.

"Hector, please," his mother said softly. Pleadingly. "Just fetch your uncle Asius."

Silence. Then —

"I'm supposed to be meeting my wife," Hector said coldly. The harsh stomping of his feet was followed by Hecuba crying out, "Hector!" and Priam calling, "Son!" For a few useless steps, they tried to follow him, but he was moving far too fast.

Stay put! Andromache warned herself. If she chased after Hector, she would have to pass through the banquet hall, where Priam and Hecuba now were. Above all, she didn't want to see *them*!

It wasn't quite noon; she could tell by the sun. If she waited a little longer, Hector's parents would leave and she could try to find her husband. She crept as close as she dared to the doorway, listening for signs of their departure.

Hecuba was crying.

You should *be crying,* thought Andromache. *You deserve to cry.*

"I can stand it if he hates us, Priam, but not if — oh, my Hector!"

Not if what? Andromache thought acidly. *Not if he stays married to that trashy Lukkana girl?*

"Ssh…" Priam soothed. "It's going to be all right."

"How?" moaned Hecuba. "And don't you dare run off and consult the stars! Not about our *son*!"

"Ssh…all right, dear. Let's go upstairs. You should lie down for a while."

Yes — upstairs! Andromache held her breath.

Two pairs of feet shuffled through the banquet hall and up the stairs. One stair — two stairs — five stairs. Once they'd reached the twelfth stair, Andromache crept out from her hiding place and tiptoed to the main door. She heaved it open, ran through, and slammed it shut, no longer caring what kind of racket she made. She was out.

ℰ〇

ON THE STREET, Andromache turned this way and that. No one. At least, no one she wanted. She wasn't surprised. She'd been held back for longer than she cared to know.

"Ector?" she called, on the off chance that he'd come back to find her.

Several heads turned, but only in idle curiosity: Trojans, eager for gossip. *Go ahead and talk about me,* she snarled silently. *That's the least of my problems!* It was almost noon, already — she would have to run to get to the stables on time.

(*What if you don't make it?*) asked the snide little Voice. (*He'll think you forgot about your meeting...or that you decided not to come.*)

Shut up! snapped Andromache, sprinting down the street. Aloud, she cried, "Ector! I'm coming!" More people were staring, now, although whether because Andromache was screaming or because she was screaming in Lukkan, she didn't know. "Ector!" she hollered, almost to spite them. *Not much farther,* she told herself. She was nearing the stables.

(*What if you're too late?*) asked the Voice. (*What if he broke down after the fight, and you find him crouched on the floor?*)

Then I'll take care of him, stupid Voice, she hissed, with more certainty than she felt. The thought made her run even harder.

Finally, she arrived at the main stables. "Ector!" she called again, but she was so winded that his name came out as a croak.

"Hey, Missy," said a familiar voice. Xanthus.

"Hector —" Andromache pleaded to the stable master. "Is he — is he —"

"Hector!" Xanthus hollered on her behalf. "She's here!"

Several horses whinnied in response to all the yelling, and then —

"Ahndromahk!" Hector was running over to her, holding her, kissing her, stroking her hair, pressing her to his chest, rocking slowly back and forth. All the while, she cried, leaving two dark circles on his tunic.

"Sssh," he said, without asking why she was so upset. "Sssh, pretty wife."

"I had to find you!"

"I've been looking for you, too."

"I'm so sorry I'm late," she blubbered. "I fell asleep out on the courtyard, and when I woke up —"

Hector stiffened. "The courtyard?"

Andromache nodded into his chest.

"Oh, Ahndromahk…we need to talk. In private."

He took her hand and led her toward the back of the stables. She followed, confused as well as relieved — Hector was calm. There were no signs of the rage and despair he'd shown earlier. Either he was putting on a show for her, or something else had happened since his stormy exit from the house.

Hector stopped in front of Buzzy, who whickered at him. "Hi Buzzy. No — no, stop — no more celery today." He sat on the floor, out of reach of the horse's mouth.

Andromache snuggled up against him.

"So, you heard all that?" he asked.

She nodded.

"Oh, my sweetheart…"

"I didn't mean to overhear!" she told him. "I was out there taking a nap, and then you and your parents were in the kitchen, and I didn't want to barge in, and —"

"No," said Hector, looking pale. "Of course you didn't. No one in their right mind would have walked into *that*. No wonder you dehydrated yourself on my clothes." He held out his tunic, wet with her tears. "The things you must have heard me say!"

"You were defending me!" Andromache protested.

"It must have sounded terrible."

"You were defending me."

Hector sighed. "Trying, anyway."

She drew closer and kissed him.

"Thanks," he said, kissing her back.

"I wouldn't mind having a Taruishan ceremony," she murmured. "I think it would be nice."

He sighed again. "You do not haff to say this."

"<u>I know. But I mean it</u>." Leaning into him, she whispered, "<u>I love you for what you said, and why you said it, but I want you to know, you were right. The wagoner was never my husband. I didn't know what the word meant, then. No matter what kind of ceremony you and I have — or don't have — *you're* my only true husband, forever</u>."

Hector squeezed her, hard.

"You look like you're feeling a little better," she said softly, squeezing him back.

He nodded. "Much better. I just had to get out of there."

"I don't blame you."

"When I left the house, I thought you were already here," he said. "I thought I was going to be late." He gave a wry smile. "You're always in the house when I think you're out of it, <u>Ahndromahk</u>. One of these days, I'll learn. I'll start looking *there*."

"Maybe there won't be too many more times we have to look for each other," said Andromache, tucking her fingers into his belt.

He sighed. "My sweetheart, you must have heard where they want me to go."

She nodded. "But you're not — right?"

"I *am*," he said. "I'm going to Santiya."

"What?" she cried. "But why? I thought you didn't want to go! You told them you wouldn't!"

"I *have* to," he said gently.

"Oh," murmured Andromache. She'd lost. His parents had won — he was leaving her, just as they'd wanted. Tears began spilling down her cheeks.

"Oh, my <u>Ahndromahk</u>!" Hector dabbed at her face with a dry corner of his tunic. "It's not that bad. It won't take long, I promise."

"How long?"

"A week — maybe a little less."

Silver streaks reappeared on her face. A week! A week without Hector, who had only just the day before become her husband! A week alone and unprotected in a house where everyone hated her! A whole week during which Hector might forget all about her!

"Not that long," Hector soothed.

The tears kept falling.

"I'll make sure Xanthus is here to entertain you," he offered.

Andromache gave a soft laugh, and Hector looked relieved.

"You really have to go?" she whispered.

He nodded.

"I don't care about gossip," she said, in a last-ditch effort to make him stay.

He held her tighter but said nothing — and she knew what that meant.

He's loved me for two years, she thought, willing herself not to cry again. *He won't forget about me in seven days*.

Hector pressed his lips to her ear. "You can care fohr Buzzy and Thisbe when I am gone?"

"You aren't riding Buzzy?"

"No, he is so tahred. And hurty. And I take not *one* hohrse there." Andromache frowned; he switched to Truvan. "There's a relay of horses. I'll stop along the way to change."

"Oh. Well, of course, I'll take care of Buzzy and Thisbe."

"You can visit to them sometime?"

"Of course. And I'll give them their wine treat, too."

Hector smiled mischievously. "And talk '*hohrse*' to them?" he asked, alluding to an early Lukkan lesson, when, in order to teach him the word '*horse*,' Andromache had neighed.

She gave him a gentle poke. "That's *still* funny to you?" she asked.

"Yes," he said. "Foreffer."

She smiled a little sadly. "When are you leaving?"

"Now. Well, after I can tell my parents," he amended.

"So soon…"

"To be *done* soon," he said firmly. "To be *back* soon, to be wiff you."

"Don't ride *too* fast!" she pleaded, thinking of the wound on his head. "Be *safe*."

"Ahndromahk," he protested. "I can rahde all rahght."

"I know." She pulled on his belt. Tears were welling once more. "I just love you…"

"Oh, pretty wife," soothed Hector. "I lahff you, too. I will be safe."

"Good," said Andromache. Sighing, she added, "I suppose it's a good thing that you'll be there to protect your uncle, on the way back." In her mind, she had an image of Hector helping a wispy, white-haired man onto a horse.

Hector snorted. "Protect!"

"What's so funny?"

"You can see, when you meet Uncle."

Andromache cuddled closer to Hector. "I can't wait to meet him," she murmured. "Because that means *you'll* be back, too."

"Soon," Hector promised. "Soon."

A few more kisses, a few more hugs, and he was gone.

Chapter 28

"Everything's going to hell." Xanthus shook his head. After Hector left, Andromache had wandered back to the main stable door, where she was now thrashing Xanthus in a game of roodles. "You'll win the next round," she said comfortingly.

"I doubt it, Missy. I doubt it."

"Oh, come on."

"How can I, when there isn't going to *be* another round?" the stable master muttered sourly. "I *knew* this was going to happen! I can see right through the likes of you — and *him*!" He pointed one stout finger at Andromache.

She looked behind her, but there was no one there. "Him?" she asked. "What him?"

Xanthus glared at her from his beady eyes. "Hector never talks to me like he did the day *you* first came to the stables. *'Bring water — now!'*" the old man simpered. "Like I'm his nitwit page!"

"Oh, *that* him," said Andromache, understanding at last.

"Eh? And what other '*him*' would I mean? Do you have any other '*hims*' hidden in your pockets?"

"No!" cried Andromache.

"I told you, everything's going to hell." The old man's tone had turned mournful.

"It isn't *that* bad, is it?" Andromache asked plaintively. Did no one in Troy feel happy for her and Hector? And what reason did Xanthus have to gripe about their marriage?

The stable master glared at her again. "You're not going to sit here and play games with an ugly old man if there's a young, good-looking one taking up all your time."

Andromache blushed and looked down. "I'll still play roodles with you," she mumbled.

"Eh? I'll believe that when I see it," snapped Xanthus. "The only reason you came here today was to play chasey-chasey with *him*. And don't get me started on the way you two were wailing at each other! You might not care, but the horses were *this close* to stampeding." He squinted one eye and held out his thumb and forefinger, barely a breath apart.

"I'm sorry!" cried Andromache, knowing that Xanthus was right — about her visit, if not about the stampede. She'd only come to the stables to find Hector…and she'd only challenged Xanthus to roodles so she could avoid going back to Hector's family.

"Hmph," grumped the stable master. "Well, now that he's gone, I don't suppose we'll have to worry about *that*! I don't suppose you'll be back here tomorrow, bawling to beat the four winds."

"I will, too! Come back, I mean, not bawl," Andromache clarified.

Xanthus gave her a haughty look. "Well, maybe I'll be here, maybe I won't. The sun's going down, Missy — you'd best skitter off home."

"Let's finish this game, anyway," she pleaded.

"Hmph!" Xanthus scowled. "I suppose you *would* want that, since you're winning."

ॐ

ANDROMACHE ENTERED the house as noiselessly as possible. She was hungry but didn't stop in the kitchen. Later, when there was less danger of running into her in-laws, she could go downstairs for a snack, but for the time being, she would stay in her room.

Her *old* room. It was quiet, now, and seemed empty. Cutie was nowhere to be seen. The events of the past three days had no doubt left the dog so confused that she didn't know where to find anyone, anymore.

Three days! Could that be all? Andromache was exhausted and couldn't imagine how much worse poor Hector was feeling, galloping off to the east on a never-ending string of horses. She hoped that he was at an inn somewhere, sleeping…something he'd done little of for the past three days.

There was a knock at the doorway, the softest little *tzit, tzit, tzit.*

Andromache gave the door a baleful look. Anyone — *anyone* — might be on the other side, and there were several people in the house that she did *not* want to see!

Tzit, tzit, tzit.

Andromache held her breath.

"Honey?" came a girlish whisper. "Are you there?"

"Oh," gasped Andromache, relieved. It was only Cassandra. "Come in."

The girl flew in, screeching, "Oh, honey!" For the few days Hector was home, Cassandra had given Andromache space and privacy. Now, she flopped on Andromache's bed and tackled her with a hug. "Finally, finally, finally, a sister, after all these years of brothers!" she sang exultantly. "I'm so happy for you! I just *love* love!"

Happy! Cassandra was happy! Someone in Hector's family was happy about the marriage! "Thank you," said Andromache, hugging the girl back.

"So, tell me!" trilled Cassandra.

"Tell you what?"

"Everything! I want to know it all — the whole story!"

Andromache drew back slightly. "You already know everything," she said, feeling no qualms about her lie. There was a long list of things she was never going to tell Hector's sister.

"There's a lot I don't know!" Cassandra insisted. "For starters, have you and Hector kissed?"

"Of course," Andromache said carefully. "You saw it — remember, when he came into the kitchen? I was holding those cups?"

"Oh, fah!" said Cassandra, waving her hand dismissively. "That's not what I mean. Have you kissed for *real?*"

Andromache looked out the window. The sun's last light was slipping down, over the horizon. With the periwinkle blue of evening came the first stars — faint, and slow, and shy.

"I'll take that as a *yes*!" Cassandra giggled. "You should see your face."

"Cassandra!" cried Andromache, blushing.

"So, when was the kiss?"

"Cassandra, seriously!"

"The day after the party?"

Andromache hesitated. "The night *of*," she said at last.

"Really!" Cassandra gasped in surprise. "So, *that's* where he disappeared to! We all thought he'd gone to sleep because his head was bothering him. Well, no, that's not quite true. Everyone *else* thought it was his head, but *I* thought he'd had a fight with his girlfriend — meaning *you*, of course, even though Mom thought I meant Penthesilea. It made sense! First, you came home looking just awful, and then *he* came home looking even worse and asked if I'd seen you. When I said you were up in your room, he ran off to take a bath, and then he hung around near the door until he disappeared. So —" Cassandra paused to ask, "*did* you have a fight?"

"Kind of," said Andromache, hedging. "But we made up."

"Oh, honey! I'm so glad!" sang the girl. "But — no, wait!"

"What?"

"If you kissed with him that night, why was he so grumpy the next morning?" Cassandra lowered her voice to a whisper. "Was the kiss — you know — *faulty*?"

"Cassandra!"

"Well?"

"There was a misunderstanding," Andromache said lightly, hoping the girl wouldn't pry further. "But we got it sorted out."

"Oh, thank goodness!" cried Cassandra. After a short pause, she added: "But the kiss? Was it —"

Andromache looked like a cherry as she howled, "No —it wasn't faulty, all right?"

Cassandra giggled. "All right. So, then, let's see — what else — oh! How long have you been in love with him, anyway?'"

"Oh, I don't —"

"At least since that soiree, right? The one where you went gollylocks?"

"Well —"

"But it was probably before that?"

Andromache laughed.

"What's so funny?"

"I don't know when, exactly! It's been a long time, but I didn't realize it until you told me."

Cassandra giggled again. "The look you gave me — like you wanted to shove me out a window!"

"I kind of did. But not as much *that* day as when you spied on us in the library."

The other girl laughed harder. "I didn't mean to, I swear!"

"Oh, I'll bet!"

"Well, maybe a little," Cassandra admitted. "I just wanted to see if he might have feelings for you after all. Ever since that soiree, I've been dying for you guys to get together!"

"I'll bet you thought we *never* would, after the night he asked you to the river with us!"

Cassandra shrieked with laughter. "I know — I wanted to smack him! What on earth was *wrong* with him?"

Giggling, Andromache defended her husband. "He was just nervous."

"How adorable!" sighed Cassandra. "He *never* gets nervous!"

"Then he's lucky," said Andromache.

"Oh, honey! What are *you* nervous about?"

Again, Andromache had a long list of answers. She chose one of the more pressing ones: "Meeting your uncle."

"Uncle? But why?"

"I've never met a king, before."

"Well, he's probably never met a Lukkan girl before!" Cassandra laughed. "He might be more nervous than you are."

Andromache rolled her eyes. "I'm serious, Cassandra! Meeting him *has* to go well. Your parents already hate me."

"No, they don't! They —"

"They don't want me to marry Hector," Andromache concluded. "That's why they sent him away."

"Oh, honey," sighed Cassandra.

"And I know your uncle and Hector are close. What if he doesn't like me, either?"

"He'll love you!"

"You have no way of knowing that."

Cassandra didn't contradict her, but she didn't concede, either. "Say," she whispered instead. "I know what would take your mind off all of this. Paris brought home a secret packet of fig-and-pistachio rolls to give to all his lady friends. He stashed it in the biggest cooking cauldron — you know, the one we only use for parties? He thought no one would look there, but guess what?" She giggled. "If you want, I can go snag the pastries. Even if he figures out who stole them, he won't dare tell on us, since he wasn't supposed to buy them in the first place. The only downside is we won't get to see his face when he figures out he's been robbed."

"I *am* a little hungry," said Andromache. And a prank on Paris sounded like just the thing to distract her from her in-law situation.

Cassandra clapped her hands. "Then it's settled! I'll be right back."

Just after the girl had left, Cutie appeared. Andromache saw her eyes first, glowing yellowish-green in the lamp light. Then the ears, standing out sideways. Then the tail.

"Cutie!" she cried. "Where've you been, girl?"

At the sound of Andromache's voice, the little dog ran in, happily snuffling the ground. She found a dried spider, ate it, and gagged on the legs.

"Come here, girl," said Andromache, half-disgusted, half-amused. "Come up on the bed, and when Cassandra gets back, you can have a fig roll. That would be better than a spider, wouldn't it? You deserve a treat! It's been a rough couple of days."

Chapter 29

Early in the morning, with the leftover pastries tucked into a basket for later, Andromache strolled down to the stables. There was no point in staying at the house, where Cassandra would be meeting with her tutors — and where Paris would be giving suspicious looks to anyone who went near the cooking cauldrons — and where their parents would be rejoicing that Hector had left Andromache behind.

Xanthus wasn't on duty at the stables. Instead, she was greeted by the nervous young guard, Thoas.

"G-g-good morning," he said, bowing awkwardly.

Andromache blinked. *'Good morning?'* And with a bow, no less? "Is — is it all right if — if I go to the back of the stables?"

"Yes, ma'am." Thoas bowed again.

First *'good morning,'* and now *'ma'am?'* Confused by his behavior, Andromache stammered on. "It's just that I promised — I promised *someone* I'd visit his — uh, the horses, and so I thought I'd — thought I'd do that."

"I can take you, ma'am."

"Oh, no! No, don't — don't go to any trouble. I know the way, I just wanted to make sure it was all right."

Thoas nodded.

"Um — so, I guess I'll go back there, then."

He nodded again.

Flustered, Andromache turned down the leftmost aisle — the one she always used, to avoid spooking Penthesilea's horse, Battleblaze. She'd gone just a few steps when she heard Thoas calling timidly after her.

"Ma'am?"

"Huh?" said Andromache, over her shoulder.

"He keeps the wine on the third shelf."

The wine! The wine for the horses! She'd almost forgotten. "Thanks," she said to Thoas, giving the boy a shy smile, which he returned.

The stables were busy, even in Hector's absence, with soldiers hurrying back and forth between the stalls and the training field. She supposed that Xanthus was out on the field. It was a place she had no wish to see, so rather than looking for him, she stayed back by Buzzy and Thisbe. All morning and well into the afternoon, she brushed them, fed them, and talked to them.

"It looks like Xanthus has been taking good care of you," she said to Buzzy. The horse's hide had several dabs of healing salve, dry but obviously new that day. "I'm sure it's not the same as when *he's* here, though. You must miss him! I know. I understand. I miss him, too." Andromache took Buzzy's long, golden face in her hands. "But don't worry. He'll be back soon, and you can go down to the river with him again. I'll go too, if that's all right with you. No, don't worry! I won't ride you. I'll just watch. I bet you're really pretty when you run through the river."

Buzzy nuzzled her side.

"Oh, I'm sorry! I don't have any celery treats with me today. I'll bring some tomorrow."

Andromache heard a snort and turned to Thisbe. "I've been ignoring you! I'm so sorry, sweetheart. Maybe tomorrow I can take you out for a walk in the pasture. You'd like that, wouldn't you? I'll ask Thoas to help me. He'll make sure I don't do anything wrong, so you won't have to worry…"

"Missy?"

Startled, Andromache turned around to see Xanthus.

"You came after all," he grumped, as though that were unfortunate news.

"I told you I would."

"Hmf! And scaring the horses again, I see." The stable master went over to Thisbe and ruffled the pony's mane.

"Scaring?" Andromache said skeptically. "She doesn't look scared to me."

"Old Thisbe knows how to hide her feelings, unlike some young turnips," said Xanthus, patting Buzzy on the shoulder.

Buzzy nipped at him.

"See what I mean?" the old man squawked. "They don't make horses like they used to."

"Do — do you want to play roodles?" asked Andromache, to change the subject.

"Eh? I suppose I could work you in." With a grunt, Xanthus added, "Since you're up here, I'm assuming your little speckled love toad hasn't returned, yet?"

Andromache cringed. *Speckled love toad?* Oh, how she wished Hector were there to hear that! "No, not yet. He said it would be about a week." *Six days, and counting,* she added to herself.

"Well, don't expect him to hurry, and don't blame him, either, with all the wedding hullaballo waiting for him on the other end! Those fool ceremonies get nuttier every year — warbling, dousing each other with water. What's next, eh?"

Giggling, Andromache said, "Prancing around with weeds on our heads."

Xanthus narrowed his eyes. "You'd better hope that's the worst they throw your way, Missy."

She giggled again. "I take it Hector was complaining to you about the wedding ceremony, before he left?"

"To me, to Lee, to anyone who didn't run the other way when he came in here, bellowing for his wife." Xanthus shook his head. "Asked us if we were deaf when we didn't tell him right away where his *wife* was — as if any of us even knew he *had* one of those!"

"Oh — I — ah —" Andromache felt embarrassed. "What did you say?"

"Eh? Told him if we weren't deaf before, he was about to make it happen!"

"I'm sorry," sighed Andromache. "That day, he was a little — I mean, he'd had a —"

"Don't you make excuses, Missy! I can handle *him*. So can Lee. Once she finally yanked it out of him that he meant *you*, and told him you weren't here — this was all before you showed up, of course — she said she hadn't heard that you two were married. She asked how he'd managed to keep the whole city quiet about your warbling and dousing and prancing. That's not normal, you see, for the city to be quiet — especially not when the commander of the army is the one doing all the warbling. *That* doesn't happen very often! So then he told us about your Lookan wedding traditions. Makes sense, I told him — sound idea, skipping all the ceremonial crap." Xanthus furrowed his giant white eyebrows in indignation. "Of course, the damn fool didn't listen to *me*, did he!"

Andromache held her breath and silently begged Xanthus to keep talking. She was dying to know what had happened in the stables, the day before, to calm Hector down and convince him to leave for Santiya.

"Oh, no!" huffed Xanthus. "He didn't listen to *me*. I suppose after what *she* said, there was no chance of him listening to *anyone*."

Andromache frowned. "She?"

"Er — er —" stammered Xanthus, who now looked more like a boiled lobster than a live one.

"What '*she*?'" asked Andromache, although there was only one possibility.

"*Perhch-chiagh*," coughed the old man.

Andromache looked away from him.

"Lee," he muttered, chastened. "Penthesilea."

Penthesilea, of course — Penthesilea, who had never been Hector's fiancée, perhaps, but who *was* in love with him. Andromache had seen the look in her eyes, just days earlier, down by the gates. She'd been devastated. Now, Andromache knew why: in that moment, Penthesilea had realized that Hector was lost to her. She might have known earlier about Hector's feelings for Andromache. Close comrades as they were, he might have let something slip or even confided in her. Then, at the gates, Andromache had made it clear that she returned Hector's love...

Turning back to Xanthus, she demanded, "What did she say to him?"

"We never did start that game of roodles, did we, Missy? Let me just get the board out, and —"

Andromache looked away from him again.

Xanthus sighed. "Well, Missy, all I can tell you is that soldiers don't always say the prettiest things." He shook his head. "That they don't, and never have. It's the one thing that hasn't gotten any worse since the old days, because it was already about as bad as it could get."

"What did she say?"

This time, Xanthus was the one who looked away. His face had turned scarlet.

"I have to go," whispered Andromache.

"Eh? But you promised me a game of roodles! You can't just promise something to an old man and then beg off."

"I have to go."

"You don't look so good." Xanthus frowned. "Maybe you should sit for a —" But before he could finish, Andromache was running for the door.

I'll try her house, she decided. She took a broad avenue that led down the hill, toward a particular neighborhood of the lower town. Once there, she veered off the main street onto a maze of twisting back alleys. She then had to turn several more times before she found what she was looking for: a narrow black door. Timidly, she knocked.

Nothing.

No one's home. Andromache wasn't sure whether to feel disappointed or relieved.

(*The door won't break! Just knock harder — or are you afraid to?*) taunted the horrid little Voice.

Andromache was in fact afraid, but she also wanted to put the Voice in the wrong. She knocked harder.

Inside, there were footsteps.

Here goes...

The door creaked open.

"Andromache?" asked Penthesilea, looking shocked. "What are you doing here? Are you all right?"

Andromache stared silently into the other woman's catlike eyes. Angry though she was, she understood the pain Penthesilea must be feeling, knowing that Hector loved someone else — that he loved *her*, Andromache.

"What's going on?" asked Penthesilea.

Andromache's throat was dry. Hector had always loved her; had Penthesilea always known? Was *that* why she'd given Andromache those occasional long, strange looks? Was *that* why she'd asked Andromache to join the army — to keep an eye on her?

"Andromache?" prodded Penthesilea.

"Wh-what did you say to my husband?" Andromache finally whispered.

Pause. "Your *what?*" Penthesilea's concern had turned to cold disdain.

"My *husband*," repeated Andromache, struggling to keep her voice from trembling. She wasn't going to cry! She *wasn't* going to let this woman belittle her! *She — wasn't — going — to — cry!* "You know — Hector."

When Penthesilea spoke, her voice was warm like metal in the rain. "Letting someone have you up against the wall doesn't make him your husband."

Andromache clapped a hand to her mouth in horror. No! That was impossible! She and Hector had been alone!

"I went to the stables, the other day," Penthesilea said stonily. "I heard sounds and thought there was a horse in trouble, so I went in to check."

Penthesilea had heard something — she'd gone in to check — she'd *seen* them! Oh, gods, she'd *seen* them! Andromache was humiliated. Still, she could have borne the shame of having been seen, if not for Penthesilea's hateful words: *'Letting someone have you up against the wall doesn't make him your husband.'* Instantly, one of the most beautiful moments of Andromache's life had been recast as something cheap. Rather than loving each other desperately, impulsively, after almost losing each other, she and Hector had been rutting. No — not even that. She'd been servicing him. *'Letting someone have you up against a wall'* went far beyond *'trysting in the library'* or even *'living in disorder.' 'Trysting'* sounded silly, but *'letting someone have you'* was tawdry. Degrading.

And I'll bet she said something even worse to Ector, thought Andromache, remembering Xanthus's beet red face. No wonder Hector had rushed off to Santiya! If his most trusted colleague could be that cruel, there was no telling what the rest of the city might say.

Andromache looked back at Penthesilea. She yearned to say something brutal — something vicious — something that would make the woman feel like *she* had just been kicked in the stomach! The best she could come up with was, "Stay away from me! I *never* want to see you again!"

With that, Andromache fled. She was crying so hard that she immediately lost her bearings, but she didn't care. Nothing mattered except getting far, far away from Penthesilea. *Bitch!* she thought, sobbing. *That bitch!*

(*And all you had to come back with was* 'Stay away from me?') sneered the Voice. (*Well, guess what — she doesn't ever want to see* you *again, either. She hates you. She hates you so much, she's made her horse hate you!*)

Andromache understood that kind of hatred. She'd experienced it, back when she thought *Lee* was Hector's fiancée. The worst *she* had done, though, was refuse to go running with Penthesilea. *She* had never attacked the other woman, or said something as cruel as '*letting someone have you.*'

Bitch! thought Andromache. *Bitch, bitch, bitch!*

Each time she thought the word, she imagined Penthesilea's face on the ground beneath her feet. She was concentrating so hard on stomping it to bits that she tripped and fell over a pile of garbage. The scabs from her days-earlier stumble tore off, and she began to bleed.

"Dammit!" she screamed, huddling to the ground. "Dammit! *Dammit!*"

Several passers-by slowed down as they neared her, but they didn't stop. *They think I'm crazy,* Andromache told herself. *Maybe they're even afraid of me. Well, good!* she thought fiercely. *I'm glad someone is!* It felt good to be feared, for once, rather than just despised.

"Move it, girl!"

Andromache looked up. A man with a pair of donkeys was waiting to get past her. She slithered back against the nearest building, and the man moved on without another word.

(*Who are you kidding?*) laughed the Voice. (*No one would ever be afraid of* you. *Those other people kept walking because they don't care about you. Go home, before you get yourself trampled.*)

Home? she thought bitterly. *What home?* The luthier's shop, which she'd never even found? Hector's house, where her in-laws loathed her? Lyrnassa, where everyone had thought she was cursed? Hurapi, the Lukkan village where her parents had died?

The Voice fell silent. For once, Andromache had managed to outsneer it. That miniscule victory gave her just enough courage to get up and start walking again.

THE TROJAN PEACE: HALF-LIGHT

Chapter 30

When Andromache finally made it home, to Hector's house, she ran right into Hecuba. Hecuba! The one person capable of making her feel worse than she already did! The one person she hated more than Penthesilea! At least Penthesilea had had a reason to be nasty; Hecuba simply enjoyed it.

"Oh, dear girl," murmured Hecuba, seeing Andromache's face. "It'll be all right."

Andromache felt herself being drawn into an awkward embrace. "No!" she shrieked, struggling free. "Leave me alone!"

"Come upstairs," Hecuba said quietly.

"No!"

"Please, Andromache...we need to talk."

Andromache didn't want to talk. She planted her feet where they were.

Hecuba sighed. "Very well, then. We'll talk here. I'm sure you won't mind Paris and Cassandra interrupting."

Andromache glowered at her with stifled rage. The woman always had *some* way of getting people to do what she wanted! "Fine," she muttered. "Whatever you say."

Hecuba nodded and marched upstairs to her bed chamber. Grudgingly, Andromache followed.

"Sit here, dear — please." Hecuba motioned to a couch. "I'll get us something to drink." She took out a jar and two cups, poured a dash of liquid into each, and handed one of the cups to Andromache.

Andromache swallowed the drink in a single gulp. Immediately, she began coughing. "This — *hack!* — isn't — *hack! hack!*

— water," she gasped. It didn't taste like Hecuba's dreadful healing tonic, either.

"No," agreed Hecuba, sitting down beside her. "It's Santiyan honeywine. Would you like another?"

Andromache nodded. She guzzled the next cup, too, but was prepared this time and didn't cough.

"I know it must be hard on you, with Hector gone again." Hecuba sighed, as though his absence hadn't been her idea in the first place. "But oh, Andromache...he needed to go."

"Away from *me*, you mean!" Andromache snarled.

"No, dear — I do *not* mean that." Hecuba poured another round of drinks. "Something's wrong with him."

"He's mad at *you*! That's what's wrong!" cried Andromache, expecting Hecuba to strike back — *wanting* her to.

Instead, the other woman sighed again. "I know," she said. "Do you think that's all it is? If you say '*yes*,' I'll believe you. You know him much better than I do, these days."

A moment earlier, Andromache would have said '*yes*,' just to make Hecuba suffer. Now, though, something was quelling her anger. It might have been Hecuba's refusal to fight, or her acceptance of Andromache as Hector's confidant. It might have been the woman's tone, which betrayed such agony and love for her son. It might have been nothing more than the calming effects of the honeywine. In any case, Andromache said, "No."

It was the truthful answer. Hector hadn't been huddling against the floor of the outpost stable because of his mother. Despite his joke, he hadn't been whimpering and screaming in his sleep because of her, either. Hecuba wasn't the reason that he'd said: *'I thought I'd finally had it.'* He'd been upset long before their argument.

Hecuba nodded. "His father and I didn't think so, either. When he wasn't at the gate — of course, we'd had word that he wasn't —" Her face crumpled briefly before she went on. "But he's always been so concerned that all the soldiers, the horses, and the gear make it inside and back to their proper places. He was always one of the last ones to leave the gate area even before he was raised to commander, let alone now. It's not like him not to oversee the re-entry. Unless —" Hecuba shifted uncomfortably. "Unless maybe — he was with you?"

Andromache took a swig of honeywine and shook her head. Stumbling upon Hector in the outpost stable was surely *not* the kind of lovers' rendezvous Hecuba had in mind…

"I didn't think so," said Hecuba, her eyes dark and sad. "I wish he had been." She touched Andromache's hand.

Andromache wrenched away. Her honeywine spilled to the ground, making a puddle that both women ignored. "No, you don't!" she shrieked. "You don't wish he'd been with me. You started crying when he said he loved me!"

"Not because of *you*, Andromache. It was because for the past two years, he's been working extremely hard to learn Lukkan." Hecuba sounded wistful.

Dumbstruck, Andromache stared. "But — but — but that was *your* idea. You *wanted* him to!" Hesitantly, she asked, "Didn't you?"

"Very much," said Hecuba. "You can't even begin to imagine! It's a long story that started before Hector was born. Let me pour you some more honeywine before I tell you. There! I come from a small country, Andromache — a small country with a rather strange history. For a reason I've forgotten or never knew in the first place, the royal family is descended from Trojan ancestors. That's why Truvan is spoken in the court. However, Santiyans outside of the royal court all speak Luwian as their native tongue, and most have also learned Hittite."

Hecuba tightened her lips. "Essentially, Santiya is a vassal state of the Hittites, obliged to fight in their wars. My brother, Asius, can tell you about that when he comes. He led a contingent to the battle of Kadesh — can you imagine, fighting the Egyptians, for all the harm they ever did us? But Hattusas called, and Santiya had to answer. The problem is, the Hittites didn't always see fit to provide protection in return, and with all of the various threats facing Santiya, my parents decided during their reign that the realm needed more security."

Hecuba coughed, interrupting herself. "Andromache, did my son tell you that back in Santiya, I was —"

"A princess," said Andromache. "He told me."

"Indeed." Hecuba nodded. "Well, my family favored reaching out to other small states, banding together for strength and security."

"Oh," said Andromache, unclear how all of this connected back to Hector's Lukkan lessons but interested enough to listen further.

"Troy was one of those small states — larger than Santiya, of course, but still tiny compared to the Hittite empire. Santiya has cultural ties to Troy, as I mentioned, but they'd faded over the years. I was sent here to revive our connection and then to approach other potential allies."

"Revive your connection to Troy?" Andromache frowned, suddenly remembering Cassandra's attempt to marry her off to Demuchus, the previous fall. "Is that why you married Priam?" It was a shocking idea. Hecuba and Priam seemed as happy a couple as her own parents had been. Andromache never would have imagined that they'd been thrown together by force.

Hecuba laughed. "In part. It all started because I'd had a fling with a Santiyan boy, back when I was Cassandra's age. A foolish fling with a foolish boy. My parents were horrified but wise enough not to protest. They knew it would only make me more determined to be with him. Anyway, I eventually caught him slobbering all over another girl, and you can imagine the state that left *me* in."

Andromache tried but failed to imagine Hecuba, young and renegade, caught up with a boy who slobbered all over people.

"I was livid," Hecuba concluded. "And ashamed. I told my parents that I was ready to do my princessly duties for the good of our country. Really, though, I just wanted to get away. I didn't feel I could show my face there, anymore. My parents took me at my word and arranged a marriage to a Trojan councilman — as I said before, to refortify old alliances. I traveled to Troy, pretending to be calm but seething inside. I'd thought they would send me to one of the nearby kingdoms, perhaps even the Hittite capital of Hattusas. I was still angry about the boy and now, on top of that, absolutely *furious* with my parents for betrothing me to a commoner."

Neither Priam nor any of the other council members were like any commoners Andromache had ever met, but she held her tongue and waited for Hecuba to go on.

"As soon as I arrived, I was taken to the council chamber. There was a man, there — an aging council member with hard, cold eyes. I started crying on the spot and yelled at everyone around me that I could never marry *him*. He was old and ugly and horrid! Just then, another man stepped into the room. He was older than me by quite a few years, but still in his prime, and most definitely eye-catching."

"Priam?" asked Andromache.

Hecuba nodded. Her cheeks had turned faintly pink. "He smiled at me and said that *he* was the intended groom — and that he would never force marriage on an unwilling person, but if it made a difference, he was younger than the other man by at least a day or two."

Andromache didn't laugh, but she gave a thin smile.

"I was mortified," said Hecuba. "The older councilman — Ucalegon — never really forgave me. But Priam was delighted by the whole scene and by me, in general. I took to him, too. He was pleasant and bright. We spoke at length about my family's concerns, which Priam already knew something about and approved. He was in favor of pursuing alliances among the small states of the region and thought that he would be able to convince the rest of the council." Hecuba smiled. "I quickly decided to follow through with marrying him."

"So you didn't really know each other," said Andromache.

"Not well at all. I'd only been in Troy a few days. But we liked and admired each other, and marriage seemed like a sensible way to further the goal of alliances."

"My parents only knew each other for a few days, too, before they got married," Andromache volunteered. "They weren't being sensible, though — they just ran off together. My mom's parents weren't too happy about it, at first."

"There were those who opposed our marriage, too," Hecuba said somberly. "Some on the city council disliked the idea of foreign royalty marrying into their power structure, as though through Priam I would single-handedly turn Troy into a monarchy!" She sniffed. "They said the only way they would allow it was if I renounced my title of *'princess.'* I agreed, if grudgingly, because by then I'd come to appreciate the way Troy was governed. My parents, on the other hand, were breathing fire over the title issue. For a while, everyone was miserable — me, Priam, my parents, and the Trojan city council."

"That sounds awful," said Andromache.

"Indeed, but we still got married, and we swore to each other on our wedding day that we would never put our children through what *we* went through. We swore that we would welcome whomever they chose for a spouse."

The tendrils of goodwill that had begun to reconnect the two women vanished instantly. Andromache opened her mouth to retort, but Hecuba cut her off.

"I know what you're thinking, dear, but if you let me finish, I think you'll see that I haven't gone back on that promise."

Defiantly, Andromache swallowed the contents of her cup. Let Hecuba try to convince her!

"I never regretted marrying Priam, even with all the turmoil surrounding our betrothal. He's always been the most wonderful man — the most wonderful husband — and I quickly grew to love him. The Trojans and Santiyans all finished by accepting our marriage.

"My life was good, here — fulfilling. Troy had no proper healers, at least none who knew the sciences of *my* country. All Santiyan princesses train as healers, you see, and our training is rigorous. My expertise was welcome. I was also named official ambassador, and was able, by this avenue and through Priam, to bring matters to the council's attention. Eventually, I realized that there would be another way to —" She interrupted herself to ask a question. "Dear, do you know how new council members are selected, when a spot opens up?"

Andromache nodded. "It's someone from the family of whoever left the council."

"Exactly. That may not be an official rule, but it's what usually ends up happening. If the member who leaves has no family, as is the case with one or two members today, someone is chosen from another council family. It's a matter of practicality. They're the only Trojans likely to have had the broad-based education required of council members.

"I knew from the beginning that Priam's children — our children — would stand an excellent chance of joining the council. I had hope that they would continue, even expand, our work on alliances. Priam and I set out to give them the tools that they would need for this — the standard course of study, plus lessons in the languages spoken by our would-be allies."

Andromache was beginning to understand. As a child, Hector had been notorious for defying his foreign language tutors. "So, you were disappointed when Hector's language lessons fell through."

"Disappointed!" Hecuba laughed bitterly. "Everything I'd worked for — and hoped for — and suffered the castigations of two countries for — just up in smoke! I was devastated, and all the more since it was Hector who balked. There was never a question of Paris joining the council. We could see from the beginning that he lacked any sort of discipline. As for Cassandra, while she's done well in her studies, I worry about those grim old council frogs devouring her if she doesn't toughen up a little." Hecuba paused.

"Then, there's Hector. He has everything a council member needs: brains, curiosity, resourcefulness. And no one would eat *him* alive. He would need to work on his tact," Hecuba admitted. "He can be a little — er, *blunt* — at times. But that's not insurmountable. The problem with Hector was that he didn't *want* to be a councilman, or do anything else that meant he'd have to sit still most of his life. He wanted to run around. Better yet, he wanted to ride around. Most of his lessons came easily. He was able to rush through them and still have much of the day to spend outside, so he put up with them. Where he finally drew the line was at languages. They took too much time, and he saw no immediate use for them.

"I can't say that *nothing* has come of Priam's and my ef forts," Hecuba went on with a sigh. "Far from it! The council began sending envoys to the states we suggested. Sometimes the members themselves even went. Most importantly, the children Hector's age and younger have received more intensive training than ever before in the languages and cultures of our neighbors. Many of *them* have spent time visiting these countries. As a result of this, Troy, Santiya, and the others have a much stronger network of alliances. Trade is booming, as well. The Achaeans have gotten bolder, of late, but so far our network has held them off. It's been a success, just not the way I'd hoped. Not with Hector. *He* was swept up by life in the military, where he could run around and ride to his heart's content."

Hecuba gave an even heavier sigh. "Of course, now he *is* involved in the alliance process, but by carrying out treaties rather than writing or negotiating them. Now, I firmly believe that the army *needs* a commander who's forceful but humane, and intelligent but daring. If Hector weren't my son —"

After taking a drink, Hecuba finished her thought: "But he *is* my son. And to see him coming home in all his states, the way he does — charred, scarred, bruised, ill, bleeding, half-eaten by lice, or sewn together like some beggar's rag! And then to feel lucky that it wasn't worse…"

Andromache, who had lowered her eyes to hide a fresh round of tears, looked up to see that Hecuba, too, was crying.

"I'm sorry. I'm so sorry." Hastily, the woman blinked and sniffed, pulling herself back together.

Andromache touched her mother-in-law's hand.

With a watery smile, Hecuba resumed speaking: "When you appeared, it was like a dream. Years had passed since Hector had driven away his last language tutor, and I had no aspiration of finding him another one. Then *you* fell from the sky! It gave me new hope. I thought there was a chance, after all that Hector had seen and been through in the military, that he might be ready for something else — and that if he could be convinced to try again with foreign languages, he might also reconsider the council.

"I certainly never would have thought to ask someone his own age to tutor him. Tutors tend to be older, of course — how else can they be expected to know more than the tutee? But then there you were, living with us, and so I asked myself, *Why not?* I thought that Hector might come to see you as a sister, and so be more cooperative for you than he had been for previous tutors. I also thought it would be good for *you*, having someone to look out for you. Hector's always been very protective of other people. He took such good care of Paris and Cassandra when they were growing up! He never had any patience for those who tried to bully them."

Andromache thought of the teenaged twins who'd hurt Cutie, and how Hector had made them shovel horse dung out of the stables. She nodded.

"I saw the signs of Hector's protectiveness right from the start," said Hecuba. "At that meeting, your first night in Troy, he was far nastier to Laoganus than he needed to be. I could tell it was a ploy to draw the council's attention away from *you*." Hecuba coughed. "I must seem naïve for not realizing the true depth of my son's feelings for you. But then, I thought he was involved with that warrior woman —"

"Penthesilea," whispered Andromache, her mouth going dry. She wished she could take another drink, but her cup was empty.

"Penthesilea," Hecuba agreed. "How was I to know that the whole time, he was actually wooing you?"

Wooing? Had Hecuba just said *wooing*? Andromache tried not to grimace.

"In any case, I blinded myself. When I saw him doing what he'd always refused to do — learn another language — I wanted so badly to believe that he'd seen reason. That he'd decided to change paths, to leave the army for a saner career, to become a councilman after all. I saw what I wanted to see. It was silly, but I'm only human." Hecuba sighed at this humbling admission and looked over at Andromache.

"I felt stupid, when he confessed his true feelings for you," the woman said slowly. "Stupid for assuming that he would join the council, stupid for assuming that he thought of you as a sister. And then, I was in despair."

"Despair," Andromache repeated softly.

"Not because I don't love *you*, Andromache," Hecuba hastened to say. "I do, very much, and I'm so sorry I said things that hurt you. I just wish…" Her voice trailed off. Her lips were trembling.

"I understand." Andromache squeezed her mother-in-law's hand again — much more tightly, this time. If she'd just spent two years believing that Hector had a plan to leave the army, only to see her hopes dashed, she would be in despair, too.

Hecuba squeezed back. "I meant what I said, Andromache. I love you. Priam loves you. We're delighted to have you as a daughter-in-law. Not that you weren't already a part of the family, but this is even more special." In a tentative voice, she added, "I hope your parents would have felt the same way — about Hector."

The words caught Andromache off guard. Her eyes filled with tears.

"Oh, dear," murmured Hecuba. "I'm so sorry. I shouldn't have —"

"No — I — it's —" Andromache choked back a sob. "He met my <u>Auntie</u> — my aunt," she whispered.

"Your aunt? Who did?"

"Hector."

"Hector met your aunt?" cried Hecuba. "When? Where?"

"In Lyrnassa. When he first became patrol captain and went to visit the villages in his sector."

Hecuba didn't answer, so Andromache went on: "He cut his leg, and she bandaged him."

"That was *her*? Your aunt was the one who bandaged my son's leg?" Hecuba's eyes were enormous, and her face was pale.

Andromache nodded.

"But — but why — what was he doing with her? Did he know her, somehow?"

Shaking her head, Andromache answered: "She was down by the stream, fetching water. He ran into her there and helped her carry the water back to her house. On the way, he fell and cut his leg, so she wrapped it for him."

"Oh — for goodness' sake!" Hecuba swallowed. "And were you — were *you* there, with her?"

"No," said Andromache. "I was out collecting herbs. She told me about it when I got back."

"Oh. I see," said Hecuba.

"She didn't know his name, though," Andromache added. "So I didn't know he was the one who'd helped her until about a year ago, when he told me *his* half of the story. We were talking about Lyrnassa, after he went on a patrol inspection there."

Hecuba, whose words had been flooding out all night, could say only, "Oh."

"<u>Auntie</u> liked him," said Andromache. "She said he was sweet. She thought he had nice manners."

"Well. I see. Well. Well." Hecuba sniffled, trying to recapture her aplomb. "That was very kind of her to take care of him, although I'm sorry she saw him in such a clumsy state. I can't imagine what he was —"

"She *liked* him," Andromache interrupted. "She would be happy. So would my parents."

Hecuba sniffled again and touched Andromache's cheek.

"Hecuba?" Andromache said softly.

"Yes, dear?"

"If you don't hate me —"

"I most assuredly do *not*!" Hecuba dabbed her still-moist eyes.

"Then why did you want him to leave?"

Hecuba cleared her throat. "*That* is yet another long story."

"I want to hear it."

"Then we'll need more of *this*." Hecuba poured honeywine into each of their cups. "Now. You know that Hector has spent a lot of time over the years with his uncle, my brother Asius?"

Andromache nodded.

"At first, it was just for visits here and there, so that Hector would feel a connection to Santiya. Then, when he got himself set on the army, Priam and I sent him to Asius. We wanted him to have the best possible training. Asius has spent his whole life in the military, and, say what you will, no one can handle horses like a Santiyan. Well, over the years, Hector and his uncle grew very close. My brother has a way with him. When Hector won't listen to anyone else, he'll listen to Asius.

"As you may or may not know by personal experience, my son can be surly at times. He doesn't tend to yell or start fights — however, when he's upset, he can make the air around him unbreathable."

Andromache nodded.

"So you *do* understand." Hecuba sighed. "I'm sorry to hear that. In any case, he got so bad a number of years ago that no one could stand to be around him. Priam and I sent him to his uncle, as much because *we* needed a break as for anything else. To our surprise, he came back a different person. Or rather, he came back his old self. Asius had worked some sort of magic on him. After that, whenever my son got a certain look in his eye, I knew it was time for a trip to Santiya."

"Have you sent him there a lot of times for — for *that*?"

"No, just a few. But it always seems to help him."

"What happened when he — I mean, why was he — why was Hector — like that?"

Hecuba snorted. "You don't honestly think he would tell his *mother*, do you?"

"I don't know," said Andromache, although she suspected not. Hector hadn't even told Hecuba about being thrown into manure when he was eight.

"Well, he wouldn't." Hecuba sniffed. "Although I have my guesses. The pattern of when he has that look is plain — even to a *woman* like me," she added sarcastically.

Andromache caught the reference to what Priam had said, that *'coming home from war could make a man realize certain things.'* No wonder Hecuba had lashed out! Perhaps she'd never fought in the army, but she still knew plenty about war. She knew the agony of seeing her son injured — the horror of realizing that people had been trying to kill him — the frustration and sadness of welcoming a different person home. She knew the fear of wondering when he would have to leave again. She knew the helplessness of waiting…waiting…waiting…

Andromache knew even more: the terror of being chased by raiders, blank-eyed and murderous. The dull sound of faraway screaming. The smell of a house on fire. The pale, waxen color of skin without blood. But for each hideous vision in her mind, Hector had to have a dozen — a hundred — a thousand — who knew? And who knew what the memories did to him? Andromache shuddered. She couldn't bear to know, or even to think about it. She was relieved when Hecuba started talking again.

"In any case," said the woman, "this time was the worst I've ever seen him. I was willing to try *anything* to help him come out of it."

Nightmares, thought Andromache. *The outpost stable*. She'd never seen Hector looking worse than at those times, either. He'd been happy, too, during his few stolen hours with her — wildly happy! — but his joy had been unstable. He'd fallen so swiftly, so suddenly, back into despair…

Hecuba went on: "But I knew that no matter *what* I tried, Asius had a better chance of helping my son than I did. Now, mind you, I've long thought marriage would be good for Hector. I thought it would do him good to have a wife — any wife! — to talk to him, comfort him, love him, and generally bring him out of the army world, even for a while. The more I pushed the idea, though, the more adamantly he refused. I should have guessed that would happen — whatever I suggest, he refuses!" Hecuba paused to give a wry smile and squeeze Andromache's hand. "Admittedly, in this case, he was right to do so. He waited for a wife he adores, rather than marrying the first girl to glance his way. I can't tell you how happy I am for both of you! And although it might seem strange to you, dear, that's the very reason I pressed Hector to spend time with Asius. I could tell from the moment he came home that he needed my brother's help — but after hearing your news, I realized the true urgency of the matter. As I said before, I'm sure that being married to you will do him worlds of good. However, this is no way to *start* a marriage. He owes it to you to sort himself out — or at least begin to — before the two of you start your life together. My brother will help him do that. I'm sorry that Hector had to be the one to fetch Asius. I truly am, dear! I just didn't see any other way. My brother needs to see Hector for himself. Once he does, he'll realize how serious the situation is and make plans to stay with us for a few months. He's a king, after all," Hecuba said as an aside. "He can't just go visiting without making proper arrangements."

Andromache nodded. She couldn't dispute *that*.

"On top of that," said Hecuba, "if someone else had gone to fetch Asius, we would have had to send a message to let my brother know the length of time he was needed and why. Otherwise, he would have come only for a few days — not long enough to make a difference for Hector. But a written message can be lost, and as for a spoken message — well, I didn't want to tell anyone else that something was wrong with Hector. I was afraid that he'd find out and would feel ashamed."

Ashamed — no, Andromache certainly didn't want Hector to feel ashamed, least of all if he was in a fragile state. She'd seen how quickly he could unravel. Wincing, she thought back to his words: *'You do not want a screamy man.'* Just as well Hecuba hadn't sent a message! As for the rest of what the woman was saying, Andromache wanted it to be true. She wanted Hector to have whatever help he needed. "Do you really think it will make things better?" she asked softly. "If Asi — if your brother stays here for a while?"

Hecuba nodded. "I do."

"And they'll be back soon?"

"Just a few more days," Hecuba said soothingly. "I know you're eager to have your husband back."

Andromache's cheeks flooded with color.

"Your face is red. We've probably had too much." Hecuba took Andromache's cup and set it on the table, along with the near-empty jar of honeywine. "There's something I've been meaning to show you," she said.

"What's that?" asked Andromache, grateful for the change of subject.

Hecuba rose from the couch to fumble through a nearby chest. "Aha!" she exclaimed in satisfaction. "Here it is." She was holding a small, linen scroll. "Here, dear — take it."

As Andromache unfurled the scroll, she saw a drawing on it: something vaguely quadrupedal, with a stick neck and an elongated head. "Did *he* draw this?"

Nodding, Hecuba replied, "Many years ago. He was such a tiny thing, with scrawny legs just like the drawing's."

With a single finger, Andromache traced the stick legs and absurdly rounded body.

"Horses were all he thought about! Long before he could ride them, he talked about them, visited them, and drew them. That's where his military career began, I suppose — his obsession with horses." Hecuba gave a wistful smile. "At the time, he was so little, we thought he'd never be much more than a scout or a messenger."

"It's a sweet picture," said Andromache.

"I suppose he'll be mortified that I gave it to his wife." Hecuba smirked. "And told her how scrawny he used to be."

Andromache flushed again and laughed — mostly with joy, at being called Hector's wife. Unlike Penthesilea, Hecuba didn't think she was ridiculous or tawdry. Hector's mother was taking her seriously.

There was a short silence, which Hecuba broke by saying, "We should have spoken sooner. Priam advised me to do so yesterday, right after Hector came to tell us he was leaving, but I couldn't find you. I suppose I didn't try very hard."

Andromache shook her head. "I'm glad it was tonight."

Chapter 31

After the string of wakeful nights she'd had, Andromache was glad to sleep late the next day. She lolled around her room with Cutie, who had herself grown lazy with the return of the summer heat. They barely stirred until late afternoon, when hunger drove them down to the kitchen.

Cutie, once fed, stretched out beneath the table and closed her eyes. Andromache gladly would have joined her, but she'd promised to check on the horses. "Do you want to come?" she asked Cutie.

The dog just lay there.

"I suppose that's for the best," sighed Andromache. "Xanthus probably wouldn't allow you in the stables, anyway." She didn't want to go down there by herself, though — not after what had happened with Penthesilea. "Maybe Cassandra would go with me."

Cassandra didn't need much coaxing. She wasn't about to miss an opportunity to visit the stables.

"I just bet I'll see something I like!" said the girl, giggling. They'd barely stepped through the door when she pounced on Thoas. The poor young guard was so bamboozled by Cassandra's flirting that he froze with a semi-conscious look on his face. Andromache dragged Cassandra away.

"Oh, he's *adorable!*" the girl squealed.

"He couldn't even talk to you."

"That's one of the things that made him so cute."

"Don't get him in trouble, Cassandra," warned Andromache. "I really like him. He's been nice to me."

"Trouble!" Cassandra heaved a sigh. "It's so unfair!"

For the next several evenings, the young women brought treats to Buzzy and Thisbe and took the horses for walks around the pasture. Later on, they took turns playing roodles with Xanthus. Cassandra had honed her balance of flirtation and strategizing to where she could make eyes at all the men yet still clobber Xanthus much of the time.

"What a world!" griped the stable master, half-fascinated, half-appalled by Cassandra.

"My turn to play you," said Andromache.

"Eh? Good! At least I can trust *you* to keep your eyes on the board, Missy!"

ﾛﾝ

ANDROMACHE LAY IN BED, cuddling with Cutie and gazing at the world outside. From her window, she could see leaves, dancing on the courtyard trees — birds, flying through the air — waves, lapping at the shore. She could see the Trojan landscape, aglow in the honey-gold light of the setting sun.

Her window had a good view. She could look down onto the courtyard, to the place where she and Hector had stretched out together in the starlight, drinking wine and hunting Lorani. She could see the bench where he'd found her, the night of the comet's appearance over Troy. She could see the door to his room, where she'd spent the night with him. Their first wedding night! Soon, they would have another. She would move out there with him, and it would be *her* room — hers and Hector's.

Looking out the window, Andromache could see her future. Hector would return in just a few days. She would throw her arms around his neck, and they would kiss, and kiss, and kiss. They would stand out on the courtyard, holding hands, wearing robes of deepest blue. *Always, always, I lahff you,* he would tell her. *Always, always!*

"Hurry back," she whispered into the breeze. "Hurry back, Ector." The sky began to darken, and the first evening star appeared. *I'll stay up all night,* she thought. *I'll watch the stars come out. I'll count them, and I won't stop counting until he comes home...*

Andromache had waited for Hector before and knew deep down that this time wouldn't be the last. The day would come when she would have to say goodbye to him again — wait for him again — fear for him again. This time, though, the waiting was joyous. She was waiting for her husband, for the celebration of their marriage. She was waiting for the sun to rise on the happiest days of her life.

PART TWO:

The Blue Dress

High summer

Chapter 32

A ndromache opened her eyes and looked out the window, expecting to see the dappled pink of morning light. In- stead, she saw midday glare. *It must be almost noon already,* she thought with dismay. She'd slept in!

Chiding herself, she leapt out of bed. The sun was now too high for her to water the plants in her garden, as she'd been planning to do, but she could at least run down to trim off the sun-browned foliage. She'd promised Hecuba to do what she could to make the place presentable for the wedding.

The wedding...

Andromache forgot about her garden plants as she drifted off on thoughts about the wedding — *their* wedding, hers and Hector's! Once Hector came back from fetching his uncle, the festivities would take place. There would be songs, and rituals, and lots of food, and dancing. When all of that was over, there would be the wedding night...

Thunk! Thunk! Thunk! Thunk! Thunk! Ka-whack! A terrible clatter just outside the door jolted Andromache out of her rever- ies. Before she could so much as gasp, the crashing sounds were followed by a knock and a stream of barking.

Cutie, thought Andromache. *But who's out there with her?* Hec- tor couldn't be back yet, could he? He'd only been gone five days, and the trip was supposed to take him a week.

"Honey?" called a breathless, girlish voice.

"Oh, hi, Cassandra," said Andromache. "I'll be right there." As soon as Andromache opened the door, she saw the source of all the crashing and understood why Cassandra sounded out of breath: the girl had been lugging a trunk up the stairs.

"Oh, honey!" sang Cassandra, obviously in high spirits. "Are you ready?"

Ready for what? "For what?" Andromache repeated aloud. She bent down to pet Cutie, who licked her hands.

"For the bridal luncheon," said Cassandra. "You know, with Mom and her friends?"

"Oh, no," groaned Andromache. Hecuba *had* mentioned something about a luncheon, where Andromache would be surrounded by a horde of Trojan ladies, come to inspect the new member of the family. "I forgot! What do I need to do?"

"Have you bathed?"

"No. I just woke up."

"Oh, dear me!" Cassandra clicked her tongue. "Well, never mind. I'll run down and get you a basin and your oils. You can take a sponge bath."

The girl hurried off, leaving the trunk behind. It had a foreboding presence. Wary of what might pop out of it, Andromache sat goggle-eyed and watched it.

In record time, Cassandra was back upstairs with the basin. "All right, honey. Here." She set it down and stepped out of the room again. "Hurry!" she cried through the door.

Obediently, Andromache scrubbed herself as quickly as she could. "All right," she called to Cassandra, when she was dressed again.

Cassandra sailed back into the room. "Oh, good! This is the fun part." Giggling excitedly, she motioned to the trunk. "Mom thought you might want something fancy to wear. She didn't know what you'd like, but luckily, one of our neighbors has five daughters, and he sent over a bunch of their dresses as a wedding gift. You get to pick one to wear for today!"

"Oh," sighed Andromache. She was going to have to pick? Oh, *terrific!* Why couldn't Hecuba have just sent something up and spared her the ignominy of choosing the wrong dress, as she was bound to do? She didn't know what to wear to a Trojan pre-wedding luncheon!

"Can I set them somewhere?" asked Cassandra. "You need to see everything before you decide."

"Sure — put them on the bed."

Cassandra scooped out the dresses. As they slithered into a heap on the bed, Andromache glimpsed a rainbow of glistening fabrics, embroidery, and beadwork.

"Oh, my, *my*," murmured Cassandra. "Yes, we're sure to find something here."

We! Andromache thought in relief. Without help, she would have been as lost as spit in the sea.

One by one, Cassandra considered each dress, *ooh-ing* and then frowning prettily as she held them up to Andromache. "I don't know…they're all gorgeous, aren't they?"

Andromache nodded. "Gorgeous." And some of the more elaborate ones looked heavier than a stack of cooking kettles. How would she ever be able to wear one all afternoon?

"What we really need is my brother's advice."

"Really?" Andromache asked dubiously. "He'd probably just call them '*uniforms*.'"

"Oh, no, not *that* brother," said Cassandra. "He'd be of no use to us. He'd gawk at you no matter *which* one you chose — or even if you showed up in a pile of rags. Don't make that face at me, it's true!" She giggled. "No, I meant Paris — he'd find the right dress for you in no time!"

"I'm sure he would," muttered Andromache. *Unless he was too busy mocking how I'd look in all the other ones!*

Cassandra sighed. "But anyway, we don't have time to track him down. Why don't you take another peek, and I'll go get some things for your hair."

"Oh, you don't have to —"

"Be right back!" chirped Cassandra. Cutie joyfully followed her.

Alone again, Andromache pawed through the dresses and surprised herself by finding one she liked. Had they not tried it, before? The cut was simple, the fabric a shimmering silver-grey, thin enough that she wouldn't swelter in the afternoon heat. She put it on and waited for Cassandra.

Moments later, the girl returned.

"Is this dress all right?" asked Andromache.

Cassandra scrutinized it. "The color looks pretty against your hair," she said diplomatically.

"But…"

"But I'm not sure it's fancy enough."

Andromache sighed. Was she really going to have to put on one of those beaded nightmares?

"No, you're right, after all," Cassandra relented. "Let's get to work on your hair. You won't want to wear it down like that in this heat."

"Oh, don't go to all the trouble. I can just braid it."

Cassandra looked crestfallen.

"Or you can do it," Andromache agreed.

With an array of hair instruments, Cassandra proceeded to twist, fuss, comb, braid, and fasten for at least half an hour. "Oh, now, look!" she finally squealed, passing Andromache her polished silver mirror. "You're stunning!"

"Um, thank you," said Andromache. The coiffure Cassandra had given her was extravagant. Tortuous. She never would have attempted it on her own. "It's beautiful. Wait —" Suddenly, Andromache was struck ill with horror that she might be left alone with the Trojan ladies. She was sure that Cutie wouldn't be welcome among them, but hopefully, at least —

"You're coming to the luncheon, right?" she asked.

"Of course, honey!" Cassandra patted her hand. "I wouldn't miss it!"

℘

ANDROMACHE FOLLOWED Cassandra to Hecuba's room, a large and pleasant place — although Andromache wasn't sure why the luncheon was going to be held there, rather than in the courtyard or the kitchen.

"Oh, stars! There you finally are, girls!" said Hecuba, when she opened the door for them. "I was beginning to wonder — well, never mind. Hmmmpf!" she sniffed, eyeing Andromache's gown. "I tell them fancy, and *this* is what they send over!"

"Should I change?" Andromache asked meekly.

"No time for that. Just run down to the kitchen, both of you, and fetch the trays of food and drink down there. I'll go with you. And hurry, my little sea stars. If any of those harridans see you carrying a tray, Andromache, I'll never hear the end of it."

The trays were full of fruits, vegetables, pistachio rolls, fig tarts, honey cakes, cheeses, and walnut bread, but no meat. Andromache wondered if the menu was standard or if it had been created especially for her. She hadn't eaten meat in years. Hecuba didn't know the real reason why, but she knew what Andromache liked and didn't like to eat. *I'll bet she planned it just for me,* thought Andromache, touched.

"March, girls, march!" barked Hecuba.

When all the trays had been brought up, Cassandra was dispatched to the door to let guests in, and Andromache was ordered upstairs, to sit. She would have preferred to mill. Of all the ways to spend an afternoon, being trapped among these ladies ranked just above licking up caterpillar droppings. She'd never really felt at home among the Trojan elite.

"Sit, dear," Hecuba implored. "Sit, for the peace of all!"

To Hecuba's manifest relief, Andromache seated herself just before the first guests arrived; and to Andromache's relief, four women came in together. Had there been just one, she would have caught the brunt of that person's attention, but in a pack, they twittered as much to each other as to her.

"Aha! Do you see? I told you!"

"You weren't exaggerating!"

"Not in the least!"

"Oh, my. Oh, my, my! But then, one must expect —"

"Have you met Andromache?" Hecuba interrupted.

"Well, of course!" chirped a merry old lark. "But back then, she was just a tutor."

"Bid everyone '*hello,*' dear," Hecuba said patiently, as though Andromache were a child. "They're here to see you."

"Hello," she croaked. She couldn't remember a single one of the women's names, but she vaguely recognized their faces from having seen them around the house. They'd attended parties or visited with Hecuba, and all of them had come to meet her during her early days in Troy — everyone had been curious about the first language tutor ever to succeed with Hector.

"Hello!" the women said in chorus. As they settled in, they placed a heap of baskets on the floor beside Andromache, murmuring all the while to each other.

"Precious little dear!"

"That color, my word!"

"Those eyes!"

"No wonder the boy —"

"Yes — no wonder!"

"Oh, don't hide your face, pretty one!" laughed the Lark. "Can't we tease you a little? Your Hector is a special pet of ours. We all helped out after he was born, when his mother was so ill." She gave Hecuba a sympathetic look.

Incensed at having to revisit that helpless hour of her life, Hecuba narrowed her eyes.

Andromache, on the other hand, took heart. She hadn't expected anyone else to suffer embarrassment at the hands of these ladies, and she was pleased to have Hecuba for company.

"We watched Hector grow," said the Lark. Laughing, she added, "And before Hecuba came to Troy, we were all half in love with Priam, of course."

Hecuba's lips pinched down to a line.

Andromache was just beginning to worry about what her mother-in-law might say, when Cassandra opened the door.

"This way," said the girl. Six more women were ushered in, all of them carrying baskets.

Andromache knew that the group's focus would now turn away from Hecuba and back to her. She breathed quickly, shallowly, preparing for the onslaught. It wasn't long in coming.

An ottery woman, sleek and bright-eyed, was the first one in the door. Andromache recognized her from her early days in Troy. Back then, the Otter had been worried that Hector was taking on too much, with Lukkan lessons on top of his new duties as commander. *When's the poor boy supposed to sleep?* she'd demanded, leaving Andromache herself to lie awake at night, wondering when Hector would quit his lessons. Now, the Otter didn't even bother to greet Andromache before saying, "You're going to be Hector's bride, then?"

Andromache nodded, trying not to look miserable about it.

"What's that you're wearing?"

A garbage sack, obviously! "A — I — uh —"

"Stand up."

Andromache didn't dare refuse.

The Otter nodded. "Mm-hmm! Well, it's cute, but take a bit of advice from one who knows. You might want to wear something more — *enhancing* — around your husband, dearie." The Otter added her basket to the growing heap.

Andromache tried to smile at the Otter but managed only a grimace. She turned to Hecuba for help.

"That was sent over by Mestor, from his daughters' stock." Hecuba sniffed. "I asked for something '*fancy*,' and this is what he came up with! Can you imagine? So like a man!"

"Men aren't the only problem. Nobody listens anymore," sighed a reedy woman twice as tall as Andromache, but stooped.

"It's not like the old days, that's for sure."

Everything's going to hell, Andromache added silently, thinking of Xanthus.

Cassandra re-entered the room with another group of women. This time, the girl sat down.

It looks like she's here to stay, thought Andromache. *Good! That must be the last of the guests, then.*

Once the new arrivals had been greeted, the Lark sang, "In any case, dress or no dress, you'll make a lovely bride, little dear."

"Guess who'd vote for '*no dress!*'" barked the Otter.

Horrorstruck, Andromache looked to Cassandra for help, but the girl's gaze was fixed on her own twiddling thumbs.

Hecuba coughed. "Please, everyone, have some water — some wine — some fruit. You first, Andromache, dear."

Grateful to Hecuba for changing the subject, Andromache accepted the cup she'd been offered. She took a small sip first, to make sure it was only water, before gulping the rest of it.

"Can you believe this, Hecuba?" chirped the Lark. "Your boy, married! I remember when he was a tiny thing, running naked through the courtyard, singing his little songs."

Andromache choked and spat her water out onto the floor. Everyone turned to stare. As delicately as she could, she covered her mouth with her elbow and tried not to laugh.

"Cassandra, dear, can you wipe up the spill, please?" Hecuba said evenly. "Thank you."

Spill? Hecuba's poise made Andromache giggle anew.

"It *is* a funny picture," admitted the Lark.

"Let the poor, sweet boy have his dignity," chided a soft-eyed woman. "All those months he went to market for me when

I was laid up with the gout, don't you remember? He deserves to have his wife think the best of him."

"Oh, come now! Why would she think less of him for running around naked? I should think she'd be pleased!"

The women shook with laughter; one or two guffawed.

Red-cheeked, Andromache sat on her couch, wishing she could escape. *If I jumped out the window, could I make it to the apple tree?*

"What always struck me about Hector was his courage," interjected the Reed. She clicked her tongue. "Such a brave boy!"

Andromache stiffened. People were always wanting to talk about Hector's skill on the battlefield, but that was the very last thing she wanted to discuss at her bridal luncheon. She tried not even to think about that part of his life. It had always filled her with terror — first *of* him, and later *for* him.

But the Reed went on to say only: "I'll never forget the day he came by and got that coven of lizards out of my house — couldn't have been more than eight or nine."

"Lizards?"

"Years old!"

Everyone laughed, including Andromache.

"He just went right up to them and grabbed them, quick as you please. And then he brought them over to me — '*Look how neat they are,*' he said, all bright-eyed." The Reed laughed. "And you know what? They were."

"Let's not forget the real Hector," chimed in another woman, and again Andromache braced herself. "He let all of our best dogs go out carousing, and two came back pregnant. There were puppies from here to the sacred oracle, and that cheeky little imp just laughed about it!"

"What I remember most are our trips to the sea shore. All the other children built the most beautiful fortresses and palaces of sand, but Hector was too fidgety. He'd spend the whole day running along the shore, and then he'd just collapse in a heap and Hecuba would have to carry him back to the city. I can still see his little legs dangling, all brown and covered in sand."

For a pleasant half-hour, Andromache was regaled with anecdotes from Hector's boyhood. She was just starting to relax and enjoy herself when the women got down to the day's main business of embarrassing her.

"Open your gifts, dearie!"

"Gifts?" she asked.

The Lark winked and nodded toward the heap of baskets. "Which one?"

"Oh, you pick. You'll have to open all of them eventually."

Andromache selected the one on top — the Reed's gift, she thought — and pulled out — what was it, exactly? She held the wad of fabric up to the light.

The women twittered.

"That's a nice one!" someone exclaimed.

"He'll like *that!*"

He? Andromache frowned. What did they mean by *he?* Unfolding the material, she finally discerned shoulder straps and the hint of a waist. She was holding a dress — through which she could clearly see the women on the other side of the room.

"Does that go under her wedding gown?" asked Cassandra.

"Oh, no. It's worn alone!"

"But it doesn't cover anything!"

"The idea isn't to conceal, dearie," the Otter explained in triumph. "It's to *enhance.*"

"Oh!" cried Cassandra, blushing a dreadful shade of purple.

The women giggled in chorus, while Andromache stuffed the dress back into its basket. Oh, how horrible the ladies were! She knew what they were up to, playing a prank on the foreign girl. They were trying to trick her into wearing that silly thing in front of Hector by telling her that he would like it, when really he would just laugh at her and think she'd lost her mind. Well, she wasn't going to fall for it! As soon as the party was over, she would hide the dress deep in a box where no one would ever see it again.

"Next!" cried the Lark.

Andromache grabbed for another gift. As she reached inside the basket, her hand grazed a suspiciously soft fabric.

"Hold it up for everyone to see!"

Meekly, Andromache obeyed.

The Lark chirped approval for the slithery dress. "Even better than the first one!"

Andromache tried to affix a certain serene, unflappable expression that she'd seen before on Hector's face; what she produced was a rictus.

"If you don't like that one, Sunshine, don't worry. You've got lots more to open!"

Looking at the pile beside her, Andromache saw that this was true. She had dozens more gifts — dozens more shameful dresses to display.

"Open mine next," said Cassandra.

Andromache's eyes widened. Cassandra? Hector's *sister* was in on it? Cassandra hadn't known about the see-through dresses, but she might have found a different way to embarrass Andromache. She'd certainly done so in the past. Tentatively, Andromache reached into the basket to find —

"A sash!" she exclaimed in relief.

Cassandra smiled. "I thought you'd like to have a blue one, now."

"Thank you," said Andromache, smiling sincerely this time. Blue was the Trojan wedding color. "It's beautiful."

"Spicy!" crowed one of the ladies. "Imagine her in *that!*"

Andromache thrust the sash back into its basket.

One by one, she opened the rest of the gifts. The women had given her oils, a hairbrush, a mirror, and lots of filmy dresses. Once the ritual humiliation was over, and a cup of wine was in her belly, Andromache relaxed once more and smiled at her benefactors. They chattered and laughed while she drifted off into a warm, comfortable, haziness…

"And wiff neery a drop in his leathery crop —"

Andromache's ears perked up. Wait — was it — no, it couldn't be! He wasn't coming back for at least another —

"He fainted fahst dead by the doooooohr."

Without excusing herself or even glancing backward, Andromache bolted for the door. Behind her, she could hear the guests making sounds of bemusement.

"What on earth?"

"What's gotten into her?"

"I think I heard Hector downstairs," said Cassandra. "He must be back."

At that, the women began to chirp excitedly.

"Was that him, singing?"

"I guess," said Hecuba, stunned. "I haven't heard him singing in years."

"Is he running around the courtyard?"

"Oho! And is he dressed like he was in the old days?"

"Come now, you vulgar old she-bat!"

Andromache was soon out of earshot of the twittering. She ran downstairs, through the banquet hall, and across the court-yard. The door to Hector's shed was ajar; he must have gone in-side. When Andromache reached the shed, though, she stopped, unsure of what she would find — what if she'd imagined every-thing, from kissing Hector, to spending the night with him, to sleeping in his arms? What if it all had been a dream, the fantasy of a lovesick mind? Or, even if it was real, what if the long ride had squelched Hector's feelings for her? Inside the shed, she might encounter a Hector who was her student, or her friend, but not her lover. Not her husband.

Sucking in a deep breath, she tiptoed to the doorway and stood there, stock-still.

"Hello?" said Hector, when her body blocked the light from outside.

"Hello."

"Pretty wife!"

Andromache's doubts vanished. She stepped inside the shed and shut the door. "I missed you!" she cried, throwing her arms around him and breathing in horses, dust, and wind.

Reluctantly, he backed away. "You shouldn't," he warned. "The road grime —"

She drew near to him once more. "I don't care!"

Again, he retreated. "But your pretty dress…"

That damned dress! It had brought Andromache nothing but grief since the moment she'd put it on. It was too plain — too boring — and now, too pretty! At her limit with the stupid thing, she pulled it over her head and threw it to the floor.

"There!" she exclaimed. "*Now* will you kiss me?"

$$\wp\mathcal{O}$$

AS SHE LAY with Hector on his old grey cloak, Andromache found herself studying the ceiling. Its wooden rafters were scored by the work of beetles; in the dim light, their tunnels looked like a strange form of writing. She shifted slightly to get a better view.

"You ahre comfohrtable?" murmured Hector.

"Mm-hmm." She kissed his shoulder. "You?"

He let out a deep sigh. "Yes."

Andromache smiled to herself. "How was the trip?" she asked.

"Too long."

"*Way* too long," she agreed. "How do you feel?"

Languorously, he answered, "I do not haff the words…"

Andromache nuzzled his bare chest. "I don't mean *that*. I mean, in general."

Hector had been so volatile before he left to fetch his uncle. Those few short days between his return with the army and his departure for Santiya had been the most wonderful of Andromache's life — but at times, they'd been dark and frightening. She could barely stand to think about how Hector had looked when she first saw him…

He was crouched on the floor of the outpost stable — he was miserable, and grimy, and covered in vomit — his eyes were hollow — his head was gashed open — he was wrenching himself out of her arms, yelling at her — 'Go away!'

She could barely stand to think about the way he'd screamed in his sleep. She could barely stand to think about Hector — her sweet, gentle Hector — yelling and swearing at his parents. Now, her best hope was that Hecuba had been right about her brother's influence over Hector…

'My brother has a way with him. When Hector won't listen to anyone else, he'll listen to Asius. I'm sure that being married to you will do Hector worlds of good, but he owes it to you to sort himself out — or at least begin to — before the two of you start your life together. My brother will help him do that.'

Andromache didn't like all the trickery that Hector's parents had used to lure him away to Santiya, but she wanted what was best for her husband. She hoped that visiting with his uncle had helped him.

"In general, I feel good, pretty wife," said Hector, in answer to her question.

Indeed, he looked good. The wound on his head was all but healed, and soon his hair would grow out enough to cover it. His eyes were soft and shining, not tight, as they'd been before his trip. Still, no matter what he said, he couldn't be trusted right at that moment. How else could he look but happy, when he was lying skin to skin with her? *I'll have to keep an eye on him*, Andromache decided. She would wait to see how he acted at more normal times.

"And you?" Hector asked softly. "You feel good?"

"Mm-hmm," she said, snuggling closer to him.

"Good." He tried to stroke her hair, but his fingers were soon tangled in the labyrinth of braids, and he wound up pulling half of them loose. "Your hair is lahke this, why?" he asked.

Andromache giggled. "There was a party for me today. All your mom's friends came over."

"Ah! So, you wear *that*?" Hector eyed her fallen dress.

Embarrassed, she said, "I know, I looked silly."

"You looked like starlight," he murmured.

The un-Hector-like comment made Andromache still more self-conscious. Blushing hotly, she changed the subject. "Anyway, I was up with those women when I heard you down here. I left a little early."

He kissed her forehead. "You ahre welcome."

"It wasn't so bad, except when they gave me tips about —"

"Ugh!" Hector grimaced "Tell me you're not serious!"

"— cooking."

Laughing, he pulled her on top of him. His skin was warm beneath hers, his arms tight around her back. Overcome with joy, she couldn't stop herself from kissing him — and kissing him — and kissing him...

"Oh, Ahndromahk," he whispered. "I miss this!"

"You mean '*missED*?'" she asked, smiling.

"Miss, missed — it is all the same when you ahre not wiff me."

Andromache kissed him again. She felt the same way. "How *is* your uncle?" she asked, thinking of the errand that had taken Hector away in the first place.

"Fine. <u>You ahre going to see him tonight, fohr the dinner.</u>"
Hector frowned. "<u>My mom — she is, ah, good to you?</u>"

Andromache nodded. "<u>She said she was sorry.</u>"

"<u>Good</u>," he said, sighing in relief. "<u>I am going to talk later
wiff her</u>."

"<u>You should.</u>"

Hector nodded. "<u>Baht first, a baff.</u>"

"<u>Oh</u>." Andromache couldn't keep the disappointment from
her voice. Their time together was ending, already! Once they
left the shed, there would be a long family dinner — longer than
usual, with Uncle there — to get through before they could be
alone again. She buried her face in Hector's shoulder.

Gently, he slid her off to the side. "I have to get up, now,
my sweetheart."

Andromache sighed. She wished she was heavier, so Hector
couldn't move her — so the two of them could stay in that moment a little longer.

ॐ

FOR THE SECOND time in an hour, Andromache lifted the
silver dress over her head and let it fall to the floor. There was
no way she could wear it to dinner! It hadn't gotten dirty, or too
terribly wrinkled. There was no rational reason whatsoever for
her to change out of it: she simply couldn't stand the idea of anyone else seeing her in it after the comment Hector had made.
The silver dress had become something private. If she wore it,
she might as well announce how she felt while lying naked in
Hector's arms.

Sighing, she sat down before the trunk of fancy dresses. Her
only recourse, as far as she could see, was to don something
flashier and say it was in honor of Uncle. He was a king, after all.
Surely she couldn't be faulted for paying homage to a king! Hecuba would probably be delighted; she hadn't liked the silver dress
in the first place.

After selecting a gown — a horrible turquoise thing, choked
with golden embroidery — Andromache contemplated her hair.

Somehow, she would have to fix the mess it had become. If she took down the remaining twists and braids to smooth them, though, she would never be able to pin them back up as Cassandra had done.

Sighing, she brushed out Cassandra's painstaking work and left her hair loose. If anyone asked, she could always claim a headache. Who knew — depending on Uncle, she might yet get one.

Feeling more or less dignified, Andromache made her way back downstairs. It seemed that the ladies had departed, leaving Hecuba and Cassandra to haul everything back to the kitchen. They were still there, tidying up.

"…I know, I didn't expect them back for at least another day or two. But there's no shortage of food, what with extras from the luncheon," Hecuba was saying. "And while we're on that subject — really, dear!" she chided, upon hearing Andromache's footsteps behind her. "Did you have to rush out like that, without even saying goodbye to everyone? They were here to see *you*!"

"Oh, Mom, nobody cared," Cassandra pooh-poohed. "They thought it was adorable — the beautiful young bride, running out to embrace her beloved." She winked at Andromache, who, at the moment, was wishing she'd chosen any color but turquoise. Turquoise! Of all the colors on earth, the one that would draw the most attention to her horrid, blushing cheeks! And *this* family was capable of uttering things far worse than '*embrace her beloved…*'

"I suppose," Hecuba admitted primly. "Well, in any case, you look lovely."

It was time for Andromache to test her excuse. "I thought it would be nice to dress up a bit more, in — in honor of Uncle."

Hecuba nodded her approval. "That was very thoughtful. He's an important man in your husband's life."

Your husband… Ever since Hecuba had explained her reasons for sending Hector to Santiya, she'd been referring to Hector as '*your husband*' instead of '*my son*.' It was either a gesture of good-will toward Andromache or a way for Hecuba to distance herself from Hector, since the two hadn't parted on good terms. *I suppose it doesn't matter*, thought Andromache. Either way, Hecuba had bought her fiction about the dress.

"Well, Asius is resting," said Hecuba, "and I sent one of the neighbor boys to the temple to find Priam. Paris said he was going upstairs to change his clothes, and —" She counted off the family members on her fingers.

"He went to the bath," Andromache supplied.

"Well then." Hecuba tightened her lips. "While we're waiting on them, we'll whip up something for dinner. Something simple, girls, since it'll just be the family."

ℰ℧

'SOMETHING SIMPLE' took up countless plates and so much room that Andromache despaired of fitting everything on the courtyard table — assuming that they managed to lug the whole feast out there in the first place!

During one of their many trips, Hector emerged.

"Oh," said Hecuba, when she saw him. "Welcome back, dear."

Sensing an awkward moment, Andromache made for the kitchen. There, she ran into Cassandra, who was staggering under the weight of a heavy cheese tray.

"Stop!" warned Andromache. "Don't go out there!"

"Why? What's wrong?"

"Your mom — and your brother."

"Which brother?"

"Which one do you think?"

"Oh!" gasped Cassandra. "Do you think they'll be there awhile?"

"I don't know."

"What did they look like?"

"I don't know."

"Do they seem mad?" Cassandra prompted patiently. "Happy? Tense? Calm?"

"I don't know!" hissed Andromache.

"I'm going to look."

"No — don't!"

"Ssh, they'll never know." Cassandra set her tray down and peeked out the window.

"So, what do you see?" asked Andromache. "What are they doing?"

"It's hard to say. I think she might be patting his arm, or maybe she's — no, she doesn't seem to be smacking him. Wait — wait — he's definitely smiling."

"Real or fake?"

"Small, but real."

Andromache sighed in relief. "Try to see if —"

"Oh, darts!" squealed Cassandra.

"What?"

"They're coming!"

"That wasn't long!"

"Quick, make it look like we were busy!" Cassandra flailed around for something to hold and came up with a round loaf of bread. She brandished it at her mother and brother as they entered the kitchen.

"Hi, little sister," said Hector. "Been baking?"

Cassandra smiled and ran to give him a hug. "Glad you're back!"

"Me, too."

"This never-ending feast!" their mother clucked. "Hector, dear, can you *please* help your wife and your sister and me carry everything outside?"

Hector smiled — a broad smile that came into being with the word '*wife.*' "Of course."

His presence, however, was more a detriment than an asset. While his family members were around, he was too busy touching Andromache's hair or slipping an arm around her waist to help much with the dinner preparations. And as soon as the others left with an armload of cups or a tray of food, he turned to sneaking long kisses and whispering to her.

"You haff a new dress."

"The other one got a little wrinkled."

Kiss. "How, I wahnder..." *Kiss, kiss.*

"I wonder!"

Kiss. Kiss, kiss. "You ahre so pretty."

"No, I'm not. I hate this dress. It's hideous and itchy."

"<u>You do not lahke it? You can then take it off, lahke the ahther</u>…" *Kiss.*

"<u>Ha, ha</u>!" *Kiss, kiss. Kiss…*

"Hector! Andromache!" barked Hecuba. "Where on earth have the two of you gone? Everyone else is here — Priam and Paris finally made it out to the courtyard. Asius is here, too, and he'd just as soon *not* have his dinner at midnight, if it's all the same to you!"

"All right—we're coming!" Hector shouted. Under his breath, he added to Andromache, "<u>As soon as *you* take your hands off my tush</u>."

Giggling, she released him, and they walked outside.

Chapter 33

The instant Andromache saw Uncle, she understood why Hector had once scoffed at the notion of having to protect him. The man was even taller than Hector and far bulkier, with his thick arms and barrel chest. When introduced to Andromache, he embraced her, pulling her off her feet and smothering her in his beard.

Cutie snarled at Uncle's perceived attack on her mama — but then, losing courage, she ran over to Hector for comfort.

Uncle laughed at Cutie and set Andromache down. "So, this is the girl who's turned my nephew to a soup!" he chortled.

Hector accepted the jab with a look of dignity, even pride. It was the exact look Andromache had earlier tried — but failed — to imitate.

"I had to get back here to see you for myself," Uncle went on. "The boy's descriptions of you weren't very informative. It was all '*shimmering*' this and '*luminous*' that. I couldn't tell if he was marrying a woman or an oil lamp."

Hector endured Paris's snickering with the same stately air. He'd never looked so regal. Andromache, on the other hand, was mortified.

"Luminous," said Priam, turning to Hecuba and smiling.

She smiled back at him. To her brother, she said, "I told you, Asius! Have you ever seen a boy so besotted?"

Andromache wished that they would find something else to talk about: how life was in Santiya, whether the river or the ferryman had been high, *anything*! Uncle, however, had other plans. He was burning to tell the story of Hector's arrival. He sat solemnly with the others while Priam gave an oration — beautiful words on the coming together of family and the joy of new be-ginnings. As soon as Priam was finished, though, Uncle launched into a discourse of his own:

"So, Sonny here shows up one day, out of nowhere, all wild-eyed, and thumps into my chambers without so much as a hello. *'Nice to see you,'* I tell him. *'What a surprise! What brings you here?'* And what does he say to me? He says, *'Get your ass on a horse!'*"

"Oh, Hector!" Hecuba chided. "Where on earth did you learn to talk like that?"

Hector shrugged.

His uncle guffawed. "Probably from me!" Resuming his sto-ry, he said: *"'And why should I get any part of me on a horse?'* I ask him. He says, *'We need to ride back to Troy so I can get married.'* You can imagine my surprise — had I heard any news of weddings? Of course not! But any fool could see there'd be no reasoning with him, so I say, *'All right, all right — go clean up, have something to eat, and then we'll head out.'* I was worried I wouldn't have time to make the proper preparations for while I was away. From the look on his face, I thought he'd be back any moment to wrestle me onto a horse. But Sonny here never came back in to see me after his bath, and when I went to look for him, I found him passed out cold in his old bedroom. When he finally wakes up, he croaks, *'How long was I out?'* and I tell him, *'A day and a half.'*"

"A day and a half?" gasped Andromache.

"That's right, little niece."

"But he's been gone five days," said Hecuba. "How long did it take you boys to ride back here?"

"We spent two nights on the road," said Hector.

"Which means you rode to Santiya in —"

"Under a day."

"Oh, for pity's sake!" Hecuba sighed. "No wonder you were tired, after riding like that!"

Hector shrugged. "I wanted to get back as soon as I could."

Touched but also worried that Hector was exhausting him-self, Andromache squeezed his hand; he let go and squeezed her thigh.

"In any case," Uncle went on. "Once he finally woke up, we didn't waste much time getting back here."

"Honestly, Asius, I hope you didn't let my son drive you to do anything *foolish*." Hecuba frowned at her brother.

"Bah!" scoffed Uncle. "I was as eager to get back here as Sonny was — I couldn't wait to see the *luminous* creature who'd inspired such a frenzy."

ℛ

THE EVENING WORE ON, with more food, more wine, more embarrassing comments, and more squeezes under the table. The moon rose high in the sky, and stars began to pop out.

Uncle seemed to have a bottomless supply of stories. Andromache had expected — and hoped for — him to be wearier, after the ride in from Santiya. Every so often, she looked longingly at Hector's room across the courtyard. She couldn't wait to walk over there with him — to shut the door behind them — to have more than a few stolen moments in his arms —

"Wake up, honey!" warbled Cassandra.

Startled, Andromache turned to face her. Cassandra was standing beside the table, not alone, but surrounded by a troupe of friends. Andromache hadn't even noticed all the girls come in, she'd been so busy thinking about —

"Come on!" sang Cassandra. "Everyone's here to keep you company. You can't spend tonight of all nights alone."

Andromache hadn't been planning to, although Cassandra's friends were hardly the company she'd had in mind.

"It's tradition to have a little party, just for girls! It's when we work on the crown and things. And then tomorrow, we'll help you get ready. You know, bathe you, style your hair…"

Hair? Bathe? Crown? Andromache was feeling stupider and stupider. "For what?"

Cassandra gestured to Hector.

"The wedding," he explained. "Do you still want it?"

"Yes, but, I —" Andromache gave him a blank look. "It's tomorrow?"

"Well, yes. That was the deal."

"What deal?"

"I told you this…"

She shook her head.

"That I'd fetch Uncle, as long as the wedding was the day after we got back here, whenever that was, auspicious or not, ready or not."

"That's true, dear," said Hecuba. "We thought he'd spoken with you."

"Really, I didn't tell you?" Hector frowned.

Andromache shook her head again. "Maybe if you got more sleep, you'd remember things like that," she muttered.

Uncle chortled.

"<u>I am sohrry</u>," said Hector, contritely covering her hand. "<u>Tomorrow, it is all rahght</u>?"

"<u>Of course</u>!" said Andromache. What an absurd question! What did it matter, which day she married the man who was, according to Lukkan custom, already her husband? Unless —

She turned to Priam. "But — *is* it auspicious?" she asked him. "Tomorrow, I mean?" Not that she believed in such things, but — just in case —

"Not to worry, little one," Priam assured her, his eyes twinkling. "Most auspicious."

"All right," said Andromache. "Then yes." To Hector, she whispered, "<u>But I don't want to go off with your sister and her friends. I want to stay with *you*. In your room</u>."

Hector's eyes darkened. He didn't look any happier than she about the traditional party for girls, but he could only shake his head somberly and say, "<u>Tomorrow</u>."

She wanted to ask him what rituals *he* would be expected to partake in, but time had expired on their private conversation.

"Come on, honey!" squealed Cassandra. "We're going to have so much fun!"

Resigned, Andromache stood and followed the girls upstairs.

℘

ONCE IN ANDROMACHE'S ROOM, the young women arranged themselves on the bed, the floor, and the clothing chest.

"So, let's get down to business," one of them said to Andromache. "Have you kissed with him, yet?"

"Well — uh — I —" Andromache stammered.

"Of course she has!" another girl interrupted. "He's *Trojan!*"

Chorus of giggles.

"How many times?" someone asked.

"I'm sorry?" said Andromache.

"How many times has he kissed you?"

"I — uh — uh —"

"Does that mean a lot?"

At least a thousand or two, thought Andromache, remembering the first night she'd spent with Hector. "I don't know."

"Where was the first place he kissed you?"

Andromache smiled to herself. Maybe there was some potential for fun, after all. "On my chest," she said demurely. From the corner of her eye, she watched the girls trying not to peek at her décolletage. They blinked. Straightened their dresses. Cleared their throats. Andromache finally felt the serene smile she'd so coveted spreading on her lips. None of the girls knew that she meant her *clothing* chest...

"Is he a good kisser?" one girl ventured to ask.

Andromache's smile disappeared into a cough.

Someone else answered: "My sister said he's pretty good."

"Rhene!" hissed the first girl.

"What?"

"Don't say that!"

"Say *what?*"

"Rhene — seriously!"

"What's the big deal?"

"She's foreign!" The hisser nodded to indicate Andromache. "She might not understand —"

"It's not like I said he was *bad!*"

"Don't worry about it," said Andromache. Did they think she was completely ignorant? She knew that all young Trojans, Hector included, crept off to dark stairwells to kiss. What was it to her? That was ages ago. Still, she couldn't resist taking a jab back at Rhene: "If *that's* what your sister said, then he must not have been trying very hard when he kissed her." Privately, Andromache added, *And if your sister is half the twit you are, I don't blame him.*

The girls didn't giggle, this time — they laughed.

Pouting, Rhene turned her back on the others. It was in this way that she found her means of exacting revenge on Andromache. "What's *this*?" she asked slyly, dangling a length of filmy fabric from her finger.

Andromache groaned. The luncheon lady dresses! Someone had brought them up to her room! Now, these girls would know about the prank the Trojan matrons had played on her — and they would no doubt want to join in.

"Oh — oh *my*!"

"Hee, hee, hee! Look at *this* one!"

"No, wait — imagine her in *this*!"

"Oh, my goodness!"

Was Hector surrounded by a similar cloud of boys, or was he alone in his room with Cutie, his self-respect intact?

"Andromache?" It was the Newbie, a girl who had recently joined Cassandra's soiree group — and who had once appreciatively murmured, *'Oh — him!'* in response to a comment about Hector...

"Yes?" Andromache asked suspiciously.

"Are you nervous about — *you know*?"

"Did someone mention making a crown?" asked Andromache, pointedly ignoring the Newbie. What was *wrong* with everyone? How she and Hector spent their wedding night was *their* business, no one else's! She was fed up with people asking questions — making comments — making jokes — giggling —

"Hee hee! You're blushing! Is that a '*yes*,' or a '*no*?'"

Again, Andromache tried to appear serene. The chirruping of the girls let her know that she'd failed.

"Look at her face!"

"She's horrified, poor thing!"

"It'll be all right. That's what my mom says."

"The crown?" Andromache insisted, her cheeks blazing red.

"Oh, fine! Here's what we have."

Andromache was disappointed to see that they'd brought laurel leaves. Hector's favorite herb, mint, would have been a better fit. *Then again, it wouldn't do for him to nibble his own headdress during the ceremony*, she thought.

"Do you know how to make a crown?"

"It can't be that hard," said Andromache. "Let me try it."

"The first step is getting the size right. You don't want it to slip over onto his neck, but you don't want it to look like a misplaced bracelet, either. How big is his head?"

"Pretty big, at times," said Andromache. Cassandra giggled.

In the end, they fashioned an oval slightly larger than Cassandra's head and embellished it with the rest of the greenery. *It'll do*, thought Andromache. *Actually, it's pretty good.*

℘

THE NEXT MORNING, the girls brought up water to bathe Andromache — as though she were so incompetent as to need help bathing, and least of all *theirs*! She did her best to stay curled in a ball while they oiled her back, washed her hair, and scrubbed her feet. The bristle brush they were using tickled her, but no matter how she kicked, the girls kept at it. She supposed that was why they descended on the bride in a throng, in case many hands were needed to restrain her during the bathing ritual. At last, when her skin was red enough to suit them, they wrapped her in a large sheet and plunked her on the bed.

The girls were hunting about for hair combs, and Andromache was trying to stay out of the way, when they heard a knock.

"It must be Paris!" cried Cassandra.

"Paris?" yelped Andromache. "What's *he* doing here?"

"He's bringing up your wedding dress. Mom had him fetch it for you."

"Tell him to leave it by the door!" hissed Andromache. "I do *not* want him in here!" The bath situation was embarrassing enough, without Paris there to jeer at her.

"Well of course, honey!" Cassandra whispered reassuringly. "It's girls only!" To her brother, she shouted, "Just leave it by the door, Paris!"

"Just leave it by the door, Paris!" he mimicked. "And never mind a '*thank you*!' Someday, I'd like one of you to go on a mission for *me*, for a change!" There was a muted thump as Andromache's wedding dress hit the door, and a terrible clamor as Paris stomped back downstairs.

"Well, let's see it!" Cassandra opened the door and seized a wad of fabric from the ground. "Oh, honey!" she gasped, unfolding it. "How beautiful!"

The dress was a warm, deep shade of blue — the color of the sea, the sky, and happiness. It looked beautiful indeed, but Andromache gave it a thorough inspection. She wanted to be sure that Paris hadn't made a hole in an awkward place or poured a foul smelling liquid onto it. "Looks good," she approved at last.

"Time to put it on!" sang Cassandra. "The guests will be here soon."

Andromache did as she was told. The girls *oohed* and *aahed* and declared the dress perfect. Privately, Andromache agreed with them: that dress, if nothing else, was her one sure way back to Hector.

Chapter 34

D uring her time in Troy, Andromache had witnessed two weddings officiated by Priam, both of which were flawless events. Serious musicians were engaged to play the wedding songs. Every ritual item was in place: a gleaming cup sat beside the spring, a delicate box filled with spices perfumed the air, and garland was hung just so. Chickens, dogs, small children, and any other creatures that might make a scene were sent elsewhere. Protocol was followed in every regard.

What was more, the bride and groom knew every gesture to make — every word to say — down to the tiniest breath. Priam always invited the couple over to run through the ceremony once or twice the evening before, so that when it came time for the actual event, their roles were polished to a high luster. As far as Andromache knew, Priam had conducted a never-ending string of perfect wedding ceremonies. That string was broken the day that his son married Andromache.

The ceremony was a disaster before it ever began. Andromache was passing through the banquet hall with Cassandra's friends when she heard Hector's voice. It was coming from outside, on the courtyard. He was *there*! She could see his head sticking out above a row of shrubbery.

Enough of this! thought Andromache, breaking through the circle of girls and sprinting toward her husband. The girls galloped after her, making hissing noises and odd, muffled shrieks. She had to get away from them! "Ector!" she called. "Please save me from them!"

Too late, she saw that Hector wasn't alone on the courtyard. The guests, already assembled, had been hidden from her view.

Her chance for a stately entrance was lost. She looked up at Hector and mouthed an apology — she'd disgraced them already! — but he seemed delighted just to see her. He gave her a radiant smile and motioned her over. As soon as she was beside him, he hugged and kissed her.

It was plainly not the appointed moment for kisses. The guests began to murmur.

Then, Andromache noticed something wrong in the courtyard. The garland, normally striking, looked limp. A paltry number of strands had been hung in strange places, too close to the ground. Hector must not have seen to it, as he ordinarily did. She supposed it would have been rude to make him decorate for his own wedding, but the whole scene suffered from the fact that he'd been given a holiday.

Garland was the least of their problems, however. Priam had arranged for Paris, rather than the usual musicians, to play the wedding songs. He'd thought that including Hector's brother would make the wedding more personal, more special. And special it was.

Paris could play the songs more beautifully than anyone else in Troy. In fact, he was almost as skilled a lutenist as Andromache's father had been. For a time, Andromache closed her eyes and drifted away on the music, imagining that her dad was the one playing the notes. The illusion was so powerful that it brought her to the brink of tears.

That's lovely, she thought, opening her eyes. *I wonder why* Priam *doesn't use him for all the other weddings*. Then, she heard it: beneath the main melody, cleverly hidden, Paris was playing the chorus of his favorite drinking song. Several of the more observant guests began to hum along in spite of themselves. When Hector finally had to cough to hold back his laughter, Paris responded by playing more boldly.

"Ahem!" Priam, too, coughed and gave each of his sons a stern look. They sobered.

Meanwhile, Andromache just stood chewing on her lower lip. She wanted to pick at her fingernails, but Hector was holding her hand.

The next mishap came when it was time for the crowns. Hector bent down to let Andromache place the greenery on his head, but as he straightened, the crown went askew. Not only did it look ridiculous, it was in danger of falling off.

Priam began chanting: "O gods on high and all around, may these crowns be a sign of your endless vitality, of the green life surging through you."

Hector's crown slipped a little more; he was now raising his eyebrows to keep it on his head. Andromache didn't know why he wasn't straightening it with his hands, unless he didn't want to draw attention to the fact that she'd gotten it on wrong in the first place.

"As we see your vigor in these crowns, so may we see it in this couple..."

I have to fix it, thought Andromache, climbing suddenly onto the wall beside the spring. She had no sooner straightened Hector's crown than a bewildered Priam stopped chanting. The guests began to twitter again — in disapproval, Andromache was sure.

Embarrassed, she leapt down from the wall in such haste that she nearly fell. Hector grabbed her around the middle to steady her, and Cutie, who thought Andromache was being attacked, barked wildly.

More twitters from the guests.

Once everyone was back in place, Priam resumed his chanting. His voice sounded tight. *Of course*, thought Andromache. *He's emotional, today — his eldest child is getting married!* When she looked up at Priam, though, she saw instead that he was holding in laughter.

The wedding was a joke, even to its officiant!

Andromache's cheeks flamed red. Her only comfort was that the worst was over — the damage had already been done to their dignity. Just then, however, Priam looked expectantly at Hector, and Hector began to chant. He easily rattled off his part, which he'd heard before in dozens of other weddings. When he fell silent, though, Andromache realized with horror that she was next. The girls had tried to teach her the words, the night before; now, though, she couldn't remember even a snippet! Priam came to her rescue by having her repeat the words after him, but over the buzzing in her ears, she could barely hear what he said.

"By all the gobs of stars above, I promise smiles of kernel love." Andromache knew she wasn't getting the words or tune right, but she chanted her part as best she could. When she finished, there was a profusion of twitters from the audience and another kiss from Hector.

The final calamity came about when Andromache had to serve Hector water from the ceremonial cup. For several breaths, she just stood before him, feeling lost. He was so tall that she wasn't sure how to do the ritual with any delicacy. The easiest thing would have been to stand on the spring's wall, but not wanting to repeat *that* gaffe, she instead rose onto her tiptoes and put the cup to his mouth. He'd barely taken a sip when she teetered, dribbling water down his chin. Aghast, she dabbed at the water with both thumbs and meanwhile dropped the cup. *Clank! Clink, clink, clank!* After ricocheting off the wall, it rolled out onto the courtyard and came to rest under a bush. Cutie leapt headlong after it, returning moments later with the cup held proudly in her jaws.

The murmurings from the guests grew louder.

Andromache looked up at Hector in apology for all of her faux pas. He beamed at her and kissed her again — not a stolen kiss this time, but a long one meant to put an end to the ceremony. It was such a nice kiss that Andromache forgot about the guests until they started roaring with laughter. Before she could even begin to wonder why they were laughing, she was torn away from Hector and forced to mingle.

"Hello, dearie! Congratulations to you! Do you remember me?" a plump woman asked. "We met here months ago, at another wedding, although it wasn't as lovely as yours."

Andromache had absolutely no idea who the woman was but didn't want to offend her. "Thank you for coming," she said. "It means so much to me."

"Congratulations!" said the next person, and the next said, "The ceremony was beautiful. I wish you a long and healthy life together." Andromache was pulled from one guest to the next. There seemed to be a thousand of them.

As she spun about, smiling, chatting, and thanking people, she overheard bits of other conversations — not all of them as complimentary as what was being said directly to her.

"I would have thought the son of the high priest could have managed a godlier wedding, and make no mistake!"

"Tut, tut! That's what happens when you rush!"

"And what *are* those things in her crown?"

"I don't know — perhaps it's a foreign custom."

Andromache hadn't actually thought to look at her crown. Now, worried about what joke Hector might have played on her, she took it off to inspect it — and gasped when she saw how beautiful it was. The green circlet was exquisitely woven, and tucked into it were several of her favorite purple flowers. The mystery of the ugly garland was solved, at any rate: Hector hadn't had time to hang it because he'd gone out to the countryside to pick flowers for her. Tenderly, she brought the crown to her face and breathed in.

She was standing there, enraptured, when a voice cooed, "Oh, what a beautiful wedding, little dear!"

Andromache recognized the Lark from the previous day's luncheon.

"The nicest once I've ever seen," said the Otter, who was standing beside her friend.

Nice? Andromache frowned. What were the ladies up to — anther prank, like the see-through dresses? Well, she was on to them! By now, she'd heard what people *really* thought about her wedding! Rushed — ungodly —

"What's wrong, Sunshine?"

"Didn't you like the ceremony?"

Muddled chanting — spilled water — a barking dog — a fallen crown —

"Well, *we* certainly enjoyed it!"

"Then why was everyone laughing?" said Andromache, before she could stop herself. She flushed, certain that the ladies would take offense at her tone, but instead, they smiled kindly at her.

"Forgive us!" chirped the Lark. "We don't often get to see couples so obviously in love with each other." Leaning in close enough to kiss Andromache's cheek, she added in a soft voice, "You have something very special, dear."

The Lark and the Otter walked away, and other guests took their place. Much as she wanted to, Andromache wasn't allowed to linger in the shadows. Everyone was eager to talk to the bride — and not least because they'd all spent three years expecting Hector to marry his fellow warrior, Penthesilea...

But Andromache didn't want to think about *her*, today of all days.

As the mingling was inevitable, Andromache didn't try to fight it. She let herself be tugged along from guest to guest to guest and, for comfort, drank a little more wine than usual. One of the few people she didn't get to talk to was her husband. He was likewise surrounded by waves of well-wishers and never quite managed to reach her, although he seemed to be trying. Each time his eyes crossed hers, he smiled and looked at her with a woozy sort of awe.

She supposed that he, too, was drinking too much.

After two solid hours, when Andromache was at her limit with socializing, she escaped to a quiet section of the courtyard. She'd only just settled down on a bench when someone touched her arm.

She stiffened. It was a touch she knew but did *not* welcome. "Hello," she said awkwardly, glad for all the wine she'd drunk. Without it, she didn't think she could have endured a tête-à-tête with Demuchus. She hadn't seen him since just after the last Trojan wedding, when he'd kissed her and asked her to marry him, and she'd fallen into spasms of maniacal laughter.

Hurriedly she scanned the crowd for Hector, who was himself cornered by a short, grey-haired woman. He smiled as Andromache caught his eye, but when he noticed Demuchus, his smile changed to a smirk. Andromache tried to motion him over; he refused her any further eye contact. *Some husband!* she thought crossly.

"You look well, Andromache," said Demuchus.

"Thank you," she said. "You, too."

He lowered his voice. "I mean, you *really* look the part." His eyes flickered meaningfully to her blue dress.

She said nothing. She didn't like his tone.

"Your gamble paid off," he added.

Frowning, she asked, "Gamble?"

"Betting your sure post as a councilman's wife against the hope of nabbing something — *better*." Again, Demuchus's gaze caressed her gown. "I hope you won't be disappointed in your ambitions."

"You aren't a councilman yet," Andromache reminded him tartly. All the same, her cheeks grew pale. Were all the other guests thinking the same thing as Demuchus? Did they see her marriage to Hector as nothing more than ambition? *Oh, gods!* she thought, her eyes flooding with tears. Was even *this* going to be spoiled for her?

Demuchus leaned in close and whispered, "Well, *he's* not really a prince, and never will be, either!"

"*His* breath doesn't smell like cadaver, either," Andromache whispered back. The words slipped out before she could stop them.

Demuchus blanched. Under his closed lips, his tongue began working its way back and forth across his teeth. Suddenly, he couldn't seem to get away fast enough. "Well," he said. "I must give my congratulations to your — ah, *husband.*"

"I'm sure he'll be pleased to see you."

Once Demuchus had turned away, Andromache darted behind a shrub and spied on his conversation with Hector. From a distance, it appeared pleasant enough. The two men talked for a long time, laughing and smiling all the while. They even clasped arms. When Demuchus finally went inside to peruse the banquet table, Andromache made her way over to Hector. She was dying to know what he and Demuchus had said to each other.

Before she could ask him, though, Hector pulled her into his arms. "I've hardly seen you, today!" he complained.

"I know." She kissed him. "I know."

"Did Xanthus ever find you? He was asking me where you were."

Andromache shook her head. "He probably couldn't see me in the horde."

"I know! It's never been quite this crazy, here. And other than Medon, Dolops, Palmys, and Thaeus — oh, have you met them, yet? My captains?" Hector scanned the courtyard until he found the group of men he was looking for. "Over there," he said, gesturing.

Andromache shook her head. "I don't think so."

"I'll have to introduce you, later. Anyway, other than them, I haven't seen most of these people in *years.* I even ran into my old Hurrian language tutor!"

"Hurrian?" asked Andromache. "How long did *that* last?"

"I don't remember, but not long." Hector grinned. "She — my Hurrian tutor — said that this marriage is poetic justice."

Andromache snorted. "Which one is she?"

"Over there." Hector pointed to a grey-haired woman, the same one he'd been chatting with when Andromache was cornered by Demuchus.

Demuchus! Although Andromache had wanted to ask about him, the thought of him now made her sigh.

"What is wrong?" asked Hector, stroking her cheek.

"I love you so much." Her face crumpled. A tear spilled out.

Hector laughed. "You lahff me? Oh, that is terrible. I am so sohrry."

"No! I love you so much, but everyone here thinks I married you for *this*." Andromache held out a length of her dress. "To have nice things. They think I'm *ambitious*."

"Ahndromahk, that is foalish. No one finks that."

"Demuchus does. He said exactly that."

Hector shook with laughter. "Demuchus?"

"What's so funny?"

"He said that? He said you married me because of *clothes*?"

"Yes."

Hector gave another whoop of laughter. "But Demuchus *hates* my clothes!"

Andromache gave in and laughed with him. It was true. Demuchus had always complained about the ratty look of Hector's tunics — the old ones that Hector prized because their worn fabric felt soft against his skin. "All right," she said. "But still, I wish you hadn't left me alone with him. You deserted me!"

"I'm sorry..." Hector's voice trailed off.

"But?" prompted Andromache.

"But it would've made things worse if I'd gone over there."

"How?" she asked. She couldn't imagine her conversation with Demuchus being any worse!

"Because, if I'd hovered around you like some overgrown moth, Demuchus would've thought I was afraid to leave you alone with him. He would've thought I was threatened by him."

Andromache sighed. "I never thought of *that*."

"See?" Hector hugged her. "I wasn't just deserting you."

She leaned into him. "What a headache, all the games men have to play."

"Oh, <u>Ahndromahk</u>!" Hector laughed. "You don't know the half of it. Xanthus brought his roodles board, and there's talk of a tournament."

Andromache frowned. "That's not really the kind of game I meant."

"In this case, I think it would be."

"What are you talking about?"

"The very worst Trojan custom of all," Hector explained. "The torturing of the married couple. We have to stay here until every last guest is gone. We have to talk to them, eat with them, play games with them, dance, or whatever else, until they decide to leave." Pause. "No matter how late it is." Pause. "And, my sweetheart, I'm afraid we're in for a very long night. Some of them have a score to settle with me."

"Torturing the married couple?" In other words, preventing them from going off to Hector's bedroom. Andromache sighed again. "You were right. That *definitely* qualifies as one of those man-games."

Hector gave her a mischievous look. "Are you saying it's only torture for the man?"

She poked him; he kissed her.

"So you're <u>*really* playing</u> roodles?" she asked. "<u>Tonight</u>?"

"<u>You can play, too.</u>"

"<u>Ector</u>!"

"<u>Yes, really</u>. I couldn't make this stuff up."

"Can't you just lose and wash out of the tournament?"

"No, I can't."

"Why not? Because it would threaten your manhood?"

"Manhood, panhood!" he scoffed. "I can't *just lose* because then they'll change the rules so the losers have to play each other. They'll make up any loophole they want so I have to stay."

"That's the stupidest thing I've ever heard."

"I know. Most Trojan women are disgusted by it and just go to bed."

With a sudden yearning for the comfort of Hector's bed, Andromache murmured, "<u>Why don't we slip over to your room for a moment or two? It's right there.</u>"

Hector shook his head. "<u>That is cheating.</u>"

"<u>Half a moment! No one would notice.</u>"

"<u>Efferyone would notice! They ahre watching us.</u>"

Andromache sighed once more; Hector kissed her again, a little longer this time.

"You can't do that, if we have to play roodles all night," she objected.

"Do what?"

"Kiss me like *that*..."

"Lahke this?" He kissed her yet again.

"There you guys are!" sang a shrill, girlish voice. "We've been searching all over for you."

Hector looked up. "Hi Cassandra," he said. "Hi, Paris."

Paris nodded to his brother. To Andromache, he said, "Hey, Hermie."

"Nice music," she muttered.

Paris gave a low bow. "It was my pleasure."

"Actually, music is why we're trying to find you," said Cassandra. "It's time for the dance!"

"Dance?" murmured Andromache.

"Oh, yes!" cried Cassandra. "The wedding dance. You and Hector have to lead it."

Dancing was one thing. Andromache had once loved dancing and could probably learn to again. Indeed, dancing with Hector was a delightful thought, especially if they were out in the countryside, under the stars. But to dance in front of everybody, where they would all see how clumsy she was and laugh at her for it? She looked up at Hector, mutely beseeching him to spare her.

"It cannot be bad," he said. "I am not bad. You remember my old nickname?"

Dancer, she thought glumly, and nodded. "But that was to make fun of you."

"Maybe," he said, shrugging.

So, he wasn't going to rescue her from *this*, either! He *liked* dancing — he'd probably been looking forward to this moment!

Hector took one of her hands, and Cassandra took the other, and between them they dragged her over to the center of the courtyard. Everyone was gathered there, ready to watch the evening's greatest spectacle. Paris grabbed his lute and began to play just as Cassandra gave Andromache a push toward Hector.

Once the dancing began, she relaxed. Hector really *was* good at it, but even if he hadn't been, he was so obviously, radiantly happy that it wouldn't have mattered. The guests murmured and twittered, just as Andromache had foreseen, but their laughter was gentle.

As the dancing proceeded, most of the guests joined in. Around her, Andromache saw half of Troy whirl past in couples or groups. The Lark and the Otter with a few other women — then Cassandra with a whole string of soiree boys, including Demuchus — then Priam and Hecuba by themselves — then Cutie nipping at everyone's heels.

Andromache giggled.

"See?" whispered Hector. "It is not bad."

"Not bad at all," she whispered back.

ᏋᎧ

LONG AFTER THE SKY HAD PASSED from blue to midnight black, a cadre of roodles players was still sitting out on the courtyard: Hector, Andromache, Paris, Xanthus, Cutie, some men Andromache didn't recognize — probably the young husbands who were seeking revenge on Hector — and, to everyone's surprise, Demuchus.

At first, Andromache had thought that Demuchus was only there to spite her, but little by little, she realized that he was enjoying himself. He looked as lighthearted as she'd ever seen him. *What on earth did he and Ector say to each other, earlier?* she wondered. Hector had refused to tell her, explaining that it was '*between boys.*' *I suppose they came to some kind of understanding. Maybe Ector complimented his poetry...*

If Demuchus was in good spirits, though, Hector was unabashedly giddy. Even his lamentable roodles performance didn't seem to bother him. He laughed his way through round after losing round, never showing the least sign of irritation or fatigue.

Andromache, on the other hand, grew sleepy as the night wore one. She eventually closed her eyes, leaned against Hector's shoulder, and just listened to the banter of the players.

"Stop trying to throw the game, Hector."

"Yeah — we're on to you."

315

"It won't get you out of here any quicker."

"Oh, hush! I'm not throwing anything."

"You're really *that* bad, tonight?"

"Yes!"

A round of laughter, including Hector's.

"His luck went to hell when his lady zonked out."

"Look at that! Poor Hermie's been stupefied."

"Poor who?"

"The bride, cankerwort."

"Poor her, nothing! Poor *Hector!*"

Cackling all around.

"I am sohrry, pretty wife," Hector whispered to Andromache. "You can sleep. Put your head on my lap."

Gratefully, she lay down.

"As if *that* will help you concentrate!" someone jeered.

"Shut up!" snapped Hector.

A chorus of guffaws.

"She's a pretty girl, Hector."

"She's a *smart* girl, not fluff-brained like most of your young lot."

"She's perfect," said Hector.

"Loooooooominous!" jeered Paris.

Hector began gently stroking her hair...

"Hector?"

Her cheek...

"Hector?!"

The half-circle of her ear...

"Hector!"

"Forget it — he's on the moon."

Cackling.

"Maybe we *should* call it a night, boys. I'm beat."

"Really?" Hector asked hopefully. His hand slipped down to Andromache's shoulder.

"Nah! You really think you'll get off that easy, after what you put *me* through?"

A longer round of cackling, mixed with a few guffaws.

"All right, all right," sighed Hector. "Just reset the board."

ᔓ

SEVERAL HOURS and a thousand jokes later, Andromache felt herself being scooped up into the air. She wrapped her arms around Hector's neck and pressed her cheek to his shoulder.

"They're gone?" she asked drowsily.

"Mm-hmm," he said. "Finally."

"How many matches did you play?"

"How many stahrs do you see?"

Andromache giggled. "Then you must be very tired," she teased. "We should get some sleep."

"Sleep!" he said scornfully. "I can sleep tomorrow." *Kiss.* "Ohr the next tomorrow." *Kiss, kiss.*

That time, Andromache didn't stop him from kissing her. They were alone out on the courtyard. No one would notice or care, now, if they slipped off to his bedroom. The torturing of the married couple was over.

Chapter 35

After the wedding, Andromache had three lazy, luxurious days with her husband. They seldom left their room, except to soak in the bath chamber, and they didn't talk to anyone except each other. No one bothered them. Far from it, the family members went out of their way to give the married couple their privacy. Baskets of food were left by the spring, but otherwise, no one even came out onto the courtyard.

Three days of calm, sleep, long talks, and loving, and then life went back to normal. Andromache hated to see the charmed days of their honeymoon come to an end, but she knew that there was no avoiding it. Hector had responsibilities that he could no longer push aside to colleagues.

On their first morning of ordinary married life, they crossed the courtyard together to eat breakfast in the kitchen. Priam, Hecuba, and Cassandra were there to greet them.

"Hello, newlyweds!" sang Cassandra.

Andromache blushed. Hector laughed and gave his wife a hearty kiss. He then made a great ceremony of settling her in, making sure that she was comfortable and furnished with a heap of breakfast delicacies before sitting down beside her.

His parents hid their laughter in a series of loud coughs; Cassandra made no effort to conceal hers. Meanwhile, equally embarrassed and touched by all the fuss, Andromache reached under the table to squeeze Hector's hand.

He squeezed back. "Do you need anything else?" he asked earnestly.

Andromache glanced at her plate, walled in by a fortress of food. What else could she possibly want? "No, thank you," she whispered.

Hector gave her a tender smile and leaned down to kiss her forehead.

Cassandra giggled. Priam smiled into his napkin.

Hecuba cleared her throat before addressing her son: "What are you up to, today, Hector dear?"

"Back to work," he said.

"Already?"

"What do you mean, '*already*'? I've been away long enough as it is."

"Well, it's not as though Troy fell apart in your absence."

"Gee — thanks."

"Your mother only means that there are people who'd be glad to help," said Priam, laughing. "You could take another day with your wife."

Hector looked at Andromache. "I could take another year," he said.

Again, her cheeks burned. Not that she didn't feel the same way, but couldn't he save such comments for when they were alone? Or at least out of earshot of that snickering Cassandra?

"But I'll have to go back sooner or later," Hector went on. "And the longer I put it off, the worse it'll be."

"That's sensible," Priam agreed.

Hecuba shrugged and rolled her eyes. "Well, since you're determined to go, be sure to meet up with your uncle Asius."

"Uncle? Where is he?"

"In the stables, I presume. He's gotten himself addicted to that silly board game you all play."

Hector laughed. "Roodles? He's down at the stables, playing roodles? That'll make Xanthus's day."

"Unless he's losing," Andromache pointed out.

"True," agreed Hector. "Too true. I'd better go and check on them." He stood to leave, kissing Andromache's lips even more emphatically than before. "<u>See you later</u>," he said. "<u>I lahff you, pretty wife</u>."

"<u>I love you</u>," she murmured back, blushing.

Hector's family stifled one last round of laughter.

After breakfast, once everyone else had left, Andromache wandered out to the courtyard. She, too, had recently been neglecting her work. Many plants were dormant in the summer heat, but her garden still needed her. *I'll be busy*, she thought, taking stock of the withered flowers, brown leaves, and spots of disease.

Cutie began yowling as a bird taunted her from high on a bush.

"Forget it!" Andromache ordered the little would-be predator. "You'll never get a bird."

Cutie wagged her tail furiously, as though she'd heard nothing but '*Get a bird*' and was prepared to do just that.

Andromache laughed. Like Cutie, she was bounding with energy. She sailed through the garden, weeding, watering, and pulling off dried leaves. Every so often, she would catch sight of Hector's — of *their* — door across the courtyard and feel a surge of joy.

He was her *husband!*

Gardening took no effort at all, that day. Her back didn't hurt, her knees didn't ache, and the water didn't slosh out of the jar she was using to carry it. Morning passed into afternoon without her even realizing it. She hoped her husband was having a similarly smooth day getting back into his own work routines.

Her husband! Andromache smiled to herself. He would be back soon; it was almost time for Lukkan lessons. *I should take a bath before he gets here*, she thought.

Dropping her last handful of weeds, Andromache ran over to Hector's room — to *their* room — to get a clean dress. Cutie went with her.

The room was much larger than Andromache's old one. It even had its own hearth. Inside, it was cool and airy. The windows, covered by gauzy curtains, let in the herb-scented breezes from the courtyard.

Andromache walked over to the bed, which was made up with soft, threadbare linens — Hector's favorite kind. He hated to sleep on rough cloth. The only time he'd ever done so was for her sake, when he'd given her his old blanket and been forced to break in a scratchy new one. *But now I've brought Stripey back to him*, she thought. *Now his bed is perfect again.*

Closing her eyes, she lay down, pressed her face to the linens, and breathed in the scents of cedar and lemon balm. She'd long associated Hector with the first smell, but the second had come as a surprise. Now, she knew that when Hector stopped at the spring every evening to splash water over his feet, he also scrubbed them thoroughly with lemon balm oil. *Cedar and lemon balm — my husband's night smell.* Her insides fluttered.

Cutie leapt up and began licking Andromache's toes.

"Hey!" cried Andromache. "All right, I'm almost ready."

She grabbed a dress and walked out to the bath chamber. There, she scrubbed her skin and rubbed in scented oil, smiling as she pictured Hector kissing her — breathing in the smell of her perfume —

Hector! He would be arriving in the library at any moment, if he wasn't there already. She would have to hurry!

Her hair still wet and dripping onto her shoulders, Andromache called for Cutie and ran to the library. It was empty. She sighed in relief and settled down on her old stool. To pass the time, she skimmed through a scroll lying on the table — a treatise on winemaking:

> *The grapes of the bunch must be inspected, one by one. If the first has rot, cast it away. If the second has rot, cast it away. If the third has rot, cast it away. If the fourth has rot —*

She dropped the scroll onto the table, thinking wryly, *If the text has rot, cast it away!* As a gardener, she supposed she ought to have been more interested, but she had her limits. She couldn't wait to show it to Hector — to watch him laugh over it.

Andromache frowned. Where was Hector, anyway? He was at least half an hour late for their lesson...

Lesson. Lesson? Lesson...Lesson! The longer Andromache turned the word over in her mind, the sillier it sounded. *A lesson.* Of *course* Hector wasn't there! He was her husband now — her *husband!* No husband, even one so tender and adoring as to build his wife a tower of breakfast foods, would want to return to the role of student. Oh, gods, how stupid of her to think he would come to the library! How stupid of her to expect him!

In fact, she thought dully, there was probably no more she could expect from him, as far as Lukkan was concerned. He had no more reason to speak it! The day he'd told her he liked it, he was secretly in love with her and needed an excuse to see her. Now, they shared a bedroom. Even if he really did like Lukkan, he had no real incentive to work hard at it. How long before he stopped learning new words? How long before he forgot the old ones?

How long till he stops calling me Ahndromahk?

&

FEELING COLD AND SOUR from her revelations, Andromache trudged down to the kitchen with Cutie. Paris and Uncle were there, bent over the age-worn roodles board.

"What's that, again?"

"Uncle! I've shown you five times, now!"

"Well, show me again. I can't let that stringy old hawk down at the stables think he can beat me."

Paris sighed. He repeated the move, but Uncle still failed to grasp it.

"Again, boy!"

Paris sat with his face smashed into his open palm and controlled the game pieces without looking.

"I was closer, that time!" Uncle boomed with satisfaction.

"About as close as *I'll* ever be to sprouting wings from my head," muttered Paris.

"Speak up!"

"I said, you *were* closer, Uncle."

"Maybe you should just let Xanthus win," hissed Andromache, immediately regretting that she'd done so. Who was *she*, to rebuke a king?

But Paris took up her cause, saying, "Good idea! Let him win, Uncle."

"And why should I do that?"

"He hates to lose."

"You think *I* like it?"

"It's *his* stable, Uncle, and his stable is like his kingdom. You wouldn't want to lose in *your* kingdom, would you?"

Uncle guffawed. "You have me there!"

Paris grinned; Andromache scowled back at him.

"What's eating *you*, tonight, Hermie?" he asked.

Uncle looked confused. "Hermie? Who's Hermie?"

"*She's* Hermie."

"I thought her name was Andromache."

"It *is*," growled Andromache. "And nothing's wrong!"

"You seem a little crabby," Paris observed. "Been too long since you —"

Andromache shot him a warning look.

"— played roodles?" he concluded, leering.

Andromache was spared the trouble of thinking up a retort when Cutie began to yip. A moment later, Hector arrived in the kitchen.

"Ahndromahk!" he cried, making straight for her.

"Ahndro-what?" Uncle frowned. "But she said her name was Andromache! I've never seen a girl with so many names."

"Our Hermie is unique," Paris said proudly.

Hector ignored the others and took Andromache in his arms. "Hello, my sweetheart," he said, kissing her.

Andromache remained stiff and didn't kiss him back.

"What's wrong?" he asked.

She didn't want to have that whole discussion in front of Uncle — and especially not Paris — but she had to give Hector *some* reason for refusing to kiss him. "I didn't think you'd get home so late," she muttered.

"But I sent you a message."

"What message?"

"Don't move!" Hector ordered Paris, who was slinking toward the door. He narrowed his eyes, adding, "And give her the message!"

"Hermie," mumbled Paris. "My brother will be home late, tonight. He said to tell you that he's sorry, and that he'll be back to grope —"

A menacing cough from Hector cut him off.

"And that he loves you," finished Paris.

Hector nodded. "That was it. Now, please excuse my brother and me for a moment."

Sensing trouble, Cutie crept out onto the courtyard.

Paris looked to Uncle for help, but Uncle laughed at him. "You got yourself into this one, young lad. I'll see you in the morning, if there's anything left of you. Good night, three-named niece. Good night, Sonny."

Hector nodded.

Paris then turned to Andromache; she glared back at him, unmoved. He'd ruined her whole evening — her first normal night as Hector's wife. Let the little brat suffer!

"Paris," said Hector. Paris gave Andromache a last reproachful look, then trudged after his brother.

While they were gone, Andromache listened intently, but she heard nothing. No screaming, no yelling, no hitting. Nevertheless, when they came back several moments later, Paris was clearly chastened.

"I'm sorry, Hermie," he mumbled, before tiptoeing upstairs.

Once Andromache was alone with Hector, she saw what she'd missed, during her fit of pique. Shadows spread from his eyes all the way to his cheek bones. His shoulders listed slightly; one was higher than the other from a knot in his neck. He even had a puffy red mosquito bite on his ear.

Oh, gods! thought Andromache. How fickle — how vain she was! Her vow to keep an eye on Hector's mood hadn't lasted a week! She hadn't been watching _him_, only thinking of herself — and to top it all off, she'd been stiff when he hugged her! "<u>Oh, Ector</u>!" she cried, throwing her arms around him.

Sighing, he let his head rest on hers. "I thought my brother would be done playing games with us, now that we're married," he muttered. "I should've known better."

"_I_ should've known you would try to send me a message," murmured Andromache, burrowing closer to him. The muscles under his skin were hard from years of physical activity and tense with the stress of that day. Gently, she squeezed his shoulders and said, "<u>You must be tired</u>…"

"Mm-hmm." Hector sighed again. "<u>So tired. There is mahch stahff to do. Stahff no one else can do rahght</u>."

Andromache turned her face to him, and he kissed her. This time, she kissed him back. "<u>Let me give you a back rub</u>," she whispered.

Hector brightened. "<u>A back rahb</u>?" he asked.

Andromache felt sick at herself for not offering to do so right away. She kissed him again. "Yes." *Kiss. Kiss.*

"Really?"

"Mm-hmm." *Kiss.*

"That is nice. You ahre nice."

"You need it." *Kiss, kiss.* "And then you need some sleep."

"Mmmm…"

Hand in hand, they left the kitchen. Hector stopped briefly at the spring to scrub his feet, and then they walked to their room. Cutie was waiting at the door.

"Hi, girl," said Hector, in response to the little dog's fawning licks. "I didn't really say '*hi*' to you, before, did I."

"You'd think she hadn't seen you in days," Andromache teased.

"It's felt about that long." Hector sighed yet again.

"Go in and lie down," Andromache said softly.

He gave her a shy look. "You do not haff to —"

"I *want* to! You're my husband."

"I know," said Hector, his eyes already less shadowed.

"I want to," she repeated.

He entered the room, threw his clothes to the floor, and lay facedown on the bed. Andromache sat beside him and placed her hands on his back. She was good at massaging sore muscles. In Lyrnassa, she'd often rubbed Auntie's back after the woman had spent the day weaving. She was out of practice, though, and besides — giving a backrub to her aunt was *nothing* like giving one to her *husband!*

Timidly, she began kneading Hector's shoulders and neck. When he sighed in contentment, she pressed harder, rubbing until the muscles in his back felt supple and his sloping shoulders were straight again. Encouraged by more soft sighs, she moved on to his arms and legs. Meanwhile, his face began to soften — to brighten — until at last, he looked as happy as he had that morning at the breakfast table.

I made him happy again. Andromache's heart leapt, and she found it hard to swallow. She felt too full inside. "I love you," she whispered, lying down beside him.

Hector wrapped his arms around her and gave her a long kiss, then another, and another, until Andromache was reassured that even Paris hadn't been able to spoil her first normal evening with her husband.

℘

NIGHT HAD FALLEN. The city was quiet. Andromache lay entwined with Hector, watching moonlight glint off the fine hairs of his forearm. The silvery light shifted with each rise and fall of her breath. It was beautiful…*he* was beautiful.

Never had she felt so safe, so happy, so thoroughly loved — and yet something, perhaps the very perfection of the moment, spurred her to ask for even more. "Ector?" she murmured.

"Hmm?"

"I missed you, today."

"I know…me too." He sighed deeply. "The days befohre today ahre so nice."

"*So* nice," she agreed, thinking of their honeymoon. "We got spoiled."

"Mm-hmm…"

"That wasn't what I meant, though."

"What, then?"

"I missed you in the library."

"Ah," said Hector.

"Ah." Andromache wove her fingers through his. "If you kept coming for lessons, would it be weird?"

He raised her hand to his lips. "I want to see you," he said. "And I lahke Lukkana. But yes, maybe it is weird to haff lessons in the library, lahke befohre."

Relieved that he didn't want to give up Lukkan, at least, she asked, "So, what should we do?"

"Maybe we can come here," he said. "Here is mohre comfohrtable as the library — *than* the library."

"Here has more airs," she teased, mimicking a phrase he'd once used.

He laughed.

"So," she said. "We'll meet here — to speak Lukkana — tomorrow afternoon?"

"Mm-hmm," he agreed.

Snuggling closer to him, she asked, "Are you sleepy?"

"Maybe a little."

Which really meant a lot. "Good night, then," she said.

"Good night, pretty wife…"

Andromache could tell the exact moment when Hector fell asleep because his feet began to twitch against hers. In recent days, she'd discovered that they always did that while he slept. She wondered if they were just so used to moving that they could no longer be still…

Twitch, twitch.

Good night, Dancer, she thought, gently touching her feet to his. *Sleep well.*

Chapter 36

Andromache awoke to the sound of footsteps shuffling about the room. "<u>Morning</u>," she murmured.

"<u>Good morning</u>," said Hector, sitting beside her. He was already dressed.

She scrutinized his face, looking for signs of lingering darkness — shadows under the eyes, gaunt cheeks, tight lips. But other than the mosquito bite, which he'd finally scratched open, she saw nothing awry.

He stroked her hair and gave her a sweet smile.

She smiled back.

"<u>You want I can bring you some breakfasts</u>?" he murmured.

Andromache shook her head. "<u>I'd rather go with you</u>." She dressed, and they went over to the kitchen. As he had the day before, Hector seated her and surrounded her with enough food for all the lower town.

While Hector was fussing over her, Uncle stumbled into the room. "Morning, you — galloping gods!" He interrupted himself. "She's not going to eat all *that*, is she?"

Andromache's cheeks reddened.

"Morning, Uncle," said Hector.

"Oh, Sonny!" The big man laughed.

Untroubled as always by the teasing, Hector sat down, his face serene. "What are you doing up so early?"

"I thought I'd take your brother down to the archery range so you'd have time to get other things done."

"Thanks," said Hector, blinking in surprise. "That would be great. You've really got to watch him, though," he warned. "He's got a thousand ways of slacking off. He pretends he's twisted his ankle, or lost his arrows. Always something."

"I'll watch him."

"And that's if he gets up on time in the first place," added Hector. "If you want, I can —"

"Sonny!" Uncle broke in. "I run a whole kingdom — you think I can't handle one lazy boy?"

"You'd be surprised," muttered Hector.

Uncle chuckled. "Let me try, anyway. Now, little niece —" He turned to Andromache, his eyes twinkling. "Could you spare just one of those breads?"

Andromache blushed again and passed the bread plate to Uncle.

ℰℐ

AFTER BREAKFAST, the day went much as the previous one had, except that it passed by in slow motion. Andromache weeded what she was certain had been three hours' worth of garden boxes, only to check the angle of the sun and discover that not even an hour had passed. Worse, the day was promising to be hot. Fiercely hot.

Cutie had no energy for hunting birds or insects. The dog did little but lie around in a pitiful heap. Each time Andromache finished one garden box and headed to the next, though, Cutie rose wearily to her feet to follow.

"You can stay in one spot," said Andromache, stroking her ears. "I love you, but you don't have to follow me."

The dog wagged her tail. The next time Andromache moved on, Cutie did the same.

Soon, the heat forced them inside. Paris was in the kitchen, back from archery lessons and a trip to the market. "How's it going, Hermie?" he asked.

"All right," she answered cautiously. He didn't seem sullen or vengeful about the incident the night before — if anything, he still looked apologetic — but with Paris, one couldn't be too careful. "How was marketing?"

He extended his arms, showing off the bounty he'd brought back with him.

"Why did you get so many pomegranates?" she asked, one eyebrow raised in suspicion.

"Uncle likes them —"

Andromache finished his thought for him: "And Hector hates them."

Paris grinned. "*Does* he?"

She rolled her eyes. "Want some help putting things away? Or maybe I could slice vegetables for dinner."

"Why, Hermie! I don't know what to say. I thought you'd be above such things, what with your upgrade in status."

"Upgrade?"

"What, you don't think it's an upgrade? Are you regretting it already?"

"Shut up, Paris."

He smirked.

"Someone has to keep an eye on you, no matter what you're doing, or you'll goof off," Andromache scolded. "And I'm back on kitchen duty, upgrade or no."

Paris mumbled, "Taskmistress!" and pretended to scowl at her, but Andromache could tell that he was pleased.

℣℥

ANDROMACHE SPENT SEVERAL HOURS making dinner and listening to Paris's gossip. His prize tidbit was the real reason behind all the pomegranates: a young, pretty vendor who sold little else. Paris also brought other news from the market — there were two merchants who'd died and one who'd been banished for pushing rocks into his figs to make them heavier.

Andromache listened avidly to his stories and decided that she would have to start marketing again. Paris would no doubt be glad for the help, and she wouldn't mind people-watching a little.

Mid-afternoon, she excused herself and went over to the bath chamber, where she soaked for a long time and carefully scrubbed her skin. Once finished, she walked to Hector's — to *their* — room and put on a clean dress. She was ready.

But it's still a little while till Ector gets back, she reminded herself. She needed something to do in the meantime. Cutie was sprawled on the floor and looked quite content, but Andromache didn't feel like napping. *I'll read a bit*, she decided. Priam and Hecuba had given her the most wonderful wedding present, a collection of tales from her home country called *Light of the Lukka Lands*. *I'll tell Ector all about it during our Lukkana lesson. No, not 'lesson,'* she corrected herself. *Lukkana time*.

As Andromache read, she hardly noticed what was going on in the stories, she was so mesmerized by the descriptions of color and light. Steep cliffs of reddish rock. Fields of crimson poppies. Soft green pines. Turquoise water. A milky lemon haze on the afternoon sky. The images might have come from her own memories, she could see them so vividly…

Just then, the tiniest *creeeak!* let her know that she wasn't alone. She looked up to see Hector watching her, a strange expression on his face. When she caught his eye, he smiled.

Cutie rushed over to greet him, yipping and leaping up on him while he bent down to rub her ears. "Hi, girl. Oh, hi," he murmured. "Yes — yes, I missed you, too." The snuffling and *schlurping* went on for several more moments until, satisfied with the welcome she'd given him, Cutie sank back down onto the floor. Hector flashed the dog a fond look, then straightened and began peeling off his tunic.

As Andromache watched him undress, she realized how artificial her little setup was. Meeting at a prescribed time and talking about prescribed topics no longer made much sense, even outside of the library. Hector had moved on — he didn't really want to sit and talk about her text, and she couldn't blame him.

She didn't want to, either, just then.

FOR A WHILE, Andromache dozed in perfect contentment with Hector's arm around her, his cheek pressed to her shoulder.

Her passage from sleep to wakefulness was slow. Gentle. Smiling contentedly, she stroked her husband's arm and ran her fingers through his hair. As she opened her eyes, though, she glimpsed Light of the Lukka Lands and felt a strange wave of nostalgia for their old library days.

"What is wrong, pretty wife?" murmured Hector. "My face hurts you?" He slipped a hand under his cheek to shield her from his stubble.

"No," she assured him. "Your face doesn't hurt."

He removed his hand. "Then why the sigh?"

"I feel a little silly."

"Why?"

She sighed again. "For thinking we could just sit and talk, anymore."

"We cannot?" Hector sounded concerned.

"You're asking *me* that? You're the one who threw all your clothes to the ground before we'd even said '*hello*.'"

Hector started to laugh.

"What's so funny?"

"Oh, Ahndromahk! I ahnderstand what you ahre saying — baht you do not ahnderstand my clothes. Always, I get naked in here."

"What!" she exclaimed. It was true that during their honeymoon, neither one of them had worn clothes, but that was more or less the point of a honeymoon. Andromache hadn't been surprised to see him undress for the massage, either, because Hector refused to lie in bed with clothes on. He'd told her on their second night together that he hated the feel of fabric bunching up under him. He'd had a reason to strip naked — or so she'd thought. Now, he was making it sound almost like a reflex! "You *always* take your clothes off at the door?"

"Yes," said Hector. "Always, I take my clothes off."

"And walk around naked?"

"Yes."

"*Every* time?"

"Most."

Andromache lowered her voice. "Not just for sleeping or — or — a roll in the hay?"

"'*A roll in the hay*?'" Hector laughed again. "This is what we jahst do?"

She poked him. "Just answer. Are you *really* always naked in here?"

"Really," he assured her. "It is my ancient habit. It feels nicer than clothes. I can relax."

Ancient habit? Andromache thought to herself. Well, why not? As a little boy, Hector had apparently been famous for streaking through the courtyard. And his preference for reading texts in his bedroom because it had '*more airs*' than the library now made sense in a whole new way! "So," she said, just to be sure, "you honestly expected to sit here with me — naked as a worm — and just *talk* to me?"

"Ahndromahk… " he said, his laughter gone. He propped himself up on an elbow to look down at her. "I came home this afternoon, and there you were, sitting in my room, reading. I've pictured that scene a thousand times, and even though I knew I might never see it, the possibility got me through some of the worst days of my life. Today, I came home, and it was *real*. I could've sat here all afternoon and just *looked* at you."

'*The worst days of my life…*' Andromache thought of Hector's despair at the outpost stable, of the way he'd screamed in his sleep. She could only imagine what '*the worst days*' had been like for him. It shocked her that he'd been able to sustain himself for so long on so little: the fantasy of a girl reading texts in his room. *It won't be like that anymore!* she promised herself. From now on, Hector wouldn't have to eke by on crumbs — she would make sure he had a feast. Tenderly, she stroked the rough skin of his cheek.

In turn, he caressed her arm, from her wrist all the way to her collar bone. "*I* would've been content just to look," he repeated, with different emphasis. "Baht then, you rahn ohffer to me and giff those kisses, fire-hot. *You* act lahke you want a roll in the hay." His fingers edged down over her collarbone and hovered there suggestively.

Blushing, Andromache said, "Well, *you* didn't exactly resist hay-rolling!"

"Why resist? I lahke it." Hector's hand then fell still, and his voice grew serious once more. "Baht now you fink we cannot talk. I do not want this."

Andromache shook her head. "I don't actually think that! I was just being silly." For so long, she'd thought of conversations with Hector — in either language, but particularly Lukkan — as something that happened in a predetermined way or not at all. That reflex would fade, though, and she wished she hadn't said anything to him. He had a stubborn look that told her he wasn't going to let the matter drop easily.

"We can haff a rule fohr no naked — and no sex — during this time," he suggested. "Anyfing so you trahst me."

No sex? How had they leapt to *that* extreme? No sex. The more Andromache thought about the idea, the drearier it sounded. Absurd, too, considering the reason Hector had proposed it: Outlawing sex might lead to *less* talking, rather than more. Some of their best conversations had come about in bed. There was no reason they couldn't talk about *Light of the Lukka Lands* or anything else they wanted while they were lying down, curled around each other. They didn't have to choose. They could have it all, in whatever order they liked. "Rules?" She grimaced. "Certainly nothing hard and fast!"

Hector blinked. "Oh — ahm — all rahght," he stammered. "No hahrd and fast sex. Only slow."

No hard and fast sex? Andromache laughed and laughed until her stomach hurt. "No hard and fast sex!" she cried.

Cutie awoke and yipped in response, making Andromache laugh even harder.

"What is fahnny?" asked Hector, looking confused.

She stifled her laughter long enough to explain: "'*Hard and fast*' is a phrase that means *strict*, as in '*Let's not have any strict rules against sex.*'"

"Oh!" Hector, too, started laughing.

"And anyway," she added, "The truth is, I don't want any rules at all."

"So, hahrd and fast sex is all rahght?" he teased.

"Mm-hmm," she murmured. "And so is slow…"

He smiled but was serious in asking, "You ahre sure?"

She nodded.

"You can always change yourself ohff mind."

"I won't change my mind," she assured him. "But there is *one* rule I'd like."

"Which one?"

334

"You have to tell me about any other weird habits you might have — besides sleeping naked and running around your room naked, I mean."

"Weird?" Hector tickled her bare sides. "I see that you sleep this way, also."

Giggling, Andromache made a grab for his hands. "Not till recently."

"Really?" he asked, letting himself be captured. "Befohre we ahre married, you sleep naked, neffer?"

"Really. Never. Until we got married, I always wore clothes to bed."

"Hmm." Hector looked skeptical.

"What, '*hmm*?'"

"It is jahst…"

"What?"

"Always, I fink you sleep naked."

"You *thought* about that?" Andromache asked in disbelief. "About me, sleeping naked?"

"Oh, Ahndromahk!" he scolded her. "Many, many times!"

"And did you — *picture* me — naked?"

"Ohff couhrse."

Andromache pursed her lips.

"What?" asked Hector. "You ahre mad?"

"No, but —"

"Baht what?"

Timidly, she asked, "How close did your picture come?"

He laughed.

"How close, Ector?"

He leaned over her and traced a line between her breasts. "Neffer, neffer can I picture somefing so pretty as you."

She groaned. "Oh, seriously!"

"What? This is true." He replaced his hand with his mouth, kissing downward until he reached her hip, which he gave a playful little bite.

Andromache began stroking his hair again. "Ector?" she murmured.

"Hmm?"

"I pictured you naked, too."

He sat up and smiled, showing off the dimple in his cheek. "You did?"

"It was because of a dream I had."

"Yes?"

"About almonds."

He laughed. "Almonds, Ahndromahk? I'm not sure that's flattering."

She poked his arm. "I was in the kitchen, and there were these almonds I was supposed to eat, but I didn't — and then you — and I…"

"We…?"

"Mm-hmm."

"In the kitchen?"

"Yes."

He leaned down to kiss her. "I lahke this dream."

"Me too."

"Almonds," he mused. "So, this is when?"

"Right after you came back with the army." She ran a hand from his forehead down to the nape of his neck. "The time your head was shaved."

At her touch, he closed his eyes and smiled.

"Ector?" she asked.

"Hmm?"

"Did you ever have any dreams? You know —" She lowered her voice. "The sexy kind?"

"Many, many," he said, wearing the same contented smile.

"What were they? I mean, what happened, in them?"

He opened his eyes, which had darkened to black.

"Tell me," she prodded. "I told *you*."

"All rahght," he agreed, leaning down for another kiss. "I can tell one dream effery day."

"How many days will it take to tell me all of them?"

Kiss. "A fousand." *Kiss, kiss, kiss.* "Maybe two fousand…"

Late summer

Chapter 37

The moon was a crescent once more. Already, a month had passed since the wedding. A month! A month of waking up next to Hector, and eating meals with him, and falling asleep beside him. In the hours they'd once spent across the table from each other in the library, they now stayed in their room. They talked about going out to the hillside or down to the river someday, but so far they hadn't done so. It was too hot, by afternoon, and their room was far too pleasant.

On those sultry afternoons, in a mix of Lukkan and Truvan, Andromache learned more of Hector's secrets. One day, he told her why he'd chosen to read *Tales of an Eastern Wanderer* during lessons…

'Why on earth did you pick that text?' she asked. 'It's the most boring thing I've ever read!'

'Exactly,' said Hector.

'What?'

'You get so lost in texts! I was hoping if I picked a boring one, you wouldn't be able to focus on it…and then you'd have to find something else to focus on.'

'Such as?'

He grinned at her; she poked him.

'Well, it almost didn't work,' he said, laughing. 'I was about to give up when you read that part about Gemasila.'

'The woman who disguised herself as a man to join the army…'

'To be wiff her lahffer,' Hector *murmured.* Kiss, kiss. *'That is the day I know fohr sure you lahff me.'*

Kiss, kiss. Kiss. *'Thank goodness for Gemasila!'*

'Ohff all peoples in all texts in all the world, she is the one I lahke best…'

Another time, Hector told Andromache that he'd kept an eye on her caterpillars, the ones she'd rescued from Priam toward the end of her first summer in Troy…

'I went to see them every day. They got bigger and bigger and then, one day, they were gone.'

'Gone?' asked Andromache.

'Well, not gone exactly,' said Hector. *'They were sleeping inside these hard, green shells. I went back every day, hoping I'd see a butterfly coming out of one — but I was always too late. I'd see the empty shell, but never a butterfly.'*

'That's too bad. I wish you could've seen one.'

'I did,' he said triumphantly. *'The very last one. When I got to the garden, the butterfly was crawling out of its shell. Its wings were all crumpled and soft, and it hung there on the shell, stretching them out.'*

'What color were the wings?'

'Black and white stripes.'

'How long did it take for the wings to stretch out?'

'I don't know. A while. It was one of the most beautiful things I've ever seen — and I never would've seen it if it weren't for you…' Kiss. Kiss, kiss, kiss.

'Ector?'

'Hmm?'

'What did you do with the sash?'

'What sash?'

'The yellow sash that the caterpillars were in.'

He laughed. *'I tried to keep it.'*

'Why?'

'Because it was yours! Because you wore it. Because then, if I had to leave the city, I could take it with me, and — '

Andromache *kissed him.* *'That's so sweet…'* Kiss, kiss.

'See?' Kiss, kiss, kiss. *'Always, I lahff you!'*

'But what happened? You said you 'tried' *to keep it.'*

'Xanthus. He happened. He find it and take it.'

'*Xanthus? But what would he want with an ugly yellow sash?*'

'*There is a sick hohrse — a hohrse wiff a hurt leg. He has to put plahnts on the leg and he need the sash to hold the plahnts there.*'

'*Plants? You mean herbs? Like a healing poultice?*'

'*Yes.*'

'*Couldn't you get the sash back later?*'

Hector's face wrinkled in disgust. '*Oh, Ahndromahk! No!*'

'*I was just kidding,*' she said, giggling.

Hector was very curious about her childhood home in the Lukka lands...

'*The rocks down in Lukká ahre really so red?*' he asked. '*Lahke in* 'Light of the Lukka Lands?'''

'*Brownish-red, I guess,*' said Andromache. '*They're striking, especially at sunset.*'

'*And the sea, it is really so blue?*'

'*Yes — it really is.*'

'*Then Lukká is a happy place,*' said Hector.

'*Yes,*' said Andromache. '*It is.*'

Other times, Hector told Andromache about his extended family. He mentioned grandparents, long dead, and cousins who had moved on. He asked about her family, too. He was especially interested in Auntie, whom he'd met once in Lyrnassa long before the village was invaded — long before he'd made Andromache's acquaintance...

'*What was she like?*'

'*What do you mean?*'

'*Well, when I met her, she seemed funny. She was kind of laughing at me. Did she tell a lot of jokes?*'

'*No, not really,*' said Andromache. '*She had to work hard. She didn't have much time for jokes.*'

'*Oh.*'

'*And she really missed my parents. My mom was her little sister.*'

Hector nodded.

'*But she was so good to me our whole time in Lyrnassa, even if we didn't laugh as much as in the old days.*'

'*I liked her,*' said Hector.

'She liked you, too.'

'I thought about her a lot, over the years. I always wondered who carried water for her on days when there wasn't a Trojan patrol passing through.'

Andromache gave him a kiss. 'Now you know.'

'Now I know…'

Their talks went on long into the night. They lay in each other's arms, looking up at the sky, searching for spots of light that were larger and hazier than the others: the Lorani. As a little girl down in the Lukka lands, Andromache had seen many such objects, but it wasn't until coming to Troy that she'd learned what they were. In Priam's library, she'd found a treatise called On Lorani, which explained all the mysteries of the night sky:

> *The Lorani swim in a vast ocean in which our earth is but a mote within a bubble of air. The fact that certain features in this ocean appear and reappear throughout the year seems to indicate that we are caught in an eddy of fantastical proportions. The celestial ocean reaches far beyond our comprehension, and most of the Lorani dwell a great distance from us. Yet we see them. We see them, and they pull at our imagination. What are these entities, whom the Achaeans call 'galaxias?' (Although it must be said that we prefer the Palaan word 'Lorani,' meaning 'cloud creature,' for which reason we have adopted this word as is into Truvan.) After much study, the conclusion has been reached that they are vast fish, or more likely sea jellies, due to their hazy appearance. Many people have stood on the seashore at night, in awe of the luminous creatures drifting on or beneath the waves. In like manner, an observer on the shore of the celestial ocean might watch the great Lorani drift serenely past each other, luminous like certain creatures in our terrestrial seas…*

The description of the Lorani matched what Andromache had often seen in the sky. Hector, however, had never been fortunate enough to spot one. He didn't believe in them, or at least pretended not to. It was an old joke of theirs...

'I think you made them up,' said Hector, after an hour or so had passed without any sign of the Lorani.

'You know I didn't!' Andromache protested. 'You've read On Lorani. *I didn't write that.'*

Hector gave her a skeptical look. 'But you believe it,' he said.

'It's convincing.'

'You're convinced that the earth is trapped inside a bubble of air?'

'And that it's floating in the celestial ocean — yes,' said Andromache. 'And that the Lorani are giant, glowing creatures who swim out there.'

'So you say,' said Hector. 'I've still never seen one...'

'They're hard to spot. If there's too much other light in the sky, theirs gets drowned out. Maybe we can try again at the new moon.'

'All right. But then we need to bring a jar of wine.'

Andromache laughed. 'Because wine makes everything look hazy, and you think that will help you find the Lorani?' Hector had tried that same trick once before.

'Exactly,' he said.

'And did that help you, the first time you tried it?' Andromache asked pertly.

Hector looked down at her, his eyes darkening to black. 'No,' he admitted. Kiss. *'Baht that night, you find me.'* Kiss, kiss.

Sometimes, Hector wasn't ready to talk when he came home. His face had a shadowed look and his shoulders were tight. In the old days, Andromache had tried to give him space when he looked like that; now, she gave him massages. They seemed to work. She would rub his shoulders until he'd relaxed and the shadows had cleared, and then he would turn toward her, his eyes soft with gratitude, and take her in his arms.

Hector's bad days didn't scare Andromache, but his nightmares did. When he awoke screaming, his eyes had a faraway, hollow look that turned her stomach to ice. It was the same look he'd had that day in the outpost stable when he'd yelled at her to *'Go away!'* Terrified that she might lose him again, she kissed him — soft little kisses on his lips and cheek and ear. *I need you, Ector. Stay with me,* she pleaded, never sure whether she said the words aloud or only thought them, because although Hector didn't an-

swer her, he seemed to understand. He kissed her back, hard —
then harder — and before she knew it they were both lying back
against the sheets, exhausted, and he was there with her again.
He was hers again. She didn't know what he saw or how to make
his nightmares stop plaguing him, but at least she could help him
come back from them. *Ector, I need you,* she pleaded each time.
Stay with me. And he always did.

The day after a bad episode, Hector invariably spent time
with Uncle. Andromache might come home from marketing to
see the two of them together, out in the garden, or Paris might
brag to her that he'd gotten out of archery practice that morning
because Hector *'had to see Uncle about something.'* Andromache never asked him what they talked about. For her, it was enough that
Hector hadn't pushed her away again — that he seemed to be
healing. She and Uncle were a team: Uncle helped Hector work
through whatever was bothering him, while she helped distract
him from it.

The moon was a crescent once more. Andromache had had
a month of getting to know Hector in new ways, a month of loving him more and more, a month of happiness that sometimes
bordered on disbelief. Still, the best part was that only a month
had passed. Their life together had barely begun.

Chapter 38

Andromache awoke before dawn when a sweet-scented breeze swept over her. "Mmm," she sighed, breathing in deeply. Hector mumbled a response. When she turned toward him, she saw that the breeze had blown a lock of hair onto his forehead. She brushed it back, thinking, *Sweet boy with hair in his face.* Aloud, she whispered, "It's a beautiful morning."

"Mmmph."

"It's still early…"

"Mm-*hmm*." That reply was a little more pointed.

"We could take a walk — take Cutie to one of the city gardens, or maybe to the wall."

At the sound of her name, Cutie thumped her tail, but she seemed as reluctant to move as Hector.

"Uncle is still taking care of archery with Paris, isn't he?" Andromache prodded.

"Mmmph."

"Then let's greet the day."

With that, Hector began laughing into his pillow, and Andromache knew she'd won.

"Greet the day!" He mimicked her voice. "Greet the day!"

She laughed back. "What's so funny about that?"

"Greet the day!" He kissed her neck.

"Stop! That tickles!"

Kiss. "Greet the day!" *Kiss, kiss.*

The kissing grew so vigorous that Cutie stirred and began licking Hector's feet.

"Hey!" he cried, lurching away from the dog. "Cut it out!"

"You know what would stop her…" Andromache hinted.

"A walk?"

"Exactly! You want to go?"

"All rahght." Hector sat up, fumbling for the clothes they'd left beside the bed. Before passing Andromache's dress to her, he warmed it against his chest.

"Thank you," she murmured shyly. He made such gestures all the time, but they still surprised and touched her.

He kissed her forehead. "You want your cloak?"

"No, thanks."

"You cannot greet the day wiff your cloak?"

"I want to feel the breeze."

Hector shook his head. "I am going to bring my cloak. You can use it, if you haff cold."

She smiled. "I won't."

They dressed and went out onto the courtyard. Cutie ran along behind them, joyously sniffing the fresh morning air.

"I've hardly ever gotten to walk through the city with you," said Andromache, when they were on the street.

"You lahke?"

The star-speckled sky was dark blue, bordered by grey. The air smelled sweetly of late summer flowers. All around, Andromache heard nothing but morning birds and the faint sounds of the breeze. She, her husband, and their dog had Troy to themselves. "Yes, I love it. It's beautiful."

"We can walk mohre in the city, ohr the cahntryside —"

"The countryside!" cried Andromache, thinking of the dry grasses and dancing winds, of the rock where she'd once sat with Hector. She hadn't been out that way since the last time with —

No, Ahndromahk!. There was no sense in spoiling the morning by thinking about *her*. "Let's go there now!"

"I cannot, this mohrning," Hector said regretfully. "I am to meet Uncle. After, I haff trainings and stahff."

"Oh."

"Baht one day, soon." He squeezed her hand and added, "In the mohrning, ohr efening, when it is not hot."

"And we can go to the river, sometime?" asked Andromache, thinking of the date they hadn't quite had, down there.

"Mm-hmm. Anyfing."

It was a beautiful morning, and she was spending it with Hector. Making plans with him. Andromache was filled with a lightheartedness she hadn't known since childhood.

"All rahght," said Hector. "We greet the day, where?"

"The walls."

They walked toward a staircase with access to the walls. Cutie, mistrusting it, stopped short at the bottom and flattened her ears.

"Come on, silly girl," coaxed Andromache. "You used to go up and down the stairs every day, back at the house!"

The little dog looked up at her, eyes wide and mournful.

"That stair is shaht, at home," said Hector.

"Shut?" asked Andromache. "You mean that it's enclosed? That it has walls?"

"Mm-hmm. This open one, it is scary."

Andromache looked again at the staircase, open on one side to the city street below — it would be all too easy for someone to fall off. Stairs like these had once figured prominently in her own nightmares. "Poor thing," she murmured to Cutie. "You don't have to come."

"She can come," said Hector, lifting Cutie up into his arms. The little dog wriggled and licked his face in delight.

They climbed the stairs. Once on top of the wall, Hector sat down with Cutie on his lap, and Andromache cuddled close to them.

"You haff cold?" murmured Hector.

"A little," she admitted. Up there, the wind was howling. "But it feels good."

"Crazy wife," he said, affectionately.

The first rays of sunlight began to show over the eastern walls.

"Hay-lo, day," said Hector.

Andromache giggled. "Hello, day."

Hector took one of Cutie's forelegs and waved it at the sun. "Hay-lo, day," he said in a squeaky voice meant to be the dog's.

Andromache rested her head on his shoulder and clutched his arm tightly — she felt so light that she was afraid of floating away, if she didn't hold onto him. "I *love* being married to you," she whispered.

❧

IT WAS MIDDAY, the hour when gardening and marketing were over and sane people found a place inside — or in the shade — to sit. Andromache and Cutie were in the kitchen, playing fetch with a piece of rope long since decommissioned by the army. When Andromache pulled on it, Cutie growled. The dog then let go, only to seize the rope again, right where Andromache was holding it.

"Ouch!" she cried, as Cutie's sharp little teeth dug into her skin. "If you're going to do *that*, then I'm not playing with you anymore. Go take a nap."

Just then, Uncle stumbled in. "Great and living gods," he sighed. "He's nuts."

Timidly, since he was, after all, a king, Andromache corrected him: "Cutie is a girl. But you're right — she's nuts."

Uncle guffawed. "Not the dog! My nephew!" He held his hand out for Cutie. Wagging her tail, the dog offered Uncle her rope. He took an end and began to pull; Cutie promptly bit his hand, just as she'd bitten Andromache's.

"Cutie!" she cried, horrified at what the penalty might be for a king-biter.

"Oh, it's all right," chortled Uncle. "My hands are like elephant leather."

"What's that?"

"You mean to tell me you've never heard of an elephant?"

Embarrassed, Andromache shook her head.

"I'll have a talk with my sister about *that*," said Uncle, scandalized. "But suffice it to say, a pipsqueak like your dog couldn't hurt an elephant. Or me." He recommended tugging on the rope, alternately growling at Cutie and laughing at her.

Relieved that Uncle wasn't upset, Andromache remembered what he'd said upon arriving. "Which nephew?"

"Pardon?"

"Which nephew is nuts?"

"Oh, well — good question! You know as well as I do that both of them are, but I meant your husband." Uncle's eyes twinkled at her.

"Oh," murmured Andromache, blushing as she always did when someone called Hector her husband. "What did he do?"

"Took me riding." Uncle groaned. "Up the hills, down the hills, faster than you can imagine."

"Are you all right?"

"All right? Am I all right, she asks! Of course I'm all right — it was the most fun I've had in years! Everyone except Sonny thinks I should just sit in my throne room and rot away. My life's been a lot duller since he took the reins of Troy's army." Uncle yanked the rope out of Cutie's jaws and threw it to the far side of the kitchen. The dog chased after it and brought it back to him.

"He used to visit you more?" asked Andromache.

"Oh, sure. He spent years with me in training — came a couple times for shorter visits, too."

"Hecu — your sister, I mean —" Andromache interrupted herself, not sure if she ought to refer to a former princess by her given name — at least not in front of her brother, the king. "She said Hector thinks a lot of you."

Uncle nodded, pleased. "And I think a lot of *him*. I wouldn't have minded having a boy like him, myself. Of course, then he'd have to be a prince, and that's his idea of hell."

Andromache looked up in surprise, and Uncle chuckled.

"Oh, I know all about it, little niece — he doesn't mince words with *me*." Uncle gave a firm nod. "The joke is on him, though, if you want to know the truth. The countries around here all think Troy has a king. They refuse to believe she doesn't, no matter what she tells the world. And since most kings in the area are also their country's high priest, you can imagine who they take for king — which means that they consider my nephew —" Uncle broke off in a chuckle. "Well, mad as hell, if he knew, I suppose. Meanwhile, Zintuhi — that's my eldest daughter — has never minded being a princess. She's filling in for me while I'm away, and I'm sure she'll do a fine job. She's a natural leader, my Zintuhi — I put her in charge of the army about a year ago, and she took right to it. Of course, she's built like her father." Uncle pointed at Andromache and guffawed. "Two of you put together *might* be as thick as one of her arms, little niece."

Andromache flushed.

"Not that someone has to be big to fight well," Uncle went on. "We have some women in the Santiyan army. They might be smaller than our men, on the whole, but that makes them smarter fighters. Just like Sonny. He started out like a twig and had to learn to fight smart." Uncle laughed. "Of course, he finally shot up, so now he's an oak who can fight smart. That's what makes him so deadly."

Andromache looked down at her hands and pretended she hadn't heard the word *deadly*.

"Yes, it's a shame we don't have more women in the army," mused Uncle, "but the ones we *do* have are first-rate warriors. A few years ago, I sent one here."

Andromache's stomach seized, then boiled. She hadn't seen the woman in ages — had hardly thought about her, although now this made twice in one day — hadn't *wanted* to think about her. She'd managed to repress the run-in they'd had at their last meeting. Now, though, every shameful detail came rushing back. She heard once again those appalling words: *'Letting someone have you up against the wall doesn't make him your husband.'* Shuddering, Andromache said the woman's name aloud. "Penthesilea."

"That's right," said Uncle. "You know her?"

"A little," Andromache croaked.

"Then you know as much as anyone does, except maybe Sonny. She's not easy for most people to know." Uncle whistled. "But one hell of a fighter!"

Andromache swallowed hard. *Terrific*, she thought. *And she hates me.*

"One of the best *I've* seen, and I've seen my share. You're too young to know much about the battle of Kadesh, but I tell you — there were more kings and warriors thrown together than there are swindlers in this city of yours, and *she* would've stood out among them."

With a gulp, Andromache whispered, "Then why did you send her here?" Oh, how much simpler things would have been, if Uncle had kept Penthesilea in Santiya! Andromache wouldn't now be the sworn enemy of her husband's colleague — his best captain — or, as the ambidextrous Hector had once put it, his left hand on the battlefield.

The battlefield…his left hand. Andromache's face went white. Hector needed his left hand! What would happen to him if he lost it? And how likely was it that he would? He'd been angry with Penthesilea when she made crude comments to *him*, but that was nothing compared to how he would feel if he learned what she'd said to Andromache. He would be furious. Maddened. Enraged. No word went far enough! He would fight with Penthesilea. Their allegiance would crack, and he would be without his left hand the next time he went out on a battlefield. And then —

No! thought Andromache. She would just have to keep that from happening.

"I'm sorry, little niece," groaned Uncle, rubbing his shoulder. "What did you just ask me?"

"Why did you send her here, to Troy?" Andromache repeated. "Didn't you need her in Santiya?"

Uncle sighed. "Of course! I wanted to keep her there. You think we like to be short on warriors, with raider camps all up and down the Munnanda Sea? But she never really fit in, there. Too much ambition for such a small country. And with the brood of daughters *I* have, she never stood much chance of rising to where she wanted to be. I was worried that if she stayed in Santiya, chafing and thwarted, she'd wind up making trouble."

Chafing and thwarted...just like she is now. Andromache's stomach twisted into an even tighter knot.

"Then Sonny came for a visit, and I had an idea. The Trojan lands are bigger than Santiya, and there's even more going on, here — especially these days, Mudders — er, I mean *Achaeans* — being what they are."

Andromache shuddered. Thinking about Mudders was even worse than thinking about Penthesilea! Mudder raiders had destroyed her former village. Mudder raiders had fought against her husband — had slashed his skin open — had bruised him — had hurt him —

Uncle went on with his story: "So I say to my nephew, *'Sonny, why don't you take Penthesilea back to Troy with you when you go?'* *'Why?'* he asks, and I say, *'Try sparring with her just once, and you'll see.'* So he did."

"Who won?" asked Andromache.

Uncle gave her a mischievous smile. "Oh, you'll have to ask your husband about *that*. But anyway, let's just say they ended up respecting each other. He agreed to bring her here, if she wanted to come, and she decided that she liked the idea of going someplace bigger. So off they went, and you know the rest."

I certainly do, thought Andromache.

"Say, niece-of-three-names — Andromache-<u>Ahndromahk</u>-Hermie — would you do me a favor?"

"Sure," she said.

"My other nutty nephew doesn't have time to coach me in snoodles, today — something about a mandatory informational meeting for all archers…"

A likely story!

"So I was wondering if you would play a match or two with me."

"Sure," Andromache said again. Anything to avoid thinking about Penthesilea.

"Great!" boomed Uncle.

ॐ

SEVERAL MATCHES LATER, Andromache escaped to her room and collapsed on the bed. All she wanted to do was close her eyes. She'd never imagined roodles could be so exhausting! Every time Uncle had made a mistake, which was often, he'd demanded that she show him where he'd gone wrong — they'd reviewed most plays three or four times. Worst of all, none of it had taken her mind off her quarrel with Penthesilea and the dangerous position Hector was now in. Hector, alone on the battlefield. Hector, without his left hand…

For comfort, Andromache reached down to pet Cutie. The little dog was lying on the floor with her muzzle between her front feet, as exhausted from playing rope as Andromache was from playing roodles.

The door creaked open.

"<u>Hello</u>," said Andromache. She looked up in time to see Hector throw his tunic to the floor as he did every day, but she felt no rush of lust — only the sick sensation of having doomed her husband.

"<u>Hay-lo, pretty wife</u>." Hector settled onto the bed beside her.

"<u>How was your day</u>?" she asked.

He hugged and kissed her. "<u>Good. Fery good.</u>"

"Uncle <u>said you went riding with him?</u>"

Hector nodded. "<u>A long rahde. A good rahde.</u>"

"A *hard* ride. He was <u>groaning, when he got back.</u>"

Snorting, Hector said, "<u>Do not listen. He lahffs to complain effen mohre than he lahffs to rahde hohrses.</u>"

Andromache smiled.

With his head tilted, Hector studied her.

"<u>What is it?</u>"

"<u>What on you? You want to rahde hohrses?</u>"

Eyes wide, Andromache shook her head. Ride? Go down to the stables, where she might see Penthesilea? Go down there with Hector, and risk starting a fight between them? They might be able to work together peaceably as long as Andromache, the source of their dispute, wasn't there. But if she showed up — if Hector noticed tension between the two women and asked what had happened —

"<u>It can be nice,</u>" Hector cajoled. "<u>You can sit inside my ahrms, befohre me on the hohrse.</u>"

Andromache gulped. That *did* sound nice...very nice. But she couldn't.

"<u>Still so scared,</u>" Hector murmured sympathetically, when she shook her head. "<u>I know, your first rahde is bad. So scary. Baht maybe in time...</u>"

Bad? Her first ride had been *horrendous* — bumping, crashing, passing out, nearly falling off, all the way from Lyrnassa to Troy. Those memories wouldn't have stopped her from riding with Hector, though. The problem was her fear of running into Penthesilea. "<u>Maybe in time,</u>" she whispered back. If enough time could ever pass to make Penthesilea stop hating her...

Hector smiled. "<u>To speak ohff hohrses,</u>" he murmured, "and the hohrse house — Xanthus, <u>he is missing you.</u>"

Andromache's stomach, which had begun to relax, knotted up again. "<u>He is?</u>" she whispered.

"Mm-hmm. <u>He yells,</u> *You're keeping your wife locked up in the house, aren't you? In my day, no one locked up their wives! The whole damn city is going to hell! Soon, we'll start keeping women in cupboards, just like all those other countries.*"

Andromache giggled in spite of herself.

"<u>Do not lahff! He is mad wiff me.</u>"

"Oh, come on! He can't *really* believe that!"

Hector shrugged. "I do not know, pretty wife. Maybe you can see him — show him you ahre not in some box."

Andromache swallowed hard — her refusal to ride horses might be understandable, but she had no good excuse for avoiding Xanthus. She liked the stable master, and Hector knew it. "I-I-" She gulped. Her voice was trembling. She hated to lie to her husband, but she saw no way around it. "I don't think I'll have time to go down there. I might have to start coaching Uncle in roodles."

Hector blinked. "Paris, he is not doing this?"

"I think Paris wants to quit," she told him. "He's annoyed at how slow your uncle is. You have to go through each play with him, over and over! Anyway, today Paris made some stupid excuse about an archery meeting, and Uncle asked me to coach him instead." She paused. "There *wasn't* an archery meeting, was there?"

Hector glowered. "No."

"I didn't think so."

"Playing roodles wiff anahther man…" Hector sighed. "Xanthus will not lahke it."

"He doesn't like *anything*."

"He lahkes *you*," countered Hector. "And if you do not go, he will yell and yell and yell at me!"

Andromache knew that this was true, and she didn't want Hector to be in trouble. "Maybe in a week or two, when Uncle is farther along," she said, hoping her answer would satisfy both her husband and the stable master.

"You ahre nice to play wiff Uncle," said Hector, stroking her hair. "I know this is not easy."

Sighing, Andromache pressed her face to Hector's chest, bare and brown. A cool evening version of the breeze that had awoken her came in through the window.

As it crept over her skin, she shivered and burrowed closer to her husband. The day's events had tarnished her early morning joy, but with Hector's arms wrapped warmly around her, she was able to forget — for a time, anyway — the stables, Xanthus, and Penthesilea.

Chapter 39

The next day wasn't as warm, and Uncle took advantage of the mild weather by paying visits to a long string of Hecuba's friends. Andromache was therefore unable to establish herself as his new roodles coach — and unable to turn the lie she'd told Hector into the truth. She felt so low that she did nothing but sit on a bench under the fig tree all day. She refused to go marketing with Paris or even walking with Cassandra, who had a rare morning free from lessons.

I'm lying to protect him, Andromache told herself. *I don't want him to have a fight with* Penthesilea *over what she said to me. She's saved his life before, he said. He needs her.*

(*How long are you going to keep lying?*) asked a snide, little Voice inside her head.

Andromache made a face. She'd been hoping that the Voice might leave her alone once she and Hector got married. *Until this blows over*, she thought, poking at the tree's roots with her toe. *Until there's no more tension between* Penthesilea *and me.*

(*That's never going to happen,*) the Voice proclaimed. (*At least, not as long as Hector is your husband.*)

Andromache sighed. She'd seen proof — a look in Penthesilea's eye — that the woman was in love with Hector.

(*That won't blow over,*) the Voice sneered. (*She'll never stop hating you —* and he's *in danger because of it.*)

With that, the Voice got the last word. Andromache had no retort. She fixed her eyes on the ground, watching as the tree's shadow gradually lengthened, reaching toward her bedroom.

ℰℐ

"HAY-LO, PRETTY WIFE."

Despite the gloom she'd been feeling all that day, Andromache's insides flooded with warmth at the sound of her husband's voice. "Hello," she said, smiling up at him.

He sat down beside her and gave her a long, wet kiss.

"Ector…" she protested. "What if someone's watching?"

The next kiss was even longer and wetter, and when it ended, Hector lay down with his head in Andromache's lap. "So, so pretty," he said, looking up at her face, framed by the fig tree. "Leaffs all around your haihr — lahke our wedding."

Andromache stroked his hair, still damp from a bath. *He's been training*, she thought, her breath catching a little. "How was your day? Tiring?"

He smiled in a satisfied way. "Yes, baht good tiring."

Slowly, languorously, she began to rub his shoulders.

"Oh, Ahndromahk, you ahre too sweet to me…" He rolled onto his stomach.

She ran her hands down his back, to his waist, then up once more.

"You gahrten, today?" he asked. Perhaps worried that she, too, might be sore, he reached down to stroke her legs. First the ankles, then the calves, then —

"No. I was too lazy." Her fingers crossed his shoulder and moved down onto his arm. As they slid over his old pink scar, he stiffened. "I'm sorry!" she cried. "Does it still hurt?"

"Not the old…"

Andromache looked down and saw a fresh bruise on his upper arm, near the scar. "How did you get *this*?"

"Not finking on what I am doing," he mumbled into her lap. "Not concentrating myself."

She imagined a club striking him in his moment of distraction and winced. "What *were* you thinking about?"

He squeezed her knee. "My lahff cabbage."

"Ector!" she scolded. Love cabbage, indeed! Hadn't he gone to the trouble of banning her from the army — of telling Penthesilea '*No effing way*' could she join — so that he wouldn't be distracted by her? The ban didn't seem to have done him much good! "Well, *don't*, next time! Be more careful."

"You ahre worff a bruise or two," he said.

She leaned down to kiss his ear.

"Pretty wife?" he said.

"Hmm?"

"Xanthus haff a message fohr you. There ahre new foals…"

Andromache shook her head.` "It's nice here. I don't want to leave." The garden was a sanctuary, and she wanted to savor the moment, there, with Hector, under the fig tree.

He nodded. "It is *so* nice, here. Always, I am so proud fohr the way you do the gahrten."

Andromache sucked in her breath. "I never knew you noticed," she whispered.

"I notice efferyfing about you." He slid his hand upward, following the curve of her calf. "*Efferyfing.*"

"Oho! By the Three-Legged Dolphin and the Three-Named Niece, it's true!" boomed a voice behind them.

Andromache fought to keep a sour look off her face. It figured! All day, when she'd been wishing that Uncle would come home, play roodles with her, and let her atone for the lie she'd told Hector, he'd stayed away. But now that she was having a quiet moment with her husband, here was Uncle, barging in. *Be nice*, she warned herself, trying to smile. *Remember what he means to Ector…*

Hector sat up. "What's true, Uncle?"

"She really *did* teach you another language, Sonny! Something beyond the swear words, I mean. I always knew you could handle those, but I thought everyone was full of wind about the rest." Unconcerned that Hector and Andromache might have been enjoying time alone together, Uncle sat down on a neighboring bench.

"She really did," said Hector.

"You must be very good indeed." Uncle nodded somberly at Andromache.

She shook her head. "Not really…he only learned it because he liked me."

Uncle guffawed. "Oh, Sonny!"

Hector slipped an arm around Andromache's waist. "Don't listen to her," he told Uncle, kissing the top of his wife's head.

"She's so good at teaching, she doesn't even know she's doing it."

Uncle gave them a thoughtful look. "That's like Sonny, here, on the training field. Have you ever watched your husband spar, young lady?"

Andromache stiffened and shook her head. Watch her husband spar? Watch him clobber people and be clobbered? Oh, no, she couldn't do *that*! She didn't want to see him fighting — she didn't even want to *think* about him fighting!

That part of his life had always been hard for her to cope with. The first time she'd ever seen Hector, he'd been dressed in battle armor, covered in someone else's blood. He'd looked like a monster — the Raider. That frightful vision of him had haunted her nightmares for months. He'd chased her down, torn her flesh, and left her to bleed until her skin turned waxy-pale — just like the corpse she'd seen long ago, in her native Lukkan village. The thought of it still made her sick.

Now, though, she was tormented by far more hideous visions. Instead of the Raider, she saw the *real* Hector — the gentle, funny Hector she'd come to know as a student, then a friend, then a husband. She saw his arm laid open to the bone — his throat slashed — his body drained of blood and left facedown on the battlefield...

No, she did *not* want to watch Hector practicing for combat!

To be sure, she was proud of him for the way he led the Trojan army. She was proud of him for riding out only to protect and defend allies, never to invade other countries. She was proud of him for saving the lives of innocents and for taking enemies prisoner rather than slaughtering them. And, his job being what it was, she wanted him to be as prepared, safe, and well-trained as possible, so that he could come home to her. She just didn't want to *watch* all the preparations.

(*Are you afraid that you'll be filled with horror if you watch him,*) jeered the Voice, (*or that you won't?*)

Andromache felt her cheeks flushing. *Shut up!* she snapped.

As usual, the Voice ignored her. (*Are you afraid he might look — sexy?*)

He's always sexy, Andromache retorted.

(*Especially after he's been training.*)

Andromache's blush deepened. She thought about how Hector was when he came home from the training field. His mood was especially playful, and everything about him exuded confidence and vigor — his voice, his eyes, his touch. In those moments, he was given to sliding his hands up her dress and planting long, wet kisses on her lips, no matter who might be around to see...

(*You've known about this quirk of his ever since that day, down in the stables.*)

Andromache knew exactly which day the Voice meant — she'd been down at the stables, bringing a lunch to Hector, when she'd overheard him taunting a colleague: *'I'm all yours, Buttercup.'* It was the first time she'd ever heard him sound cocky, and although she wouldn't have admitted it to herself at the time, the tone had stirred something inside her.

(*You were hot for him because he knew he could clobber that other guy,*) said the Voice.

I was 'hot' for him because of his confidence! Andromache corrected. Confidence was sexy. She couldn't help that! No matter what gave Hector such a feeling — playing roodles, reading, riding horses — she would respond to it.

(*Too bad it's only training that does the trick.*)

Andromache sighed. The Voice was right. Only training affected Hector quite that way. She supposed it was because he'd once been small, and he'd had to work hard to excel at combat. Reading had come too easily for him to take much pride in it. Hector liked challenges — he'd said as much.

(*And you like how he feels afterward,*) the Voice concluded. (*But as long as you don't see it happening, you can enjoy the effects without accepting the cause. You can pretend that that Hector has no part in your life.*)

Before Andromache could respond to the Voice, Uncle — who'd been gaping at her in astonishment ever since she shook her head — interjected a question of his own: "You've *never* watched Sonny spar? Why not?"

The Voice got in another jab: (*Are you afraid you'll like what you see?*)

Andromache caught her breath. *Why haven't you watched him spar? Are you afraid you'll like what you see?* The questions wove around each other, leaving her unsure which one she was supposed to answer. Not that she wanted to answer either one...

Hector loyally spoke for her: "Because, Uncle, the training field gets too crowded. She's had some bad experiences with crowds." He gave her a comforting squeeze.

Feeling very small, Andromache closed her eyes.

"Oh," said Uncle. "Well, I can sympathize. Crowds give *me* headaches, too. Take today — your mother's friends are something else, Sonny! I've never heard such gabble, and I've lived among both soldiers and daughters."

Hector laughed. "They like to talk, that's for sure."

"You're telling *me*! The only worse gossip I've ever met is that stable master of yours, but at least there's only *one* of him."

Hector laughed again. "Speaking of Xanthus, I heard you talked my wife into being your roodles coach."

Guiltily, Andromache looked downward. She'd never actually spoken to Uncle about this. Would he out her, or would he play along?

To her relief, Uncle nodded. He seemed to accept the arrangement without question. "She's a good teacher."

"I *told* you!" Hector exclaimed.

"And incredibly patient, too." With a guffaw, Uncle added, "She'd have to be, to put up with *you*, Sonny!"

Chapter 40

Andromache was awakened by a kiss on her shoulder.

"'<u>Lo</u>," she mumbled.

"<u>Hay-lo, my pretty wife</u>." Hector played with her braid, using it to tickle her nose.

"'<u>M'napping</u>…" she protested, still half asleep. A day split between the garden and the roodles board had left her utterly exhausted.

"<u>A good idea</u>."

Hector lay down beside her. She knew at once that he had no plans for sleeping, though, because he'd climbed into bed fully dressed. *He's up to something*, she thought warily.

Before long, he confirmed her suspicions: "<u>There is a new hohrse at the hohrse house</u>," he said. "<u>A little girl, so gentle</u>."

Andromache cringed. The more Hector asked to teach her to ride, the worse she felt. It was something personal, something he treasured, like Lukkan was to her. He wanted so badly to share it with her…

"<u>You ahre still scared?</u>" he murmured. "<u>It can be all rahght. I am going to hold you — you ahre not going to fall</u>."

"<u>I know</u>," she whispered, hating herself. She'd lied to Hector, hidden things from him, and now he thought she didn't trust him. She was as low as low could be.

He hugged her. "<u>Then come</u>."

She shook her head.

"<u>Why not?</u>" he asked. "<u>Somefing is weird, Ahndromahk. Befohre, you lahff the hohrses and the hohrse house</u>."

Finally, she broke down. She couldn't stand it anymore. "<u>I don't want to see *her*</u>," she whispered.

"Her? Who — the hohrse?"

"Penthesilea."

"Oh."

Hector sounded so strange that Andromache turned over to face him. "What is it?"

"She's gone."

Andromache blinked. "Gone?"

Hector nodded.

"Since when?"

"Since before our Trojan wedding."

Andromache had never asked why Penthesilea wasn't at their ceremony — the reason had seemed obvious. She'd never imagined that the woman might simply be gone. Now that she thought about it, though, it made sense. Surely Uncle would have mentioned seeing Penthesilea, if she'd still been in Troy. He knew her, and knew that Andromache knew her. Yet he'd only spoken of her as part of his past. "Why did she leave?"

"Oh, Troy was starting to feel small to her. She didn't like knowing that she'd always be second in command, as long as I'm here. She wanted to go somewhere that needed a leader." Hector's eyes shifted around as he spoke; his tone was unnaturally light.

"You're lying to me," accused Andromache, adding to herself, *And not very well*. Having just come clean to him, she felt justified in demanding the truth.

Hector sighed. "Ahndromahk…"

"What is it?"

"All right. She and I had a — *disagreement* — right before I went to Uncle's."

"She called me your whore," Andromache clarified. "Or something to that effect."

Hector sat up. His eyes were glittering. "Where did you hear that?" he fumed. "Did Xanthus tell you that? If he did, I'll —"

"Ssssh — no. Xanthus told me you'd seen her before you left, but that's all he would say, so I went and talked to her myself. *She's* the one who told me."

His face white with rage, Hector said, "I'm so sorry!"

"I'm fine," Andromache assured him. Then she started to cry.

"My sweetheart!" he exclaimed. "<u>Ahndromahk — come here. Come here.</u>" He pulled her into his arms and stroked her hair. "<u>She cannot talk to you lahke that, now. Do not worry.</u>"

Andromache sobbed even harder. "I — don't — care — what — she — c-c-calls — me!"

"Then what?"

"You — w-w-won't — be — safe — anymore!" she wailed. Things were happening just as she'd feared! Hector's colleague was gone. Because of *her*, he'd lost his left arm!

"I won't be safe?"

"There's — no one — to — protect you!"

"What do you mean, protect me?" He wiped her tears away with his thumb.

Andromache took a few deep, shuddering breaths and tried to pull herself together enough to explain. "You need her — on the field — next to you," she reminded him, sniffling. "You said — she's your — left hand. You put — your life — in *her* hands."

"Oh!" said Hector, understanding. "You mean protect me during —"

Andromache hid her face in his chest and started crying again. He would have no one beside him, anymore. He would be alone, undefended, and it was all *her* fault. She'd doomed her own husband!

"Don't, my sweetheart, don't," murmured Hector, kissing her hair. "<u>It is all rahght.</u>"

She shook her head. It was *not* all right! It would *never* be all right!

"Sssh — listen. When I said that, I didn't mean she was literally next to me."

"You — didn't?" Andromache hiccupped.

Hector shook his head. "Maybe it was like that in the beginning, but Lee and I haven't fought together in a long time. We mix stronger people with weaker, and since she and I are both pretty good, we aren't near each other. If I said she was my left hand, it's because I trusted her to lead another section of the army."

Looking up from his chest, Andromache asked, "So she really wasn't next to you?"

"No," said Hector. "Whether she's on the field or not won't make any difference in how safe I am, <u>Ahndromahk</u>. I promise."

Andromache sighed. Her arms, which had been clutching Hector, went slack, and she let her body relax. His words weren't much of a comfort — he hadn't been *that* safe to begin with, as his scars testified! — but at least he wouldn't be any worse off. "Did you — did you *order* her to leave?" she asked tentatively.

Hector shook his head once more. "I would've tried to fix things so that we could work together again. She was a good colleague, a friend. No — it was Lee's decision to leave. She didn't want to be here, anymore. But she said she'd help if Troy ever needed an ally, and I promised her the same."

"You left each other on good terms…"

Hector nodded. "We've had disagreements before, sometimes about you. What she said to me — I know she meant it in your best interest. She didn't think that I was doing everything I could to protect you, and she called me on it. I respect her for that." A dark shadow crossed his face. "But I can't respect her for saying it to *you*."

"I know why she did," whispered Andromache. "And why she *really* promised to help you if you need her."

"Why?"

"She's in love with you."

Hector shook his head.

"Yes, she is. I *know*."

"You fink this why?"

"Because of the look on her face, when she realized that *I'm* in love with you." Andromache gulped. "And then there was the look on her face after she saw us in the stables…"

Hector's cheeks went white again. "I am so sohrry, pretty wife. So sohrry! That day, I tell effery one, '*You can go home. You can go away.*' Then *you* ahre there, wiff me, and I fink —"

"You thought we were alone," Andromache finished.

Hector nodded. "I was so stupid."

"Not stupid. Just a little —"

"Carried off?" he suggested.

She smiled. "Carried *away*. We both were. But my point is, if anyone else had walked in on us there, they would have made fun of us, or been disgusted, or felt embarrassed. Penthesilea was *pissed*." Andromache thought of the woman's cruel look. "Because she loves you."

As he had before, Hector shook his head.

"How can you be sure?"

"I jahst know."

"How?"

He paused, searching for the right words. "Lee is too much lahke me to lahff me."

Andromache didn't have the first idea of what he meant by that. As far as she could tell, Penthesilea was nothing like Hector, except that both of them were warriors. He was gentle, and warm, and open, whereas she was harsh — distant — cruel.

For a long moment, Andromache looked into Hector's eyes. "I still say she left because she loves you, and she couldn't stand to be here now that we're married."

He gazed back and didn't blink. "Then we mahst agree on a disagree," he said, moving his fingers through her hair.

Andromache closed her eyes. "I'm sorry you lost your work partner," she whispered.

"Me too. Baht the city is going to be all rahght. So am I. So is Lee."

"And she'll always be your ally?"

"Always."

They fell silent.

"Ector?" murmured Andromache, after a moment or two.

"Hmm?"

"Who won?"

"What?"

"When you sparred with Penthesilea, back in Santiya, when you first met…who won? Uncle wouldn't tell me."

Hector smiled. "At first, she is winning. I fight stupid. I fink she cannot fight good, becahse she is a woman. So stupid!" His smile turned rueful. "So then I fight fohr real — and then I am winning —"

"So you won?"

He shook his head. "We fight mohre. No one is winning. And then —"

"And then?"

"And then it begins to rain. Hahrd. We go inside. We haff some wine wiff Uncle." Shrugging, Hector said, "That is all. A weird fight."

"Did you ever have a rematch?"

"No. It did not matter."

Andromache smiled. Tenderly, she traced the line of Hector's collarbone. "<u>All right</u>," she murmured.

"<u>What, all rahght</u>?"

"<u>You can teach me to ride horses</u>."

"<u>You ahre serious</u>?" he whispered.

She nodded.

He gave a joyous laugh.

"<u>Tomorrow</u>," she said firmly, before he could suggest going down there that evening.

He nodded. "<u>Tomorrow</u>."

Chapter 41

"Just step here."

"I don't want to step on you."

"You're stepping on my knew, not on *me*."

"Your knee is a part of you, isn't it?"

"And *you're* stalling — aren't you!"

"Is that a horse pun? *Stalling?*"

Hector gave Andromache a look of disgust before seizing her around the waist and tickling her. "I'll stall *you*!" he said.

She giggled and sank halfway to the floor.

"Oh, no," he protested. "Don't go limp! Come on! Thoas can't wait around all day."

Andromache looked at the young man patiently holding the reins of Hector's horse, Buzzy. He hadn't laughed at her once. Biting her bottom lip, she straightened up. "All right. I won't stall anymore."

"Good," said Hector. "Step here."

She stepped onto his knee.

"Now grab on, up there."

She took the mane in her hands.

"Now hold on while I give you a boost." Hector put both hands under her bottom and thrust upward while she pulled, and before she knew it, she was sitting on top of Buzzy. She held her breath, but the horse didn't bolt or buck. He didn't seem to mind that she was there. Once she was solidly astride, Hector climbed up behind her, much more elegantly than she had; he used a stool.

Andromache poked his thigh. "<u>You just made me get on that way so you could feel me up</u>!"

He settled in with his arms around her waist. "So what?" he murmured in her ear. Aloud, he said, "Thanks, Thoas. I'll take the reins, now. My wife and I are going riding."

The young guard nodded and gave the reins to Hector, who took them in one hand. With the other, he continued holding on to Andromache. She looked back over at Thoas and saw that he was smiling.

As Hector guided Buzzy outside, Andromache turned to face forward. She felt a sudden rush of panic. Why did they have to move? Why couldn't they just stand still, this time, and chat with the kindly stable guard? She couldn't ride a horse! The idea was ridiculous! What was Hector thinking? He was delusional if he thought she wasn't going to fall off!

"You all rahght?" asked Hector. "You ahre so stiff."

"It's just —" She sighed. "Are you sure this is safe?"

"Safe? Why not?"

"Because—maybe together we weigh too much for poor Buzzy."

"You weigh noffing," scoffed Hector. "We ahre safe."

As they proceeded onto the city streets, Andromache found herself relaxing. Hector fell into the rhythm of Buzzy's gait with movements so smooth they seemed unconscious. *He's beautiful,* she thought with a pang. Pressed to him, atop the horse, she felt as though they all were one creature. She knew the illusion would end the instant he asked her to ride a horse alone, but she was glad, even for a little while, for the chance to know her husband this way.

"Hey, Pronous!" Hector's voice rang in her ear; he was calling out to a man on their right. "This is my wife, Andromache."

"So, the rumors are true! My nephew said you got married."

Hector tightened his arm around Andromache's waist; behind her, she could feel him nodding emphatically.

Pronous cackled. "Are you sure you know what you're getting into, young lady?"

Afraid to move, Andromache gave a hesitant smile. "I think so."

The man laughed even harder, as though she'd made the wittiest of jokes. "Well, may the stars shine on both of you!"

"And on you." Hector nudged Buzzy with his heels and they started off again.

"Who's that?" asked Andromache.

"An ahncle ohff Dolops."

Dolops, she knew, was one of Hector's captains. She'd seen him at a few welcome-home parties and met him at the wedding.

Almost instantly, they slowed again. "Hey, there!" Hector called to another passer-by.

"Hey, yourself. Who's that up there with you?"

"My wife — Andromache," Hector said proudly.

"Pleased to meet you, Andromache." The man nodded to her. "A fine man you've married! A fine man."

"Thank you." The response was awkward, but she didn't know what else to say. As she and Hector started out once more, she asked, "And who was *he*?"

"I buy breads from him."

"Oh." Andromache had only traveled through the city with Hector a handful of times, but he'd never been chatty. His behavior today was extraordinary.

As he slowed to greet a third person — this time, a middle-aged woman — Andromache finally understood what he was up to, and why he'd been so eager for her to go riding with him. He was showing her off to people who, for whatever reason, hadn't been able to come to the wedding.

"Hello, Iphis!" he exclaimed.

"Hello — why, Hector, is that you?"

"It's me — and my *wife*."

"Hello, dearie," said Iphis. "What's your name?"

"Andromache," she answered, turning back to see Hector's face. He was beaming.

Iphis laughed softly. "May the stars continue to rain happiness on you."

"And on you," said Hector. To Andromache, he whispered, "She is the sister ohff the man who makes our wine jahrs."

Andromache nuzzled Hector's arm with her cheek. "I love you, too," she whispered back, wishing that she had someone to show *him* off to — her old neighbors in the Lukka lands, or even the ones in Lyrnassa.

He kissed the top of her head, and they continued onward. Andromache soon lost track of all the people they met, there were so many of them. One benefit to the stops was that, in the course of the slow, gentle ride, she grew used to the feel of the horse beneath her. By the time they got back to the stables, her nervousness had largely passed.

Xanthus, who had taken over for Thoas, was there to meet them. Andromache had a flash of inspiration. It wasn't quite what she'd had in mind, but close enough.

"Xanthus!" she called out.

"Eh? Is that you, Missy?"

"Yes — and I'd like you to meet my husband."

The stable master scowled at both of them. "I'm glad to see he's let you out of the cupboard."

Chapter 42

"Your turn," said Xanthus. He was playing a game of roodles with Andromache while she waited for her second riding lesson.

She hesitated for a moment, considering several options before moving one of her pieces. Too late, she saw her mistake.

"I roodle you!" crowed Xanthus as he swooped in to conquer her side of the board. "You're playing like crap, Missy."

The stable master was right. He'd already beaten her three times that day and was, as a result, abominably cheerful. Andromache would have loved to trounce him, just once, but how was she supposed to concentrate, when every guard or soldier who passed by smiled at her or saluted her — to say nothing of the three who had offered her water? Never had she garnered this much attention at the stables!

A beefy, middle-aged man lumbered by, giving Andromache a nod that could almost have passed for a bow.

Unable to stand it anymore, she hissed to Xanthus, "What's up with them?"

"Eh? Up with who?"

"Everyone here! They're being so weird to me! They're smiling, and bowing, and —"

"Well, of course they are! You're their new favorite person."

"Me? Why?"

"Because, Missy — you've put their boss in a good mood."

Andromache felt the inevitable red creeping into her cheeks.

"Not that he's ever been a dragon, mind you, and don't let anyone tell you otherwise! But these past few weeks —" Xanthus chuckled. "It's like someone put wine in his grain."

Andromache's blush deepened.

"So," said the stable master, eagerly rubbing his hands together. "Care to extend your losing streak?"

"All right," sighed Andromache. "Set up the board."

૪૭

WHEN HECTOR ARRIVED for their riding lesson, he led Andromache down the middle aisle of the stables. Until recently, Penthesilea's horse, Battleblaze, had had a stall there, and, knowing that Battleblaze was terrified of her, Andromache had always used the outer aisles. *I don't have to worry about that anymore*, she thought. *I can go down any aisle I want*. The realization gave her no joy, though — no relief, no sense of victory over Penthesilea and her grudge-bearing horse. Instead, Andromache just felt guilty that Hector had lost his best captain. His friend.

"Here." Hector stopped beside a stall that held a small, dark brown mare. He smiled and introduced Andromache to her. "This is Frondsia."

Andromache was prepared. She held out a piece of celery to the horse and murmured, "Hello, Frondsia."

The little mare accepted the treat.

"There!" said Hector. "You'll be friends, now."

Nodding, Andromache stroked Frondsia's neck.

"Are you ready?" asked Hector. "To ride, I mean."

Andromache swallowed hard. Was she ready? She wasn't sure, but at least Frondsia hadn't bucked, spooked, or whinnied in terror. That seemed a good omen. "Ready," she whispered.

Hector smiled and opened the door to Frondsia's stall.

Chapter 43

Andromache awoke to the sound of Cutie, yipping in the kitchen. She groaned. She was far too tired to investigate. All afternoon, she'd been riding Frondsia around the pasture. Alone. No one had been with her on the riding blanket. True, Hector had been holding the horse's reins the entire time and had never her let her go faster than a walk, but Andromache had ended the day mentally and physically exhausted. She and Hector had gone straight home for an evening nap.

Cutie barked again: "Yip! Yip! Maaaawrooo, yip! Yap!"

"I can see what is her problem," mumbled Hector.

"I'll go, too."

"You do not haff to."

"I'm hungry, anyway."

"Me, too." Pause. "And then maybe after, we can haff some almonds…"

Andromache laughed and gave her husband a kiss. Ever since she'd told him about her sexy dream, they'd used *almonds* as a sort of code word. "We'd better hurry, then."

They retrieved their clothing from the floor, dressed, and walked out onto the courtyard. More yips rang forth from the kitchen.

"What's that crazy dog up to?" grumbled Hector, still groggy. His hair was even more tousled than usual.

"I'm afraid to know." Andromache took his hand as they peered through the doorway.

The truth was more astonishing than either of them could have imagined: Cutie was barking as Uncle played a boisterous match of roodles with — of all people — Demuchus.

Hector rubbed his eyes, as though he didn't quite believe what he was seeing.

"You'll never understand the game," chided Demuchus. "You don't think the right way. You're a *monarchist.*"

"No, I'm a *monarch!*" Uncle guffawed.

Cutie, noticing Andromache and Hector at the door, barked a welcome at them and began weaving around their legs.

"Sonny! Little niece! Come in, come in. I was just playing roodles with Gemuchus, here."

"*De*-muchus," the young man haughtily corrected.

"I like this guy!" boomed Uncle. With one meaty hand he slapped Demuchus on the back. Demuchus's head bobbed dangerously close to the table, but he seemed unhurt. "Is he a good friend of yours, Sonny?"

Hector was wearing a bemused but placid expression. Demuchus, on the other hand, looked worried. "Yes," said Hector, sitting down at the table.

Andromache slid in beside him.

"We were hoping you would both come," said Demuchus, his face relaxing.

"Quite so. I've hardly gotten to see you, little niece," said Uncle. To Demuchus, he added, "Sonny here has been keeping her —"

Please, please don't say 'busy!' thought Andromache.

"— to himself."

"Well, that's only natural," Demuchus averred. "They have a remarkably tight bond."

Andromache frowned. What Demuchus had said was neither untrue nor offensive, but it bothered her somehow. She looked up at Hector. He shrugged.

"They've been spending hours together, each day, since long before the wedding," Demuchus added.

"Now, about that," said Uncle, furrowing his thick brows. "Sonny told me all about when they first got together —"

Andromache gave Hector a ferocious poke under the table and hissed, "You blabbed what we did up in my bedroom?"

"No!" Hector hissed back. "Not *that!*"

"— but precious little detail about what led up to it."

"She's been his Lukkan tutor for over two years, now," said Demuchus. "The first language tutor ever to succeed."

"Yes, yes. I knew that much."

"What more is there to know? The many hours they spent together had just the effect one might expect on a young man and woman of their ilk."

Ilk? thought Andromache.

"Ilk?" asked Uncle.

"Their age, level of intelligence —"

"I see."

"— their relative attractiveness compared to ideal beauty."

Uncle squinted. "I don't know. She's *got* to be closer to that than Sonny — have you ever seen his mug on a bad morning?"

Tilting his head solemnly, Demuchus pondered. "Perhaps. But the point is, they are both *approximately* the same distance away."

Uncle gave his nephew a skeptical look; Hector smiled back at him.

"Then there's the question of their upbringings," Demuchus went on. "Her largely rural childhood complements his, spent in the city. It's a classic case of opposites cleaving to each other."

In horror, Andromache looked at Hector. *Cleaving?* she mouthed.

He shrugged again.

"Hmm," mused Uncle. "If you ask me, it's a classic case of Sonny wanting to do the opposite of what everyone expected — and by that, I mean booting his language teacher out the door."

"I'm not so sure," said Demuchus, shaking his head. "You cannot deny that the men in his family line have a predilection for foreign women."

"Now *that's* true!" Uncle agreed. "You've nailed that one, Demuchus, my boy."

"Paris had better hope so," Hector chimed in. "I don't think there are any Trojan women who'd want him."

All the while, Andromache kept silent. She was appalled. Long ago, Demuchus had told her that he wanted to study her empirically; he seemed at last to have fulfilled that wish. Somehow, despite her refusal to marry him, he'd managed to become an expert in her!

Having concluded his list of observations, Demuchus made a proposition to Hector and Andromache: "Would the two of you accept my challenge to a match of team roodles, so that I might show your uncle the niceties of that form?"

"What do you think?" asked Hector.

Andromache shrugged.

Demuchus set up the board.

After Andromache and Hector had won two matches, they switched teams. Andromache claimed Uncle as her partner, and together, they won the next two matches.

Demuchus gave Hector a look of disgust. "I thought you were supposed to be good at this game."

"I *am*."

"We lost to a neophyte — a *royalist* neophyte!"

"A *royal* neophyte," corrected Uncle, chortling.

"My wife is an excellent player," said Hector.

Demuchus's eyes narrowed to slits. "Your wife — so *that's* the problem!"

"What?"

"You've been letting her win!"

"No, I haven't."

Andromache's mouth fell open. Had Hector let her win, the few times they'd played each other? As soon as she asked herself the question, she knew that it was true. To be sure, she'd learned roodles quickly, and she usually played well enough to beat Xanthus or Cassandra. Still, she should have known better than to think she could beat Hector in an honest match. Hector, whose very life depended on strategizing! *That* explained why Paris had once refused to play on Hector's team, against her! "You've been letting me win!" she cried.

"Not exactly," mumbled Hector, looking sheepish. "Maybe letting myself lose..."

"I can't believe it!" She shot him a look of betrayal. "You let me think I was *good*."

"You *are* good," he assured her. "You *are*."

Andromache glowered at him. "Stay and play, if you want, but I'm *not* going to be your roodles charity case anymore!" She stormed out onto the courtyard.

"Your wife is pretty steamed, Sonny!" Uncle chuckled from inside.

"My wife is *pissed*," amended Hector, sounding — of all things! — delighted at being in trouble with her, as though that somehow solidified them as a couple. "I'd better go find her."

His odd reaction startled Andromache out of her anger. By the time he found her, she was calm enough to let him put his arms around her.

"I'm sorry," he said, kissing her. "I just hated the thought of beating you. It made me sick."

"*That's* why you let me win?"

He nodded.

"Well, don't! I don't care if you're better at roodles."

Still abashed, Hector said, "All right. I'm sorry."

She leaned against him, returning his embrace. "It was all worth it, for the look on Demuchus's face," she murmured. "He thought he'd win for sure, on *your* team..."

"Poohr bastahrd." Hector laughed.

Andromache smiled but then grew pensive. "Ector?"

"Hmm?"

"Don't you hate him, anymore?"

"Why hate him?"

"I can think of a couple reasons." *For throwing you into a manure pile when you were eight*, she thought but didn't say. *More recently, for kissing me.*

"Ancient reasons," said Hector, brushing aside the grimmer moments of his past with Demuchus.

"So, what — are you friends, now?" asked Andromache.

"Maybe."

"But you never got to punch him."

"Pahnch?"

"You know, that time you and I were out in the countryside, together, and you told me what Demuchus did to you when you were little? You said that even after everything that happened, you could've been friends with him if only you'd gotten to punch him, once."

Hector laughed. "Oh, yes—I remember, now. Baht maybe I want to no mohre." He hugged Andromache tightly and kissed the top of her head.

She hugged him back. His magnanimity astounded her. She couldn't imagine herself playing a cordial match of roodles with Penthesilea, if that woman were suddenly to reappear...

Against her stomach, Hector's started growling. They'd been too distracted by the gaming to eat. "Are you still hungry?" she asked.

He nodded. "I am raffenous."

"Me, too." She gave him a coy smile. "And I wouldn't mind some almonds…"

"Now?" Hector's face was eager. "Or after mohre games ohff roodles?"

Andromache thought for a moment. "After," she decided. "Whoever wins decides how many times we have almonds."

That way, at least, Hector would have incentive to play his best.

Chapter 44

After that night, Demuchus became a regular visitor to the house. In entering the kitchen, Andromache was never sure, if he would be there, so she made a habit of peeking in before she stepped through the door. No matter how Hector's attitude toward Demuchus had changed, there were some days *she* couldn't bear to spend time with him.

All the same, she had to admit that Demuchus had solved one of their ongoing problems: who would coach Uncle in roodles. Neither she nor Paris wanted to do it, and while Cassandra might have, the girl had entered a new phase of her studies that left her ensconced in the library. No one had seen much of her in months. In any case, Demuchus was ideally suited to the task, and Uncle seemed delighted by him. The two spent hours bent over the roodles board. Some evenings, Andromache and Hector played matches against them, and she could tell that Uncle was improving.

While they played, they had lively conversations. Demuchus usually started them off with comments on one or another text he was reading. Andromache supposed that he missed going to soirees, those study sessions for young Trojans where he'd once reigned as king of the debate. In her kitchen, though, he found a very different sort of audience. Andromache could barely tolerate him, after all the odious things he'd done to her and Hector. Uncle adored Demuchus, but not in the polite way of the soiree-goers. Uncle was frank — good-natured — loud. And then there was Hector, who relished saying odd things just to see how people would react...

'You can't honestly believe that northland snakes breathe fire!' sneered Demuchus, as they were discussing a treatise on agriculture in countries bordering the Munnanda Sea.

'It's not about belief,' Hector said calmly. 'I'm telling you what was in the text. The northland farmer who was interviewed said he lost two whole fields of grain to a fire — but there were no clouds that day, which rules out lightning as a cause.'

'A neighbor must have started it — a careless boy, or someone with a grudge.'

'The farmer had no neighbors.'

'A traveler, then.'

'But no one was passing through.'

'Perhaps he started it himself, for attention.'

'And lose an entire year's work? That doesn't make sense.'

'It makes more sense than snakes breathing fire!'

'The fact is that the only unusual thing to happen the day of the fire was that a whole line of snakes was seen fleeing the field.'

'The text never claims that they were responsible for the fire!'

'No, it doesn't,' Hector agreed. 'But from what it does claim, we can rule out everything else.'

Hector could make even the most absurd conclusions sound irrefutable — and Demuchus, who wasn't used to absurdity, didn't know how to counter it. After such discussions, he would leave the house in a froth, vowing never again to waste his time debating texts there. Yet night after night, he would come back to do just that. There was no harm, no sting, to Hector's cheekiness, and Demuchus seemed determined to outflank him.

Meanwhile, Andromache found herself joining the discussions. Back in the old soiree days, she'd rarely said a word. The erudite group had made her feel foolish. Now Uncle, and even more so Hector, changed the dynamic for her. Hector had once told her that she was smarter than the other members of the soiree group. *'You fink new ideas,'* he'd said. *'Those peoples, they haff no new ideas. They repeat fings from texts. From older peoples. To sound mohre smahrt.'* He might have been trying to flatter her — he'd secretly been in love with her at the time — but regardless, with him beside her, Andromache was her brightest, most confident self. She could even quash Demuchus…

'The council is in despair,' Demuchus proclaimed.

'Why now?' Hector asked mildly.

'Because I informed them that their plan to levy taxes on blisterlet is likely to fail.'

'Why?' asked Hector. 'Because no one in their right mind would want to buy it?'

'Of course people want to buy it!' said Demuchus, aggrieved.

'I'd buy some from you, lad!' Uncle said comfortingly. 'What is it, again?'

'It's an herb,' Andromache broke in. 'People use it to make sleeping potions.'

'Ah!' said Uncle. 'That's more my sister's domain. Myself, I've never had trouble sleeping.'

'Then you're among the fortunate few,' sighed Demuchus, implying that he himself endured frequent white nights.

'If there's so much need for blisterlet, why would the tax fail?' asked Hector.

'Because — the conditions here are unsuitable for growing sufficient quantities.'

Andromache snorted.

'It's true!' said Demuchus. 'I've read several treatises on the cultivation of blisterlet, and all of them assert that the light conditions in our land are disadvantageous. Blisterlet is native to the coastal region southeast of here, you know.'

'Of course I know,' Andromache said curtly. 'I come from there, re-member?'

'Coming from there doesn't mean that you're fully versed in the botani-cal arts of that region, nor in the sun cycles!'

'Well, I'm plenty well versed in growing things, and I'm telling you, your treatises are wrong.'

'Wrong!' Demuchus was too stunned to say more.

'Wrong,' Andromache repeated. 'There's no problem with the light here, as far as those plants are concerned.'

'Then why do three most learned scholars say otherwise?'

Andromache thought for a moment. 'Did they check how wet the soil was?'

Demuchus pursed his pouchy lips. 'They may not have,' he admitted.

'There's the problem,' said Andromache. 'Blisterlet doesn't tolerate flooding. As long as you make sure the soil has a proper moisture level, the plants should grow just fine, here.'

Demuchus gave her a look of respect mixed with suspicion. 'I'll set a few of our best gardeners on the task, to test your — supposition. If you're right, who knows? The council may ask you to write a treatise of your own.'

'You should be so lucky, little niece!' Uncle chuckled. 'That sounds like a rip-roaring good time!'

Andromache smiled.

Hector stared at her. He'd been staring the whole time, and his eyes were very black. He looked like he wanted to pounce on her. 'Oh, my wife!' he said later, when they were back in their room. 'My brilliant wife. By all the gods, you're sexy…'

🙚

ANDROMACHE FELT LESS THAN SEXY on horseback, but she was improving. Hector still didn't have her ride beyond the stable pasture, and he never left her side when she was on horseback, but he'd given the reins over to her. She was responsible for telling Frondsia where to go, and how fast.

The new stage scared Andromache. She loved horses more than ever, and she loved Hector more than ever, but her favorite part of each riding lesson came at the end, when she and her husband brushed the horses, petted them, and fed them treats.

Hector was unfailingly patient as a teacher. He never rushed Andromache or showed irritation with her. He could even sense when she needed a break from riding lessons.

"Want to rahn, instead ohff rahde?" he asked one day, when the weather was just pleasantly warm. "We can go out to the cahntryside."

"Oh, I'd love to!" said Andromache. She hadn't gone running out in the countryside since before their wedding, and she'd never gone running with *him*. Even so, she had one misgiving: to reach the countryside, they would first have to go to a little outpost stable, where the tunnel leading out of Troy was hidden. The previous winter, Andromache had often used this tunnel to go running with Penthesilea, but the last time she'd been to the outpost stable, she'd found Hector there…

He was crouched on the floor — his clothes were filthy — his eyes were hollow and faraway. 'Go away,' he growled at her. 'Go away!'...

She was nervous about seeing the place again, but Hector didn't give her time to fret. With his hand warm in hers and a sunny smile on his face, he led her into the stable, through the tunnel, and out to the wild country beyond.

It was a magical day, the kind that could carry a person through weeks of rain and gloom. The whole hillside was alive. A scattering of summer flowers — among which were Andromache's beloved purple blooms — waved about on the breeze. Butterflies and birds filled the air with color — with song — while squirrels scampered up and down the scrub oaks.

Best of all, though, was the tortoise. Andromache shrieked in pleasure when she saw it. Hector, who was behind her, didn't know why she was shrieking and hastily caught up with her.

"What's wrong?"

"Look!" She pointed at the tortoise.

"Oh." Hector relaxed.

"I've never seen one out here, before!" Andromache's voice had dropped to an awed whisper. "I guess it was too cold, back when I used to go running. Oh, she's beautiful!"

"Why don't we sit for a while?" said Hector.

Andromache nodded. They sat with their arms around each other and watched the tortoise grazing on tiny pink blossoms.

"She's slower than *you*," teased Andromache, after a while.

"Me? Slow?" asked Hector.

"*I* was in the lead this whole time," she reminded him. Gently squeezing his thigh, she added, "Even with your long legs."

He snorted. "I *want* to rahn behind."

"Why, to protect me from squirrels and tortoises?"

"No." Hector's eyes were black. "To *look* at you."

The tortoise was promptly forgotten — and by the time Andromache and Hector remembered her, she had moved on.

They slowly made their way back to the gateway cottage, which concealed the outer end of the tunnel. At the door, Hector stopped short. Andromache looked down and saw a wispy snake, no thicker than her little finger. It was coiled and ready to strike.

"Troy has a new guard!" Hector laughed. "I guess we'll have to stay out here."

"That's fine with me," said Andromache. "We could go on a Lorani hunt when it gets dark."

"I wish." Hector sighed. "I have a night patrol…"

Andromache fell silent. No wonder Hector had offered to skip their riding lesson in favor of something she liked more — he'd wanted to take away the sting of their first night apart since the wedding. She grasped his hand tightly in hers, and together they stepped around the snake.

Early autumn

Chapter 45

Dusk was falling, the dinner dishes were washed and put away, and Andromache was sitting in the kitchen with Paris, listening to the jangling of his lute. One of his regular taverns would soon be hosting a competition for lutenists, and Paris was desperate to win — so desperate, in fact, that for weeks, he'd been practicing the same three Trojan drinking songs over, and over, and over. His family had grown to hate the music and now fled whenever Paris strummed the opening lines.

Only Andromache could still bear to listen: Paris's lute was her grandfather's handiwork and sounded very much like the lutes her dad had made. Interestingly, hers was the only criticism that Paris would accept, anyway. She wondered if Hector had told him who her dad and grandfather had been — if that was why he gave her more respect than he gave the others.

"You need to take that section faster," Andromache advised him.

"Faster?" Paris held up his hand and wiggled his fingers at her. "These are called '*fingers*,' Hermie, not '*whirlwinds*.'"

"You're supposed to be playing a dance, not a dirge," she retorted.

He frowned. "Maybe a *little* faster…"

"Take a break," she suggested. "Then try it again."

"There *are* no breaks when the stakes are this high," he said haughtily.

Andromache shrugged and walked across the kitchen to pour herself a cup of water. While she was over there, the music broke off abruptly.

"Hi, Mom," said Paris.

"Hello, Paris, dear. It's sounding — well, lovely."

"Thanks."

"If only you could apply yourself this way to something *loftier*. Hymns, perhaps." Hecuba sighed. "But never mind that. Do you know where your brother is?"

"Probably off in some dark room, feeling Hermie up."

Andromache flushed. "I'm right here, nitwit," she snapped from the other side of the kitchen. "I've been here the whole time, and you know it!"

"Paris!" howled Hecuba. "Take that filthy mouth of yours out to the bath chamber for a thorough scrubbing!"

Paris left, although he headed upstairs rather than toward the bath chamber. Andromache supposed that he'd decided to practice some more.

"I didn't see you, dear," Hecuba apologized. "Otherwise I would have asked *you*."

"Hector's got another night patrol training," said Andromache, in response to Hecuba's earlier question. Her cheeks were still the color of wine.

"Did he take my brother with him?"

"I think so."

Hecuba rolled her eyes. "Well, Asius is certainly enjoying his vacation in Troy. I can't swear it won't be the death of him, but that's his choice. *You're* the one I'm concerned about, to tell the truth, dear."

"Me?" asked Andromache.

"Are you finding enough to do these days?"

Andromache nodded. The garden kept her busy. Between vegetables for the kitchen and herbs for Hecuba's healing mixtures, not to mention all the ornamental flowers, there was always something needing her attention. Once the weather turned cool, there would be even more for her to do. In the meantime, she'd been thinking about starting another weaving project and tackling a few of the new texts Priam had collected over the summer. She spent as much time with Hector as his schedule would allow, either in their room, or in the stables, or in the

kitchen playing roodles. With all of those activities, plus marketing, cooking, and taking care of Cutie, not to mention keeping
Paris on task, Andromache's days were full.

"Not that marriage isn't delightful, but that doesn't mean
you can't have other pursuits," Hecuba opined. "Your husband
certainly does. I do — I never practiced the healing arts as much
in Santiya as I did after marrying Priam."

Andromache looked up at her. "You didn't?"

"No, indeed. As a princess, I was taught them, of course,
but unfortunately, I was too flighty to put them to use until I
came here. In any case, I've been thinking about you, and how
you have in essence lost your Lukkan pupil. Even if you and my
son spend more time together than ever, it's not as though you
have to plan lessons, these days."

"I guess not," Andromache said cautiously. She mistrusted
where Hecuba was leading the conversation.

"I thought your days might be dragging a bit, of late," Hecuba went on. "And it just so happens that one of my friends has
a grandson — nine or ten years old — who is about ready to
begin instruction in a foreign language."

"She — your friend — wants Lukkan for her grandson?"

"Indeed — that's her first choice." Sighing, Hecuba added,
"She thinks it must be the easiest of all available languages, if
Hector managed to learn it."

Andromache laughed.

"So, what do you say, dear?"

Andromache could think of worse things than teaching a
child — teaching Demuchus, for example! — but she wasn't
overjoyed by the idea, either. Starting over at *I like dogs*...with
someone who had no ulterior motive for learning, and who
might therefore make her life very difficult...just as her own
husband had done with *his* other tutors...

"I don't know," she said dubiously. "I'll think about it."

In truth, she wasn't sure what to make of Hecuba's offer.
The woman had long championed foreign language instruction,
with the goal of strengthening ties among Troy and its neighbors. She was passionate about the cause, yet that evening, she
hadn't once mentioned Troy's future. Her main concern had
been her daughter-in-law.

She must think I'm bored, mused Andromache. Perhaps it was because nearly everyone in Hecuba's family led high profile lives; ambassador, healer, council member, high priest, commander, and council-member-in-training were just some of the posts they held. Hecuba probably couldn't even imagine someone shrinking from the public eye. She probably couldn't understand why anyone would prefer the company of dogs, plants, horses, and a few cherished people.

But Andromache liked her quiet place in Troy. She loved her life, and she certainly wasn't *bored*! If Hecuba had asked her to teach the little boy because the city was short on language tutors, she wouldn't have hesitated. As it was, though…

I won't do it because of her, Andromache told herself. *I'll only do it if I want to*.

𝕭

"YOU AHRE GOING TO DO THIS?" asked Hector, when Andromache told him about his mother's proposition.

"I don't know," she said. She was no closer to a decision. "I don't know much about kids — I've never really been around them."

"They ahre lahke any person," said Hector, shrugging.

"You've spent time with kids?" she asked in surprise.

"My brahther and sister."

"Well, of course *them*!" Hector was years older than his two siblings.

"Neighbor kids too," he added.

"Do you think I could do it? Tutor this boy?"

"Ohff couhrse. You can do anyfing."

"You *have* to say that…"

Hector smiled. "What worries you?"

"With you, teaching was easy. You *wanted* to learn it — to impress me."

Pause. "So, it has worked? You ahre impressed?"

"I don't know," Andromache teased. "You were never very good at speaking in the past...and I think you've gotten worse since the wedding."

In a monotone, Hector recited the first such words he'd ever tried to learn: "I feeded my hohrse. I seed Dad. I eated breakfast. I learned many foalish words."

Andromache giggled. "Exactly."

"Maybe the kid can want to impress, you, too," suggested Hector.

Andromache thought back to the times long ago when she'd practiced reading with her dad. Once, she'd wanted so badly to please him that she'd stayed up late, looking ahead in the text that they were reading — but she'd sat too close to the fire and singed her dad's precious scroll. He'd awoken in the middle of the night to the sound of her weeping...

'What's wrong, little Cricket?' he asked.

When she showed him the text, he looked somber but said only, 'It's all right. We can still read it. Don't cry. Don't cry — here, climb up here.'

She crawled into the bed, between her mom and dad, and fell asleep.

She then thought back to Hector's first lesson, how hard he'd struggled to say the phrase, *'Lahff ees a bahkoff gotsheet.'* She thought of how she'd insulted his accent and how he'd laughed it off — of how he'd spoken to her in his mind whenever he was away from her. Working with him, like working with her dad, had been about so much more than just the transmission of a language.

Andromache knew then what her answer would be. She hoped that Hecuba's friend wouldn't be too disappointed.

Chapter 46

On what was perhaps the last mild evening of the year, the family gathered on the courtyard to celebrate the prize Paris had won. Everyone was chattering cheerfully — everyone except Paris, who had a moldy look.

"Second place," he muttered, over and over. "Second place! Damn judge must have been bribed."

"Oh, Paris," sighed Priam.

"No, Dad, seriously! Wait, I'll play it for you, and you can tell me if it deserves *second place*."

"You deserved first place," said Cassandra.

"Thank you, Songbird."

"Now, can you please play something *different?*"

Paris made a face at his sister.

"That's all we've been hearing for *weeks*," she moaned. "My history tutor was furious with me because I hadn't learned the first twelve kings of Hanigalbat — and do you know why? All I could think of was — *jangle jangle twaaaaaanagle jangle twangle twinga twiiiiiiiiiiiiing!*" Cassandra broke into an imitation of her brother's most overplayed tune.

"Oh, boo-hoo, Songbird," snapped Paris. "It's not like your tutor gave you *second place!*"

Andromache smiled in perfect contentment. The evening sky above them was a deep, rich, blue. She was sitting in Hector's arms, stroking Cutie with her feet. She was watching, but not participating in, one of Paris's most memorable tantrums. She was surrounded by people she loved, and who loved her. It was one of those moments she knew would be with her forever.

"The courtyard looks lovely," said Priam, to change the subject. "Lovelier than I ever could have imagined."

Hector, from behind Andromache, wove the fingers of both his hands through hers. "The gardener makes the difference."

Paris, still sour, grimaced. "Look, man, you've got her. Do you have to keep flirting with her all the time?"

"I never got to flirt with her before," said Hector, crossing his arms so that he and Andromache were embraced. "There's a buildup."

"No, you *chose* not to flirt. The window has closed."

"Married people can flirt, Paris," said their father. "Your mother and I flirt."

"Oh, *Dad* —"

"No, really. Watch." Priam raised his voice to get his wife's attention. "Hecuba, my dear?"

Hecuba turned away from Uncle, with whom she'd been talking. "Yes? What is it?"

"I can't stop thinking about the meeting last night. You had everyone riveted."

Hecuba's cheeks flushed. "Thank you. That's sweet of you to say, Priam."

"You had *me* riveted..."

"Oh *gak*, Dad!"

Andromache giggled, and so did Cassandra. Uncle chortled. Hecuba, now frankly red in the face, laughed with them.

"In any case," said Priam, a serene smile on his lips, "the fact remains that our courtyard is a thing of beauty. I wish I could say the same for the temple gardens," he finished sadly.

Andromache's ears perked up.

"Whatever do you mean, Priam?" asked Hecuba.

"They've been let go, lately. The sacred herb bed is looking rather like a patch of dried seaweed."

Hecuba clucked in disapproval.

"I'm afraid the young priests don't have the same connection to the earth that my generation does — and my generation doesn't have the young priests' knees." Priam rubbed his joints and sighed. "The result is a shambles where there ought to be abundance."

"I could help," Andromache said timidly. "If you want, I mean."

When she saw both Priam and Hecuba beaming in response, she suspected that they'd been angling all along for her offer of help. They were plainly still worried that she didn't have enough to do, especially now that she'd declined to give Lukkan lessons.

"What a lovely idea!" said Hecuba.

"Are you sure, little one?"

Andromache nodded. "I mean, I couldn't do much, until the rainy season. But I could weed a little, and make plans for what to plant…"

"Wonderful!" said Priam. "Why don't you come with me tomorrow, so I can show you around?"

"Do not be late," Hector murmured in her ear. "You mahst not offend the sacred herb."

Cautiously, so as not to be seen by the others, Andromache pulled her hand away from Hector's and poked him in the ribs. She knew all too well the danger of his quips, and she didn't want to spend her first day on the job lost in a fit of hysterical laughter.

Chapter 47

P riam hadn't been exaggerating the sad state of the temple gardens. Sacred shrubs grew every which way, resembling nothing so much as sea urchins. As for the sacred herbs, they hadn't been properly watered in months — if ever. The peaked little plants huddled miserably in their boxes, their leaves too dry even to supplicate. Whatever sacred task they were supposed to be doing, Andromache couldn't imagine that they were up to it.

"I don't know," she whispered doubtfully to Priam. "I don't know if I can save them. I might have to transplant new ones from our courtyard." To her, the sacred herb looked like ordinary oregano, and that was what she envisioned transplanting. Being rooted in the temple would no doubt confer sacredness to the plant...

"Anything, little one," Priam urged. "Anything at all. You have my full and unreserved permission to do what you think needs to be done, and I will help you in any way I can."

Once Priam had gone into the building, Andromache knelt beside a large box, pursing her lips. The plants within had only been saved by the luxuriant fig tree above them — and even with the mercy of that shade, their future looked doubtful. Still, she'd promised to try, so she watered them, weeded them, and picked off the weakest stems and leaves. When she was finished, the bed at least looked tidy.

By then, the sun was too high for her to do any more watering, so she moved on to the beds in the shade of the temple building and began to weed them. Inside, the priests were at work; she caught occasional snippets of their conversation.

"The stars would never allow it," said one priest.

Allow what? thought Andromache.

"You mean they cannot stop it," a different priest amended. "That's blasphemy!"

"I meant that they *cannot* in the sense that they *would not*, under any circumstances, choose to intervene in the course of human events — even something so vast as empire-building."

The first priest grunted. "As though one such as *you* knows the will of the stars." He seemed, however, to have retracted his charge of blasphemy.

Andromache wondered how the two priests would react to *her* knowledge of the night sky. They must never have read *On Lorani*, or they would know that the stars were not all-powerful deities, but one of many types of creatures swimming through the celestial ocean.

Thinking about the Lorani made her wonder whether infinitely tiny worlds were floating in bubbles beneath the waves of the terrestrial sea, and if for them the earth's luminous sea animals were like stars and Lorani. If she took a gulp of sea water, would she accidentally be swallowing a host of miniscule worlds, populated by infinitesimal Hectors and Andromaches?

The idea left her dizzy — and, perversely, thirsty. The pool in the garden ought to be safe. It was fresh water, not salt, and had no colonies of glowing creatures. She could drink it without fear of swallowing miniature versions of herself. She cupped her hand and dipped it into the pool, bringing the water to her lips.

"Little one!" cried Priam.

Afraid that she must have transgressed, Andromache spat her mouthful of water onto the ground.

"You're still here," Priam said gravely.

"I'm sorry," she whispered. Had she also broken a rule dictating the hours of temple gardening?

"I promised my son that I would send you back home before now. He knows how hot this particular courtyard can be and is afraid you'll overdo it."

Oh — that. Relieved that she hadn't caused offense against the temple, Andromache assured Priam, "I feel fine. He's overprotective." Which, in all honesty, didn't bother her. She liked that Hector worried about her.

"That *is* his way, especially where you're concerned," Priam agreed with a smile. "But it's also true that the heat catches up to you before you realize it…here, most of all. Whoever planned this courtyard was more concerned with tile arrangement than with the planting of trees."

"Oh," said Andromache. "I didn't — I didn't think —"

"Don't be upset! The fault is mine, if indeed there's fault to be had. You look well enough, I'd say — the stars be praised — but come, have some water, just to be on the safe side."

Priam led her to a patch of shade near an olive tree, which was, like the fig, hardy enough to flourish even through years of neglect. A jar of water and several cups were sitting beneath it on a table.

"What do you think of the temple?" asked Priam, pouring two cups of water.

"It's pretty," said Andromache. "Calm."

"Then the priests must have been exceptionally agreeable today." Priam laughed. "Usually, they spend the day bickering."

"I heard a little of that," she admitted.

"What were they on about?"

"Whether or not the stars intervene in human affairs."

"Ah. And did they reach a consensus?"

"I guess — that the stars *could*, if they wanted to."

Priam took a long drink. "You don't sound convinced."

Andromache shifted uncomfortably. "I don't know much about the stars…"

"Nor do any of us, when you come right down to it. Go on, little one."

"I read — read somewhere —" she didn't want to name the text, on the off chance that Priam would deem it blasphemous and get rid of it. He might have obtained it without first reading it. "— that stars and the other things up in the sky are really animals, like glowing jellyfish floating in a giant sea."

Priam nodded. "You must be referring to a treatise called *On Lorani.*"

"Yes," she whispered.

"Fascinating text. To me, the exact nature of the stars is interesting but unimportant. You're surprised, little one? But it's true. Priests, like all people, think about the stars in whatever way they find most approachable. We old priests use the words '*stars*' and '*gods*' interchangeably to mean something beyond ourselves — ineffable light. I always saw them as offering signs and guidance, but not favors. The light is there, providing the exterior prompting we humans sometimes need in order to access our own wisdom, as well as our gratitude. Indeed, the highest purpose of our religion is to give thanks for all that we have in life. If there are animals up in the sky who hear our words of thankfulness — or even if there's nothing of intelligence up there at all — no matter. The important thing is to speak these words. But back to *On Lorani*...I do have some objections to what the text puts forth. For instance, the stars move around in such regular paths year to year, whereas animals move about randomly. It's impossible to predict the path of a fish, unless there's a niblet nearby."

"They might be caught in an eddy," argued Andromache. "That's what the text said."

"True," said Priam. "I'd forgotten about that argument."

"Also," she went on, feeling braver, "some animals migrate. Storks come the same time every year, and so do eagles. What if the stars and Lorani do that? They're so far away that to us, it looks like they go to *exactly* the same place, when actually they just go *pretty close* to it. To us, their paths might look more regular than they really are."

"Well said." Priam nodded with respect. "I should have you present these ideas to the priests, little one. But tell me, what would the author of *On Lorani* say about what my priests were discussing — the intervention of the stars, whatever they might be?"

This was an easy question: "The stars and Lorani wouldn't intervene in human affairs because they don't even know we're here. Our whole world is too small for them to see. They could swallow us and never know it. Maybe *we'd* never know it."

Again, Priam nodded. "You may be right, little one. I confess to thinking less about signs, these days. I always believed in their intentional presence, a message from the powers beyond us, but more and more I've been leaning away from that line of thought. In any case, many of my older colleagues would accept your explanation for the lights out in the night sky. Our generation is concerned only with wondering at and showing appreciation for the marvels of the universe. For that, it hardly matters whether the stars are human-like gods, gigantic animals, or something else entirely."

Andromache broke in: "Hector once told me that there's a fallen star in the temple, and it's made of some kind of metal."

"Iron," said Priam. "We do indeed have a lump of iron that fell from the sky. It's most intriguing, although I couldn't say for certain that it's a star. Hector made a leap to call it that. In any case, the young priests want to take our religion in a strange direction — making petitions, mostly, and not for things like tranquility or happiness, but for wealth and power. And since great animals and lumps of metal are not likely to listen to petitions, these priests prefer to think of the stars as human-like deities." As Priam finished speaking, he snorted.

"What is it?" asked Andromache.

"Can you imagine <u>Cutie</u>, hovering around up there, listening to requests for riches, wine, or love?" Priam laughed. His laughter sounded much like Hector's, although older and a little worn down around the edges.

Andromache thought about what her father-in-law had said. Looking back, she found that she couldn't remember him ever asking the stars for anything, not in a single one of his orations. He expressed thankfulness for all of the good things in his life. He extolled the beauty of the earth and the best, most peaceful impulses of its inhabitants. What he never did, though, was make demands. Feeling a deeper than ever appreciation for him, she took his hand and squeezed it. He squeezed back.

"So, little one," he said. "According to the priests, what exactly would the stars not intervene on?"

"Empire-building, I guess."

Priam's face turned suddenly grave, even sad, as he looked at her.

Andromache lowered her eyes, not wanting to know why his expression had changed. She didn't want to think about sadness — she'd had her fill of it, and what she wanted now was joy. "Hector will be home, soon," she said softly. "I was hoping to take a bath before he got there."

"Of course, dear," said Priam. "You should go. It looks like you've already done good work!"

"I finished one bed and started on another."

"Please don't feel you have to rush. Things move slowly, here, despite the young priests. And let me know if there's anything you need."

"Well —"

"Ask it."

"It's just —" Andromache sighed. Her parents hadn't been devout. Temples and rituals were new to her. So far, her one real experience with religion had been the Lyrnassans shunning her and calling her cursed. She'd unknowingly violated their taboo on blood, and they'd made her pay forever after. "I guess I'm a little afraid," she said.

"Of what?" Priam asked gently.

"Of — of — I don't know — offending someone, or breaking a rule, or —"

The priest laughed. "Is that why I saw you spit out the other water?"

Andromache blushed. "I-I didn't know if it was sacred, or something. You stopped me from drinking it."

"It doesn't taste very good, so we usually bring in water from the city cisterns."

"Oh."

"You're a sweet girl," said Priam, smiling fondly at her. He kissed her forehead. "I'm glad you married my son."

Chapter 48

E very morning, when Hector set out for the stables or the training field, Andromache walked down to the temple. As she'd warned Priam, she wasn't able to do much more at first than some weeding and trimming, but even that little bit of work made a big difference. The gardens looked cared-for — loved.

Once the autumn rains came, she began gardening in earnest. She planted new seeds and transplanted herbs and flowers from her own courtyard. Slowly, a haze of green came over the temple gardens.

Still shy, Andromache nodded politely to the priests but seldom spoke to them. They treated her in the same formal way. Several times, though, she overheard them making appreciative comments about the gardens, and their praise filled her with a warm sense of pride.

The end of summer had other compensations, not least of which was Hector's lighter schedule. He would still be holding trainings throughout the winter, and there were the stables to look after and other on-going projects, but overall, his work life slowed down during the rainy months. Andromache saw more of him than ever. He didn't have as many tasks to do during the hours they were apart, and he was better rested when they were together.

On foul weather days, they stayed inside to read and discuss texts. Whenever the rain let up, though, they spent time together outdoors. They took Cutie for walks out in the countryside or rode horses — and not just in the pasture behind the stables, either! Hector had begun leading Andromache on rides around the city.

One especially lovely day, Hector suggested a trip down to the river Scamander. "We neffer get to see it."

Andromache nodded, thinking back to that spring day when they'd planned to walk along the river together — and how, before they could go, Hector had been called away with the army. "That sounds wonderful," she said.

They went to the stables to fetch Buzzy, who, according to Hector, loved splashing in the river.

"What about Frondsia?" asked Andromache.

"She lahkes not the water," Hector explained. "She is too scary — *scared*."

"And Thisbe?" Andromache gave the grizzled old pony a wistful look.

"She is too old. It is too fahr fohr her."

"Poor thing." Andromache stroked Thisbe's soft cheek. "I'll bring you a treat, when we get back."

The little pony whickered gently, but Buzzy wasn't near as docile. He pranced and kicked up his heels.

"Does he know where we're going?" asked Andromache.

Hector nodded. "I fink so. He is smahrt, and he lahffs the riffer."

To get to the river, they had to pass through Troy's outer market, which sprawled in an arc between the main gates and the harbor. Andromache had been there once before, the day she and Hector had buried her dog, Muka, in the sea. She remembered it as a frightful place, teeming with merchants and deckhands who jostled her pitilessly. She'd fallen down amidst all the chaos and might have been trampled, had Hector not come back to rescue her.

Now that she was used to navigating the crowded streets of Troy, though, the outer market didn't scare her. She and Hector chatted happily as they passed through it and out to the river Scamander.

As soon as Buzzy was in sight of the water, he strained at his lead. Hector laughed and let him go. He and Andromache watched the horse galloping through the shallows, splashing water and tossing his head in the rainbow droplets of spray.

"See?" said Hector. "He looks lahke a baby hohrse."

Buzzy charged over to them and butted Hector's shoulder. He shook out his mane, showering them with mist.

"Buzzy!" Hector scolded. "Quit it, will you?"

Andromache came to the horse's defense. "He *loves* you," she said firmly, stroking Buzzy's golden hide. "He's showing off for you."

Hector laughed.

"He *is*!"

"Wiff his *haihr*?" Hector shook out his own hair, making several stray locks fall in his face. "This is to show lahff?"

"Now *you*, quit!" Andromache said with a giggle.

"Sit?" asked Hector, pretending not to hear her right. "We can do this." He found a rock to sit on and pulled her down onto his lap. They cuddled together, warm and happy, watching Buzzy make a few more passes through the river.

"Ector?"

"Hmm?"

"Did you know Buzzy as a foal?"

"Mm-hmm."

"Is this really what he was like? You said he looked like a *'baby horse*,' just now, but I didn't know if you meant —"

"Yes, he is lahke this," Hector answered. "Full ohff energies. Crazy. Baht he does not lahke me."

"He didn't like you?" Andromache was surprised. "But he loves you so much, now."

"I know," said Hector. "I bring to him apples —"

"And wine," Andromache interrupted.

"And wine." Hector laughed. "Mahch wine. I stand by him. I talk to him wiff a quiet voice. It takes a long time, baht finally he trahst me. He lahff me."

Andromache pursed her lips. "Buzzy liked *me* right away," she said pertly.

"Ah," said Hector, smiling. "Ohff couhrse that is true. *You* speak hohrse."

She poked him on the shoulder. He caught her hand, and then before she knew it they were kissing — and kissing — and kissing — for so long that Buzzy finally came over to them and nipped at Hector's arm. The horse seemed ready to go back to the city, or else he was upset that he'd lost his audience.

"Oh, Ahndromahk..." Hector sighed into her hair. "Some-day, I promise, I'll bring you here without a chaperone."

She smiled. "It's all right. I liked watching Buzzy — and I'd love to come back with him, sometime."

AND SO THEY DID, whenever the weather allowed. Along with Buzzy, they started bringing Cutie, who fell instantly in love with the river. They always took those walks at sunset, when the gold of the western sky matched the gold of Buzzy's hide, and the waters of the river and the sea were a deep, dark blue.

Late autumn

Chapter 49

Andromache sighed and pawed one last time through her clothing chest. It was a beautiful late fall day, clear and auspicious — wedding weather. All morning, the family had been setting up for the event, and she'd only just been released by Hecuba...

'Go on, dear. Get dressed,' said Hecuba. 'No, boys — not you! I need you to run out and fetch a few jars of the coastal wine. We were supposed to get a shipment, but it never arrived. I can only assume the delivery man drank it on the way up here, thirsty lout! Oh, if only I could — '

Glad for her dismissal, Andromache had crept out mid-rant and gone to her room to change clothes. However, nothing there appealed to her.

"What should I wear, Cutie? My white dress, my tan dress, my other tan dress, or my grey one?" It didn't matter, of course. No matter which dress she chose, she would once again be a dead leaf in the garden of colors worn by Cassandra's friends. Drab little Andromache...

Andromache paused mid-sigh. She *did* have other dresses, now that she thought about it! She hadn't worn them, or even looked at them, since before the wedding, but she still had the chest full of gowns sent over by Mestor, the neighbor with five daughters. "Should I wear something *fancy*?" she asked Cutie.

The dog yipped.

"All right, then — I think I will." Andromache looked around the room and saw the chest tucked neatly under a table. She pulled it out, opened the lid — and gasped.

It was the wrong chest. Before her sat the gossamer dresses she'd been given at her bridal luncheon. Those dresses! She'd forgotten all about them. She knelt, grabbed one at random — it seemed to be vaguely blue in color — and held it up to the light.

Completely transparent! Neither a dress, nor a naked body, the thing was a foolish parody of both. She imagined parading around in it while Hector laughed himself sick. Did Hecuba's friends think she was *that* stupid, that she would fall for their prank?

Andromache looked thoughtfully at the dress. Then again, why not? She and Hector could *both* have a good laugh at the expense of those ladies! Together, they could poke fun at all the tricks played on Trojan brides and grooms — from the pre-wedding sleepover, to the torturing of the married couple, to this. It was a wedding day, after all!

Hastily, she slipped the filmy blue gown over her head and slid under the blanket. She'd barely settled herself when Hector arrived.

"Hay-lo, pretty wife," he said. "Hay-lo, Cutie."

The little dog pranced around him, but Andromache stayed in bed. "Hello," she said.

"Oh, no. You feel sick?"

"No."

"You ahre in bed." Concerned, Hector sat beside Andromache and stroked her hair.

"Just catching a quick nap before the wedding," she said.

He groaned. "The wedding! I do not want to go. I am so tired."

"I know."

"Baht we mahst get ready. Mom is in the kitchen — 'Hector, hurry up! Must you always disgrace us with your tardiness? And don't get me started on Andromache. She was always punctual before marrying you!'"

It was the perfect opening. "Actually, I'm ready to go." Andromache kicked off the blanket and sat up.

Hector gawked at her. He said nothing.

She rose to a kneeling position. "What do you think?"

402

Eyes wide, Hector gasped out a very dry: "What — thees?"

"Isn't it silly?" Andromache laughed. "It was a present from one of your mom's friends, just before the wedding. I had to sit there and open basket after basket of these things. The ladies were trying to fool me into thinking they were sexy, so I'd wear one for you — and you'd laugh at me. It was their little joke on the bride. I forgot all about the stupid things until today. What do you think? Do you like this one, or should I go with another color?"

"Ah-ee lahke eet," whispered Hector, his accent thicker than it had been in years.

"It's really something," Andromache said sarcastically. She held the skirt out for display.

Still not laughing, Hector caught a fold of the dress between his thumb and forefinger. "So soft…" He dropped his hand to her thigh; the heat of his skin seeped down to hers through the gauzy fabric of the dress.

It was Andromache's turn to gasp. "You really *do* like it," she murmured.

Hector sucked in his breath. His hand moved to her hip, and then around to her bottom. "Ah-ee lahke eet," he croaked.

"But I just thought it was funny," she protested.

Hector's hand slid down to her knee — slipped under the hem of the dress — eased upward once more to her thigh. They both watched its progress through the faintly blue haze of the dress. "Thees dress ees not fahnny," he said. "Eet ees   uh — *naughty.*"

"Naughty," Andromache murmured.

"Naughty…" whispered Hector. Then, his hands were all over her, hot and arousing — he was pulling the dress off her shoulders, sliding it up her legs — he was biting her neck — he was grabbing her —

"Hector! Andromache!" Hecuba hollered from across the courtyard. "The guests will be here any moment!"

"Aaaagh!" Hector cried in disgust. He rolled off the bed and kicked one of his sandals. It struck the wall with a loud *thwack*!

Andromache watched the spectacle in amazement. She'd never seen her husband so wild.

"You!" he gasped, pointing at her. "Help me!"

"Help you, what?"

"Help me think of something disgusting — something *not* sexy — so I can go out there without —"

"Embarrassing yourself?" Giggling, Andromache took a sly peek just below his waist.

"It's not funny!"

"It's a *little* funny."

"Your sense of humor is a *little* off, tonight," he shot back.

"All right, all right — oh, wait I know!" she cried. "Herb bread!"

"Herb bread?"

"Remember that time before we were married, when we were sitting on the stairs together, and I touched your arm and — well, you liked it?"

Hector narrowed his eyes. "So?"

"So," said Andromache. "After that, we talked about herb bread, and it must have worked. I mean, you got up and left — remember?"

Hector let out a hoarse laugh. "I remember."

"Hector! Andromache!" barked Hecuba. "I mean it! Get out here, *now!*"

"All *right!*" Hector bellowed back, through the window. Under his breath, Andromache could hear him muttering, "Herb bread. Herb bread. Herb bread."

Hastily, she threw on the grey dress — it was long and loose enough that no one would know she was wearing a sheer blue one beneath it. No one, that is, except Hector.

ᏙᎧ

IN WHAT SEEMED like a flashback to her own wedding, Andromache was torn away from Hector right after the ceremony.

There must be some taboo against spouses talking to each other, she reflected. *At parties, they're supposed to mingle with the guests. And mingle*, she thought wearily. *And mingle — and mingle.*

Now that she was Hector's wife, Andromache found herself unable to hide in the corners. Everyone wanted to greet her, and more than a few wanted to chat. They asked about her riding lessons and wondered how she was getting along with '*King Asius.*' Several hinted that she must feel a special kinship to him, which made her wonder if the rumors about her supposed royal birth — rampant during her first year in Troy — had been revived.

While Andromache spoke politely to all of the guests, she wasn't genuinely happy to see anyone until the Lark and the Otter found her. She liked those two women. They'd been kind to her, comforting her about her own disastrous wedding ceremony — and she had no more reason to be wary of them, now that she knew the filmy dresses weren't a joke.

"Hello, little dear!" warbled the Lark.

"Hello," said Andromache.

"We were just talking about you."

"We were," the Otter agreed.

"Oh, really? Why?"

"This wedding was nothing compared to yours, Sunshine."

"But this one was perfect!" Andromache protested.

The Otter made a moue of disapproval. "Perfect except for the bride and groom, who were as much fun to watch as a pair of boulders," she grumbled. "But enough about them. Are *you* enjoying married life?"

"Yes," said Andromache, nodding emphatically. She loved her new life — the kissing, and the cuddling, and the talking at all hours. She loved running over to Hector when he came home and throwing her arms around his neck. She loved going to bed with him, and waking up with him, and everything in between. She *loved* being married!

The two women laughed at the vehemence of her '*yes.*'

"Now, *that's* how a bride *should* look!" barked the Otter.

"Indeed," sang the Lark. "And so should the groom. Yours certainly does, dearie. He's eyeing you as we speak!"

Andromache peered over at Hector and saw that it was true. What the Lark hadn't noticed — although she would certainly have approved if she *had* — was that Hector was staring largely at Andromache's shoulder. He was trying, she felt sure, to catch a glimpse of her gauzy blue dress.

"And who can blame him for staring?" the Lark went on. "You're radiant, little dear."

"And *he's* looking healthy for the first time in years," said the Otter. "You've been good for each other, Sunshine — that's obvious."

"We're glad to see it!" sang the Lark. "You deserve every happiness, both of you."

"Every happiness," the Otter repeated firmly.

With that benediction, the two women strolled off in search of Hecuba, and Andromache was left at the mercy of Cassandra's friends, whom she hadn't seen since her own wedding. She was worried, at first, that they would ask embarrassing, overly personal questions, but they turned out to be more interested in Lukkan wedding customs than in bedroom gossip. Interested, and also incredulous.

"No," she had to tell them, at least seven times. "The Lukkan ceremony *really* doesn't require flowing water."

Each time, they gasped or clucked their tongues in disapproval. Andromache didn't have the heart to tell them that in the Lukka lands, there were no wedding ceremonies at all.

$$\wp$$

ONCE THE DANCING STARTED, Andromache made for the back stairwell. *To hell with Taruishan taboos — I want my husband!* With luck, he would be there, in their old meeting place —

And he was. "Ector," she murmured.

He wrapped an arm around her and buried his face in her stomach. "Pretty wife." The words came out muffled.

She sat down on his lap. "I'm glad I caught you before you went out to torture the married couple."

"Fohrget them! I want only *you*!" And then he kissed her — and kissed her — and kissed her —

"Shouldn't we go further up the stairs, if we're going to do that?" she whispered. "This is where teenagers go to kiss, right — the Make-Out stairs?"

"We're not teenagers," said Hector, kissing her again. His fingers crept under the shoulder of her grey dress, feeling for the shimmery blue one. "Let's just go to our room."

Andromache drew back from him.

"What is it?"

"I never got to be a teenager," she said wistfully.

Hector gave her a thoughtful look, shifted her off his lap, stood, and took her hand. "Come on," he said, pulling her up the stairs after him. "Hurry, before someone sees us."

He steered her to the darkest corner of the second floor alcove. She took his hips in her hands.

"No," he murmured, moving her hands upward. "Above the waist only."

Andromache snorted. "There's a rule?"

"Lots of rules," he explained. "Teenagers need rules."

"Oh," she said.

They leaned toward each other.

"My name's Sarcho," whispered Hector, in a nasal little voice.

Andromache giggled.

"What's yours?"

She giggled again. "Shut up!"

"What a pretty name. Will you kiss with me, Shaddup?"

"I guess...*Sarcho*."

With a superfluity of spit, and his tongue slopping around her mouth like an oyster in a shell, Hector kissed her. The kiss was even viler than Demuchus's had been. Andromache pushed him away, and then, for good measure, swatted him. Laughing, he made a half-hearted attempt to block her.

"That was awful!" she accused.

"I'm sorry." Hector laughed again and caught her hands in his. He sat down, pulling her gently to the ground with him. "I'm sorry, Ahndromahk...but you *said* you wanted a teenager kiss."

"Well, I take it back!" She shuddered. "I can see why you wanted to go back to our room, rather than reliving *that*."

Hector gazed at her from very dark eyes. "There are other reasons I wanted to go back..."

Andromache's face grew hot at the thought of his hands moving under her sheer blue dress. She supposed that he'd been having the same thought all night; the repulsive kiss he'd given her was no doubt payback for her teasing.

"But you're right," he went on. "Being a teenager *sucked*."

"I always thought it seemed like fun, here in Troy," said Andromache.

Hector scoffed. "Fun? With all those girls gabbling in their stupid groups, rating your kissing, making marks on their little score cards? I was a nervous wreck for at least five or six years."

Andromache laughed.

"I'm serious!" said Hector. "But of course, you don't dare *not* kiss them, because then they say even worse things — that you must have bad breath, or even the lip twitch."

Andromache laughed harder. "They don't say that!"

"They *do*! Paris is what he is because, years ago, some girl asked him to kiss with her, and when he refused, she spread a rumor around the whole city that his tongue was covered in fur. After that, he never turned anyone down — in fact, he didn't wait to be asked — but it wasn't easy to recover from a furry tongue."

By now, tears were streaming down Andromache's cheeks.

Hector looked around the alcove, sighed dramatically, and said, "This place is a cesspool of my old nightmares."

"Oh, come on!" Andromache chided. "I bet all the girls were lining up to kiss you."

"Are you kidding me?" He raised a withering eyebrow. "I looked like I was eight until I was at least eighteen, Ahndromahk! What I got were the pity-kissers — the biters — the eaters of garlic."

Andromache shrieked in laughter. "Stop — please, Hector! Biters?"

"I'm *serious*!"

"Well, is that such a bad thing?" she asked, through more giggles. "You bite *me*, sometimes. You bit me tonight."

"Oh, Ahndromahk!" he scolded. "That's not what I mean! Have your lips ever bled because of me? Have you ever felt like you were making out with a sea urchin?"

"A sea urchin?" she gasped. She was laughing too hard to say more.

"It's the truth!" he insisted.

"And w-what did the s-sea urchins say about *you*?"

He smiled. "That anyone who kissed with me got green teeth."

"What?" cried Andromache. Green teeth sounded every bit as frightful as a furry tongue.

"Because of my mint habit," he explained. "I told you, Trojan girls are cruel. They look for any weakness and exploit it. But I always thought, better Green Teeth Boy than Bad Breath Boy."

Andromache's laughing fit passed. She slipped her fingers through Hector's belt, murmuring, "I don't mind green teeth."

"No?" He gave her a kiss — a real one, of the type that had once made her slide off her clothing chest. There was nowhere to fall, this time, since she was already on the ground, so she pressed in closer to him. In the midst of all the kissing, her grey dress bunched up, leaving the diaphanous blue one exposed.

Hector stopped kissing her to stare at her legs. Very softly, he moaned, "Herb bread."

Andromache had never felt so sexy. She decided on the spot that she'd had enough of the alcove, enough of being a teenager. She was ready to go back to being Hector's wife. "Forget the herb bread," she murmured. "My old room is just at the top of this staircase…"

Winter

Chapter 50

Andromache had begun a new weaving project. Her previous one, the green and white striped cloth, had been claimed by Hector before she could make it into anything. For months, she'd lost track of it, and then, one day, she'd seen it folded neatly on a shelf near Buzzy's stall...

> *'What's that doing here?' she asked Hector.*
> *'A blanket,' he said. 'Fohr night patrols.'*
> *'Why don't you just take one of our other blankets?' she asked. 'That thing isn't even finished. And it's so small — it can't possibly cover you.'*
> *'You maked it,' he said, as though this one fact outweighed all other considerations.*
> *She blushed and mumbled, 'At least let me make you a new one that's the right size.'*

The next day, Andromache had started weaving a new blanket for Hector. She was still wary of flower patterns, after her disastrous first attempt, but she decided to try a motif of pale green vines set on a background of rich brown. So far, the vines didn't look bad — they were recognizably botanical. Besides, she knew that no matter how ugly the blanket turned out to be, Hector would treasure it.

The brown cloth grew as slowly as the others had — even though Andromache's weaving skills had improved — because she spent less time in the loom room than she had the previous two winters and more time at the stables. Even on days when it was too rainy to go out riding, she brought treats for the horses and played roodles with Xanthus. Uncle liked to go as well, to test his hard-won gaming skills against the grumpy stable master.

For Andromache, those visits were fun but disconcerting. She'd never gotten used to the soldiers' deferential treatment. Before her marriage to Hector, they'd barely noticed her; now, she couldn't pat Frondsia or make a single move of her game piece without some man bowing to her or offering her water.

"Just enjoy it, little niece!" Uncle counseled her, one day. "What's the harm in letting them fawn over you, a bit?"

"Eh? The harm?" Xanthus muttered. "I suppose there isn't any, when this city is already a slough of toadies and flatterers. Not much further down for it to go, if you ask —"

"I roodle you!" crowed Uncle. "I *roodle* you!" He looked at Andromache for confirmation. "Right?"

After inspecting the board, she nodded.

"That's the way of royalty," grumbled Xanthus. "Distracting people, interrupting them — then moving in for the kill." He sulked back into his carapace and couldn't be coaxed out for the rest of the day.

Most evenings, Andromache and Hector lounged around the kitchen, playing more matches of roodles. Cassandra and Paris occasionally joined them, but their usual companions were Uncle and Demuchus.

Hector kept his promise not to let Andromache win. As a result, she could no longer beat him, but she'd gotten very, very good. After playing against him, she found herself taking fewer moves than ever to win against Xanthus, Cassandra, Paris, or Uncle. She wasn't sure how she would have fared against Demuchus, because she never consented to play him one-on-one. His presence in her kitchen was something she tolerated but didn't encourage — all the more because of his latest project. Having apparently learned all he cared to know about Andromache, Demuchus had moved on to other subjects...

'I have at last decided on a topic for my final writings,' Demuchus announced one evening, as though they'd all been breathlessly awaiting that news. He and Hector were in the middle of a game of roodles.

'Final writings?' Uncle frowned. 'Are those where you write down who gets what when you croak?'

'Indeed they are not,' Demuchus huffed in outrage.

'If you want to be on the council, you have to write a treatise, first,' explained Hector. 'Something useful and interesting to Troy as a whole.'

'Oh, I see,' said Uncle. 'So, what are you writing about, Demuchus, my boy?'

Demuchus inhaled. 'I've selected a title...' He paused to heighten the tension of the moment. 'On the Command of Armies.'

For once, he got the exact response he'd hoped for — shocked silence. Hector was the one to break it. 'Really?' he said.

'Indeed. The council library has an excellent collection of texts for me to consult, although I might add that it's a topic I'm not unfamiliar with myself, as former first bowman of the northeast tower — '

'What?' asked Andromache, in disbelief.

'It's true,' said Hector. 'I heard he was good.'

Demuchus bowed his head graciously. 'But, close at hand, I have several resources even more knowledgeable than myself.' He nodded to Uncle and Hector. 'That is, of course, depending on whether or not you grant interviews to me...'

'Well, I will,' boomed Uncle. 'I could tell you stories that would flatten your nose.'

Covering his nose protectively, Demuchus thanked Uncle and turned to Hector.

'Sure,' said Hector. He looked surprised but flattered.

'Excellent!' Demuchus exclaimed. 'I'm most excited about the project. No one can say it isn't of use to the city, what with all the trouble those Achae — '

'I roodle you,' said Hector, with sudden ferocity.

Uncle whistled, while Demuchus and Andromache gaped. None of them had seen the attack coming.

Hector took Andromache's hand, under the table. Gently, he laced his fingers through hers and squeezed.

'Knowledgeable, indeed,' murmured Demuchus.

Hector ignored him. 'Do you know how to reset the board, Uncle?'

'Do I know? Of course I know, Sonny! What, do you think I left half my brain back in Santiya?'

'You said you wanted to travel light,' said Hector, shrugging.

'All I meant was I didn't want to get roped into bringing seventy-seven cases of honeywine for your mother, like last time...'

Andromache found Demuchus much easier to endure with Hector there. Even so, she felt happiest at the end of each night, when Demuchus returned to his own house, leaving her and her husband free to walk across the courtyard to their bedroom. The air outside chilled them. They had no choice, once they got to their room, but to cuddle under the blanket until they were warm again. To talk about texts they'd been reading or discussions Andromache had had with Priam about the Lorani. To doze off. To give each other massages. To kiss — and kiss — and kiss.

Chapter 51

Andromache hurried out of the dyer's shop and headed for home. In her right hand, she was carrying a basket full of thread. It felt heavy — promisingly heavy. *This should be enough*, she thought, before correcting herself: *No, it has to be*...

Time was short. No matter how she argued or begged, Hector had categorically refused to abandon the old, skimpy, green-and-white cloth. She had dreadful images of him huddling beneath it while out on patrol. His determination both touched and horrified her, and she knew the only way to break it was to finish his new blanket. *I'll just have to work faster*, she thought, stepping into the entry hall. *Or else spend more time on it — starting now*.

From just outside the kitchen, though, she heard Hector's voice. He sounded unusually serious.

"...I know, but they haven't gone past the fringes."

"You've been lucky."

"It's not *luck*!"

"I didn't mean it like that, Sonny. I know you've worked your asses off to keep it that way."

"Damn right. Besides, I don't care what people are saying. Troy isn't Kadesh, Uncle — and the Mudders aren't the Egyptians, out empire-building."

Empire-building? Andromache was startled by the return of that phrase, which she'd heard at the temple. Had the priests been talking about the Egyptians, then? Or the Mudders?

"The Hittites are concerned about them," said Uncle.

"About the *Mudders?*" Hector sniffed disdainfully. "They're completely disorganized!"

"That could change. I've seen it happen before."

"What do you suggest, then?"

"First of all, you might consider enlarging and repairing the defensive trench around the lower town. And then, there's that stretch of the western citadel wall. You need to shore it up, Sonny, or at least deploy more archers there, on watch."

"You think I don't know that? I've told Laoganus —"

"That's your co-commander, right?"

"Exactly."

"And what did he think?"

"The old ass won't listen to a word I say."

"That's not stable, Sonny — commanders who won't listen to each other."

"I know that, too, Uncle, but he's not going to change."

"Make him change."

"You think it's that easy? I'm not a king, remember? He's not going to do what I say just because I can out-bellow him."

"There are other ways —"

"Like *what?*" Hector's voice was sharp — raw. "You think I'm just going to *assassinate* him? Is that it?"

From the series of scuffling sounds that followed, Andromache could only assume that Hector had flown up out of his seat and was pacing around the room. Helplessly, she listened to sound of his feet. If they'd been alone in their bedroom, if Hector had simply awoken from a nightmare, she would have known what to do. *I need you, Ector — stay with me,* she would have implored. She would have covered his face with kisses, and before long they would have been lying back, exhausted, in each other's arms.

Now, though, she felt lost. It was the middle of the day, and Hector was fully conscious, and Uncle was there.

"Sonny! Hector! Calm down, boy. Calm down. Sit!" barked Uncle.

Hector sat. He was breathing hard.

"I meant you could talk to your parents — have them exert pressure."

"He likes them about as much as he likes me." Hector's voice still sounded ragged, but more normal than before. Andromache sighed in relief.

"Maybe," said Uncle. "But couldn't they talk to some of the other council members? Wrestle up a coalition, or something?"

Hector laughed. It was a black laugh, but reassuring compared to his earlier sharp cry. "Wrestle up a coalition?"

"Well, you can't expect me to know the jargon, Sonny. As you pointed out, all *I* have to do is bellow."

Hector laughed again. "And you do it well."

Deciding that this was a good a moment to join them, Andromache ran in and wrapped her arms around Hector's neck from behind. She squeezed a little too hard, making him grunt. "<u>Hey, there</u>," she whispered in his ear.

"<u>Hi, pretty wife</u>." He gave her forearm a kiss.

"Little niece," said Uncle. "Want to join us for a cup of honeywine?"

Andromache hesitated. "Do you want me to? I didn't mean to interrupt, if —"

Hector hugged her arms, and Uncle passed a cup over to her. Their invitation was clear. Andromache sat down next to her husband, so close that their sides were touching, and took a large swallow of the honeywine. "Oh!" she exclaimed, coughing.

The two men laughed.

"That'll set your gullet straight!" boomed Uncle.

Andromache, whose gullet was in open rebellion, coughed again.

"It gets better after the first drink or two," Hector said soothingly.

That, Andromache knew, from the jar of honeywine she and Hecuba had once polished off together. She'd just forgotten how strong the stuff was. Cautiously, she took another sip and managed not to cough.

"What do you think?" asked Uncle.

"It's nice," said Andromache.

Hector hugged her.

"Then you'll have to come visit, sometime soon. My country doesn't do a lot of useful things, but we do make excellent honeywine."

Visit? Andromache frowned. "Are you leaving?"

"Soon. I've been away a long time, already." Uncle chuckled. "I've got to make sure my wife hasn't forgotten me."

"I wouldn't worry too much about *that*," teased Hector.

While the two men laughed, Andromache frowned again. "Are you riding him back?" she asked Hector, trying to hide her dread. They'd been married for six months — for six months, he'd been home. She'd forgotten how to go a whole day without talking to him, and she hated to fall asleep when he wasn't beside her. Each time he had a night patrol training, she clung to him the whole night after. She couldn't imagine spending five or six days without him.

There was no chance that he would ask her to come along, either. She wasn't yet competent enough on horseback to take such a long ride — especially not on relay horses, who might not be as gentle as Frondsia. And even with all the time that had passed, and all the changes in her life, Andromache still didn't want to be hauled around in a wagon. She didn't want to be re-minded of the wagoner — that foul old man whom she had, for a time, called her husband...

Uncle soothed her fears: "Two of my daughters are coming to get me. They've never been to Troy, and my sister hasn't seen them since they were little girls, when she came to drop Sonny off for a visit. Come to think of it, he was almost as small as they were, then, even if he *was* a lot older."

Hector made a face at Uncle.

"Oh," said Andromache, snuggling closer to her husband. He hugged her again.

"They should be here any day now," added Uncle. "I told them to come around the full moon, so we could all have an ex-cuse to party. Not that my sister needs much of an excuse." He chuckled and threw back his last swallow of honeywine.

"I'll miss you," murmured Andromache. It was true. She liked Uncle's loud, large presence.

"None of that, little niece. None of that. Why don't you get out the roodles board, Sonny? Demuchus has been showing me some moves, and I bet I can thrash you — even if that cunning wife of yours helps you cheat."

"That, I'd like to see!" Hector smiled, but it was a poignant smile. Andromache knew that she wouldn't be alone in missing Uncle.

Chapter 52

"Paris, straighten up, I say! I won't have my country people taking *my* son for a hunchback!"

Paris sighed. "It's just our cousins, Mom. Who cares what they think?"

Hecuba gritted her teeth. "*I* do. And if I know Santiyan royalty, they'll have an entourage. So straighten up!"

"It's not enough that you made me buy cuttlefish for them? Cuttlefish!"

"Well, it's not as though I could ask Andromache to fetch it. She doesn't eat meat."

Silently, Andromache gave thanks for that fact. She'd never seen food as revolting as the cuttlefish that Paris had brought home from market.

"*That* is not meat," argued Paris. "*That* is what sick people cough up and spit out."

Hecuba turned green. "It's my nieces' favorite dish, and you're at least going to try it."

"Hector can have my share."

"No, I can't."

"And why not?"

"I don't want to offend my wife," Hector said smugly.

Andromache giggled, and Paris glowered menacingly at both of them.

"What are you afraid of?" taunted Hector, wiggling his fingers like tentacles. "That the suckers will stick onto your tongue while you chew?"

Paris clamped his lips firmly together, which made Hector laugh.

"Oh, that's enough out of both of you," Hecuba scolded. "Any moment now, your father will be back with the guests."

"So — until they get here, we're supposed to just stand around?" groused Paris.

"By all means, make yourself useful in the kitchen!"

Paris sat down on the bench behind him, letting his back slouch into an arc.

"Straighten up, for the love of —"

"Mom!" trilled a girlish voice from near the main door. "Hector! Andromache! Paris! They're here — they're all here!"

Cutie, who'd been sleeping, stood up on high alert.

"Well, show them in!" cried Hecuba. "Don't just leave them milling at the doorway!"

"All right!" Cassandra danced into the banquet hall and was immediately pounced on by Cutie. "Hi, girl! Hi! Oh, yes, you missed me! You missed me, didn't you?"

Next came Uncle, flanked by two girls somewhat younger than Cassandra. He had an arm around each, and, as they entered the room, Andromache heard them whispering to him.

"You were right, Papa."

"Yes, you were right. It's different —"

"Yes, different —"

"But nice."

Hecuba swept over to her nieces and embraced them. "Oh, girls! It's been too long! You're grown, already — and here I thought you were still tiny chicks. Down, Cutie. Down, I say! For pity's sake, Andromache — Hector! — when *will* your dog learn that hugging is not an act of aggression?"

Andromache picked the little dog up. "You can't just nip like that," she whispered. "They weren't hurting each other, you silly dog."

"You've met my dog, Cutie," Hector was saying to his cousins. "This is my wife, Andromache." He put his arm around her waist.

At his touch, she looked up — just in time to catch the silly grin saying '*wife*' had brought to his face. She wanted to hug him for it, but her arms were full of Cutie.

Meanwhile, the girls began to coo over Andromache:

"We heard about you!"

"Yes, when Hector came for our Papa he told us about you."

"Except all he could say was how pretty you are."

"Yes — that was *all* he said!"

Andromache blushed.

"He didn't tell us what you looked like, though —"

"In what *way* you were pretty —"

"Except he called you lum —"

"All right, all right." Hector cut them off, but of course Andromache knew what they'd been about to say, since Uncle, too, had teased him for calling her '*luminous.*' She kissed his shoulder; meanwhile, Cutie licked her on the chin.

The cousins giggled.

"Your dog is cute."

"Very cute."

"Especially —"

"Yes, especially —"

This time, again, Andromache knew how to complete their thought: "Her ears." It was the only possibility. At the moment, Cutie's red-brown ears were standing straight out from her head.

The cousins nodded. "Her ears," they agreed in unison, before chattering on:

"Is she friendly?"

"Can we pet her?"

"Sure," said Andromache.

Both girls sank their fingers into Cutie's fur. The little dog reached one of her forelegs out toward them, and they laughed in delight. After petting Cutie for another moment or two, they danced over to greet Paris. Cutie wriggled out of Andromache's grasp and ran after them.

"<u>Your cousins — they're nice</u>," Andromache whispered to Hector. "<u>But — but — but</u> —"

"<u>I know</u>," he whispered back. "<u>They ahre twins — I do not know them apahrt.</u>"

"<u>They seem funny, too. You told me once that princesses can't be funny.</u>"

After a moment's reflection, Hector explained, "They aren't princesses — they're *twin*cesses."

Andromache groaned. The sound caught in her throat as she saw two women moving toward her. Both looked to be a decade or so older than her, and both were dressed in gowns far too fancy to have made the trip in from Santiya. They must have stopped somewhere — the public baths, perhaps — to change before coming to the house.

They had plainly wanted to make a certain type of entrance.

"Why, hello, Prince," said one, bowing to Hector.

The other woman, too, made a bow. "It's good to see you again, Prince," she said.

Grimacing slightly, Hector bowed back to them.

Prince? thought Andromache.

"This is my wife, Andromache," said Hector, introducing her to the women. His hand moved back to her waist.

When the women snickered, Andromache assumed that Hector was grinning, again.

He finished the introduction, saying to her, "And these are Arinna and Ninatta, two ladies of Uncle's court."

"Pleased to meet you," said Andromache, bowing as best she could. Certain that she would never remember the ladies' full names, she dubbed them Rinnie and Ninnie.

The women bowed gracefully. "Pleased to meet you," said Rinnie.

"We're here to keep an eye on your cousins, Prince," said Ninnie, smiling coyly.

"Then you must be very busy," said Hector.

"Oh, no," said Rinnie. "They're good girls."

With a sly glance, Ninnie murmured, "You look different, Prince."

Prince, Prince, Prince, Andromache thought in irritation. Why did the women have to keep calling him that? Hector wasn't a prince — he'd made that very clear. And why did Ninnie have to use that syrupy voice, like she was flirting with him?

Flirting? Oh, gods, she probably *was* flirting with him! All the ladies of the court had probably flirted with him on his visits to Santiya. As the king's nephew, he would have been a prime target for flirting.

(*Or maybe more,*) the snide Voice suggested.

Andromache's insides froze. *Or maybe more.* Young women, pretty women, elegant women in fine dresses. Hector must have met dozens of them there, far from his mother's watchful eye — far from the innocence of Troy, where young people's trysts went no further than stairway kissing, and where even that had strict rules of decorum.

Was *that* why these two ladies had laughed when Hector introduced Andromache as his wife — not because of his grin, but because of *her* appearance? Because she was short and covered in dog hair? Because she was ridiculous, in comparison to the Santiyan girls they knew Hector had known?

Other than Penthesilea, Andromache had never given much thought to the women who might have passed through Hector's life. He'd never given her reason to. He was so tender, so devoted, so utterly in love with her.

(*But then, there's the way he kisses you,*) the Voice jeered.

Andromache thought of the spine-melting love kisses Hector gave her. Why was the Voice trying to turn *that* against her? *What's wrong with* that? she asked hotly. *Why should* that *upset me?*

(*Because,*) said the Voice. (*You know how awful his teenage kisses were — which means that he must have had a* lot *of practice making out before he met you.*)

Andromache tried to ignore what the Voice was saying. After all, any women there might have been were in Hector's distant past. They were nothing but vapor and shadow…

But no, that wasn't right. They *had* been mere shadow. Now, they were taking shape, becoming real. Suffocatingly real. Andromache was having trouble breathing. She huddled closer to Hector, even knowing that to do so made her look threatened — like some hovering, overgrown moth.

"Not for a few days," said Hector, in response to whatever question the women had asked while Andromache was fretting. He squeezed her hand absently, oblivious to her distress.

"Then you simply must take us out tomorrow, Prince!" said Ninnie.

Sounding surprised, Hector said, "I could, but I thought you'd want to rest, after your trip."

"You know we ride every day, Prince!" Rinnie laughed. "Besides, what other chance will we have to see your charming countryside?" Turning to Andromache, she added, "You ride, too, don't you, dear?"

Miserably, Andromache nodded. The last thing she wanted was to gallop around the hills with these women, next to whom she would inevitably look awkward, but she could hardly claim not to ride when Hector was standing right there. "A little," she said.

"Well, then you'll come, too!" said Rinnie.

"Delightful." Ninnie smiled. "Tomorrow, then."

Hector looked dubious about the idea but said nothing.

Andromache scowled. What was Hector's problem? Was he embarrassed, thinking of how she would look, riding alongside the stately Santiyans? Or had he been planning to relive old memories while on the next day's ride — memories that would be spoiled by the presence of his *wife*? Well, too bad for him! She was *going*! "Tomorrow," she croaked.

"But now, Prince," said Ninnie. "We really must say hello to your mother."

Again, the two ladies exchanged graceful bows with Hector.

"Enjoy your house," blurted Andromache. When the women furrowed their brows in confusion, she blushingly said: "I mean, enjoy your stay at *our* house."

Well done, she rebuked herself, as Rinnie and Ninnie walked away. *What's next, shooting wine out of your nose at dinner? How many more humiliating stories are you going to give them to share with the women of Uncle's court?*

Deep down, Andromache feared that she'd just asked a very dangerous question.

∞

PRIAM OPENED DINNER that evening with an oration on welcoming guests into the heart and home. Once he'd finished speaking, everyone began to eat. The gathering was far too large for a single conversation, so Cassandra chatted with her cousins while the two Santiyan ladies talked to Priam. Hector, Hecuba, and Uncle formed their own little group, which left Andromache with Paris.

As though he'd divined her insecurities and wanted to punish her for teasing him about the cuttlefish, Paris spent the meal listing off all the ravishing women who might have made the journey from Santiya in place of the two — as he saw it — mediocre ones who actually had.

"You wouldn't catch me in a stairwell with either of *them*," he muttered.

Andromache glowered at him. While listening to Paris make his tally of the Santiyan court beauties, she'd reflexively pictured each woman kissing her husband. She suspected that Paris knew this and hated him for it. "You'd never get *them* into a stairwell because they know about your furry tongue," she snarled.

Paris's eyes widened, and his smirk, for once, disappeared. "Take that back, or I swear, I'll —"

"You'll *what?*"

Steaming with fury, Paris lobbed a piece of cuttlefish in her direction. She flinched.

"What's wrong?" asked Hector, turning toward her. As his eyes fixed on the quivering blob of cuttlefish, he muttered, "I see. Well, little brother, Uncle's leaving in a few days."

"So?"

"So, it's back to *me* as your archery coach. Uncle has obviously been letting you slack off, as I can only guess that you were aiming *that* —" He pointed to the blob. "At my wife's head."

"My aim is fine, as you're about to find out!" Paris raised another hunk of cuttlefish, using this one to menace his brother.

Hector countered with a piece snatched from Uncle's plate.

"Boys!" cried Hecuba, noticing their face-off. "Lower those at once! Where's your dignity?"

Everyone at the table was now staring at them. The two Santiyan ladies twittered to each other.

Chuckling, Uncle brandished his own hunk of cuttlefish and asked, "Is this another Trojan game, like *joodles?*"

Hector laughed. "Yes, Uncle, but it's one even *you* might be good at."

Uncle launched the blob he was holding and hit Hector square on the nose. "Not bad, eh, Sonny?"

Hecuba sighed in disgust. "A pack of tomfool children!" she muttered.

"Sorry, Mom."

"Sorry, Sis."

"Sorry."

After the squabble, everyone settled back into their previous conversations — everyone except Paris, who refused to speak to Andromache. It was, for her, the one bright spot in an otherwise abominable evening.

Chapter 53

A ndromache was lying facedown on the bed, trying not to cry. Her backside was sore — although not as sore as her pride. Riding with the Santiyan ladies had been far worse than she'd ever imagined it could be. The whole time, she'd bounced mercilessly up and down, which was in itself enough to bring tears to her eyes. Next to the elegant Santiyans, she'd looked coarse and oafish.

That was nothing, however, compared to what had happened after Rinnie's horse nipped Frondsia on the rump. Andromache shuddered at the memory...

Frondsia bolted and Andromache, unable to control her, was carried far out into the countryside. The others chased her down, cornering Frondsia and forcing her to stop. As soon as Andromache managed to slither off the horse, Hector hauled her up onto Buzzy, with him, and rode headlong back to Troy. He was silent — stiff — positively reeking disappointment, even anger. Because I humiliated him, she thought. After all the riding lessons he'd given her, she'd failed — and by looking like a fool, she'd made him look like a fool. He didn't speak to her the whole way home...

The bedroom door crashed open.

"Ahndromahk?"

"Hmmph," she muttered.

"There you are!" cried Hector. "I went into the kitchen to look for Mom, and when I turned around, you were gone!"

"Hrmph mrmph." It was true. As soon as they were home and Hector's back was turned, Andromache had slunk off. And no wonder! He still sounded angry...

Hector flopped down onto the bed beside her. He kissed her between the shoulder blades, on the neck, on the ear. He knelt over her, surrounding her with his arms. "That was scary," he murmured. *Kiss.* "So scary." *Kiss, kiss.* "So scary, pretty wife."

Scary? thought Andromache. She looked over her shoulder at him and saw that his eyes were bloodshot and shadowed; his hair was exceptionally mussed, as though he'd pulled it half out of his head. He was a wreck. "You were worried?" she asked.

Hector stared at her as though she were insane. "Yes, ohff couhrse!"

All at once Andromache began laughing, while at the same time crying tears of relief. "You were worried!"

"Yes!"

"Oh, you silly man!" she cried. "I was fine. I just had to wait for Frondsia to stop. I couldn't make her do it."

"Stupid, stupid hohrse!" Hector growled. "I hate her!"

"That other horse bit her. It wasn't her fault."

"She huhrt you!"

"Just a little bruise," said Andromache, patting her backside. "It already feels better."

Hector nuzzled Andromache's ear.

"I-I thought you were mad at me," she said. "For looking stupid in front of everyone."

"Mad?" he asked, sounding indignant. "Not mad, you crazy woman — *terrified!*"

"You didn't say anything on the ride back…"

"You were *hurt*," Hector said gravely. "To take you home, *that* was the impohrtant. Talk can wait." Looking sheepish, he added in Truvan, "I'm sorry, my sweetheart. I can see why you misunderstood. I've trained myself never to look scared because in the army, it's better to look mad. Sometimes the training just takes over." He frowned. "If I was mad about anything, it was that I just *knew* something like this would happen! I hate big riding parties, with all different experience levels mixed together!"

So that's why he didn't want me to go! thought Andromache. She rolled over onto her back, took Hector's still-worried face in her hands, and kissed him. "Silly man! You sweet, silly man!"

He kissed her back, hard — as hard as he had that long ago day in the stables.

છ

"YOU'VE DONE WELL for yourself, Princess," said Rinnie. She, Ninnie and Hecuba were sitting in Hecuba's room, sipping tisane — or perhaps it was honeywine. Andromache, who had run upstairs to fetch the roodles board, heard their voices and paused outside the half-closed door to listen.

"You, *have*, Princess," Ninnie agreed.

"Sssssh! You can't let anyone hear you call me that," hissed Hecuba. All the same, Andromache could tell that Hecuba rather liked hearing the title, if only for nostalgia's sake.

"Sorry — Lady Hecuba. You have a lovely house."

"It's as large as the palace," Ninnie chimed in.

"Oh, heavens, no," Hecuba demurred.

"It *is!*" cried Rinnie. "And the gardens are infinitely better. That's plain to see, even if it isn't quite spring, yet."

"That's all my daughter-in-law's doing. Priam used to tend them as much as his priestly duties allowed, but once Andromache moved in, she took over for him. He has her working down at the temple, too."

"We know — he showed us, on the way up to your house. He seems very proud of her."

"He is. We all are. Honestly, I don't know how I managed to make even the simplest healing poultice before she came here! She can get almost anything to grow. She has a magic touch."

Andromache flushed with pleasure at the compliment.

"And not just with herbs," teased Rinnie. "I thought your son was going to pop open when he introduced her as his wife, yesterday — and tonight, he couldn't keep his eyes off her."

"Or his *hands*," Ninnie added slyly.

Hecuba sighed. "He wasn't doing anything — *untoward* — was he?"

"Goodness, no!" cried Rinnie. "He was adorable. He almost spilled the serving dish when she passed it to him because he was so busy trying to touch her hand."

"It wouldn't be the first time!" Hecuba laughed. "You definitely don't want to be sitting near them if there's a stew going around."

Andromache blushed again, this time in embarrassment.

"He was touching more than her hand when you sent them off for more wine cups," purred Ninnie.

"Ninatta! Don't be crude!" cried Rinnie.

"Oh, relax — I only meant a little kissing. He pounced on her just as soon as they were in the corner."

The color in Andromache's cheeks deepened. She supposed the kiss *had* been rather intense, but not without reason. Hector was still shaken from what had happened earlier. His need to touch her was understandable! And why had that nosy woman been watching them, anyway? It wasn't *her* business, whether or not they kissed!

"I wasn't thinking when I sent them there," admitted Hecuba, although she sounded pleased rather than upset. "They can't help themselves. You should see them in the morning, before work: *I'll miss you…I'll be thinking about you all day,*" she simpered. "Every day it's the same, except sometimes Hector throws in how smart and pretty Andromache is. I never thought I'd hear *him* saying that kind of thing."

The women giggled — Rinnie did, anyway. Ninnie's laugh was more of a sly cackle than a giggle. "Your girl doesn't seem to mind," she said.

Mind? Why would she mind? She *loved* being adored by her husband — and if their scenes elicited the occasional giggles, groans, smiles, winks, or eye-rolls, so what! The world could just look the other way!

"It's nice to see a couple still in the touchy-feely phase," said Rinnie.

'Phase?' Andromache frowned. What did she mean, *'phase?'* True, not all couples were as demonstrative as she and Hector — his parents, for one, had a much more stately way of showing affection — but they were different people. They couldn't be expected to act the same way. None of that meant that she and Hector were in a *phase!*

"They've been married for six months, right?" Rinnie went on.

"Maybe a bit more."

"Six months! An eternity. I had dresses a thousand times prettier than your girl's, hair combs, jewels…" Rinnie sighed. "Still, I couldn't even hold my husband's eye for six *weeks* — and his eye wasn't all that stopped working." She switched suddenly to Luwian: "~~His desire went a little *soft*, if you know what I mean~~."

Although Andromache couldn't speak Luwian, it was close enough to Lukkan for her to understand. There was no mistaking what Rinnie meant.

The other women murmured knowingly.

"~~His troubles may have had nothing to do with you~~," soothed Hecuba. "~~Sometimes, things just don't work right~~."

"~~I know~~," said Rinnie. She sighed again. "~~I never asked him why. Talking about it just would have embarrassed him and made everything worse. You know how men are! Anyway, I can only assume he lost interest in me. '*Things*' never worked for me again, except once, just long enough to make an heir~~."

"~~Mine started out that way~~," Ninnie volunteered. "~~Not because of me, though…he was just too old and fat to hold up the firebrand. But then, I didn't marry him for his talents in the bedroom. That's what lovers are for~~."

Hecuba sniffed in disapproval, but Rinnie giggled. "~~Well, the Prince certainly isn't old or fat~~," she said.

"~~Indeed not~~," purred Ninnie. "~~I foresee a long line of girls trying to turn his eye away from his wife…and some are bound to succeed, even if the poor thing *does* get some hair combs, jewels, or other tricks to heighten her charms~~."

The day before, with her self-confidence at low ebb, such a statement might have sent Andromache scuttling back to her room. Tonight, though, she had no doubt — she and Hector weren't like other couples, whose fires for each other died out. Her skin was still hot from everything they'd done in their bedroom that afternoon. She was tingling all over with thoughts of what they would do later, after everyone else had gone to sleep. Tricks like the see-through dresses were fun, but she didn't *need* them to hold Hector's eye! Any other women there might once have been were back in the shadows of the past — where they belonged.

"My son waited long enough to marry Andromache," said Hecuba, indicating her displeasure with the conversation by switching back to Truvan. "I can't imagine he's in a hurry to be done with her."

"Oh, but they always are, eventually, when the novelty wears off."

"His father isn't done with *me*, Ninatta!" Hecuba declared.

Andromache cringed. The information was far too personal for her liking. All the same, she couldn't help taking comfort in it.

"Trojan men may be different," Ninnie conceded.

"Well, that's wonderful news for you, Princess," said Rinnie. "You'll have lots of grandbabies."

"Sssh! Stop calling me that." Hecuba's protest sounded even less convincing than before.

"Do you think there's one on the way, yet?"

"How should I know?" Hecuba snorted. "If not, I'm sure it's not for lack of trying."

The ladies laughed.

Andromache flushed. First she was in danger of losing Hector's eye, and now she was spending *too much* time in the bedroom with him? Well, why shouldn't she? They loved each other. They enjoyed each other. There was nothing wrong with that! *'It's not for lack of trying,'* indeed!

As Andromache reflected on the words, though, her indignation turned to unease. Why *hadn't* she gotten pregnant, yet? She liked to think that it was the universe's way of evening things out — that after all the trauma she and Hector had suffered, they were being granted some quiet time together before their lives were taken over by a squalling, vomiting infant.

On the other hand, maybe something was wrong with her. Maybe that episode with the wagoner all those years ago had hurt her insides…

Andromache squeezed her eyes shut. She *wouldn't* let a silly comment shred her confidence again! What was done was done, and she couldn't let it bother her. Hector had married her because he loved her, not for the babies he imagined having with her. He'd never even *mentioned* babies! He —

"Sometimes it takes a while." Hecuba's voice, now serious, interrupted Andromache's thoughts. "Sometimes there are — difficulties."

Difficulties. Andromache shuddered. Like Hecuba, she knew all about such difficulties — and she didn't want to think about them.

The other women, too, fell silent.

"Well," said Rinnie, coughing delicately. "After everything, just look at your children. Hector is a dear, of course. I haven't had much of a chance to chat with your other son, this time —"

"Just as well," muttered Hecuba.

"— but your girl is charming."

"Cassandra is delighted to have her cousins here. I hope she doesn't chatter them to death."

"Don't worry — they'll get her first," Ninnie said grimly. "And there are two of *them*."

"Oh, now! They're good girls!" clucked Rinnie. To Hecuba, she said, "Are you going to miss your brother, the king, Prin — I mean, Lady Hecuba?"

"I will. It's hard for us to get away and visit each other, these days. But I think my son will miss him more."

"They've always been close, haven't they?" said Rinnie.

"Very," said Hecuba.

"Then the Prince will have to bring his charming little wife for a visit," suggested Ninnie.

'*Little wife — charming little wife,*' Andromache muttered to herself. '*The novelty always wears off. Prince, Prince, Prince.*' Oh, she knew someone *she* wasn't going to miss, once the Santiyans left!

"Perhaps," said Hecuba. "Perhaps he will."

"I don't know that we'll ever be back *here*," sighed Rinnie.

"Then stay longer — stay an extra week or two. Our house is your house."

"I wish we could, but the queen is missing her husband. She wants us back as soon as possible, which means we'll be leaving day after tomorrow."

"I understand," said Hecuba.

From the other side of the doorway, Andromache breathed a sigh of relief.

Chapter 54

Cassandra moaned.

"What's wrong?" asked Andromache.

"I can't believe they're leaving tomorrow!"

"Your cousins?"

The girl nodded, her eyes downcast. Never one to remain unhappy for long, though, she said, "But we've hatched all sorts of plans, for once I'm on the council. I think I've made more progress in three days than most council members make in a decade!" She picked up a lamp from the pile Hecuba had left for them. "*And* we get to have a party tonight!"

Andromache smiled. "Maybe you could visit your cousins in Santiya even before you join the council."

Cassandra's face fell once more. "I can't ride that far," she sighed. Listlessly, she set her lamp on a table, nudging it this way and that.

"Well, then I'll bet they'll come back here," said Andromache, trying to help her sister-in-law cheer up. "They can't have much to do in their own country, anyway, since they're seventeenth and eighteenth in line for the throne."

Cassandra laughed. "They don't have *that* many sisters."

"You know what I mean."

"I do." Cassandra smiled a mischievous smile. "What do you think would happen if the throne came to them — do you think they'd share it?" She giggled at the thought.

"They could wear one kingly robe —"

"And one crown."

Andromache paused. "Does Uncle really wear a crown?"

"I don't know…you should ask Hector."

"Then we'll have to wait till he gets back. He's out riding."

"With Uncle?"

"Mm-hmm."

"Do you think they'll make it back for the party?"

Andromache reached for a lamp. "Uncle wouldn't miss it. There's going to be a roodles tournament."

"I heard. Demuchus is in charge of it."

"I still can't believe they're friends." Andromache sniffed.

"I know! After all the fuss Demuchus has made about monarchies, now he'll be visiting one!"

"Visiting?"

"He's planning to go see Uncle in a few months. He wants to interview Uncle for his treatise, *On the Command of Armies*, and maybe even learn Luwian while he's there. He says it's a diplomatic and scholarly mission, but if you ask me..." Cassandra smiled. "Well, Uncle *is* a lot of fun to be around."

"He sure is," Andromache agreed. She wondered if Hecuba knew what Cassandra and Demuchus were planning. If not, the woman would be delighted to learn that her dreams for the Trojan city council were coming true, despite Hector's refusal to join it. The younger generations were devoting themselves to diplomacy, to strengthening ties with nearby countries. Yes, Hecuba would be pleased...

Andromache smiled privately before saying to Cassandra, "Anyway, that solves your problem of how to get to Santiya. I can't believe Demuchus would ride all that way on horseback, either. I bet he'll travel by cart, and maybe you could tag along with him."

Cassandra brightened. "I hadn't thought of that!"

The girl was dancing as she and Andromache finished decorating for Uncle's farewell party.

Chapter 55

The next morning, Andromache, Hector, and Hector's entire family accompanied the Santiyans to the main gates. "The stars guide you on your journey," said Priam.

With a guffaw, Uncle said, "I don't plan to travel at night, if it's all the same to you." He slapped his brother-in-law on the back.

Priam smiled. "Then may the road signs guide you instead, brother."

Uncle laughed again. "I was worried when my sister sent word that her husband would be joining the priesthood — and for real, mind you! Not like me, where I step into the solstice ceremonies twice a year and try not to wreck things. But you're all right, Priam. You're all right."

Meanwhile, Cassandra and her cousins were exchanging a twittery farewell, and Hector was standing beside the ladies of the court.

Prince, Prince, Prince, Andromache thought venomously, but she gritted her teeth and forced herself not to hover around him. Instead, she tried to think about all the ways that Hector showed his love for her — and about the cool, detached farewell he was giving the Santiyan ladies...

As Andromache watched, four arms flew around her waist.

"Come visit us sometime!" said one of the twincesses.

"Anytime!"

"Papa always leaves Hector's old room empty —"

"So there's always a place for you."

"And you can bring your dog!"

"All right," said Andromache. "It was so nice to meet you."

"Goodbye, now!"

"Goodbye!"

"We still have to give a hug —"

"To Aunt Hecuba!"

As the girls rushed off, the ladies of the court came toward Andromache.

"I wish you a safe trip back," she said politely.

"And *we* hope you don't wait too long before visiting," said Rinnie.

"Although you might want to hire an ox cart to bring you, or at least get a little more practice riding, before you come," suggested Ninnie. "I say this for your own good, my pet. Our terrain is far less forgiving than yours — and I'd hate for you to have an accident."

Andromache affixed the serene smile she'd learned from Hector. "Don't worry. If I ride there, I'll just share my husband's horse." She knew the retort sounded childish and insecure, but she didn't care. It felt good.

Uncle rescued her from the ladies. "Little niece...it's been a true pleasure," he said, kissing her cheek and pulling her into a bear hug. Her feet were dangling in the air.

"For me, too," said Andromache, her voice muffled by his shoulder.

"Take good care of Sonny, for me," he said, setting her down again.

She nodded. "I will."

Just as Uncle was about to turn away, he leaned in to kiss her other cheek. "And make sure you go down to watch him on the training field. You won't be sorry."

Andromache nodded again, although she had no plans to do as Uncle asked.

The Santiyan party climbed onto their horses. As they rode away, Andromache moved over to Hector and slipped her arm through his.

"It's a fair trade," he said softly, for her ears only.

"What is?" she whispered back.

"I'll miss having Uncle here," he began, "but I don't think I could've taken another day of those women. I'd forgotten how obnoxious Santiyans can be."

Delighted, Andromache kissed him. "Whatever you say —
Prince," she teased.

"If you ever call me that again," muttered Hector, "I'll —"

"You'll *what?*"

He touched his nose to hers. "I'll throw cuttlefish at you."

Late winter

Chapter 56

After Uncle's departure, Andromache prepared herself for the worst — a collapse in Hector's emotional state. He hadn't had a nightmare in weeks, but she knew that they could dwindle, only to resurge. Hers had certainly done so during her first year in Troy.

And, if Hector's nightmares came back, Andromache was now the only help he had. Uncle wasn't there to talk with him afterward. What if those talks had really made the difference for Hector, more so than being with Andromache? Or what if he needed both?

The night Uncle left Troy, Andromache lay awake, worrying about what would happen to her husband. Beside her, Hector slept in perfect peace — other than his feet, which, as usual, were twitching.

That's just one night, though, she told herself. *Tomorrow, who knows?*

But as one peaceful night followed the next, and the next, Andromache relaxed. However Uncle had helped Hector — and however being married to her was helping him — the results seemed to be lasting.

JUST AS LASTING was the presence of Demuchus in their lives. Andromache had fervently hoped he would stop visiting once his roodles tutee left Troy. Instead, he still came over nightly to play roodles and conduct his mini-soirees. Andromache could barely tolerate those visits.

One evening, at her limit with Demuchus, she stayed in the kitchen only as long as courtesy demanded before escaping to her room. When Hector came out later, he made as little noise as possible. He even hissed a curse at the squeaky door and whispered, "I am sohrry," when he found Andromache awake.

"I wasn't sleeping," she reassured him.

"Oh." He frowned. "Then you leaffed why?"

"I can only stand so much of Demuchus."

"Oh, Ahndromahk…" Hector laughed softly.

"And I need kisses to take away the bad taste he leaves in my mouth."

Hector laughed again but obligingly gave her a kiss.

"*Lots* of kisses!" she insisted. "And maybe almonds."

"Almonds?" *Kiss. Kiss, kiss.* "You know that's going to make me want to invite him back," Hector teased.

Andromache drew her husband close and murmured, "You know you don't need *him* as an excuse."

Demuchus's visits continued, night after night — and on those occasions when Andromache left early, Hector seldom waited long to join her.

Chapter 57

"You want to do what, this afternoon, after trainings?" Hector murmured sleepily.

"Hmmm — I don't know," said Andromache. She wanted to ask for a riding lesson, but she knew what he would say; ever since the Frondsia incident, he'd refused even to consider resuming lessons, no matter how she pleaded. She knew that she could have gone riding without him — Thoas or even Xanthus would have helped her — but the point was to ride *with* Hector, to share in his favorite activity. The last time she'd asked him was three days earlier...

'Are you kidding me?' he exclaimed. 'I didn't want you to go on that trail ride, but I didn't say anything, and look what happened. I'm not going to make that *mistake again!"*

'I told you,' she said. 'What happened was a fluke! That other horse bit Frondsia on the rump. How would you feel if someone bit you there?'

He made a face at her.

'Besides,' she argued. 'Riding lessons were your *idea.'*

'I know. I have some pretty dumb ideas, sometimes.' Muttering, he added, 'Like bringing that nag up here in the first place. I thought she was calm! I guess that was just in the pasture, where she didn't have room to show her true colors.'

'I suppose she's happier now,' said Andromache.

Unwilling to look at Frondsia every day after what had happened, Hector had taken her to live on one of Priam's farms, where there was a large herd of horses. He'd left orders that she be well-treated but never, ever, brought back to Troy.

'The foreman's a good guy,' said Hector. 'And when I left, that stupid horse was doing just what she likes best — running frantically up and down hills. But at least no one was on her back, this time.'

'I could start over,' Andromache suggested. 'With a different horse.'

Hector changed the subject...

The next day, though, he'd compromised. Together, they'd taken Buzzy out galloping across the plains, with Andromache in front and Hector's arms around her. Andromache had never imagined that the world could look so fast...

"You ahre smiling," said Hector.

"I know," she said. "I was thinking about the ride we took the other day."

He kissed her. "We can go again."

"All right," she said, and then she kissed him back, harder.

The kissing went rapidly from warm to torrid — at which point Hector groaned.

"What's wrong?"

"Kissing," he said. "Bad idea."

"Why?" she asked.

"Paris."

"Oh." Andromache frowned. "What did he do?"

"Noffing," sighed Hector. "We haff the archeries."

"Archery practice..." Andromache, too, sighed. "It was nice of Uncle to take that over while he was here."

"Mmmm," Hector murmured in agreement. "I had not to leaff this bed..."

"You don't have to, today, either." Andromache leaned in to give him another kiss. "Stay."

Hector eagerly succumbed to her kisses. Too soon, though, he groaned again. "Ugh...Paris."

"No — no Paris!" whispered Andromache, wrapping her leg around her husband's. "He wouldn't care, anyway, you know. He'd rather sleep."

Hector let his head fall to her shoulder. "I can't start that. He'll beg out every day."

"So?"

"So, what kind of commander am I, if I can't even keep my stupid brother in line?"

"He's the worst of the bunch!" *Kiss, kiss.* "Everyone knows that." *Kiss.* "No one would judge you." *Kiss, kiss...*

"<u>Ahndromahk</u>," Hector protested.

Andromache sighed. By now, she was half-crazy with lust, and there was only one way she was going to let Hector leave. "All right," she said. "Go meet your stupid brother! But then, no riding Buzzy this afternoon. Come home, instead. Right after training." Right after training...when he would be in one of his playful, energetic, swaggering moods. She would be there waiting for him — wearing her naughtiest see-through dress! — and the combination —

Hector was nodding. "All right."

"I mean *right* after," she warned him. "Don't stop at the bath house first."

"Yuck!" he protested, grimacing. "You don't want that, trust me! And if you don't trust *me*, trust my mom. She won't let me back in the house like that."

"Oh, she won't even see you," said Andromache. "And you won't be dirty for long — I'll have a bath ready for you."

"In *here?*"

"Well, we have a hearth and a kettle."

Hector looked dubious. "It's easier for me just to go to the public baths."

"<u>No, Ector</u>!" Andromache insisted. "<u>*Here.* If you have to leave now, then I want you back as soon as possible, so I can give you a bath</u>!"

Pause. "<u>All rahght</u>," he agreed.

She slid her leg off his waist, releasing him.

WHEN THE SUN was high, Andromache began preparations for the promised bath. For all the pressure she'd put on Hector, she was now feeling nervous. She'd never given anyone a bath, before, and had a vision of the afternoon ending in disaster.

<u>Just do the opposite of what</u> Cassandra's <u>friends did to you before the wedding</u>, she told herself. Where they'd scrubbed her flesh raw,

she would gently sponge Hector's back and arms — rub cedar oil into his damp skin — all the while, giving him peeks of her dress — *through* her dress —

Andromache sighed. First, she would have to lug firewood into their room. _A lot of firewood_, she decided, _so there's no danger of having to run out during the bath to fetch more_. "Hey, girl!" she called aloud to Cutie. "Want to come with?" The dog ran joyfully after her, and together they went out to the woodpile and back.

Andromache was making her second trip when she heard a groan behind her:

"Oh, Hermie," said Paris. "I'm not sure I want to know…"

"Good," snapped Andromache. "Then don't ask."

"All right, all right. You win. I have to know! Are you blocking off the windows, so my brother can't get in? Are you building a boat? Are you —"

"I'm building a *fire*," Andromache hissed. "For bath water."

Paris's face froze, mid-mock. "For *you?*"

She shook her head.

"Lucky bastard," he muttered. "*I* should get married."

"Good luck with that," Andromache retorted.

Paris frowned thoughtfully. "You want some help with the firewood?" he asked.

Surprised, Andromache nodded and said, "Thanks. That would be great." She could only guess why Paris had decided to help her — perhaps Hector had gone easy on him during archery practice, and he was showing his gratitude, or perhaps it was just the right phase of the moon — but she wasn't going to turn him down.

Paris wordlessly moved firewood across the courtyard and even hauled water without being asked. When the work was done, he wandered off, still silent and strangely pensive.

Andromache soon forgot about Paris in the midst of all her other tasks. Once she'd fetched coals from the kitchen hearth, she went back to the bedroom, started a fire, and set a small kettle of water over it to heat. Cutie curled up nearby. "Find a warm spot?" murmured Andromache. "I'm surprised you need it, with all that fur! But I'm glad you're comfy."

When the water was hot, Andromache poured it into the large bathing kettle, added some cold water, and stepped in. _Not bad_, she thought, glad to have had a practice run before Hector came home. Hurriedly, she scrubbed, dried off, and rubbed in scented oil.

I'll just put some more water on, she thought, when her own bath was done. *There! Now it's time for me to get ready.* She reached under the bed, feeling for the basket where her gauzy dresses were stored. *Here it is! Maybe today I'll try the white one...*

She slipped it on, pulled her bathing robe over it, and curled up on the bed to wait.

And wait.

And wait.

When the door finally squeaked open — she didn't know how much later — it startled her from a light sleep.

"Hey," said Hector, sounding not playful, but sheepish.

Andromache's eyes popped open. Immediately, she saw the reason for his tone: he wasn't the least bit sweaty or grimy.

"You stopped at the public baths!" she accused.

He sighed. "I know."

"Why didn't you want *my* bath?"

"Ahndromahk, you have no idea how gross —"

"I went to a lot of work," she interrupted, sniffling. "*You* have no idea how hard it was to lug all this *stupid* wood in here, even with your *stupid* brother's help, and now it's all for *nothing!*"

"No! I want your baff!" Hector implored. "All day, it is all I want!"

"But you cleaned up before you even got here!"

"A first step — I do not want to disgahst you during *your* baff."

"What's the point of a double bath?"

"What is the point to come home and disgahst you, pretty wife?"

"Well, you *wouldn't* have," she said defiantly. "I don't care about a little dirt and sweat."

"Not a little — a *lot.*"

"Whatever!" she huffed. "This was a stupid idea."

"No! It is not!"

"I'll just put this stuff away." Andromache reached for two thick cloths to grab the kettle. "Far away, in the back of the storage shed!"

"No!" Hector caught her hand. "Next time, I will do rahght. Next time, I will be in sahch filff when I come home!"

Andromache gave in and laughed. "You promise?"

"Yes! Yes!" he said eagerly.

"All right." She wrapped her arms around him.

Hector held her tightly and, after a few moments, when it seemed safe to do so, he kissed her.

She kissed him back. And kissed him, and kissed him. She knew it was a good kiss, too, from the way he melted against her.

§

THAT EVENING WAS SO DELIGHTFUL, in the end, that Andromache went on to offer many more baths. Each time, Hector arrived home with a token layer of dirt, one that he'd obviously applied after cleaning up at the public bath house. She pretended not to notice. He'd always been particular about matters of cleanliness, and if washing before he saw her was that important to him, she would let him. The habit wasn't worth fighting about — at least not as long as he came home on time, with a glint in his eye.

Chapter 58

"This is going to be so much fun!" sang Cassandra. She took Andromache's hand and began to swing it. Hector gave his sister an indulgent smile; Andromache snorted. They were making their way through the city streets toward Demuchus's house, a journey that was, for Andromache, awash in unpleasant memories. *Fun* was not the word she would have chosen to describe a dinner party with Demuchus.

"I'm so glad you and Demuchus are friends, now!" Cassandra said to Hector. "And I was right all along about a marriage to Andromache healing the rift between you — I was just wrong about *who* should marry her."

Andromache snorted again; Hector laughed.

"We're here!" cried Cassandra, rapping on the door.

A servant opened it. Andromache couldn't be sure, but she thought he was the same man who had antagonized her after her ill-fated kiss with Demuchus. Certainly, he was looking down his nose at her. Unable to do likewise to Cassandra and Hector, who were taller, he asked, "Can I help you?" His grudging tone told them that he was hoping for an answer of '*No.*'

Andromache longed to poke his puckering little mouth, but Hector smiled warmly and said, "We're here to see Demuchus."

"One moment." The man disappeared.

"Doesn't he know we're coming?" Andromache whispered to the others. "Demuchus, I mean. He could've opened the door for us himself and avoided this stupid little ceremony."

"What makes you think he *wants* to avoid a ceremony?" asked Hector, his eyebrow raised.

"Be nice — please!" begged Cassandra.

"Oh, Cassandra, take it easy — I'm not being mean. I like Demuchus. But ask him yourself if he would ever purposefully avoid a —"

Hector was interrupted by a thin, genteel voice: "Good evening, honored guests."

"Good evening!" trilled Cassandra.

"Hello," said Hector.

Andromache muttered a reluctant, "Hey."

"Come in, come in." Motioning for his guests to follow him, Demuchus glided off.

Andromache looked around as they walked. Nothing in the house had changed since her soiree days, unless perhaps there was an additional vase or two. *Mudder vases,* she thought with disdain. She couldn't imagine collecting them, no matter how beautiful they were.

Demuchus finally stopped in an immense, high-ceilinged room. "I thought we might dine in the banquet hall," he said. "The portico will admit just enough of the salubrious evening air."

Hector coughed; Cassandra shot him a warning look.

"Here we are, then," said Demuchus, gesturing toward the table. "Won't you take a seat?"

Andromache had never seen Demuchus's banquet hall before, as his soirees had always been held outside. The room was even larger than that of her in-laws, but it had a somber, even gloomy, air. It was a room that frowned on merriment. Outside, the courtyard looked as bleak as Andromache remembered.

"My lord," murmured the servant.

"Yes?" said Demuchus.

"The dinner is ready."

"Thank you. Bring it out, then."

Andromache snorted. Despite the ferocity with which Demuchus had always railed against monarchies, he ran his own household unabashedly as king.

Moments later, the servant returned with a platter of roast partridge. He walked around the table, serving a large portion of the dish to everyone. Andromache hadn't eaten meat since she was twelve or thirteen. She didn't even like to have it on her plate, but this time, there was no way out — she would just have to accept the glistening lump of partridge and try her best not to think about it.

Cassandra gave her a sympathetic look, and Hector gently squeezed her hand under the table.

The servant left briefly to retrieve a basket and a bowl. He then made another round of the table, this time ladling out vegetables and distributing bread.

"Please — enjoy," urged Demuchus, pouring wine for each of them. He then took a bite, smacking his lips appreciatively on the partridge.

Andromache erected a partition of bread to block off the meat. Once her vegetables were safe, she began eating — and discovered that the food was delicious. When interspersed with sips of the cool, effervescent wine, it rivaled even Paris's cuisine. Perhaps she'd been wrong to think —

Demuchus cleared his throat. Andromache looked up to see that he was staring at her.

"Is the food not to your liking?" he asked coolly.

"Huh?" she said.

"You're not eating anything."

Andromache took a bite of vegetables and chewed hurriedly. "I *am*," she said. "And it tastes very good."

"But you're not eating the main dish," Demuchus objected.

"Let it go," murmured Hector.

Andromache wasn't sure if he was talking to her or to Demuchus — although, if he'd meant to advise *her*, she reasoned, he probably would have spoken in Lukkan.

As for Demuchus, either he didn't hear the comment, or he ignored it. "What's wrong with the partridge?"

Andromache sighed. Against all odds, the evening had been enjoyable up to now. She hated to ruin it by telling Demuchus the truth, but she simply *couldn't* bring herself to chew and swallow the meat.

"Oh, my word, Demuchus!" sang Cassandra. "I never noticed the exact shade of your wall plaster, before. It's really lovely, you know! Darker than ours. I always liked the nice light tan we have, but this color suits your house better, don't you think?"

"Just tell me — *is it not to your liking?*" asked Demuchus, ignoring Cassandra and homing in on Andromache, who finally gave up trying to be polite. With Demuchus, as she'd discovered long ago, a direct approach was best.

"Not really," she said.

Demuchus's eyes widened. His cheeks puffed out.

"Andromache doesn't eat meat," said Hector, trying to soften the blow. "She hasn't for years."

"Well!" huffed Demuchus. "How *rude* of me, to put a plate of it before you, then."

Wary of escalating the affair, Andromache looked down. She wasn't sure what irked Demuchus more — a guest refusing to eat his food, or having himself failed to discover this key fact about her during his empirical study.

Demuchus clapped his hands, and the servant appeared. "Take that away," ordered Demuchus, pointing to Andromache's plate. "Fix up a bowl of mushroom stew for her ladyship."

Her ladyship? Andromache was about to make a truly nasty retort, when, just in time, Hector took her hand and squeezed it. She coughed back her words.

"Now you're choking? Dear me," Demuchus said frostily. "I'm sorry you find the meal so appalling."

"Oh, relax," said Hector. "*I'll* take some more."

"So will I!" said Cassandra.

Demuchus passed the serving dish their way. He then collected their cups, which he filled with a generous second helping of wine.

Andromache pushed her cup over to him as well. At home, she would simply have reached for the wine jar in the middle of the table, but at Demuchus's house, reaching wasn't an option. The jar remained beside him, and cups were refilled only when he deemed it appropriate.

Evidently, Andromache's moment had not yet come. Even once her cup was sitting right in front of Demuchus, he pointedly ignored it. "May I have some more wine, please?" she asked him.

"I chose this wine because it complements the flavor of the partridge," Demuchus said with dignity. "It is simply *wasted* on bread and mushrooms."

Her jaw dropped. "You're not going to give me any more?"

Demuchus pursed his pouchy lips and folded his hands on the table.

"Here — take mine," said Hector, pushing his cup over to Andromache.

"No," she protested.

"Please!" He winked at her.

"All right."

As soon as Andromache was holding his cup, he took the empty one and gave it back to Demuchus. "May I please have some more?"

Sourly, Demuchus poured out the wine. He had no grounds for refusing Hector, who had partaken of the roast partridge.

Just then, two sets of footsteps — one limping, the other marching — rang out on the banquet hall floor. The strident set belonged to the servant, who wordlessly gave a bowl of mushroom stew to Andromache before marching back to the kitchen.

The tottering set belonged to Demuchus's uncle, Ucalegon, whom Andromache had never met — or, more accurately, to whom she had never been introduced. As soon as he spoke, she recognized the harsh, white voice that had interrogated her on her first night in Troy.

"My lord commander Hector," he said, without bidding anyone '*good evening*.' "I need to speak with you, in private. Council matters."

"But Uncle," Demuchus protested. "We're having dinner."

The old man turned a glassy eye on his nephew. "Dinner can wait."

"It's all right," Hector said to Demuchus. "I won't be long."

Andromache could tell by her husband's stiffening posture that he didn't like Ucalegon very much, and she could see why. The man was as dry and abrasive as sand. In spite of all the tension that evening, she began to feel sorry for Demuchus, having to grow up with only Ucalegon for comfort or affection. No wonder he was so stunted.

Once Hector had left, Cassandra tried to revive the conversation. "Do you know of a text called *On Jirandibur*?" she asked.

Demuchus nodded slightly.

"Well, it's *so* hard! Every time I think I've grasped the meaning of the words, I read one more that negates everything that came before it. Do you have any suggestions?"

Earlier that week, Andromache had heard Cassandra confidently discussing the same text with her father. If she was asking for Demuchus's help now, it could only be to coax him out of his ill humor.

Demuchus, however, refused to acknowledge her question. Instead, he turned to stare in the direction taken by Ucalegon. "Council matters," he muttered. "As though I have no right to hear them. As though *you* have no right." He nodded to Cassandra. "Both of us shall one day be members. Even *you* —" Grudgingly, he indicated Andromache. "You have no hope of joining the council yourself, but as wife to one of Troy's commanders, you, too, have a right to hear the conversation."

Andromache shrugged. She didn't care about missing the conversation. Hector would fill her in on it later, if she asked him to. "Well, what can we do about it?"

"We can finish dinner," Cassandra said bravely.

"I'm afraid I've lost my appetite." Demuchus crossed his arms in front of himself and laid them on the table.

Andromache looked at Cassandra, who looked back at her. Were they supposed to follow Demuchus's lead? The mushroom stew smelled delicious, and Andromache longed to try it, but she was afraid of breaking any more mealtime taboos. As one, both women assumed the same posture as Demuchus.

They waited in silence for Hector to return. They waited — and waited — and waited. Finally, just when Andromache was beginning to fear that her arms might petrify, she heard her husband's familiar step.

"Hector!" she cried, turning toward him. "What took you so long?"

Even through his smile, his expression looked grim. "I lost my way back to the banquet hall. I'd forgotten how big your house is, Demuchus."

Demuchus gave the compliment a tight-lipped smile.

"Were you all waiting for me?" asked Hector. "Your plates are still full."

"We thought it would be nicer to eat when everyone was here, together," said Cassandra.

"You didn't have to do that!"

"It'll be cold, by now," Demuchus complained.

"Cold partridge is a delicacy in some countries," said Cassandra, touching his hand.

Demuchus gave her a look of surprised gratitude.

Once Hector had sat down again, they all turned back to their food. The mood had been spoiled, though, and they ate more out of courtesy than hunger.

"I have an early morning, tomorrow," Hector finally said, to excuse them. "Thank you so much for the dinner, Demuchus. We'll have to do it again."

"Yes!" cried Cassandra. "Maybe at our house, next time."

"Thanks for the stew," said Andromache, wanting to end the evening on a gracious note. "You didn't have to do that."

"On the contrary," snipped Demuchus. "You obliged me to."

Once more, Hector squeezed Andromache's hand. She took a deep breath and nodded farewell to Demuchus.

The walk home was decidedly more sober than the walk out had been. At the door, Cassandra split off, saying, "Goodness, I had no idea how late it was! And I still have to study for a while, if I'm to be of any use during lessons, tomorrow. I'm supposed to have all the major midland lakes and rivers memorized, and I just *know* I'm going to mix up a few of them!"

"Maybe you should put a map under your pillow while you sleep," teased Hector.

"Hmm," said Cassandra, considering the idea. "Maybe."

Hector laughed. "Goodnight, little sister."

"Goodnight!" Giving each of them a hug, first, she walked upstairs.

Hector wrapped an arm around Andromache. "<u>You ahre sleepy</u>?" he asked.

She nodded. She was ready for bed.

"<u>Me, too</u>," said Hector, and indeed he must have been. Although he stopped at the spring, as usual, he scrubbed his feet in a slow, half-hearted way. He seemed to be drifting, rather than walking, as they crossed the courtyard to their bedroom.

When they opened the door, they saw that Cutie, too, was weary. The little dog looked up at them and gave a few feeble wags of her tail.

"<u>Oh</u>!" cooed Andromache. "<u>She can't even get up to say '*Hi*.' Hello, baby. Oh, hi, there, puppy</u>." She sank down to the floor beside the little dog.

Cutie wriggled closer to Andromache. Her eyelids drooped shut.

Hector, too, sat down, murmuring, "<u>Oh, you ahre so sleepy — so sleepy</u>." He leaned over so that his nose was almost touching Cutie's; the dog flicked her tongue out to lick his lips. "Yuck!" he protested.

Andromache laughed. "<u>What did you expect?</u>"

"<u>Not tongues. I do not want to kiss wiff her</u>." Hector pulled the little dog onto his lap and stroked her flank, saying, "<u>Ha, ha! You cannot get me, now. You want to, baht you cannot. The tongue, it is not quite long enahff. Ha, ha</u>."

Andromache leaned against him. "<u>Ector?</u>"

"Hmm?"

"<u>What did</u> Demuchus's <u>uncle say to you?</u>"

"<u>Oh</u>." Hector's voice lost its teasing tone. "<u>He tell me, 'Go to the next meeting.</u>'"

Remembering previous times when Hector had gone to a council meeting — and had then, shortly afterward, left with the army for weeks on end — Andromache looked up at him in horror. "Are you leaving?"

His eyes met hers and softened. He reached out to stroke her hair. "<u>No, pretty wife. Not now</u>."

"<u>Some time?</u>" she whispered.

He sighed. "<u>I do not know. Maybe</u>."

Andromache gulped back a sob. She shouldn't have been surprised. Their marriage had changed nothing about the ways of the outside world.

"<u>Baht not now</u>," Hector said again, soothingly. He leaned down to kiss her. She clutched him tightly, moving halfway onto his lap and squashing Cutie in the process. When the little dog scolded them with a low moan, they laughed.

"<u>We ahre bothering you, Cutie?</u>" Hector asked their pet. "<u>So sohrry. Oh, so sohrry</u>."

Andromache fondled the dog's ears. "<u>What's the meeting about, then?</u>"

"<u>It is fohr to make better the fence</u>."

"<u>What fence? Do you mean the walls?</u>" she asked, remembering the conversation she'd overheard between Hector and Uncle.

"<u>Oh</u>." Hector laughed. "<u>Kind ohff. I want to say 'defenses.'</u>"

"Defenses," said Andromache. "<u>But that doesn't sound like a bad thing…</u>"

"It is not."

"Then why were you so — so —" She broke off, unsure how to finish her thought.

"Irritated?"

"I guess. Why were you so irritated when you got back to the table?"

"Becahse, that ahncle, he is not nice. I do not lahke to talk wiff him."

"Oh. Me, too." Andromache shuddered. "He's awful. I remember him — or his voice, anyway, from *that night* — the night I came here…"

Hector hugged her closer. "You remember?"

She nodded, whispering, "I feel really bad for Demuchus."

"I know," said Hector. "Effen wiff his silly wine games."

Andromache snorted. Now that she was home, she could see the humor in the evening. "Can you believe that? I've never heard of such a thing, refusing a guest wine because she wasn't eating the right food!"

"Demuchus is —" Hector hunted through his brain for the right word. "Unique."

"Exactly!"

Hector looked so pleased with himself that she giggled.

"What?" he asked.

"You're cute."

"No, no," he said, but too late to stop the dimple from appearing in his cheek.

Andromache touched it. "I was thinking that all night."

"What, that my face is full ohff stahbbles?"

Andromache smiled again, remembering how Hector had managed to procure the wine for her without treating Demuchus unkindly. "No, that you're cute. That you're sweet, even to Demuchus. That I love you. That I'm happier than I could ever say to be your wife." Her hands found his, and she interlaced their fingers.

Hector leaned in to kiss her. She could smell the wine on his breath — wine laced with mint. "I lahff you, too, my pretty wife, and I am so happy, too. Baht —"

"But what?"

"Baht my tush is sohre."

"Oh." Andromache laughed. "You want to go to bed?"

"Please yes."

When they moved over to the bed, Cutie hopped up with them. She curled into a ball and lay there, content. Meanwhile, Andromache and Hector slipped under the blanket and threw their clothes to the floor.

"Better?" asked Andromache, snuggling close.

"Mmmm...mm-hmm."

"Good. I like your tush. I don't want it to be sore."

"I lahke your tush, too," murmured Hector, sliding his hand downward from her back to her thighs.

A breeze blew in through the window. It was cool, but far greener than any wind blowing over Demuchus's barren courtyard. Maybe, if Andromache ever finished working on the temple garden, she would offer to help Demuchus with his. He had so little beauty in his life...

As Andromache inhaled, the smells of earth and rain-fed plants from outside mixed with the scents of her husband's skin: cedar, mint, and lemon balm. "Ector?" she whispered.

"Hmm?"

"Tell me a love secret."

He kissed her. "All rahght. Tonight —" *Kiss, kiss.*

"Yes?"

"I eat no bird at dinner."

Andromache laughed. "Are you serious?"

"Mm-hmm," said Hector. "I hided those bites ahnder my bread. I remember what you say once about Demuchus, how he smells lahke '*sweat and lamb.*' You hate his meat breaff. And I want your kisses mohre than I want bird."

Andromache giggled. "So, *you* didn't deserve to drink the wine, either!"

Hector shook his head. "I'm an outlaw," he whispered. "Just like you."

"But you *do* deserve the kisses," she murmured. "As many as you want."

Early spring

Chapter 59

Andromache awoke to a sudden blast of cold air as her blanket was torn off. Beside her, Hector was sitting up, swearing, rubbing his forehead.

"<u>Ector</u>?" she asked. "<u>What's wrong</u>?" Had he heard a sound outside, or had he had a —

"<u>Bad dream</u>," he muttered.

She leaned into him, kissing him softly on the lips. *I need you, Ector...*

"<u>I am in a meeting</u>," he whispered. "<u>A council meeting</u>."

"<u>In your dream</u>?"

"<u>Yes. I cannot leaff. That is the bad pahrt ohff the dream</u>." Hector forced a laugh — a pasty, yellowish-grey laugh.

Andromache didn't laugh with him. Whatever had woken him up, it wasn't a nightmare about the Trojan council. Those meetings irritated and exhausted him, but they didn't terrify him. For her sake, he was trying to make a joke. A pasty, yellowish-grey joke...

"Sssh," she murmured in his ear.

He shuddered.

"Sssh...<u>don't</u>." *Ector, I need you. Stay with me.*

THE NEXT MORNING, Hector seemed normal again. As they were finishing their breakfast, Paris slunk down, and Hector exchanged the usual round of taunts with him before dragging him off to the archery range.

After their practice, Andromache met up with Paris to go marketing. "How was archery, today?" she asked.

He shrugged.

"Good? Bad? About like usual?" she probed. She wanted to find out how Hector was faring, without Uncle there to talk to.

"It's always a delight, Hermie," Paris said dryly. "There's no way I'd rather spend the early morning than with my brother breathing down my neck." He leered at her. "Now that I say that, maybe *you* should take up archery — you might like it."

"Shut up, Paris," she muttered, relieved all the same that he'd made one of his typical dirty jokes. To her, that meant he hadn't noticed anything strange about Hector.

When the marketing purchases were all neatly stored away, though, Andromache packed a lunch and went down to the stables to check on her husband for herself.

"H-he's not in, yet, ma'am," said Thoas. "He went with X-Xanthus to measure the throwing range."

"I'll just wait back by his horses," said Andromache.

Thoas nodded. "I'll tell him, ma'am."

Buzzy and Thisbe were as happy as ever to see her, especially when she pulled two radishes out of her basket.

"<u>You guys are hungry, today</u>," she murmured, setting her basket on the ground and giving each horse a radish. "<u>Haven't you eaten, yet? Well, that's all right. I'll feed you.</u>"

Andromache measured grain into their feed troughs. After a moment's hesitation, she added a splash of wine. "<u>There</u>," she said. "<u>That should take care of you.</u>"

Two arms embraced her from behind. "<u>And what on me?</u>"

"<u>Ector!</u>" Andromache turned around to hug and kiss him.

"<u>Mmm, that is nice.</u>" He kissed her back. "<u>Baht the wine? You save some fohr me?</u>"

He was teasing her! He was making a real joke! Andromache laughed and shook her head. "<u>None for you</u>," she said pertly. "<u>The horses drank it all.</u>"

"<u>Greedy hohrses</u>," he complained.

"<u>You'll have to make do with kisses.</u>" *Kiss, kiss, kiss.*

"Mmm…" *Kiss, kiss.* "If I mahst." *Kiss…*

"Well, not *just* kisses," murmured Andromache.

"What else?" *Kiss.* "What else, pretty wife?"

Andromache giggled. "I brought you a lunch."

"A lahnch!" Hector poked her. "That is all?"

She giggled again and pointed to the basket at her feet.

"Huh…" said Hector, furrowing his eyebrows.

"What?"

"That basket — it looks familiar, sitting on the ground, like that."

Andromache blushed. She could just imagine how surprised Hector had been, that long ago day when he'd passed by Buzzy's stall to discover an overturned lunch basket and apricots strewn about on the floor. She still hadn't told him about her role in that adventure — although, judging by his face, he already suspected her. "You're imagining things," she said.

"Am I imagining the food in that basket?" he asked.

She laughed. "No…that's real."

"Good. I'm starved."

They decided to sit by the door with Xanthus while Hector ate. The old stable master naturally insisted on playing a game of roodles — and then, when Andromache beat him, another. And another.

"You're cheating, aren't you, Missy! You think you can just sit there and fool an old man?"

"No!" she cried indignantly. "I'm just — I'm just playing well, today."

"Prove it — play *him*!" Xanthus pointed at Hector, who seemed to have drifted off.

Hector blinked. "What?"

"It's a slow day around here," argued Xanthus. "Let your wife play you, to prove she's not cheating me."

"Oh. All right," said Hector.

He reset the board and made his first move. Andromache countered. Within seven moves — an unheard-of number — she'd routed him.

"Fine, Missy," grumped Xanthus. "You proved your point."

But Andromache wasn't happy at all. "You promised," she rebuked Hector.

"Huh?" he asked, looking first at her, then at the board, to which she was gesturing in annoyance. "Oh."

"You *promised!*"

"Oh!" he said again, understanding, this time. "Pretty wife, I try to win! Honest."

"You did?" Andromache asked suspiciously.

Hector nodded.

"Oh," she said. Knowing that he'd kept his promise unsettled her; she'd never beaten Hector in an honest game of roodles. Something was wrong with him. "I'm sorry."

He came around the table to give her a kiss. "No, do not be. You play better, today. That is all."

Andromache hugged him tightly. "All right," she said. Still, she decided not to play him again for a while. Her victory had an unpleasant taste.

ℂ

TWO NIGHTS LATER, Hector awoke screaming, "The stables! The stables!"

"Ector, what —"

"They're on fire! They're burning! *Buzzy!*"

"Sssh," soothed Andromache. "You just had a —"

"They're *burning!*" Hector yelled at her. "I have to go down there."

"I'll go with you."

Barely stopping to throw clothes on, they raced out of the house and down in the direction of the stables. It was all Andromache could do to keep Hector in sight, his legs were so long and he was running with such desperation. Her lungs felt like they were filling with sand...

When she arrived, panting, at the stables, she saw that they were unburned. Hector was standing at the door. He turned toward her, his eyes hollow and bleak.

"I'm so sorry," he moaned.

"Sssh..." Andromache wrapped her arms around him. "It's all right." *I need you, Ector. Stay with me.*

"I'm *so* sorry." He was shaking.

"It was better to check. How could you know, otherwise?"

"You told me." He rubbed his forehead. "I didn't believe you."

"I know what it's like," she reminded him. "I know how real they can seem."

He sighed.

"Do you want to go back to the house?" she asked.

Hector looked once more at the stables, reassuring himself that all was well, and nodded.

Andromache took his hand. He seemed to be having the resurgence in nightmares that she'd so dreaded. She could only hope her help would be enough for him.

At home, neither wanted to go back to their bedroom, so they instead took a lamp and crept up to the weaving room. Hector's new brown blanket was coming along nicely. "Do you like it, so far?" Andromache asked shyly.

Hector rubbed the cloth between his thumb and forefinger. "So mahch, Ahndromahk," he murmured. "I do not deserff it. Sahch a blanket…sahch a wife."

She kissed him. "It's not done, yet. It needs to be longer."

"I can watch you make it?"

"Now?"

Hector nodded.

"All right," said Andromache. She stood before the loom and began working the threads. In and out, back and forth, over and under, again and again. A short while later, when she turned around to glance at Hector, she saw that he was asleep.

Chapter 60

"Where's Hector?" called a voice from outside, on the courtyard.

"It must be time to torture the married couple," said Andromache. The house was once again full of guests; after she and Hector got married, quite a few young Trojan couples had decided to do likewise. "Are they going to have a roodles tournament?"

Hector shrank into the shadows. All night, he'd been withdrawn and agitated. He'd hardly spoken to anyone, except a few council members, and those conversations hadn't looked pleasant. Hoping to cheer him up, Andromache had lured him into the stairwell to repeat a few items of gossip that the Lark and the Otter had shared with her. Hector hadn't listened to a word of it. Throughout her stories, he'd done nothing but gaze wistfully at her.

"Are you still thinking about the dream?" she asked timidly. The night before, Hector had woken up gasping and trying to thrash his legs, which were pinned down by Cutie. After shoving the dog roughly to the floor, he'd turned over to bury his face in Andromache's chest...

They were taking you!' he cried.
'Who was?'
'I don't know! I don't know, but they were dragging you away — and I was chained to a wall — and there was nothing I could do!'
'Sssssh...I'm here,' she murmured. 'I'm here, and I'm safe. We're both safe.'
'I know.'

'It wasn't real.'

'I know. Baht it feels real.'

'I know,' said Andromache, tightening her arms around him. 'Sssh, I know.' Outside, she could hear a growl of thunder. She wondered if that sound had somehow sparked Hector's nightmare. Go away, she thought at the storm. Leave us alone. Leave him alone! Once the rumbling receded, she let go of Hector and bent down to the floor. 'Cutie,' she said. 'Come on. Come back up here. He didn't mean it.'

The dog flattened her ears and gave Hector a sick look.

'Oh, little girl,' he said sadly. 'Come here.' He held his hand out to her, and she licked it.

'I'll forgive you,' said Andromache, in the squeaky voice they used to impersonate Cutie. 'Your hand is too salty for me to stay mad at you.'

Hector gave a dry laugh. He lifted Cutie back onto the bed and the three of them lay cuddled close until morning.

Hector shook his head. "Not the dream."

"Then what's wrong?"

"Hector!" called the voice from the courtyard, more insistently this time. "Where are you? We need your help!"

Hector's face was blank.

"You should go," said Andromache.

"Hector, come on! Where are you?"

Hector took Andromache's hand. "You want a walk?" he asked softly.

She frowned. "You're not going out to the courtyard?"

He shook his head. "I want a walk."

"All right."

Holding hands, they hurried to the door before any of the other guests could stop them.

"Where do you want to go?" asked Andromache, once they were on the street.

Hector thought for a moment. "The sea," he said finally. Turning an earnest look on her, he asked, "You lahke the sea, rahght?"

Even as Andromache nodded, her stomach was icing over. She loved the sea, but the only time she'd been there with Hector was to bury her dog, Muka. Why wasn't he taking her somewhere they'd made happy memories?

Hector tightened his grip on her hand and quickened his pace until Andromache found herself jogging to keep up. As they raced through the streets, they passed few people. Most of Troy was probably up at *their* house, for the wedding, and everyone else was at home, or in a tavern. The only person she or Hector spoke to was the guard at the lower gate.

"Morys!" called Hector. "We need to go through."

Morys opened the gate.

Even the outer market was quiet at this hour — so quiet as to be creepy. Andromache drew closer to Hector, who'd slowed his pace somewhat.

"It is all rahght, pretty wife," he murmured, slipping his arm around her. "I am here. You ahre safe." It was almost a reprisal of their conversation the night before.

"Where exactly are we going?"

"The sea."

"I know, but —"

"By the riffer?"

Andromache nodded.

They walked down to the shore, near the mouth of the river Scamander, southwest of where they'd buried Muka. When Hector reached the water's edge, he sat down on a large, flat rock. Andromache sat beside him. In front of them, the water surged and boiled, its ferocity a remnant of the previous day's storm. Wind had torn through the cloud cover, leaving a bright sky over the rushing waves.

"Ector?" asked Andromache, squeezing his hand. "What's wrong?"

He said nothing but just kept staring out to sea.

"Please…you can tell me."

With a heavy sigh, he answered, "Stahff is going to happen."

"Stuff?"

"Stahff."

Andromache's stomach turned to ice. So, this was it. Hector would be leaving. It all made sense, now — the tense conversations with the council members, Hector's strange behavior. He'd been dreading the moment when he had to tell her. "When?" she whispered.

"Soon."

Andromache joined him in staring out to sea. It was dark, but she knew that a host of luminous creatures must be out there somewhere, either pulled down by the lashing of the waves near shore or floating in deeper water, where the sea was still. Too far out for her to see.

Muka, too, was beyond her reach. Months and months ago, some other storm had torn her from the blanket in which she was buried. She'd gone to ride the deep currents, and the fish had cleaned her bones.

Andromache wiped a flood of tears from her eyes.

She wanted to be in the sea. She wanted to be out where the creatures were, to feel the waves pulling at her skin. Lowering her feet into the water, she took a step, and then another, before Hector caught her hand.

"What are you doing?" he demanded.

"My feet are hot." Her eyes were hot; so was her hand, locked in Hector's. The rest of her was ice.

"Stay by me — please, Ahndromahk."

She allowed herself to be drawn back onto the rock. *'Stay by me'* — her magic words, or almost. The words that called Hector back from his nightmares. What if she said them now? *'Stay by me — please, Ector!'* Would he do it? Or were those words powerless in the world that they'd now entered?

With his arms wrapped tightly around her, Hector lay down on the rock. Now, they were facing the sky. It didn't look much different from the sea — both had a sheen of water over them. Andromache blinked twice, rapidly, and the sheen disappeared from the sky.

"It is pretty, here," said Hector.

Andromache nodded. She hated it all.

"Ahndromahk…say something."

What was she supposed to say?

"Ahndromahk?"

"Hmm?"

"You won't go outside the walls while I'm gone, will you? I don't want to think about you out there, alone…"

To think about her out there, alone — to be distracted — to wind up with bruises, or worse —

Andromache started to shake. "I won't go out there," she whispered.

"Thank you."

She wished there were something she could ask of *him* to make herself feel better, but nothing came to her. "Ector?" she finally said.

"Hmm?"

"Walk through the waves with me."

Hector nodded and sat up, sliding his feet into the sea. For hours, Andromache walked with him, her hand in his, their legs stirring the water into eddies each time they took a step. Eddies — swirls — like those that swept the Lorani on their dance around the sky…

Chapter 61

Normally, Andromache would have been thrilled to see Hector burst through their bedroom door and throw back the lock — such ferocity on his part would have meant an extreme state of lust. The day after their conversation by the sea, however, she knew the gesture had a very different meaning.

"Oh," she said softly, or maybe she just mouthed it. She wasn't sure any sound had come out. She looked at the floor, thinking over and over again the same stupid thought: *He can't leave yet — I haven't finished his blanket.*

While her eyes were downcast, Hector came over to her. He wrapped his arms around her, kissing her hair, then her mouth.

She didn't kiss back.

"Ahndromahk…" He kissed her again.

This time, she moved her lips against his, but without any feeling.

"Please," he implored her.

It was a piteous sound. Andromache had never heard Hector begging, before. She supposed that he'd never had reason to. Now, though, the macabre thought that this time might be their last left her unable to make love with him.

"Ahndromahk — please." Gently, he touched her. "Please. Maybe it is long befohre we ahre together, again."

She started to cry.

"*Please,*" whispered Hector.

Andromache looked up to see a ghost of the expression he'd been wearing in the outpost stable, when she'd found him kneeling in vomit. All he wanted were a few moments of sweetness and comfort before he left, to help him forget what was to come. It was so little to ask...

Slowly, she removed her clothes and lay down. Hector did the same. He held her close and began kissing her.

Andromache could barely stand it. His skin was too hot; his breathing, too loud. She could hear too clearly the sounds his throat made when he swallowed. His arms were too tight — they were crushing her. Almost at once, she wriggled away.

Hector let her go. His fingers combed several times through the ends of her hair; his hand closed into a loose fist, then released. "It is the hour," he murmured.

Andromache let out a strangled cry. Too late, she clung to him, desperately kissing his face, his arms, his chest, his neck, his hands, his hair — any part of him that she could reach.

For a moment, he let her...but then, he pulled away.

She wasn't supposed to cry, now. Andromache knew that. Hector's parting image of her shouldn't be a weepy, red-faced, sodden wife, yet here she was, making a mess of their farewell. But she couldn't help herself. She didn't *want* a farewell! They'd only just started their life together, and now — and who knew? — and it wasn't *fair*, and —

"Ahndromahk," whispered Hector.

She looked up to see that he was dressed again. She opened her mouth to tell him everything she needed to say, but this time she was certain that no words came out.

"I know," he said. "I lahff you."

Then he was gone.

Shortly after, from inside the house, Andromache heard Cutie's angry shrieks of goodbye.

ANDROMACHE LAY CURLED in a miserable ball. She was lost to the world, lost to time, out of touch with everything around her until Cutie scratched at the door. Andromache let her in with a whispered, "Hey girl," and crept back to bed.

Equally despondent, Cutie hopped up beside her and lay down without squirming, scratching, or licking. For hours, they huddled together on the bed. Andromache stayed on Hector's side, her face buried in the sheets where he'd so recently been. Cutie nestled into the crook of Andromache's legs.

As they lay there, Andromache imagined that she'd been sent back in time to her first few days in Troy, when she'd done nothing but cry and cling to Muka. That long-ago agony seemed so small in comparison to the present one that she took comfort in the illusion — at least until it was shattered by a hint of cedar, mint, or lemon balm.

Night fell. With the fading of light came the heightening of sound. Scraping sounds…brushing sounds. Were they plants, moving in the wind? Mice, scuttling around? Or were they the sandaled footsteps of a marauder, sneaking out to her room, knowing that she was alone?

Above her, the curtain rustled. Andromache looked up just long enough to see that something solid was there before reburying her face in the pillow. What *was* it? *Who* was it? If she stayed still, maybe it would go away.

Instead, the rustling persisted, then grew louder — loud enough that Cutie barked.

Andromache let out a shriek and batted the curtain as hard as she could. A startled bird cheeped and flew away.

Cutie barked several more times.

"Just — a — bird," gasped Andromache, whose heart was still fluttering.

Cutie readied herself to spring off the bed: she knew what a '*bird*' was and wanted to chase it.

"I'm not letting you out," said Andromache. "I'm not letting you leave me here, alone!"

After a small moan or two of protest, Cutie lay back down and let Andromache hold her.

JUST BEFORE DAWN, Andromache sank into a sleep just deep enough for dreams....

She was in a tunnel, the one leading under the city walls to the country-side. She was climbing up the stairway to the exit. Then the stairs began cracking beneath her, and she fell down to the tunnel floor. She tried to go back to the other end of the tunnel, but it had been filled in with dirt. The dirt was still being pushed in toward her — it was about to engulf her —

Andromache awoke out of breath, certain that she was going to suffocate. Instinctively, she reached out for Hector, but instead of landing on warm flesh, her hand sank through the air. The sensation gave her a sickening jolt, similar to when the stairs had given way beneath her in the dream.

She opened her eyes and realized that she was lying on Hector's side of the bed; she'd reached out toward the open air of the room. Her own side of the bed was empty. It made sense. *She* felt empty.

Since marrying Hector, Andromache hadn't had that many nightmares. The few times she did, Hector had held and soothed her until the dreams faded. Now, she had no one to comfort her except Cutie, who apparently hadn't forgotten about the bird from the night before and was pacing in front of the door.

The sun was up.

"All right," grumbled Andromache. "I'll let you out, now, I guess. And thanks a lot." As she opened the door, Cutie gave a sharp bark and ran over to the spring, where someone was filling a water jar. When Cutie saw that it was Hecuba, not Hector, her joy fell off slightly, but she still gave the woman's feet a thorough licking.

"Hello. Yes, hello. Yes, I'm happy to see you, too. Now, take your tongue off my toes and get a drink," said Hecuba. Her voice carried through the clear air of the courtyard. "Where's your mama?" Hecuba spun around to see Andromache, hovering at the door to her room. "Hello, dear," she called.

"Hello," said Andromache.

Hecuba walked over to her. "It's going to be lovely day," she said, as though nothing was awry.

Andromache nodded dully.

"Not as cool as the past few days," added her mother-in-law.

Which meant that Hector would now be sweating under the weight of his armor. The shield would be chafing his arm.

"Not as cool." Hecuba shook her head. "But dry, at least."

As Hector rode toward wherever he was going, he would be inhaling the dust kicked up by a thousand horses. His mouth would be parched. His lips would crack.

Hecuba frowned. "Do you think you'll go down to the temple gardens, today, dear?"

And listen to the priests arguing about war and the will of the gods? Not likely. In fact, Andromache wasn't going to leave the house at all. She wasn't even going to open the door to let guests in — guests would want to talk about Hector's military prowess, and she was in no mood to listen.

"Dear?" prodded Hecuba.

Andromache shook her head in answer to her mother-in-law's question.

"Well, that's all right. Maybe another day."

Maybe — or maybe *not*.

Hecuba cleared her throat. "I was thinking…" she began.

Andromache looked up.

"I was thinking," the woman said again. "That is, Priam and I were thinking — that you might like to stay in the main house for a while. You're so far from everyone else, out here. Everyone except your little monster, that is." Cutie had put her front paws up on Hecuba, and the woman was petting her fondly.

Andromache considered the proposal. Last night had been a torment. Would tonight be any different? Except for the occasional evenings when Hector had patrol training, going to sleep had become something Andromache did only with her husband beside her, touching her. Most often, they both slept on their sides. If they were facing each other, they held hands, and she fell asleep to the warmth of his breath on her cheek. If they were back-to-back, she felt his spine against hers. On chilly nights, he curled around her with his arm encircling her. That was her favorite way to sleep, intimate and safe.

Her nights were going to be lonely until Hector came back. Having other people down the hall wouldn't change that. Besides, Andromache would have to lie on clean sheets, freshly laundered, smelling only of flower oils...

"Thank you," she said softly. "But I think I'll stay out here."

"Very well." Hecuba nodded. "Then would you at least like to come up to my room for a sip or two of honeywine?"

Andromache hesitated. "Can I bring <u>Cutie</u>?" she murmured.

"Of course," said Hecuba. "But she'll have to content herself with water. She's silly enough as it is, without a belly full of wine."

Chapter 62

Two evenings later, Andromache was in the kitchen, picking at a plate of dried apricots. She was in a very cranky mood.

Out at the main door, she heard a knock — or, rather, three polite, insistent taps. She ignored the sound. Whoever was out there, she didn't care — she didn't want to see anyone.

Tap, tap, tap. After a delicate pause, *tap, tap, tap.* The sound promised to go on all night.

Go ahead and tap, Andromache thought sourly. *I can outwait you*. If she knew nothing else, she knew how to wait. She was becoming an expert at it.

Tap, tap, tap.

"Very well!" called Hecuba, with an ill grace to match Andromache's own. She marched down the front stairs and over to the door. Opening it, she said, "Oh." Her voice held a mixture of surprise and misgiving. "Come in, then. I'll track down Cassandra for you."

There was a muffled reply.

"Oh." Hecuba now sounded stiff. "Well, I believe she's in the kitchen."

The kitchen? Andromache sucked in her breath. She would have just enough time to leave, if she ran…but then she would make a liar of Hecuba. Pinned down by guilt, she stayed, awaiting her guest. Dreading him, or her.

"Good evening," said a familiar voice.

Andromache frowned. Demuchus! If not the very last person she'd been expecting, he was at least close to the bottom of the list. He hovered near the table, waiting to be asked to seat himself. "What are you doing here?" she demanded.

"I'm here to play roodles," he said, removing a game board from beneath his arm and setting it before her, on the table.

Andromache knew the board only too well. Demuchus always brought his own; he didn't trust theirs. "Well, in case you haven't heard, Hector's not here."

Finally, Demuchus sat, although he still hadn't been asked to do so. "I'm here to play roodles with *you*. And I must apologize for being so rude as to ask, but since you haven't offered, I would very much like something to drink."

Andromache bristled. "All we have is water."

"Ah!" he exclaimed, brightening. "You must mean water from the wellspring out on the courtyard! The most exquisite water in the city."

Wellspring! The word made Andromache seethe with irritation. Why did he have to call it a wellspring? Why couldn't he just say spring, like everyone else? She took as long as she could, fetching him the water, to put off going back to the table. Eventually, though, she had no choice but to set the cup down before Demuchus.

"So," he sighed, after an exceptionally loud gulp of water. "Which color would you like to be?"

"I don't *want* to play roodles!" snapped Andromache, thinking, *And least of all with you!*

"But you *must*," spluttered Demuchus.

"Says who?"

"Says your husband."

"I told you — *he's not here!*"

"I know that," Demuchus said soothingly.

As usual, his attempts to calm Andromache had the opposite effect: "Then why are *you* here?" she cried out.

"I promised your husband that I would come over to play roodles with you during his absence."

"You promised my husband — to come over *here* — and play roodles with *me?*"

"Indeed," said Demuchus with great dignity. "And I do not break my promises."

"Well," said Andromache, rising to her feet. "I'll speak to *my husband* as soon as he gets home and explain to him that it wasn't your fault the promise was broken."

"But he wanted to make sure you had company. He didn't want you to be lonely."

Something sincere broke through Demuchus's stuffiness — true liking of Hector, the desire to fulfill a promise made to a friend — and with it, Andromache's fury collapsed. What had Hector been *thinking*? How could he expect her not to be lonely? "I don't want to play roodles," she repeated, her voice cracking.

"Andromache —"

She held up her hand. "I'm not doing it, so you can put that board away." When Demuchus made no move to do so, she did it for him. The look of shame and failure crossing his face as the roodles board closed led her, for the second time that evening, to act out of guilt. "But I was thinking…your courtyard garden needs some work. Tomorrow evening, I'll come over to tend it for a while. I'll bring Cassandra, and you can both keep me company. Play roodles with her, if you want. That way, you can keep your promise — the spirit of it, anyway."

Demuchus sniffed angrily at her suggestion. "I will *not* have Hector's wife at my house, working like a *servant*."

"*Hector's wife* can do whatever she wants!" Andromache retorted. Her words had a haughty tone she hadn't intended and didn't like. Demuchus, on the other hand, seemed to respond to it.

"Agreed," he said. "However, I'll only allow it on the condition that you and Cassandra come to dinner, first."

Andromache sighed. She'd thought to spend an hour, maximum, at Demuchus's house. This was shaping up to be a much longer outing. But what could she do? It had been her idea, more or less. "Agreed."

Once Demuchus had left, Hecuba marched into the kitchen. It was beneath her dignity as a former princess to linger with her ear pressed to doorways, but plainly, she'd wanted to. In her eyes, nothing could redeem Demuchus for having once used *her* courtyard to force a kiss on Andromache.

"What did *he* want?" asked Hecuba, coming straight to the point.

"To play roodles," Andromache said tiredly.

Her mother-in-law sniffed. "Why on earth would he think you'd want to do *that*?"

"I guess Hector made him promise to entertain me while he's gone," sighed Andromache. Her eyes were prickling with tears again.

"Oh, my girl," murmured Hecuba, smoothing Andromache's hair. "It won't be long. He'll be back soon."

Andromache nodded, although she put no trust in those standard words of comfort. Hecuba had no real notion of when Hector would be home —

Andromache straightened. Or *did* she? Hecuba was married to a council member, after all, and was herself an ambassador! "Do you know where he went?"

"He didn't tell you?"

"I didn't ask." That question had been one of many things locking her throat down just before her husband left.

"South," answered Hecuba.

"South?" Hector had gone south once before, just after their Lorani hunt, just before she realized that she loved him...

"South," Hecuba confirmed. "Troy has a number of allies down that way. They need help. They've been getting raided."

"By — by —"

"By the Achaeans."

Mudders! Andromache's stomach knotted. "The ones who attacked Lyrnassa."

"Yes," said Hecuba. "That was the closest they've ever been to Troy." She sighed heavily. "And we can't have them coming any closer."

Andromache's head was swimming. She thought of Hector, wearing his Raider armor as he had in Lyrnassa, once again facing the Mudders. Looming over them — streaked with gore — hacked open, leaking dark blood — stumbling —

"You're shivering," said Hecuba. "Would you like a tisane?"

"A tisane would be nice," whispered Andromache. "Maybe rose petal, or linden blossom?" Anything but mint. Mint would make her cry.

As Hecuba set about making their drinks, she returned to the subject of Demuchus. "In any case, Andromache, dear, don't feel bad about sending that cad away. Your husband has some rather —" She coughed. "*Original* — ideas, sometimes, and you can't be expected to comply with all of them."

"I told Demuchus that Cassandra and I would come over, tomorrow. The plants on his courtyard are in even worse shape than the ones at the temple."

"You're going to *garden* for him?"

Andromache nodded.

"Well. You do what you have to do." Hecuba gave a sharp nod and repeated herself: "You do what you have to do."

Chapter 63

Before going to Demuchus's house, Andromache and Cassandra stopped by the stables.

"I want to see Thisbe," Andromache explained. "She's missing Buzzy right now."

"Oh, the poor little thing!" murmured Cassandra.

Thisbe greeted them with her usual gentle whickering. Never as greedy as her golden friend, she didn't butt her head against Andromache's arm but waited patiently for a radish treat. When she'd finished crunching, Andromache led her out into the early spring sunshine. The pony shook her mane and trotted pertly around the pasture.

"She looks happy," said Cassandra. "She's showing off for us."

Andromache nodded. "She loves the attention. I need to come down here more often."

"Any time you want to, I'll come with." Cassandra took Andromache's hand, but she was looking elsewhere: one of the few remaining young men had caught her eye. "Must be one of the archers under that other commander. I'll have to ask Paris about him," she muttered to herself.

As they were leaving, Andromache turned to Thoas, who was guarding the door. "Is Xanthus around?" she asked.

"N-no, ma'am," he said.

"Can you please tell him '*hi*' for me?"

"I — I'll tell him, ma'am."

"Thank you, Thoas."

Cassandra smiled winsomely at the young guard. He blushed and looked away.

"I told you not to tease him," hissed Andromache.

"Yes, ma'am!" Cassandra giggled.

Andromache poked the girl's ribs with her elbow.

"Oh, don't be mad at me," sighed Cassandra. "I can't help myself! Everyone's looking cute, today. I've had so much reading to do, lately, that it's been *forever* since I've kissed with anyone!"

Andromache didn't answer. She was lost in shame. Days earlier, *she'd* had the chance to kiss with someone — someone she loved, too, not just a random cute boy — someone who was leaving, to return no one knew when — and she'd sat there with wooden lips. Stone lips. Who was *she* to criticize Cassandra, or anyone else, on the subject of kissing?

"Let me know if you're coming back down here," Cassandra pleaded. "It's worth a try, don't you think? Even if they *are* all scared of my brother?"

With the word '*brother*,' the girl let out a small sigh and then fell silent. Neither she nor Andromache spoke again until they'd reached Demuchus's house.

Once they were sitting with Demuchus, though — out on his courtyard, since the weather that evening was mild — Cassandra's merriment returned. Because of her, the three of them managed to have a reasonably enjoyable dinner. Demuchus even refilled Andromache's wine cup without being asked.

Andromache drifted in and out of the conversation. Whenever she lost focus, she inspected the plant life out on the courtyard. There was very little to see — just three scrawny trees and a few solemn pots of herbs. It would never be lush, there, but by trimming off the dead foliage, she could at least make the place look less funereal.

Dinner ended. Andromache fled to the herbs, while Cassandra and Demuchus continued their conversation. Andromache was half listening to their thoughts on the importation of spices when a white voice sliced through the courtyard air:

"A word, boy."

Ucalegon was glowering at them. He fixed Cassandra with his stony eyes and nodded toward the hall of vases, indicating that she was to go there. She darted inside.

The old man then turned to Demuchus. "What is *she* doing?" he demanded, pointing at Andromache. "And why are *you* allowing it? What would her husband think?"

Andromache and Demuchus exchanged a look of shame. Deep down, Andromache knew that Hector liked for her to garden. He liked anything that made her happy. But something hard in Ucalegon's voice reduced her to the pitiful heap she'd been when she came to Troy. She was demeaning herself and bringing shame upon her husband while he was away...

Away—away to danger, blood, and smoke — away without even a kiss from her — away without hearing from her that she loved him. She was an even more disgraceful wife than Ucalegon would ever know.

Before Demuchus could answer his uncle, Andromache ran into the house to find Cassandra.

The girl was huddled awkwardly beside a vase half as tall as she was.

"I have to go," whispered Andromache. "You can stay, if you want, but —"

"No, honey. Of course I'll go with you. Are you all right?" Cassandra looked at her with concern.

"Fine — just — just tired," stammered Andromache. She took Cassandra's hand. "Please, let's go."

"Did that horrible man yell at you?" asked Cassandra, once they were safely on the street.

"No, he — the three of us were being too loud, I guess."

"He gets worse every year!" sighed the girl. "Poor, poor Demuchus."

"Poor Demuchus."

"Maybe I'll invite him over, tomorrow. He wanted to take a look at one of our texts, anyway — a rare treatise on spices. Demuchus said he didn't realize we had it in our library. I knew, of course, but I had no idea he'd be so keen to read it. I mean, who doesn't like *eating* spices, right? But that doesn't necessarily make them all that interesting to read about, except — oh, honey! What's wrong?"

Andromache was weeping openly, now. "I don't know."

"*I* do," said Cassandra, wrapping an arm around her.

Andromache leaned against the girl and tried to stop sobbing. She couldn't.

"Just let it out," counseled Cassandra.

"I-I don't know what to do!" wailed Andromache. "Every time someone mentions him — every time I even *think* about him — I just —"

"Honey, honey, honey…it's all *right!*"

"This is stupid." Andromache wiped her nose. "He'd be so mad at me."

"He wouldn't be mad at you! Don't be silly."

"Look at me! I'm a wreck! I was a wreck when he left — I never even told him —" Andromache's face crumpled. "That I love him."

"Goodness, gracious! He knows *that*," said Cassandra.

"I'm a rotten wife!"

"You are *not!*"

"I *am!* And I don't know what to —"

"Come here." Cassandra held Andromache tighter. After a moment or two, the girl said, "Here's what we'll do. When we get home, we'll go to the library. I think I know some texts that might help you. They're full of stories about all of history's most famous wives and lovers, and they're sure to have some useful advice!"

Andromache wiped away the last of her tears. Suddenly, she felt more shocked than sad. "Cassandra!" she gasped. "How do you know so much about those texts? Is there some advice *you've* been looking for?"

The girl's cheeks turned pink. "As a future member of the council, it's my responsibility to familiarize myself with *all* of our library's texts. You never know when one might be useful."

"You never know," Andromache agreed, giving Cassandra a thoughtful look. "You never know."

LONG INTO THE NIGHT, Andromache read story after story and poem after poem about all the great love heroines of the past. Despite Cassandra's assurances, though, the women's stories only made her feel worse. All of them stoically awaited the return of their husband or lover, enduring months, even years of deprivation without ever shedding a tear. A scant four days had passed since Hector's departure, and Andromache had already wept a minor lake over him. Feeling more inadequate than ever, she heaped the texts onto the table beside her bed.

All night, they watched over her — a rebuke in wood and clay.

Chapter 64

For the next two weeks, haunted by loneliness and a sense of failure, Andromache spent each morning down in the lower town. There, she searched for some last vestige of the master luthier's shop.

The master luthier's shop — her grandfather's shop — the place where her dad had grown up. Her grandfather was dead, and the shop long gone, yet Andromache knew that the building was still down there. Hector had told her so…

Over the past year, she'd set out many times to find it, never sure how she might recognize it. By a piece of the old sign? By a feeling deep inside her? Nothing had worked, but the truth was, she didn't really want to find the place. While searching, she'd had visions of her father and the life he might have led. She'd seen him as a little boy, running around the streets, and as an adolescent, learning the art of lute-making. Part of her feared losing those visions if she ever set eyes on the real shop.

She hadn't been back to the luthier's quarter since her Trojan wedding, but now, she went every day. As though to make up for lost time, she sank deeper into the dream world than she'd ever been before.

Her visions were always the same, now, set on an alternate life's path: her dad had never been disinherited, had never left Troy. Instead, her mom had come there from the Lukka lands to live in the luthier's shop. Andromache's parents were still alive, comfortably middle-aged, and every day, she and Hector went down to visit them. Her mom showed them the beautiful new blankets, scarves, and cloaks she'd woven from Trojan wool. Her dad requested texts to borrow from Priam's library. Then, after they'd chatted for a while, her mom brought out a quince tart — Andromache's favorite — and her dad strummed his lute. His playing sounded remarkably like Paris's, but older. Deeper. While he played, Hector put his arms around Andromache, and her parents smiled to see their girl so happy...

Inevitably, some sound disturbed her daydream: a chicken, outraged at being doused with water, or a rowdy child, spinning down the street like a whirlwind. When that happened, Andromache moved on to another street, another door.

She tried to avoid passing Penthesilea's door. Despite what Hector had said, Andromache still felt that she'd put him in danger by causing the rift with his comrade. She wondered where Penthesilea had gone and wished that things had turned out differently, not only for Hector's sake, but also for her own. Penthesilea had called her '*tough.*' No one else had ever said that, and Andromache didn't believe it — especially not in recent days! — but maybe spending time with Penthesilea would have made it true.

If nothing else, Andromache might have had another friend. Penthesilea had begun to talk a little during their long ago runs through the Trojan countryside. Andromache had learned just how similar their backgrounds were — they were both exiles, both orphans, both survivors of raids. Indeed, Penthesilea was the very person Andromache might have become, if her life had taken just one or two different turns. They had so many things in common...

(*You had* too *much in common,*) the Voice corrected. (*You were in love with the same man.*)

Andromache had no energy to fight the Voice. Besides, it was pointless to lament the friendship she'd never had with Penthesilea. Even if things had ended differently between them, the woman wouldn't have been in Troy right now. She would have been with Hector, serving as his left hand in the army.

Aside from those lonely morning rambles and occasional trips to the temple gardens, the only place Andromache felt like visiting was the stable. There, she walked and groomed Thisbe and did her best to play roodles with Xanthus, but she couldn't concentrate on the game, and he didn't have the heart to beat her.

In between outings, she stayed busy with quiet activities — reading, gardening, or cooking. When guests stopped by, though, she dropped whatever she was doing to flee. Once, she even sat in the bath chamber for four hours rather than passing by the group of girls who had come over to study on the courtyard with Cassandra. She knew what the visitors would say to her — and it was a conversation she wanted at all costs to avoid.

Out of love for Hector, and also out of sympathy, she made an exception for Demuchus. She wanted to help him escape Ucalegon's house for a while; what was more, she didn't want him to suffer the same sense of failure that was gnawing at her. Her sympathy had its limits, though: she insisted that Cassandra stay with her so she wouldn't have to face Demuchus alone. The girl was only too happy to oblige. Demuchus was her future colleague and she seized any opportunity to talk to him.

Much as the soiree groups always had, Cassandra and Demuchus discussed works of literature, scholarly treatises, and histories. Now, though, they looked at everything through the lens of diplomacy. They debated how the information in a given text might help them strengthen ties to other countries. They compared notes on conversations they'd had with the twincesses and Uncle.

Andromache seldom interjected anything, but she didn't tune Cassandra and Demuchus out, either. She was frankly impressed with them. They were beginning to sound like real council members with solid plans for Troy, instead of idle youths entertaining themselves. Over the course of those evening visits, she realized that Cassandra wasn't really a girl, anymore. Something in her had crystallized, and she was now a young woman, an adult ready to engage in adult matters.

Once Cassandra and Demuchus had wrapped up their discussion for the evening, Andromache faced the hardest part of her day: crossing the courtyard out to her lonely bedroom.

Cutie went with her. The dog watched as, every night, Andromache performed a strange new set of rituals. She opened the lid of the largest clothing chest, took out Hector's tunics one by one, pressed them to her face, and replaced them in the chest. She next checked the foot of the bed to make sure that his two spare sets of sandals were there, lined up to interlock with hers. She touched her fingertips to the impressions left by his toes.

Then, with the sandals in place, she climbed over them and lay down on the bed.

On the bad nights, which were many, she succumbed to the morbid thought that Hector's side of the bed would never again be warmed by him. It would remain cold and empty — empty, except for dust blowing in the window of the room that once had been his. Cutie would look expectantly at the door every time it squeaked, only to be crushed over and over when Hector didn't appear. They would never see him again, not even his broken, mutilated body...

On better nights, Andromache imagined conversations with Hector. She missed his voice — it was the first part of him she'd really known. She could almost hear it, husky and soft, asking her about '*vay-getables*' or calling her '*pretty wife.*' Was he storing up things to tell her, the way she was? Already, she had dozens of anecdotes to share with him.

For the moment of his return, though, she had bigger plans. To make up for not telling him she loved him before he left, she would do something even grander — recite a passage from one of the library's great love poems.

She'd skimmed through the texts, trying to find one she liked. Some were absurd:

> *Your arms, O my love, have the burnished gleam of sandalwood. As sweetly as incense do they smell when they embrace me. I fly the majestic heights on opalescent wings...*

Andromache had discarded that text without reading any further. Hector would laugh himself sick over *opalescent* — that is, if either of them could make it past *burnished sandalwood.* Other poems weren't bad:

> *You are the safe harbor to the ship of my heart. You guard it, keep it, surround it, hide it, no matter how the storm rages. A thousand rushing waves you send back, one after the other, until the winds pass and the sea is calm once more...*

Andromache had read through the poem several times, finally deciding that it was just what she wanted. It expressed her feelings for Hector far more beautifully than she could have managed on her own. Whenever she felt hopeful about Hector's return, she worked on memorizing the words.

No matter what kind of night Andromache was having — one where she despaired of ever seeing Hector again, or one where she made plans for his homecoming — she tossed and turned for a long time, only to be plagued by nightmares once she finally fell asleep.

Some of the dreams were merely sad. Hecuba arranged a beautiful bowl of fruit that no one ever ate and that slowly molded over, then desiccated. Other dreams were frightening. Violent. From those, Andromache awoke in a sweat, with Cutie standing over her, panting worriedly.

In the morning, before doing anything else, Andromache checked the sandals. If one of Hector's was missing, she would always find it deep in whatever nest Cutie had made for herself. Andromache would put his footwear back in place, then slip on her own sandals and wander down to the luthier's quarter.

After two weeks of those rituals and routines, Andromache realized that she was no longer constantly on the brink of tears. She contained her crying to the bad nights, with only Cutie there to witness her red face and slick nose. She felt a little more dignified, if still far short of the stoic grace achieved by all the legendary heroines. Secretly, though, Andromache wondered if they, too, had had a dog stashed away in their bedrooms — if they, too, had wept into the creature's flank at night, so they could make it through the day without crying.

Chapter 65

Andromache knelt down in the temple garden, doggedly plucking weed after weed from among the tender shoots of sacred herb. *I just did this bed yesterday!* she thought in frustration. She flung the weeds to the ground, wishing their demise could be more dramatic. *Schluup, plop, schluup, plop.*

Crash!

Andromache looked up at the temple building, where the sound had come from. Startled but curious, she crept closer to the building, peered in through the window, and saw her least favorite priest — a bulbous young man who spent his days loudly praising the deity of war.

Andromache despised him and suspected that Priam did, too; as she well knew, her father-in-law didn't believe in specific gods for specific purposes. While Troy's army was away, though, the young priest was allowed to run rampant. Perhaps it was to offer comfort to those Trojans who *did* believe in a separate war god. Then again, perhaps Priam was hedging his bets — allowing the young priest to do his work, just in case he really *could* intervene on the army's behalf. On Hector's behalf.

Either way, that day, the priest of war wasn't looking as sanctimonious as usual.

When Andromache peered in through the window, she saw that the *crash!* had come from a shattered jar. The priest must have dropped it, spilling sacred unguents all over his feet. Oil oozed over the hairy filthiness of his toes and left a slick behind him as he slunk away. He found a scrap of wool cloth to clean himself with, but, before he did, Andromache saw him dip a single finger into the oil on his foot — and then *taste* it.

She collapsed to the ground in spasms. Knowing that she mustn't laugh aloud — because if the priest realized that she'd seen him, he would be furious! — just heightened her state of hilarity. Each time she pictured that thick, knobby finger descending into the oil, she doubled over in a feigned coughing fit.

Her spluttering went on for a quarter of an hour. Other priests began ducking their heads out to check on her, and finally someone sent for Priam.

"What's wrong, little one?" he asked. "You were fine this morning."

Again, Andromache saw the finger, lowering inexorably into the oil. "I — *cough* — must have — *cough* — breathed in some — *cough, cough* — dust."

Priam shook his head gravely. "It sounds serious. Drink some water, and then I'm sending you home. And please, little one, tell my wife exactly what happened. She may have a tonic to recommend for you, or perhaps an oil salve — oh, dear me!"

The word *'oil'* had sent Andromache into another gasping fit.

"Iamenus!" Priam called for a younger priest. "Please walk my daughter-in-law home. She isn't well."

As soon as Andromache was away from her escort, she dissolved into laughter. How she wished that Hector were home, so she could tell him the story! He delighted in that sort of thing. She imagined his eyes lighting up as she described the priest's sacrilegious sampling of the — how would Hector phrase it? *'God oils,'* perhaps?

God oils! By that point, Andromache had laughed so much that her stomach was cramping, but she took it as a sign of progress that the thought of Hector speaking Lukkan made her want to laugh instead of cry.

That night was a good night. She recited the poem from memory almost all the way through and imagined giving Hector two thousand — no, three thousand! — kisses just as soon as he returned. When she pressed her face to his pillow, she had to breathe a little more deeply to catch the scents of cedar, mint, and lemon balm, but they were there, and they comforted her.

૪つ

ANDROMACHE AWOKE with her same stomach cramp the next morning and wondered if she'd been laughing in her sleep. She couldn't remember having had any funny dreams, but there was no other explanation for the cramping. As long as nothing funny happened that day, the cramps would no doubt ease.

Better stay away from the temple, then, she thought.

The day was dull, offering no reason for laughter, but Andromache's stomach cramp only intensified. All through the afternoon and evening it grew worse, so much so that she couldn't sleep. The aching in her abdomen kept her awake.

Somewhere in the night, Andromache began to realize what was happening, and the next morning confirmed it: her cycle had returned. She felt silly for not recognizing the cramps sooner, but then, the time between her cycles had always been long. It was understandable to forget a particular sensation after five or six weeks, especially the most recent weeks, with all the drama of Hector having nightmares, then leaving with the army —

Ector leaving — the day he left —

Andromache doubled over, wrenched by a new type of pain. She cried and cried all morning and long into the afternoon.

૪つ

EVENTUALLY, CASSANDRA CAME looking for her. "Andromache?" she murmured through the door. "Honey?"

Andromache didn't answer.

"Mom says you haven't been up, yet. She sent me to check on you."

Still, Andromache said nothing. She didn't even move.

"I'm coming in, honey."

The door creaked open.

"Oh, no!" cried Cassandra, seeing Andromache curled up in a ball. "What's wrong?"

"Cramps," mumbled Andromache.

"Oh, poor girl…"

"Mmph."

"Want me to rub your back? Or get a tonic from Mom?"

"No." In truth, Andromache was hardly feeling the cramps anymore. What did the physical pain matter, compared to what it meant?

Andromache had never thought much about babies — only once, when the Santiyan ladies were there, and their comments hadn't made her *yearn* for a baby. If one came, so be it; if not, she was more than happy just to have her husband. Now, though, she didn't have her husband, and today was a very bad day. She saw the army coming back without Hector. The house, without Hector. Her future stretching out, dry and dusty, without Hector. His scent — the last vestige of him — fading from their bed, until there was nothing left.

She thought of the day he'd left, of the small comfort she hadn't been able to give him. Only now did she see what she'd denied herself. It would have happened that time. She was *sure* of it! If only she hadn't broken down, she would have a baby growing inside her, now…Hector's baby, and hers. She wouldn't be alone, and her future wouldn't be utterly devoid of *him*. And if, on the other hand, he *did* come home, it would have been to a joyous surprise — the rounding of her belly. *Would have been…*

"Do you want something to eat, or a text to read?" offered Cassandra. "Or I could stay with you, if you want."

Andromache shook her head. A text — as though she cared about texts!

"Well, if it's all right, I'll go tell Mom why you're not up and about, then. She's convinced you have a deadly plant disease — something about inhaling bark mold at the temple?"

Had it really been just days since Andromache had laughed herself sick over the priest and his oil? How meaningless all of that was! "No," she murmured.

"'*No*,' I can't tell her you have cramps?" asked Cassandra.

"'*No*,' I don't have a plant disease," said Andromache.

"Phew! That's a relief." Cassandra sighed. "I'll let her know you'll be all right in a day or two."

"Sure," said Andromache. But she would never be all right — *never*.

"And I'll come back in a little while with food," Cassandra added.

Andromache shook her head.

"You're not hungry?" asked the girl.

Andromache shook her head again.

"You might be, later."

Even knowing that she wouldn't be, Andromache didn't protest further. She was too tired to argue with Cassandra. "All right," she said. "That's fine."

Once Cassandra had left, Cutie crawled out from under the bed. She was holding Hector's sandal in her jaws.

"Hi, sweetie," said Andromache, taking the sandal. It was slick with dog saliva, but Cutie hadn't damaged it. Not even a little. "Good girl! You were nice to Daddy's shoe."

Cutie wagged her tail.

Andromache tucked the sandal under her pillow and pulled Cutie to her chest. The little dog didn't protest. Like Muka before her, she allowed herself be squeezed in Andromache's time of misery.

Mid-spring into late spring

Chapter 66

"That's the wrong shelf, Hermie," said Paris. "*Plates* go there, not radishes."

Andromache shrugged. "Whoever needs the radishes will find them."

"Well, *I'm* the one who's going to need them, and I'm telling you, they'll rot and turn to sludge before I ever look for them on the plate shelf."

"You'd have to be blind to miss them."

"And *you* —" Paris pointed at her with a leafy stalk of celery "— would have to be crazy to put them there. Radishes have *never* gone on that shelf!"

"Fine! Put them wherever you want! Put them up your —"

"Whoa, Hermie! Take it easy! You know, you've *really* been short, lately."

Andromache glared at him, although she knew he was right. Ever since the coming of her cycle, she'd been in a full-on depression. She'd given up all of her activities except visiting Thisbe. She avoided going to the stables when Xanthus was on duty and gave poor Thoas nothing but curt nods. When Demuchus stopped by, she made sure to be in bed, and she *had* been rather brusque with all the family members.

Just as she was about to apologize, Paris interrupted: "Never mind. You've always been short. That's probably why you put the radishes on the plate shelf — you can't reach the right one."

"Shut *up!*" cried Andromache. "Just shut up, before I throw this radish at your stupid mouth!"

"I'll give you my whole next month's allowance if you can hit me — mouth or otherwise," taunted Paris.

"I'd gladly *pay* a month's allowance to try!"

"So, go ahead."

"All right!" Andromache raised her arm, radish in hand. She was taking aim, ready to launch the vegetable, when Cassandra ran into the room.

"Honey!" cried the girl. "You have to come!"

"Just a moment!"

"No, *now!*" Cassandra insisted. "They're back! They're here!"

Immediately, Andromache knew what she meant. The world began to spin; the radish slipped from her hand.

"Come on!" Cassandra was dragging her by the arm, out the door. Once on the street, Andromache began to run. She sprinted to the city wall, leaving Cassandra to follow as best she could.

By the time Andromache had climbed up to the viewing platform on the wall, the main city gates were open. Soldiers had begun to file in. None of them were on horseback, though, and none of them were wearing orange cloaks. Andromache picked at her cuticles.

"There you are!" panted Cassandra. "My brother wasn't lying, when he said how fast you could run. Phew! I'm about to pass out, here, and —"

"Ssssh," said Andromache. "Let's watch."

More and more waves of soldiers swept in through the main gate. Their clothes were a uniform grey-brown color, heavy with the dust of the road. Andromache tore a strip of dry skin from her thumb, which began to bleed. She swore softly and sucked on it.

"There he is!" squealed Cassandra. "No — wait — never mind."

When the blood didn't stop flowing, Andromache wrapped her thumb in a fold of her dress. Why, oh why, hadn't she made Hector promise to come in *first?* She knew he would have argued that it wouldn't be right, shoving in ahead of his soldiers, but if she'd pressed him, he would have relented. She would *know* by now — she wouldn't be left here to wonder, to pick at her fingers and bleed. "Do you see him now?" she asked.

Cassandra shook her head.

Maybe he went back to the outpost stable, thought Andromache, with a wave of dread. *Maybe he's sick again. Maybe I should —*

"There!" trilled Cassandra. This time, her voice was sure. "He just came in."

Andromache looked where Cassandra was pointing and saw the telltale flash of vomit orange — which was, so said Hector, the color of his commander's cloak. She then recognized Hector's bearing, the way he held himself on his horse. While Cassandra laughed and cheered and even sang to the people around them, Andromache silently watched her husband. His return, like his departure, was leaving her too full of emotions to speak.

❧

ONCE THEY'D SPOTTED HECTOR, the two women ran home to prepare for his welcome-back party. The radish was still lying on the kitchen floor, where Andromache had dropped it. She scooped it up and placed it on the proper shelf.

"That's a good first step," said Cassandra, "but we have a lot more to do before the guests arrive!"

Andromache set about cleaning and organizing. Meanwhile, her heart fluttered around inside her as though it meant to soar straight up to the Lorani. *Ector's home! Ector's home! Ector's home!* she sang to herself with each lamp she set out, each floor she swept. Not much longer, and he would be hugging her! A few moments more, and she would be reciting her poem! How did it go, again? Something about a harbor —

"Hello, there, girls!" cried Hecuba. "My! Haven't you been busy — and thank goodness for that, since we'll be short a pair of hands! Priam is off arranging for a delivery of wine — six dozen jars! As though we'll ever drink that much, let alone on a single night! But he insists." Even in chiding Priam, Hecuba looked radiant.

"I think everything's ready, Mom."

"I'm sure you're right, Cassandra, dear — the place looks marvelous. Still, I'll have a look around, to be sure. You girls, run along to your baths!" Hecuba made a shooing motion.

Cassandra turned to Andromache. "You can go first," she offered.

"I'll just take a bath in my room," said Andromache.

"That's a good idea. Oh, honey!" Cassandra threw her arms around Andromache's waist. "I'm so happy for you!"

Andromache laughed. "Me, too."

"Hey," said Cassandra. "When I'm finished bathing, I can come out and do your hair."

"All right, if there's time." Andromache hoped there would be. She wanted to look her best. "Just knock first, in case I'm still in the bath."

"All right! See you!"

"See you."

Andromache took coals from the kitchen hearth and went out to her bedroom. There, she found Cutie, asleep on the floor. "Hey, sweetie! Daddy's coming home — yes, Daddy's coming home!"

The little dog went straight from bleary to frenzied. She ran around in circles, yipping sharp little barks.

"All right — all right, enough. Sssh, settle down. We have lots to do before he gets here." Andromache started a fire in her hearth and then went out to the spring for water. Cutie followed. Hearing noises in the banquet hall, she ran over to investigate.

Andromache knew that she should chase after Cutie — if the dog wasn't locked away before the guests arrived, Hecuba would hit the roof! — but she wanted to bathe first, so she went back to her room. There, she put water over the fire, stripped off her clothes, and gathered her bath oils. As she moved around the room, the bed caught her eye. *I won't be sleeping there alone, tonight,* she thought, feeling giddy.

When the water was ready, Andromache poured it into the large bathing kettle and climbed in. She'd just finished washing her hair when she heard Cutie yipping furiously over in the banquet hall. *Dammit!* she thought. *I'd better hurry!*

Then, mercifully, the barking stopped. Andromache sighed, relieved that she would have a little more time to get ready. She could rub in her bath oil, choose a dress to wear —

Squeeeeak!

Dammit! she thought again. That sound was the bedroom door! Hadn't she told Cassandra to knock? Huddling down, she hollered, "I'm not ready, yet! Just give me a moment, all right?"

"All rahght."

Andromache gasped and leapt out of the kettle. Hector was standing just inside the door, smiling his a sweet smile. She flung herself at him — hugged him — kissed him. His lips felt new, as though they'd never before touched hers. At the same time, they felt wonderfully familiar. So did his rough cheeks — his arms — his hair, still damp from a bath and smelling freshly of cedar. Hector was back — *her* Hector!

"You have — put my heart — with ships," she blubbered, trying to remember the first line of the poem she'd planned to recite for him.

Hector laughed. "What?"

"You have sent — a raging wave — a *thousand* —" It was no use. "I love you!" she cried instead, amidst a torrent of kisses. "I love you. I love you. I love you!"

"I lahff you, too. Oh, Ahndromahk." He pressed his face to her wet hair. "I miss you."

Andromache laughed and cried at the same time. "No, you missED me! You can't miss me now — I'm right here."

"I know." Hector hugged her even closer.

"Oh, no…" Andromache wedged her hands up between their torsos, pushing him slightly away. "I'm getting your clothes all wet! I'm so sor —"

Hector started kissing her again, this time with his tongue as well as his lips, and Andromache melted against him. She was suddenly very aware of her nakedness.

"No sohrries," he murmured, sliding his hands over her slippery bottom and pulling her hips in to his.

She moaned softly.

"Fife weeks," he croaked. "Teuh days — seffen hours —"

"Till — when?"

"Wiffout *yeuh*…"

Andromache loosened his belt and pushed his tunic up over his chest. Five weeks without each other…so long. *Too* long!

"And also —" Hector threw his tunic to the floor. His eyes were as black and bright as she'd ever seen them. "Eet ees how long yeuh need sleep, after tonight…"

Then, they were on the bed, devouring each other. Dimly, Andromache hoped that no one would come out to bother them with stupid party business, but then Hector was inside her, and she forgot about everything outside of the two of them. His face above hers was beautiful. He was beautiful, with his eyes closed, his mouth half-open. She touched his lips. He sucked her finger into his mouth. "<u>I love you</u>," she murmured, over and over. "<u>I love you, Ector. I love you…</u>"

Andromache didn't realize that she was crying until Hector went still.

"<u>Ahndromahk?</u>" he asked hoarsely. "What's wrong?"

"<u>Don't stop!</u>" she pleaded.

"<u>You're not hurt?</u>"

"<u>No. Don't stop!</u>"

Hector did as he was told. But as soon as they were lying back against the sheets, holding each other, he asked once more, "<u>You ahre all rahght?</u>"

"<u>Yes</u>," murmured Andromache. "<u>Beyond all right.</u>"

"<u>Baht befohre, you ahre crying.</u>"

"<u>Because I'm *happy*</u>," she said, smiling in a way that threatened more tears at any moment. After the emptiness of the past five weeks, she was now too full of emotions to handle them without crying. "<u>So happy. You?</u>"

"<u>Oh, pretty wife…I am deep blue happy.</u>"

Andromache smiled, thinking of their wedding clothes. For a Trojan, there was no higher level of happiness than deep blue. "<u>Ector?</u>"

"Hmm?"

"<u>I love you</u>," she said, for the thousandth time that day.

"<u>I lahff you, too</u>," he said, although he now sounded a little confused.

"<u>I didn't tell you before you left</u>," she explained, her throat tightening. "<u>I couldn't — I just — I —</u>"

"Sssh," he murmured. "<u>I knowed it. I knowed.</u>"

"<u>But I — I mess it up every time!</u>"

"<u>Effery?</u>"

"<u>The other time you left — I couldn't tell you then, either! You know, out in your shed? Before we were — before we had — I mean, it was the night we were supposed to walk down by the river together, but you got called away, and we couldn't. You</u>"

were packing up, and I went out to your shed — that's why I went out there, to tell you I loved you, but I got all —"

"Sssh…I knowed then, too," soothed Hector, stroking her hair. "You told me wiff your eyes."

Andromache snuggled closer to him. Outside, on the courtyard, she could hear the first guests arriving. "They're here," she said. "I guess we'll have to wait till later to wear each other out."

"No one is here," argued Hector. "I hear noffing."

"I hear their feet. They're coming closer — soon, they'll be at our door."

"Let them."

"Ector…" Andromache squirmed. "They're probably wondering where we are — or worse, they *know*. They'll start talking about us."

"And say what? That we love each other? That we missed each other?"

"You haven't heard it all." Andromache sighed. "They say a lot more than *that*."

Hector laughed. "So, you think we should get dressed and go out there, then."

"At least until the guests have had more wine…"

"All right, my sweetheart," he said, releasing her.

Andromache slid out of bed and threw on the first clean dress she could find. Hector followed more slowly. The tunic he'd worn home was still wet from when she'd hugged him, and he didn't seem to know what to wear instead. "I don't even remember what I have, anymore," he said.

As he knelt down to poke through his clothing chest, Andromache quietly looked him over for hidden wounds. He had a few small scrapes — some shield-chafing on his arm — a minor bruise or two. Nothing serious. Reassured, she just stood there, torn between watching him further and throwing herself into his arms.

"Do *you* remember what I have?" he asked her.

Remember? Had she not brought his clothes out to touch them every night while he was gone? "Six or seven old, ratty tunics," she whispered.

He laughed. "Aaaaaah," he sighed, pulling each one from the chest. "I'd forgotten what it was like to wear real clothes."

498

The thought of him enduring weeks and weeks of his rough army tunic, when he so delighted in soft fabrics, again brought Andromache to tears. "Pick the best one," she murmured. "The softest."

Hector took his time running the fabric through his fingers. "This one," he finally decided, holding up a whitish tunic that, to her, was indistinguishable from the others.

She watched as he got dressed — watched the fabric slide over his honey-brown skin — watched his hands loop the belt just so —

Hector turned toward her then and caught her staring. They both froze; neither spoke. His dark eyes fixed on hers, and she couldn't look away — couldn't swallow — couldn't breathe — couldn't —

"Ahndromahk…"

The word was almost too soft to hear, but it broke the intensity of the moment just enough to release her. She ran over to Hector, burying her face in his shoulder — breathing him in — holding onto him until the too-full feeling passed.

"Don't let anyone tear you away from me, tonight."

She shook her head.

The sounds coming from the courtyard grew more insistent. Andromache relaxed her hold on Hector. He kissed her forehead, looked toward the foot of the bed, and frowned. "Ahndromahk?" he murmured.

"Hmm?"

"Do you know where my other sandal is?"

℘

THE PARTY WAS MUCH like all the others had been, with hordes of guests, an oration by Priam, and free-flowing wine. Unlike those other parties, though, Andromache managed to stay beside Hector for the entire evening. She clung to him, and he to her.

The Lark and the Otter spotted them and ran over, cooing. "Hello, little dear!" they cried, kissing Andromache's cheek and pinching Hector's. "Welcome back, boy! Welcome back."

"Thank you, Hecamede — Castianira!" Hector smiled at the women. "I'm glad you could come."

"You'll be gladder when we leave, and you can be alone with your wife," the Otter decreed.

Beneath the lock of hair that had fallen over his face, Hector's eyes were darkening. His dimple was coming out. "Maybe," he said impishly.

Andromache tried hard not to think about the color of her cheeks.

Delighted, the Lark sang, "That's as it should be! We'll be sure to make it out of here at a decent hour."

"And we'll drag along as much of this riffraff as we can, Sunshine," barked the Otter. "You can count on us."

Naturally, most of the guests were more interested in seeing Hector than Andromache, but all the girls who wanted to exchange kisses with him — and all the neighbors who wanted to thwack him on the back or cup his cheek — had to work around her. She was drowned in the scent of as many perfumes and scratched by as many whiskery cheeks as she had been on her Trojan wedding day.

Still, even she was nowhere near as sociable as Demuchus. Early on, he'd sidled over to Hector and said solemnly: *The promise is fulfilled.'* Just as solemnly, Hector had clasped Demuchus's arm. After that bizarre exchange, Demuchus had begun sailing in and out amongst the many guests, asking after their well-being as though he were a child of the house. He was still busy making his rounds long after Hector and Andromache had crept over to the stairs to take a break. While they sat there, they watched him.

"Are you comfortable, Thymoetes?" asked Demuchus. "If you find it too warm in here, I could show you out to the courtyard. There's a bank of crimson flowers near the wellspring that you simply mustn't miss, in any case."

"Wellspring!" hissed Andromache.

"You'd think he was the host," whispered Hector.

"<u>Oho</u>!" said Andromache. "<u>That's *your* fault</u>."

"<u>*My* fault? Why</u>?"

"What do you mean, why? '*The promise is fulfilled*,'" she simpered, in her best impression of Demuchus.

Hector laughed.

"It's not funny! He's been over here at least every other night. No wonder he thinks he owns the place! What possessed you to make him promise to play roodles with me?"

Hector leaned down and kissed her, hard. "He was the only one I could think of who's stubborn enough to visit you even if you told him not to," he said. "I thought maybe you'd feel less lonely if there was someone around to distract you. Was I wrong, my sweetheart? If I was, I'm sorry."

Andromache didn't answer. She wanted another kiss. And then another, and another...

"Ahndromahk..." murmured Hector.

"We could go up to my old room..."

"I want to go to *our* room."

Andromache looked over at the courtyard, but dozens of guests were still out there, blocking their exit. "Then we'll have to wait."

Hector nodded, and they went back to watching Demuchus.

℘

"IS THE WINE TO YOUR LIKING?" Demuchus asked a guest. Another two hours had passed, and the young future councilman showed no sign of tiring. "It was acquired from a special shipment. There's none like it on earth — who else but Melanippus would have thought to add in a measure of sea slug ink?"

Andromache, who had been sipping a cup of the wine, spat her mouthful to the ground. Hector snorted and spread the liquid out with his toe.

"Sea slug ink?" Andromache whispered in horror. "Did I hear him right?"

"I am sohrry, pretty wife — baht yes." Hector cuddled her close. "Lahke I always tell you, these parties ahre crazy."

Andromache nodded. "You're right."

"So," said Hector, clearing his throat. "I think that you want no mohre wine…"

Andromache shook her head vehemently.

"And you do not want to talk to any mohre peoples?"

Again, Andromache shook her head.

"Then let's go," said Hector. "To bed, I mean."

Andromache looked around and saw that most of the guests were gone. At last, she and her husband could slip out to their room. "Sounds good," she murmured, brushing the stray lock of hair out of Hector's face. "Then you can finally get some sleep."

"Sleep!" he said scornfully.

"Yes, sleep. You're tired."

"Fife weeks!" he said, with burning eyes. "Two days —"

"And seven hours — I know!" She laughed. "But if you need —"

"I need no sleep," he said, sounding haughty. "I need *you*."

What Hector said wasn't quite true — he *did* need sleep, but he was able to put it off until long after the party had ended. The only sound outside was the chirping of crickets when Andromache at last laid her head on his chest and closed her eyes. It was, she thought, an unusual way for them to sleep, but that night, nothing else would do.

Chapter 67

ndromache awoke still pressed to Hector's side. "G'mahning," he said as soon as she stirred. Andromache sighed happily and hugged him. "Have you been awake long?" she asked.

Hector shook his head. "Jahst a little."

"You should go back to sleep. You must be exhausted."

He shook his head again. "I jahst want to look at you. You ahre so beautiful," he murmured, spreading his hand out over her ribs. "Always, you ahre pretty, but *now*..."

"You forgot what I looked like," she teased.

He shook his head. "You ahre different."

He's probably right, thought Andromache. Lately, she hadn't gone running in the exercise arena or even walked around the city. Instead, she'd sat for hours in the kitchen, huddling by the hearth and eating honey cakes —fig rolls — walnut bread. She'd eaten more than she wanted, perhaps to fill the hollowness inside her or perhaps simply because the food was there. Either way, if Hector noticed a difference in her, it was most likely flab. Feeling shy, she tried to curl in around herself; Hector's hand stopped her.

"Want to go for a walk?" she asked, writhing a little.

"You ahre joking?"

"No."

"No to you, then," said Hector. "I do not want a walk." He leaned down and began kissing her stomach. After only a moment or two, though, he stopped kissing to look back at her face.

"What are you thinking about?" she asked softly.

"Lost kisses." He sighed. "Lost time. It is all too mahch..."

Andromache nodded. She understood how it was, having intense and unpredictable emotions. The day before had been a wild ride from fury, to dread, to joy, to lust, to wistfulness, and back to joy. But now, she and Hector could pace themselves. They could take time with their feelings. "<u>Why don't we just talk for a while</u>?" she suggested. "<u>Or I could tell you a story</u>."

"<u>Which stohry</u>?" he asked.

"<u>How about '*The priest who tasted the sacred oil*?</u>'"

"<u>Oh, Ahndromahk</u>!" Hector laughed. "<u>I cannot wait to hear it</u>."

℘

LATER THAT DAY, they went down to the stables. Xanthus greeted them at the door. "Well, well — look who's back." His voice was gruff, but he patted Hector warmly on the arm.

"Good to see you," said Hector, smiling. "It would've been nice to see you last night, too."

"Eh? At that party of yours? Wasn't it enough that I went to your wedding? You know I have no use for that kind of thing — or you *would* know, if you ever listened to a word I say! You should have your ears buffed out!"

"I'll look into it," Hector promised.

"And look who else finally dragged her sorry self in." Xanthus scowled at Andromache and muttered something under his breath about '*dereliction of duty*.'

"Finally?" asked Hector.

"I've missed a few days," said Andromache. Hurriedly, she added, "I came in to see Thisbe! I just didn't stay for roodles."

"Oh," said Hector.

Xanthus's thick, white eyebrows knitted together in a frown. "A few days, eh?" he growled. "Try a few *weeks*! Young people have no sense of time, anymore."

"I'll come tomorrow!" Andromache promised.

"Don't do me any favors, Missy," Xanthus said coldly.

Hector coughed. "I just wanted to check on the horses."

Xanthus turned his glare on Hector. "Eh? The horses? You think I don't know what to do with the horses? As if I weren't the one to teach *you* about horses?"

"All right!" said Hector, holding up his hands in surrender. "We'll just go see Buzzy."

"Hrmph."

They were allowed to pass.

"Boy — his temper has really gone to hell!" murmured Hector, when they were out of earshot of the stable master.

"Oh, don't joke about it," moaned Andromache. "He hates me, and he's right to. I should've come to see him, more."

Hector laughed. "He does not hate you! He lahkes you. He misses you. I can ahnderstand."

"You have nicer ways of showing it." She turned slightly toward him, just in time to see the dimple appear on his cheek.

When they reached the far end of the stables, she saw that Buzzy and Thisbe had been put in a single enclosure. The two horses were standing with their necks draped over each other, and they didn't move apart, not even to sniff Hector's pockets for treats.

Chapter 68

For a few more days, Andromache enjoyed the slow return to normalcy that she'd been hoping for. She and Hector worked most of the day at their various occupations — which, for her, included placating Xanthus with many games of roodles — but met up in the afternoon for a few cozy hours in their bedroom. After dinner, they took Cutie for a walk or chatted with the other family members.

On the fourth day after Hector's homecoming, though, the pattern changed.

"I'll be a little late, this afternoon," he said. "I have to go to a council meeting."

"What!" cried Andromache. Her face drained of color. "But you just — you just —"

"It's only routine business. I'm not going anywhere."

"Oh," she said, relaxing. She remembered, now — at some point after every military campaign, Hector made a presentation to the council. This must be that meeting. "It sounds like you might miss dinner, so why don't you meet me in the kitchen, afterward? We can have a snack."

Hector raised an eyebrow. "Almonds?"

Andromache blushed and poked him in the ribs.

ROUTINE OR NOT, the meeting went unusually long, that night. When Hector finally came home, Andromache was asleep at the kitchen table. She awoke to him shaking her shoulder.

"Ahndromahk…"

"Oh!"

"Sssh — it's just me."

"Oh." Her head felt thick, dumb. She had to blink several times before she could focus on Hector. He looked as tired as she felt, or even more so. "Are you hungry?" she asked.

"Not really."

"Do you want to go to bed, then?"

He nodded.

The cool night air of the courtyard revived Andromache, so that she was fully awake by the time they reached the spring. Hector, on the other hand, drifted past it. "Aren't you going to stop?" she asked.

"Oh. That's right." He sat down on the wall and gave his feet a listless scrubbing. He seemed to be moving through water rather than air.

Andromache frowned. "Are you feeling all right?"

"Just tired."

Despite his fatigue, once they were lying in bed, Hector had trouble falling asleep. All his tossing, and turning, and sighing reduced their blanket to a pitiful wad.

Andromache straightened the covers. She wished that Hector would turn onto his other side and curl up to her the way he usually did on chilly nights. Instead of complaining, though, she slid her arm around him, snuggled close, and kissed his neck. His shoulder. His back.

"Ahndromahk — please," he said.

As in, '*Please stop.*'

Inside, Andromache was reeling. In all the time they'd been together, Hector had never rebuffed an offer for loving, not unless he was late for an archery lesson, and even those occasions were rare. Tonight, he had nowhere else to be — and *he'd* been the one to bring up '*almonds*,' earlier! Had the council meeting put him out of the mood? If so, she couldn't blame him, but she *could* try to put him back in it. She kissed his neck again, murmuring softly, "Maybe it'll help you sleep."

"I can't."

Andromache froze. Thanks to the conversation she'd over-heard between Hecuba and the Santiyans, she had an idea about what Hector couldn't do. She'd understood what those women had meant by '~~desire going soft~~' and '~~things just not working right~~.' That had never been a problem before, with Hector, but at least it ex-plained his distance. He was ashamed, and he didn't want to re-veal his shame by trying — and failing — to make love with her. Hector didn't deal well with shame; the first time he'd screamed in his sleep beside her, he'd all but shattered.

"Oh," Andromache said softly. She wanted to comfort him, to tell him that all she really cared about was having him home and getting to sleep beside him again, but she was afraid to say anything. The one Santiyan, Rinnie, had said that talking about this particular problem only embarrassed men. Afraid of driving Hector away, Andromache let the matter drop. "Let me give you a massage, then."

"I don't know…"

Andromache sucked in her breath. Hector *loved* massages! He'd never turned one down, before — not unless he wanted to give one to her, instead. "I *want* to," she insisted.

Pause. "Whatever."

Since he hadn't said '*no*,' Andromache placed her hands on his back and began to knead. The muscles there were as tense as she'd ever felt them. She moved up to his shoulders and neck and then down to his legs, rubbing first hard and then gently. Usually, when she did this, Hector would moan and sigh in bliss, but that night he never made a sound. He almost seemed to be asleep, except that his feet were still.

Finishing the massage with a final long stroke up his spine, Andromache lay down beside him, her back pressed to his. She couldn't fall asleep. Sometime during the massage, two or three hornets had crept into her stomach. They began to buzz around…

Chapter 69

A ndromache awoke to a cold, vacant space in the bed beside her. She frowned, rubbing the sleep from her eyes. Even once they cleared, she could scarcely see her surroundings in the pre-dawn light. Where was Hector? It was too early for him to be meeting with Paris, too early for him to be working down at the stables. Had another nightmare sent him running around the city? Or was he just out, taking a walk? Why hadn't he asked her along, then? She loved morning walks! Why hadn't he at least kissed her goodbye?

Another hornet buzzed in to join its comrades.

He probably tried to wake me up, but I was sleeping too soundly, she told herself.

It was a reasonable explanation, and she was more or less satisfied with it until Hector failed to appear in the late afternoon, at their old Lukkan hour. *He's got a lot to do to catch up, after being away*, she thought. *Remember how it was, just after the wedding?*

(*After the wedding, he at least tried to send you a message,*) sneered the Voice.

Andromache closed her eyes in dismay. She hadn't heard the Voice in a long time; she'd hoped it had found someone else to bother.

(*After the wedding, he may have come home late, but the first thing he did when he got there was kiss you. Let's just see if he does that tonight.*)

Why wouldn't *he?* Andromache thought indignantly. *He's my husband. He loves me!*

As it sometimes had in the past, the Voice smirked.

෪

THAT NIGHT, Hector came home even later than he had the night before, and when he found Andromache waiting for him in the kitchen, he barely acknowledged her.

"Hi," she said.

"Hi."

"You had to work pretty late…"

"I know." He offered no explanation for why.

"Did you try sending a message by your brother, again?" she asked.

"What?"

"Paris — your brother — he always loses the messages you send with him."

Hector didn't answer.

"*Loses* — that's probably not the right word. I think he likes to start fights."

"Maybe…"

"You've had a rough day," Andromache said sympathetically, wrapping her arms around Hector's waist. "Let's go to bed."

Hector responded with a tepid, flat, little squeeze. Another hornet or two joined those already buzzing around Andromache's stomach.

Out on the courtyard, Hector stopped at the spring. He sat on the wall, took a brush, and scrubbed until his feet were red and raw. Even then, he didn't set the brush down.

"Hector — stop!" Andromache protested, when she saw that he wasn't going to do so on his own.

"Oh," he said, dropping the brush.

They walked the rest of the way out to their room. Hector slipped his clothes off near the door, as usual, and folded them into a careful pile that he placed on top of the clothing chest. He then lay down on the bed.

Cutie was already there, at the foot end. She thumped her tail in greeting, and Hector ruffled her ears.

So, the dog rates higher than the wife, now, Andromache thought bitterly. She sat on the edge of the bed, hoping to feel a hand on her back — to hear an apology — anything! — but once Hector was under the blanket, he didn't move.

Andromache wanted to scream at him but managed to stay calm. *He's still embarrassed, Ahndromahk,* she told herself. *He's probably worried that any touching at all will lead to kissing, and then you'll want to have sex with him, and he won't be able to, and he'll feel stupid in front of you. Just give him space till* ~~'things are working,'~~ *again.*

She removed her own clothing and slid under the blanket, curling around Hector's back the way he'd so often curled around hers.

Don't forget how patient he was with you when you were cringing through your first year of lessons — let alone those times when you picked on his accent and tried to make him miserable. He probably wanted to yell at you, but he didn't. He was kind to you. He loved you. You can do the same for him.

Andromache slid an arm about her husband's waist.

The other thing to remember is that he just came back from a campaign. He's always strange after he's been away. And this time, Uncle isn't here to help him recover. If he needs time, give it to him — especially if he's embarrassed, on top of everything else.

"I love you," she whispered into Hector's shoulder.

No answer.

Andromache told herself that he was already asleep.

Chapter 70

Hector came home even later the next night. Andromache, who had been dozing at the kitchen table, was startled awake by his footsteps.

"What happened?" she shrieked when she saw him.

"What do you mean?"

"Your hair!" Hector's hair was gone again, completely shaven. "Did you have —" Andromache lowered her voice. "Hair bugs again?"

"No." Hector sighed. "I just got sick of it."

Andromache slouched against the table. He wasn't sick of his hair, she was sure — he just didn't want her to be able to brush it from his face. He wanted to remove any impulse that she might have to touch him.

That's stupid! she told herself, as another hornet stirred inside her. *All day, he's training and working in the stables. He just doesn't want hair in his eyes all the time*.

The Voice smiled knowingly and said, (*That never bothered him before*.)

Without the hair, Hector's eyes and nose looked stark — severe. The scar on his temple, which Andromache had almost forgotten about, glared forth, jagged and purple.

As they sat near the spring, that night, she didn't stop him from scouring his feet. She wore her dress to bed, and he didn't notice.

Lying in the dark beside her husband's motionless form, Andromache wondered what had happened to her. At one point in her life, she'd stood up to Hector. She'd picked fights with him and risked angering him. Had she grown weak? It was possible; she hadn't been that strong to begin with. But she suspected the deeper truth was that she didn't *want* to fight him — she wanted to love him. She understood now why he'd refused to fight with her, during her early days in Troy, back when *he* wanted to love *her.*

That night, a few more hornets found their way into her stomach, and the swarm began working on its nest.

Chapter 71

For a time, Andromache wondered if Hector had lied to her about the last council meeting — if he *was*, after all, going to be sent away again, and that was why he was acting so strangely. She soon rejected that idea, though. Day followed day, one after the next, and Hector remained in the city. All the same, she saw very little of him — and even when he was home, he seemed far away.

Andromache wanted to be supportive. She wanted Hector to know how much she loved him. Merely thinking about him, though — let alone being around him — sapped her strength. Left her listless.

One by one, she gave up her activities.

The day she stopped gardening at the temple, she told Priam that her hands were getting too dry — too cracked — and she showed him her tortured cuticles as proof.

"Oh, dear," he said. "No, you mustn't be gardening, in *that* state! Not here, and not at home, either. Take a break from it, little one, for as long as you need — and be sure to show those hands to my wife."

Next came Paris. Andromache told him that she wasn't going to the market because, on her last trip there, she'd gotten a foot rash.

"Your feet look fine to me," he said suspiciously.

"Of course they do!" she snapped. "The rash cleared up, and I don't want it back!"

"Whatever, Hermie," sighed Paris. "Just let me borrow your dog."

"She can go if she wants," said Andromache.

Xanthus was an easier companion to shake than either Paris or Priam. She didn't need excuses; she just had to avoid him. She knew what it would cost her, when and if she ever went back to playing roodles with him, but, for the moment, she had bigger problems.

Once Andromache had stripped her life of activities, she felt empty but also relieved. She no longer had to waste energy digging in the earth, wrangling Paris, or mollifying Xanthus. She could devote herself entirely to getting through the rotten patch with Hector.

No one asked her why she never left the house, anymore. The family members were all too busy to notice. Cassandra had entered another season of heavy reading and was spending most of her time in the library. As for Priam and Hecuba, when they were home at all, they seemed to be in the grips of their own, private argument. Andromache had overheard just a snippet — *'How could you approve that, Priam?'* followed by *'How could I not?'* Andromache didn't know what had been approved, but it must have been controversial. Even when Hecuba and Priam weren't together, their manner was stiff and huffy. Neither paid attention to anything around them, including Andromache's withdrawal from her life in Troy.

Neither commented on Hector, or asked why he was avoiding the house. Perhaps they simply hadn't noticed.

Chapter 72

One morning, Andromache awoke to find not an empty space, but Hector, still asleep. He was there! Her luck was changing! The wait was over, and life would now go back to normal. Hardly daring to breathe, she reached under the bed for one of her see-through gowns and writhed her way into it. She'd seen how Hector reacted to those gowns! He wouldn't be able to resist her, especially not in the morning, when he was comfortable and warm with sleep.

"Ector," she murmured, wrapping her arm around him. "I'm so glad you're here. I love you. I want you so much! I —"

Hector shoved her roughly aside. "I'm late," he mumbled, almost falling over in his haste to leave their bed. "I'm late."

"For *what?*" demanded Andromache, not just frustrated, now, but also humiliated. Her eyes were filling with tears, and her stomach was a frenzy of buzzing.

Hector turned back toward her, his look indescribable. He, too, had somehow been hurt by this. "I'm late," was all he said before stumbling out the door.

Then don't come back, Andromache thought at him, her tears welling thicker and faster until the door was a blur she could no longer see. *Don't bother coming back*. Andromache's voice broke as she said the words aloud: "Don't come back!"

This wasn't like before, when Hector had had his occasional rough days or dark dreams. Then, he's sought comfort in *her*, through kisses, or talking, or loving. Now, she wasn't enough to make him happy. She could no longer distract him from his darkness, and why? The answer was obvious: Hector had fallen out of love with her. He didn't want her anymore. Whether or not '~~things were working~~' for him, they weren't going to work with *her*. She'd lost his eye, and no amount of jewels or hair combs could ever bring it back.

The women from Santiya had said this would happen, and she hadn't believed them. She *certainly* never would have dreamed that love could end so suddenly, like the snuffing of a candle. *Ector is different*, she'd told herself. *I'm different — we're different!* But either she'd been wrong, or something had changed.

Something changed! Andromache pinched her thighs and stomach hard enough to leave a mark. Here was her problem! When he first came home, Hector had pretended to like the new softness of her body, but he hadn't been able to lie to her for long. Hard and narrow was how he liked her — she was hideous to him, now. And that tormented look he'd given her? The reason for it was obvious! He felt guilty because he'd once cared about her; he didn't want to hurt her by revealing his disgust.

The hornets inside her flew in circles, faster and faster. They lowered their abdomens and began to sting.

Andromache closed her eyes, thinking strangely of Thisbe. Hector had always shown affection for the pony, but also, she now thought, a certain contempt. *'She is lahke a plant,'* he'd said. Always waiting, always still and calm, never moving. Dull.

Screw you! thought Andromache, in the direction Hector had taken. She lashed out at the love texts still stacked on the bedside table, not caring if the precious objects were damaged. *Screw you!*

With that, she threw on the first short running dress she could find and sprinted down to the exercise arena, where she ran lap upon lap upon lap. *Screw you!* She didn't stop until the sun was high and she was on the verge of collapsing.

As she walked home, her legs felt like jelly, but imagining them tight and toned kept her moving. She took a circuitous route back to the citadel and, before re-entering it, stopped by the stables to visit Thisbe.

Andromache was glad to discover that Buzzy wasn't in the enclosure. She didn't want to see Buzzy — didn't want to see Buzzy's owner — didn't want to see anyone but Thisbe. She'd slipped into the stables while Thoas had his back turned.

"You're not a plant," she whispered to the pony. "You're a good girl. I'll walk you out in the pasture tomorrow, I promise."

Thisbe nibbled on Andromache's dress and delicately licked dried salt from her arm.

Again, Andromache felt the stinging of tears. "And I'll bring you a treat. I promise that, too."

The faithful little pony whickered in response.

Tears rolled down Andromache's cheeks. She hugged Thisbe's head to her chest and buried her own face in the animal's mane. Then, from behind her, Andromache heard footsteps. *Is it Buzzy?* she wondered, turning around.

"Oh, ma'am, I'm — I'm — sorry to bother you," said Thoas. "I heard a noise, and I —"

Not trusting herself to speak, Andromache just nodded.

"Do you want me to find —"

She shook her head. Thoas and Xanthus had been among the first to witness Hector's love for her; she couldn't bear for either of them to see his disdain. "I was just leaving."

∾

AT HOME, Andromache took a long bath, imagining all the while that she was adrift in the celestial ocean. If she moved her hands just right, they swirled the water into currents — currents like those that swept the Lorani out to the farthest reaches of the universe.

Andromache followed them. Up there, there were no hornets...no sweating...no aching head or lungs or legs. No tears. No misery. Just a host of beautiful creatures. Glowing. Luminous. *Luminous.* Once, Hector had called *her* luminous —

A nasty thought jolted her suddenly earthward: she'd told Hector not to come back! He might not have heard her, but she'd said the words aloud, and that was what counted. They couldn't be unsaid.

I didn't mean it, Andromache thought out to him, in panic. *Come back. Please come back!* She dried off, dressed, and ran to the kitchen to see if he was there. He wasn't. *Please! I didn't mean it.*

An hour passed. He didn't come. She was alone.

Come back! Come back! she thought with growing urgency. She felt light-headed and wondered if she'd made herself heat-sick by running outside all morning.

(*You're hungry,*) the snide Voice told her.

Andromache ignored it. Whatever she did, she wasn't going to eat. If Hector was already sickened by her, she wasn't going to make the problem worse by gobbling down a big meal. Not only would eating fatten *her*, it would give the hornets something to feed off of — and the treacherous Voice knew it.

(*What does it matter? He's not coming back, anyway — you told him not to.*)

"Shut up!"

"Hermie?" said Paris, entering the kitchen. "Are you all right?" His normally sly face was concerned.

"I'm fine," whispered Andromache. "I — I — must have dozed off."

"You don't look so good."

The tears started again. "Thanks."

"Oh, Hermie, take it easy. I meant you look like you need a nap."

"Maybe."

"I can help you to your room, if you want," said Paris, offering his arm.

Andromache was ashamed, both because she looked unstable enough to need an arm and because she wanted it so badly. If Paris put his arm around her waist for a few moments, she could imagine it was —

"I don't need any help," she said brusquely.

"All right, all right." Paris held up his hands. "Forgive me for offering! It's just — well, you look like a leech sucked all your juices out."

"Thank *you*, Paris," snapped Andromache, hoping he could tell which word she wanted to say in place of '*thank.*' "I wasn't sure just how hideous I looked, but now I know. Thank you! *Thank — you!*"

"I'm sorry, Hermie. Hey — I'm sorry, Andromache." He put his arm around her shoulders.

Andromache was momentarily startled out of her misery. She must have made quite an impression on Paris. He'd *never* called her by her real name, not once in the nearly three years she'd lived in Troy.

"Is there something you want to talk about?" His grey eyes weren't mocking, but worried.

Slowly, Andromache shook her head. She did — she very badly did want to talk to somebody, to get advice — but Paris was the wrong person, if the right person even existed. She had to live with Paris. She couldn't let him know about her most intimate problems. Her shame.

"At least let me get you some water," he said.

"It's all right."

"I want to." Hastily, Paris fetched her a cup of water with rose petals and honey.

"I shouldn't have yelled," she mumbled, sipping the water.

"Pfft," he said, waving a hand. "You call that yelling? Your voice is as little as you are."

By teasing her, Paris had meant to make her smile, but she couldn't. She felt too empty. There was a time when Hector had teased her, had tried to make her smile...

"Thanks for the drink," she whispered to Paris.

"Do you want something stronger? Or, I could get my lute and play a few songs for you."

Blinking back tears, Andromache shook her head. The lute would only remind her of her family, of that other home she'd lost. "I'll just go out to the room," she said. "Good night."

It was barely evening, but Paris didn't challenge her farewell. "Good night."

Back in the room — *The room*, Andromache thought glumly, *not my room, or our room* — she saw the collection of love poems scattered pitifully on the floor. Ashamed of her outburst, she re-stacked them and placed them in a chest, along with her sheer and shimmery wedding gowns. She would never again open that chest. The texts would be safe, there. Untroubled.

Andromache lay down on the bed with Cutie beside her. Much as she wanted to stay awake until Hector came back — supposing he did — she fell asleep almost immediately.

ॐ

HOURS LATER, she awakened once more to the sound of Hector screaming. He had indeed come home and was now in the grips of a nightmare. Forgetting all of the recent strain between them, she threw her arms around him, murmuring, "Ssssh, Ector — it's all right. I'm here. I love you. It's all right."

"No!" he cried.

"Please, Ector..." His cheeks were wet. She could feel it. He was —

"No!" He leapt out of bed and disappeared into the night.

He was lost to her. Andromache's stomach heaved. It knotted and twisted, making one last stand against the full onslaught of the hornets, but, inevitably, it succumbed. Hordes of insects swarmed in, stinging her, filling her with their buzzing wings and their poison —

Then, Cutie was barking at her — howling at her — licking her hands, which Andromache realized she'd been using to claw at her own stomach.

"Go away," she whimpered to Cutie, but the dog wouldn't leave. She stuck her snout in Andromache's face and licked her cheeks.

"All right," sighed Andromache, hugging Cutie. "All right." She pulled the dog awkwardly down beside her.

For the next few hours, Andromache pictured the great Lorani out in the celestial ocean and the miniature ones floating down in the earthly seas. Thinking about the creatures brought her comfort. How beautiful, how peaceful, it would be to float among them, to be enveloped by their light...

Chapter 73

S o began a dismal routine. Clinging to a last shred of hope that Hector might notice her again, Andromache ran every morning down at the exercise arena. Afterward, when she was certain that Hector and Xanthus would be on the training field, she went to the stables to see Thisbe. Poor, little waiting Thisbe — Andromache's animal double.

The pony seemed more forsaken every day. Her mane had lost its shine; her eyes had lost their luster. She seldom nibbled at Andromache's dress.

"Why are you so sad, girl?" asked Andromache, although she had her suspicions. Buzzy hadn't been in his stall much, lately: *'H-he's out on the training field, Ma'am,'* Thoas had told her, although she hadn't asked. *'S-sometimes Xanthus takes the horses out, so they get used to the s-sounds.'*

"You never know, he might have to go away again," Andromache murmured to Thisbe. "You wouldn't want him to be scared, would you? He needs to practice…"

(*Yes,* Buzzy *needs to practice,*) said the horrid little Voice.

Andromache frowned. Why was *it* chiming in on that?

(Buzzy *has to spend lots of time away from* Thisbe, *even though he doesn't want to,*) the Voice went on. (*He doesn't* choose *to leave her by herself, and he doesn't enjoy it, either — which is more than I can say for his owner.*)

What are you talking about? Andromache muttered. As far as she could tell, Hector wasn't enjoying much of anything, lately.

(*Isn't it obvious?*) The Voice paused, reveling in the thrill of what it was about to say. (*Your husband has a lover.*)

That's not true! cried Andromache, feeling sick at the thought.

(*You heard that* Santiyan — Ninnie. *She said it was bound to happen eventually.*)

What does she know?

(*Plenty! She's taken lovers herself.*)

Ector wouldn't do that!

(*Why not? How can you be so sure? Because of the tender way he's been treating you, lately? He's gone all the time, and even when he's home, he hardly notices you.*)

That — that's only because '~~things aren't working~~,' Andromache said desperately, refusing to let the Voice win.

(*They haven't been working with you,*) retorted the Voice. (*With his lover, on the other hand...*)

The hornets rallied, stinging Andromache's insides into a swollen, weeping mass. *No!* she screamed. *That's not true!*

(*Fool,*) the Voice sneered back. (*You poor, blind fool.*)

Andromache collapsed from the hot pain of the stings. The Voice was right. It was right! Everything made sense, now — Hector's fatigue, his strange hours, his lack of interest in *her*. The doubt first introduced by Rinnie and Ninnie bubbled forth again, more violently, this time. Why hadn't she seen it earlier?

You poor blind fool...

৪৩

FOR THE REST of the day, Andromache barely stirred from her bed. She just lay there, wondering what she was like. Perhaps even littler and lither than Andromache herself. Or perhaps, regretting the fact that he hadn't chosen Penthesilea in the first place, Hector had taken up with someone tall and beautiful, with copper hair and silver eyes. Someone queen-like. Radiant.

Next to a radiant woman, a luminous one disappeared.

৪৩

LATE THAT NIGHT, as Hector lay down beside her, Andromache breathed in carefully to see if he'd carried any strange smells with him.

Cedar — lemon balm — mint. No smell of roses, no lilies, no hyacinth. Nothing that shouldn't be there. She breathed in again, to be sure, but the only scents were those of her husband.

(*Fool! What about his clothes?*)

The Voice was right — Andromache would have to check. Warily, she slid out of bed and over to the clothing chest. There, she breathed into Hector's just-worn tunic.

Cedar — lemon balm — mint. The only other smells she caught were sweat, dust, and horses. Hector's work smells.

Feeling silly, Andromache crept back into bed. She propped herself up on an elbow, looking down at her husband, ashamed by her untrusting thoughts. As she watched him sleeping, though, doubt took over once more.

(*He could've changed clothes,*) said the Voice. (*You can't tell his tunics apart, and he knows it.*) He might even have left his other tunic at *her* house — on *her* floor — beside *her* bed —

Andromache choked down a sob. Simply smelling his clothes wouldn't tell her anything. If she wanted to find out who he was meeting every day, she would have to follow him.

Chapter 74

E arly the next morning, when the city was still wrapped in fog, Hector left their bedroom. Andromache crept after him, opening the door slowly so it wouldn't squeak and leaving it ajar. Cutie looked up at her but lay back down almost instantly. The dog had grown used to early morning departures.

The street outside was empty. Andromache cringed to hear her feet tap against the cobblestones, but Hector never turned around. He moved forward, unhurried, although not dawdling either, and not looking around him. He was quiet but not furtive and seemed unconcerned that someone might be watching.

Brazen! thought Andromache, although another part of her, deep down, wondered if he might instead be innocent.

As Hector unknowingly led her through Troy, she realized that he was walking toward the sculpture garden — a meeting place for lovers, she knew, although typically in the evening. *She must be someone very special, if she's willing to come here so early,* Andromache thought bitterly.

She waited a moment before following Hector through the door. She would lose him briefly, but the garden was small. It wouldn't be hard to find him again.

Once inside, she tiptoed around, hiding behind blocks and trees, alert to the danger of being discovered. After suffering Hector's abandonment for weeks, now, a strange, detached part of her felt almost excited by the chase — by the prospect of catching him in the act. He would be unable to deny it; he would be unable to slink off into the morning shadows. He would have to look her in the eye and see the agony he'd caused her.

Andromache was so lost in thoughts of justice that she almost walked right past Hector. He was on the ground in the far northwest corner, his knees pulled to his chest, his eyes staring into the void. He looked as though a whole parade of Uncle's fabled elephants could have lumbered by without his noticing.

Frowning, Andromache ducked behind a sculpture, the one of Commander Atymnius. She waited for almost two hours, but Hector didn't move — except occasionally to rub his forehead — and no one came to join him. Finally, when sounds from the other side of the garden wall suggested that the city was coming to life, Hector sighed, stood up, and left.

Was he sighing because his lover hadn't come? Had *she* forsaken him? Would he go to her now?

Still keeping her distance, Andromache followed him. He went straight to the stables. Her stomach, which had been tensed against the constant onslaught of hornets, relaxed a little: there was no way he would risk meeting a woman *there*! Everyone there knew Andromache — and even though Xanthus was no doubt furious with her for avoiding him, she was sure that he would pepper Hector with horse clods before letting him bring a paramour anywhere near the stables. As long as Hector was there, Andromache felt safe.

℘

HECTOR DIDN'T reappear from the stables until late in the evening. He looked worn and stooped.

Andromache hardened her heart against him. She *wouldn't* notice, *wouldn't* care! Not after what he was putting *her* through. Besides, she had other business to attend to — she had to follow him again, to see where he'd been spending the evening hours.

Just as he had that morning, Hector led her to the sculpture garden. He then sat there, hugging his knees and staring into space while night fell around him.

Andromache felt increasingly nauseous and confused. The scene before her was somehow more disquieting than if a woman had slunk through the darkness to perch on Hector's lap and stick her tongue in his mouth.

I have to get home...

Andromache picked her way carefully across the garden. Although she made no noise as she pulled the door shut behind her, she felt certain that Hector wouldn't have noticed if she'd slammed it.

ℰↄ

THE NEXT FOUR DAYS passed in much the same way: Hector went to the sculpture garden, and Andromache followed him. No one else was ever up there, and he never seemed to be expecting anyone. He thought he was alone.

With all that she'd witnessed, Andromache could no longer believe that Hector had taken a lover. He'd neither replaced her nor been unfaithful to her. He simply didn't love her anymore.

In those quiet moments, late at night, when he came back from his second daily trip to the sculpture garden, Andromache longed to ask him '*why*' — to ask him what she'd done, that he would prefer sitting alone down there to being with her — to tell him that she still loved him — to ask him what she could do to make him love *her* again — but the silence between them had gone on for so long that she was unable to break it.

Chapter 75

The spring weather was unstable — warm one day, cool the next — and the fifth morning of Andromache's spying mission brought a chilly wind.

Hector arose at his now-typical hour. Less out of interest than habit, Andromache donned a cloak and followed him. Hector, she noticed, wasn't wearing a cloak. He didn't seem to feel the chill as he walked to the sculpture garden, but once he was sitting still, he began to shiver. Rather than leaving, though, or even moving around for a while, he just sat there.

Andromache had never seen anything so lonely as her husband, shivering in the cold wind of the seaside sculpture garden. *Go to him,* she told herself. *Wrap him in your cloak. Wrap him in your arms. He needs you.*

Just as Andromache was about to heed this thought, another Voice chimed in: (*He doesn't need or want you. If he did, he would've asked you to come here with him. He's here to get away from you.*)

But he's —

(*And don't forget how many weeks he's left* you *shivering in your bed. He doesn't care how cold* you *are.*)

It was true. Hector *had* done that. He *didn't* care that she was suffering.

(*If he'd wanted to be warm, he could've stayed in bed with* you.)

Andromache looked at Hector, trembling with cold. Shivering. Doing nothing to help himself. She looked away. So be it — if he was determined to freeze, then she would let him.

ℰↄ

HECTOR CLIMBED into bed early that night. He was still shivering. *He probably never thawed from this morning*, thought Andromache. *But I'll bet he still went back to that sculpture garden tonight*. She pictured him huddled, cold, and alone, and was racked with remorse. *He could've frozen! He could've died!* How could she have left him there? Was she that empty? However agonizing the past five weeks had been, Hector was her husband, not her enemy. He'd suffered far worse from her without complaint. How could she have left him? What was wrong with her?

She began to cry quietly. "<u>You're so cold</u>," she murmured, sliding her arm around his waist from behind. "<u>You're so cold</u>." Tears poured down her cheeks. "<u>I love you, Ector</u>..."

To her surprise, Hector turned over and returned the cuddle. "<u>Always you crying when you say that</u>," he teased, brushing the droplets off her lashes.

It was as though a stone figure had come suddenly to life. He was teasing her! He was *touching* her! How long had it been since he'd done either? Andromache couldn't remember, but it felt so good and familiar — being near him felt so good and familiar — that, impulsively, she kissed him. *Ector, I need you. Stay with me*.

He kissed her back.

I need you. Stay with me. Her magic words! That was what she should have been saying all along! He'd always listened to those words. How could she have forgotten? She kissed him again, harder, and began running her hands all over his naked body. He smelled good — felt good — tasted good. She wanted to have him closer. She wanted to have him *now* —

"<u>Yeuh wearing thees, why</u>?" Hector, as urgent as she, was yanking at her night dress.

"<u>I don't know</u>!" She ripped off the dress and plastered herself to him. Sweat beaded up on her chest and upper lip and her heart hammered as though she'd never been with him before. He sucked hard on her nipples; she bit him on the shoulder and dug her fingernails into his back. She was ready! *He* was —

Abruptly, Hector stopped and pressed his face to the curve between her breasts. "I wanted to gut those boys that hurt you and Cutie," he croaked. "I wanted to do everything you said."

Andromache stiffened. Those boys — Cutie's tormentors — the ones who'd been dangling the little puppy by her leg, two years earlier — the ones who'd given Andromache a black eye when she'd taken Cutie from them. Hector had been furious.

'Something has to be done about those boys,' he'd growled. *'Consequences! This is* my *city, and I'm not going to stand by and let that kind of thing happen, here!'*

The threat had terrified Andromache. The next day, when Hector had assured her that the boys wouldn't be bothering any more puppies, she'd cried: *'I told you to leave them alone — not* gut *them!'*

It had been a horrible thing to say — an unjust, undeserved, awful thing to say. As she later found out, all Hector had done to the boys was force them to muck out the stables. Andromache still hated herself for what she'd said to him.

Just then, though, she hated Hector more. What was *wrong* with him? When they were lying in bed together, he was supposed to confess love secrets! He could have told her that he used to watch for a light in her room on the nights she went to soirees, or that he used to look down her dress during Lukkan lessons. He was *not* supposed to bring up a fight they'd had long ago! He was *not* supposed to talk about gutting people while he was making love with her!

Nothing for weeks, and now *this?*

She had to get away. If she didn't, she would suffocate. With a grunt, she wrenched herself out from under him and lay on her side, facing away. "So *what?*" she hissed. "You *didn't* hurt them. Xanthus told me everything."

"No," Hector agreed softly. "I didn't hurt them."

Those were the last words either of them spoke, that night. Andromache lay motionless on her side of the bed, picturing herself in a bubble among the great, luminous Lorani. She imagined being sucked into one of them, traveling through its glowing depths, being eaten by its light. She drifted from those thoughts into sleep before waking once more to the sounds of Hector leaving their bed. As far as she could tell, it was the middle of the night.

Andromache didn't follow him. Instead, she put her hand to the hollow where he'd just been. The sheets were cooling beneath her touch, the scent of cedar dissipating. How long would it take for the last trace to disappear, if he never came back to their bed? Longer than a month, she was sure, but perhaps no more than two...

Andromache's eyes snapped open. *Two months? Oh, gods — no! Not now!*

Two months. That was how long it had been since her last cycle. She should have had another one since then; two months was too long, even for her. Her cycle hadn't been so late since —

Andromache thought of the wagoner and shuddered.

Not now! It must have been the night of Hector's return, or shortly after. He'd stopped loving her within days of coming home.

Not now! Why now? I can't do this! Two months ago, if Andromache had found out that she was pregnant, she would have wept with delight. Now, she felt sick. Desolate.

Why now? Her already-swollen eyes filled with tears. Now was not the time for this! She couldn't even handle her husband, let alone a baby! She hadn't thought about babies since Hector's return — at first, because she was so focused on the joy of being with him, and then, later, out of misery. *Not now!*

Would he even want it? Would he even be around for it, or would sitting in the sculpture garden keep him too busy? Would she spend all day alone in their room with an infant — cleaning it, rocking it, and trying to hush its wailing? Poor, lonely infant, abandoned by its father...

I don't want a baby now, she thought, sobbing at the memory of how she'd longed for one, just two months earlier. How her life had changed, since then! *I don't want a baby with* him*!*

Andromache curled into a ball, wrapping her arms around her knees. She felt even more desolate than Hector had looked, down in the sculpture garden.

Chapter 76

Faster — faster — faster!
Andromache was down at the exercise arena, running lap after desperate lap. She no longer cared about flab. Her figure would soon be obliterated — not that Hector would notice, anyway. After that one ill-fated attempt to make love with her, he'd gone back to avoiding her. He hadn't tried to explain himself, hadn't tried to kiss or touch her again. He might as well have been a stranger. Andromache had given up trying to understand his behavior. What did his reasons matter? He'd deserted her, and she hated him for it. *I hate him! I don't want a baby with him!* They were atrocious thoughts — diseased thoughts — and running was the only way she had to cope with the pain they were causing her.

Running also helped her escape the house. The house meant family, and in recent days, the family members had started noticing her again. They'd noticed her withdrawal, her lethargy, and her blank face, and they'd started asking questions:

What's wrong? Are you all right? Are you sick? Do you need a tonic? You should lie down. You should eat something. You should drink something. You should chew pomegranate seeds. You should soak your feet. You should wrap them in damp moss.

The day before, in the kitchen, she'd run afoul of Hecuba…

'What's wrong?' the woman asked.

'Nothing,' said Andromache. She was hot, sweaty, and dizzy from her run and knew that she looked terrible. 'I'm fine.'

'Are you sure? With the adjustments, lately…'

Whatever Hecuba meant by "adjustments," Andromache didn't want to hear another word about it. 'I'm fine,' she insisted.

Hecuba narrowed her eyes. 'My son said you didn't look well.'

Andromache's knees buckled. 'Hector?' she asked pleadingly.

'Paris.'

'Oh.' How far she'd sunk, that Paris now cared more about her than Hector did!

'I'm inclined to agree with him. Your color is off.'

'I was running,' Andromache said defensively.

Hecuba frowned. 'You might be overdoing it.'

'I'm fine!' snapped Andromache, in a tone that she'd never used on her mother-in-law.

Hecuba backed down. 'All right. But let me know, dear, if you need anything.'

Down in the exercise arena, Andromache didn't have to endure that kind of conversation. No one there approached her. No one even knew who she was because most Trojans didn't recognize her outside of the house. No one realized that she was Hector's wife.

His rejected wife, carrying his rejected baby.

Andromache picked up her pace. Women had survived this before — there was the Santiyan lady, Rinnie, for instance. But Rinnie had probably had parents, brothers, and sisters around her…aunts, uncles, and grandparents to console her. For Andromache, though, Hector was *everything*. He was her whole family. Everyone else was gone.

The air turned red and thick. Andromache wobbled on her feet. Who would be there to pick her up, if she fell? Hector, who had saved her more than once, was lost to her. So was Auntie. Andromache had dragged her body out to sea years ago. As for her mom, her dad —

Andromache frowned. Her dad…

She handed her dad the text she'd borrowed from Priam's library. 'You'll love it, Dad! I promise.'

'On Lorani?' he asked skeptically. 'What's it about, Little Cricket?'

Smiling, Andromache shook her head. 'I don't want to spoil it for you.'

'Are you two hungry, yet?' asked Andromache's mom. She was holding a quince tart.
  'Oh, Mom — my favorite!'
  'I know, Ahndromahk. Did you think I would forget?'
  'No, Mom. Of course not. Never…'

Andromache shook her head. Doubt was gnawing at her. Where *were* her parents — had they really died, long ago, down in the Lukka lands? Or were they here, in Troy, living in the luthier's quarter? She could see them — she could see them so clearly! She'd even taken Hector to visit them, back when he still loved her.

Or had that been a dream?

Her brain felt too heavy. She couldn't remember. She had to find out.

Only half aware of what she was doing, Andromache ran out of the exercise arena and through the city streets, turning finally onto a small alleyway where she'd once made frequent trips. She looked, and there it was — the luthier's shop! How *could* she have missed it, all those other times? It was right there, bright and welcoming! Paris had been wrong. They'd all been wrong. Her family wasn't dead.

She reached out and knocked once, then again, on the narrow black door. "Mom! Dad!" she called. No one answered. Once more, she rapped on the —

Black door…

Then, she understood. This wasn't the luthier's shop, but Penthesilea's house, empty for many months, since before Andromache's Trojan wedding. This place had no connection to her family, yet it, too, could have been her home. What would her life have been like, if she'd accepted Penthesilea's offer of lodging? If she hadn't stayed at Hector's house — tutored him — fallen in love with him — married him — been abandoned by him? And what if she'd joined the army when Penthesilea asked her to? Would she have grown so tough that nothing could hurt her?

She'd been tough, once— *'Stay away from me! I never want to see you again!'* she'd screamed. She'd been tough enough that day to drive Penthesilea of Troy.

Oh, how she hated herself for that moment of toughness! If only she'd shown compassion, instead! Perhaps the two women would have reconciled in time, just as Hector and Demuchus had done. Perhaps now, Andromache would have had someone to turn to — someone outside of Hector's family — someone who understood the misery she was feeling.

For, despite all of Hector's protests, Andromache had never stopped believing that Penthesilea was in love with him. She'd loved him and been rejected by him. An orphan, an exile, an outsider, a castoff — her life was Andromache's life. If only Andromache had shown some compassion...

And gratitude, Andromache told herself. *I should've shown some gratitude.* Penthesilea had been the one to bring her to Troy instead of Thebe. Penthesilea had believed that she was strong enough to make it. Penthesilea had offered her options, although Andromache had been too foolish to accept them. Even that last day, just before their fight, Penthesilea's reflex had been to ask, *'Are you all right?'* However little they knew each other, there was a connection between them. Surely in time they would have reconciled, if Andromache hadn't lashed out with all her hurt and anger and driven Penthesilea away.

Andromache pressed her hand to the narrow black door. She wished she could tell Penthesilea that she was sorry, but it was too late. The woman was long gone.

Feeling dizzy, Andromache leaned against the door and shut her eyes. She was surprised that her body didn't pass through the door, it was so light. So nebulous.

Unlike her body, her mind felt thick. *I should probably get home.* The thought came slowly — honey oozing down a finger. When the word '*home*' finally reached the bottom, what Andromache saw was not Hector's house, nor his garden, nor their room. It was neither Penthesilea's house, nor the mysterious luthier's shop, nor the shack Andromache had shared with Auntie in Lyrnassa. Instead, she saw the little Lukkan cottage where she'd once lived with her parents. She saw the pine trees — heard the whisper of their needles in the wind — smelled the wildflowers that grew in the clearings. She felt happy. She began to walk back there — or rather, to float.

Chapter 77

Far away, Cutie was howling and Hector was screaming. "Mama! Mama!" he screamed. "Mama, help!"

There was a rustling of footsteps from somewhere beyond them.

"Mamaaaaaaaa!" Strident and shrill, he held the last syllable for what seemed like an hour, but Andromache's notions of time were fuzzy. Everything was fuzzy, except for Hector's hand, on her chest. The other, on her shoulder. Those were solid. Uncomfortably solid. They were —

"Mama!" Hector screamed again. "Mamaaaa! Maaaaaaa-maaaaaaaaaa!"

"What is it, Hector — oh!" His mother interrupted herself with a gasp of horror. "Oh, *gods*!"

"Help!" pleaded Hector. "Mama, please — help her! *Help* her!"

"What *happened*?"

"I don't know — I don't know! — I came out — she was here — oh, Mama, all the blood — all the blood! All the —"

"Calm down!" Hecuba switched abruptly to healer mode. "I'm going to help her. But I need *you* to calm down."

Andromache felt two more hands on her body.

"Her heart's beating…and she's breathing." There was sudden warmth near Andromache's face as Hecuba leaned over her. Then, on her hand, another warmth — the soft slickness of a dog's tongue. "Shoo!" said Hecuba to Cutie.

"All the blood!" Hector wasn't screaming, anymore, but moaning.

"I know. I see it. Did she fall?"

"I don't know." His hands were limp. Impossibly heavy.

"Just in case, I need to feel her head." Hecuba traced circles all over Andromache's scalp. "It's not coming from here."

"There's so much…"

"I know! We have to find the source." Hecuba searched on, maneuvering around the inert masses that were Hector's hands. "I think she rolled over, and that's why she's covered in it."

"It smells like a battlefield…"

"Focus, Hector! Help me get her off her side so I can find where this blood is coming from, or else go get someone who will!"

The two larger hands stirred to life and pulled at Andromache's hip and shoulder. She came to rest on her back, her thigh touching Hector's knee. Vainly, she whimpered and tried to roll back onto her side.

"<u>Ahndromahk</u>?" cried Hector, in response to the voluntary movement.

She didn't answer.

"Oh," his mother said quietly. "Oh…the poor girl…"

"What is it? What's wrong with her?"

"Then you didn't know?"

"Know what?"

Pause. "That she was pregnant."

Hector was silent.

"Oh. Well, sometimes women don't tell until they're sure. I didn't tell your father about Paris or Cassandra, either, right away. After what had happened…"

Silence.

"After the miscarriages, I mean," murmured Hecuba.

Hector still said nothing.

"I think the bleeding's stopped, but I need to check."

Andromache's legs were pried apart — she was being prodded, inspected, and no one was saying anything. It went on for hours, maybe a day.

"Thank goodness!" sighed Hecuba, gently brushing the hair off Andromache's forehead. "She's not bleeding much, anymore — if at all. She's in shock, though, poor little thing. That's probably why she's not saying anything. Go find your sister — she and I will clean Andromache up and put her to bed."

Finally, Hector spoke. "I'm going to wash her," he said.

"Sweet boy," murmured his mother. "She might — she might prefer to have a woman do it."

"I'm going to wash her," he repeated.

His mother sighed but said only, "I'll bring water to your room."

"All right."

"Make sure to keep her warm, Hector."

"All right."

Andromache felt herself being lifted, pressed to something solid — Hector's chest — and then she was floating again. One arm released her, briefly, and she heard the familiar squeak of their bedroom door. So, that's where they were. That's where she'd landed, after floating away from Penthesilea's house...

Just inside the doorway, Hector sat on the ground, cradling Andromache so that her head rested on his shoulder. She felt him so keenly — his arms around her — his legs beneath her — his chest pressed to her side — his warm breath on her ear. This was the last time she would ever feel him. Soon, it would all be taken away.

She began to shudder. Hector tightened his arms, tried to warm her —

There was a knock.

"Come in."

"I'll just set it here, right next to you." There were scraping sounds. Sloshing sounds. A basin being set on the ground.

"Thank you."

"I brought some cloths, too..."

"Thank you."

"Hector — if you need *anything* — I'm here. We're all here."

"Thank you."

The door closed again. There were more sloshing sounds, and then Andromache felt something being slipped under her dress, between her legs. A damp cloth. She cried out and tried feebly to curl into a ball.

"Oh, Ahndromahk," whispered Hector. "That hurt you?"

She didn't answer. It hadn't — not really. She just couldn't stand for him to —

"I am sohrry." For a few moments, he just held her. When it seemed that she'd calmed down, he ran another damp cloth over her neck, washing the sweat and blood from her body. She lay still. As he began to pull the dress off her shoulders, though, she twisted back in on herself. He didn't try to unbend her but instead sponged off her arms and hair. His hands were even gentler than his mother's.

One last kindness, thought Andromache, as she began to dry heave.

"<u>Ahndromahk</u>," Hector whispered again. "Sssssh — <u>it is all rahght</u>."

She shook her head. "You're going to leave me, now," she finally managed to croak.

Hector threw the cloth to the floor and wrapped his arms and legs around her. "Never," he said, his face buried in her hair. "Never — I love you." He kissed her ear, her cheek, her neck, her shoulders.

Andromache clung to her knees and whimpered, "Yes, you will. I wished away our baby."

Whatever pain or confusion her words might have caused Hector, he pushed it aside for later. "You can't wish away a baby, <u>Ahndromahk</u>," he said, enveloping her rounded form. "It doesn't work that way."

"It does!" she shrieked. "I've done it before! Years ago, with the wagoner's!" She tensed, preparing to be heaved to the floor, now that Hector knew what a monster she was.

To her surprise, he held her even tighter. "Is that what he did to you?" he whispered, outraged. "He left you out there, after this happened to you?"

She was on the cliffs above Lyrnassa, begging the wagoner not to go, not to leave her and Auntie — she was crying as she watched the wagon bump along, away from the coast — she was shambling down to Lyrnassa — she was weak and covered in blood —

She was breathing too fast! She was going to pass out —

Hector caught her arms before she could pull at her hair, as she'd been about to do. "<u>Neffer. Neffer, pretty wife. Neffer, my Ahndromahk</u>," he murmured.

She broke into sobs.

For what felt like hours to her still-fuzzy brain, Andromache sobbed and wept, emptying herself of all the hornets that had been nesting inside her. They tried to sting her as they were expelled, but their poison didn't hurt as it once had.

Silently, Hector held her until her wailing stopped and her breathing slowed.

"I can take this?" he asked, pulling gently at her soiled dress.

Andromache nodded. She uncurled enough for him to slide it up her legs and hips. He maneuvered her arms through and pulled the garment over her head. She heard it thud against the ground.

Hector then retrieved the wash cloth and finished bathing her. The whole time, she clung to one of his arms, so his work was one-handed and slow. Several more hours — at least, that was what she thought — passed before he finally placed the soft cloth back in the basin.

"You need sleep," he murmured, gathering her once more in his arms and carrying her to the bed. He took out fresh, clean clothes for her, dressed her, placed a bandage between her legs, and laid her on her side.

"No!" she cried as he drew back from her.

"I am going to be there," he said softly. "One moment."

She heard him opening the door and dragging something in — a fresh basin of water, she supposed, left by his mother. Then came the quiet sounds of cloth against stone as Hector scrubbed the floor. Muffled splashes as he bathed. Rustlings as he changed clothes. A squeak as the door was opened once again. Several dull thumps as all their dirty things flew out onto the courtyard. When this was done, Hector came to bed and lay behind her, wrapping his arm around her. She drifted off to sleep.

WHEN ANDROMACHE OPENED her eyes once more, the room was dark. Night must have fallen. Hector was still there, behind her — in fact, he didn't seem to have moved.

"Ector," she whispered. "Are you awake?"

"Yes, pretty wife." He leaned over her. "You need something? Water?" His voice was pinched with concern.

Water. That sounded good. She nodded. "Please. Water."

Hector sat up and poured her a cup from the jar beside their bed.

Andromache, too, tried to sit up.

"No, I can help you." He held her half-upright while she drank, then helped her lie down again. After replacing the cup, he stretched out beside her, now facing her. Looking into her eyes...

Andromache started to cry. "I'm so sorry," she whispered. "So sorry..."

"No, Ahndromahk —"

"I'm so sorry about our baby."

"You did noffing wrong. Noffing."

"Yes, I did!" She switched to Truvan to make sure that he understood. "I *told* you, I wished it away —"

"And *I* told *you* that it doesn't work like that."

"I wished away the wagoner's!" she insisted, sniffling and wiping her eyes. "I thought ,and thought, and *thought* about how I couldn't stand to have his baby inside me — and then it was gone."

"That's coincidence," said Hector. His throat sounded tight.

"I still thought it," whispered Andromache, looking at Hector's face, so close to hers.

His eyes were full of sorrow. "Why did you think it?" he whispered back. Both of them knew he wasn't asking about the wagoner's baby.

"I saw you in the sculpture garden," she said.

Hector stopped breathing.

Andromache went on: "I followed you. You were leaving so early, every morning, and you didn't tell me why." She paused. "I thought you were screwing some other woman."

"Oh, Ahndromahk!" His voice broke. "Never. *Never!*"

"Well, you weren't screwing *me*," she shot back.

He closed his eyes and rubbed at his forehead.

"What was I supposed to think?"

"Not *that!*" The tone of Hector's voice was half-anguished, half-reproachful. "You're the only woman in the world. I would *never —*"

"I know," Andromache whispered. "I followed you for a week, and all you did was sit there on the ground, freezing to death." She began to sob again at the memory. "I saw you shivering. I had a cloak on, but I didn't go over to you. I didn't wrap it around you or sit next to you — I just let you freeze. I let you freeze! I let you *freeze!*"

"Sssh," said Hector, once again removing her hands from her hair.

"I left you there! You could've frozen, and I didn't care. I just —"

"Sssh…"

"I was so, so mad at you!" she sobbed. "I *hated* you! You could've stayed in bed, so warm, with me, but instead you went to the sculpture garden and froze. You wanted to be *there* more than you wanted *me*. You didn't want to talk to me, or kiss me, or make love with me —"

"Ahndromahk —"

"What? It's true!" Her voice rose to a wail. "You only tried *once*, and we both know how that ended! That was the day I realized I was pregnant." She gave a bitter little moan. "You didn't want me, anymore. I knew you wouldn't want our baby, either, and I'd be all alone."

"I wanted you." Hector closed his eyes. "Oh, Ahndromahk, so much! And I wanted her —"

"You were *gone* all the time!" cried Andromache.

"I know."

"Every morning."

"I know."

"For hours."

"I know."

"And every night, too."

"I know! I know! I *know!*" Hector snapped. "And I wasn't here when you were bleeding to death! And I made you not want *my* baby inside you!"

Stunned by the depth of self-hatred in his voice, Andromache burrowed closer to him. "I didn't mean it," she whispered, kissing him over and over, dousing his face with her tears. "I never meant it. I was just scared. I wanted our baby so much, Ector. I did, I wanted our baby. I —"

"I know," said Hector. "I know." He turned onto his back, pulled her head to his chest, and let her cry herself to sleep.

❦

THE NEXT TIME Andromache awoke, she had to pee. She tried, ever so softly, to slip out from under Hector's arm, but the moment she stirred —

"Ahndromahk?" His arm tightened around her.

"I'll be right back."

"From where?"

Andromache felt a strange urge to laugh. She had to pee but was trapped by Hector — how terrifying this same problem had once seemed to her! And what a fool she'd been! "I have to pee," she said flatly.

"Oh," said Hector. "Let me help you."

"I can do it."

"You shouldn't be up."

"Well, I don't want to wet the bed."

"I mean, I'll hold you."

"Ector — I can sit on the basin."

"What if you fall while you're on it? What if you start to —" He shuddered.

Remembering the screams she'd heard — *'Mama! Mamaaa!'* — Andromache gave in and put her arms around his neck. "All right."

He held her steady over the basin while she used one hand to pull her dress up over her hips. She was very glad, now, to have Hector to cling to. Her mind was clearer than it had been, but her body still felt wobbly, especially her legs.

Afterward, however, she asked that he set her on the floor with a bowl of clean water and turn his back. He obliged but insisted on carrying her to the bed when she was finished washing.

"Be right back," he said, drawing the blanket over her legs.

Andromache watched him carry all the dirty things out to the courtyard. During one of his trips, water sloshed out of the bowl and onto the floor, which he then had to clean again. In all the drudgery, he never complained. "You really love me," she whispered, when he finally lay down beside her.

"So much," he agreed, kissing her forehead. "So very much."

"Then why did you stop talking to me?"

"You fell asleep, my sweetheart."

"No — not just now. Before."

Silence.

"Why did you stop talking to me? Why did you stop wanting to be with me? Did I do something wrong?"

Hector closed his eyes and shook his head.

"Then what is it?" whispered Andromache. "Please, <u>Ector</u>. Tell me."

"I *couldn't* talk to you, <u>Ahndromahk</u>," he sighed. "I couldn't even *look* at you. I couldn't stand to see the look in your eyes when you knew."

"Knew what?"

"Oh, gods!"

"Knew *what*?"

"That I'm a monster — a murderer."

"<u>Ector</u>!" she exclaimed, startled. "I would *never* —"

"You did when you first got here," he interrupted. "When you first came to Troy, that's how you looked at me."

Tears of guilt and sorrow welled in her eyes. He'd known, all along! He'd known about her fear of the blood-soaked Raider — he'd known about the horror she held him in — he'd known that she saw him as a monster. "I was sick, then," she whispered. "And scared. And alone. I didn't know you! When I was little, raiders were always coming to the Lukka lands and killing people — I saw it! I saw bodies with all their blood gone. And I thought you were — I didn't *know* you, or what you were like. Oh, <u>Ector</u>, I'm so sorry — so sorry! — so —"

"Sssh, don't cry," he murmured. "I don't blame you. Please, <u>Ahndromahk</u>, I understood. I understand. I know what you saw the day we met, above Lyrnassa. I know what soldiers look like at the end of the day —"

"<u>And *I* know better, now</u>," she said, kissing him. "<u>I know *you*. You're gentle.</u>" *Kiss.* "<u>You're warm.</u>" *Kiss.* "<u>You're</u> —"

"A murderer," finished Hector. His voice was flat and grey.

Andromache's lower lip began to tremble. "I *know* you've had to kill people," she whispered. "I fell in love with you knowing that." Not that she'd ever said so, or thought to reassure him! "I've known it since the day we met. You had to kill Mudders to save the Lyrnassans."

"That's not what I mean." Hector was rubbing the old scar on his temple. "I didn't *want* to kill any of them. I had to stop them, but I didn't want to kill them. I took as many prisoners as I could."

"I know," said Andromache. "I know. I heard."

"I know how to kill," Hector went on. "And I'm not afraid to do it, but I don't like it."

"Of course you don't."

"Killing is a last resort, when you're out of other choices, but even then, it's bad. You understand, Ahndromahk. I know you do. After you killed that goat, you could never eat meat again."

Andromache thought of the baby goat she'd found while out walking in the mountains of the Lukka lands...

The little creature was screaming in pain — his belly was torn open, and there was nothing she could do to save him. She took a rock in her hand — crack — crack! The screaming stopped. There was blood all over her, and she was running, running, running back home to her parents...

"You're right," she said softly. "I know how bad it is."

"Even when you have to," he repeated. "But what you did doesn't make you a murderer. You didn't *want* to kill that goat."

'You didn't want to kill that goat.' Again, her eyes filled with tears. The words echoed what Hector had said, the last time they'd tried to make love: *'I wanted to gut those boys — I wanted to do everything you said.'* Whatever it was he'd needed to tell her, she hadn't let him. "That night when we were —" She swallowed hard. "You started to say something about those boys who hurt Cutie. You were trying to talk to me."

"Ahndromahk..."

"I shut you down."

"It's not your fault." Again, Hector rubbed his temple. "I wasn't trying very hard. I was tired, and cold, and I just wanted my life back. I wanted to forget everything. I didn't really want to tell you."

She gently took his hand and kissed it. "Tell me what, Ector? Please, I'm listening. What didn't you want to tell me?"

Hector pulled away. "What I really was. What you were really married to. I couldn't be with you if I didn't tell you. I couldn't

stand to dirty you with any more lies. But once I told you —"
He rubbed his temple harshly.

"Ector, stop!" Andromache grabbed for his hand.

"The look on your face —"

"Please, Ector!"

"It seemed better to stay away from you..."

"Please — tell me!" she said. "Tell me what you think you were lying about. Tell me why you're so upset."

Hector seemed to cave in on himself. He reached again for his temple — ran his finger along the old scar there.

Of all the scars on his body, that was the one Andromache hated the most. It reminded her of the day she'd found Hector in the outpost stable, huddled and filthy, a gash on his forehead — the day when she'd told him she loved him, and he'd yelled at her to *'Go away!'*

That gash...she'd never asked Hector about it. Once it had healed and his hair had grown out to cover it, she'd let herself forget. What good did thinking about it do? Better just to move on. Hector never mentioned it, either. Every so often, he rubbed the scar, but Andromache had always just assumed that he was drawn to the odd texture, like a rough patch on the road might catch one's sandal. She hadn't seen any deeper meaning behind the gesture — at least, not until now.

"What happened?" she whispered. "When you got that cut, I mean?"

Hector closed his eyes. "It is hot. I take off the — the —" He drew a helmet in the air around his head.

"Helmet."

"Yes, helmet. Not long," he assured her. "Only fohr to wipe off the sweat. It stings me in the eyes." In Truvan, he added, "I know it sounds stupid. It *was* stupid! I knew better. I knew not to take it off — a rookie mistake. But my head was somewhere else, that day. I was mad. I didn't want to be there. I kept thinking, *'I shouldn't be here!'* And then, there was all that fucking sweat! I thought if I could just get that fucking sweat out of my eyes..."

Andromache saw her husband, surrounded by enemies. He was hot and sweaty — he needed a moment to breathe, to wipe his eyes.

"A rock hits me. Here." Hector pointed to the scar.

Andromache winced as the stone sliced into her husband's forehead — as the thin skin tore — as blood welled up in a crooked line.

"I look up. This guy is smiling." Hector's voice was bitter. "Lahffing."

A hulking brute, streaked in gore, his mouth gaping open in a black, rotten smile as he drew her husband's blood — laughing as blood poured into Hector's eyes — his warm, dark eyes! — and burned them.

"I feel stupid. And mad. So mad! I go crazy."

Andromache was crazy, too. Her blood was on fire.

"I fink, *'No mohre lahffing. You can cry!'*"

She saw her husband, enraged — boiling —

"So I kill him," finished Hector. "And I *want* to."

"You *had* to!" cried Andromache, her voice sharp. "It was you or him!"

"I *want* to," Hector insisted. His eyes were hard. "I hate him. I do not stop. Always befohre, I stop. If I can, I stop. I say, *'Be my prisoner.'* And most guys want to be my prisoner. They do not want to die."

It was true. Priam had told her long ago how prisoners were treated in Troy — they were ransomed or else given a place to live and integrated into society. It wasn't a bad lot in life, to be taken prisoner by a Trojan.

"Sometimes, they ask me," said Hector. "They *ask* to be my prisoner. I ask, ohr they ask. Baht not him." Hector's voice was hoarse. "I do not stop. I do not ask."

Andromache gripped his arm. "Ector...did *he*?"

"Did he what?"

"Did *he* ask? Did he *want* to be your prisoner?"

"I do not know." Hector rubbed the scar again. "I do not know, I do not care. I kill him. He is the captain. He is dead, and his guys ahre scared. I go after them — mohre and mohre and mohre. They rahn. I chase them. I get many — my soldiers follow — they fink this is my stretegy — and *they* get many — and then it is done — and there is so mahch blood — and I am so crazy, so crazy..."

Andromache saw her husband, confused — exhausted — covered in blood. Tears ran down her cheeks.

"It is so stupid, what I do!" cried Hector. "Stupid to take off the helmet. Stupid to get mad. Stupid to — to —" Unable to find the word he wanted, he switched once more to Truvan. "I never should've charged. The way I fight — the way we've always fought in Troy! — is to hold a line. Make the enemy get tired of it all and give up. We're a wall, not a spear. Once in a while, you might *have* to attack, but you don't do it just because some guy pisses you off." He rubbed the scar on his forehead. "I don't know where my head was! If my soldiers hadn't followed me —"

"But they did!" Andromache broke in, not wanting to think about the outcome if Hector had wound up alone, in the middle of the Mudder horde. "They followed you."

"I was lucky."

"They're well-trained," she argued. "And loyal."

"I was *lucky*," he insisted. "Luckier than I deserved."

"Ector!" she gasped. "You don't mean that!"

"Yes!" he said. "It is bad, what I do. It is bad to haff no prisoners."

"But you didn't ask those Mudders to invade!" Andromache protested. "They could've stayed home instead of starting a fight. Raiders are scum, Ector."

"Still, it is bad, *wanting* to kill them."

"You snapped," said Andromache. "Anyone can snap under pressure."

"If I can snap one time, I can snap again," Hector argued. "This is how I feel, when the battle is done. This is how I feel, when we rahde home. I feel dirty. I feel stupid, and crazy, and bad, and ahgly. I want to be alone…"

"But instead, I found you," said Andromache in a low voice.

"And I say, *'Go away!'*" Hector finished her thought. "I do not want you to be wiff a murderer."

"Stop calling yourself that!"

"I am explaining how I feel that night."

"Well, if that's how you felt, why did you come to my room at all?"

"To tell you I am sohrry," said Hector. "To tell you noffing is your fault." He swallowed hard. "Baht then —"

"But *then*," Andromache echoed. *Then — then.* How sweet *then* had been…

"You ahre holding me — lahffing me — kissing me. It is all I want fohr years." Hector pressed his forehead to hers and held her close. "It is so good, you know?"

"I know."

"Wiff you, I am so happy."

Andromache remembered the joy on his face, that night. "I know," she said.

"When I snap, when I go crazy, I fink I can neffer be happy again. Baht wiff you, I am happy."

"Deep blue happy," she murmured.

He nodded. "So strong a happy, it can make the bad stahff go away. I fink, *I can be a good commander again. I can be a good man again...*" He sighed. "Baht then I still see that guy — the guy wiff the rock."

"Your nightmares," whispered Andromache, thinking of the first few nights she'd spent with Hector.

He nodded. "I haff trahble to fohrget him."

"Your parents knew that something was wrong," she said. "That's why they tricked you into fetching Uncle. They wanted him to help you, before the wedding."

"Mom tells you this?" asked Hector, with a curious look.

"Mm-hmm. While you were away, we talked about a few things. She said you went to Uncle other times, too, and came back feeling more —" Andromache paused. "Yourself."

"On that, she is rahght," said Hector. "Baht my parents do not trick me. I *want* to go. I *want* to see Uncle. I *want* help befohre the wedding."

"You did *not*!" Andromache objected. "You were shouting at them, refusing to go —"

"Yes." Pause. "And then I see Penthesilea."

"Yes." Andromache knew *that* story as well as he did. "And she called me a whore, and then you fetched Uncle for the ceremony so no one else would call me that."

"Yes," said Hector. "And no. She call you that, and I am mad. So, so mad. *Too* mad. I want to hit her." He stopped to let his words sink in. "To *hit* her! To hit her fohr a word. I know it is a bad word, baht I do not hit people, Ahndromahk. That is not me. Then, I see that I am getting too mad, too easy. Wiff her, wiff Mom and Dad — effen wiff you." He paused again. "I know then I need Uncle. You see, he knows stahff. He is in the ahrmy, too. He is lahke me. He has seen it all."

And no one else in Hector's life had seen that kind of thing. No one else understood.

"The first time he helps me," said Hector, "I am jahst a boy. Eighteen, nineteen. I am mad and weird and haff trahble to fohrget stahff."

Hector didn't elaborate on '*stuff*' this time, either, but Andromache could imagine. She had memories of her own: the acrid smell of smoke. The cracking of a rock against a skull. Torn flesh, like meat. The yielding of bone. She knew how sensations could linger. She could imagine the horrors in Hector's mind, things no one should ever have to know…

Gore, spurting into his mouth — flesh, splitting under his hand — the reek of guts torn open — cries for help that he couldn't answer — a comrade, a friend, lying facedown on the sand —

"At first, the ahrmy is so fahn," Hector went on. "I can rahde hohrses. I can practice fight. Always, I lahke the practice fights! They ahre fahn. They ahre exciting. I stahrt out bad, baht I work hahrd and get good."

Good? No, Andromache knew that '*good*' didn't cut it. Hector was the *best*, the best in all of Troy, the greatest warrior Troy had ever seen. Of course he liked sparring! Who wouldn't want to be the best at something?

"I fink the ahrmy is so fahn! Then, when I am eighteen or nineteen, I go to a *real* fight. The real fight is different. Hohrrible. So hohrrible, I cannot say."

But Andromache could imagine what he wasn't saying…

The crunch of bones under an axe — the screams of a broken-legged horse — the sickly smell of putrefying flesh —

"So hohrrible, Ahndromahk!" Hector repeated. "I go to the real fight, and I come back mad and weird, and Uncle make me tell him *efferyfing*. One time, I tell it. I face it. Then I mahst build a wall ohff rocks around it so I cannot see it. He teach me to do this."

"You built a wall around the bad memories in your mind?"

Hector nodded.

"Did that work?"

"Yes," he said. "Mostly, yes. Maybe somefing slips out, baht it does not hurt so bad."

His black laugh, thought Andromache. *It helps keep the memories from hurting.* She reached out to touch her husband's arm.

Hector paused. "You ahre all rahght?" he asked softly.

Andromache nodded. In truth, she was *not* all right, in ways she couldn't even begin to think about, but she didn't want him to stop talking. It had been so long since they'd talked! "Why did you stay in the army, if it's so horrible?" she asked.

"Becahse someone mahst do it. Always, there ahre enemies, efferywhere. I tell myself, *'Better me than someone who likes to start trouble.'* I can be calm. I can listen to good advice. I can help my soldiers. I can help them do their best. I can help them come home. That is why I stay, and that is why I lead. I am a good leader." His voice, which up till then had sounded proud, broke. "I *was* a good leader."

"Ector —" Andromache protested.

But he interrupted her, insisting on the past time: "*Was.*"

His face was set in a stubborn way, and Andromache could see that there was no point in arguing. "You never finished telling me about your uncle," she said instead. "What exactly did he say about that man — the man with the rock?"

"He say I remember it wrong," Hector admitted. "Maybe the battle is going on too long. Maybe it is time fohr attacking. And maybe those soldiers do not want to be prisoners."

"Ah!" crowed Andromache. "You were being too hard on yourself! You just did what you *had* to do!"

"I know you want this fohr true," Hector said gently. "So does Uncle. But I did *mohre*, mohre than I had to do."

"You even said, you don't remember what happened."

"I remember enough."

"So, even Uncle couldn't help you, this time," Andromache murmured in dismay. How silly she'd been to think that Hector could be fixed, just like that, as though he were a cracked board or a fraying cloth. Minds didn't work that way. She should have known better!

But Hector contradicted her: "Yes, he help! He tell me:

'Even if you're right, it was only once. Forget about that man, Sonny! Think about your wife, instead — think about how much you love her. Focus on her. Make a new start with her. Love her, and let her love you. She deserves that.'"

Hector's voice softened. "I know that he is rahght, pretty wife, and I want all this fohr you. I tell myself:

'Don't be stupid, Hector. Take it. Take everything she's giving you, and be happy. Forget about the man who laughed at you. You went crazy once, but you'll never do it again. Forget about that man! It might take a long time, but you can do it. Forget about him — and never tell _Ahndromahk_, because she'll stop loving you if she finds out...'"

Tears welled in Andromache's eyes. "Oh, Ector! I wouldn't — I _won't_ —"

"So I fohrget," said Hector, cutting her off. "Little by little. I build a wall around him."

But somewhere along the line, he'd apparently stopped forgetting. "Did something happen, the last time you were away?" she whispered. "Something that made you remember him? Is that why you started going down to the sculpture garden?"

Hector shook his head. "Noffing happens."

"Nothing?"

"A normal fight, yes. Noffing _crazy_ happens. I do the necessary, that is all." He sounded grim — because, after all, even '_the necessary_' was so atrocious that most people tried not to think about it, let alone do it — but he also sounded proud. "The fight is safe."

"'_Safe?_'" Andromache echoed, in disbelief.

"Mohre safe — less risky," Hector clarified. "We hold a line. We send back enemies. When they rahn, we let them rahn. They come back. We hold. They rahn. We stay to be sure they do not come back again." He paused. "I am proud ohff my guys. It is hahrd to sit still. Baht they do it. We do it rahght."

"They did what you asked," said Andromache. "I _told_ you — they're well-trained. They're loyal." _They love you_, she added to herself, thinking of Thoas, of Xanthus, of the others she'd come to know, the ones whose brash jawing changed to murmurs of respect when Hector came near.

"They do well," he said simply. "We win. We come home."

Andromache thought back through all he'd said, but something was missing. Either her mind was going fuzzy again, or he still hadn't come to the heart of his story. "That's a good thing, isn't it?" she asked. "Good that you won — and *how* you won?"

"Yes," he said.

"Then I don't understand! Right after you came home, everything changed. The night you gave your report was when you stopped loving me!"

His arms were tight around her. "I did not — I did *not*!"

"You stopped loving me," she repeated. "You never stayed with me. You left me…" They'd been around this point before. Or was this the first time? Had the night started over? Andromache moaned. She couldn't endure it. She couldn't stand living through this night again.

"I need time alone," said Hector, from very far away. "I am not myself."

Andromache knew why he sounded distant. He was back in time, in her room, the first night he'd ever come to her. He was telling her why he'd gone to the outpost stable instead of staying with the army, at the gates. She didn't know how to get back there with him — but she didn't *want* to be alone again! — especially not *here*, in the unbearable present! — she needed —

"Sssh, my Ahndromahk," soothed Hector. His arms trembled with her sobbing. "Rest now."

"No!" Her head began to clear, again. She wasn't ready to rest. *He's talking about now, not then,* she told herself. *He's talking about when he went to the sculpture garden.* "Why did you need time alone? What were you thinking about?"

Hector paused. "About the ahncle ohff Demuchus."

Andromache shook her head — it *must* have gone muddy again! Had Hector said —

"Ucalegon," he clarified.

Andromache was suddenly, fully, awake. Her body stiffened with dislike. "What does *he* have to do with anything?"

"You know that pahrty, wiff Demuchus? At his house?"

Andromache nodded. "Ucalegon took you away, that night. You were gone a long time."

"Yes. That night, he talks about the fight — when I kill the man wiff the rock."

"What?" asked Andromache. "Why?"

"Becahse he is reading the text ohff Demuchus."

Andromache frowned. "Text?"

"*On the Command of Armies*," Hector explained.

"Oh, the treatise!" said Andromache, remembering. "Demuchus's council treatise. He studied you."

Hector nodded. "I talk to him. I tell him some stahff."

Andromache tensed. "You talked to *Demuchus*? You told *him* things? When you wouldn't talk to *me*?" Uncle was one thing — she could understand why Hector would talk to *him*. But why *Demuchus*?

"No, no," Hector said hastily, switching to Truvan so there would be no misunderstanding. "I told him about some generic concepts — how a defensive line works, how a charge works, how you can use the landscape to your advantage. That sort of thing."

"Oh," said Andromache, relaxing once more.

"When I told Demuchus about charges, I stressed how risky they were and why they should be avoided, if possible. I gave him a little overview of that battle — the one with the man who laughed at me. I didn't tell Demuchus why I attacked, just that, in hindsight, it had been a dangerous thing to do. Ucalegon read that passage. He read between the lines and understood more than I told Demuchus. That's why he wanted to talk to me."

"Oh," Andromache said again. "Did he like what you said?"

Hector shook his head. "He thought I'd interpreted the battle all wrong, and that attacking had been the right move. But he liked that I knew about attacks and how to carry them out." Hector's voice turned white and sharp:

"*You have it in you to become the kind of commander we need. I've known it since the day you rode into Lyrnassa and beat back that shipload of Achaean raider filth...*"

His imitation of Ucalegon was so perfect that Andromache shrank from him.

"*Those Achaeans underestimated you. They thought you would waste time with our standard channels, setting up defenses and sending back to Troy for aid. You showed them, boy! — and you showed them again in your most recent campaign. That's what we need against the Achaeans. Swift attacks. No more caution, no more waiting. Do it that way every time! No more prisoners — kill as many as you can. I've lived among the Achaeans, and there's only one thing they understand — force. The more ruthless you are, the better. The only prisoners they take are women, and believe me, the women would be better off dead. You know what I mean, boy! The Achaeans can't be bought off the way we've bought off the Hittites all these years. Just do what they do. Kill them — slaughter them — murder them — "*

"Stop!" Andromache pleaded. "<u>Ector</u>, stop! Calm down."

He was panting.

"Ssssssh…" She rubbed his neck until his breathing slowed.

"I'm sorry," said Hector.

Andromache shook her head. "You have nothing to be sorry about! What did you say to that horrible man?"

Hector gave a nasty laugh. "That *he* could go do all that slaughtering, if he wanted to, if he could even hold a spear upright —"

"Good for you!" Andromache whispered fiercely. "Good for *you*!"

"He was pissed," said Hector. "But not as pissed then as when I came back to Troy, this last time. He found out that I hadn't ordered any attacks — hadn't chased any of the Achaeans when they retreated. He asked to see me right before the general council meeting:

What did I tell you, boy? How many times did you repulse them? If you'd counterattacked and killed them, you would have shortened the battle by weeks. Not to mention the future. They'll invade again, all over our lands. Maybe Troy itself. They have no reason not to. They were testing you, to see if you meant what you told them last time. You failed."

"You did *not*!" Andromache hissed in outrage.

Hector was rubbing his scar again. She caught his wrist to stop him.

"You did right, <u>Ector</u>," she said. "You did *right*."

He snorted. "Ucalegon didn't think so. He said the Achaeans would think I'm a coward."

"You're *not*!"

Again, Hector laughed, still more nastily than before. "I know. That's the kind of stupid taunt people always throw at each other, and I've heard it too many times to take the bait. I told him to fuck off."

"Good!" cried Andromache, squeezing his hand. "I'm glad you said that! I *hate* him!"

"Me, too," said Hector, but his rage seemed to have faded. He'd gone strangely limp. "But then he just stared at me..."

Andromache could see those marble eyes — hard, just like the voice —

"He stared at me. Then he said:

'You'll see. Don't listen to me! Keep holding your line, repelling a few here and there instead of killing them. You'll see. You'll see them come back in hordes. There are thousands upon thousands of Achaeans, and they want to build an empire. I've seen them; so will you. You'll see them trample over everything you love — your city, your people. Your wife. They'll drag her off in chains. She'll be a slave — another man's plaything — that is, unless he doesn't like her. Then, he'll just slit her open and let her blood pour out..."

With those words, Hector broke down and started sobbing in Andromache's arms.

"Sssh," she murmured, stroking his hair. "Ssssssssh..."

"He — he made me see all my worst nightmares, and I —"

"Ssssh..." Andromache held Hector close and kissed him; all she wanted was to comfort him. As his trembling slowed, though, she began to seethe. She *hated* Ucalegon, that monster — playing on her husband's love for her! "I hate him," she whispered. "I hate him for what he said to you! He had no right! Oh, Ector, you should've come straight home, so we could talk —"

Slowly, Hector drew back from her. He looked calmer, if still upset. "I had to go to the council meeting," he said.

"Ector," she scolded gently. "Your report could've waited."

He shook his head. "My report wasn't the real issue."

"Then what was?"

"Laoganus."

"Laoganus? The other commander?" Andromache frowned. She knew Laoganus only from his voice, a blustery voice hollering at Hector her first night in Troy. "What about him?"

"He got sick while I was gone."

"With what?"

"I don't know — some kind of fever." In a low voice, Hector added, "I heard he went blind."

"What? That's awful!"

"I know. I haven't gone to see him, and I won't unless he asks for me. I don't think he will — I don't think he would want that."

Andromache shook her head. She couldn't imagine a sick, blind Laoganus asking to visit with his young rival. He hadn't been happy three years earlier, when Hector was given command of half the army. "I'm sorry," she said to Hector. "I know you didn't always get along, but —"

"I know." He hugged her, his face pressed to her hair. "It's horrible. I don't know if that part is true or just a rumor, but it's true enough that he's sick — too sick to serve as commander. So, the council had to figure out what to do about his post. Ucalegon saw the whole thing as an opportunity to push his own agenda." Once more, Hector mimicked Ucalegon's voice:

" *'Events such as these are a reminder that we must from time to time review our policies. The world is always changing, and we must be ready. I cannot stress this enough in the case of the Achaeans. We've grown careless, watching them raid our allies' shores. We've let ourselves be fooled about their ultimate goal. No more! Hear it now, from me — the Achaeans want an empire. They want to enrich themselves on the very trade routes that have brought wealth to Troy. They mean to take our city, sooner or later, and we must be prepared to stop them.'* "

Andromache scoffed. "The man is obsessed!" she said caustically. "I hope the other council members told him the same thing you did!"

Hector hesitated.

"They believed him?" she asked, feeling a twinge of fear.

"They agreed that the Achaeans are a concern —"

Andromache blanched.

"— but everyone says that," Hector added hastily. "Even Uncle said it."

And bickering temple priests, Andromache thought to herself. *And Cassandra's friends.* "Is everyone right?" she whispered.

"Oh, my sweetheart…listen, there have been some Achaean raids near us, but those bands were small and scattered. They'd be crazy to attack a city as strong as Troy."

"But the council —"

"They have to plan for the worst, that's all," Hector said gently. "Just because you prepare for the worst doesn't mean it will happen."

"I suppose that's true," said Andromache, though her stomach clenched once more in fear. Hector might tell her anything to keep her from worrying. "What else did that awful man say?"

"That it was time to revamp Troy's army. That there should be a supreme commander again, in case decisions ever have to be made quickly. The council agreed to appoint one."

Andromache frowned at Hector. "You?"

He looked away.

"You never even *told* me!" she cried. Although, now that she knew, a lot of things made sense. Those times when Hecuba had spoken of '*adjustments*,' she must have meant Hector's promotion. She must have thought Andromache knew. Then, too, there was the ongoing quarrel between Hecuba and Priam: Hecuba, who hadn't wanted her son approved, and Priam, who'd felt compelled to give his nod. At the time, their rift had seemed unimportant, compared to Andromache's private anguish. She'd never dreamed that their problems might be linked.

"I couldn't tell you," said Hector. "It was part of everything I couldn't talk to you about."

"What do you mean?"

"Ucalegon was the one who nominated me for the post."

"He *what?*" exclaimed Andromache. "After yelling at you? After saying those disgusting things about me?"

"He nominated me," confirmed Hector. "He wanted me specifically. He said I'd be perfect for the times we were facing. He said I had control over the troops but wasn't afraid to flout the old rules if necessary. Because of what happened in Lyrnassa," Hector explained. "The council had to agree with that, since that was why they'd promoted me to commander in the first place."

Andromache nodded.

"Frankly, I didn't have a problem with it either. But what came next was another story. Ucalegon said:

Laoganus — praise be to the stars for his service — was more bluster than follow-through. Hector is isn't like that. He's effective. Aggressive. He's proven himself capable of ridding the country of Achaeans."

"He was still talking about Lyrnassa," said Andromache.

"Yes," Hector agreed. "But even more, he was talking about the time I went crazy, when I killed and took no prisoners. He was arguing that Troy's army should be led by a murderer."

"He didn't call you *that!*" Andromache was stunned. "Not even *he* would say *that!*"

"No," said Hector. "Not in so many words. But he talked on, and on, and on about all those things that I'd been trying so hard to forget."

"Oh <u>Ector</u>! I hate him!"

"The council didn't hate his speech," said Hector. "They approved me unanimously. I guess Ucalegon convinced them."

"No!" cried Andromache. "That's not why they wanted you. Do you really think your *dad* would listen to him? You're a good leader, <u>Ector</u>. They trust you — that's why they approved you. What that horrible man said had nothing to do with it!"

Hector sighed. "I don't know. I tried to talk to them. I reminded them that at Lyrnassa, the Achaean raiders had attacked first — that's why we went down there. I said that we never pick fights with any landing party, on the chance that they're only there to trade or take in water. I said that if the council chose me as supreme commander, I would use Troy's old methods, and my army would serve as a wall, holding a line.

"Ucalegon answered that based on what had happened in Lyrnassa, our policy should be to meet every Achaean ship with spears, not walls. That we should attack them immediately, without waiting to hear why they're there. That we shouldn't wait to test his theories until Achaean raiders are swarming past our bedroom windows."

Hector's voice broke. "He stared at me when he said that, <u>Ahndromahk</u>. That's when everything started crumbling. I saw only two paths open to me, and both were horrendous. I could start killing, and slaughtering, and murdering as a first step instead of a last resort. Oh, <u>Ahndromahk</u>! — don't you see how much worse that would be than before, when I killed the laughing man and his followers? That was one time. That was me, snapping once. I had a chance of moving forward from that. But Ucalegon wanted me to change my whole approach to battle. There would be no end to it, not until I was dead."

"Don't say that!" cried Andromache.

"But it's true. And not only that, you'd hate me for it! You'd look at me, and know what I was, and want to retch."

"Ector!" she pleaded.

"The other choice was *not* doing what Ucalegon said," Hector went on. "But if I ignored him, I'd have to risk watching you be dragged away, or —" He shuddered. "Or killed. No matter what I did, I'd lose you somehow. Of course, there was never really any choice. There's nothing I wouldn't do to save your life, even if it made you hate me —"

He broke off yet again. "That night, all those walls in my head started collapsing. First the one that had the laughing man behind it, then all the others. *All* of them! I remembered things I didn't know I knew. Things from years ago. Awful things. Sickening things. They were like thousands of rocks, falling on top of my head. I tried to duck them, for a while, but it was too much, and I finally stopped trying…"

Hector stared blankly at his hands. "Whenever I went to the sculpture garden, I thought about my past, and my future, which were pretty much the same thing. There was no hope, just a head full of hideous things and the promise of more to come. I saw how wrong I'd been to think I could have a new start. Once I murdered the laughing man, my path was set — there was no turning back."

He paused. "I thought about you, too," he said, looking into Andromache's eyes. "How I was dragging you down with me — how I wished I'd never gone to your room that first night."

"Ector!" she protested, but he went on.

"I regretted marrying you and dragging you down into all this filth. You could've been the wife of a farmer — someone who grew grapes and vegetables with you. I wished —" Hector's voice cracked. "That the *real* rock had hit my head harder. Done the job."

Andromache burst into tears. Her stomach was heaving. She was going to be sick — she was going to hurl all over the place, all over Hector, all over the floor he'd just washed clean —

"Ssssh…" Hector held her close, stroking her hair to soothe her. "Ssssh…I'm sorry. Oh, <u>Ahndromahk</u>, I shouldn't have said that…"

"I don't *want* a grape farmer!" Andromache screamed. She could feel reality thinning around her again. "All they talk about is grape rot — don't you remember?" Sobbing, she quoted the text: '*If the first has rot, cast it away. If the second has rot, cast it away. If the third has rot —* '"

"Please," Hector begged. "Please, calm down."

"Oh, gods! I never showed you that text!" sobbed Andromache. "I wanted to! I thought we could laugh —"

"<u>Ahndromahk</u>, stop."

Hector's arms tightened around her to the point where they almost hurt. He was restraining her. He thought she was crazy. She *was* crazy — she'd been reaching for her hair, again.

"<u>I don't want a grape farmer,</u>" she whimpered, sinking into his chest. There, she wept, and sobbed, and let herself be rocked.

"<u>Ahndromahk</u>…" said Hector, when she was quiet once more. "<u>Oh, Ahndromahk!</u> I'm sorry."

"I know," she whispered.

"I felt lost. And scared."

"I know."

"I was going insane — I mean that, <u>Ahndromahk</u>. I was so scared about what might happen that it was hard to be around you."

"It was hard *not* to be around *you*," she countered.

"I thought you'd be better off —"

"I *wasn't.*"

"I know," said Hector, his voice breaking again.

Andromache looked at him. In the dim light of the room, she could see that his cheeks were wet. She tried to imagine how she'd looked to him, crumpled on the ground, covered in blood. She tried to imagine how the reverse scene would have looked to her…

Fighting back tears of her own, she buried her face in his shoulder and hugged him fiercely. She had a right to be furious with him — to hate him, even — for abandoning her, no matter how scared he'd been. She had a right, but she was weary of anger. She was weary, and weak, and sad, and she just wanted to be with her husband. She wanted him to hold her. She wanted to soothe *him* — she was as much to blame as he was. He had a right to hate her, too, for how stupid and selfish she'd been! She, of all people, should have recognized the signs of his fear.

They were subtle, even misleading. The day of Muka's burial, when he was afraid Andromache might throw herself into the sea, he'd been stiff with her. Down at the stables, when he was scared she would succumb to heat-sickness, he'd grown angry. And out in the hills, after Frondsia had carried her off, he hadn't said a word to her. He'd seemed furious, mortified — anything but frightened. *'I'm so sorry, my sweetheart,'* he'd said, later. *'I can see why you misunderstood. I've trained myself never to look scared because in the army, it's better to look mad. Sometimes the training just takes over...'*

After all the time they'd spent together, Andromache should have known what it meant for Hector not to talk to her. She'd been too stupid, too wrapped up in herself, to see that her husband was shattering.

A small sob escaped.

"Ahndromahk?" murmured Hector. "You ahre all rahght?"

"Y-yes."

"You ahre comfohrtable?"

"Pretty much."

"You do not hurt?"

She shivered.

"Ahndromahk?"

"A little cramping," she whispered. *And I'm empty...*

"You want to turn?"

She nodded. Hector helped her turn onto her other side.

"Sleep," he murmured. "Sleep a little. I will be wiff you." He lay on his side so he was curled around her, the way she liked best. "I will not leaff you..."

Andromache closed her eyes. She was nearly asleep when a thought jolted her. "Ector!" she cried.

"What is wrong?"

"You said '*she.*' You said '*her.*'"

"What? When?"

"Earlier. About the baby. You called the baby '*her.*'"

"I did?"

Andromache nodded. "How did you know?" she croaked. For, when his words had finally hit her, just then, she'd known them to be true. Andromache had *seen* her — a laughing little girl, her long hair blowing in the breeze, her tiny hand tucked into a much larger one. "How did you *know*? I didn't even know. I called her *it*, and —"

"Ahndromahk," Hector interrupted. "I didn't know. I didn't know, either — I just —" He sighed. "Girls are sweeter, that's all. I was hoping..."

"Oh." As Andromache watched, another child joined the first — a little boy, running around naked, catching lizards and singing little songs. He was as clear to her as the girl. Andromache wanted to hug both of them to her, but she knew that if she tried to touch them, they would vanish. Instead, she stroked her husband's arm. "Boys are just as sweet," she told him. "But you were right. She's a girl. I see her..."

Chapter 78

Light was streaming in through the cracks between the curtains — strong light, late morning at least. Andromache reached back to touch the bed behind her. It was empty, as it had been every morning for weeks and weeks.

It was a dream, she thought. Her reconciliation with Hector, the way he'd held her, everything he'd said to her: all of those things were fantasies. Her heart sank down into the floor — or rather, part of it sank. Another part hurtled desperately skyward. If the conversation was a dream, then the little girl she'd seen wasn't lost, after all!

Andromache gasped. She brought her hand back around to her belly, feverishly touching it. *Are you there?* she thought. *Please be there!*

But, as she shifted, she became aware of a cloth between her thighs. *The bandage,* she remembered. She hadn't dreamed *that*— her baby was gone.

"Ector!" she screamed.

Nothing.

"Ector! Ector! Ector!" She shrieked his name until it came out as nothing more than a broken sob. "Ector…"

Just when Andromache believed that she'd lost everything, and that only the worst parts of yesterday had been true, the door crashed open and Hector burst through. His eyes were wild as he ran to her.

"What's wrong?" he asked hoarsely.

"I didn't know where you were!" she sobbed.

"Ssssh, Ahndromahk." Hector took her in his arms. "I am here, now. I am here."

"You left —"

"Sssssh," he soothed, rocking slowly back and forth. "Only fohr water." He kissed her hair. "Our jahr, it is empty. "

"Oh." She nestled against his shoulder and tried to collect herself.

"And broken, now," he added. "The jar. I dropped it, when you —" He hugged her tightly. "I thought you were hurt."

"Just scared," she said.

He kissed her hair again. "You want somefing to eat?"

She shook her head.

"There is a tray outside the door. I can get it."

Andromache tightened her hold. She didn't want to let go of him.

"You need somefing," he pleaded. "Water, anyway. The tray has a little jahr."

Sighing, she released him. Hector slid off the bed and back over to the door. He returned almost instantly with a heaping tray of food.

"Did your mom leave all that?" whispered Andromache.

"I fink so."

"That was nice…"

Hector sat beside her. "You want some fruits, maybe?" he murmured. "Stew?"

Andromache swallowed hard. Her throat was coated in dust. "All right."

He handed her a piece of bread dipped in stew and watched her choke down a bite. "Good?" he asked. His eyes were bright with worry.

"Good." She set the bread back down on the tray.

Hector took it and tasted the stew for himself. "Mmm," he agreed. "Good."

Andromache rested her head on his shoulder. She felt inexpressibly tired.

"You want somefing else?" he asked, holding up a slice of dried apple.

After one obedient bite, she gently pushed his hand away. "I guess I'm not hungry."

Pause. "I can eat?"

"Of course."

Hector pulled the tray over. "I ran into Mom before, at the spring," he said, once he'd polished off a handful of dried apple slices and the remainder of the stew. "She wants to see you."

Andromache's heart began to pound. She wasn't ready for the family, for what they would say! The girl she'd lost was Hector's baby — their granddaughter, their niece. She couldn't look them in the eye.

"She wants to make sure that you're all right," Hector added. "To make sure you're healing."

Andromache shook her head. "Only you! I only want you." She'd *just* gotten him back! All she wanted was to fall asleep beside him, with his arm around her — to wake up and feel him near her. They still had so much to talk about. They'd hardly begun to talk about *her*. Their little girl...

The last thing she wanted was to see Hector's mother — have her legs ripped apart — be inspected. Judged. Told, *You're sick, Andromache. You're putrefying. And you deserve it.*

Quiet tears streaked down her face. Hector brushed them away.

"Ahndromahk?" he whispered. "I need to go. Jahst a little moment and then I am back."

She nodded.

He slipped out the door, and true to his word, was soon back — unexpectedly laden with another, larger, tray of food.

"Ector?" she asked, frowning. "What's all this about?"

"I told Mom '*Not today*.' She said that's fine —" He nodded to the tray. "As long as you eat — and drink — and don't have a fever."

Fever was a legitimate concern, after some of the crazy things Andromache had said and thought the night before. She felt saner, now, though. The danger of fever had passed. And she didn't feel hungry at all. Still, if eating was the price for keeping Hecuba away, she would do it. Sighing in defeat, she took a handful of figs and ate them.

"Good?" asked Hector.

Andromache nodded. They tasted like clay.

Hector brushed a loose hair off her cheek. "Ahndromahk?"

"Hmm?"

"I know you don't want my mom, but could you handle a different visitor?"

She stiffened. "Who?"

"Wait." Hector rose from the bed, opened the door and whistled.

Cutie flew in.

"Go help your mama," said Hector.

Cutie leapt onto the bed, and Andromache hugged the little dog so tightly that she grunted. Far from minding, though, Cutie reveled in the attention. She was a white blur of joy — wriggling, arching her back, licking Andromache's face and hands.

"Hi, baby," Andromache murmured to Cutie. To Hector, she scolded, "*She's* not a visitor. This is her room, too."

Hector sat beside them and caressed Cutie's ears. The dog gave his chin a swipe before gleefully writhing her way into Andromache's lap.

"Good grief," said Andromache.

"She's been worried about you."

"I guess so!"

Hector rubbed Cutie's smooth head and whispered, "She led me to you…"

Andromache blinked. "Oh," she said.

"Mom and I were down at the stables, checking on an injured horse. She'd forgotten her oil kit, though, so we came back here to fetch it. '*You go get the oils from the kitchen,*' she told me. '*I'll run up to my room. We might need some dried snapwort, too, and all my stores are up there.*' While I was in the kitchen, I heard Cutie. She was just barking, barking, barking, out —" Hector gulped once, then again. "Out where you were, on the courtyard. I thought she was barking at birds," he added. "You know how she gets."

Andromache nodded.

"But she just kept going and going, so I went out there to see what the matter was." His voice was thick and hoarse. "She saved you."

Andromache hugged the spotted little creature. "She's a good girl."

Hector nodded. Cleared his throat. Looked away.

Andromache took his hand and held it.

"You want I can read to you?" he asked.

She nodded. "I'd like that."

"You haff somefing down here?"

Andromache thought of the love poems and texts she'd hidden in her clothing chest. As much as she loved Hector, in that moment, none of them seemed right. But there was another text, one she'd brought down a few weeks earlier, as a token of happier times…

"Yes," she answered. "It's on top of the table by the door."

Hector fetched the text, laughing softly when he saw the title. "*On Lorani?*"

"It's my favorite."

"Effen if Lorani ahre not real?" he teased gently.

"They're real," Andromache insisted, in accordance with their old joke. "They're there. I've seen them." She leaned back against Hector's chest, while Cutie lay down with her chin on Andromache's thigh. Hector began reading:

> "*The Lorani swim in a vast ocean in which our earth is but a mote within a bubble of air. The fact that certain features in this ocean appear and reappear throughout the year seems to indicate that we are caught in an eddy of fantastical proportions. The celestial ocean reaches far beyond our comprehension, and most of the Lorani dwell a great distance from us. Yet we see them. We see them, and they pull at our imagination…*"

ℰↄ

ANDROMACHE SLEPT all afternoon. When she awoke to silver starlight shining in around the curtains, Hector was still there, lying beside her.

"Hay-lo, pretty wife," he murmured, stroking her hair.

"Hello." She yawned.

"You sleep all rahght?"

"Mm-hmm." She hadn't had any dreams. Her sleep had been black and peaceful.

"You hahngry?"

Knowing the penalty for not eating, Andromache sat up and dutifully choked down a few bites of bread. One of the mouthfuls was dry, the other soggy — both, unpalatable — but she ate them. "I slept all day," she said.

"You can sleep all you want."

"Have *you* slept?"

Hector hesitated, then shook his head.

"Not —" Andromache cleared her throat. "Not since —"

He shook his head again.

"Ector — for pity's sake, don't do that! I'm fine."

A third time, he shook his head. "We don't know that you're fine…" The way his voice trailed off was a hint.

Andromache sighed. "If I let her come tomorrow, will you promise to get some sleep?"

"Tomorrow," he agreed. "After Mom sees you."

Andromache stiffened.

"What's wrong? Am I hurting you?" He stopped stroking her hair and looked down at her.

"No!" she said. "It's just —"

"Just what, my sweetheart?"

"What's she going to do to me?"

"Oh, Ahndromahk!" he scolded gently. "She just wants to check on you. She does this all the time, for women all over the city. She's a healer. You know that."

"I know."

"Then what are you nervous about?"

Andromache looked away from Hector's face. "Is she mad?" she finally murmured.

He lay down beside her and held her close. "She loves you."

"I know she wanted grandbabies." Andromache was breathing faster. Her eyes were brimming over with tears. "I heard her telling the Santiyan ladies. And I *had* her grandbaby and I —"

"Don't," whispered Hector. His voice was agony to hear.

"I'm sorry — I'm sorry —" Andromache kissed him on his cheeks, his eyes, his forehead. "I'm sorry —"

"Sssh…" murmured Hector, brushing her hair behind her ear. She wanted very much to ask him if he'd seen their girl, like she had, but his face was closed. It could wait.

Chapter 79

At the sound of a knock on the door the next morning, Andromache began to cry. All through the night, she'd dreamed of babies lost in pools of water — babies sent away in baskets — babies swept like dust, out of the house — babies taken away by ants and buried under the earth. Her nerves were shattered.

"I'll stay with you," whispered Hector, kissing her forehead. He then stood to open the door for his mother.

Hecuba came into the room. "Good morning, dear," she said, smiling.

"Good morning," murmured Andromache.

"How are you feeling?"

"All right." Privately, Andromache added, *Except for all the babies I got rid of last night*...

"My son brought you something to eat, yesterday?"

"Yes. Thank you for making up the tray."

"Of course, dear," said Hecuba. "You need to eat."

Andromache nodded.

Hecuba cleared her throat. "I'm assuming he also told you why I wanted to come..."

"Yes."

"Then would it be all right if I examined you?" After a pause, Hecuba added. "We'd all feel so much better, if we knew that you're healing."

Andromache nodded again.

"Good." Hecuba frowned. "Hector, dear?"

"Hmm?"

"Why don't you fetch your wife some breakfast?"

"No!" shrieked Andromache, reaching for Hector's hand.

"She wants me to stay, Mom."

Hecuba pursed her lips. "I see. Well, it's as you both decide, of course."

Hector nodded; Andromache clung to him.

"It's as you both decide," the older woman repeated. "Lie back, then, dear. I'm just going to roll up your dress…"

As Andromache felt her ankles — then calves — then knees — laid bare, she imagined what Hector was seeing. His wife, her flesh pale from inactivity and bumpy from the cool air. The flesh that had once driven him wild with passion, now subjected to his mother's scrutiny…

"Stop!" she screeched.

Hecuba stopped. "Did that hurt, dear?"

Andromache shook her head. "No, it's just — <u>Ector</u>?"

"What is it, my sweetheart?"

"You have to go."

"What? But you said —"

"I changed my mind."

"Are you sure?"

"Please, go."

"All right." Hector stood to leave. "I'll be right outside, if you need me."

"Why don't you go get her some breakfast, like I said before?" urged Hecuba.

"I'll be right outside, if you need me," Hector repeated.

Hecuba waited till the door was shut, then sighed. "It's better this way. This would take forever if he was in here, fussing over you, getting in the way."

Fussing. Such a flimsy word for what Hector had been doing, the past two days! On top of the endless cleaning and worrying, he hadn't even let himself sleep, and —

Hecuba broke in gently: "Are you really doing all right, dear?"

Andromache gave the barest of nods.

"You don't have to be. I stayed in bed for days — I didn't move at all."

Andromache felt her hemline being pushed up from her knees. The bandage was then moved away from her thighs.

"Especially the first time," Hecuba went on. "It was frightening — sad — black. Everyone had advice, of course. Every neighbor, every family member, every passer-by…and none of it was worth anything. You won't have to go through that. We'll keep everyone away till you say you want visitors. Cassandra's in a regular frenzy because I told her she's not to bother you until you or your husband personally tells her it's all right, but never you mind. She could use a lesson in restraint, especially when it comes to socializing. The way that girl gads about! I've never seen the like. My husband won't bother you, either. He's at the temple, of course. He hasn't budged from there since he heard the news. I suspect he's spent most of his time walking through the gardens — he loves what you've done down there, dear! In between walks, he's been praying. I don't really know what good it does — don't tell *him* I said that! — but it comforts him, and it can't do any harm. Then, there's Paris — he's been moping around, griping about having to market by himself, moaning that life is unfair and this is just the latest proof. No one ever called *him* selfless, to be sure, but that said, I peeked in his baskets, yesterday, and he'd brought back nothing but *your* favorite foods. So, once again, you need to eat, dear — if not for your own good, then so my poor younger son will feel he's accomplished something…"

As Hecuba spoke, she palpated Andromache's abdomen and examined her body. "No more blood has leaked out, has it?" she finally asked.

Andromache shook her head.

"Well. I've seen a thousand women in a similar state, and as far as I can tell, you're going to be fine," said Hecuba, looking sorrowful nonetheless. "I just don't think the time was right for a baby."

Andromache curled up on her side and started crying. "I wanted her," she moaned. "I wanted her so much! I wanted her! I *wanted* —" Her voice broke off. She was sobbing. Shaking.

"Ssssh…I know," murmured Hecuba, stroking Andromache's hair. "There was nothing you could do." Hecuba's touch was gentle. It reminded Andromache of her own mother's hand, smoothing her hair when she was sick or hurt. Hecuba had the same kind of hands: small but forceful, they could soothe injuries or whisk away fevers with one stroke.

Andromache wondered if her own hands would have been like that, one day…

The door squeaked.

"How is she?" Hector asked anxiously.

"She's going be fine, dear."

He let out a long breath.

"I'll mix up a tonic for her to drink several times a day," said Hecuba. "Other than that, we'll just have to make sure she eats enough and gets plenty of rest. She's such a tiny thing! We don't want her getting frail on top of everything else."

"All right."

"There's nothing wrong with her, as far as I can see. Like I told her, the time just wasn't right for a baby."

"All right."

"Now, as for *you*!" Hecuba said to her son. "You look terrible. Get some sleep. You and your wife aren't alone against the world — but if you were, you wouldn't be able to help her like *that*."

"All right, Mom."

"Well, then — I promised your wife she wouldn't have to suffer through visitors, so I'll be going, but let me know if you need anything. Anything at all."

"Mom?"

"Yes, dear?"

"Thank you."

Andromache heard the soft sounds of several cheek kisses. Then, the door squeaked again, and Hecuba was gone.

න

THE NEXT TIME Andromache awoke, Hector, too was gone. Her first instinct was to scream for him, but she fought it back. *He's in the house, finding food. Or maybe he's just getting some fresh air.* She sat up and pulled the curtains aside. Out on the courtyard, she saw Hector and Paris, each carrying a basin of fresh water. They were talking to each other. As they neared her room, she caught the tail end of their conversation.

"Oh — and mom's right, by the way," said Paris. "You look like shit. You're caving in on yourself."

"You look like a nice bread, puffed up in the oven," Hector retorted. He sounded grumpy, but Andromache could tell by his face that he was more pleased than annoyed by the ribbing. It was a sign of normalcy.

"Ha, ha. That's a good one."

"I thought so." Hector paused. "Hey, little brother?"

"Hmm?"

"Thanks for helping with the water."

"Any time. My life's delight is to haul things for people."

"All right, all right. Just bring it in."

Paris stopped abruptly. "I'll leave it by the door — I don't want to wake her up."

Hector nodded. "Thanks."

The door squeaked again. Hector carried in both basins, one at a time, and then turned toward the bed.

"Hello," Andromache said softly.

"My sweetheart! You're awake!"

Even as he smiled at her, Andromache could see that his mom and brother were right. He looked terrible. Gaunt, grey, drawn — the past few days had taken a visible toll. He sat down beside her, touching her hand lightly — hesitantly, as though he wasn't sure he was supposed to.

"Your mom said I'm all right," she murmured.

"I know." Hector looked at her, his eyes awash in love and pain. "I'm so glad you let her see you."

"Me too. She was really nice to me."

"I knew she would be! She loves you."

"She loves *you*, too." Andromache paused. "I heard what she told you, that you should go easier on yourself. And she's right. Please, Ector — get some sleep!"

He sighed.

"You promised you would, if I let her see me."

"Ahndromahk —"

"Just for a while," she coaxed. "I feel a lot better, honest."

"But —"

"Lay down." She pushed on his shoulder. "You have to! I mean it, Ector."

With a soft sigh, Hector obeyed. He lay down beside her, his forehead touching her thigh. "Sleep, now," said Andromache. "Sleep…" Silently, she added, *It's my turn to keep watch.*

In moments, Hector's feet were twitching. Andromache adjusted the blanket around him. He looked uncomfortable. He'd been wearing clothes continuously ever since the miscarriage — either because his constant trips in and out made nudity impractical, or because he no longer wanted to be naked around her. She hoped it was the former. If she came through this only to be treated like some fragile little vase, cherished but untouchable…

She sighed. She couldn't let herself think about that, at least not yet. It was too soon to worry about *that*. Both she and her husband *were* fragile, now, and in shock. They needed time to get strong again.

Hector moaned in his sleep.

A nightmare? wondered Andromache. "Ssssssssh," she murmured, smoothing his hair. "I'm here. I need you. Stay with me." Her fingertips brushed against the scar on his forehead, and reflexively, she shuddered. How she hated that scar! She hated everything it represented — the danger Hector had been in during the battle, the way he'd punished himself afterward. In more ways than one, that wound had almost destroyed him.

He gave another soft moan.

"Sssh…it's all right," whispered Andromache. A murderer! He'd actually called himself a *murderer*! She still couldn't believe it. Murderers killed unarmed teenagers and took revenge on childhood bullies. They attacked blameless villages, setting fire to the houses and slaughtering the inhabitants. They chased little girls and mothers up hillsides. They drained men of blood and left their waxy-pale corpses facedown on the earth. They preyed on the weak, or on moments of weakness.

Hector wasn't like that! If he killed anyone, they were armed men — raiders, attacking an ally of Troy. The man with the rock had invaded a strange land, and Hector had stopped him. That was it.

Andromache felt helpless. She wished that she could take it all away from him, all the shame and hurt…

(*How very good of you,*) the snide little Voice interjected. (*He wouldn't even* have *it if it weren't for you.*)

Andromache closed her eyes against the pain — the Voice was right! No matter what, Hector would have ugly memories, but she'd been the one to turn them into shame. Instead of accepting his warrior side, she'd tried her best to ignore it. She'd never talked to him about that part of his life. She'd never expressed interest in his campaigns. She'd never gone to watch him on the training field. She'd never asked him more than a cursory *'How was your day?'* For all he knew, she still saw that part of him as monstrous, just as she had the day they met, when he was covered with someone else's blood. He had no way of knowing that her feelings had changed…

(*Have they?*) the Voice asked spitefully.

Of course they have! Andromache wasn't scared of Hector, anymore — she was scared *for* him.

(*Yes,*) the Voice agreed. (*You're scared for — how do you phrase it? — the* real *Hector.*)

Andromache's stomach churned.

(*As for that other person…when it comes to him, you're just like the villagers from Lyrnash.*)

The villagers — the people who'd shunned her — who'd looked upon her with horror when she arrived in Lyrnassa, covered in the blood of her first miscarriage. They'd never asked her what happened; it didn't really matter. To them, blood was the sign of an angry god. They'd allowed her to stay, but in all the years she lived there, their feelings of suspicion toward her had never changed.

(*You're just like them, the way you shun part of him,*) the Voice went on. (*It doesn't matter how noble the army's cause is, you still don't want to think of him the way he was that day.*)

Andromache winced. Her Hector, the *real* Hector — who was that person to her? Hector, in his plain white tunic. Hector, clean and laughing — that was the *real* Hector! Hector, riding horses, playing roodles, reading texts, petting Cutie — loving his wife. Her Hector — the *real* Hector — had nothing to do with blood and gore. Not for any reason! Those things belonged to some shadow Hector — a fake, a simulacrum…

(*And as long as you make sure never to see him looking like a warrior, you can believe all of that.*)

Oh, gods! moaned Andromache. The dreadful little Voice was right.

(*You've been shunning part of who he is,*) gloated the Voice. (*And he's known it all along.*)

Known? It was worse than that. Hector hadn't just known — he'd helped Andromache deceive herself. He'd protected her from any mention of war, violently roodling Demuchus or plying Uncle with honeywine in order to change the subject. He'd never even let her see him after combat practice, at least not until he'd washed off the dirt and sweat that came from sparring.

(*You're just like the city sculptors,*) sneered the Voice, and Andromache knew what it meant. She was just like the city sculptors, deciding which parts of Hector were ugly and removing them. No wonder Hector had been drawn to the sculpture garden! He'd sat there, wishing that he could be like the carving of Commander Atymnius, smooth and pure, his defects scoured away. He'd sat there, thinking that such a Hector was the only one Andromache could love...

She choked back a sob. She *hated* those sculptures! She *hated* that place and would never go back!

(*It's too late,*) said the Voice. (*You already hurt him.*)

I hurt him, Andromache agreed. She'd hurt Hector, and he'd hurt her, and neither of them could change that. But there was so much more she understood, now, and she refused to believe that it was too late for them, no matter what the Voice said. They'd broken each other, but not, she thought — she hoped — beyond repair.

Hector's feet twitched again — his poor, raw feet, cracked from the vicious scrubbings he'd been giving them, lately. His poor feet...she could help *them*, at least. All she needed was a little oil to rub into them.

Slowly, she slid her legs toward the edge of the bed.

"Ahndromahk?" murmured Hector, reaching out for her. "What's wrong?"

Such a light sleeper! Andromache sighed — his feet would have to wait. "Nothing," she said. "Just getting comfortable."

"Oh. All rahght..."

Gently, she stroked his warm, brown skin until he fell back to sleep.

Chapter 80

Hector groaned softly, yawned, and opened his eyes to look up at Andromache.

"Hi," she murmured.

"Hi." He blinked several times and yawned again. "I am outside how long?"

"Outside? No — you've been here the whole time."

Hector squinted at her, frowning, until he realized that she was teasing. Blearily, he pressed his face to her leg. "Do not mock my Lukkana. I am only half-waked."

"You were *out* for a long time," she said, stroking his hair. "I don't know how long, but I think it's pretty late, now."

He looked up at her again. "How ahre you?" he asked.

She sighed. "Ector?"

"What is it?"

"I feel icky."

"Icky?"

"Gross. Disgusting."

"Oh, my pretty wife, you ahre not —"

"I'd really, really like a bath, one with warm water and bath oil. But I know you're tired, and —"

"Ahndromahk, stop. That is why Paris and I, we bring this water."

"So you *do* think I'm icky!"

"Oh, Ahndromahk!"

"Well, you *said* —"

"I know you lahke baffs. That is why I bring water."

"Oh."

"You want I can make hot the water?"

578

Without warning, Andromache began to cry again.

"What is it?" asked Hector, reaching up to brush the tears from her cheek.

"Ugh!" she exclaimed. "I don't even know what's wrong with me! I can't stop crying."

"Ahndromahk," he said gently. "You jahst —"

"I know, I know, I know!" she interrupted, trying to collect herself. "But I wasn't thinking about *her*. I was thinking about how sweet you are to me."

Hector sat up and kissed her forehead. "I am going to make hot the water. Then I am going to giff a baff to you." He rolled out of bed, smoothing his tunic in wordless distaste. It must have bunched up under him in bed — and all for *her*.

Quietly, Andromache sniffled.

Once the water was set over the hearth to heat, Hector returned to the bed. "You can put your ahrms around my neck."

"I can walk, Ector."

"I know. Baht you can get into the tahb?"

Andromache looked at the kettle's tall sides and shook her head.

"So, you can put your ahrms around my neck."

She did so, pressing her cheek to Hector's shoulder while he carried her to the bath.

"You can sit here," he said, depositing her in the tub. "And get ready. I am going to put on some linen."

Confused at first — he was already wearing clothes, wasn't he? — Andromache quickly realized that he'd meant he was going to change the linens on their bed. She felt the beginnings of another round of tears, this one brought on by his thoughtfulness. *Enough!* she snapped at herself. *He told you to get ready.* Get ready. What had he meant by that? Unless he had a very strange bath in mind, it could only mean taking off her dress.

Andromache hugged her knees. She'd never been shy about taking off her clothes in front of Hector, at least not after the first time, but everything had changed in recent days. She was his invalid, now, not his wife. Her body could inspire only pity...

"You ahre weahring this dress for the baff?" asked Hector, interrupting her lugubrious thoughts.

She nodded dully and made up a lie. "I can't get it off."

"Oh, pretty wife! Why do you not say this?" He rushed over and gently removed her dress, tossing it to the ground. "The water is finished, not too hot," he said. "I can bring it."

"All right. Thank you." Now naked, Andromache clutched her knees still more tightly. The water might be ready, but she wasn't sure that *she* was.

"First, I clean your hair?" asked Hector. The small kettle of warm water was on the floor beside him. In his hand, he held a cup.

Andromache nodded and clamped her eyes shut. Water began pouring over the crown of her head, streaming down her back and face. Abruptly, it stopped again.

"It is hot enahff?" asked Hector.

"Perfect," she assured him.

He poured out more water and began massaging her scalp. When her hair was done, he gathered it and moved it across her left shoulder so that her back was bare. He poured another cupful of water over her and smoothed away the rivulets. As the water trickled down her arms and into the tub, though, his hands stopped moving.

"You ahre beautiful," he sighed.

Andromache caught her breath.

"Always, I lahff your shoulders."

"My shoulders!" She gave a soft laugh that sounded like a wheeze. Of all the parts of her for him to love — her *shoulders?*

"Yes," he said. "I lahke when you wear the dresses ohff my sister."

"You mean back when I first got here?"

"Mm-hmm," said Hector. "These dresses ahre too big fohr you. Always, they fall from your shoulder. Always, you put them back…baht still, I get a peek."

Andromache let her jaw drop in mock accusation. "You ogled me!"

"So?" Hector kissed the nape of her neck and picked up the cup. Gently, he poured warm water over her arms — her stomach — her legs. When he'd finished, he said once again, "You can put your ahrms around my neck."

Andromache did as he asked. He lifted her out of the tub and set her down beside it, on a thick cloth. She lay there, eyes closed, as Hector retrieved her bottle of bath oil and began rubbing it into her skin.

"It is fahnny," he said.

Funny? Andromache had begun to relax after the '*beautiful shoulders*' comment, but funny wasn't a word she wanted to hear when Hector was touching her naked body. Warily, she asked, "What's funny?"

"This oil. It smells rahght only on you. Sometimes, befohre we ahre married, I go into the baff chamber. I smell this oil, and it smells pretty —" He shook his head. "But neffer is it rahght wiffout *you*."

Andromache's heart swelled, and her vision grew blurry. *Stop! No more crying!* But these, at least, were happy tears.

"A clean dress," said Hector, when he was done rubbing in the oil. He held the garment over her head and lowered it onto her.

"Thank you," she said softly.

"Now — you ahre to be in bed."

"I'll walk."

"I can help."

Andromache could tell by his tone that he would be hurt if she refused. "All right." Leaning on her husband, she tottered over to the bed and burrowed under the fresh sheets. Hector wrapped Stripey the blanket around her.

"Be rahght back," he whispered, with a light kiss on her ear.

Andromache watched him empty the kettle, pour in fresh water, disrobe, and briskly wash himself. "Ector?"

Without stopping, he answered, "Hmm?"

"You know how you noticed my shoulders?"

He smiled. "Mm-hmm."

"I noticed *your* ankles."

"What on them?"

"They're comforting."

This time, he stopped washing to laugh. "Comfohrting?"

"Mm-hmm."

He laughed again — his golden laugh, as warm as ever, if a little worn down around the edges. Andromache was honestly surprised to hear it, after all they'd just been through. But then, she wondered if the darkness Hector had known was what made his laugh so radiant, and his joy so vivid, in the first place — if life and laughter, fun and love, were more beautiful to him than to most people because of what he had to compare those things to.

Hector finished bathing, climbed out of the kettle, dried off, and put on clean clothes. Even then, he didn't rest, but instead hauled another pile of dirty clothes and sheets onto the courtyard. He came back only to scoop out his bath water and carry the first of the small basins outside, as well.

For Andromache, the series of movements symbolized Hector's life. From cleaning the Chute, to scrubbing blood off the floor, to killing invaders, he did the dirtiest, hardest, worst, most painful jobs without complaining. It wasn't that he didn't notice the filth — his raw feet and hands proved otherwise — but he did those things despite it.

Her lungs hurt. Her heart ached. She loved him so much! Once more, tears began rolling down her cheeks. "Ector?"

"Sssh…you should sleep. I'll be right there," he murmured, lifting the second small basin.

"I really want a baby with you."

Hector spun around in horror, spilling water all over the floor. "NO!" he cried.

"You don't want a baby with me?" whispered Andromache. Her tears, which had sprung from a deep, sweet emotion, turned bitter.

"You have no idea what you looked like, the other day!" Hector's eyes were blazing, now. "That was the worst thing I've ever seen in my whole life, and I'd rather die than have to see it again!"

"Ector!" she protested.

"I mean it!"

"It wouldn't be that way."

"You don't know that! You can't control it!"

Andromache swallowed hard. Hector's face was growing blurry again.

"Oh, my sweetheart," he said softly, coming over to the bed and pulling her into his arms. "I'm sorry — I shouldn't have yelled."

"It's all right." She wiped her eyes on his shoulder.

"It's just — you have no idea! There's *no way* I'll risk —"

"What, so we're never going to have sex again?" Andromache interrupted.

Hector reeled under the blow but didn't buckle. "No."

"<u>Ector</u>!"

"What?"

"I'm *not* never having sex with you again!" she cried. "And I want a baby with you!"

He buried his face in his hands.

"<u>I'm sorry</u>," whispered Andromache, wrapping her arms around him. "<u>Ector, I'm so sorry. I shouldn't have said that. It's all right. Sssh, it's all right. We don't have to decide right now</u>…"

"I need to clean up, now," he said, breaking free from her embrace.

For a few horrible moments, Andromache thought the rift between them was reopening, and that all the progress they'd made had come undone. She would live out her days alone — unloved — unwanted —

Hector hurriedly mopped the floor before returning to bed. Once there, he lay down and pulled Andromache close.

Crying tears of relief, she clung to him.

"<u>Ahndromahk</u>?" he murmured.

"Hmm?"

"<u>Please, you mahst ahnderstand, it is you that I want most. Wiffout you</u> —"

"<u>I understand.</u>"

Pause. "<u>The ahtller night</u> —" Pause. "<u>You see her?</u>"

Andromache nodded. "<u>She was holding your hand.</u>"

Hector kissed her. They both fell asleep.

Chapter 81

Thyme. Oregano. Mint. The sharp scent of earth.

The breeze was cool on Andromache's cheek. She heard wings, the rustle of leaves — things were moving out on the courtyard. Slowly, she slid her legs to the edge of the bed.

"What's wrong?" Hector demanded.

Andromache swallowed her amazement. How had he heard her? He'd been fast asleep!

"Ahndromahk?" he prodded.

"Nothing — I just —" She bit her cheek gently to moisten her mouth, dry from sleep. "I just wanted to go outside."

"Oh," he said, sounding relieved. "I can help."

"I want to walk."

"I know it, pretty wife. I can help."

Andromache thought once more of the way he'd screamed after finding her out on the courtyard, and she knew it would be cruel to refuse his help. "Thank you," she murmured.

Together, they stepped outside. Andromache shivered at the touch of the cool morning air.

"I can get your cloak," offered Hector.

"Thank you," Andromache said again. While Hector went back into their room, she glanced over the courtyard, wondering where exactly she'd fallen. She had no memory of that moment; she didn't even remember coming home. Had it been by the fig tree? By the spring?

"Here," said Hector, returning with the cloak. As he draped it tenderly over her shoulders, their eyes met. Andromache almost took a step back. She was shocked by the depth of the hollows in his cheeks, the shadows ringing his eyes. Even Paris had understated just how awful he looked! She must not have seen it, in the dim light of their room…

"Somefing is wrong?" asked Hector, when he noticed her frowning.

"Just a leg cramp," she lied.

"You haff need to be careful, my pretty wife," he scolded gently.

"I will," she said, leaning against him. "Maybe we should have breakfast out here."

"You ahre hahngry?" Hector's voice was cautiously hopeful.

Andromache nodded. She *was* hungry — a little, anyway. The thought of simple foods didn't make her stomach turn.

"We can sit where?" he asked.

"You pick." She was afraid to choose. She might unwittingly steer them toward the very spot where she'd fallen.

"By the apple trees?" he suggested.

Pink blossoms had been raining down, leaving a silken, aromatic carpet on the courtyard. "That's beautiful," she said.

They walked over to a bench beneath the apple trees.

"You sit," said Hector. "I can bring foods."

"Thank you." Andromache held his hand and gaze for a lingering moment before he disappeared into the kitchen.

The breeze picked up, tossing the branches over Andromache's head. She loosened her hair and let it fly about, the way the little girl's had been doing. She looked down at the ground. There was no sign of blood…

When Hector came back, moments later, Andromache's hair was windblown and wild. A tear was running down each cheek. "Oh, pretty wife," he murmured, seeing her face. He set the food at her feet and put his arms around her.

"I know!" she wailed. "It's pathetic! You must be so sick of me, crying all the time — but I can't turn it off! I don't know how."

"Sssh, Ahndromahk." He kissed the top of her head. "I am sick ohff you *neffer*! And I lahff you *becahse* you can cry."

"What!" She scoffed. "Why on earth would you love *that*?"

"You haff a soft heart." Kiss. "You rescue caterpillahrs and pahppies." *Kiss, kiss.* "Many times, you haff been hurt, baht you ahre not hahrd inside. You can still feel. You can still cry." *Kiss, kiss.* "I lahff you fohr this. I lahff your soft heart."

Hector's words and kisses touched Andromache so deeply that she found herself in tears once again. "Oh, for pity's sake!" she blubbered into his chest. "I've *got* to stop this, before I dry up!"

"Lahke this?" Hector let go of her, leaned down, and picked up a dried, shriveled fig.

Andromache wheezed. *Is that my new laugh?* she wondered, hoping not. It wasn't a pleasant sound. "Yes. Like that."

Hector smiled. "You ahre still hahngry?" he asked.

"Yes," said Andromache. "But not for figs."

"Then what is your delahght?"

She wheezed again.

"What?"

"I like the way you talk. It's cute."

Smiling again, Hector chose two honey cakes and a handful of dried apricots from the tray.

"Perfect," said Andromache.

While they ate, they watched the happenings in the garden. The plants and passing insects were unimaginably lovely, with their waving stems, and legs, and lacy wings. Andromache had seen them all a thousand times before, but they'd never been as beautiful as they were that morning.

"Look!" she cried. Two brownish birds were chasing each other around the garden, squawking and flapping as they hopped from shrub to shrub. "They're in love," she said. "Or *he* is, anyway. She doesn't seem convinced."

"Mahch lahck!" Hector called out to the bird doing most of the chasing.

Andromache wistfully watched the little birds. Soon, they would mate and lay eggs in their nest. The mother bird — or maybe both parents, she wasn't sure — would guard the eggs zealously, lashing out with beak and claws at anyone who dared step too close to the nest. Birds were good parents...

She didn't realize that yet another tear had fallen until Hector brushed it away. She crumpled against him.

"You ahre seeing her?" he whispered in her ear.

"I did earlier," she murmured back. "Her hair was blowing in the breeze. She was laughing —" Her voice broke.

A rain of petals fell onto Hector's lap, soft pink against his battered tunic. Andromache touched one. It molded to the tip of her finger.

Hector cleared his throat suddenly. "Hi, little sister," he said.

Andromache looked up to see Cassandra nearby, hovering like a nervous ghost.

The young woman hesitated. "Is it — I mean — are you — can I —"

Andromache nodded just as Hector said, "Come on over."

"I wasn't sure," said Cassandra. "Mom was so adamant — *'Don't bother your brother or his wife, Cassandra.'* It's been the anthem in the house for days, now, as though I'm about to go bang pots outside your window, or something. I mean, seriously! She must think I'm soft in the head!"

Andromache wheezed.

Cassandra gave her a ginger hug. "Oh, honey! I'm so glad to see you up and about! We've been so worried — oh! But I'm not supposed to say that, am I?"

"Why not?" asked Hector. "Say it. Give her an incentive to keep eating." He grabbed the wizened fig and wiggled it right in Andromache's face.

As she watched the motions of the absurd little fruit, Andromache gave a rusty laugh — not her normal laugh, but not a wheeze, either.

Cassandra, too, laughed, although she sounded unsure. "If you want, I can have Paris bring you some *real* food, later."

Hector launched the fig at his sister. It was a feeble throw, easily dodged, but for a moment Andromache felt like life was back to normal, and she was grateful.

Cassandra's smile faded. Looking awkwardly at the ground, she said, "Well, I should probably run up to the library…"

"What are you working on?" asked Andromache.

"A fascinating treatise on the properties of stones — and it really made me start watching my feet, let me tell you! I had *no idea* about all the terrible things that could happen if you stepped crosswise over a hunk of cinnabar!"

"Happy reading," Andromache said softly.

"We'll be careful of the rocks," Hector added.

"I certainly hope so," said Cassandra, her face sober. "All right, then. I'm off." Instead of leaving, though, she turned once more to Andromache. "Honey?"

"Hmm?"

"If you're out, later, maybe we could play a game, or read together, or have a snack, or something? Or maybe tomorrow, or —"

"I'd like that," said Andromache. She wasn't sure that this was true, but she wanted to try, for Cassandra's sake. For Hector's sake. For her own sake.

Cassandra left for the library. As Andromache watched her go, she squeezed her husband's hand. "Ector?"

"Hmm?"

"What's happening with the army, these days?"

He shrugged.

"It's just, you haven't been to the stables, or the field...you haven't left the house in days."

"You need me here."

Andromache looked up through the branches of the tree above them. "You're right," she murmured. "I *did*."

Hector nodded, missing or ignoring the fact that she'd spoken in the past.

"How's Buzzy?" she asked. "How's Thisbe?"

Although Hector's face looked pained, he said only, "Xanthus can care fohr them."

Silence, except for the whispering leaves and the still-frisky pair of birds.

"Ector?"

"Hmm?"

"You can go back to work. When you said you'd never leave me again, I didn't take it literally." Or, if she had at the time, she was slowly coming back to her senses.

Hector sighed.

"I know they need you," said Andromache.

"People can fill in."

"I know it'll get messier and messier the longer you stay away...and then you'll have to bring home boxes of ropes for me to untangle."

He gave her a thin smile.

"Ector...it's all right."

"No, my sweetheart — it's *not*. How do I know you'll be safe while I'm not here?"

"I'll be fine — if it makes you feel better, I won't leave the house."

He gave her a look. "And the house is so safe?"

Andromache winced. She could still hear Hector screaming, *'Mama! Mama, help her!'*

Hector nodded, satisfied that she'd understood his point.

She tried a different tack. "Then I'll stay with someone — Paris, or Cassandra, or your parents. You won't have anything to worry about."

"<u>Ahndromahk</u> —"

"You'll have to go back to work *sometime*, won't you?"

"I don't know."

"What do you mean?"

"I don't know."

"Are you going to quit?"

"I don't know."

Andromache caught her breath. He was serious! She hadn't been. She *never* would have dreamed that Hector might actually quit!

"I love this city," he said. "I want to serve Troy somehow. I want to be useful. But there are other ways for me to serve besides leading the army."

Andromache felt dizzy. If what he said was true, it would mean the end of her worst fears. She would never again have to imagine him hurt or dying on a battlefield far from home. "What would you want to do?"

"I don't know."

"You could be an ambassador," she said tentatively, thinking of what Hecuba had always envisioned for Hector. "You could raise more allies for Troy."

"Maybe," he said.

Encouraged, Andromache went on: "You could go down to the Lukka lands. You'd have an advantage there, since you speak Lukkan. They'd trust you."

"That's an idea."

"Oh, <u>Ector</u>! You could do anything!" cried Andromache. "You could! Maybe someday you'd want to join the council, after all!"

Hector gave a bitter laugh. "If only I'd joined it a year ago…"

Andromache blinked back tears. Her hope turned to ashes. Not like *this*! He couldn't quit the army like *this*, his head bowed in shame. The thought broke her heart. "<u>Ector</u>," she whispered.

No response.

"<u>Ector</u>, Ucalegon <u>made you think that you were stuck between two impossible choices, but that's not true — that was never true</u>."

Silence.

"<u>You can do what's necessary and no more</u>," she said. "<u>Just like you always have</u>."

He turned toward her.

"<u>Just like you *always* have</u>," she repeated.

"<u>And what if the necessary changes?</u>" he asked. "<u>What if mohre is necessary? What if</u> Ucalegon <u>is right, and Taruisha needs mohre spears than walls?</u>"

Andromache knew what he was picturing — Mudders rampaging through the streets. Mudders, tearing past their bedroom. Mudders, dragging her away. She touched his hand. "<u>I love you</u>," she said. "<u>I trust you completely</u>."

He sighed. "<u>Then tell me — what do I do?</u>"

"<u>Serve the city however you think you're most needed</u>," she said softly, looking down.

Hector drew his toes through a pile of fallen petals, leaving strange, wavy lines behind him.

"<u>Just promise me one thing, Ector</u>," she whispered.

"<u>Yes, pretty wife?</u>"

"<u>Promise me you won't choose for the wrong reasons</u>." She swallowed, knowing how difficult the words would be to say. "<u>Don't not go back to the army because you think you don't deserve to, or because you think that I won't want you, anymore. I know your heart. There's nothing you would ever do that would make me not love you</u>."

Hector kissed her and gave her a long, tender look. "You know that's too many '*woulds*' and '*nots*' for me to understand," he finally said.

Andromache against his shoulder and touched her foot to his on the carpet of velvety blossoms. Eyes closed, she sat there, drinking in the sunshine and the feel of Hector's skin against her own...

When at last she opened her eyes, she saw that the pair of birds had flown away.

Chapter 82

By the time a week had passed, Andromache was taking only an occasional nap during the day, and her appetite had more or less returned. Each morning, she, Hector, and Cutie strolled through the courtyard gardens, pulling weeds and watching insects buzz among the flowers.

Most afternoons, they played roodles against Cassandra and Paris. Although Andromache didn't always want to see her in-laws, she knew that these visits were good for her. Cassandra's chatter and Paris's gossip reminded her that there was life outside her grief for the little girl.

She needed reminders. Her sorrow was ever-present, and almost anything could cause it to spill over. One day, while tidying, she'd caught sight of *On Lorani* and thought about all the texts the little girl would never read. Her visit to the weaving room had been even worse. She'd gone up there to finish Hector's brown blanket — she was so close! — but after one look at the loom, she'd started whimpering...

'*My mom taught me how to weave*...'
Hector nodded. '*I remember.*'
'*I'll never get to teach* her*!*'

She'd dissolved into tears, and Hector had gathered her in his arms and carried her down to their bedroom.

As time passed, though, while Andromache's grief didn't diminish, her crying spells grew less frequent. One night, she was stunned to realize that she'd made it all day without shedding a single tear. The guilt she felt at that fact almost made her cry, but she managed to hold it back.

The next day, Hector left the house for the first time. After much sighing and clearing of his throat, he went down to the stables to check on Buzzy and Thisbe. He returned a mere fraction of an hour later, his face ashen, as though he expected to find Andromache lying once more in a pool of blood. When, instead, he saw her smiling at him from under the apple tree, he ran over to her and hugged her fiercely.

After that, he returned bit by bit to his normal routines — a patrol here, a training there, a ride in between. Eventually, he was gone much of the day, but unlike before, he checked in at home every few hours. His face was always drawn when he first looked out onto the courtyard, but as soon as Andromache smiled at him from beside a garden box, or ran over to throw her arms around him, color flooded to his cheeks. His eyes began to shine again. He came back to life.

Andromache, too, loved those moments of reunion with Hector, but she also found that she needed time apart from him. It gave her a chance to be with the little girl. Softly, she sang the old childhood songs that she and Hector had known:

> *'Time to take the horse to the old tin alley*
> *Time to walk the foxes past the old tin door.*
> *Hey! With the pretty goat, hand it up slowly!*
> *Hey! With the hen and the cockerels four.'*

> *'Sunny, sunny, sunny meadow,*
> *Grasses tall, grasses high,*
> *All around the sunny meadow,*
> *Crickets jumping by and by.'*

When Andromache wasn't singing, she talked to the little girl. She told her that she had truly wanted her and always would. She explained that when she'd thought 'not now,' she'd been feeling very scared and alone — and that people often thought, said, or did terrible things when they felt that way.

Andromache never spoke or sang to the little girl in front of Hector. She worried that he might think she was wallowing in grief, or even going mad. Careful as she was, though, one morning, Priam came home unexpectedly and caught her murmuring the lyrics.

"I'm sorry, little one," he said when he saw her reddening cheeks. "I didn't mean to disturb you."

"I — I was just —" Andromache looked down and whispered, "I was singing to the baby." She didn't know why she'd told him — perhaps it was because Priam had always put her at ease, right from the first moment their eyes had met.

"That's a good idea," he said.

Andromache looked up again. "It is?"

Priam nodded. "It is, if it helps *you*."

"It's not — crazy?"

"I shouldn't think so," said Priam, sitting down beside her and pulling a weed.

"Oh! I haven't been taking care of things the way I should," Andromache apologized.

"The garden will survive." Priam smiled. "Look at how well it bounced back, after years of my neglect."

Andromache smiled wanly. She pulled a weed of her own, sighed, and let the plant fall to the ground.

"Little one?"

Andromache sighed again. Something was bothering her. Despite all the terrible thoughts she'd had while she and Hector weren't speaking, she'd never truly wanted to lose their little girl. No — those thoughts had come from the despair of believing she'd lost her husband.

With the wagoner, however, everything had been different. She'd *wanted* that baby to disappear.

Oh, she'd had reason. No one could have argued otherwise! Her thirteen-year-old self had been racked with sorrow. She'd just lost her parents, her home — a baby would have been too much for her, especially a baby with the wagoner. The monster! Only a monster would have put a girl in that position — tricked her, used her, and thrown her away. But in spite of everything, she couldn't help feeling guilty.

The Lyrnassans had always believed that she was being punished for something...

She was stumbling down the hill — her dress was soaked in blood — the villagers were shrinking back in horror — they were muttering to each other — 'Don't touch her!' — 'The gods have cursed her!' — 'Don't you see? She's covered in blood!'

What if they'd been right all along? What if the gods were angry with her? What if Hecuba was wrong about why Andromache had miscarried the little girl? What if that had happened not because the timing was wrong for her body, but because she was being punished? What if the author of On Lorani was wrong — what if Priam was wrong — about the nature of the stars? What if they really were human-like deities? Vengeful deities? What if they'd punished her for her thoughts about the wagoner's baby by taking Hector's baby, too? What if they continued to punish her, taking any and all future babies that she and Hector might have had together?

With a long, deep breath, Andromache asked the question at the heart of her recent worries: "Why do people die? Not how — *why*. Is it a punishment? On the people who are left, I mean?"

Priam took her hand. "It feels like it."

She nodded.

"But let me ask you something," he said gently. "How old were you when your parents died?"

Andromache swallowed hard. "Thirteen," she mumbled.

"What could a girl of thirteen possibly have done to deserve that kind of punishment?"

I killed a baby goat, she thought. *I watched two people making love inside their tent.* Those were the worst things her youthful self had done. But, as Hector had pointed out, she'd killed that goat out of mercy — and the couple in the tent had never known or cared that she was outside. It made no sense that she should be punished for those things. Certainly not by having her parents taken away! "So there's no reason why people die, then?" she murmured to Priam. "It just happens?"

"That's my belief."

"And you don't think I'm cursed?"

"Oh, my child, no!" The old priest squeezed her hand.

Gratefully, she squeezed back.

"Of late, I find myself more and more intrigued by your *On Lorani* text," said Priam. "Someday soon, we should discuss it again, in even greater depth."

"Hector doesn't believe in the Lorani," whispered Andromache. "He's never seen one."

Priam laughed. "Well, you'll have to show him one! Then he can come to our discussion, too."

Andromache smiled. "I will," she said. "I promise." For a long while, she sat there quietly with Priam, pulling weeds and watching Cutie pounce on passing insects.

Chapter 83

"Your shoulders are really tight."

Hector groaned in response.

Andromache rubbed harder. "Were you out on the training field all day?"

"Most ohff it."

She paused. "Did — did you spar?"

"Mm-hmm."

She resumed kneading. "How did it go?"

"All rahght."

"Did you win?"

"Ohff couhrse."

Again, Andromache's hands went still. "What do you mean, *'of course*? Isn't that a little arrogant?"

"No," said Hector.

She snorted. "It sounds arrogant to me."

"Maybe. Baht I haff not losed in years."

"Years?" she repeated, not sure he'd said the proper unit of time. He'd been known to confuse them. "As in the time it takes to go from one summer to the next?"

"Years."

Her mouth gaped open. "How many years?"

"I do not know. Many."

Andromache pressed the heel of her hand into his back. Hector groaned again. "Yes — there."

She pressed harder, moving her hand in small circles. "Many years," she said. "I believe you, but how?"

"How?"

"How did you get to be so good? Was it because of all the training you got in Santiya?"

Hector laughed.

"What's so funny?"

"Pahrt, it is that training. Yes. And I can use boff hands the same. This surprises ahther fighters. Baht also —" He laughed again, making Andromache laugh with him this time.

"What is it?" she demanded, tickling him. "Tell me."

"All rahght. You remember I haff a bad stahrt wiff women, yes?"

Andromache smiled, picturing a spindly teenaged Hector, unpopular with the girls on the Make-Out stairs. "I remember."

"Baht still, I *lahke* women, a lot. And I want to do fings wiff women. Ouch!"

"Sorry," said Andromache. She supposed she might have pressed a *little* too hard….Gritting her teeth, she asked, "What does liking women have to do with sparring?"

"All that energy had to go somewhere, Ahndromahk," said Hector.

She stopped short. "What?"

"I put it into training — and training — and training some more, until I got good," he explained.

Andromache lay down beside him. "So good you haven't lost in years?"

"Yes."

"That's a lot of energy, Ector."

"Tell me about it."

"And you never used *any* of it off of the training field?"

"I won't say *none*," he said cautiously. "But very, very little."

"Oh." Andromache pinched her lips together and reminded herself that it didn't matter, anyway, how much energy Hector had spent on other girls. That was in the past, and she cared only about the present. The future.

"I never had as much energy as when *you* came to Troy," he went on, smiling mischievously. "And *all* of that went into training, until…well, you know."

Andromache smiled back. "I know."

Hector reached out to stroke her hip. She took his hand and played with the fingers, spreading them out like a sea star on her belly. "You must have trained pretty hard today, as sore as you are," she murmured.

"*Very* hard," he agreed.

Andromache caught her breath. It had been a long, long time since Hector had given her one of his fiery kisses, but he now looked like he was about to. He leaned in toward her...

Finally! she thought. *Kiss me — please, kiss me!* She understood why he'd been avoiding that type of kiss, but she missed it so much! She would have given almost anything for a night of Hector's lips against hers — his tongue touching hers — their bodies pressed against each other, yielding and hot —

But his kiss was barely long enough to warm her before he drew back again.

Andromache sighed, and Hector looked away.

"Do *you* want a back rub?" he mumbled in apology.

She swallowed hard. "Thanks," she said. "That would be nice."

Chapter 84

"Ahndromahk?" Hector asked one morning.

"Hmm?"

"Are you feeling all right?"

"Yes," said Andromache, frowning. "Why? Do I look sick? Is something —"

"No!" Hector said hastily. "I was just wondering if you'd mind having guests tonight."

"I don't mind," she said automatically, but the fact that he'd asked gave her pause. "Unless — who are they?"

Hector's face was hard to read. "It's a surprise."

"I don't know..." Andromache had learned to be wary of surprises.

"It'll be fine. I promise."

"All right," she said. "I trust you."

Her trust faltered when, that evening, Hector ushered in the unthinkable combination of Xanthus and Demuchus.

Xanthus was a welcome sight. She dove straight into the old man's lobstery embrace, and he gave her a tentative hug. "Hi, there, Missy. Good to see you up and about." He seemed to bear her no ill will for the way she'd neglected him, during her rough patch with Hector.

"I've missed you!" she cried.

"Eh? Well, when I heard you couldn't come to the stables for a while, I thought I'd —"

She squeezed him again, and he squeezed back, this time.

Demuchus coughed. Andromache gave him a chilly nod. She had nothing to say to Demuchus. It was *his* uncle who had tormented Hector — *his* stupid treatise that had made Ucalegon want to talk to Hector in the first place! Demuchus had no business coming to her house!

"Let's go sit on the courtyard," said Hector. "It's a nice night. We can play a match or two of roodles."

"I brought my board," said Demuchus.

"Good! Then —"

"We'll meet you out there," Andromache interrupted. "I need to have a word with my husband, first."

"Oh — of course," said Demuchus, taking Xanthus by the elbow.

The old man swatted his hand. "Eh? So, you think I don't know the way? As if I wasn't here for the wedding? As if there were a thousand ways a man could get out to the courtyard, from here, anyway? Young people, these days!"

"Please forgive me for wanting to help an elder gentleman!" huffed Demuchus.

Stiffly, they both marched out to the courtyard.

"You'd better make this fast," whispered Hector. "Or one of them might leave here with a roodles board smashed over his head."

Andromache didn't laugh. "Why is *he* here?"

Hector sighed. "They were both worried about you."

"*He* doesn't get to worry about me!" she fumed. "Not after what his uncle —"

Hector put his arms around her. "Ahndromahk…"

"I *hate* that guy!"

"I know. I do also…"

Andromache stiffened. "But?"

"Baht Demuchus is not the one to say that stahff."

She bit her lip.

"I want no more enemies, Ahndromahk." Hector's voice was weary. "I want friends."

Sighing deeply, she argued, "But Demuchus is so — so — so —" She struggled to find the right word to describe her one-time suitor. "So Demuchus!"

"I know it," Hector agreed. "Baht he is all rahght. He is all rahght."

Andromache looked away. She couldn't just forget about everything that had happened. On the other hand, she wanted to make her husband happy.

"Ahndromahk?" he prodded gently.

From the courtyard, she heard cackling, a sure sign that Xanthus was on the cusp of victory. "All right," said Andromache. "Demuchus can stay, as long as I get to watch you guys trounce him. So help me, if you don't play your best, tonight —"

Hector smiled. "I will, pretty wife." He held out his hand, and together they went to join their guests.

Summer

Chapter 85

Andromache chose the worst possible season for her first trip outside of the house: high summer. Hector argued and railed against it in every way he knew, but she was determined. She'd been cooped up for far too long and needed some air.

"In the morning," she coaxed. "Or in the evening, when it's cool."

Reluctantly, he accompanied her on a short morning walk around the citadel, following a route that avoided the sculpture garden. When that went well, he agreed to a longer stroll the next morning. The evening after that, they went to a play with Cassandra, and the following night, all three of them played roodles with Xanthus, down in the stables.

From then on, Andromache gradually fell back into her old activities — although now, she was never alone outside the house. Hector walked her to the temple gardens, where Priam met her and sat with her. Cassandra escorted her to plays and concerts when Hector couldn't come, and Hecuba made trips with her to buy thread so that she could finally finish the brown blanket.

Even Paris shared in the babysitting duties.

"I want to go marketing," she told him, one night. "Can I tag along with you, tomorrow?"

"Sure, Hermie."

The next day, though, Paris was a nervous wreck. From the moment they stepped outside the house, his eyes never stopped darting around; he even shrieked once or twice.

"What's wrong with you?" asked Andromache.

"What's *wrong* with me?" Paris shot back. "Do you have any idea the lecture your *husband* gave me, before we left? Do you have any idea what will happen to me if I don't bring you back in one piece, Hermie?"

Andromache smiled and tucked her arm into his. "Well, then you'd better be careful. I want to go to both of the markets, today."

"Both?"

"Regular and herb."

"The herb market?" Paris groaned.

Andromache nodded. "And while we're down in that area, there's an old shop I want to see."

The luthier's shop. Until now, she hadn't dared set eyes on it. The visions she'd seen of her dad as a little boy — as a teenager — as a middle-aged man, living with her mother — had seemed so real. So beautiful. She'd been afraid to let her fantasies go, afraid to let them unravel in the face of reality...

Now, she was finally ready. Paris would know where to find the luthier's shop — his own instrument had been made there. "There's an old shop I want to see," she repeated. "And you're just the person to take me there."

Paris raised an eyebrow. "I have to admit, I'm intrigued. But don't even think about giving me the slip."

Andromache laughed. She didn't mind all the extra vigilance. She knew it would wane eventually — if nothing else, when the weather turned cool again and there was no question of her getting heat-sick. Meanwhile, she had a whole household of people looking out for her. Caring for her. Loving her.

The next night, they even held a family dinner to welcome her back to health, although it was disguised as a midsummer festival, in case she didn't want to be the center of attention. Andromache wasn't fooled, though: nowhere, in any of the dishes, was there a single scrap of meat.

Chapter 86

Despite the high heat, Hector was spending much of his time on the training field. He'd never taken on such a merciless regimen, not even during Andromache's first two years in the city. He was so full of energy, she began to hope that he might back out of his stupid vow never to have sex with her again.

She wished he would hurry. She missed it all so much! She missed the pleasure, the closeness, the joy on Hector's face, the talks afterward. He was most with her — most *hers* — in those moments. She was sure that Hector missed it, too, but he could be horribly stubborn, especially when he was afraid for her. After the Frondsia incident, no amount of coaxing had led him to restart riding lessons, and Andromache feared a similar obstinacy now.

It would have been one thing if sex were impossible. If Hector's lower half were somehow injured — if ~~'things weren't working'~~ and would never work again — Andromache would have said farewell to sex without a second thought. But in this case, Hector's top half, not his bottom half, was the problem. He was still scared of what might happen if Andromache got pregnant again. Never mind that his own mother had pronounced her healthy; he couldn't bring himself to take the risk.

Andromache believed that time would soothe his fear, but he'd held out much longer than she'd expected. Her patience was wearing thin. She wanted their old life back — their old ways of being together. She wanted a baby with him, too, or at least the possibility. Every so often, when she was drifting off to sleep, she saw the little girl. It was hard to watch her laughing and not run over to her, or hug her...

Andromache wanted another chance.

Hector, however, staunchly kept his oath. If a family member happened to mention almonds, he refused to meet Andromache's eye. He wore clothes to bed. He held her and kissed her, but never in a way that might lead to more. *Comfort kisses,* she thought disdainfully. *All he ever gives me are comfort kisses.*

Night after night, hoping to break his resolve, she pressed her body close to his. She cuddled against him, stroked him, and gave him kisses. He never responded as she hoped, but she kept trying. *I can be stubborn, too,* she thought.

Then came a night so hot that snuggling was unbearable. Vanquished by the weather, and by her husband's misplaced fortitude, Andromache retreated to her side of the bed. *I might as well sleep on the floor,* she thought bitterly. *It wouldn't matter to him, anyway.*

It came as some comfort that Hector seemed as miserable as she was. He flopped about on the linens, vainly searching for a cool place. "This sucks," he finally complained.

"It *does* suck," sighed Andromache, thinking, *More than you know.*

"Let's go out," said Hector.

"Out? Where?"

"Well..." He thought for a moment. "What if we went on a Lorani hunt? A real one, out in the countryside. We could take Cutie with us."

"I don't know." Andromache frowned. While she liked the idea of escaping their room, she had a sullen urge to balk. Why give Hector what *he* wanted when he wouldn't do the same for her?

Hector's brow furrowed in concern. "Is that too far?"

"No!" she exclaimed. The last thing she needed was for him to think she was weak! "No, I just —" She blurted out the first excuse that came to mind. "My dress is all rumpled."

"Oh," he said. "No one will see it. No one but me, I mean."

And who cares how I look in front of you, right? she thought sourly. "I want to change."

He shrugged. "All right."

Andromache plunged an arm deep into her clothing chest, felt around for a dress, hauled it out, and changed into it. "All right," she said. "Let's go."

Hector didn't respond. He was staring at her.

"What is it?" she asked.

"Isn't that the dress you were wearing when —" His words broke off, but Andromache could have sworn she saw a glint in his eye.

She looked down, surprised to see which dress she'd pulled out of the chest: it was the silvery gown from her bridal luncheon. The dress that Hector had said looked like starlight. The dress that she'd slipped out of to stand naked in his arms. *He remembers it*, she thought, her bitterness ebbing away. *He likes it*. For the first time that night, she smiled.

Hand in hand, with Cutie beside them, they strolled through the city streets. Andromache felt much better than she had in their bedroom. With every step, silky fabric brushed against her legs. *It's brushing against* his *legs too*, she thought. The dress would bring her luck — and to think, she'd almost refused to go out for a walk!

"Almost there," said Hector when they reached the outpost stable.

Inside, Andromache staggered under a wave of memories. She saw Hector, crouched on the floor, pushing her away, rubbing the gash on his forehead. That gash! She thought about everything it meant. A man with a rock...a black-mouthed man who had laughed, who had made her husband bleed. A man who had almost —

Her feet slowed, but Hector's didn't — and since she was connected to him, she kept moving forward. He squeezed her hand; she clutched his. He took a lamp in his other hand. As they walked through the tunnel, tears rolled down Andromache's cheeks. How feeble happiness had become! Moments earlier, she'd been flirting with Hector, enjoying the wind and the swish of her dress. Now, black thoughts were invading again. The fragility of life, the permanence of death...

Just forget it, Andromache told herself. *He's here. You're here together. Don't ruin it*. Torn between gratitude and sorrow, she tightened her grip on Hector's hand until her fingers were shaking.

They passed from the gateway cottage out into the countryside. Slowly, they walked toward the large, flat rock where they'd first officially become friends. As Andromache breathed in, she caught the scent of her favorite purple flowers — the ones used to make her bath oil and her wedding crown. She smiled, and the lingering dark thoughts faded.

"This is better already," sighed Hector, lying down on the rock.

"More airs," teased Andromache.

He smiled and pulled her down beside him. She snuggled close. Out there, on the hillside, the wind made it cool enough for them to touch.

"What exactly should I be looking for?" asked Hector.

"The Lorani look like stars, but bigger and fuzzier."

"Like that? Is that one, there?"

Andromache pressed closer to him, squinted, and followed his finger with her eye. "No, that's just a star behind a cloud."

"What about *that*?"

"Maybe…wait! No, not that one either."

They went back to gazing at the sky, its deep, velvet darkness split by a ribbon of silver. Cutie, who'd been happily exploring the hillside, leapt up beside them and lay down. All was still and quiet. Little by little, Andromache found herself nodding — drifting off — giving in to the gentle tug of sleep—

"There!" Hector suddenly exclaimed. "I haff one!"

Andromache opened her eyes to see that he was pointing up and to his left. As she looked, her heart began to pound. "That's it!" she cried, grasping his other hand. "Oh, Ector! Isn't it just beautiful!"

"It is small," he said.

"No!" Andromache shook her head vehemently. "It's not small, it's just far away. That's why they're so hard to find."

"Ahndromahk!" Hector laughed. "Do not worry. Any size, I lahff it. It is so pretty." He squeezed her hand. "Lahke you."

A thrill ran through her as she lay beside him, inhaling the sweet scent of mint. Hector's breath was coming as fast as her own. She was glad for her dress, glowing faintly in the starlight. She was glad that Hector had called her pretty.

For a long while, they quietly watched the luminescent creature. It didn't seem to move, although Andromache knew that she wouldn't be able to tell, from as far away as they were. Only if she were in the celestial ocean, close to the giant creature —

But she didn't *want* to be up there. Rolling onto her side, she wrapped an arm around her husband.

Hector squeezed her hand. "So," he said. "You saw these all the time, when you were a kid?"

"All the time."

"And you didn't even have any wine to make things look blurrier!"

"Says who?" she retorted.

Hector blinked. "I just thought — since you were ten or something —"

"Nine."

"Nine?"

"Maybe even eight."

"And your parents just let you have wine?"

"No-o-o…my friend and I kind of stole it."

"*You* stole?" asked Hector, incredulous.

"My friend's parents had plenty to spare. They never missed it."

"You stole — and got drunk! — when you were eight or nine?"

"Well, not *drunk* exactly. Just a little tipsy. We never pinched too much at a time."

Laughing, Hector said, "I never really thought of you as a mischief-maker."

"Well, I was," said Andromache. Impulsively, flirtatiously, she added, "I still am."

"Yes," murmured Hector. Pause. "You ahre…"

Andromache drew a sharp breath. She hadn't imagined it, before, the glint in Hector's eye — and now it had traveled to his voice. His fingers, too, awoke and began caressing their way up her arm.

"You know the first time we were out here together?" she whispered, as his fingertips burrowed under the shoulder of her dress. "The day you showed me how to get through the tunnel?"

"Mm-hmm…"

"I felt really close to you that day."

"Me, too."

"You could've kissed me."

609

"Oh, Ahndromahk!" he scolded. "That is no good time fohr a kiss."

"Why not?"

"Well, for one thing, until that day, you didn't even know we were *friends*," said Hector. "It seemed like a bad time to spring a romance on you. I was afraid you'd start running away, again."

Andromache poked him in the arm.

"Besides," he said, laughing. "I'd just confessed to being thrown in shit when I was a little boy! It wasn't really my sexiest moment." Now, on the other hand, Hector was plainly feeling sexy. His voice was lower and huskier than usual; his fingers had ventured out onto her collar bone. There, they hesitated, unsure whether to head up, toward her neck, or down.

Andromache didn't breathe. *Down,* she pleaded with the fingers. *Go down.* She wanted them inside her dress, warm against her breasts, skimming their way over her stomach. *Please, go down!*

In spite of all her silent pleading, the fingers stopped. They retreated to her shoulder and remained there, slack, quiescent, and demure.

"I lahff you," whispered Hector.

"I love you, too," said Andromache. She kissed Hector's shoulder and lay back against the rock, trying to hide her disappointment. They'd been so close! What had stopped him? Was he still scared of hurting her, or was something else the matter? *Just be patient,* she told herself. *He deserves that. He waited years for you.*

"It is there still?" asked Hector. "The Lorani?"

Squinting upwards, Andromache found the hazy patch of light once more. "There," she pointed. "It's still there."

Chapter 87

"See you later, pretty wife."

Andromache felt a soft kiss on her forehead. She opened her eyes to see Hector silhouetted against the window. It was morning. "See you later," she said, reaching for his hand and kissing it.

On his way out, he stopped to pet Cutie. "Bye, little girl. Take good care of your mama." The dog thumped her tail in response, then the door squeaked, and Hector was gone.

Andromache sighed. She and Hector hadn't even kissed, out on the hillside, but something had happened. She felt closer to him than ever and wanted desperately to be with him.

(*You can be, if you really want to,*) the sneering little Voice told her.

As always, it was right.

(*So — do you want to, or not?*) it challenged.

Andromache crawled out of bed. She dressed quickly and crossed over to the main house. Cutie followed, her eyes bright and eager.

"What are *you* so excited about, today?" asked Andromache. "Eating? Catching flies? Breathing?"

Cutie crouched down, tail wagging, ready to spring up at the slightest motion from her mama.

"Not now. We can play later," Andromache said guiltily. "I have to go out, and you have to stay here. Be a good girl."

As Andromache rushed out, she refused to look at the bleak little creature behind her. She knew that the sight of Cutie's eyes, misty with hurt, or her ears, folded back against her head, might be enough to keep her from leaving the house.

Cutie gave a heart-rending moan. If it had been a word, it would have spanned eleven syllables, each of them thick with betrayal. Ever since the miscarriage, she and Andromache had been almost inseparable.

"I'm sorry — I'll be back soon," whispered Andromache, slamming the door shut behind her. Her eyes filled with tears. In truth, she didn't know how long she would be gone. Moments, if she wimped out; hours, perhaps, if she didn't. *Stop crying. Cutie will be fine*, she told herself. *Now, go*.

Because it was hot, she went slowly. She didn't want to risk heat-sickness. She plodded down the city streets, past the houses of their neighbors, through the portal of the upper citadel, toward the stables. They seemed particularly far away, today. She was just beginning to worry that someone had moved them, horses and all, when she arrived at the familiar door.

She didn't walk inside, as she'd so often done before, to visit with Buzzy, Thisbe, or Xanthus. Instead, she followed the stables' outside wall until she came to a gap. There, she stopped to peer in.

Chaos. Hordes of people. Clanks and dull thuds.

Andromache recoiled, trembling. Back at the house, this had seemed like a good idea, but now she wasn't so sure. *Maybe tomorrow*, she told herself. *For today, maybe it's enough that I came down here*.

(*Maybe tomorrow*...) sneered the Voice.

Andromache took one step inside. She'd never been to the training field, before. Should she go left? Right? Straight ahead? A man behind her settled the question by pushing her roughly to the left.

The stands were now just ahead of her. Weaving her way strategically among the spectators, she managed to find a place several rows up from the bottom. She sat down — took a deep, almost painful, breath — and turned toward the field.

Men — as well as a few women — were out there in pairs and trios, batting away at each other with clubs, dulled swords, and staves.

Refusing to let herself shudder, Andromache scanned the field for her husband. Meanwhile, the other spectators hollered and bawled for their favorite combatants.

"Go, Epistor!"

"You can do better than that, Dryops!"

"That's it, Hypsenor! Keep it coming…keep it coming! Don't let up! You've got him — I mean, *her*!"

"Dammit, Elasus! And to think, I wagered my best rooster on you! You owe me a rooster, Elasus!"

Andromache's eyes leapt from one group to the next as the shouts erupted around her. *Which one is Elasus?* she wondered. *And why would anyone wager a rooster? And where on earth is my husband?* She'd come here to watch *him*, after all, not his underlings. If she couldn't find him, she might as well squirm her way back to the exit. She could wait for him in the peace of the garden, maybe have a bath ready for him. He loved baths after training! Yes, she would just duck home and —

One more look around, Ahndromahk, she told herself firmly. *Or that stupid Voice will never let you forget it.*

At last, she spotted Hector, surrounded by a throng of other soldiers. He seemed to be coaching them, though, not sparring with them. Andromache wasn't sure whether to be pleased or disappointed, so she just kept watching.

The people around her were a sea of heat. Sweat pooled under her arms — between her breasts — behind her knees — in the small of her back. Soon, it would soak through her dress, making her look like she'd fallen into the sea.

Maybe I should go home and take a bath, she thought, fanning herself. Just then, though, she noticed Hector approaching a pair of unruly swordsmen. He tried — presumably — to help them focus their energy. He spoke to them, demonstrated movements with his own sword, and adjusted the fighters' positions, but nothing seemed to help. Finally, disgusted, he called for one of his captains: "Medon!"

Medon ran over.

"Now *watch*!" Hector growled.

As he and Medon engaged, Andromache forgot about the sweltering heat. She watched — and watched — and watched. She couldn't take her eyes off her husband. Now she could see why the family'sguests had always raved about him, had tried to cajole her into going down to the field. She could see why Uncle had praised his skill, and why the Newbie had uttered such a rapturous, 'Oh — *him!*' Hector was fleet. Fluid. Beautiful. He was as beautiful there on the field as he was while running up the hill, or riding Buzzy — as beautiful there as he was in the library, or in their bedroom. His eyes and his arms were everywhere at once, and he never seemed to tire.

Andromache elbowed her way down to the first row. She was now quite close to him.

The sparring had evolved beyond a mere demonstration. Hector and Medon were showing off, enjoying themselves — playing, as Cassandra had always said. At the same time, neither wanted to lose, so their sparring grew more and more intense. The crowd roared. Everyone — *everyone* — had come hoping to watch Hector.

Andromache had no doubt whatsoever about the outcome of the match. Her husband was clearly going to win! "Ector!" she cheered, in her excitement. By chance, she shouted right when most of the other spectators were silent, and her voice carried out onto the field.

Hector turned sharply toward her, his eyes wide with surprise — and then pain, as he was hit by a blow he hadn't seen coming. "Stop!" Andromache heard him bellow to Medon.

"Give up?" the man jeered.

"You wish," snapped Hector. He looked over at Andromache, whom Medon now noticed and recognized. He nodded politely to her and then busied himself with the two soldiers he and Hector had supposedly been teaching.

Meanwhile, Hector ran over to his wife. "Ahndromahk," he whispered.

She threw her arms around him. He was filthy! The dust from the field was making a mud with his sweat, and his whole skin was dripping — soaking through her already-sodden dress — but she didn't care.

"What are you doing here?" he whispered.

"Watching you."

"Watching me get clobbered, you mean!"

"It was my fault. I distracted you."

"Yes. You ahre making me to look bad. You mahst go."

Andromache shook her head. "I want to stay."

"Ahndromahk," Hector protested, his face growing solemn. "I do not want to fight this guy befohre you."

"Why?"

"Becahse — he is good. I am going to —" He broke off, looking ashamed. "Be scary."

"I want to watch you," she whispered.

He sighed.

Andromache pulled away slightly and looked at him, thinking how beautiful he was. "I want to watch you."

Her words — or maybe her look, or maybe her tone — had a strange and wonderful effect on Hector. He smiled, and when he did, his dimple came out.

"I want to watch you," she persisted. Her own voice had grown thick; her insides were fluttering.

"If you go now," he said, pretending to bargain, "I will do anyfing you ask, howeffer icky. I will scrahb the Chute — I will take prickle weeds out ohff the gahrden — anyfing!"

Andromache smiled and leaned in close to his ear. "If you let me stay, I'll do anything *you* ask...however naughty."

Hector paused. "Stay," he finally whispered, rubbing the delicate skin of her wrist with his thumb. "Baht no mohre than an hour."

"Why? So I don't get too much sun?"

"Yes — baht also —" His voice had a slight swagger to it. "You ahre going to need a long nap, befohre I come home."

Andromache's skin began to tingle. "What about you?" she murmured. "Won't *you* be tired?"

Hector shook his head. "Do not worry on me. I am going to be fine."

"As long as you think about herb bread," she teased, glancing slyly at his lap. "And not my naughty see-through dresses."

"Herb bread — not naughty dresses," Hector agreed. He gave her a last decorous peck on the cheek and stood to rejoin Medon. Before leaving, though, he cast a mischievous look back over his shoulder. "Ahndromahk?"

"Yes?"

"You can wear the blue one?"

Blue — the color of the sea, the sky, and happiness. It felt right. She would wear the blue dress.

Epilogue

Andromache sighed in relief. Finally, he was asleep! She'd tried everything — *everything!* — but he'd spit up twice during '*Old Tin Alley*,' and '*The Cricket Song*' had only made him scream. Bouncing had further enraged him. It had been a move of desperation, laying him on Hector's chest, but their son was now quietly rising and falling like a pelican on the waves.

"Ahndromahk," whispered Hector, after a moment or two. "What do I do now?"

"Nothing!" she hissed. "If he wakes up and starts screaming again, I'll rip my ears off. Or his. Please, Ector — please don't move! I'll do anything you want…"

"Anything?" he whispered, a gleam in his eye.

She laughed softly. "Anything."

"I wouldn't mind a foot rub."

Andromache blinked. That was *it?* "All right," she whispered. "If Cutie will make room for me."

The dog, curled up at the end of the bed, wagged her tail.

"I'll take that as a yes," murmured Andromache. She moved down beside Cutie and took Hector's feet in her lap. They were long, bony, and callused — and, as always after he'd stopped at the spring to scrub them, they smelled faintly of lemon balm. She began rubbing.

"That feels good," sighed Hector. "Later, I can return the favor…"

There was silence for such a long time that Andromache finally looked over to see whether Hector, too, had fallen asleep. He hadn't — he was smiling at her.

"What is it?" she whispered.

"Ahndromahk," he murmured. "Ahndromahk — you haff been the joy ohff my lahff."

Her fingers tensed around his toes. "Are."

"What?"

Andromache shook her head. "You're still mixing up your past and present." Hector had promised to work harder at distinguishing the two so that he wouldn't confuse their baby. Now, though, he was overusing the past time words — perhaps to make up for his old habit of ignoring them. He meant well, but sometimes Andromache found the results unsettling. *Maybe I'll ask him to go back to his old ways*, she thought. *We'll have plenty of time, later, to straighten Mander out.* Aloud, she said to Hector, "You should have said, 'You are *the joy of my life*.'"

"You ahre rahght, pretty wife. I am sohrry." In apology, he locked his big toe around her index finger.

"It's all right," she whispered, massaging his instep with her thumb. "You're the joy of my life, too." Reconsidering, she added, "You and the little ones." She nodded toward Cutie, then the baby, asleep on Hector's chest.

Hector smiled and whispered, "He is heavy."

"You think so? His dad's a lot worse!"

Again, Hector flexed his big toe.

Andromache squeezed back one last time and lay down beside her husband. She wished their son was heavier still. Heavier than Hector, heavier than the whole house — so heavy that he could keep them in that moment forever.

The baby shifted. Hector groaned dramatically, murmuring, "Careful there, Mandrake."

"Oh no!" scolded Andromache. "Not you, too!"

"Not me, what?"

"Calling our son Mandrake! It's bad enough that Paris does it — your brother and his stupid nicknames!"

Hector laughed. "Mandrake, son of Hermie."

"It's not funny!"

"A little fahnny."

"Oh, really? What if Mander grows up thinking that *that's* his real name?"

"Then I can tell him, '*No, son. It is wohrse. You ahre named fohr a riffer*.'"

"There's nothing wrong with that," Andromache retorted. "Skamahnder is a nice name. Besides, we *had* to call him that! The river is where he was conceived."

"Ah," said Hector, a smug look on his face. "Ohff where, we cannot be sure."

Andromache gave him a poke that was more like a caress. "Maybe. But none of that gives Paris the right to nickname our son! Especially not when he says Mander is *weird*!"

"Mander chews on my belt," said Hector. "That *is* weird."

"He's teething!" whispered Andromache, in defense of their son. "He *has* to chew things! And you should be flattered that he chose your belt. It's his way of showing that he loves you."

As if to prove her point, the sleeping baby took a handful of Hector's tunic and clutched it. "My little weird son!" murmured Hector, stroking Mander's tiny hand. "You can haff my belt, and anyfing else you want…"

Andromache soon felt the telltale twitching of Hector's feet against her own — he, too, had drifted off. Gently, she rose up onto her elbow and looked down at her sleeping family. Everything about the scene before her filled her with a joy so deep that it was almost painful. There was the ray of sunlight falling across Hector's face; the baby's fist, now closed around his finger; Cutie, snuggled warmly beside them. *My loves,* thought Andromache, smiling. *My loves.*

It was an enchanted moment.

The Old Woman from Thebe

(Recorded by Thorro, scribe of Awarna, commissioned to collect the stories of immigrants to the Lukka lands)

Only a fool would rush toward a doomed city — or so I would have said, before I met Penthesilea. But she was no fool.

How could someone like *me* know Penthesilea, you might ask? I wouldn't blame you for wondering that. I've wondered it, too. I know how I look — old, and bent, and grey. How could *I* be a companion to a warrior like *her*? The only answer I can give you is that in this world, things are always happening in ways you wouldn't expect.

Take how I met her. She found me the night the raiders came to Thebe. I was serving wine in the tavern, like usual, when they broke down the door. Just broke it right down! And that was only the beginning. Once they were inside, they turned the tables over, smashed the wine jars, and took the gold. Now, I heard tell of raiders going back to Thebe, after I'd left, and doing even worse things. I'm sorry to say that I believe it all. I'd believe anything I heard about *them*.

When the raiders came into the tavern, I hid behind a table as quick as I could. One of them found me. He spoke my home language, but I could tell he was foreign. He sounded funny, you know? He yelled at me, over and over — '*Get out, you stupid old sow!*' — as though *that* would make me want to come to him! Finally, he got sick of yelling. He grabbed my ankle and started pulling me out from my hiding place.

I still had a cup of wine in my hand — I'd been about to serve it to the young Wintusi boy when the raiders came. Isn't it funny, the things you remember? After all I've forgotten, I can still picture that Wintusi boy's ears. He had the funniest ears, pointed at the top, and I wasn't the only one to notice. There were some who took those ears for proof he was a wood satyr. Me, I say that's nonsense. If he'd been a wood satyr, the girls would have been swarming all over him, but no woman ever looked at him twice, as far as I know.

Anyway, back to my story. I had a cup of wine in my hand, and I threw it at the man who was attacking me. What else can an old woman do, when a big brute is pulling on her ankle?

That was when I saw *her*. Penthesilea. I'd been watching her all night, of course — couldn't help it. Not many like *her* came into our tavern. It wasn't so much that she was beautiful, although I suppose she was. No, it was more that she had a way about her, like she was in charge and no one was going to tell her what to do. And then, there she was, standing behind the brute that had my ankle. After my cup hit him, she clocked him, too, and down he went. Didn't get back up again. She reached her hand out to me, and I left with her. I never looked back!

I didn't know anything about her, then. I didn't know that she'd been living in Troy, for the past few years, or that she was trying to find a new place to settle when she found me. I didn't know why she was in Thebe — still don't, for that matter. She never told me why she went *there*, not even after we'd been together for years and she was like a daughter to me.

She asked me if I minded traveling east, away from the sea. Minded? As if I cared where I went! Once those raiders gutted the tavern, I had nothing. I was surprised she wanted me to go with her, old and useless as I am, but she took me. I was the first of her strays. We went east and north, toward the Munnanda Sea. We stopped for a while in one of the midland countries, where Penthesilea knew the king. He had a strange name, Asimus or Aslius or something like that. I can't quite remember — it's not as clear to me as the Wintusi boy's ears! But I have to say, I wasn't surprised to find out that Penthesilea knew a king. We stayed with him a few months, and then we kept going — east and north.

While we were on the road, Penthesilea gathered in more strays. All of them were women or girls hurt by men. Penthesilea taught us how to defend ourselves. Anyone can defend herself, she said — even an old woman with a wine cup. When we got to the mountains, she decided it would be a good place to stay. She gave us more training with weapons — things we found or made ourselves, like rocks, or staves, or clubs. She taught us not to be helpless. Not to be victims.

No one but me knew why she took in so many strays. She talked to me more than she talked to most people. It started on the day when she told me I reminded her of her mother — had this look on her face like she was about to crack apart. Now, I worked in a tavern all my life, so I know that when people look like that, it's best just to let them talk, or not talk, as they see fit. They usually talk. Penthesilea did. She told me she'd been born up north of Thebe, along the straits, but raiders came and took her and her mother as slaves. She never said what happened to her father. I knew, of course — *everyone* knows what raiders do to men.

The raiders took her and her mother to the Munnanda Sea. Penthesilea never said much about her life with the raiders, but I heard enough to know that they hurt her. I know that her mother died, and that Penthesilea blamed herself for it. I also know that Penthesilea killed her master. He got what he deserved, if you ask me, but of course she had to run away, afterward. She ran southwest and eventually wound up in the midland country I mentioned before, the one with King Asimus or Aslius. She told me that he was the first good man she'd ever met.

She said that most men were brutal and violent, and women didn't know how to defend themselves. She felt it was her mission to teach them. Some men might be good, she said, but too many of them aren't, so women have to know how to fight back.

She said you even have to defend yourself against the good men — and that they can be the most dangerous of all.

Anyway, Penthesilea took us in and taught us how not to be helpless. We became her army, and she was our queen.

There weren't any men living out in the mountains with us. Our group only got bigger when Penthesilea found more strays. Sometimes, one or another woman didn't want to join us, and she took it pretty hard. No one but me seemed to notice. She'd get that look on her face, like she was barely holding it together. I'm only an old woman, and I don't know much, but I know when someone's feeling bad about her past. Maybe she was thinking about her mother, or maybe something else. She never told me. She just kept building our group.

One of the women was Palaan, and she called us '*Ha-mazin.*' She said it meant '*wild women.*' I don't know if that's true. I don't speak Palaan. But it's true enough that we were wild. We lived in tents. We had little gardens and hunted for meat. There was talk of building a more permanent settlement, with proper houses — maybe even a tavern! — but we never got around to it. Penthesilea went riding back to Troy before we could.

Troy. When Penthesilea heard that Troy was in trouble — that midland king sent word to her — she took some of her best women and flew out west to help. I begged her not to go. Told her it was a lost cause, if that many raiders were attacking the place. Look what a dozen raiders did to my tavern in Thebe, and the messenger from King Asimus — no, King *Aslius*, I'm almost certain of it! — said there were *thousands* of raiders at Troy! I told Penthesilea she should just stay in the mountains, with us. She didn't listen to me, though. No one listens to old women.

We stayed up there in the mountains for a while, after she left, but there came a time when we couldn't do it, anymore. She'd taken the best women with her. The rest of us weren't very good at living on our own. A few women left, and then a few more. I was all for staying — what if Penthesilea came back, and I wasn't there? But then finally there were only four or five of us left, and the others talked me into leaving with them. What else could I do? I couldn't live up there in the mountains by myself. And the truth is, I never really expected Penthesilea to come back, anyway.

The women — the ones I left with — brought me here, to Awarna. The best thing about this place is there are still some people here who speak my home language. They moved down to the Lukka lands years ago for the sun and the pines and the bright blue sea. It's a pretty place, I'll grant you that, but I didn't come here for any of that. I just went where other people were going. An old woman can't always pick where she gets to live.

It's worked out well enough, for me. I'm back in a tavern. How do you like that? All that traveling, all that time in the mountains, and here I am, right back where I started! I cook now, though — I don't serve wine. I told the owner I was done dealing with drunk men, and he said that was fine.

Yes, Awarna is a nice place. Life here is easy, compared to living out in the wilds, but there are times I miss it. I miss *her*, Penthesilea. I never saw her again, after the day she left for Troy...

I wish I'd tried harder to keep her from going, but nothing would stop her! She said she had people there she needed to help. She said she had to honor a pact she'd made with Hector. They'd sworn to help each other if either was in danger.

Now, when she said '*Hector*,' I knew who she meant. Everyone in Thebe knew him. He was almost a local boy, for us, from the time he spent running a patrol in our area. He was the talk of all the old tavern chin-wags! Every time they watched him spar, they came in afterward, grumbling about his opponents:

If I'd been on the field, he never would've tricked me into looking away. Only an idiot would fall for that. And so what if he can switch hands during a sword fight? That's no excuse. I could've disarmed him, anyway!'

It made me laugh to hear them talk, the fools! If twenty of them had ganged up on Hector, they still couldn't have beaten him. I kept my mouth shut, though, and served them their wine, because that was my job. But can you imagine those fat, old windbags trying to fight against Hector? The pride of Troy? If you ask me, their brains were rotted right through from all their years of drinking too much wine!

Anyway, when Penthesilea mentioned Hector, I knew who she meant. She said the two of them had fought together in the army, back when she lived in Troy. If you can believe it, she told me that she was even part of his patrol once, the one that came to Thebe. The old windbags in my tavern always said there was a woman in that group, one who never took off her helmet or told anyone her name. I didn't believe them. Who would? Like I said before, their brains were rotted through. But it looks like they were right, just that once.

Where was I? Oh, Hector. Penthesilea told me that he was a good man — and that she'd promised to help him if he ever needed her.

I couldn't tell you exactly what she thought of him, but she had a funny look on her face when she told me about him. I knew she wasn't riding off to Troy just because of some pact. If she'd been an ordinary woman, I would have guessed that she was in love with him. Penthesilea wasn't ordinary, though, and it was hard for me to imagine her in love with any man, after everything she went through as a young girl. But then, if she had fallen in love with a man — even a good one — I could see her wanting to get away from him. Maybe that's why she left Troy in the first place.

Then again, maybe her funny look had nothing to do with love. Sometimes friends part on bad terms and spend the rest of their lives regretting it — that's why I made sure to hug Penthesilea before she left, so she knew we were on good terms, even though I thought she was crazy for leaving and told her so. I don't think I could sleep at night, now, if I hadn't hugged her that day…

But I was talking about Penthesilea and Hector. The thing I never understood was that she said '*people*.' She said she had '*people*' in Troy. Not a friend, not a lover — not a single person at all. *People.* Penthesilea never used words she didn't mean, not like some do. If she said '*people*,' then she meant '*people*.' It wasn't just Hector that she was running back for.

That's all I know. Penthesilea never talked much about her days in Troy. I just hope she found what she was looking for, when she rode back there. I hope she got another chance to see the people she cared about. A second chance is what we all want, in life. Old as I am, that's what she gave me.

Geography of *The Trojan Peace*

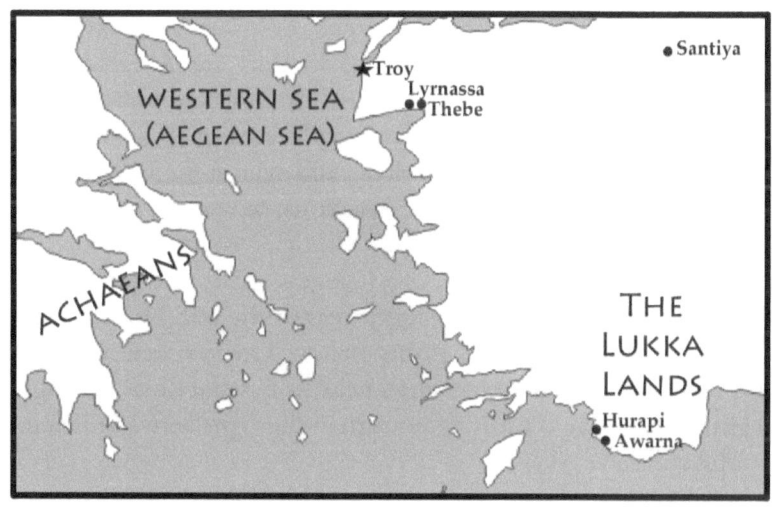

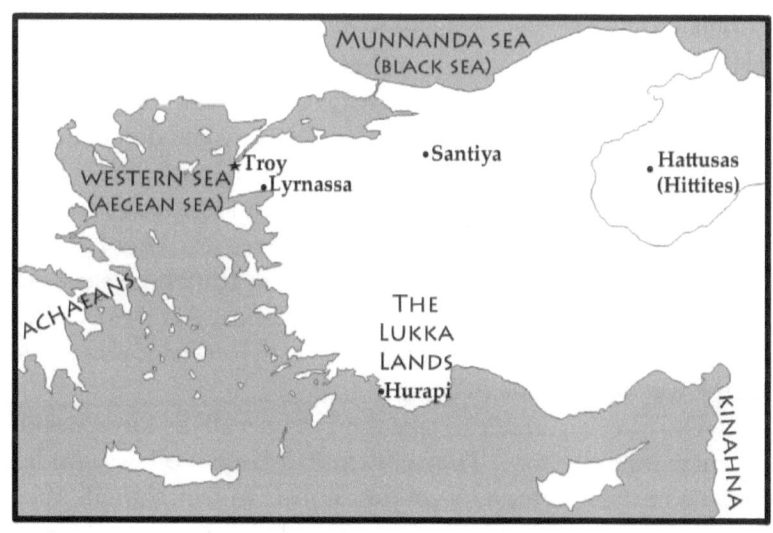

Brief Summary of the Trojan War

Paris, prince of Troy, abducts Helen, queen of Sparta, and takes her back to Troy. Helen's husband, Menelaus, and his brother, Agamemnon, amass a great army of all the kings and warriors of Greece, notably Odysseus, Achilles, Ajax, Patroclus, and Nestor. In Homer's *Iliad*, the Greeks are referred to as Achaeans or Danaans. The Trojans, often called Dardans, assemble their own army. They call in allies from all over Thrace and Anatolia (modern-day Turkey), and even as far away as Lycia (the Lukka lands) to the south. Amazons, or warrior women, are also among their allies.

For ten years, the Greeks lay siege to Troy and raid nearby cities. The *Iliad* begins in the tenth year of the war. Homer's epic recounts fighting on the plains below Troy as well as at the Greek ships, which are beached nearby. Several duels are highlighted, but none is more famous than the fight between Hector and Achilles.

Hector is a Trojan prince, Paris's brother, and the supreme commander of the Trojan army. He's the greatest of all the Trojan warriors. Achilles, in turn, is the greatest of all the Greek warriors. After Hector kills Patroclus, Achilles's companion, Achilles vows revenge. Achilles wins the duel. After killing Hector, he lashes Hector's body to his chariot and drags the body three times around the walls of Troy. He continues to do so each day, for many days in a row, in order to shame and desecrate the Trojan hero. Priam, Hector's father, eventually retrieves his son's body from Achilles, and the *Iliad* ends with Hector's funeral.

Other texts take up where the *Iliad* leaves off. After Hector's funeral, the fighting continues. More heroes from both sides die, including Penthesilea, queen of the Amazons. Achilles is killed by Paris. In general, though, Hector's death foreshadows the end of the war and the fall of Troy.

The Greeks, unable to take the Trojan walls by force, decide to enter them by ruse. They construct a large, hollow wooden horse and then pretend to sail for Greece. In fact, though, their ships are hidden behind the nearby island of Tenedos, and Greek warriors are concealed within the horse. This horse, which is viewed as an offering to the sea god, Poseidon, is brought within the walls of Troy. That night, the Greeks slip out, signal to the rest of the army, open the gates, and begin sacking and burning the city.

Troy is utterly demolished. The Trojan men are killed, as are some of the babies — notably Scamandrius (also known as Astyanax), the son of Hector and his wife, Andromache. The Trojan women — including Andromache, Hecuba (Hector's mother), and Cassandra (Hector's sister) — are dragged off as trophies of war. Helen is reunited with her husband, Menelaus.

Author's Note

The Trojan Peace: First Light and *The Trojan Peace: Half-Light* began as a single novel. I wrote it because no matter where I was or what I was doing, I couldn't stop thinking about certain characters from the Trojan War legend, namely Andromache and Hector. I first encountered them in the play, *Andromaque*, by Jean Racine. Right away, they captured my heart. I read everything I could about them, including works by Homer, Euripides, and Jean Giraudoux. Since those works pertained largely to the Trojan War and its aftermath, I also imagined what might have happened *before* — how exactly Andromache might have met Hector, and what their life might have been like in quieter times. After several years of this, I started writing down the stories that were in my head. Why not? I was always thinking about them, anyway. But what was it that I found so compelling about these two characters?

Laughter and tears

Homer's *Iliad* is a tale of war — rage — destruction — the fall of a city. Even so, it's also a tale of love. I don't mean Paris and Helen; theirs was an ill-thought-out affair. By the time Helen appears in the *Iliad*, she's longing for her husband, Menelaus; for her family; and for her home in Sparta (3.167-69). She despises Paris and refuses to return to his bed until the goddess Aphrodite threatens her (3.480). [Note: all citations of the *Iliad* refer to the Robert Fagles translation.]

No, if the *Iliad* is a tale of love, it's because of Hector and Andromache.

What makes their relationship unique? Doomed lovers always inspire sympathy, and readers of the *Iliad* know from the outset that Andromache will lose Hector to the war. His death is foreshadowed throughout the poem. Andromache even begins mourning him as soon as he rejoins the battle, long before he dies (6.597). Ill-fated couples are common enough, though. Romeo and Juliet, even Paris and Helen — none of these romances were destined to end well. What sets Hector and Andromache apart from the others is the maturity and substance of their love for each other.

Andromache and Hector are a literary rarity: a happily married couple. They speak together only once in all twenty-four books of the *Iliad*, but their conversation in Book Six is heartbreakingly tender. By this point in the story, fighting has already been fierce down on the plains below Troy. Hector has returned to the city, briefly, to relay several messages. He looks all over for his wife and finally finds her at the Scaean Gates. There, Andromache begs him not to rejoin the battle; he tells her that he must. She starts crying; he tries to soothe her. He tells her that no one is more important to him than she is. The idea of her being taken captive and hauled off into slavery is more appalling to him than anything else that might happen to Troy or even to his family (6.530-6.555). Then, in the midst of this touching scene, Hector reaches out for their baby, Scamandrius — but Scamandrius is horrified by the sight of his father's helmet and starts screaming.

What do Hector and Andromache do? They laugh. They laugh, and then Hector removes his helmet, takes Scamandrius in his arms, and kisses him. It's a moment of ordinary humanity in a world tumbling toward horror. It's also an illustration of extraordinary love: two people who can laugh together even at the worst of times.

In this scene at the Scaean Gates, Hector and Andromache show their truest natures. Yes, Hector is a warrior — a great warrior and a killer of Achaeans. He's even covered in battlefield filth when he and Andromache meet at the ramparts (Hector mentions his gruesome state when he first comes back to Troy, in verse 6.316). Later, at Hector's funeral, Andromache will remember what a ferocious fighter he was (24.867-70). It must be said, however, that war has come to *him*. He has no choice but to fight off the invaders as best he can, despite the fact that where he truly belongs is with his family.

After parting from her husband, Andromache keeps looking back toward him. Likewise, Hector doesn't rush back into battle, but dawdles. They're both reluctant to leave the place of their last meeting. Even once Hector is again fighting the Achaeans, he thinks about his wife. He remembers how she had sometimes teased him by giving wine first to his horses, and only then to him (8.210-16). Then, as he kills the Achaean hero Patroclus, Hector taunts the dying man, saying that now, Patroclus won't have the chance to drag Trojan women off into slavery (16.967-70). Hector doesn't speak Andromache's name, here, but I can't help reading those lines in Book Sixteen as an echo of Book Six.

As warriors go, Hector is cool-headed. When his brother, Paris, offers to challenge Menelaus to a duel — and thus potentially end the war — Hector leaps at the chance. He rushes into no-man's-land and orders his men to stand down (3.93-97). Later, even after the war has re-ignited, he still listens to reason. Several times he's won over by plans that offer "less danger, more success" (12:98 and 13:865). Yet he also makes risky decisions. Against the recommendation of his advisor, Polydamas, he insists on attacking the Achaean army at their ships (12:281). A bloody battle ensues, during which Hector says:

> *"So fight by the ships, all together. And that comrade*
> *who meets his death and destiny, speared or stabbed,*
> *let him die! He dies fighting for fatherland —*
> *no dishonor there!*
> *He'll leave behind him wife and sons unscathed..."* (15.574-78)

Although personal glory is on Hector's mind during this battle, the fate of his wife is, too. Perhaps the latter as much as the former explains why the levelheaded Hector is motivated to launch risky, audacious, even foolhardy initiatives by the end. At very least, he'll go down knowing he tried everything he could.

Throughout the epic, Andromache is equally occupied by thoughts of Hector. During Hector's duel with Achilles, not knowing that her husband is running — and then fighting — for his life, she prepares a bath for him (22.519). The gesture is intimate. Tender. She imagines him coming home and relaxing. It seems to be a scene they've lived many times, a profoundly ordinary domestic scene. Then, when she learns that her husband has been killed, the knowledge nearly destroys her (22.540). She wails — runs around — shrieks — faints — throws her crown, a marriage gift, to the ground. Hector clearly meant everything to her.

In some of the *Iliad*'s last lines, at Hector's funeral, Andromache grieves over how young her husband had been. She laments that now, he would not die in bed, beside her — that they would never have the chance to exchange a few last, loving words (24.875). *That* was the death that should have been his. *That* was the world that he should have belonged to, a world of tenderness and laughter, of shared tears and shared joy.

In a poem filled with godlike heroes, Andromache and Hector stand out as beautifully — and terribly — human.

Changes

The Trojan Peace: Half-Light contains several departures from the Trojan War legends. First, the son of Andromache and Hector is traditionally known as Astyanax or Scamandrius (after the river Scamander, near Troy). In *The Trojan Peace*, he's instead called Skamahnder, a Lukkanized form of the name.

A more noticeable change is to the timeline. The *Iliad* takes place in the tenth year of the Greek siege on Troy. In the epic poem, Scamandrius is only a baby. He must therefore have been born during the siege. By contrast, in *The Trojan Peace*, Scamander is born before any siege on Troy has taken place. However, readers can — if they choose — still see a ten-year timeline. Several characters mention years of Achaean raids on Trojan allies and then on Trojan territory. These raids began before Andromache's arrival in Troy. Ten years might well elapse between the first of these raids and the end of *The Trojan Peace*. On the other hand, the legendary *'ten years'* could be taken as hyperbole rather than an exact amount of time. I leave this choice up to the reader. Helen is also absent from *The Trojan Peace*. The event or situation that finally sparked the siege of Troy is left in obscurity. Readers are free to imagine whatever cause they find most likely: trade wars, expansionism, or even the abduction of a beautiful woman.

Details of note

As in *The Trojan Peace: First Light*, all elements of Trojan ritual come from my imagination. So do all songs and texts. The battle of Kadesh, however, was a real historical conflict between the Hittite empire under Muwatalli II and the Egyptian empire under Ramses II. The battle took place in 1274 BCE.

There are three other items I wanted to highlight. First, the title of Part One is *The Tamer of Horses*. In the *Iliad*, 'tamer of horses' is an epithet commonly used for Hector. Second, as I mentioned in my previous Author's Note, the Munnanda Sea is the name I use for what we now call the Black Sea. According to one online dictionary, '*Munnanda*' comes from the Hittite language and is translated as '*hidden*' (Puhvel 153-55). Finally, the '*fire mountain*' and '*ice palace*' that Andromache and Hector discuss refer to real places in southern Turkey. The '*fire mountain*' is the Chimaera, a coastal mountain where pockets of gas naturally ignite and burn. It looks as though dozens of campfires have been set across the mountainside. According to legend, the Chimaera is the home of the winged horse, Pegasus. In mythology, Chimaera is also the name of a monster killed by Bellerophon (with the help of Pegasus). The monster was part lion, part goat, and part snake — and he breathed fire. The '*ice palace*' refers to Pamukkale, a terraced mound of travertine deposited by hot springs. Pamukkale lies some 200 miles inland from the coast.

I'll end this note with a last word on languages. In the course of learning French and German, I made an interesting discovery: things that were emotionally hard to talk about in my native language were much easier to say in a foreign language. The struggles of finding the right word provided an emotional distance, or a shield. In my mind, the same is true for Hector.

Sources

Askin, Mustafa. Troy: With Legends, Facts and New Developments. Rev. ed. Antalya (Turkey): Keskin Color Kartpostalcilik, 2010.

Benoît de Sainte-Maure. Le Roman de Troie. Ed. and Tr. Emmanuèle Baumgartner and Françoise Vielliard. Paris: Livre de Poche, 1998.

Blamey, Marjorie and Christopher Grey-Wilson. Wild Flowers of the Mediterranean. 2nd ed. London: A & C Black, 2008.

Blondel, Jacques, James Aronson, Jean-Yves Bodiou and Gilles Boeuf. The Mediterranean Region: Biological Diversity in Space and Time. 2nd ed. Oxford: Oxford UP, 2010.

Cimok, Fatih. Les Hittites. Tr. Marion Feildel. Istanbul: A Turizm Yayinlari, 2010.

Cunliffe, Barry. Europe Between the Oceans. New Haven: Yale UP, 2008.

Fields, Nic. Troy c. 1700-1250 BC. 2008 ed. Oxford: Osprey Publishing, 2008.

Homer. The Iliad. Tr. Robert Fagles. New York: Penguin Classics, 1990.

Homer. The Iliad. Tr. Robert Fitzgerald. 2004 ed. New York: Farrar, Straus and Giroux, 2004.

Homer. The Odyssey. Tr. Robert Fagles. 2006 ed. New York: Penguin Books, 2006.

Korfmann, Manfred O. Troia/Wilusa: Guidebook. Trans. Jean D. Carpenter Efe. 2005 ed. Çannakale (Turkey): Çannakale-Tübingen Troia Vakfi, 2005.

Melchert, H. Craig. "Lycian." In The Ancient Languages of Asia Minor. Ed. Roger D. Woodard. Cambridge (UK): Cambridge UP, 2008.

Lalande, Bernard. "Notice." In Andromaque. Jean Racine. Paris: Librairie Larousse, 1959.

Map of the Eastern Mediterranean. Original at http://www.d-maps.com/carte.php?num_car=3160&lang=en

Puhvel, Jaan. Hittite Etymological Dictionary: Vol. 3 Words beginning with H. In Trends in Linguistics Documentation 5. Berlin: Mouton de Gruyter, 1991. Accessed online 8-31-2014. http://books.google.com/books?id=kghtOX_crPMC&pg=P

A155&lpg=PA155&dq=munnanda+hittite+words&source=
bl&ots=Qs2ICti_xj&sig=W5UPZH93O9X1QSRYERtht2n
hi5k&hl=en&sa=X&ei=CUN_UI-iC-
Tq0gHrtoC4DQ&sqi=2&ved=0CB0Q6AEwAA#v=onepag
e&q=munnanda%20hittite%20words&f=false

Racine, Jean. Andromaque. Paris: Librairie Larousse, 1959.

Smith, Duane. "The Canaanites Were in Canaan." Abnormal Interests: A few thoughts on things that interest me (blog). Posted 9-10-2006. Accessed 8-31-2014. http://www.telecomtally.com/blog/2006/09/the_canaanites.html

Sterry, Paul. Collins Complete Guide to Mediterranean Wildlife. London: Harper Collins, 2000.

Virgil. The Aeneid. Tr. Robert Fagles. 2008 ed. New York: Penguin Books, 2008.

Wood, Michael. In Search of the Trojan War. 1998 ed. Berkeley: University of California Press, 1998.

Woodard, Roger D., ed. The Ancient Languages of Asia Minor. Cambridge (UK): Cambridge UP, 2008.

Acknowledgments

The Trojan Peace has been a labor of love for the past eight years. I have many people to thank for helping me throughout this process.

First and foremost, I must thank Marc Nelson. You're my husband — my love — my best friend in the world — my fellow dreamer — my fellow traveler — my favorite conversation partner — my everything. Thank you for giving me space in the early stages of this project, when I refused to tell you what I was working on. Thank you for reading early drafts of *The Trojan Peace* and giving me feedback. Thank you for always believing in my characters, even when I was frustrated with them. Talking about them with you has helped bring them to life — you have supported me in ways that only a fellow artist would be able to do. There is a lot of you in *The Trojan Peace*, more than you — or perhaps even I — know. Thank you for your laughter, your passion, your willingness to listen, and of course, your love of animals. Thank you for wrangling my computer when I was ready to smash it against the wall. Thank you for gazing at the stars with me. Last but certainly not least, thank you for your beautiful paintings. Ever since I started writing *The Trojan Peace*, I dreamed of having your artwork on the cover. Thank you for making that dream a reality.

Thank you to my parents, Bob and Karen Bartelt, for always encouraging me to appreciate and explore the wonders of the world. Some of my earliest memories involve hiking through the mountains of southwestern Montana and marveling at the geysers in Yellowstone National Park. You took our family to many fascinating places when I was a child; later, you supported my wish to study abroad in France and East Asia. These adventures –all of them — have had a lasting impact on my curiosity, creativity, and willingness to try new things. I also want to thank you for teaching me tenacity, without which writing a book would be impossible. Thank you for your patience, your keen intelligence, and your love. I would need many more pages to list all that I admire about you.

Thank you to my brother, Erik Bartelt, for inspiring me to visit Turkey. Before you went there in 2011, I'd never thought of Troy as a modern-day travel destination! I'd also never dreamed that Turkey would become one of my favorite places in the world. I started writing *The Trojan Peace* long before either you or I visited Turkey, but going there — seeing those legendary landscapes first-hand — has definitely informed my writing. Thank you for opening that door for me, and thank you for everything else that makes you the best brother I could ever imagine.

Thank you to Tom Mayer for encouraging me to write. I think your exact words were, "What? You want to go to grad school for *French*?! Are you crazy? Why don't you write fiction?" Nevertheless, you gave me the letter of recommendation that I'd asked for. I learned so much and had so many wonderful experiences during grad school, yet in the end, I realized that you were right — academia was not for me. I'll never know what you would have thought of *The Trojan Peace*, but I can't thank you enough for that first little push. Thank you also for everything you taught me about close readings of texts and careful structuring of arguments. I may never again encounter another mind as fine as yours.

Thank you to Josh Shepherd and Nikki Dyke for reading early versions of *The Trojan Peace* and sharing their thoughts with me. A fresh eye is invaluable for finding mistakes and pointing out strengths and weaknesses. I'm truly grateful for the time you spent reading my work and helping me improve it.

Thank you to Adrienne Bashista for preparing my CIP data block for me.

Thank you to all the teachers and professors who contributed to my education. I never took a class that wasn't somehow interesting and valuable. It can be difficult for someone who loves science, math, music, literature, languages, history, and everything else to find a path in life; it can be difficult to focus. However, these diverse areas of interest have also been an asset — I've drawn from all of them while writing *The Trojan Peace*.

I'd like to thank a few professors in particular: Professor Hope, for sensitizing me to the rhythms and sonorities of poetry; Professor Laronde, for exposing me to the theories and practices of translation; Professor Heilenman, for sharing her knowledge of language acquisition; Professor Racevskis, for his detailed and thoughtful critiques; Professor Guentner, for giving me a background in aesthetics; Professor Curtius, for her instruction regarding *la créolisation*; Professor Ungar, for his line-by-line analysis of *Le Cimetière Marin*; and Professor Thomas, for securing me a teaching position in France.

Thank you to my Lyle family. You've truly been a bedrock of support for me throughout the past eight years — often in ways you never realized. Your kindness, patience, caring, and compassion show every day in all you do. Thank you for the hugs, for the laughter, and for keeping me grounded.

Lastly, I must say thank you to Luke, my little cattle dog, my very own Cutie. You're a constant source of joy, sweetness, and love. You've snuggled in my lap while I'm writing; you've licked away my tears of frustration; you've taken walks with me whenever I needed a break. You make the world a better place. Thank you for being so innocently, purely, and perfectly yourself.

Also by Jill Bartelt

The Trojan Peace: First Light
The Trojan Peace: Half-Light

Available in print and digital formats

Connect with Jill Bartelt via her author page
on www.calymenepress.com

Connect with Marc Nelson

www.marcnelsonart.com

On Twitter: @Marcnelsonart

www.ingramcontent.com/pod-product-compliance
Lightning Source LLC
Chambersburg PA
CBHW022231020726
47496CB00004B/853